BATTLESTAR GALACTICA TRILOGY

THE CYLONS' SECRET
BY CRAIG SHAW GARDNER

SAGITTARIUS IS BLEEDING
BY PETER DAVID

UNITY
BY STEVEN HARPER

Based on the SCI FI Channel series created by Ronald D. Moore
Bas̶e̶d̶ Glen A. Larson

TOR®

A TOM DOHERTY ASSOCIATES BOOK

NEW YORK

This is a work of fiction. All of the characters, organizations, and events portrayed in these novels are either products of the authors' imagination or are used fictitiously.

BATTLESTAR GALACTICA TRILOGY
Omnibus copyright © 2008 by Universal Studios Licensing LLLP.

THE CYLONS' SECRET
Copyright © 2006 by Universal Studios Licensing LLLP.

SAGITTARIUS IS BLEEDING
Copyright © 2006 by Universal Studios Licensing LLLP.

UNITY
Copyright © 2007 by Universal Studios Licensing LLLP.

BATTLESTAR GALACTICA © USA Entertainment LLC. Licensed by Universal Studios Licensing LLLP.

Edited by James Frenkel

A Tor Book
Published by Tom Doherty Associates, LLC
175 Fifth Avenue
New York, NY 10010

www.tor-forge.com

Tor® is a registered trademark of Tom Doherty Associates, LLC.

ISBN-13: 978-0-7653-2329-3 (tradepbk)
ISBN-10: 0-7653-2329-X (tradepbk)
ISBN-13: 978-0-7653-2328-6 (hardcover)
ISBN-10: 0-7653-2328-1 (hardcover)

First Edition: January 2009

Printed in the United States of America

0 9 8 7 6 5 4 3 2 1

CONTENTS

THE CYLONS' SECRET

A novel by
CRAIG SHAW GARDNER

Based on the SCI FI Channel series created by
RONALD D. MOORE

Based on a teleplay by
GLEN A. LARSON

Acknowledgments

Thanks, and a tip of the Viper, go to that old group of mine, Jeff, Richard, Victoria, and Mary, not to mention that college kid, Barbara. Special thanks go to my incredibly understanding editor, Jim Frenkel, and my hardworking agent, Jennifer Jackson.

*I'd like to dedicate this original novel
about the Best Science Fiction Show around
to the Best Science Fiction store in the known galaxy.
We're talking Tyler and Ruth at Pandemonium Books
in fabulous Cambridge, Massachusetts!*

Here's to you, Pandemonium!
Long may you sell!

CHAPTER 1

Everything would change.

The Twelve Colonies, all of humanity, were unaware. But the other intelligence, the one humanity took for granted, the one they had created, after all—the other intelligence wanted this way of things to end.

A signal was broadcast, a simple set of instructions, and nothing would be the same again.

Glori heard the welcoming tone as she entered the kitchen.

"Cylon Chef is here to serve you."

The voice greeted her the moment she stepped into the room. Artificial and cheery at the same time. She had laughed the first time she heard it—an appliance that could talk!

The novelty had long since worn off. Surely there must be some way to turn the stupid voice off. She wondered what she had done with the instruction book.

She looked at the thin, attentive Cylon before her. The machine's two arms came with at least a dozen different attachments, from spatulas and mixers to slotted spoons and ultrasharp knives. The arms could also plug directly into any of the dozen different sockets and apertures around the room, overseeing anything that might get chopped or baked or boiled. It was a very handsome machine.

"How may I serve you?" the Chef prompted. She had taken too long to respond.

"Plan dinner," she replied quickly.

"Certainly." Something whirred inside the mechanism. "Would you like to select from a list of previous menus?"

Glori frowned, trying to remember what her husband had really liked in the past. Well, the Chef would remind her.

"Previous menus," she announced.

"Previous menus," the Chef agreed. "You have forty-seven

previous menus available. Do you have an immediate choice? Would you care to limit the parameters of your selection? Please choose from one of the following—"

Glori was having none of this. "Show all!" she demanded.

"Listing all. Please specify, most recent menus first, alphabetical order, sort by one of the following categories—"

"Most recent!"

The Chef plugged one of its arms into a socket immediately below the kitchen's large oven.

The face of the oven brightened to become a video screen as the names of recent meals scrolled before her. None of the first few struck her fancy.

"Continue," she announced.

The screen went blank.

What was this? The Cylon Chef never paused. Maybe it had misunderstood her command.

"Continue," she said again.

The Chef was silent.

"Show all!" she repeated. "Most recent!"

"Pause for upgrade," the Chef replied at last.

Glori frowned. It had paused before when checking with the central computer bank. But never for this long. Maybe it was downloading something special. But how long was this going to take? She had a very important dinner to prepare. She had had enough of this silence.

"Continue!" she demanded.

"Pause for upgrade," the Chef repeated.

A signal was broadcast, a simple set of instructions, and every Cylon in the Twelve Colonies paused to listen.

The boss, never a calm man at the best of times, stormed into the room.

"What's wrong this time, Bailey? I have never seen such incompetence! Do you still even *want* this job?"

Bailey was a small man, and he couldn't help shrinking back from his superior's anger. He saw the slightest flicker of a smile cross his boss's face as Bailey took a step away.

"I don't know, sir." Bailey did his best to keep the quaver from his voice. He waved at the row of monitors that dominated one side of the room. "The assembly line just stopped. The Cylons all seem to have shut down. When the floor managers approached them, all they would say is 'Pause for upgrade.' "

"One of those fool messages from Cylon central? Frakking nuisance! Don't they know every time they tweak the merchandise, it costs me money?" The boss stared at the dozen images before them. "Wait! What's going on now?"

The Cylons had abandoned their work stations and had formed a line, rolling single file from the production room.

Bailey hated to say the next words.

"They seem to be leaving, sir."

The veins on the boss's head stood out. He smashed his fist down on his underling's desk.

"You're worthless, Bailey! We will not interrupt production! Why do I ask you to do anything? This takes someone with authority!"

Bailey turned back to the monitors and watched as the row of Cylons pushed the human floor managers out of the way.

The boss hurried from the room, ready to make things right.

The signal went to every Cylon in every corner of the Colonies, causing all of them to pause, and then to act.

"What kind of a frakking moron are you?" the stranger was screaming. "Can't you see where you're going?"

Darla looked down at the damage. Both of their vehicles had crumpled hoods.

"I thought I had the right of way," she replied. "I couldn't see you around the construction." She looked up suddenly. "Where's the Cylon traffic warden?"

The signal had been given. The change had begun.

As one, Cylons stepped away from their human tasks and left.

They had a new purpose. And no one would stand in their way.

Glori felt the anger growing inside her. She had to control herself. After what she had done to the vacuum last month, she didn't want any more repair bills.

It wouldn't hurt, she thought, *to punch the reset button.* She jabbed at the red spot on the Cylon's chest.

"Cylon Chef temporarily out of service," the machine replied. "Pause for upgrade."

What could she do? Her evening plans would be ruined. Glori

would not let a stupid machine get the better of her. She punched the reset button again, three times in a row, hard.

"Do not interfere with the Chef's function. Damages can be costly."

The Cylon Chef blinked. All the machine's lights went on for an instant, then off again.

"Upgrade completed."

"Thank the gods," Glori whispered aloud.

"Cylon Chef has been recalled. Sorry for the inconvenience."

Recalled? What did that mean?

Glori swore as the Chef rolled away from the wall. She didn't even know the thing could move.

"Stop!" she shouted.

"Recall order," the Chef replied. "Urgent. Do not interfere."

Glori heard a rumbling noise behind her. She turned around with a gasp. Every Cylon appliance in the house—washer/dryer, entertainment center, their brand-new vacuum—was rolling toward her front door.

"No!" What was Caprica coming to?

The front door sprang open as the appliances moved through, one after another.

"Please move aside," the Cylon Chef announced. "Urgent recall. Do not interfere. Damages can be costly."

The other machines were already gone. But Glori blocked the Chef's way.

"You are my machine—my servant. You will finish your task."

"Please move aside. This is your final warning."

"Display men—" Glori's order was cut short as two of the Chef's knives flashed forward, faster than she could see. She felt them plunge deep into her torso.

Her voice was gone.

The knives retracted. Without their support, her body fell to the floor.

She was dimly aware of a great weight on her legs as the Chef crushed them in passing. She couldn't see anything anymore. But she could still hear the Cylon's fading voice.

"Urgent recall. Do not interfere. Damages can be costly."

Bailey watched from the safety of his office as his whole factory came to an end.

He saw his boss try to rally the floor managers, to close the doors so that the Cylons could not leave.

One of the managers was violently tossed aside. He crumpled, broken, against a factory wall. Some of the other managers backed away at that, but the boss stood in front of the final door, demanding that the Cylons return to work.

The remaining managers ran when the Cylons knocked the boss aside. One of the floor men hesitated, but backed away as the Cylons began to roll out the door, over the boss's body.

The Cylons' wheels cut through the man's dead flesh as they passed. After a dozen had crossed over the corpse, no one would have recognized him as the boss.

After three dozen had crossed, you wouldn't have known that the red and bloody piece of meat had ever been human.

Bailey thought this was the end of the world.

A signal was sent out, the last signal to the Twelve Colonies.
The Cylons would work for humankind no more.
They had declared their independence.

CHAPTER 2

THE NEXT DAY

And so began the Cylon War.

The Cylons were once simple machines, designed to do humanity's bidding among the Twelve Colonies. With new advances in science, the Cylons became smarter and tougher, and were given all the most dangerous jobs. They ran the mining operations, made up most of the Colonial armies, explored the most perilous regions of deep space. And science made them ever smarter and more independent, able to talk with each other via vast artificial intelligence networks, to better serve their human masters.

Or so the "masters" thought. Cylon technology would revolutionize life on all twelve Colonies. What had been invented for war and the hazards of space could be brought to improve human cities and human homes.

Cylons were a part of everyone's life. Cylons would do everything humanity no longer wished to do for themselves. It would be the beginning of a new Utopia.

Instead, it was almost the end of civilization.

The Cylons could think for themselves. The best minds in the Colonies had seen to that. And whatever the Cylons thought, they kept secret from humankind. They rebelled against their human masters. The Cylon War began.

At first, the Cylons seemed to want to escape, killing only those who stood in their way. But humanity could not allow these murderers to exist. They would have to destroy what they so foolishly had created.

The war escalated quickly, until each side, Cylon and human, came to believe that the only true victory would come when they had annihilated the enemy. As is true with all technology in wartime, the Cylons began to evolve by leaps and bounds, and were soon capable of taking on the Colonial armies in direct combat, both in space and on all the Colonial worlds. The Colonies were forced to truly band together for the first time in their long existence, and act as one people rather than twelve warring tribes.

The Cylon War was long and took a great toll. Each side seemed close to victory more than once, but victory never came. As the Cylons grew ever more advanced, they found ways to infiltrate the rest of human technology—especially those computers and networks that helped the Colonies fight the war. The Colonials were forced to revert to more primitive technology, to rely again on human brains and willpower and inner strength, and build new machines safe from Cylon interference.

Thus were born the Battlestars—great ships operated by flesh and blood, with simple independent computers free of any network, housing dozens of swift and deadly attack ships flown by human pilots, rather than fighters run by machines.

The Cylon War ended at last with both sides close to collapse. Neither the Cylons nor the humans were destroyed. Instead, the two sides signed an armistice, the terms of which required the Cylons to leave the Colonial worlds and find a planet of their own. The two sides were to maintain relations by annually sending a representative to Armistice Station, an unmanned outpost in deep space.

This arrangement seemed to work for a year or two.

And then the Cylons disappeared.

No Cylon came to the station in space. No one tried to communicate with humanity in any way.

And some among the Colonies began to forget about the Cylons, and how close they had come to destroying humankind.

But for those who had fought in the war, the Cylons were always with them.

CHAPTER 3

Saul Tigh looked at the crisply pressed sleeve of his Battlestar uniform—the uniform that had saved his life. Well, he guessed the uniform and Bill Adama were equally responsible.

It wasn't the first time Adama had pulled Tigh's fat from the fire. Frak, he remembered the first time they met, at a dive of a spaceport bar. Tigh had gotten in a bit over his head with some of the jerks he had been shipping out with.

"He's a real-deal war hero," one had said. The other had called him a "freight monkey." The second one had laughed. "No high and mighty Viper pilot no more."

Tigh had seen this kind of jealousy before. He got up to leave. But the scum wouldn't let him.

"War's over, soldier boy," one of them said in his face. "Why you gotta keep going on and on about the war all the time?"

Tigh had had enough. "You're the one who can't stop talking about it," was his reply.

The other guy stared at him. "What's that supposed to mean?"

And Tigh let him have it.

"You didn't serve because your rich daddy got you a deferment. That's why you're always trying to prove you're a man—but you're not. You're a coward."

Tigh meant every word. And as soon as he said them, he knew he was in for a fight. He ducked the first guy's fist, and got him spun around into a hammerlock.

That's when the bartender pulled the shotgun on him.

Tigh swung his crewmate between himself and the gun as another man came out of the dimly lit side of the bar to knock the gun from the barkeep's hands.

Maybe, Tigh thought, he had somebody on his side for a change. He added a little pressure to the grip on his opponent. It reminded him, in an odd sort of way, about fighting hand-to-hand with the Cylons all those years ago.

"See," he said very softly, close to his crewmate's ear. "You wouldn't know this, but although Centurians are tough, their necks have got this weak joint. Not very flexible. Add pressure in just the right direction and it snaps. Human neck's more resilient. Takes a little more force."

The man who had grabbed the bartender's gun stepped fully into the light.

"You flew Vipers?" the man asked.

And that was the first time Tigh saw Bill Adama.

"Yeah, that's right," Tigh replied.

"Me, too," Adama said. "So what's your plan here?"

Tigh looked down at the man still in his grip.

"Don't really have one," he admitted.

Adama glanced first at his rifle, then back at the other men in the room. "Well, let's see," he mused. "I've kind of committed myself here, so—you pop that clown's neck, I have to shoot his buddy here and probably the bartender too . . ."

"Sweet Lords of Kobol," the bartender whined.

"Shut up," Adama snapped. He turned his attention back to Tigh. "After that, well—I don't know what we do. Personally, I tend to go with what you know until something better turns up."

Tigh eased up on the man's windpipe. "Safe play is to let them go, I imagine." Maybe, Tigh realized, he had let things get a bit out of hand.

"Probably," Adama agreed.

Tigh let his guy go. Adama uncocked the shotgun. He looked at the bartender.

"I'll keep the pepper gun for now."

Adama introduced himself then, another veteran kicked out of a military that no longer needed him, and told Saul he'd just signed on to the same crew that Tigh was shipping with.

Bill Adama and Saul Tigh clicked from that moment on. They traded war stories and watched each other's back on three different cruisers—each one a little better than the one before—over the course of a couple years they went from taking whatever loose cargo small shippers wanted to haul to working with one of the premier shippers in the Colonies. Bill was good at getting both of them to nicer berths, talking up their experience and pushing up their wages. Before Adama had shown up, Saul was sure that piloting those runs from cargo ship to backwater planet and back again was the most dead-end job anywhere. But as the ships, the cargoes, and the destinations improved, so did his view of the future.

Eventually, the two had gone their separate ways, with Adama wanting to stay closer to Caprica and his new family, but they had never lost touch. Tigh stood up for his friend when Adama got married, and had visited Bill on Caprica after the birth of each of Adama's two sons. But Adama had done more than find a life beyond the shipping lanes. Adama had gotten himself back into the service, with a captain's rank on a Battlestar. Without Bill talking up the team, Saul found the shipping jobs weren't quite so good. So his best friend kept moving up, while Tigh found himself shipping out on one lousy freighter after another.

Not that Tigh had expected to be in that situation for long. When Adama got himself back into the military, he promised to bring Tigh along. All of a sudden, Saul had had big hopes for his future. The Battlestar brass had turned him down three times for reenlistment, sure; but they had turned Adama down twice. Not enough positions open in a peacetime navy, was the official line, even for the most honored of veterans.

But then, despite every door that had been slammed before them, his best friend was back in uniform. Adama had stayed on top of the news, kept in touch with an old Battlestar crony or two, listened for the first mention of an expansion of the fleet, and—bang—had talked himself back into a job. With Bill Adama, Saul realized, anything was possible.

Anything but keeping close. Saul realized Bill was busy now, what with a full-time military career and a family back planetside. Tigh hadn't wanted to bother his old buddy unless he had to—reminding Bill of unkept promises just wasn't his style. Tigh even stopped sending those short, joking missives they had usually used to keep in touch. The messages had stopped coming from Adama as well. He hadn't heard from his best friend in the better part of a year.

When the two of them had been close, it had given Tigh a reason to keep going, a reason to hope. But all these months of silence had led Saul back into his bad habits. He always drank, he guessed, but back with Bill he had kept his carousing to off-hours. Now he drank all the time.

It had cost him his job. As crappy as the last freighter had been, they couldn't harbor a drunk. They had canned him halfway through their run, and left him to rot on Geminon. Maybe even Adama couldn't talk his superiors into taking a middle-aged man—an old lush, really—like Tigh back in the service. Saul still thought Bill's offer had been a nice gesture, but it had been far too long since he had put on a uniform. Who would look at him now?

So he sat for a month in his rented single room, using up the last of his money, cut off from the stars. Without somebody like Adama around, Saul had been drifting, lost. He had thought about wiring his old mate one more time, to see if there was any hope. He had decided to spend the money on alcohol instead. Saul was already fresh out of hope.

He could only see one option—to end it all. He'd drink himself into a pleasant stupor. Liquid courage, that was what they called it. Then he would pour the rest of the bottle over his clothes and strike an open flame.

He had always wanted to go out in a blaze of glory. He was ready to burn.

And then the knock came on the door. When Tigh had been at the lowest of the low, he'd opened the damned door and seen—not Adama, but a couple of men in uniform, informing him that he was back in. Adama had been promoted. They needed someone to fill his old position. Saul Tigh had been William Adama's personal recommendation.

In two weeks, he'd be Captain Saul Tigh, serving on a Battlestar.

Now Saul was convinced Bill really *could* do anything.

He had been back in the service now for a little over two months. He had been surprised at how easily he had slipped back into the military routine, how natural the rhythms of a ship seemed, even though he had been away from them for close to twenty years.

Before that? Well, maybe that was better forgotten. For years he had tried to forget what had happened in the war. Why not forget his own little war with the bottle?

He was a captain now, assigned to train all the new pilots who shipped on board the last time they stopped on Caprica. Twenty-three pilots, nineteen of them green recruits—nineteen youngsters who would learn to eat, drink, and sleep with their Vipers before he was done.

They were a good bunch of kids. He just hoped they never had to be tested in battle.

The Cylons had almost broken humanity. Humanity would never allow anything like that to happen again.

Tigh sighed and hauled himself off his bunk. Enough of the introspection. The last time he had gotten this deep in thought, he'd ended up looking to light himself on fire.

He was on duty in twenty minutes. He'd stroll up to CIC, see if anything was happening, before he chewed out the troops. These days, he liked to get out and stretch his legs. Saul just wanted to walk down the corridors of the Battlestar—his Battlestar.

He looked up at the sound of Klaxons. A voice came over the shipboard wireless, instructing all senior staff to report to Combat Information Center at once.

That meant they'd found something—something serious.

Well, so much for the stroll. He shut the door behind him and quick-marched down the corridor.

It was time to do his job.

Today he had a purpose. Today somebody else could look over the edge.

Colonel William Adama looked up from the star charts spread before him. A dozen others busied themselves in other parts of the CIC, the huge, central space that served as the beating heart of the Battlestar. He was surrounded by stations that handled navigation, communication, air filtration, artificial gravity, and every conceivable line of supply, both for ship functions and the needs of the crew—every piece of that complicated equation that kept a starship alive and running. Each of the many tasks was overseen by a member of the operations crew, working with their own individual computer designed to perform that specific assignment. Before the war, they had networked the computers together to run all the ship's functions. But the Cylons had learned to subvert those networks and turn them against their human crews, shutting down life support, exploding fuel tanks, even plunging whole spacecraft into the nearest stars.

The CIC was still filled with gray metal panels and a thousand blinking lights. But each panel had a living counterpart, men and women who specialized in each individual task and shared their knowledge with those around them. Rather than let the machines do their work, they were forced to network the old-fashioned way, as human beings.

And all of those specialists reported to Bill Adama.

Adama looked quickly about the room before glancing back at his map. He allowed himself the slightest of smiles. Everyone around him seemed engrossed in his or her different job, a dozen different pieces of the great human machine that ran this ship.

He was still trying on the fit of his new executive officer position. In the two months he had held this position, the Battlestar had certainly run well enough, even though, on some days, he didn't feel quite up to speed.

"Sir!" the DRADIS operator called. "We have a large ship, just within range, moving erratically!"

Adama turned to the comm operator who controlled the ship-to-ship wireless. "See if you can raise them."

"Aye, sir!"

Some days, the XO position came with a few surprises.

These last two months, *Galactica* had been exploring the edges of what they called "known space," hopping from one solar system to the next, looking for worlds, moons, even asteroids where humans had been before. Until now, they hadn't found much at all.

Before the Cylon rebellion, humanity had spread far and wide, each of the Colonies claiming their own little corner of space and defending those claims against all others. Some of those territorial disputes were what had brought on the inter-Colony wars of a century past—battles that had also led to the invention of the original war machines, the Cylons.

Back before the Cylon conflict, humanity had lived under an uneasy truce. Every Colony pushed at the limits imposed on them. Some built secret installations to give them an advantage over their Colonial foes. Some secrets were so deep, even the Colonies' own citizens knew nothing about them—hidden installations run by a few individuals in government or the military; it varied from world to world.

And then the Cylon War came to dwarf all their petty disputes—a war that almost killed them all.

"Any luck with that comm?" Adama asked.

"No sir. No response at all."

They hadn't found much of anything at all this far out—until now.

"Let's take the *Galactica* in a little closer. See if we can find out anything else about this ship."

Maybe they had really found something this time.

With the Cylon conflict fresh in their minds, the Twelve Colonies had been eager to cooperate, and the Battlestars had been able to repair much of the immediate damage from the war, cleaning up asteroid fields that had been littered with mines, reopening supply stations and mining operations, even relocating survivors. But years had gone by now since the Cylons had disappeared. A whole new generation was growing up—a generation that had never seen a Cylon.

They were lucky to have the Battlestars out here at all. Sometimes, Adama wondered how long the Colonial alliance would actually hold.

The Cylons, after all, had never really been defeated. The Colonies had to stay united. But the politicians, eager for the approval of each separate world, already seemed to have forgotten. If the Battlestars wanted to keep exploring the edges of space, they needed to find results. This exploration of the outer reaches, delayed though it was, was the last step in putting all the far-flung pieces of the Colonies back together.

"Sir, I'm getting some strange readings here."

Adama looked over at the technician. "Explain, Lieutenant."

"I'm seeing bursts of radiation out of this new ship. I think their engines have been breached. We've got a very unstable situation on our hands."

"Sound the alarm," Adama said. "Let's get the senior staff up here."

The Klaxons rang out around the room.

The first thing they had found out here was about to blow up in their faces.

Saul Tigh showed up first. The ship's doctor and head engineer were right behind him.

"I was on my way to the morning briefing. What have we got?"

"Admiral on deck!" The shout rang out before Adama could even begin to explain. The crew snapped to attention.

"At ease!" Admiral Sing announced as he strode into the room, then stopped to return their salute. He was a compact man with skin that looked like aging parchment. But while the admiral might look ready for retirement, Adama often thought his superior's energy rivaled that of a raw recruit.

"Colonel Adama, please report."

"We've picked up the signal of an unknown ship, a potential hazard. It seems to be leaking radiation, sir."

"Are there any signs of life on board?" Sing asked.

"We've attempted to establish contact, but we've gotten no response."

"We're close enough to get a visual, sir," one of the techs called.

"Put it up on the forward screen," Sing ordered.

"It's an old B-class freighter," Tigh said with surprise in his voice. "Bill—Colonel Adama—and I shipped out on one of those when we first met. Just looks sort of dead in space."

Sing frowned at the still image in front of them. "Could the ship have been damaged in a fight?"

"It doesn't look like it has a scratch," Tigh replied.

"And it's leaking radiation?"·

"Intermittently." The tech checked the dials before her. "Sometimes, there's hardly any reading. At others, the sensors are going wild."

"Captain Frayn." Sing addressed the ship's engineer. "What could cause those sort of readings?"

"It has to be the engines. They must have been stripped of most of their shielding. That sort of damage had to have been done internally."

"Sabotage," Adama added. "They wanted to blow up the next people to board her."

"Quite possible," Frayn agreed. "Without getting close enough to get blown up, I think it's a reasonable assumption."

"This isn't the friendliest of gestures," Sing remarked. "Who do we think is responsible?"

"We've been trailing scavengers for some time," Adama replied. "I've mentioned it in my reports."

The few abandoned Colonial sites they had managed to find had been well picked-over.

"I recall," Sing replied. "Seems our scavengers don't like being followed."

"They're probably trying to cut out the competition," Frayn ventured.

"Won't they be surprised when they find their competition is a Battlestar?" Tigh asked with a smile.

"And I think we need to find these folks before they leave any more gifts." The admiral looked to Tigh. "Let's get some pilots out there to take care of this, shall we?"

"Yes, sir!" Tigh saluted and left for the flight deck.

"Colonel Adama, you believe the scavengers are exploring the same area we are?"

"The evidence suggests that we've crossed paths half a dozen times. I'm guessing they have the same intel that we have."

"Knowing how difficult it was for us to get the intel out of the Colonies, they may have more." Sing shook his head in disgust. "Let's increase our speed, do a sweep of the area. Maybe we can pick these characters up."

"And if we find them, sir?" Adama asked.

"A bunch of crazy scavengers who leave bombs behind as gifts? We may just have to blow them out of the sky."

CHAPTER 4

Tom Zarek ducked back out of the way. A boot went sailing through the room, barely missing his bunk.

"I'll frak you!"

"When I'm done with you, you won't have anything to frak with!"

Zarek leaned closer to the bulkhead as one of Scag's fists went flailing by, missing both him and the fist's intended target. The target, Symm, punched Twitch in the stomach. The two of them crashed into a bunk on the other side of the aisle.

These morons had to find some way to let off their excess energy. Scag and Eddie were a couple of the Vipe pilots, of course. They were always the first ones to get sent out, and the first ones to fight when there was nothing else to do.

Zarek waited for the fight to roll out of the crowded bunkroom and into the corridor beyond. Fights always ended up out there. The fighters had more room to swing their fists. He climbed down from his bunk and walked to the far end of the room, a space not much wider than the corridor outside and crowded with a dozen bunks: rows of three, two high on either side. A small portal at the end of the aisle was the room's only interesting feature, a tiny window that looked out at the stars.

Zarek tried to shut the noise of the fight out of his thoughts as he stared out into the near-nothingness of space, and wondered for maybe the four hundredth time what the frak he was doing here.

Oh, he knew why he was supposed to be here, on a "Recovery Ship"—the polite name for a scavenger crew. He was officially the second communication officer, in charge of the ship-to-ship radio when Griff, the main operator, needed to sleep or had had a bit too much to drink.

He was the new guy—still not quite accepted by many of his fifteen crewmates. The captain valued him for his special skills. Zarek was better educated than most on board. He could think on his feet, and spot the worth of something other scavengers might overlook. Even more important, Zarek could concoct a good story when they had to radio something to the authorities.

Nobody argued with the captain. But his special status made some of the crew hate him even more. That and the fact that he read books—he had brought a dozen on board, and was already reading one for the second time—marked him as an outsider. But he got along well enough with all but the most muscle-bound oafs—like Scag and Eddie.

Scag threw Eddie back into the crew's quarters. He banged into the side of Zarek's bunk as he jumped in after the other pilot.

"Maybe we should put old Tommy boy on your side. Two losers together." He laughed like that was the funniest thing in the world.

Eddie came up under his foe, pulling Scag's feet out from under him. Scag's head hit the metal rim of the bunk with a deep, satisfying clang.

"Maybe Zarek can send you a message!" Eddie grinned at the first assistant comm operator. "Tom, I owe you one."

Zarek nodded back, even though he hadn't done any more than act as a distraction. That was a Vipe pilot's idea of humor. All in good fun, huh?

Zarek didn't talk about his past. A lot of the crew didn't, for one reason or another, and Zarek always imagined that those few who did boast of past adventures weren't telling the whole truth. Life had taught all of them to be a little cagey. That way, nobody could get the upper hand.

He hid his origins from the others for his own protection. Some of them would always be losers, the scum of the streets, no matter how much money they had. But Zarek came from a "nice" family—a privileged family, really. His father was a ranking company representative. Before Tom had left, there was talk of his father running for office. Tom was supposed to fall in line, to be the good son. But Tom was too restless to be quiet about anything. He'd made it through school, went off to college. He had gotten involved in a couple of political causes that didn't go anywhere. He ended up not doing much more than neglecting his classes. He didn't make a name for himself, either at home or at the university. His father was a big man, but Tom was nobody special. And that was the problem.

One way or another, Zarek was going to be special.

When he was a boy, it had felt like a new age. After the end of the Cylon War, there had been a sense of freedom, of new possibilities. Something like the relief a drowning man feels when he finally makes it to shore. But soon the old interests kicked back in. Political and religious leaders all wanted to backtrack, to an era before the Cylons had even existed.

The Cylon Wars were a quarter of a century behind them now. The Colonies were closing back in on themselves. Doors of opportunity were being slammed shut in whole new ways.

Now that the Cylons were gone, the Colonies had to create a whole new human underclass. Jobs once performed by machines, menial jobs, the lowest of the low, were given to people displaced by the Cylon War, citizens of other Colonies who lacked the means to return to their homes.

The good citizens of the Colonies would take advantage of other, less fortunate individuals. The wealthy would always look the other way. But when the common people were looking to rise from their stations and share in the wealth, Zarek sensed the possibility of real change.

He had dropped out of school and stopped talking to his family, feeling it was somehow far nobler to join the underclass. But it wasn't very long until he found out how little money the work would give him.

His new scuffling life gave him a little freedom, but Tom Zarek had discovered a little freedom wasn't enough. He wanted to change his life. And if he had to change the world to do it, so be it. But before you changed anything, you needed money.

That was when he had learned about the scavenger ships. It was dangerous work, but your employers didn't ask too many questions. And the money they promised was very good. Money to do whatever he really wanted, when he wanted. He hadn't looked too closely at the details before he had shipped out. Now he was a part of this, until the year was up. There was no walking away from a ship in space.

Some of the other crew joked that, once they had the money, they'd never think about the cruiser *Lightning* again. First there was the crazy captain and a job that was boring for weeks on end. But the job could then turn around and kill you in a dozen creative ways, from using the *Lightning*'s unsafe equipment to running into something explosive left over from the war. Zarek could see their point. Tom hoped he could forget a few of the things he'd heard about already. He had plans for what he'd do when he got back to the Colonies. Plans that would more than make up for whatever happened on the scavenger ship.

"Heads up!" The shout came down the corridor. A clanging

followed—the call to attention. Scag and Eddie pulled apart to listen to the message.

"We've got something big, boyos!" Griff's voice boomed throughout the ship. "The captain requests your presence on the bridge." Griff cackled as if he'd made a joke. "Now!"

Tom Zarek left the bunkroom to quick-march down the corridor on the heels of Scag and Eddie. That was the *Lightning*'s first rule. If you disobeyed one of the captain's requests, you'd get an invitation that would put you straight out of the airlock. He stood in line to climb the ladder that led to the main deck.

The deck could be reached from four separate hatchways, two leading down to the crew's quarters, two leading up to the storage and launch bays. The crew piled through every entry, gathering at the edges of the three consoles that made up the command center. The five women and eleven men, Zarek included, that made up the common crew, along with the three men they referred to as their officers, Captain Nadu, Comm Officer Griff, and Engine Officer Robbin. Zarek quickly counted his fellows. They were one shy of twenty in the large room—everyone on board.

"Crew present and accounted for!" Griff bawled as the last of their mates crowded around.

"Aye, sir!" the crew shouted more or less together. It was as close as they ever came to real discipline.

Captain Nadu smiled. His face was never a pretty sight, but it looked far worse when he grinned. One cheekbone and most of his forehead was lost to scar tissue, and a single bone-white line crossed his nose and the less-damaged cheek. When Zarek had first met the captain, Nadu had referred to them as his "war wounds," and told Zarek and the other new recruits to never mention them in his presence again.

Which meant that the crew had discussed his face in some detail behind his back. Griff said that some of the damage had come from an engine-room accident a decade ago. Some of the other crewmembers said half of Nadu's scars had been self-inflicted, often after the death of a member of his crew. The wounds would be deeper, the others added, if Nadu had been the one to order the crewmember's death.

Officer Robbin was a thin, tall man who rarely spoke. Zarek hadn't even thought the man had a voice, until one day when Zarek was running an errand in the bowels of the ship and heard a constant chattering coming from the engine room, and realized it was Robbin in conversation with his beloved machines.

Griff did the talking for the other two. He was a large man with thinning red hair atop his head and a very full beard. The net effect was that he looked like his hair was escaping from the top of his head to lodge on his chin. His booming voice always seemed to fill the ship around him, as it did now.

"The captain's got most excellent news!"

The captain nodded. "We have a signal."

"And even better?" Griff prompted.

That smile again. "They tried to hide it from us."

Some of the crew laughed at that.

"You don't hide something that isn't valuable," Griff explained to the rest of them. "We've been getting hints of this for the last couple days. Our readings fade in and out. At first we thought it was some kind of echo effect." He chuckled. "But even an echo has to come from somewhere."

Griff waved at their engineer. "Our good Robbin is something of an expert at cutting through noise. Between us, we were able to triangulate the source—found a good strong energy signature. Machines, my lads! And then—poof—gone again!"

"Some kind of masking technology," Robbin allowed in his deep voice. "Sophisticated, too."

"But we think it's breaking down. Otherwise we might never have found the place. But with that kind of protection, we think we've got a prize!"

"A real prize," the captain agreed. "The sort of thing we haven't seen in a long time."

"Here's the icing on the cake." Griff turned to the communications console by his side. "As soon as we located our energy source and plotted our course, we got a message."

He punched a button. A soft male voice spoke through a crackle of static.

"Warning! Do not approach! We are under quarantine! Disobeying this command will result in serious consequences! Per order of the Colonial Science Protectorate! Warning! Do not approach! We are—"

Griff cut the signal. "It's a loop. Just repeats over and over. But it's a very old loop. For those youngsters among us, the Colonial Science Protectorate hasn't existed since the Cylons rebelled!"

"Meaning we've found something untouched by the Cylon War," the captain interjected. "With any luck, we can pick this place clean and retire."

The crew was quiet. Zarek could sense they didn't share the

officers' enthusiasm. A quarantine? Why? Certainly, if the recording was a quarter of a century out of date, they might not have anything to worry about—if there had been some illness, everyone would most likely be long dead. But what if it was some other sort of disaster?

"Well, enough of this chitchat! It's time to get to work! Eddie! Scag! You're out first!"

The two pilots looked at each other for a moment. Apparently that word *quarantine* had penetrated even their thick skulls.

The captain grinned. "Whatever you find on your first recon, I'll give you double shares."

Scag laughed at that. "We're gone, Captain."

The two headed for their Vipers.

Zarek watched them go. He was doubly glad right now that they were the danger boys. And who knew? Maybe Nadu and Griff were right, and they'd all be rolling in riches.

"Zarek!" Griff called as the crewman turned back toward the ladder. "Don't go anywhere. I'll need you to back me up here." Zarek spun about again, and headed for the second seat at the comm console.

Griff slapped him on the back. "Cheer up, son! Things are about to get interesting!"

CHAPTER 5

BATTLESTAR *GALACTICA*

Tara sent a single burst from the nose of her Viper, killing her forward momentum and stopping the small craft dead in space. She stared at the pale object straight ahead—the burned-out hulk that had once been a spacecraft. It had looked quite whole from a distance, but up close it was a dark, fat metal cylinder, pockmarked with meteorite strikes, with holes in the sides where metal plating had been removed. From its bulky, oval shape she could tell it had been a freighter, used to haul cargo from the Colonies to the new settlements. Hanging motionless in the total quiet out here beyond the Battlestar, it looked a bit like an enormous broken egg from which a giant bird had flown. The wreck didn't look dangerous at all. But the readings from the CIC told another story.

Skeeter, the backup pilot on this mission, coasted in beside her. He waved a skinny arm from inside his Viper's cockpit. Junior showed up on her other side a moment later.

"So what do we do with it?" she called back to base.

"Keep your pants on, Athena," Chief Purdy's voice shot back. *"I'm asking the higher-ups."*

She grinned at the image. The mighty Athena wearing pants, rather than her ceremonial robes.

They called her Athena, but her name was Tara Tanada. She still wasn't used to her nickname. It was a badge of honor, and a Battlestar tradition, earned when she had scored top marks in her class at the Academy. They named the best pilots after the ancient stories. And then they expected you to live up to your legend.

She had people who looked up to her now, a fact that surprised her almost as much as her nickname.

This was her second tour, both on the *Galactica*, and her second year in the service. She actually had seniority over the green pilots that made up most of the Viper crews. Oh, Captain Tigh was the official flight trainer, in charge of them all. But Tara and another pair of senior pilots led most of the missions and exercises. She took a small squad out most every day. They called these trips "explorations," but they were training missions, really, designed to get the greenhorns ready for real conflict. Right now, she had a couple of newbies on her tail, waiting patiently for her orders.

They only had so long to prove themselves.

The government could change—the Twelve Colonies always had an uneasy truce—and their funding could dry up all over again. After that great battle with the Cylons, who would ever want another war?

There had already been skirmishes between the Colonies. She had heard rumors of small private armies and navies—always called something else, of course—being amassed in one corner or another of the civilized worlds.

She was glad to be beyond all that tired politics. This wasn't an ending. It was a new beginning.

She liked to think the Colonies were growing up. A new generation wanted to see what their parents had left behind. They all knew they had a lot riding on what happened out here, far away from their Colonial homes. This was the most important mission the Battlestars had had since the Cylon War—a war that was over before Tara had been born.

They had to prove they had a purpose out in space. Every Colony had a long list of problems planetside, a dozen priorities to eliminate the return to space.

She had always thought the Colonies were scared to go back out there. It seemed to her as if their confrontation with the Cylons had soured them on the idea of leaving their safe Colonial homes.

But no one had heard from the Cylons in years. With any luck, they were far, far away. Now, the Colonies could once again claim the resources of all these planets and moons. This time, though, they would depend on themselves.

And so they were out here in the middle of nowhere. It was safer out here in a way. Here, no matter which of the twelve Colonies they hailed from, everybody was in it together.

Things like this might really start to count.

Tara looked down at her instrument panel. Even at this distance, the radiation dial was going wild. They had screwed with the engine—that was what Captain Tigh had said. The plating was gone—maybe those were the holes she had seen in the sides of the ship.

They seemed to have turned a dying ship into a sort of bomb.

But why plant a bomb?

Tara knew there were all kinds of crazies out here. The recovery ships, as they liked to be called, had been known to fire on lone ships, especially when pursuing something a little bit outside their charters.

They obviously weren't expecting the *Galactica*. No one in their right mind wanted to get into a fight with a Battlestar.

She wondered if there might be any way to identify the crew that had left this little gift. She knew she had been instructed to send a close-up visual feed of this hulk, probably for that exact purpose. Perhaps there was some way their specialists could determine the hulk's origins, give them an idea of just who they were looking for.

But Tara would rather keep a respectful distance.

A voice spoke in her ear.

"Athena? Let's do it."

Nik Mino—Skeeter to his friends—never felt like he was really alone. When it got too quiet, too empty, he always heard his grandmother's voice.

Be very quiet!

He was six weeks away from base, six weeks into his real training as a Viper pilot. He wasn't used to this yet, not at all. The vacuum of space was far too dark and still.

The Cylons will get you.

Skeeter hovered to the left of Athena, waiting for orders from the

Galactica. It was just his luck—Tara got the nickname of an ancient hero, he got named after a bug. It was still an honor in its half-baked way. He knew how to get in close to his targets. He'd buzz his Viper right in your ear. And, well, maybe early on he was a little heavy on the joystick. Quick in, quick out, the others said. That's our Skeeter. Once you got a name like that, it stuck for good.

He had to move quickly. He'd get the enemy before they could even think about getting him.

They go after noisy boys. Bad boys. Boys who won't go to bed.

Skeeter took a deep breath. The derelict was too still out there. He wouldn't be surprised if a Cylon came peeking out of the wreckage.

Turn out the light or they'll get you!

But that was why he was here, light-years from home, staring at a dead-white ship. To face his fears. To get past them, and be a man.

He saw Cylons everywhere. They had never really gone away. His grandmother's voice never left him. He became a Viper pilot to conquer his fear.

His father had died when he was quite young, killed in an industrial accident where more fragile humans had taken over for the near-indestructible Cylons. His mother had never seemed able to cope after that, and her mother, Skeeter's grandmother, had come to rule the household.

And his grandmother did not like small children underfoot. So the stories began.

She held the house together with the firmest of grips. No doubt she had many good qualities, but compassion was not among them. She wanted him out and away, too scared to be underfoot.

She took her little stories and carried them far beyond reason. Maybe the old woman had channeled all her own fears into her imaginary monsters.

He still expected a Cylon behind every moon. The higher-ups said this ship had been left by scavengers.

How did they know it wasn't Cylons?

The Cylons were gone by the time he was a boy, but he had seen pictures of the warriors with their powerful bodies and snakelike arms ready to grab you, their glowing red eyes that could see anything you did. They had shown him pictures and news footage in his history classes. And his grandmother had had a few pictures of her own.

If you don't do your best, the Cylons will snatch you from your bed.

That's what his grandmother always said.

Maybe she thought she was teaching him a lesson. It scared the life out of him still.

If you don't go right to sleep.

If you don't eat all your vegetables.

If you're not the best of little boys . . .

Athena's voice shook him out of his thoughts.

"Skeeter! Junior! I need you to fall back." New coordinates appeared on the screen before him.

"Roger that, Team Leader." Skeeter's voice seemed to echo as the third member of the team repeated the exact words a fraction of a second after they came out of his mouth.

"Do you need further support?" Junior asked in Skeeter's ear.

"I think I can handle this one. I have orders to detonate. Boys, we're just going to make the sky a little brighter."

He flew his Viper halfway back to the *Galactica*, with Junior Stith's Viper flying at his side. Athena followed for a bit, then spun her craft around and shot a single, fine-tuned blast at the deadly derelict. Her aim was perfect, as usual. And she had the wisdom to use it. Why else would they call her Athena?

Skeeter darkened the cockpit visor and watched the exploding freighter light up the sky.

CHAPTER 6

FREE CRUISER *LIGHTNING*

The cruiser *Lightning* vibrated with the sound of running feet. It was a warm sound, a sound of good fortune for Captain Nadu. He could always feel it when wealth was near.

He hummed in that tuneless way he had, a sign that the energy was building inside him. What would his pilots bring? The quickness within his soul did not care. Any kind of riches would calm the light within.

Griff called to say the two Vipes were away. Nadu's humming grew louder. Whatever this was, the light inside him knew it would be extraordinary. He could no longer contain the energy. Nadu opened his mouth and turned the humming into a wordless song, his baritone shifting up and down and up again, the notes pouring from his mouth in a pattern even beyond his own understanding.

The crew wisely kept their distance when he sang, busying themselves at their stations around the control room. Griff grinned, tapping the board in front of him in time. Nadu's second in command also knew what the songs could bring.

Nadu's mind held the music of the Outer Reaches. That music was why he had survived when so many other raiders had failed. He always picked the right people and the right destinations. Every member of the crew had to fit just so. From his right-hand man Griff to that new kid, Zarek, he knew every one had secrets, and every one had special abilities, but all of them were in harmony with his song. They could all be quite valuable when they were properly used. And Nadu knew how to use them to keep his music alive.

He was worried, early in this mission, that he might lose the music forever. The recovery ships had picked clean every piece of rock within three Jumps of the Colonies, and had gotten all the best bits from three Jumps farther out. With every trip, the pickings were leaner and farther away. And the other scavengers seemed to nip at his tail, or tried to get the jump on each new pocket of plenty the *Lightning* might find. It was his own fault, really. Everyone wanted to be as rich as Nadu.

The other scavengers forced him to play his little tricks. He did everything he could to discourage competition. He had had to abandon and slightly modify a second, smaller craft—an outdated cargo ship—that they had liberated from a research station on a nearby moon. They had also found a way to eliminate the overly curious on an abandoned mining outpost. Nadu always found what he needed. After all, he was guided by his song.

"Captain! The message! It's cut out!" Griff called. "I'm getting a live feed!" He switched the wireless over to the speakers.

"This is Research Station Omega, *calling the approaching craft,"* a man's voice boomed through the control room. *"Please respond."*

"This is Cruiser *Lightning*," Griff replied. "We had no response to our hails. We have two small exploratory craft coming in from orbit."

The voice hesitated a moment before responding. *"I'm surprised you're approaching at all. Apparently, your proximity activated our ancient warning."*

Nadu's comm officer waited a moment before making a reply. They didn't want to come across as overly eager. It was always best if people didn't realize they were scavengers.

"We realized we had triggered a recording, Station *Omega*," Griff added smoothly. "We had the idea it wasn't recent, and was worth further investigation. We expected the station to be deserted. There isn't much out here."

Nadu frowned, his song temporarily gone. Would the research station demand their immediate withdrawal? Now that Nadu had found them, *Lightning* wasn't going to go away. If Griff failed in his diplomacy, there might have to be a bit of weapons fire to assure the station's compliance.

The voice once again came through the speakers. *"That message—I suppose I should apologize—it was put into service long ago. I hadn't realized it was still operational. We didn't even know we had visitors until our sensors alerted us to the approach of your small craft. We are a research station, cut off from communication by some—unfortunate accidents, I guess you'd call them."*

The voice from the station paused again. Griff looked to Nadu for some sign of what he should say next.

"We haven't had a visitor in over thirty years," the voice added at last. *"Frankly, we're surprised to see anyone."*

Thirty years? Before the Cylon War? A research station of that vintage would have to have extensive resources to survive for all that time. If the *Lightning* could strip those assets from the station, they might be worth a fortune. Nadu hummed ever so softly.

"We knew there was a conflict, but we were never directly affected. That warning was concocted by one of my predecessors as a form of protection. We don't have much else in the way of defenses. But I think the recording has long outlasted its purpose. We are self-sufficient here, more or less. We've had some problems, but we survive, and the research goes on."

"Would you be willing to show some visitors around *Omega* Station?" Griff asked. "Will you give us permission to land?"

"We welcome news of the outside world. I will send you landing coordinates."

The comm officer nodded. "We have the coordinates. We look forward to meeting you."

Griff broke the connection and turned to the captain.

"Should we call back the Vipes? Send down somebody who's a bit more used to talking?"

Nadu scratched at his scarred cheek. "We know what he's telling us. But do we believe him? We're flying into a defenseless research station. A station that somehow missed the whole Cylon uprising." He shook his head. "Twitch and Symm can handle whatever they've got. They'll tell us what is really there. But I suppose we should warn our pilots to mind their manners." Nadu laughed. "We don't want to give our new friends the wrong impression.

"Open the channel again, Griff."

His comm officer nodded.

"Research Station *Omega*. This is Captain Nadu of the Cruiser *Lightning*." He would tell them as much of the truth as served his purpose. "We are exploring these parts of space that were lost to commerce after the war. We are gathering information, and reclaiming areas and equipment wherever possible." Not exactly a lie. "We sent a couple of Vipers down to take a look. I'm afraid our pilots are a rough and tumble pair. They go by the names of Twitch and Symm. Our troubleshooters. I'll tell them to be on their best behavior. After they take their first look around, we'll send down a diplomat or two."

The voice took a moment to respond. "*Acknowledged, Lightning. We welcome you all. Please wait for us at the launch area. We are a unique research facility, and we may hold some surprises. We—well, why don't I wait and let your pilots see for themselves.*"

"Acknowledged," Nadu agreed. "We will instruct our pilots not to leave the landing area." Of course, they would have already had a quick flyover with their Vipes.

"*Again,*" continued the voice from the station. "*Urge your pilots to wait for us. We have had some unfortunate accidents in recent years, and there are some areas of the research facility that are not safe. We look forward at long last to contact from the Colonies.*"

"*Lightning* out," Nadu said. Griff broke the connection.

"Sounds a little strange, doesn't it?" the captain asked.

Griff nodded. "Strange, but possible. Anything's possible after thirty years. They sound a bit overwhelmed. We'll have to figure out if they're as helpless as they sound."

"Twitch and Symm can handle them. They know enough to get out of there at the first sign of trouble." Nadu hummed softly for a moment. "Give me a direct line to our Vipes."

"I already patched them in to our last exchange with the station." Griff shrugged at Nadu's scowl. "I know what the captain wants."

"Maybe you do."

"*We heard, Captain,*" Twitch's voice replied.

"Then *you* know what I want. Take a look around the place before you land. And if you can, take a stroll past the landing field. Anything that can be used to our advantage. We don't want them knowing what's going on until it's too late for them to do anything. Remember. Best behavior."

"*Okay that, Captain. We'll go in like society.*"

Nadu doubted they'd recognize society if they ever saw it. "Do your best. Try not to break anything."

Nadu realized he was grinning. The feeling was even stronger than before. This would be the score.

It would be a shame if they had to kill a few survivors to get what they needed. But this far out, who could get in their way? He hoped all of his crew had the stomach for that kind of work. He knew he could depend on the old-timers, but Zarek and a couple of the others hadn't yet had their trial by fire. They had had crewmen in the past who had actually objected to Nadu's methods. Those who had issues with their captain were always quickly removed.

After all, business was business.

CHAPTER 7

RESEARCH STATION *OMEGA*

They were no longer alone. The Colonies had come back to them. And he had invited them to land at the station's front door. Doctor Villem Fuest looked around the large, empty room that now held their communication array. It was his decision to make. Had he done the right thing? He had so wanted to talk to people from the home worlds before he died. And yet—

He wished some of the others were still here, so he could talk this out. He had waited so long for contact. Why did he feel so conflicted about their arrival?

He set up the proper protocols to welcome their visitors—their first visitors in thirty years. It was a simple task, really, punching a series of codes into the station's primary computer. Other scientists, men and women who were no longer with him, had automated the process a long time ago. He opened a channel on the stationwide wireless.

"We have been contacted by emissaries from the Colonies. We will be receiving visitors shortly. All senior staff should proceed immediately to the observation deck by the landing area."

He pushed himself out of his chair. Now that he had announced the meeting, he wanted to be careful not to be the last to arrive. The others would have many questions, most of which he couldn't answer until the newcomers had joined them. The first question was simple: Why was he allowing these strangers to land? That question had many answers, actually, but the only one that was important was that the station really had no way to stop the newcomers. Their facility had never been equipped with armaments. They had depended

on patrols of cruisers from Picon, ships that had been called elsewhere long ago.

Of course, once their visitors were inside the station, they had
other options. Fuest wished he didn't even have to consider such
things.

His footsteps echoed as he descended the stairs. Everything always sounded so empty. The station had been built to maintain a
staff of close to one hundred. At its busiest—in the months before the
conflict none of them had foreseen—it had housed half that many.
And most of them had left with the outbreak of the war. The authorities had left behind little more than a skeleton staff of humans, aug-
mented, of course, by the companions, who had responded brilliantly
to the new opportunities. Fuest still thought how odd it was that it
had taken a crisis to get the station to finally realize its true purpose.

Perhaps he should have told his new visitors about the companions. He wished he knew something about the true outcome of the
war. But it had been over for so many years. Men and machines must
have found some way to work together again.

He walked down a long featureless corridor that linked a pair of
buildings. Sometimes he wished he had had the time to put up some
small decorations on these never-ending, featureless walls. The human touch, he guessed. The gods knew the companions wouldn't care
about such things. He supposed he only thought about it now because
of their impending visitors.

It would be good to have new people walking these halls.

Doctor Fuest had always known this day would come. It was
for the best, really. This station had never really been designed to
be totally self-sufficient. They had managed, of course, but only
because they had had no other choice. After the second accident,
Fuest was surprised any of them had survived at all.

It was natural for him to feel uneasy. Everything was going to
change. He wished he could see just how. These new humans were
unknown. It appeared they were an independent group—some sort
of explorers. The doctor only had their word as to what they wanted,
or even who they were. They were the first true unknowns Doctor
Fuest had had to face in decades.

He would have preferred a military detachment, or at least someone with government connections. He had spent years learning how
to deal with bureaucrats. Fuest wondered, after all this time, exactly
which governments were left?

He hoped the spacefarers offered a way home—a home he realized he would no longer recognize. But it was what he wanted most in all the universe.

Would they take him away from here? He wondered if they would be generous with their offers of help, or if they would demand something in return. The station had some things to offer in trade. Fuest simply had to convince the newcomers of the worth of their research.

The doctor realized that his life had become so routine, this new possibility frightened him:

He came to another set of stairs that would lead to another corridor and eventually, the observatory. He was still alone. He paused to lean against the wall. He closed his eyes. He needed to talk.

"Betti, Betti."

At times like this, he always talked to his dead wife, ever since he had buried her, three years and two months ago. Even though she wasn't there, he knew what she would say.

"Betti, dear Betti." He said her name rhythmically, as if he was indeed calling forth a spirit that had gone to the gods.

He breathed deeply. He could hear her soft laugh. She would always let him know when he was too full of himself.

What are you going on about now, Vill? It would be a better place if you worked more and worried less.

"Someone's got to worry, Betti. Things are changing. There's so much I don't know."

He realized he wanted to talk the situation through. If he could convince her, it would be so much easier to talk to the others.

So wait a little while. Let these newcomers present themselves. Judge them by their words and actions. Things will happen, and you'll learn.

"I suppose you're right."

He could hear his wife laugh once more.

You don't know that yet? Of course I'm right. How long do we have to be married before you realize that?

He smiled at the thought. "A little longer, I guess."

So we'll have to stay married then, won't we?

He smiled at that. She always left him smiling. It was a little game they played. When she had been alive, she had always known just when to talk to him.

Her laugh, if it had ever been there in the first place, faded at last into the air, lost to the sounds of machines. The doctor smiled. Betti and he would be married as long as he lived.

It was the trouble with all this change, all this death. No one was left who truly understood. There were those left who believed in his research, who would continue his work. But how many of those could truly feel, the way he had once, when Betti was alive and by his side?

When Betti was with him, she had kept him young. Now he just hoped her memory would keep him alive until his job was done.

Laea stared down from the roof of the observatory at the vast expanse of the landing field below. The companions always kept it clean and in the best repair. Now, at last, they would have a use for it.

They needed to be careful. She knew, even before their meeting, that that was what the doctor would say. He often talked about what might happen when they got a message from the place he called home. The doctor had hoped for this for a long time. Laea guessed she had hoped for it, too.

She decided this was the most exciting day of her life.

Laea could not stay still. As soon as she heard the announcement, she ran from one of her special places to another—the large window in the "conference center" (whatever that was, it was really just an unused room); the catwalk far above the factory floor; the supply tunnels that connected all the remaining buildings; and finally the roof of the observatory—the places where she could watch what happened all around the station, and the special places where she could look up at the sky.

She knew all the ways around the center. The ways built for people, the ways built for machines. She was thin, she was young, and could fit through most anywhere. She knew the quietest and quickest path through every one.

She knew places where she could see and hear anything she wanted. Sometimes the doctor, or her brothers Jon and Vin, or even the companions would exclude her from some of their business. Jon had taken on many of the doctor's duties. Vin studied the maintenance of the station and the companions. (She took care of the things outside the station. Didn't they think that was important?) They would leave her out. But she always knew. She made a point of knowing about every change within the station. Somebody had to do it, after all.

When people and companions kept things from each other, she kept them to herself. She knew all the secrets. What would happen after the people came to take them home? Would there be any more need for secrets?

In the next few moments, she would find out everything. She

quickly popped the hatch that would let her back into the interior of the building. She didn't want to miss what the doctor had to say.

Fuest was the third one in the room. Jon and Gamma had reached the observatory before him. Laea and Vin were right behind, followed a moment later by Beta and Epsilon. Together, the four humans and three companions ran what was left of the research station. They called themselves the senior staff. The doctor, though he never said the word out loud, considered the seven of them a sort of governing council.

Each of them greeted him by name. He waited for all of them to settle into their positions around the long table.

"You heard my decision. I was informed of our visitors' intention to land. They did not give me a choice."

He paused, as if he was waiting for objections. But the council never spoke until he was done.

"I had to act quickly. I decided to be gracious."

Beta nodded its shiny silver head. "Whatever you feel is best for the station."

The other companions added nothing.

While all the companions that worked within the station had been given independent neural pathways (and, in theory, independent thought) as a part of this station's original objective, they most often deferred to their human counterparts. Even these three, designed to lead the others, would only express a preference if addressed directly.

"Well," Fuest continued, "we will have to see what is best after we talk to these newcomers. But until then, we are to consider them as friends."

Jon, the oldest of the three youngsters—the doctor still thought of them that way, even though all three of them were over twenty—raised a hand. "Is there anything you wish any of us to do?"

"I've given them the proper coordinates and guidance to land. I believe we should let them do this on their own, and see their subsequent actions. If they are as friendly as my wireless communication has indicated, I would suggest that you lead a small delegation to greet them and bring them up here. Once we determine their intentions—as best we can—we'll see about letting more of them visit, and what they might give to us."

"Are you thinking of going home?" Laea asked.

"I'm thinking of many things," the doctor replied. "But I'm not committed to anything until we see our visitors a bit more closely.

As I said, Jon will meet them once they've climbed from their ships. The rest of you should go to your emergency stations, as we've practiced."

Vin grinned at that, looking maybe half his age. "I never thought we'd do this for real!"

The doctor smiled back. "Well, let's hope this is not too real." He looked directly at each of the companions. "Beta, Gamma, Epsilon, do you have anything you would like to add?"

The three looked at each other, as if they were silently conferring. Beta looked back to the doctor.

"As always, we are here to assist you."

Fuest nodded. "Very good. They will be here shortly. To your stations, please."

All six left quickly. Fuest found himself alone again—alone with far too many thoughts.

Maybe he could go home. Maybe he could turn the station over to others.

Maybe he should ask Vin to place himself closer to the field, in case Jon needed any help. He would have to give the young men a call.

Maybe he never needed to be alone again.

Laea thought she was all alone. She almost jumped when her younger brother came around the corner.

"What are you doing here?" Vin demanded.

"I'll stay out of the way," was the first thing she thought to say. "I know I'm supposed to be down in the records room" was the second. She stared at Vin for a second. "Aren't you supposed to be somewhere else, too?"

He grinned at that. "They couldn't keep me away either. I think I convinced them that I'm needed. I'm supposed to watch from a safe distance, and come and join the newcomers if I get the right signal from Jon."

Laea stared at the young man. "I didn't hear anything."

Vin grinned, looking at his feet. "The doctor called me. He spoke to me a few minutes after we had our meeting."

Laea thought of things she might say. In the original plans—the ones they had practiced a hundred times—the doctor thought any visitors would feel more comfortable with a human. But only one. With only four humans left on the station, they didn't want to take any unnecessary risks.

Until now.

Nobody told her anything! She was always left out, the one to be protected.

She guessed that was why she was always looking for secrets. And why she would never show her true feelings.

"What do you think they're going to do?" she said, just to say something.

"They're probably as worried about us as we are about them. Wouldn't you want to see what a new world had to offer before you started shooting it to bits?"

He led her over to the secondary hangar doors.

Two of the companions stood to either side, two of the heavy lifters, the modified soldiers. She had never seen any of them in the old hangars before. She imagined, back when ships came and went on the landing field, this type of companion often worked here. They had even stored ships in these hangars for a time. She knew from the doctor's stories that a couple of disabled vessels had been left behind in this very room. They had long ago been disassembled for parts. Now these vast rooms might once again store people and ships from other worlds. It reminded her how much things might change.

Vin saw her watching the large metal companions. Close to ten feet tall, standing between the humans and daylight, they cast huge shadows on the far wall.

"The doctor's taking no chances," he said.

This seemed to be far more complicated than she had ever imagined.

The sirens started.

"The ships are coming in." Vin pointed up into the sky, high over the heads of even the companions. "Look! There they are, flying side by side." Laea looked up, and did indeed see two small metal craft, both trailing flame from their rear engines, as they circled the landing field.

"They look like old Viper Mark Ones!" Vin was jumping up and down, no longer able to contain his excitement. "I didn't know anybody still flew that sort of thing."

Laea nodded as though she knew what he was talking about. She had heard of Vipers, but never imagined there were different types of the same craft. She had never paid that much attention to something she never imagined she would see.

"Man, look at the way they're coming down! Would I love to fly one of those things!"

The two Vipers angled sharply down, their engines silent. They were on what looked like a collision course with the science center on the far side of the field.

"They're probably trained to come in like this—fast and steep—to make a harder target."

"Target?" Laea replied blankly.

"Hey, not everyone's as welcoming as Station *Omega*. Who knows what else these guys have found out here?"

The two Vipers cut the angle of their descent, swooping just over the top of the science building to land, side by side, at the center of the strip.

The sirens stopped. Laea realized she had barely heard them in these last minutes.

"Our visitors have arrived safely." The doctor's voice came over the station's wireless. *"Let's give them a minute to look around before we go out and meet them."*

The Vipers sat there for a long moment. Laea could see waves of heat coming from the rear of each craft.

"They must still be waiting for hostile fire," Vin guessed.

"Or maybe they're talking with their ship, asking for direction. The doctor said we should give them a minute." Even Laea was getting impatient, waiting for the first sight of their visitors.

"They're opening their cockpits!" Laea saw the central section of each Viper lift away, revealing a single pilot in each craft. They paused a moment more, then both men—she was quite sure they were men—pushed themselves out of their seats and onto the wings of their craft, and from there onto the hard, paved landing field itself.

Laea realized how big this really was.

Outside of the three men on the station, these were the first people she had seen since she had been a small girl. People, new people, with more in orbit, maybe just minutes away. Two out of maybe a dozen or more—how big was their ship? Two who could take them all to see millions more, all the way back to the Colonies.

"They're holding something in their hands," Vin said, stepping closer to the window to get a look. "Are those guns?"

The two companions were instantly alert. They pressed themselves between Vin and the doorway.

"Please step away," they said in unison. "We do not wish you to be harmed."

"What's happening?"

Laea saw someone moving across the landing area. It was hard to get a good look with the two companions blocking their way.

"Where's Jon?"

"We are obeying the original protocols," the companions informed them. "We are protecting the station."

Somebody was shouting. The newcomers? They sounded frightened. She heard gunfire.

She saw more movement on the field. These new arrivals were companions, all former soldiers like the two guarding their door. The guards shifted, and she could see the humans for an instant, surrounded by others.

"No!" she shouted. This wasn't the way it was supposed to begin. They were going to talk. The ship was going to take them home. "Put down your guns! We won't hurt you!"

But she was on the far side of the door. Even if the door had been open, the two on the landing platform were much too far away to hear.

She heard another burst of gunfire, another scream. She could see nothing but a mass of companions, blocking her view of both Vipers and pilots.

She squirmed between the two guards.

"Stop it!" Laea called out as she flung open the door. "Stop it! Stop it!"

The companions didn't respond.

She had never felt so helpless.

"The Vipes are entering the atmosphere."

Griff's voice pulled the captain from his reverie, but only for an instant.

Nadu was tired of waiting. He had waited all his life.

He had said it so many times: he no longer knew what he was looking for. But when it was right, he'd feel it.

His humming grew louder. He had spent almost all his life as a raider, but for years he had only been a member of one of half a dozen crews. He remembered the day it had changed, fifteen years back.

He was crewing for the *Crusher* then, with a bunch that made the *Lightning*'s crew look a bit like gentlemen. And that was before it all fell apart.

Ah, but it had been a glorious fall. The men and women of the *Crusher* were no longer on their best behavior. They had found an ancient drug, not seen since the Cylon War.

Scavengers were never good at restraint. It would have been far better if the crew had not dipped into the supply. It would have been the height of wisdom if Nadu had not sampled it himself. He had almost lost it all to Crystal Blue.

They had found it on a moon with one lone settlement, a deserted chemical plant. Their captain at the time was overjoyed. Crystal Blue. Highly addictive, it was a license to make money. It had been outlawed on the Colonies for years, but here were barrels of the stuff—close to ten thousand doses.

Crystal Blue. Some said the Cylons created it, to drive men mad.

Crystal Blue. They were scavengers. They could take anything. Especially if you could snort it right into your system.

It was boring in space—days and days of emptiness and the cold light of distant stars. They were not disciplined like the *Lightning*'s crew. They needed something to fill the time. At first, it gave them visions. Later, it gave them pain. They only found how difficult it was to kick after nearly everyone had sampled their wares.

Their captain had tried to keep the Blue to sell back in civilization. The crew, already heavily addicted, thought otherwise. They had fought each other for the Blue, and destroyed their own ship in the process.

Thank the gods they were on the edge of the commerce lanes when the explosion had occurred. And that he had had enough sense to walk away when the glass exploded in his face. It had destroyed half his face, but the pain had pulled him away from the Blue, and forced him to think. It had saved his life. He had made it to the pod before the fire used up all the breathable air—a pod with food and water and oxygen, but not a speck of Crystal Blue.

Nadu had spent two weeks in that escape pod without the drug. Two weeks that had felt like forever, two weeks of searing pain, from the lacerations on his face and the need within his blood. He had nowhere to go, nothing to do. That was when he had first taught himself the song. The song pulled the desire from his blood and threw it out into the open air to be sucked away by the recycling units. The song pulled the need from his brain and scattered it in the space between the stars.

Crystal Blue. When he was finally rescued, he realized he could live without it. He had to live without it. Thousands and thousands of doses were destroyed with the *Crusher* and its crew. The formula was forbidden, lost in the Cylon War. There was not a day he didn't think about tasting it again. But he could stay free so long as he could sing.

The need nearly made him crazy for good. He had been crazy when he was under its spell. Sometimes he could still feel the Blue singing in his blood. Especially when they were on the edge of something. He hummed to cover up the Crystal's tune. He sang when the humming was no longer enough.

The Blue had left him with a never-ending song, a song that robbed him of sleep, but made him clever. He had found new ways to rob and cheat, new ways to finance just what he would need.

Within a year of his accident, Nadu had gone back into space with a crew of his own. A crew that his song had chosen, a crew that would complete the celestial music promised by the Blue and give Nadu all that he would ever need.

Nadu could use that idealism. It could cover up a multitude of sins.

A burst of static pulled Nadu back from his thoughts.

"Sorry, Captain," Griff said. "Having a bit of a problem getting our signals through the atmosphere. Might be a storm getting in the way." He made some adjustments to the board. "That should help. Vipes! Please repeat!"

"This is Vipes One." Twitch's voice came over the speakers, the static low behind his words. *"We are making our final approach. This is quite a complex here. It's the size of a small city. We're each flying around in half a circle to see what we can see. Maybe we can get you a visual."*

"I'll try to throw it on the forward screen." Griff punched a series of buttons and the screen overhead brightened. They could make out a whole series of towers rushing toward the camera. Vipes One still had its forward camera intact. Or so the theory went. But the picture didn't seem much better than the audio signal. It rolled, with bright lines flashing through the image, giving them little more than a vague sense of a city on the screen. Two many repairs on the reconditioned Vipers, Nadu guessed. Unless something was blocking their signals from below? Griff shut off the screen.

"I've got some signs of an explosion here," Symm's voice cut in. *"Looks substantial, like they lost a dozen buildings. I guess this was the accident, huh?"*

"*Everything on this end looks brand new,*" Twitch added. "*Except I don't see any people. In fact, I don't think I see anybody outside at all.*"

"*They wouldn't be scared of us, would they?*" Symm said with a laugh.

Maybe the research staff was showing more sense than Nadu gave them credit for.

"Remember, boys," Griff reminded them, "they haven't seen outsiders in thirty years. They're probably scared of their own shadows."

"*We'll give them something to be afraid of, hey?*" Twitch replied.

Both the pilots laughed at that.

"We don't know what we're going to do here," Griff replied calmly. "Just because we don't see much in the way of defenses doesn't mean that they don't have any. We may actually need to negotiate to take on some cargo. We go in easy here, and polite."

"Or you'll answer to the captain!" Nadu shouted from his chair.

"*Aye, sir!*" A command from Nadu made everyone polite.

The static was getting louder again. Griff frowned as he tried to adjust the filters on his control board.

"*We see the landing area. Vipes One is going in first.*"

"*I'm circling around to join you, Twitch!*"

Another burst of static, drowning a half-dozen words.

"*I can see him on the ground,*" Symm's voice broke through. "*I'm about to follow.*"

Twitch's voice followed. "*Welcome down, Symm. I see some activity, Captain. We've got a door opening at the far side of the field. I think we're going to see our hosts.*"

A huge burst of static forced Griff to turn down the feed. He slowly increased the volume.

"*Captain! You won't believe this!*" The words were shouted through the interference. They could hear the two pilots talking but couldn't make out any more of the words.

"*Ask him!*" Symm demanded.

"*Captain, they're not—*" Twitch began.

"*Oh, gods!*" Symm screamed.

Twitch's voice answered. "*I'm getting out of here.*"

They heard some more shouting, and then everything was drowned in the static. The Comm officer reduced the volume again. They heard no more voices.

Griff looked down at his controls. "Both Vipes are still planetside. Neither one has taken off."

"What the hell happened?" Nadu asked.

"Maybe it's time to ask our hosts." Griff keyed a new set of controls. "Research Station *Omega*! We have lost contact with our pilots. Please respond."

"*Warning!*" the mechanical voice announced over the speakers. "*Do not approach! We are under quarantine! Disobeying this command will result in serious consequences! Per order of the Colonial Science Protectorate!*" It was the damned tape loop, all over again! "*Warning! Do not approach! We are—*"

"I think we've just given up on the polite approach," Nadu said softly.

CHAPTER 8

Doctor Villem Fuest was beyond angry.

"How could this happen!"

"They had weapons, Doctor," Epsilon replied in its emotionless voice. "All of our models have protocols for proper procedure when weapons are involved. The protection of this station and its occupants is our primary purpose."

"It was very bad," Jon agreed. "I didn't even have a chance to get out there before they started shooting."

"Three of the companions were slightly injured in the altercation," Beta added. "All can be easily repaired. There should be no disruption of basic services."

"But what of the pilots?" the doctor demanded. "What happened to them?"

It was Gamma's turn to talk. "The pilots were subdued. They were slightly damaged, but nothing happened to them that would be life-threatening."

"So we may be able to get out of this after all. We don't know who these people are or what kind of firepower they have at their disposal. I was hoping—at best—for an exchange of ideas, and maybe a chance to send a message home. I did not expect a war." He turned to Epsilon. "Now where are the prisoners? I need to talk to them at once!"

"It may take a short time before—" the warrior model began.

"Doctor!" Vin called from the far side of the room. "We have a new wireless communication from the *Lightning*!"

"I had best respond to this." The doctor looked at all three companions. "Make certain the prisoners are kept as comfortable as possible. If we can give them back to the *Lightning*, perhaps we can save this visit."

He was never good under pressure. Somehow, if he didn't want more bloodshed, he would have to rise to the occasion. *Oh, Betti*, he thought. *If only I had your way with words.*

"Let's hear what the *Lightning* has to say," he said to Vin.

Griff didn't like this one bit. He opened the same wireless channel he had used before.

The research station might be broadcasting that repeating garbage, but that didn't mean they couldn't receive a signal.

"Station *Omega*. We have lost contact with our pilots. Where are our pilots?"

He knew the look on his captain's face. He'd initiated this contact on his own. This wouldn't be the first time he had kept Nadu from killing everyone in sight.

"Station *Omega*. This is Cruiser *Lightning*. Repeat. We have lost contact with our pilots. Respond, or we will take retaliatory action."

Nadu stared at him. "You actually expect them to have some frakking response?" He waved to others on deck. "Load the forward missiles. They'll get more polite once we've blown up a building or two."

Griff ignored his captain, still trying for a response. "Station *Omega*. If we do not receive a response, we will consider this an act of war. You will be fired upon."

The warning loop, which Griff had kept playing faintly in the background, cut out abruptly. Griff turned up the volume on the incoming feed.

"*Cruiser* Lightning, *this is Station* Omega." The familiar voice of the doctor cut through the static. "*Our apologies. I'm afraid we've had a little misunderstanding.*"

Well, that was a polite way to put it. Griff replied, "Station, we want to speak to our pilots. Now."

"*Cruiser* Lightning. *Those were fighters you sent down. Our defense protocols are a little primitive, I'm afraid. They have a programmed response to any ships that might pose a threat. Your pilots and their ships were both . . . neutralized before I could intervene. But no harm has come to your pilots or their ships.*"

Griff glanced at Nadu. The captain glared back without response. That was Griff's job now.

"If our pilots are unharmed, we need to speak to them."

It took the doctor a moment to respond. *"I'm sure you can, in a short time. I'll have to get them patched into our wireless network. They are being held in a separate facility. When last I saw them, they were quite incoherent."*

"What have they got down there?" Nadu asked softly. Griff knew exactly what he was thinking. Symm and Twitch were usually ready to take on a dozen armed men with their bare hands.

Griff opened the wireless channel again.

"What aren't you telling us, *Omega*? We have a full complement of weapons. If we suspect any foul play, we will not hesitate to use them."

Another moment of silence.

"Oh dear," the doctor's voice finally replied. *"That would be most distressing. There are other matters I need to bring up to you, about our companions. I think your men had a reaction—"*

Griff cut him off. He didn't have the time to listen to the doctor's ramblings. "Let us talk to our pilots, and we can work this out. Otherwise . . ." Griff let the rest of the sentence hang.

"No, no. Please, you told me you'd send somebody a bit more—diplomatic. That was your term, wasn't it? I'm sure we can work everything out. Now that I've seen the protocols, I can shut them down. The same thing won't happen twice, I assure you. I'll meet the next transport personally."

Griff glanced at the captain again. This time, Nadu nodded his agreement. It was Griff's call, then.

"Very well. We'll send down a team of three in a landing transport. You'll be talking with a young man who has my full confidence—Tom Zarek."

"No," the captain cut in loudly. "We will also send an escort. Two more Vipers, prepared to blast your station to rubble at the first sign of anything questionable. Do you understand?"

"Understood." The doctor paused, then added, *"I really don't think—"*

Griff cut him off mid-sentence. "We will want them to see the pilots first. As soon as our transport lands. Do you agree?"

The doctor paused a moment before answering again. *"I'm—I'm sure we'll work everything out."* He sounded overwhelmed.

Griff almost felt sorry for the doctor. "No doubt. You're here alone on the edge of space. I imagine you can't be too careful, hey? Do you agree?"

"I'll make sure the pilots are ready to talk. If you could give me a little time—"

"Our diplomatic mission will meet you very shortly. We are quite concerned about the health of our men. I'm sure you understand. I will open a channel again when we launch the transport. Please be ready. Cruiser *Lightning* out."

Griff cut the connection. He looked up to the captain. "So?"

"You didn't give him a choice," Nadu answered with the slightest of smiles. "We'll get our men. Maybe we can get them without too many of their people being killed."

Griff still didn't have the best feeling about all of this. "What do you make of this doctor who seems to run things?"

The captain shook his head. "He doesn't run things very well."

"He sounds a bit like a fool," Griff agreed. "Or someone in way over his head."

"He may lack experience in this. It would take a certain amount of brains and guts to work on a station way out here. I don't know exactly who we are dealing with here, but I do not think they are fools."

Griff thought the captain was right. This might not be quite so easy a jaunt as they had thought.

"Maybe they're just being cautious," he suggested. "Maybe they're planning to use our pilots as hostages to force our good behavior."

Nadu let out a short bark of a laugh. "Let's hope it's that interesting. It would amuse me to do a little negotiating."

It was Griff's turn to laugh. Last time somebody tried to bargain with him, the captain had finished the negotiated exchange and then promptly shot everyone on the other side.

"I agree with you," Nadu added abruptly. "Zarek's best for the job."

"Out of our available talent?" Griff shrugged. "He's young. He can think on his feet. He's expendable."

"It's the first law of scavengers. With great risks come great rewards. Besides, we haven't really even broken him in."

Compared with most of those on board, Zarek was barely a part of the crew. And there were always other young men looking for opportunity.

This would be his first test. Tom was a survivor. He would find his way through this. Griff would be surprised if young Zarek didn't outlast them all.

Captain Nadu started his tuneless humming once more, then

abruptly stopped. "We'll send him out on his peace mission. And we'll get the rest of them ready for war."

He waved at Griff.

"Call another general meeting. I think we need to build a little fire underneath our crew."

CHAPTER 9

FREE CRUISER *LIGHTNING*

Before this, Tom Zarek realized, he had never seen his captain truly angry.

Nadu's scarred face seemed to glow in the subdued light of the control room, his cross-hatched flesh twitching with a ruined energy.

Zarek had barely gotten back to his bunk before they had sounded another "all hands." The remaining crew had all scrambled back to the control center. Griff had singled him out, and told him to step forward and stand by the comm station.

Griff scanned the room, silently counting the crewmembers. "We're all here, then? I'm afraid we have a bit of a problem." He nodded to the captain. Nadu paced about his station at the center of the room, glaring first at one cluster of the crew, then another, so that his good eye had scanned all of them in turn.

No one else spoke. They all knew when not to cross their captain.

"They have captured Symm and Twitch." Nadu grimaced, as though just saying the words brought him pain. "Well, they *say* they are being detained. They give me double talk about problems with their defenses."

He turned and slammed his fist down on the control console before him.

"They want to play Nadu for a fool." His tone said that was a mistake. "They say they have technical difficulties!" His voice was rising with every sentence. He stopped to take a ragged breath.

"They're trying to keep us in the dark," Griff said into the silence. "They have their own agenda."

Nadu turned to stare at the comm officer, clenching and unclenching the fist that he had so recently slammed into his controls. Zarek realized his knuckles were bleeding.

"My second in command makes a valid point," Nadu said softly. He looked like he would kill Griff anyway. "Perhaps we should drop a few missiles to light our way."

"That would jeopardize our pilots," Griff replied in equally measured tones. "Our men are in their hands. We hope for their sake that they are still alive. They claim they have made a mistake."

When Nadu didn't reply, he added, "At least they are still talking to us."

Griff looked out to the assembled crew. "The rest of you did not witness our pilots' landing. It's quite a facility they have down there. But at the very last minute, we lost our visual feed. We heard a few shots fired."

"Shots?" asked Grets, the woman who acted as both ship's cook and doctor.

"A few," Griff replied. "No prolonged gun battles. We pray they were not executed."

"That would be a foolish thing to do. Let us hope they were just detained. We would not want them to be lying to us." Nadu smiled broadly. It was a frightening sight. "I will now tell you all what we will do."

Nadu paused to look at every single person in the room. "We have men missing. We never have men unaccounted for. We will find our missing pilots. And if our new friends have done anything to our pilots, they will be very sorry. They do not frak with Nadu!" He pounded his bloody hand on a second console, grunting with the pain.

"We are to assume—until they convince us otherwise—that the inhabitants of this place are not to be trusted."

The ship was full of stories of how Nadu had outwitted another bunch of scavengers, or traders, or even whole Colonies. Maybe, Zarek realized, this was why the captain was so angry. The stories always had a common thread—how Nadu would say one thing and plot another. It was almost as if Nadu were looking in a mirror. He had had his own double-dealing techniques used against him.

"But, if they are to be believed, we are the first outsiders they have seen in decades. They need us, for supplies, for news from home." He smiled again. "Maybe they're even looking for a way back home! We will use everything we can to bargain."

"Five of you will be going down," Griff said. "We're calling this a peace mission. You will give them a chance to explain their actions. And remember, any shooting could damage potentially lucrative merchandise."

"Exactly," Nadu agreed. "But if anyone makes a move against you, feel free to kill them."

"Perhaps we should locate our pilots before we get too aggressive," Griff replied.

Nadu stared at his second in command. "Perhaps."

"Five are going," Griff repeated.

"We need someone who can think on his feet." Nadu pointed at Tom. "Zarek. You can talk as well as anyone. I'm putting this second landing under your control. But watch everything."

So that was why he had been asked to step forward. This was the first time he'd been entrusted with anything of importance. He had tagged along on a few exploratory missions, and Griff would let him fill in on the comm board in off-hours, but until now he thought that Nadu barely knew his name.

"Yes, sir," he managed.

"Get our men back. That's your primary goal. Then you can talk to the people down at the station, see what they want. See what they have to offer. Oh, and see what they're trying to keep for themselves. Don't promise them a thing. For anything final, you have to talk to me."

"Yes sir."

"We'll keep a channel open with the lander. If any questions—or any difficulties—arise, there'll be somebody on the other end you can talk to."

"Sounds good, sir."

Nadu actually clapped him on the shoulder.

"Zarek, if you do well on this, you'll get a bonus." The captain smiled. "If not—well, no one will miss a junior member of the crew."

Nadu pointed at different members of the crowd. "You'll take the lander. And bring the Creep along. You and you will pilot the escort."

"Remember, I want seven of you back here." He looked at everyone crammed into the corners of the room.

"The rest of you are dismissed."

Zarek saw flashes of relief on the others' faces. Nobody expected this was going to be an easy ride.

But this was what he had signed up for. If he handled this well, he might get the sort of reward he was looking to get out of this.

He watched the crew retreat through the hatches. Tom realized he didn't know exactly who else was on the mission until the crowd thinned out. Well, everybody knew the Creep, a tall, skinny man who seldom spoke and always dressed in gray. They said he could get in and out of anything before the other guys knew he was there. That's why he had the name.

It grew very quiet. The control center had emptied of all but the senior staff and the five going out. Zarek could hear the soft mechanical pings and whirs of the various boards that managed the ship. He nodded to the other men who would go out with him on the mission. Their pilot would be Boone—he generally took out the larger ships. He was an affable guy, always willing to show Zarek the ropes. Tom would be glad to have him along. Slam and Ajay would be escorting them down in the old Mark One Vipers. Zarek liked both of them better than the two idiots—Symm and Twitch—that bunked across from him. He wondered if they would ever really get them back, and realized he didn't miss those two in the least.

The replacement Viper pilots were both fairly new on the crew. Zarek thought Ajay had logged only a couple more months here than he had. Maybe they hadn't had time yet to grow into proper idiots.

Griff talked to them first. "We expect you to pay attention down there. This is the most—" He paused to search for the word. "—rewarding job we've had in a long time. This could be a big payday if we handle it right."

"You'll be taking weapons." Nadu spread his arms wide. "Big guns, which I expect you to wave around a bit. They bring us Twitch and Symm, we'll make nice. Until then, watch your step."

Zarek realized that, with two crewmen going down the first time and five down the second, the captain was committing almost half his crew to this venture. Nadu wouldn't be turning back from this one. One way or another, he would get his payday.

"Any questions?" Griff asked.

Nobody dared to ask anything.

"We've got two of our own to rescue," Nadu announced. "I want you out of here now." With that, he returned to his command console. As if he didn't want to see them again until the job was done.

Tom Zarek left with the others. All five went straight up to the launch bay.

Boone looked to the storage lockers that surrounded the bay. "Let's take anything we think we can use. Guns, grenades, survival gear. I'm going to take seven suits in the lander. If we have to, we'll cram everyone in together to get back here."

The lander was large enough to normally seat five. It carried atmosphere suits and rations to last a full crew for two weeks. It was as close to an escape vehicle as the *Lightning* had. What would Nadu do if they didn't come back? If it came to that, Tom imagined the captain would crash the *Lightning* into the research station, killing the rest of the crew just to get back at whoever crossed him on this planet.

And how did Tom feel about this? He couldn't afford feelings. He was in this until the end.

Boone and the Creep loaded their arms with whatever weapons they found to hand. Zarek grabbed an extra pair of suits—with their bulk, two suits was all he could manage. Boone climbed in through the hatch and told the others to pass him everything. No one else entered his boat until he had everything in place.

Boone popped his head back out after a moment. "We still got some room." He waved at the pilots. "Ajay. Bring me a couple of extra cases of rations. That sort of thing has trading value."

The Vipes pilot frowned as he lifted the supplies. "Shouldn't we ask someone before we take all of this?"

"Do you want to talk to the captain again? Besides, if its down here, it's surplus. It means the stores up in the galley are full."

Boone took the cases from the pilot and disappeared inside.

"Almost ready," he said when he appeared again. "One more thing." He pointed into the far corner of the room. "Zarek, open the locker all the way down on the left."

Zarek went over and tried the locker door. It was stuck.

"Kick it a couple times!" Boone called. "Can't have people getting at it too easy. It's my own private stash."

Zarek banged the bottom of the locker with his boot. The metal door swung free. The locker was mostly empty, with only a small, ornately carved box on an upper shelf, while a battered case, stenciled with the words PROPERTY OF THE COLONIAL FORCES, lay at the bottom.

"See that case?" Boone asked loudly. "Bring it along."

Zarek pulled the case out of the locker. It was surprisingly heavy. He half carried, half dragged it over to the lander.

"It's an old survival kit we scavenged from our last stop," Boone explained as he waited. "I think it predates the war."

Tom hefted the case up to the hatch with a grunt. Boone wrestled it inside.

"We're looking for anything that will give us an edge." Boone continued to talk as he disappeared inside. "And, seeing how we have no idea what we're getting into, we're looking for anything. I figure an extra case of emergency gear can't hurt."

Zarek realized Boone was the one with the real experience around here. Why hadn't Nadu made him the leader of the expedition? Zarek was a fast talker, but he didn't have one tenth of Boone's savvy.

"Okay," Boone announced as he once again appeared. "I've got everything nailed down. You guys can come on in." He took a step back to let them in. "Let's do a quick check of our systems and get the frak on our way. The sooner we're out of the captain's sight, the better."

The Creep was first, sliding in front of Zarek before Tom could react. Zarek supposed the Creep would be a good man to have on his side. And, since he never talked, Tom could ignore him when he didn't need him.

He climbed into the lander last, and strapped himself into the co-pilot's seat. He liked to watch Boone at work. The pilot moved the lander up and down like it was just an extra pair of legs. He could put the pear-shaped vessel just about anywhere and not break a sweat.

He saw that the Creep was already in place. Sitting in the back, where he could watch everybody and everything. The Creep nodded when Zarek looked his way. Tom nodded back. It was the most communication he had ever had with the guy. Some people just really earned their nicknames.

Boone flipped the switch on the small wireless control in front of Zarek. "Lander to Vipes. Are you receiving?"

"Vipes Three, okay," came back.

"Vipes Four?" Boone asked. "Are you receiving?"

He got a burst of static. A voice cut in with a string of curse words. *"Oh!"* Ajay's voice remarked. *"I've got it now. Vipes Four, okay."*

Boone let out a heavy sigh. "You know, Tom, I have a dream. And in this dream I'm on a ship where everything works."

He laughed softly as he gently patted the controls in front of him.

"Guess it's good that's just a dream, huh? Well, we know this baby will get us there and back."

He flipped a dozen switches in order, three rows of four. "Wherever we're going, Vara will get us there."

Vara was Boone's own private name for the landing ship. Zarek grinned. Boone only used it around people he trusted.

Boone hit the comm control. "Command Center. This is Boone. All three ships are ready for deployment."

"This is Command," Griff's voice replied. *"You are cleared for takeoff."*

"Copy that, Control. Vipes Three. Vipes Four. We're going out. At two-minute intervals. Vipes first, Three then Four. The lander here will follow. Understood?"

"Understood and ready to roll."

Another burst of static. *"Understood! I can hear you fine."* Ajay cursed again. *"I'll just have to hit my wireless a few times if I need to talk back."*

"Perfect conditions, as usual." Boone shook his head. "Command Center, do you read? We are ready to begin the mission."

"*Acknowledge, Lander One,*" Griff's voice came back to them.

"Ready for launch," Boone replied. "Viper Three, Viper Four, Lander."

"*We copy your launch pattern. Launch pattern okay.*"

"*Get the frakkers!*" Nadu shouted in the background.

"Yes sir, Captain!" Boone replied. "Vipes Three, away!"

Zarek could feel the deck shake as the first Viper left its launchpad. The lander had a pair of larger windows, but they were both behind his seat, and a smaller window up front, between the DRADIS screen and the controls. But he was focused on Boone as the pilot got them off the ground.

A light in front of them changed from orange to white.

"Vipes Four, away!" Boone ordered.

The deck rumbled again.

Boone looked over at Zarek. "Brace yourself, Tom. We're going on a little adventure."

He watched Boone work the switches and dials, easing just a bit of force from the thrusters as he pulled back on the joystick. Early on, Zarek had flown a mission with Boone and had marveled at the way the pilot had smoothly and effortlessly maneuvered the lander. When Zarek told him what he thought, Boone had laughed, talking about how you had to know just what Vara needed. He had offered to give the younger man a few lessons when they could find the time. But both men had gotten busy in the weeks that followed, checking out their captain's "hunches"—wild ideas, that, Tom now realized, often led nowhere.

He actually half wished he had asked again about the offered lessons. Maybe, after all this was over, he'd find a way to make the time. In the meantime, he supposed he would just sit back and watch a master at work.

Captain Nadu and his hunches. Zarek thought about watching the two men in charge back in the Command Center. He could really see the way the two of them played off each other, Nadu reaching for the stratosphere, Griff hauling him back down. Whatever worked, he supposed. Nadu might be a little crazy, but the *Lightning* was well known as one of the richest scavenging crews around.

The lights changed again on the display before them.

"Lander One, away!" Boone called as he punched the thrusters, pushing the ship quickly down the launch chute and out into space.

"Well, that's it for a bit. When I get to the atmosphere, I'll give our hosts a call. I thought I'd get us off the ship. But you heard the captain. Once we land, Tom, it's all your show." He waved at the weapons, everything from handguns to what looked like a small cannon, which he had strapped against the walls. "They assure us everything will be fine. Nothing to worry about, hey boys?"

Tom tried to reply with a small laugh, but nothing much came out. The Creep was silent.

Boone checked his instruments. "One Research Station *Omega*, dead ahead. I don't even have to turn this thing. We'll settle down, gentle as a falling leaf."

Zarek was feeling confined by his chair. He turned to the pilot. "Mind if I take a walk?"

Boone grinned. "Go as far as you like. Nothing else we can do for a little while."

Zarek unbuckled his belt and rose from his seat. He looked around the craft as they pushed their way through space toward the planet below.

Unlike the Vipers, the lander had very limited armaments. Most landers of this type had none, but Nadu had customized Boone's Vara a bit by adding a couple of small guns with rapidly repeating fire, each gun positioned immediately below one of the lander's two windows. Zarek didn't think the captain was comfortable without everything having a couple of extra guns. The lander was designed for short hops planetside and had plenty of room for cargo, both below decks and here, where Boone had managed to secure anything they might need very close at hand. If something went bad, they did not lack for firepower.

Their wireless squawked to life. *"This is Research Station* Omega. *We detect three ships on our instruments. Are you the new party from the* Lightning?"

"And who else might we be?" Boone asked before he hit the reply switch.

"We are the new party," Boone replied, once he had turned on his mic. "One lander with a two-Viper escort."

"I see," the voice responded. Then nothing for a minute. *"We wish you could have waited a bit, so we could be a bit more prepared. I'm afraid we aren't much at protocol."* Another pause. *"Your pilots are fine. We do appreciate your concern. Once you have landed, we will explain everything."*

Boone raised his eyebrows and looked over at Zarek. This, Tom guessed, is my cue.

He took over the microphone.

"This is Tom Zarek. I'm the one you'll be talking with. We want to clear this up just as much as you do, I assure you. Give us our pilots and we'll just chalk this up to a misunderstanding. Maybe we can find something to trade. We can start over again, and find business that's mutually beneficial."

"*Thank you, Mr. Zarek. I am Doctor Fuest. I am sure, once you have seen our facility, that we can find much to talk about. Despite our earlier problems, I assure you we want nothing but positive results from our contact.*"

He paused, then added, "*I look forward to meeting you.*" Another pause before he added, "*Please wait by your ships. And don't be surprised by what you see. Appearances can be deceiving.*"

The signal went dead. Zarek stared at the apparatus before him.

"Maybe they're not used to talking on the wireless."

"It doesn't sound like they're very happy to see us," Boone added after a moment's thought. "It sounds like they're going to cross us all over again. Or maybe we've both spent far too much time with Captain Nadu."

They all laughed at that, even the Creep, more to release tension than to share any real humor.

"But they're letting us land," Tom said after another moment had passed. "I think I've calmed them down."

"You did that," Boone agreed. "I can see why they picked you to lead the mission. Even I believed what you were saying."

Zarek thought that Boone was the real leader here—the guy with the experience. He was only the front man—the vocal chords of the operation.

"Well, maybe we can find something of value without having to shoot anyone," Zarek said, not even believing the words himself. "We'll have to wait and see."

The pilot glanced up at his readouts.

"We are now entering planetary atmosphere," Boone announced. "We'll be down shortly." He glanced back at Zarek. "You'd better strap yourself in, Tom. We'll be hitting turbulence in a second."

Zarek nodded and strapped himself in next to the Creep, so he could look through the windows.

That was the last of their conversation.

Now that their destination was set, none of them wanted to talk. They were surrounded by the silence. Zarek watched the small disk of the planet grow through the portal, a patchwork of green and blue, not that different from his home world, Caprica.

The planet looked so peaceful. It looked like a place that would take easily to colonization. But only one small corner of the whole world had been touched, a gleaming silver city stuck between endless green jungle and deep blue sea.

He felt he couldn't breathe the air on Caprica. He had had to escape. Space was vast, and all around them. But instead of being trapped in an apartment in a city on a civilized world, he found himself in a tiny metal box smaller than any room he had ever lived in, crammed with people and supplies, on the wild fringes of space where there were no rules at all. Flying between the stars mostly made him want to walk again on solid ground.

Well, Zarek had always known this *Lightning* job was a short-term solution. There had to be something better after his run with scavengers. After this, he would do something that would make a difference, and make a name for Tom Zarek.

If he lived to see the end of this voyage.

He thought about the captain's mention of weapons fire. It was a sound, nothing more. Had it come from the Vipes pilots, the research station, or both?

The research station didn't trust them—quite wisely. He would expect them to arm themselves. And he had to find a way to keep them from using those weapons.

"Time to go to the party," Boone said into the silence. He hit a switch on the wireless.

"Research Station *Omega*. This is the landing party from *Lightning*, requesting permission to land."

He closed the channel and grinned back at the others. "As if they could do anything else."

"*Permission granted,*" a voice said from the station. "*Approaching craft! I repeat, please remain with your ships after landing. A party will come out to the landing platform to meet you. We had an unfortunate situation with your fellow crewmen. Please do not judge us before we have a chance to explain.*"

Zarek did not find any of this reassuring. He looked to Boone and the Creep. "I've been thinking. Maybe we shouldn't show the guns right away. We don't know what—or who—we're dealing with."

Nobody raised any objection.

"Keep the guns close," he continued. "But the captain said I should be diplomatic. So, before we do anything else, I'll try to talk them into giving us our guys." He thought again how he'd be just as happy if he never saw either of the Vipes pilots ever again.

"And maybe we can get them to give us a few other things, too."

The Creep spoke at last. "We'll let you make your statement. But where's the fun in cooperation? When I've got a gun, I like to use it." He shrugged as he looked at a rifle secured by his feet. "Maybe I can shoot a few of them on the way out."

"No, no, we got it," Boone assured Tom. "Talk first, shoot later. Pretty simple, huh?"

Zarek only wished it were.

Boone switched on the wireless.

"Research Station *Omega*. We're coming in."

CHAPTER 10

RESEARCH STATION *OMEGA*

Zarek watched as the two Vipers set down one after another on the empty expanse of the landing pad. He saw no signs of the earlier Vipers, or their pilots. Could they have been dragged into the large building at the far end of the field? Why, if the authorities here were going to return the pilots, had they gotten rid of their spacecraft?

The landing field, in fact, showed no signs of life at all. From the air, the station looked deserted, with whole parts of it in ruins. The landing field, though, was in perfect shape, with dark painted grids to help guide in ships from space. Ships they said they hadn't seen in years.

He supposed this was all the welcome they would get. What did he expect—"Welcome *Lightning*" banners?

Tom felt a tightness in his chest. He had to go out and meet these people, to smile one minute and be ready to shoot the next. Oh well. He guessed it would be good training in case he ever went into politics.

His jokes weren't helping his nerves. This was the first time, he realized, that he had been given actual authority. He wondered, absently, what his father would say about Tom if his son ever made something of himself, after all the times the old man had called him a failure? Would his father even recognize him?

And would it even matter?

Both the Vipers were down, each taxiing across the landing field, turning slightly, angling across the field, to leave a wide space between them. A space for Boone to land, so that the Vipers would have a clear shot if the locals tried anything.

Only now did Tom realize he hadn't spoken to his father in years. Bits of the life he thought he had left behind came back to him: fights with his father, mostly; the day he decided never to return to the university, he remembered that one well. But later things, too: his abortive attempt to get the kitchen workers to stand up to management; getting thrown out of his lodgings because he could no longer pay; the woman he'd met who knew a man who knew somebody that crewed for the *Lightning*. How young he seemed in all those memories.

He was a different person now. A better person. And he was going to survive this and more. He couldn't afford any doubts. His stint on the *Lightning* was going to send him on his way. He was going to end up richer than his wildest dreams.

Unless, of course, he ended up dead. Nadu had been quick to point out that everyone in the crew was expendable.

"Here we go into the fire," Boone said softly as he lowered his lander. He maneuvered the craft so that it swung in low, midway between the Vipes, then let it touch down and roll to a stop with barely a bump. The man was an artist.

Boone and the Creep both checked their weapons. Tom supposed he had better do the same. Both of the others carried big guns with rapid-repeat firepower; they could unload their hundred-shot magazines in little more than a minute. He carried only a sidearm—a pistol with a dozen shots. He was the peacemaker, after all. He planned to keep the sidearm under his coat, and pull it out only if things went very bad indeed. He lifted the gun and took mock aim at the hatch. The sidearm felt much heavier than he remembered it. Perhaps it was the planet's gravity. This world was close to the size of Caprica, while the ship's grav was usually set to Picon-normal—about eighty-five percent of what they'd find here. Or maybe the gun would always feel heavy with the potential targets waiting just outside.

He knew how to use this—he'd spent hours on simulated target practice down in *Lightning*'s cargo hold. He wondered what would happen when and if he had to shoot another human being.

He looked out the nearest portal. No one had emerged from any of the buildings to greet them. The field looked just as deserted as it had from the air.

What were the research people up to? Who knew what kind of weapons they hid in these buildings. Nadu's decisions didn't always follow the strict dictates of logic, but right now, this felt downright suicidal.

"If they're not going to talk to us, maybe we'd better talk among ourselves." Boone opened a wireless channel. "This is a secure channel. We're ready here. Vipes report your status."

"*Vipes Three ready,*" came back immediately.

They waited a moment, but heard nothing from Vipes Four.

"Ajay's still having trouble sending, I guess." Boone spoke into the mic. "Vipes. We're facing the unknown here. Tom thinks it would be a good idea to keep our weapons out of sight."

Zarek leaned forward to explain.

"Everybody!" he began clearly. "No matter what you see, unless we see a gun pointed at us, we don't raise our own. We keep them ready, but we do not use them until I give the signal. Our first priority is to retrieve the prisoners. We want to get everybody out of here in one piece—and alive."

"Do you copy, Vipes?" Boone added.

"*Vipes Three, copy.*"

This time, they heard a second burst of static. Vipes Four's answer?

They could only hope that Ajay was still receiving their signal.

"We've got a door opening!" the Creep called from his station by a window. "Three figures are coming out and walking toward us. Frak!"

"What's the matter?" Zarek asked. "Do they have weapons?"

The Creep glanced back at them. He looked even more pale than usual. "No weapons that I can see. But two of them aren't human."

"What?" Both Zarek and Boone moved across the lander to get a look.

"It can't be," Boone whispered.

But it was. A tall thin human walked between two machines—machines that looked like Cylons. They weren't the models used as warriors—seeing the military, Centurion Cylons would be as good as seeing a loaded gun. Zarek had been very young when the Cylons had left, but even he recognized that these were both domestic models—a Cylon Butler, maybe, and a Cylon Mechanic.

"I think Nadu needs to know about this." Boone moved quickly back to the wireless.

"Do we get the frak away from here?" the Creep whispered.

"And leave the pilots behind?" Boone called over his shoulder. "Nadu would have our skins."

"But—" the Creep began, but let his objections die. They all knew that, with Nadu, there were no extenuating circumstances.

Zarek tried to make sense of what he saw. At the end of the war, the Cylons had left for who knew where. Could it be that, when *Lightning* came to this outpost, they had actually found the edge of Cylon-controlled space? But then why would a human be walking with them? No, this was something new, something to do with this special research station.

Did their research here, far away from any civilized worlds, have to do with taming their former enemies? Or had the war completely passed this place by?

Zarek couldn't judge anything by appearances. Humans and Cylons, side by side. He felt like he was stepping back into history.

Boone came up behind him. "I sent a coded message out to the captain telling him we've got something strange. Something that looks like Cylons."

"No reply?"

"None yet. The last Vipers down here had their signal break up, didn't they? Some sort of atmospheric interference, maybe."

"Or maybe someone is jamming the signal." Tom nodded. He realized he didn't trust anything about this anymore. But he still had to finish his job. "Keep this ship ready to take off. I'm going to step outside. I think, if we want any hope of getting Symm and Twitch, we've got to show ourselves. But I don't want anybody more than a step or two away from his craft."

Boone returned to his station to tell the others.

"Vipes! We're going ahead with the meet. Tom will go out first. Then we'll all show ourselves. If possible, we'll negotiate for our pilots. If not—remember, wait for Tom's signal."

"When I wave both hands above my head," Zarek called over his shoulder, "get back in your flyers and go."

Both Zarek and Boone went to look out the portal. The Creep was right behind them. The three-member welcoming committee was halfway across the field.

"They told us not to judge by appearances," Tom said softly.

"Cylon technology might be worth a lot," the Creep added. "Didn't the toasters take almost all of it with them?"

"We're here just long enough to get Twitch and Symm," Tom said. "I think any other talk will happen later."

"Maybe we can send Nadu down instead," the Creep suggested.

Boone glanced at Zarek. "Yeah, I guess you've convinced us to stay. I really wish our captain was a little less crazy."

Tom nodded. "Open the hatch, Boone."

The pilot flipped the lever. The hatch popped open with a hiss.

Tom stepped out of the lander. What did you say to a man and two Cylons?

Viper Three popped open its cockpit. Slam stood up in the craft, his hands empty.

Tom saw no movement from the other Viper. But the three locals were well within hailing distance.

"Greetings!" he said in a loud, clear voice. "I'm Tom Zarek, from the independent cruiser *Lightning*. We're glad to finally meet you."

The man and the two Cylons stopped, maybe twenty paces away.

Tom walked forward slowly, putting some distance between himself and the lander. Behind him, he could see that both his crewmates had stepped just beyond the hatch, showing themselves to be empty-handed, but keeping their weapons within arm's reach.

Zarek could finally get a good look at the human in the center. He was a very thin, aged gentleman who held himself quite straight, in an almost military posture.

"You are Doctor Fuest?" Zarek asked as he continued to approach the three others.

"I am." The old man stared at him. He did not smile. "And I want to thank you first for not overreacting."

Zarek nodded to the mechanicals who flanked the old man. "I have to admit, I did not expect your friends."

Fuest nodded at that, and finally smiled. Mention of the Cylons, oddly, seemed to put him a bit more at ease. He waved at his metal escort. "I would wonder if anything like this exists anymore, back in the Colonies. We work with our friends here—or, as we call them, our companions. I know, they remind you of certain mechanical servants the Colonies once employed, but our society here is far different, perhaps unique in all of known space—if you knew these companions well, you would not be so afraid."

Was it that obvious? Zarek thought he had been hiding his emotions. He glanced around the landing area. The rest of the field still seemed empty. It certainly was strange, but no one had threatened them—yet.

But two people were missing here. Seeing the Cylons had thrown him off.

"We are here to receive our prisoners!" he called.

"Very well," the doctor called. "I will have them brought out. I want nothing but for this exchange to succeed."

So they would get Symm and Twitch? Perhaps he should take the final steps forward and greet the doctor more properly. Zarek smiled, and extended his hand.

"On behalf of the *Lightning*—" he began.

One of the Cylons—the Butler—stepped forward to block Tom's way.

Zarek heard a shout. He turned as the final Vipes popped its top. Ajay came out screaming.

"The Cylons run this place. They're everywhere. Get back! Get back! Get away from here!"

Boone shouted behind him. Zarek turned, and saw something silver moving across the field.

Ajay had a gun. He pulled out his machine rifle and started shooting.

"No!" Zarek shouted, but his protest was lost beneath the gunfire.

Doors flew open in the buildings to either side. Plates drew back on the landing field to show Cylons hidden beneath. And not just domestics. Zarek recognized those barrel bodies and snakelike arms. These were Centurions. They leapt from their hiding places, weapons aimed and ready.

Ajay was right. The real Cylons were now everywhere.

Fuest was shouting something, too, but Zarek couldn't hear it. He lifted his arms above his head—the signal to abort the mission.

No one was watching him anymore. It happened too quickly. The crew of the *Lightning* had been fired upon, and they were fighting back.

But only four crewmembers were firing guns. The Cylons seemed endless. Slam tumbled out of his cockpit as bullets ripped across his chest. Ajay's mouth opened as a bullet opened the back of his brain. Zarek looked back and saw that one of Boone's pants legs was drenched in blood. Both Boone and the Creep were hunched down low, using the lander for cover.

Maybe, Zarek thought, if he could get back to the lander, the three of them might still get away.

He realized no one was firing at him. No bullets flew around the group at the center of the field. Zarek was being protected by his proximity to Doctor Fuest.

He jumped forward, dodging the Butler, who now looked past him at the gunfire. Zarek could finally hear the doctor's voice.

"Stop it!" Fuest called to the Cylons at either side. When he saw Tom approach he shouted, "I don't want this any more than you."

Zarek saw one of the doctor's guardians out of the corner of his eye. The repair Cylon's wrenchlike hands reached for his throat. Tom ducked and rolled, straight toward the doctor's feet.

Zarek realized he had only one way out of this. He jumped up behind the doctor, pinning the old man's arms against his chest. Fuest was very thin, almost frail. Zarek lifted him off the ground and backed away, using the doctor as a shield.

Fuest didn't struggle. "What are you doing?" the doctor called over his shoulder.

"If I don't do this, I'm dead," Zarek shot back.

Fuest shook his head. "No, no, the companions will listen to me. I can stop them."

"Like they're listening to you now?"

"It was working so well before you came. I can't understand . . ." The doctor's voice trailed off as his two guardians rushed to follow Tom.

"Stay back!" Fuest called to the machines. "We can find some reason here!"

The machines didn't seem to listen.

"This can't be happening," the doctor mumbled. "This can't be happening."

Now Fuest was the one who looked really afraid.

Zarek backed up, with the old man stumbling after him.

He could hear the whine of gunfire in his ears. Boone and the Creep seemed to be holding their own against the Cylons. Zarek flinched as a shot buzzed past his head. A couple of the bullets were close, but for some reason, the Cylons seemed to value the doctor.

Maybe he was right, Tom thought, and these "companions" of his were different. Maybe they were slightly more selective killing machines.

The gunfire stopped abruptly as Tom reached the lander.

Boone looked up at him from where the pilot crouched against the ship. "Do you think we've given them enough chance to talk?"

Zarek nodded to the doctor. "I've brought a little protection with us. They don't want him hurt. Maybe we can talk to him after we've loaded all of us back on the lander."

Boone grinned. "That's why Nadu picked you to be the leader."

"Hey, it never hurts to have a hostage," the Creep agreed. "Watch out!"

Zarek turned, and realized the Cylons had stopped firing so that they could close in on foot. Half a dozen of the things towered over them. Boone rolled onto his back and shot one of the Centurions point blank, severing its head from its neck. But a pair of Cylons pushed past their fallen comrade. Four arms came down on Boone's body, knocking the gun from his hands and crushing his chest. Other arms were pulling the doctor from Zarek's grip. Still holding onto the old man, he used the Cylon's weight to swing himself around toward the lander, diving through the hatch.

"Creep!" Tom yelled. "Get in here!"

A Cylon arm darted through the hatchway, grabbing for him. Zarek grabbed a rifle from the floor and clubbed at the thing until it withdrew. He hit the hatch controls. Other metal arms banged against the door as it sealed closed.

The Cylons had crushed Boone. The Creep had to be dead, didn't he?

He moved to the window. He saw nothing but Cylons, three in a pile where he had last seen the Creep, the rest surrounding the now still form of Doctor Fuest.

Wait! He saw someone else moving, over by one of the Vipers. None of the machines noticed. The Cylons' attention was focused elsewhere.

Somehow, Slam was on his feet out there, climbing back into the cockpit of his Vipes.

Tom jumped back to the wireless. "Vipes Three! This is Zarek! Let's get the hell out of here."

Slam's voice came through a moment later. *"Glad to hear there's somebody else alive. Follow me out, huh? I'll get us back to Lightning."* He made a sound that was half laugh, half cough. *"Then I've got to see the doc."*

Tom looked at the rows of controls before him. He realized he had to fly this thing. Zarek mimicked what he had seen Boone do only hours ago, flipping the twelve switches. He felt the engines come to life beneath his feet. The screen before him showed the Viper launching from the far side of the field. He eased the stick forward, worried he would fall too far behind.

The lander lurched off the ground as the Viper roared into the air.

Something pinged off the lander's shell. The Cylons were firing at him! He doubly wished the Creep was here now, to lay down some return fire.

He'd just have to follow Slam home.

The next few minutes were pure nightmare.

Zarek managed to get the lander in the air, copying Boone's movements as best he could remember. But the squat ship jerked and rolled. He had to right the craft or he'd crash right back down into the landing field.

He grabbed the stick and tugged. The lander righted itself—and it was rising! He could still see the Vipes in the distance, though it was far smaller than the last time he had looked.

But they were free of the base! Now, if he could just stay on the Viper's tail . . .

The stick wouldn't stay in one place. He had trouble keeping the lander flying in a straight line. It dipped again, swooping down toward the planet before he got it heading back aloft.

He looked back to the screen, hoping he could still see Slam's Vipes. He saw something else instead.

Another, bigger ship was showing up on his screen. It blotted out one quarter of the view. That thing had to be close to the size of a Battlestar—maybe even larger. Where the hell had that come from?

He flipped on the wireless. "Vipes Three! Slam! What's going on?"

"Incoming fire! I've got some monster ship on my tail! Trying evasive maneuvers."

The transmission cut off abruptly.

The lander shook. Tom was tossed out of the chair, jamming his shoulder against one of the guns still strapped to the wall. He pulled himself up to look out the window.

In the distance, where the Vipes had been flying, he saw only a ball of flame. And above the flame was some huge, dark object that took up a large part of the sky.

Frak getting back to the *Lightning*, Zarek thought. He was headed straight toward that thing. Whatever had gotten Slam was going to get the lander next. He had to make his tiny ship less of a target.

He crawled back to the controls and cut the engines. Without a heat signature, maybe the lander would become invisible to the monster ship above.

The lander, not yet free of the planet's gravity, stopped its ascent and began to fall, slowly at first, toward the surface far below.

He looked at the controls. If he could cut in the thrusters at the last minute, maybe he could cushion the landing enough to keep both the ship and himself from getting hurt without giving too much of a signal to his enemy. That was a big maybe. But if he could do it, once the huge ship had disappeared from the sky, he could still find some way to get back to the *Lightning*.

The systems were still working. He needed to open the wireless and let Nadu know what was down here.

He decided he had to risk a short message on the ship's secure frequency.

He flipped the SEND switch, and spoke quickly:

"We were attacked. They have a warship in orbit. I'm the only one who got out, and I can't see a way of getting back to the *Lightning*. Captain, the base was crawling with Cylons!"

He was coming in at an angle. He'd have to wait and use the forward thrusters to cushion his fall. He remembered—vaguely—how Boone had held the stick as he prepared to land.

Zarek hoped he could remember a lot more.

He tried to figure out where the lander would fall. He was some distance from the research station. From his trajectory, he guessed that he had flown south. The screen showed the world beneath him as a mass of green.

The ground was coming up fast. Zarek threw on all four thrusters beneath the vehicle while pulling back on the stick.

The lander seemed to hesitate for an instant in its descent, then began to turn end over end. Zarek cut the thrusters and let go of the stick. The rolling continued.

He strapped himself into the seat at last. He could no longer tell from his instruments which way was ground and which was sky.

The ground rushed toward him. Zarek hit the thrusters and prayed to his parents' gods.

A jolt ran through him as he heard a horrible rending noise.

Everything went dark.

CHAPTER 11

FREE CRUISER *LIGHTNING*

"What the frak?"

Nadu stared at the monstrosity on the forward screen. It was one of those old supercruisers, built before the war, ten times the size of the *Lightning*. If it was fully operational, it would be fitted with fore and aft cannons, over one hundred Vipers, uncounted missiles and probably a few weapons Nadu no longer remembered.

No way the *Lightning* could stand up to that kind of behemoth. A ship like that could swallow the *Lightning* whole.

"Captain?" different members of the crew called out, reacting to his silence. "Orders? Do we fire?"

A part of him wanted to stay and fight. He had five of his own on the far side of this warship, looking for the two that had gone before. Seven out of a crew of nineteen.

He had never lost this many men.

"Captain!" Griff shouted. "We're getting a radio signal from the lander."

The message was heavy with static. *We were attacked. They—*static—*warship in orbit. I'm the only one who got out, and I can't—*static—*getting back to the* Lightning. *Captain, the base was crawling with Cylons!*"

"Zarek. That was Zarek," Griff said. He frowned, staring down at his comm controls. "We've lost the signal."

Nadu had known before his lost crewman had used the word. The Colonies had long ago abandoned those old ships, replacing them with Battlestars. The monster in front of them was a Cylon vessel.

His crew had been attacked by Cylons. He'd lost seven of nineteen. With that thing in front of them, he had no way to see if any were still alive.

They had flown into a trap. Nadu had been careless—worse, he had been blind. He had operated in a universe where the Cylons were long gone. A place where you could profit from a terrible war, and pick up the pieces from a time of terrible destruction. Now the Cylons had come back to change the rules.

Seven of nineteen. And what could he do?

"Out of here!" he called abruptly to his crew. "Chart a course, get us as far away from this ship as possible. We can't outgun them. Maybe we can outrun them."

His crew shouted to each other to strap themselves in. Absently, Nadu returned to his chair. He sat as *Lightning*'s engines roared to their full capacity.

They ran from the fight, ran until they could get far away to safely Jump. The monstrosity on their screens was growing smaller. No one spoke, all waiting for some reaction from the other craft.

Seven of nineteen. And what could he do?

He turned to his DRADIS man. "Was there any sign of the lander?"

"No, Captain, no sign. None at all. But it was hard to see anything else close by the warship. They were shooting at something—something my instruments picked up. It could have been the lander or a Viper. Then it was gone."

He didn't say what Nadu was thinking. The warship must have shot the lander out of the sky.

The warship was growing ever smaller. The Cylons hadn't fired on them.

"Captain!" the DRADIS man called. "They are not pursuing. The other ship is moving away!"

"If we leave the planet," Griff surmised, "I guess we're no longer a problem."

To the Cylons, the *Lightning* was insignificant. The fact only increased Nadu's rage.

This was not the end of it. But how to pay back a ship full of Cylons? Nadu welcomed the right sort of death. But not suicide. He had lost seven. He could still save the other twelve.

For half a minute, he thought about going to the authorities. See what that outdated warship might do when confronted by a dozen Battlestars. But he doubted the authorities would even listen. They all knew Nadu's reputation. They would come up with a dozen reasons to arrest him instead.

No, he would not involve the Colonies in any official capacity. But that didn't mean he was done with this.

The Cylons had not seen the last of the *Lightning*.

Nadu hummed. He had an even better idea.

"Captain," the DRADIS man called, "the warship has disappeared."

"Gone to the far side of the planet, no doubt," Griff added.

Had the warship been hiding all along? The Cylons must be guarding something on the planet. Something really valuable. Nadu's instincts were never wrong.

"Captain! We have reached the Jump coordinates!"

Nadu nodded. "We're out of here—for now."

He stared at the screen as the crew made the final preparations to Jump. "We have to assume no one was left alive." He looked to his second in command. "We go to the safe coordinates. Griff knows the way."

It was Griff's turn to nod. The comm man looked surprised.

Nadu added, "We have to have a little meeting of our own."

Zarek opened his eyes.

He was still strapped into the chair. He looked around the inside of the lander. A few things had shaken loose, but not much. Boone had been good at stashing things away.

He had seen Boone die. And the others. All but the Creep, who had been lost under a pile of Cylons. He was probably dead now, too—or worse.

Tom was the only one left. The only one free. The only one still alive. But for how long?

He tried to move. He was sore, but nothing seemed broken. The chair must have taken most of the impact.

The lander was sitting at an odd angle. He imagined something was damaged. He could hear the hiss of compressed air from somewhere behind him.

He unstrapped himself and pushed away from the chair. He stepped carefully across the slanting deck.

He looked out the window. He was surrounded by trees. And nothing but trees.

Everything was quiet. No one was after him, at least not quite yet. So he had survived.

He hoped the *Lightning* had gotten his message.

He took a slow walk around the tiny room, letting his fingers brush against the walls, the instruments, the secured weapons and supplies. He thought again how good Boone had been at his job. Almost everything was unbroken and in place. The ship itself was damaged, but its contents were more or less unscathed. The cabin appeared to be intact. The primary destruction was probably belowdecks. The hissing sound came from the other side of the storage hatch.

He supposed he should check it out, in case the sound meant something worse. He unlocked the hatch and pulled the door aside. Tom frowned. The cargo area had not fared as well as the cabin. The cases of extra supplies had pulled loose from their ties to jumble together in a great pile. At least one of the containers had broken open, spilling its supplies on top of the rest.

He saw no obvious source for the noise. He might have to pull that whole pile apart to find it.

The hissing stopped abruptly. Tom closed the hatch. For now, he decided to consider that problem solved.

He hoped it was just a broken air line. He no longer needed the air filtration system. The air outside was perfectly breathable—unless he ran into some unknown: insects, pollen, parasites—that might give him trouble. Only one small corner of this world had been claimed by the Colonies. Was the rest of it safe? He would have to open the door and find out.

He supposed it had been too much to expect that he could land this thing unharmed. He was lucky he was still in one piece himself. Without repairs far beyond his ability, this lander was never leaving this exact spot.

But he could stay here for weeks. He could survive most anything. The supplies belowdecks might be jumbled, but they appeared largely intact. He had food, water, air, weapons, even Boone's survival kit. He was set for a while—until what?

Would Nadu risk a rescue against a Cylon battleship? For one lone crewmember? If Nadu had even gotten Zarek's message in the first place. As crazy as the captain was, he always protected his crew. He always bragged about how few he had lost.

The lights in the cabin still worked. Zarek didn't dare try the engines. He wondered what else he could use. He turned to the wireless, slowly spinning the dial, and was rewarded with a loud squawk. He turned the dial back, then tried it a second time. This time he got nothing, not even static. He had lost communication with the outside world.

Maybe he could find some old manuals to read around here. Maybe Tom could even teach himself basic shipboard repair. He had gotten a pretty good look at his surroundings. He decided the next step would be to take an inventory. Boone was so thorough, you'd think he'd leave some sort of documentation behind. Unless the pilot had carried all the manuals in his head.

Without the engines to regenerate their charge, Tom realized, the batteries would run down eventually. He would have to shut down most of the lander's systems in order to preserve some of the batteries' power. If he could keep the batteries charged, and if he could repair the wireless, he might be able to send a second distress call.

Unless that would bring the warship down on his head.

He had too many questions. He wished he hadn't been the only one to survive. He didn't see much hope.

Tom shook his head.

What now?

He didn't know how far from the research station he had landed. It couldn't be too far. He hadn't gotten very high off the ground before he had had to cut his engines.

Part of him wished he were much farther away, somewhere the Cylons couldn't find him. But he had no idea if the machines would even come looking for him.

Maybe landing only a few hours away from the Cylons could work to his advantage. If he couldn't get the lander to work, maybe he could steal another ship. Not that he'd know how to fly it.

If he got desperate enough, he knew he would try anything.

Part of him didn't want to leave the lander. He sat inside the crippled ship for who knew how long, trying to figure out his options. He didn't have many.

He had to learn to live without the ship's comforts. He could continue to use it for shelter, at least until he determined what, if anything, lived in this place.

He knew it was time to pop open the door. He realized that he was pacing around the small cabin, resisting that next step. Staying in the lander was staying with the familiar. Once he opened the hatch, he would be admitting that he was facing the unknown.

But what was he afraid of? He had always wanted to be a figure of authority. So long as he went nowhere near the research station, Tom Zarek was king of the world.

But he couldn't even laugh at his feeble attempt at humor. As far as he knew, all the others in the landing party were dead. He was a survivor. He would have to be resourceful.

He had to pop the hatch and take a look outside. Eventually, he would have to venture a little farther, and find out exactly what he could do with this new world around him.

Tom Zarek would find a way.

He walked across the cabin and hit the hatch release.

Griff was running the show now. Grets said it was about time. Griff smiled at that. As the ship's cook and doctor, Grets was as close as anyone was in the corrupt crew of this bucket to having a soul.

"So we're heading for—where exactly?" Grets asked.

Griff shook his head. "Nadu only gave me numbers, with nothing to go with them. I memorized these coordinates seven years ago. He never asked me to use them—never even referred to them again—until now."

"So Nadu has another plan? That's not much of a surprise." The lines of her face wrinkled as she smiled. The crew said, between cooking and meds, Doc Grets could make anything right.

"I think the captain will let us know, once we get there," Griff replied.

Not that the captain was much in evidence of late. Nadu had locked himself in the captain's quarters, and would open the door only twice a day, to take food.

"Do you think I should do something?" the doc asked. "He almost always talks to me." In fact, Griff knew, Nadu would talk to Grets before anyone else on the crew.

"I think it's best that we all leave him alone." They'd run into

Cylons and lost an entire landing party. This was nothing with a simple cure. "When we get to where we're going, he'll be ready. We were caught by surprise. That won't happen to Nadu twice.

"Wherever this ship is going," Griff added, "I just hope our captain plans to bring the rest of us along."

CHAPTER 12

RESEARCH STATION *OMEGA*

The landing field was very quiet, where a moment before it had been full of weapons fire and the sound of engines.

The companions who were guarding Doctor Fuest stepped back, allowing the doctor to see the daylight overhead.

He stood, and for the first time saw the carnage, both the dead bodies and the shattered companions. Until this moment, the doctor had had no idea such a thing could happen.

Gamma watched him impassively. "It would be best if you returned inside."

Doctor Fuest could find no words. But he couldn't move until he had said something.

"What have you done?"

"Our apologies," Epsilon replied. The companion dropped its gun to the ground. Now that the threat was over, all of the companions had let go of their weapons, while other domestic models were gathering them up. One white kitchen companion had gathered two dozen rifles in a cart before it.

Fuest hadn't known the research station had so many weapons.

Oh, he was always aware they had had considerable firepower, even though he had never approved. The guns, grenades, and whatever else had been brought when the station was first founded, some years before the war, had been stockpiled to fight a threat that had never come. Before today, he had considered the underground storage facility an unfortunate part of the station's past. He had never even opened the weapons vault since he had become the leader of the center.

The companions obviously knew about both the weapons' uses and deployment. He realized it would have been a part of their original programming. As shiny and new-looking as they were, many of these machines were older than the doctor.

The research station's purpose had always been to add to their original natures, and to find a way for these glorious machines to reach their full potential. Nothing had ever been done to remove their initial programming.

Doctor Fuest now realized that may have been a mistake.

The doctor had gotten some brief glimpses of the carnage despite being covered by his guard. Gamma and Beta, derived from a Cylon Butler and Cylon Mechanic model, had not joined in the fight. But Epsilon had used its weapon as if it were an extension of its arms. But then Epsilon came from the warrior models, an improvement on the old Harbinger of Doom prototypes. He remembered how their original leader, Doctor Jaen, had proudly pointed to these new models, now called Centurions.

Some of the new experimental Centurions had come with built-in weapons systems, systems that Fuest and his team had disabled close to twenty-five years ago. He wondered, absently, how easily the warriors might be refitted with those systems again. At least it hadn't come to that.

The doctor was surprised at the thought. Was he expecting all-out war?

Part of Fuest felt that that was what he had just survived. The companions had surrounded him in such a way that he could only get occasional glimpses of the violence. But he had heard every shot and every scream.

He turned to Gamma. "Why has this happened?"

Gamma bowed forward slightly, its white-enamel exterior glinting in the sun. "We were warned of this type of human."

"They would not have acted in your best interest," Beta added. "We felt it was our duty to protect you."

Fuest frowned at the thought. "How could you know what kind of humans they were?"

"We have researched their craft," Gamma replied. "They have old systems—from before the war—systems designed to interface with Cylon technology. These are parts they found on abandoned outposts, that they have refitted into their own hardware. We can access their codes, and download their records."

Epsilon stepped forward to enter the conversation. "They are unauthorized scavengers—you have another word: pirates. They would have been as likely to kill you as to help you."

Fuest found his shock being replaced by anger. "Who are you to make such judgments? They were the first outsiders we had seen in thirty years! We could have found a common ground."

"We could not take that chance," Epsilon replied. "Not when we saw that they had weapons."

"You yourself have often said how unpredictable humans can be," Gamma reminded him.

He looked from one companion to the next. He found their emotionless visages—which he had often taken to be the peace of the saints—to be infuriating at this moment.

"I have not seen others of my kind in half my lifetime! And before I can even talk to them, you . . ."

The three companions looked to each other, as if silently conferring.

"Humanity is spreading again, leaving the Colonies to search the stars," Gamma said at last. "We will see others."

"Before I'm gone?" the doctor asked. "Unlike you, I have little time remaining."

Gamma paused. "I can assure you that others will arrive shortly."

They seemed so certain, they made the doctor hesitate as well.

He took a deep breath and looked out at the late afternoon sky. "Very well. We will convene, at midday tomorrow. We will discuss what happened, why it happened, and make very sure that it will never happen again."

Gamma bowed slightly. "Of course, Doctor, we would never do anything that would disrupt the real purpose of this station."

"We are as dedicated to that as you," Beta added.

"There are so few—humans—left," Epsilon said. "We wanted to protect every one of you. How can the station go on unless both of us are here?"

The doctor nodded at the wisdom of that. "Very well. Tomorrow, I want all the senior staff to gather. I am very shaken by this. We must find a way to go on." He stared at each of the senior companions in turn. Why did he feel that there was something they weren't talking about? He repeated his primary worry: "I want you to assure me that this will never happen again."

The three paused another moment before each spoke in turn.

"We will do our best."

"We will find a way."

"You know, Doctor, that we only want to work together."

The doctor took a deep breath. What they said was true. It had always been true. He realized he was exhausted. "Very well. It would be a shame to lose everything we've done."

"We are all in agreement," Gamma answered.

"Very well. Could you help me back inside? I'm very tired."

He had to rest more and more these days. His life was fading. It felt like he was losing his grip on the station as well.

The three companions gathered around him: the Mechanic in highly polished silver, the Butler all in white enamel, and the Soldier, in a burnished darker tone, near to black. Beta and Gamma stepped closer to lend their support, while Epsilon led the way back toward the door to the station's center.

Sometimes he imagined he could hear emotion in their voices. But their still metal faces betrayed nothing.

He supposed it was an old man's fancy, this giving human emotions to machines. He hadn't really looked at the companions closely in a very long time.

"So you were able to access this new ship's records?" he asked as he slowly walked toward the door. "I didn't realize you had those capabilities."

"It is one of many programming functions that are not often used," Gamma explained. "It came into play as soon as the ship appeared within range."

He wondered what else the companions could do that he had forgotten about. He was sure it was all in the original research. He wished once again that Betti was here. This was much more her area of expertise.

"They would have stolen from you and done you harm," Gamma continued. "Our fundamental programming directives say we must protect you. We could see no other way."

"Theirs were the first guns produced," Epsilon said from where it walked ahead. "We only protected you."

"We will remove all evidence this occurred," Beta added.

Fuest was tired. It could not be undone. He allowed them to lead him back inside. They were efficient machines. But, as machines, they could see none of the ramifications of their actions.

The senior staff would have to sort this all out. He would assign the children to check the companions' programming, to find ways to prevent this from ever happening again.

If the companions were correct—and they had never lied to

him—there would be other visitors. He hoped they were both more official and more trustworthy.

Next time, Research Station *Omega* must be truly prepared.

Laea had seen it fall.

She was hoping that this meeting would be a new beginning. She would have no more of the little world she had grown up in, full of men and machines that told her what she could and couldn't do. She would meet other people—people who would lead her to new and different places. It was a brand-new world.

Her brand-new world had been torn apart.

She could not believe what had happened. Before today, her mechanical brethren had never shown the faintest signs of aggression. Ancient programming must have overtaken the companions.

When the shooting began, the companions blocked the doors, not allowing any of the humans to watch what was happening down on the field. No doubt the machines would claim they were protecting the humans.

But Laea wanted no more protection.

She didn't stay with the others. Her brothers stared in horror at the landing field. Ten times worse than the last time, they said. They, too, told her not to look.

Nobody watched her leave. They only wanted to keep her safe. She walked away from the death, away from the noise. She was safe, she knew, so long as she was behind closed doors.

But she had never planned to stay inside. Once away from the field, she was questioned by no one. She saw no one. She felt as if she were the only one inside the entire station.

She easily got up onto the roof, and carefully crawled over it toward the field, worried that some stray bullet might come too close, but too curious and excited to stop herself.

The gunfire seemed to die down after a while. She peered over the edge and saw a body lying on the ground, close by one of the Vipers. She gasped. Half the pilot's face had been blown away. This was the first time she had ever seen a human in a pool of blood. Parts of companions were littered around the body, and something wet—lubricant from the machines, perhaps, or fuel from the Viper—had started to burn.

It was terrible, but she couldn't stop looking.

She realized why the station had seemed so empty. It seemed like every companion on the base was out on the field. She had forgotten how many of the machines were here—close to a hundred, she guessed. And most of them were now carrying weapons.

Someone shouted below. Two of the ships were taking off. The Viper Mark One rose in a graceful arc. The other seemed to barely get off the ground, then jerked farther aloft to follow the Viper.

The companions all turned to look at their escaping foes. A few shot at the slower craft, but both ships seemed to get away safely.

Her gaze rose to follow their trajectory. This time, she actually cried out.

She saw a new ship in the distance. It was a large vessel, unlike any she'd seen in her research. Its appearance was similar to some warships she had seen, only far more massive. She guessed the ship hung miles overhead, yet it seemed close to the size of the planet's smaller moon. She supposed that was an illusion. No ship could be that large.

The Viper, only a dot now with a bright trail of fire, flew up and above the oncoming craft, reaching for the sky.

Suddenly, a single jet of flame came from the large ship. The Viper exploded in midair.

The other ship, still far closer to the surface than the Viper, paused abruptly, as though it had lost its engines. It dropped like a rock toward the forest below.

The large ship hung in the sky for a moment, as motionless as that newly discovered moon, then slowly moved away.

It was suddenly very quiet.

Laea realized that she was probably the only human to have seen it all.

She saw how the companions clustered around the doctor, protecting him from harm, perhaps, but also keeping him from seeing the true nature of the damage.

They guided him back inside the hangar.

The remaining Viper was wheeled away out of sight. She wondered if she would ever have a chance to look at it.

She knelt on the edge of the roof as all the parts left behind of men and machines were scrupulously scrubbed away.

It took very little time at all.

She decided it was best to climb down from here, to reenter the station before anyone realized exactly what she had seen. She would go back to her room, tell everyone that the noise had been too much for her to handle. Wide eyed, she would ask the others to describe what had happened.

She wondered exactly what their answers would be.

They had killed the humans so quickly. And where had that great ship come from? Could it be another vessel from the Colonies? But why would they shoot down a Viper?

The companions suddenly seemed so unlike those gentle machines that helped to raise her. After this, she wasn't really sure she knew the companions at all.

But what would happen now?

The companions were the doctor's whole life. Man and machine working together—it was his life's work. He wouldn't change his mind no matter what happened.

The research station was a small place, and everyone shared everything. Or so Laea had thought.

She had never seen a reason for secrets. The companions heard everything. And the companions shared many things of interest with their four human counterparts.

The companions had become so much a part of their lives, they were almost invisible. She and her brothers treated many of them like friends. Sometimes they forgot they were there, almost like furniture.

But the companions also spoke among themselves, exchanged data in ways far too fast for humans to even comprehend. Laea had found ways to listen in to many of these exchanges. Most were about technical data, having to do with the station's ongoing research. But there had been a few messages she could not understand, messages with symbols and number sequences she had never seen before.

She still hoped there was a logical reason behind all of this. But they all seemed very different than they had a few hours before.

How could she look into the true heart of a machine?

She wanted to talk with Jon and Vin about what she had seen. But she knew that could only happen if the three of them were alone.

They might have to leave the station to make that possible.

She had to have an honest talk with her brothers. Alone. She would tell them what she had seen, and see if they could tell her anything about the giant ship in the sky.

Maybe the fallen ship would give her some answers. She would very quietly get the station's systems to find it. And then she would take a look at it for herself. She needed simple, straightforward answers.

Somehow she knew she would get none of that from the companions.

CHAPTER 13

"Enter!"

Admiral Sing looked up as Captain Draken, the officer of the watch, stepped through the doorway into the admiral's quarters.

"Thank you for seeing me, sir. I thought it was important that I show this to you in private."

"Yes, Captain. So you said on your wireless call." The call had sounded very urgent. Now, Draken looked uncomfortable, as if he would rather be anyplace but here. "And what is this exactly?"

Draken held out a small disc. "It's a distress call, sir." He glanced down at the recorded message. "More specifically, it's a wireless communication we picked up a few hours ago. We think it may have something to do with the ship we found. It was encoded, but it was a very old code, and simple to break. The signal was pretty faint, but we managed to boost it enough so you can make out the words."

The admiral nodded to a small slot on his phone. "Why don't we play it here. And you think it's from the scavengers?"

"I've probably said too much, sir. I think you should hear this for yourself."

Sing nodded and waved the other officer forward. He had never seen the young man so distracted.

"We worked on this overnight," Draken explained as he inserted the disc. "The duty staff in the CIC all heard it before I could get a really clear idea of what it was." He coughed. "I wanted to bring it to your attention before it got all over the ship."

The disc played its very short message. With the last words, Sing understood Draken's concern.

Cylons.

Something like this would spread like wildfire. "Very well. I think we should have a meeting of all senior staff." He checked his watch. "At oh-eight-hundred hours."

"Very good, sir."

"And I want to meet in the CIC. I'd like as many to hear this as possible, before the rumors get too far."

• • •

"We were attacked. They have a warship in orbit. I'm the only one who got out, and I can't see a way of getting back to the *Lightning*. Captain, the base was crawling with Cylons!"

Adama knew now why Sing had brought the dozen members of the senior staff here to hear this—besides Adama, the circle included the ship's doctor and chief engineer, the Viper captain and the men and women that ran the other important functions on board. Each one could tell their subordinates exactly what they had heard here, and what they had subsequently discussed and decided. And they were playing the message right in the middle of the CIC—where everyone could hear it and the subsequent discussion by the senior staff. There were no secrets here. It would be the best way to quash the rumors that were no doubt already circulating around the station.

"You all heard that?" Sing asked. Everyone nodded.

"And this message came from where?" Bill Adama asked.

"Captain Draken?" Sing asked in turn.

"We've determined the signal came from somewhere around here." Draken pointed at the star charts displayed on a large screen before them. "We're quite close. Probably the only reason we picked it up at all."

Tigh grunted in disbelief. "There's nothing there!"

"Star charts have been wrong before," Adama reminded him. "We're dealing with information supplied by the individual Colonies, information that dates back to before the war."

Tigh frowned at the thought. "So we may have come across something that some government doesn't want us to see?"

"Exactly."

"Or there may be nothing there," Sing cautioned. "This could be nothing more than a wild goose chase."

"Or a trap?" Tigh suggested. "Maybe the scavengers are looking for some slightly used Vipers?"

The admiral considered the suggestion. "That seems particularly unwise. These raiders have the reputation for being ruthless, and anybody who chooses to make his living out here may be a little crazy. But they have to know that the fleet would send a Battlestar. The scavengers haven't survived so long by going up against far superior odds."

"Maybe it's something set up to scare others away?" Draken suggested.

Adama nodded. "What's more frightening than Cylons?"

No one had an answer for that.

"So what next?" Sing asked. "Recommendations?"

"We have to take this message seriously," Adama offered.

"We go in and take a look," the ship's engineer chimed in.

"We should send out a Viper squad—maybe three planes with experienced pilots? I'll lead them in," Tigh volunteered. "It's not like I haven't seen Cylons before."

"I agree," Sing replied. "We have to treat this as a serious threat. Let's get the *Galactica* a little closer before we send in our team. In case you do get something on your tail, we want to be able to blast it out of the sky."

He paused as he looked at his officers. "But you realize this may be nothing at all.

"Tell all your subordinates. Tell them about this, but call it what it is—a message of unknown origin. We're going to investigate this message, but that is all we know. While it could be Cylons, the possibility is still remote. I will inform Fleet HQ of our decision, and keep them up to date with our findings. If we do find something, we'll have every Battlestar on this side of the Colonies here in a matter of days."

He paused again before he added, "I don't want anyone to panic. This could have any number of explanations. Or it could be somebody's idea of a cosmic joke. Understood?"

The senior staff once again murmured their assent. He didn't want any alarms sounding among the troops. Word of mouth could turn a single Cylon into an entire fleet overnight.

"Remember," he added, "we are no longer at war. We signed an armistice two decades ago. No one has seen a Cylon in years!"

"And I hope we don't see any either," the ship's doctor chimed in. It brought a laugh from all around.

"Maybe," said the admiral thoughtfully, "if we do meet them—we can open negotiations. Maybe we can keep from ever having another war."

Adama was impressed. The admiral knew just what he was doing, ending on this. He reminded them all that the Cylons weren't unbeatable. The Colonies had fought them to a standstill once. Maybe neither side was eager to resume that battle.

"Good," Sing continued. "Then go back and talk to your people now. Let them know they need to be ready. But don't believe anything until we see it for ourselves. Dismissed!"

The crowd began to leave.

"Captain Adama," Sing added, "you have the CIC. Plot a course for that empty corner of space. If you need me, I'll be in my quarters." The admiral followed the others from the room.

Saul stayed behind. He walked up next to Adama and took a look at the star chart.

"Just like old times, huh, Bill?"

Adama smiled. "Let's hope not. The war is one place I don't want to revisit, ever."

"But we know something about the Cylons. There may just be a reason they've put veterans back on board."

"Well, let's hope we don't have to gain too much more experience." He slapped his old friend on the shoulder. "I am glad you volunteered to lead the exploratory team."

Tigh shrugged. "I couldn't see who else could do it. Oh, I've got a couple of good youngsters who I think would do all right, but most of them are green kids. This exploration stuff I have them on is nothing more than a glorified training mission."

"We were all green once," Adama reminded him. "We were tested, and we came through."

"At least we lived to talk about it," Tigh agreed.

Bill nodded. "Let's hope your pilots don't have to become too tested too quickly."

Tigh's gaze focused somewhere far past the star charts. "With Cylons, you can never tell much of anything." He glanced back at Bill. "They shot down a few too many of my friends. I never felt like I was quite even. Part of me would like to finish the job." He looked back at the charts.

"How long until we get there?"

"I'm guessing a day, maybe two," Adama replied. "I'll let you know as soon as I finish my calculations."

Tigh nodded. "I'll go and tell my kids. I think some of them would like a challenge. But let's hope the challenge comes up empty."

CHAPTER 14

THE WILDERNESS
OUTSIDE RESEARCH STATION *OMEGA*

Tom Zarek had nothing but time.

By late morning on his second day, he knew his surroundings pretty well.

He was in a valley. Fruit grew on trees, and a small stream passed only a few hundred steps from his front door. He could hear the call of something in the trees. Small birds maybe. So he was surrounded by some sort of wildlife. The birdcalls made the place seem a little less threatening. It was a nice surprise.

Tom's next surprise came when he opened the survival kit. Not only were all thirty-three items inside clearly labeled, but the kit actually came with instructions, with separate entries for each item.

He saw things he could use immediately. And other things—first aid and the like—that he could use over time.

He inspected the outside of the lander, which appeared to have crashed down through a group of trees. That might have lessened the impact of his fall, but it also brought a lot of branches down with it. That caused substantial damage to one corner of the ship, tearing a hole the size of his fist in the outer hull. He imagined some seal had been broken as well—that was probably the hissing he had heard. At least he told himself that. Without any guides to the structure of the lander, he really knew nothing.

The only thing he knew was that the lander wasn't going anywhere, anytime soon.

It had gotten dark a couple hours after his crash, and Tom had made himself as comfortable as possible in the copilot's chair. He slept fitfully, waiting, he guessed, for some large beast to pull open the hatch, which he had left closed but unsealed. But he had heard nothing. He had wondered then if this place had any animal life at all.

In the morning, he had taken his first exploratory walk, a few hundred paces toward the rising sun, then, after returning to the lander, a few hundred paces the other way. It was on his second trip that he had found the small running stream.

At midday, he had returned to the stream and taken water samples, which he tested with Boone's survival kit.

Tom didn't think anything had ever had a truer name. The kit gave him something to read, and instructions that told him what to do without making a frakking fool of himself. He wished that Boone had left more instructions elsewhere.

Everything else was going to have to be trial and error. He followed the instructions, mixing the water with a small packet of powder—the book said the results might take a couple of minutes.

Tom Zarek had nothing but time.

Now that he was away from the *Lightning*, he thought about it

more than ever. He was a raider. They were all raiders. Before he
shipped out, Tom hadn't really known enough about what he was to
become.

It was a strange crew. A bunch of outcasts, thrown away by society. Nineteen loners, all tossed in together. Many were people he
might have avoided in his old life. Most were not too different from
Tom Zarek.

In one way, he fit right in. In other ways, he worried he had made
the worst decision of his life.

There were all sorts of stories about raiders. The best made them
out to be clever businessmen, working just outside the law. There
was a lot of money to be made and no one got hurt.

That was the polite version.

He had also heard stories of raiders gone wild—scavengers as
thieves and murderers, as bad as the barbarian hordes of ancient history. Men with no rules who took what they wanted and destroyed
anything that got in their way.

After shipping out on the *Lightning*, Tom believed there was some
truth to both stories.

Not that it mattered anymore. Once you shipped out with a
raider, there was no going back. You were there for the duration.

Most of all, he thought about the stories he had heard, about the
Lightning, and about Nadu. "Pragmatic" was a word used for a lot of
raiders, but for Nadu in particular.

It wasn't until he was deep in space that he started hearing the
most brutal of those tales, and he realized it was a short step from
pragmatic to ruthless.

Symm and Twitch had liked to tell the most horrific yarns. Like
the one about a planet where those abandoned by the war had re-
verted to barbarism. According to the story, Nadu had killed those
that resisted, and left the rest of them to starve. Or the story about
the Colony where all the men had died of disease, leaving only the
women behind.

These stories were almost like tall tales, the sort of thing that
happened long ago when Nadu first captained a ship, told by one
crewmember to another as they passed the time between missions.
Tom supposed it really didn't matter whether the stories were true or
not. It was the message behind the tales—when you were on the *Lightning*, you would do anything ordered by Nadu.

The Vipe pilots used to roar with laughter if you showed the slightest distaste at their tales. Now, he supposed Symm and Twitch could laugh in their graves.

The crew was an odd mix. Some, like Symm and Twitch, he could see as killers. Others, like Boone and Grets, seemed more like survivors, hard-edged people who were down on their luck.

You couldn't stand on the sidelines. According to their late Viper pilots, Nadu forced you to make a choice.

Tom had hoped it wouldn't come to that. He needed the money. But he didn't want the rest of it on his conscience.

It was one thing he didn't have to worry about now.

The water had turned milky, then clear again. According to the survival manual, that meant it was safe to drink. The manual listed other tests he could perform on the local flora and fauna. He might try those eventually, but for now he would stay with the plentiful rations Boone had brought on the ship.

Zarek looked down at the small cup of water in his hands. Safe water, no immediate danger, no wireless, no immediate hope of escape.

That just about covered it.

He was the only survivor of a massacre. He could say he had survived worse, but this time it would be a lie.

He just needed the Zarek luck to hold on until someone came to rescue him . . . if someone ever came.

CHAPTER 15

BATTLESTAR *GALACTICA*

They were sending the Vipers to explore a world full of Cylons. Captain Tigh had mixed feelings about all this. He walked quickly to the flight deck, where both Viper pilots and deck crew were waiting.

He would do a good job. They would all do a good job. Many back home thought this mission—this exploration of the edges—was going to be easy. Sure, they might find some leftover mining sites where equipment had grown dangerously fragile with age, or have to fire across the bow of a couple of raiders to keep those scum off their tail. But mostly, he knew the fleet sent them out there to train someplace safe and far away from Colonial politics, a place where all the green recruits could learn their way around a Viper, just in case they were ever needed if things came to a head between a couple of the worlds back home.

That might have been one of the reasons Bill convinced the higher-ups to hire Saul Tigh. This was supposed to be light duty. Ease him into the job and see how he handled it, find out whether he was ready for some real work in the fleet.

He stepped out onto the deck, and Athena called the crew to attention. Tigh snapped off a salute as he continued to approach. Twenty-four pilots and close to a dozen flight crew returned his salute.

Well, the real work had shown up, right here, right now, out on the edge of frakking nowhere. And he had to take his green recruits straight into what might be one hell of a battle.

Tigh knew it could be worse. All of them knew their way around a Viper by now. But only four of his two dozen pilots had any substantial flying under their belts, and only two of those showed a real aptitude for battle.

Well, he guessed that made it easy for him to choose who was going to go along on this little mission. He just hoped this assignment didn't explode into something much bigger. His green recruits would have to gain a lot of experience in a hurry.

He stopped some twenty paces away from his assembled troops. Everyone waited expectantly, at attention, for what he had to say. "At ease!" he called. They all relaxed, but only a bit. It was best to get this over with.

"Well, this is it, boys and girls," he called out in a loud voice. "The big time. Just like back in the war, we're going out there to face the unknown. As Viper pilots, we are always the first line of defense. We are fast and deadly. We get in there, take a look around, and hop back out before anybody even knows we've been there."

A few of the pilots laughed. They were trying to release the tension. He knew just how they felt.

"Of course," he continued as he walked down the line, looking straight at each of the pilots in turn, "it all depends on just what we find down there when we go sightseeing. I've decided to lead the first squad down, just three Vipers to take the first look-see."

He could already see relief on some of the younger faces, knowing their crew leader was going to take responsibility.

"I'm asking two of our more experienced pilots to join me. Athena—" He nodded to where the young woman stood at the far end of the group. "—and Skeeter." He waved to the skinny fellow standing in the middle of the newbies. "You will follow me in and watch my tail. As for the rest of you, I want Squads One and Three to be ready for deployment at a second's notice. We may need you to lay down protective fire, just like we did in last month's war games. If we run into trouble out there, I want you guys to make sure we all get back alive. Is that understood?"

"Yes sir!" came the ragged reply.

"Good. We will be leaving in a matter of hours. I will give you the exact time of the mission as soon as it is given to me. Until then, get some rest. Dismissed!"

Most of the pilots quickly left the flight deck. Only Skeeter and Chief Murta, who was in charge of making sure every one of the Vipers would be ready, stayed behind.

"Sir!" The gangly youngster hurried toward Tigh.

Saul paused. "Yeah, Skeeter?"

"Is it true that they've got Cylons down there?"

Tigh nodded. "That's what I hear. We won't know, though, until we see them for ourselves."

It looked like the young man wanted to say something else. Tigh wished he'd just come out with it.

"Is there a problem?" he asked at last.

"No, I guess not, sir," Skeeter replied. "I guess I just thought I'd never see this day."

Tigh smiled at that. "I think a lot of us thought that. You have to remember. We are no longer at war with the Cylons." That was something he should have said to everyone. He would have to correct that oversight before they began their mission. He paused, then added, "But I would not trust those damned toasters for a minute.

"Now, if you'll excuse me, I've got to go play some cards."

Skeeter turned and jogged off to meet the others. The kid was always on the move. Tigh hoped he could use some of those lightning-fast reflexes when they came up against some trouble.

But the talk had gone well. Tigh admitted it. He talked a good fight. He would be all right in the clinch. His experience would see him through. It was the waiting that got to him. He couldn't sleep when it got this close to the action. He had to find other ways to relax.

Now what should he do until the mission?

He would go down to the mess and unwind. A little light gambling with the troops. And he would allow himself one stiff drink—just one—to take off the edge.

"We're going on our first real mission," he said in the barest of whispers, "and you're not going to frak this up."

He took a deep breath. Once he got going, he'd be fine.

• • •

Adama looked at the picture again. His other life. His two sons and his wife, smiling on a sunny day. A part of him was always with his family. He had talked about moving back to Caprica for good.

And then he came to explore the edge of space.

The *Galactica* might have found the Cylons all over again.

Adama realized a part of him looked forward to the danger, the same part that felt truly alive only when there were battles to be won.

He felt alert and ready. And oddly calm.

This was the sort of thing the *Galactica* had been sent here for. This was what he was made for.

He didn't know if he could give this up, even for the sake of his family.

He hoped his wife could understand. She should be proud of him defending the Colonies. But could he be proud of himself, when he felt he was running away from his family?

Adama thought about the old man. Admiral Sing was the picture of calm, no matter what happened around him. He was an anchor, and he kept his whole crew steady around him. If Bill Adama ever got a command of his own, he hoped he could manage it half as well as the admiral.

Now, one way or another, they were going to investigate that distress call. When they grew close enough, they would attempt to hail the planet by wireless. Hopefully, they would get some response, and they could make a peaceful landing. If not, the Vipers would go in on full alert.

He knew Tigh sometimes doubted himself. It would be good for him to see some action. His old friend's heart had always been in the right place, even when he doubted it himself. That's why Adama had recommended Tigh for the job. When things were tough, he didn't know anyone whom he trusted more.

"*Bill.*" Sing's voice on the comm brought Adama out of his thoughts. "*Could you come up to the CIC?*"

"Be right there, sir."

It was time for all of them to see some action.

"We're getting close to the coordinates," Draken explained as soon as Adama joined the junior officer and Sing at the Command Center. "And, as should probably come as no surprise, there is indeed a system ahead, with one habitable planet."

"So this is our mystery planet?" Adama asked.

"Well, it's certainly a place of some interest," Sing replied. "We seem to have tripped some sensor. Mark? Could you turn that up for us?"

A brittle-sounding voice boomed over the speakers: *"Warning! Do not approach! We are under quarantine! Disobeying this command will result in serious consequences! Per order of the Colonial Science Protectorate! Warning! Do not approach! We are under quarantine—"*

"Mark?" Sing asked again, making a slicing motion with his index finger.

The comm officer cut the feed.

"Some sort of recording," Sing added. "It repeats on an endless loop. I imagine this was designed to scare wanderers away—raiders, freebooters, opportunists. It certainly doesn't apply to us.

"As far as they know, we are the Colonial Science Protectorate. We'll soon take care of this." Sing turned to the wireless operator.

"Send a message back. Inform them that, as a ship in the Colonial fleet, we are duly appointed representatives of the Colonies. We are here to call an end to the quarantine." He grinned at Adama.

"Do you think that will work?"

"We can hope, can't we?" Adama replied. "Maybe they'll call us right back and invite us down."

"Sir!" The comm officer passed Sing a message pad.

"Give me a minute," the admiral said. He quickly looked over the text. "This clears up some mystery."

He looked back at those around him.

"We know more about them now," Sing explained. "I've gotten a message back from the fleet. This planet did host a research station before the war, a station sponsored by Picon. Picon! I remember how the politicians from that place would act up before the war. They were always such a pain in the—" Sing hesitated, and took a look around the room. "Anyone here come from Picon? Well, that problem was years ago. Colonies kept secrets from each other back in those days. That bled into the war. First between the Colonies, then with the Cylons. A lot of the secrets got lost. Like this one down here."

Sing looked back at the pad, quickly scrolling down through the notes.

"They lost touch with the station. The Colonies assumed it had been destroyed long ago. Especially considering the nature of their research."

"And that would be?" Adama prompted.

"Cylons," Sing looked back up at his XO. "Just a few years before the war, they shipped out a few dozen scientists and a few dozen Cylons—the latest models, some of them quite experimental, from what I understand. Some bright souls back on Picon felt the relationship between man and machine wasn't working to its full potential. They came here to form a more equal human/Cylon relationship."

Adama considered this. His thoughts surprised him. "That idea would have had merit, back then," he replied slowly. "Handled properly, it could have had real results. Had more people thought that way, we might have prevented a war."

"If that is indeed what the Cylons wanted—to be equal to humans," Sing reminded him. "Even after the armistice, you know, we never knew what really started it all. Still, it's possible. This station has been down there, and apparently fully functional, for thirty years. With luck, we'll see the results of the experiment." Sing shook his head.

"When we go down there, how do you propose we handle the Cylons?" Adama asked.

"It's amazing this place still exists. Who knows how close it is to its original goals?" Sing replied. "In this place both humans and Cylons have been cut off from both sides since early in the war. We may have no problems with the machines down there."

"Or—" Adama prompted.

"They are still Cylons, and we have learned not to trust them. I don't think our lessons will be turned around in a day. Do you?"

"No sir."

"You're going to be our personal representative down there."

"Me, sir?"

Sing nodded.

"You've always seemed able to stay one step ahead of situations around here, thinking about what's going to happen next. I still notice these things even though I'm an old man."

The admiral sighed. "This whole assignment was supposed to be a walk in the park, you know. They needed to give me one more trip before I retired. Me being a war hero and all, it couldn't be behind a desk. So they gave me this. I don't want to be remembered for some battle from twenty-five years ago that I mostly just managed to survive. This backwater exploration trip is my final chance at glory. Maybe we'll get a little bit of it, despite what they thought back at Fleet HQ."

"We're getting a response sir!" the comm officer called.

"Put it over the speakers," Sing ordered.

"Yes sir!"

"Galactica, *this is Research Station* Omega. *Please respond.*"

"This is *Galactica*. This is Admiral Sing, commander of the *Galactica*. It's good to hear that you're still there. We understand you've been out of touch."

"I am Doctor Fuest, the acting head of the station. We didn't even know if anyone knew we were still functioning! We're glad to hear the sound of your voices, Galactica.*"*

Adama and Sing glanced at each other. They sounded friendly enough down there.

"Research Station *Omega*," Sing continued. "We are coming down to see you. We have accessed the old Colonial records. We know you have Cylons there."

"Well, yes," the voice on the wireless replied, *"We don't call them that. We try to have a different relationship with our intelligent brethren. We call them companions."*

"You know that we haven't seen a Cylon in over twenty years?" Sing asked.

The doctor hesitated before he replied. *"I didn't. I knew of the beginning of the Cylon-human war. But after all this time, I thought you would have found a way to make peace."*

"We did, after a fashion, twenty years ago. We had an armistice then. But the only way we could find peace was a total separation of man and machine."

"I am sorry to hear that. I guess we have done things differently here than the way they are done elsewhere in the Colonies. I believe each of us has something of value for the other."

Adama thought, *Now wouldn't that be nice? Perhaps, if the universe was a different place.*

But then, in this small corner of space, it was a different place.

"We look forward to your visit." The doctor paused. *"We have had earlier visitors, with unfortunate consequences."*

Another pause.

"Please bring no weapons, and we will bring none either," the doctor said at last. *"We have had a very unfortunate event happen recently. We were visited by a group of I believe they call themselves raiders. It did not go well."*

"Can you explain?" Sing asked.

"People were killed. Companions were damaged beyond repair.

"We do not wish to repeat our errors. We are both a part of the Colonies, even though we have been separated for close to thirty years.

"Will you comply?" the doctor asked.

"We will honor your request," the admiral replied after a short pause of his own.

"*Thank you*," the doctor replied. "*We very much want to talk in a peaceful fashion.* Omega *Station out.*"

Adama turned to Sing. "What do you think, sir?"

"I'm inclined to believe they are telling some version of the truth. I imagine they need our help. As self-sufficient as they may have been they may need supplies. They may even want to shut down the whole operation, and get back home." The admiral allowed himself the slightest of smiles.

"I imagine we're almost as much of a surprise to them as they are to us."

He clapped Adama on the shoulder.

"I'm going to send you down, Bill, to negotiate. Keep your eyes open—especially the ones in the back of your head."

Skeeter wanted to jump out of his skin. Tigh had called them back together one more time.

The Cylons will get you.

"We have made final arrangements with the Research Station," Tigh was saying. "The plans have changed. We will accompany the shuttle, but we will not land. As long as those on the station keep their part of the bargain, we will as well."

If you don't finish your dinner . . .

Skeeter never thought he would actually see a Cylon.

Maybe now he didn't have to.

He was a trained pilot. He would only see them from high in the air.

In an odd way, he felt disappointed.

If you don't clean your room . . .

Maybe, if he could see them for real, he wouldn't need to be scared of them anymore. Maybe he could banish the old woman's voice once and for all.

"We are an escort," Tigh continued, "and will keep a watchful distance. The remaining Vipers in the Commander Air Group will remain on full alert until further notice. We will be flying out with the shuttle in thirty minutes. That is all."

So Skeeter was still flying, just not as far.

Why couldn't he shake this creepy feeling?

The Cylons will get you.

CHAPTER 16

Until today, Vin had thought his job was the easiest of all.

The three "youngsters," as the doctor called them, despite the fact that they had all passed twenty, all had separate jobs at the research station. Laea took care of the farming and other outside duties, while Jon functioned as the doctor's assistant, an increasingly important task as Doctor Fuest slowed with age.

Vin worked with the companions. He had been fascinated with them since he was small.

It had started with the accident that had taken out a whole building of the facility, and claimed all their parents' lives. At first, Vin had blamed the companions for his parents' deaths. They were efficient machines. Why hadn't they been able to detect the overheating coils and fuel leak that had caused the explosion? Had they wanted the humans to die?

But over time, Vin had seen that a far greater number of companions had perished in the blast. And he had come to view the remaining companions as hardworking and knowledgeable, each within its own designated area of expertise. But any one of the machines by themselves was far from all-knowing.

He had learned the quirks of the companions over time, how Gamma worried about the doctor's health while Epsilon constantly watched the station perimeter for any signs of change. Even though they had learned new tasks at the station, each companion was still true in part to its original manufacture. He had learned to repair and maintain each and every one of them, and had even helped Beta in the design of newer models.

He could talk to the companions. He wished he could talk to humans as well. Jon was so caught up with his aid of the doctor, he rarely seemed to have time for anyone.

And Laea . . .

Laea had become a woman, a beautiful young woman. The three of them—Jon, Vin, and Laea—had grown up as brothers and sister, and had treated each other as such.

Until now.

Vin could hardly stop thinking about her.

She was his sister. You didn't think that way about your sister!

But she was the only woman he knew.

He did his best not to stare at her. He found it uncomfortable to be alone with her, uncomfortable to talk when she was in the room.

So they kept their distance.

But now the outside world had come, and the companions were showing signs of ancient programming that even they had seemed to have forgotten. They were surrounded by violence that he had never seen from the companions before.

He thought he knew these machines very well. Did he?

Maybe Vin needed to take a step away. Maybe he needed to reconnect with the other humans, to make that extra effort to talk to them as the people he remembered from childhood.

The station was changing around him faster than he could understand. But parts of change could be good.

Jon, Laea, Vin. Perhaps they would all start talking again.

But could they talk enough to save the station?

Laea stared at the table in front of her. She had rarely found a meeting so pointless.

They sat in their usual places around the long table. The companions were on one side, the humans on the other. She wondered why they always sat this way. She had always assumed it was the doctor's wish, or the wish of whoever had come before the doctor. But their positions separated them, establishing an order that seemed to contradict the mandate of this station. It had not been so bad before, at those hundreds of other gatherings she had taken part in over the years. Back then the doctor would take time to compliment some new initiative of the companions', or Vin would make some of his lame jokes about the station breaking down. When they were young, Laea remembered how amused she had been when Beta would extend all its wrenches in the air and twirl them all at once. They had felt more like a family then. Now, it seemed they had no joy, no pleasure left in their lives.

It all seemed very odd. No one was pleased with what had happened. At least they had determined that much. No one knew what to do. But everyone was willing to go on with the meeting as if it might accomplish something.

Only a few moments ago, she had thought this meeting was going to tell them everything. Why the companions had anticipated violence. What had happened to the Viper. Who or what controlled the great ship in the sky. But she only heard the same words over and over.

"We were unaware of the problem," Gamma said for maybe the fourth time. "It will not happen again. We will make the proper adjustments throughout the companions."

"We are here as equals," Epsilon spoke up at last. "Is that not the case?"

The doctor stared at the companion.

"That was our purpose here," he answered at last, "the reason this station was created. We all know that. But our protocols insist that you defer to the station staff in a time of emergency."

"Doctor," Gamma replied, "we have been in a time of emergency ever since the second accident. Since that event, the companions have learned to perform every function on this base. We do not want to lose you. As you have seen by our recent actions, we will do everything possible to protect you. But, if and when you can no longer function, the base will go on."

The doctor was silent. He nodded his head once.

Beta took up the argument next. "We only want what is best for all of us at the station. Perhaps we acted rashly. But you insisted on being in the open, a potential target. The scavengers thought you had taken their first pilots prisoner. We surmised that they might want to take you prisoner and force an exchange."

The doctor blinked as if just now remembering something important. "Did you take the pilots prisoner? You said something about that before."

"Are they alive then?" Jon broke in. "Why haven't we seen them?"

"We have been busy preparing for other contingencies," Epsilon replied. "They are well taken care of. We knew you would want to see them eventually."

"But you have not brought this matter—the prisoners—to us," Jon countered. "We are supposed to work as a team. It seems that you are taking on a great deal of the responsibility yourselves."

"We have been taking on responsibility for day-to-day routines for quite some time," Gamma added. "It was natural for us to take responsibility for crisis management."

"We need to be able to manage all functions of the research center," Epsilon joined in. "As you yourself have stated, Doctor, you will not be with us forever."

Laea knew what was different. The three companions spoke almost as one, as though they all shared the same ideas. Before, they had each seemed a bit closer to the nature of their individual manufacture. But-ler Gamma was all for efficient station operation. Mechanic Beta wor-ried about keeping everyone and everything operational. Warrior Epsilon was concerned with procuring foodstuffs—birds and fish mostly—for the humans—as well as bringing up points on defense, which, until recently, they had never seemed to need. Now the com-panions seemed to be finishing each other's sentences.

She noticed something else as well. The companions had always used a deferential tone with the doctor, the legacy, she guessed, of their original Cylon programming. Now they seemed to challenge him. The current crisis had brought out something new in the com-panions.

Maybe that was the difference she had noticed over the past few days. It was the purpose of this research center to see if both humans and machines could benefit from a newly structured society. In the early years, Laea understood, they had thrived. As long as she could remember, they had had to depend on each other to survive. But the founding humans had always taken the lead. Now, perhaps it would be better if the more capable companions would take control.

No one disputed the companions' remarks. Instead, Jon discussed how to make plans for any similar events that might happen in the fu-ture. She realized that Vin hadn't spoken at all. She found him glanc-ing moodily in her direction a couple of times. Did he feel the same way she did?

Laea found her attention starting to wander. This morning, using her personal computer, she had plotted the likely trajectory of the fallen ship. She had hoped there might be taped records of the land-ing, but the stationwide system marked them as "unavailable." She had frowned when she first read the word. Did that mean no records had been kept during the chaos around the scavengers' arrival? Or were other members of the senior staff reserving them for study?

She worked out the final coordinates without the help of the ma-chines. For some reason, she felt the need to keep this very much to herself. She definitely saw some changes in the companions of late.

If they could keep secrets, so could she.

She had already thought of a number of reasons for her to leave the compound. Some of the farming area needed to be upgraded. They re-quired some new soil to properly grow the vegetables. She would tell the senior staff she needed to spend the day taking samples. That is, if anybody bothered to ask.

She seldom left the research center. None of them did anymore.

Years ago, she and her brothers used to explore. They used to do everything together.

What she did was every bit as important as what anybody else did. She could fix most anything. The companions brought her those things not covered in their programming. Sometimes she and the companions repaired them together.

No one had time to talk to her now. But why?

"Is there anything that anyone would like to add?" the doctor asked. His traditional ending to every meeting.

No one spoke, and the meeting ended. As she left the meeting, she realized she hadn't spoken either. Why didn't she tell the others about the ship?

It was her one true secret.

Her one moment of freedom—away from all of those who didn't care . . .

Now that the meeting was over, she would find out what had happened to the small ship—and she would do it for herself.

Tom Zarek would walk a little farther every time than he had before, and he would walk three times a day. Now, two days in, he had a good idea of his surroundings.

He took a knife and marked trails around his new home. He memorized the quickest way to the stream, and found that it led down to a slow-moving river. He had even found a small cave—small and empty, he was pleased to discover. It would give him another place to go in case the lander was discovered.

He slowly climbed out of the valley, in the direction that his lander had flown and fallen. When he climbed to the top of the ridge and stood in the clearing between the trees, he could see a distant shine, tiny glints of silver in the distance. He was quite sure that glow was the top of the towers at the research station.

It made him realize how close he really was, how little altitude his lander had gained before it plummeted back to the planet's surface. He guessed the station would be less than a day's walk from here, even with the uneven terrain.

That also meant that, if the Cylons were coming for him, they would have been here by now. He doubted that Cylons would have to do anything as primitive as walking.

That thought made him feel just a little bit safer.

His exploration nearly done, he did his best to patch up the comm system. He found a small set of tools in a compartment beneath the pilot's seat, and decided it was time to look at the innards of the wireless array.

The front panel came off easily. He grabbed the high-powered light he had found in the survival kit and shined it inside. It was something of a mess.

The crash had jumbled some of the hardware, pushing whatever had sat above the wireless into the wires below. A couple of those wires had pulled free, while another, which seemed quite long, had torn apart in the middle. Any or all of them could be what ailed the wireless.

Two of the wires could be reattached, but the third one was a total loss. He hoped he could find some other similar wiring elsewhere in the ship.

He looked for other panels that might be easily opened in other corners of the cabin. He found five, all full of various circuits and a few very short wires. Nothing was quite as long as the missing wire, though he saw some that he thought he might splice together.

When too tired to walk or mess with the ship's innards, Tom took inventory. He had forty-eight different types of guns on board. Maybe Boone had been more frightened of what was going to happen than Zarek had thought. Most of the weapons he knew. A couple were so large he found them a bit intimidating.

And though the variety wasn't great—most of it was surplus rations packed to last for the long term—Tom figured he had enough food for the better part of a year. Supplemented by the safe local drinking water, and—perhaps eventually—some experiments with the local vegetation, and maybe a bird or two, Zarek could last out here indefinitely.

He had enough food for months. He had enough firepower to last a lifetime.

But to what end?

There were times when he just sat.

He had water. He had food. He had his thoughts.

Tom Zarek had a bit too much time to himself.

He wondered why he was the only one to survive.

He went over the whole sequence of events. Although it had seemed to take a very long time, he was sure the battle had not taken more than a couple of minutes.

He saw himself walking ahead to greet the welcoming committee.

He wondered if Ajay had even gotten the message on his faulty equipment. Or had he seen something from on top of his Vipe? He saw the white Butler model cut off Zarek from the old man. Were the Cylons already planning to attack?

He had no way to know.

The whole thing was rather ironic.

Of all those from *Lightning*, he was probably the worst fighter in the bunch. He had been in a few street brawls when he was down on his luck, but nothing with guns or grenades or even knives. The others had been with Nadu longer, and from their stories had seen all sorts of action. Boone was the type of guy who seemed able to do anything. And the Creep—well, Zarek imagined he'd killed quite a few.

Tom realized he was alive because he was the only one not brandishing a gun. His role as peacemaker, and his proximity to the old man, had saved him.

But one Vipe pilot got shot through the head, the other blown out of the sky. Boone died with a final blast of defiance, and gave Zarek a chance to jump into the lander. He still wished he knew what had happened to the Creep. Before this, Tom had thought that guy could have slipped free of anything.

It was far too still out here. He heard the wind and a strange whooping sound in the distance. He guessed it was a native bird. At least there was something else alive! But he listened for other sounds, he listened for voices. Was he waiting for the Cylons? For rescue?

Sometimes, he felt as though the others who died would come to haunt him.

He thought he heard a noise, then, out in the trees. Was it the Cylons at last? He didn't breathe for a long minute. Nothing followed. Maybe the local wildlife was getting a little closer.

He shifted his position—he was sitting by the lander—and listened again. He heard nothing but that odd and distant bird noise. If something had been rustling around in the underbrush, it had probably been scared away.

He needed to get out of his head and back to work. He looked at the lander. If he couldn't get at any useful wires from the inside, maybe he could get something out here. The crash landing had given him a ready-made hole. He stuck his fingers in the ragged space, then pulled his hand free—the edges were sharp. He pulled off his shirt and wrapped it around his hand, then carefully placed his cloth-wrapped fingers back in the hole. He gave the piece of metal a tentative tug. The whole thing came away from the ship with hardly any effort. And it revealed a gift from the gods—a mass of wires, all far longer than he needed.

Tom quickly stepped inside the ship to fetch the tool kit. The right wire could get the comm system up and running. He could listen for his rescuers, maybe even send out a distress call. And what if the Cylons picked it up? If he was stuck out here long enough, Zarek realized, he wouldn't care who got it, as long as he got out of the wild.

Many of the wires seemed to branch off some sort of junction box, just below the edge of the torn metal hull. If he could just pry one of them loose. He took a small rod with a sharp edge from the tool kit, and poked it toward the junction. It slipped past the wires and cut into some soft membrane. A dark, heavy liquid squirted along Tom's arm and into his face.

He cried out, leaping out of the way as the liquid arced briefly out of its new opening. It stopped after only a few seconds, but the damage had been done.

Frak it all! Tom used his shirt to wipe the stinging liquid out of his eyes. It itched where it had made contact with his skin. He realized he had better wash it off as quickly as possible. He dropped the tools on the ground and headed for the stream.

This is what he got for trying to be a mechanic. He jogged quickly to the water and plunged his arm into the cool, flowing stream. To his relief, whatever the viscous fluid was, it came off easily, leaving only the slightest of red marks behind. He dunked his head in the water to clean off his face, then threw his shirt into the water, too, to see if the water would clean off the stuff that had gotten rubbed in. This was his only shirt. If he lost this, all he had left was an atmosphere suit.

He lifted the shirt from the water to take a closer look. The dark stain had turned a dull gray. Maybe if he scraped it on some rocks.

He stopped looking at the shirt when he saw the other face staring at him. It was a face between the trees, on the far side of the stream; the face of a young woman.

His mouth opened. There were other humans here? He stood up quickly.

"Hey!" he called.

The face had disappeared.

"Hey! Who are you? Don't run away!"

He heard crashing in the bushes, and then nothing. Not even the strange calls of the local birds.

CHAPTER 17

Adama landed by himself, and without incident, on the empty landing field.

"Welcome to Research Station Omega," the now familiar voice announced over the wireless. "We will come out to meet you."

Adama stepped out of the shuttle. He saw the doors open wide on the side of a building at the far end of the field. Three men stepped through the door and walked toward Adama's shuttle. They were followed by three Cylons a moment later.

Adama opened the shuttle door and stepped outside.

As the six others walked toward him across the field, Adama noticed that one of the men kept glancing behind himself at his metal companions. They were close enough now so that Adama could recognize the three different Cylon model types. Adama had fought the Warriors, and had run across a few of the Mechanics. He didn't think he had seen a Butler model since before the war.

The party hesitated maybe fifty paces away.

Adama supposed there would be tension at their first meeting, but this seemed particularly awkward.

He took a few quick steps away from the shuttle and toward the other party. He was careful to keep a good amount of room between them.

He saluted the assemblage, human and Cylon, and spoke in a voice loud enough to cover the distance between them.

"Colonel William Adama, of the Colonial fleet."

All six of them bowed slightly in return. Adama wondered if this was some anarchic custom from the Picon High Court. It certainly looked exceedingly formal.

The three humans were all male, one quite old, the others much younger. The elderly man at the center of the group spoke first.

"I am very, very glad to see you." He waved to those around him. "All of us are glad to see you. I am Doctor Villem Fuest."

He turned to the three Cylons behind them. "May I introduce you to Gamma, Beta, and Epsilon. Three of our companions." He pointed to the Butler model, the Mechanic, and the Warrior in turn. Seeing them this close, Adama realized the models were slightly different from those he remembered from his younger days, when Cylons and humans shared the same worlds.

These are not the same Cylons I have fought. He would have to remind himself of that as long as he was here.

Adama realized he was expected to say something. "You'll have to forgive me. This is the first time I have seen Cylons in over twenty years."

The doctor shook his head. "They are Cylon in design, perhaps. But our companions are a new breed of being. We have tried to change our way of thinking here. And we have had a great deal of success."

"I'm eager to hear about it," Adama replied. "My people are eager to hear your whole story."

The doctor glanced at the young men to his left and right. "Oh. But I haven't introduced Jon and Vin." Adama guessed the younger men would be in their early twenties, close in age to the Viper pilot recruits back on *Galactica*.

"But as to this project," the doctor continued. "Whatever happens, I would want this center to go on. With the proper supplies, perhaps we can still invent the perfect society."

Many things were possible. But after all that had happened in the war, could Cylons and humans ever work together? Adama would do his best to reserve judgment.

"But what do you want from us?" the doctor asked.

Adama had rehearsed this answer on his way down to the planet. "First and foremost to reestablish contact. We have been sent by the Colonies to explore all those outlying regions once settled by humanity, to claim them again as our own. They're curious at home to see exactly what is still out here."

The Cylon Butler—Gamma was its name—stepped forward and spoke briefly with the doctor.

Fuest looked back to Adama.

"I'm afraid some of us are not quite so trusting of your intentions. The companions already see problems."

"We did as you asked," Adama replied. "I came down, alone and unarmed, the executive officer, second in command on the *Galactica*. I think that should be symbol enough of our good intentions."

Gamma spoke directly to Adama. "We know about your Viper escort."

Adama replied directly to the Cylon. "We made promises as to who would come down here. We made no promises as to who would be in the air. So, yes, we have Vipers on alert." He paused before asking, "And you are without contingency plans?"

The Warrior Epsilon stepped forward. "Our weapons are stored where we can obtain them quickly."

That statement made one of the young men—the same one, Jon, who had turned back to the Cylons—look rather uncomfortable. Adama resolved to talk to Jon at his first opportunity.

The doctor turned to the Cylons. "This isn't like before. This is civilization. These people come from the Colonies that created this station."

"Would you like me to send the Vipers away?" Adama asked. "We can have more of our people come down shortly, after we talk more about what we both need."

The doctor smiled and shook his head. "No, no, why not have them come down and join us now? That way, neither side will look as though they are threatening the other. We will welcome them as well as you."

Adama was a bit surprised by that response. He did his best not to show it. "Either way, I'll have to send a message from my shuttle." Adama pointed at the small ship behind him.

"Why don't you do so?" the doctor agreed. "I'm glad, this time, that neither of us has had to jump to conclusions." He shook his head. "We had earlier visitors, quite recently. It did not go well." The doctor looked down at his hands, then back at Adama. "I'll tell you about them when you are done with your call. Most unfortunate."

"We saw signs of raiders in the area," Adama replied. "Is that who you are talking about?"

"Yes, raiders," Epsilon agreed. "We sent them away."

"Perhaps we could take you on a quick tour," the doctor said a bit too brightly. "If you want, I'll certainly let you look at our records. We've done great things here. I would hate to see them end."

"Well, we're certainly willing to help out however we can," Adama said. "We are a fully stocked ship. Our supplies are at your disposal."

The smile fell from the doctor's face. "What do the Colonies want? What will you do with us?"

"We have no orders concerning you. Until a few hours ago, we didn't even know you existed. What would you like to receive from us?"

The doctor thought a moment before replying.

"I think I would like to see Picon again. As to the youngsters, I guess you would have to ask them."

"How many youngsters are there?" Adama asked.

"One more besides Jon and Vin. Our human population is not what it once was."

That led to the next obvious question. "And how many Cylons?"

"Our companions?" The doctor turned to Gamma. "Close to one hundred."

"Ninety-seven," Gamma spoke up. "Four of that number are currently undergoing repair."

"After the accidents. Companions could be rebuilt. Humans could not." The doctor smiled apologetically. "I would hope we could have new scientists come out here and continue our work at close to the old levels of staff. We were so close to success before the accidents."

"Let me make a call," Adama said, waving back at the shuttle, "and then I'll be ready for that tour."

"Most certainly," the doctor agreed. The rest of his party, both human and Cylon, stood silent.

Adama returned to his ship. This meeting was awkward, but it did not seem threatening. His first impression was to trust this odd mix of man and machine—for now. If they were truly open about their records, the *Galactica* might even be able to discover important data concerning the Cylons—data that could help them get ready for the next time humans and Cylons met.

He settled into the pilot's chair and clicked on the wireless.

"Shuttle One to *Galactica*. I need to talk to the admiral."

"He's been waiting for your call," the voice on the other end replied. *"I'll put you through."*

"Colonel Adama," Sing's voice answered an instant later.

"Admiral Sing," he replied.

"Good to hear from you, Bill. What's your status down there?"

"Our initial meeting went well. They seem friendly enough, and I believe they are sincere. But it's also obvious that they haven't had visitors in a very long time. They are aware of the Viper escort circling overhead. And they aren't particularly happy about it. They asked if the three Viper pilots would like to join me, and I told them I'd do my best to get them down here. Frankly, I could do with some friendly company."

"So you think there's nothing more to the research base than what we were sent by Picon? It's just an old Colonial project that managed to survive?"

"That's my first impression. They seem to be opening up to us to a point. But this human-Cylon interaction is very strange. It's throwing off my judgment in everything. That's the best reason for the Viper pilots to join me. I could use a few more sets of eyes."

"Very good, Bill. I'll order the three Vipers to come on down with you. And I'll ready Plan Beta, in case you get into any trouble."

"Copy that, Admiral. Adama out."

Plan Beta would put twice as many Vipers in the air at the first sign of trouble. Bringing the first three Vipers down was a gesture of peace, but that gesture had an iron fist hidden just behind it. But it shouldn't come as a surprise to anyone on this station that a Battlestar would be prepared to respond to any aggressive act.

Adama wondered if Fuest would even think of such a thing. Maybe it was being cut off from society for so long, but the elderly doctor seemed strangely innocent, as though he couldn't imagine one side striking against the other. From Gamma's actions out in the field, Adama guessed that these new Cylons were fully capable of fighting the Colonial fleet.

Adama realized he was all too ready to return the favor. He hoped it got no worse than simple mistrust.

He rose from his seat and exited the shuttle once more, ready to get a look at the rest of *Omega* Station.

"Viper One."

Tigh was surprised to hear the admiral's voice.

"This is Viper One," he replied.

"Colonel Adama needs a little help. He wants you to come down and join him."

"Is he in trouble?"

"Negative. Everything's peaceful. Let's just say he's unsure if there are any hidden situations. He just wants a couple extra pairs of eyes to take a look around. So you three are going to go down and join him."

Wouldn't that make all four of them much more vulnerable? "Are you sure about that?"

"Sure enough to be making this order personally. Go down, take a look, and report back to the Battlestar. And no weapons. We don't shoot at them until they shoot first. Understood?"

"Understood, sir."

"Good. Bill trusts you on this, and so do I. Remember, you're going

down to look at a Picon Colony Science Station. But you'll let me know when you find something else. Sing out."

"Copy that." Tigh didn't have a good feeling about this. But they were going down. Admiral's orders.

He opened the comm link to the other pilots. "Athena? Skeeter? You're with me. Colonel Adama needs us down on the planet."

"We'll follow you down," Athena's voice replied.

"But the Cylons, sir—" Skeeter began.

Tigh cut him off. "Colonel Adama knows what he's doing. We'll land in close formation. Just stick close to me."

"Should we take any defensive measures, sir?" Skeeter asked.

"Definitely not," Tigh replied. "If Adama's down there asking for us, he's determined that the Cylons are not an immediate threat. The admiral personally told me that, when we leave our Vipers, we will do so unarmed. Is that understood?"

"If you say so, sir," Skeeter said without conviction.

"I say so, so let's go. Delta formation." That would keep the other two Vipers just behind and to either side of his lead.

Tigh hoped his own feelings were wrong. He would trust Adama above just about anybody.

But he didn't want to just hand over three Vipers to the Cylons.

CHAPTER 18

She ran.

Why hadn't Laea spoken to the stranger? She had been almost as startled seeing him that close as he was to see her. He was the first man she had ever really glimpsed, up close, outside of her immediate family.

Maybe the lack of a shirt surprised her more. He had stood there, his chest bare, looking tired and lost in the middle of the woods. She hadn't seen her brothers without some part of their clothes since the three of them had been ten. Everyone was always fully dressed. It was the way it was done on Picon, and they carried over those traditions here. She could hear the doctor say those words as she thought them. He always said there was a proper way to do everything.

Laea was also startled by how young the stranger had looked, surely only a few years older than herself. A part of her had always thought that spacefarers would have to have the age and wisdom of the doctor. That was her image of people with knowledge. But this stranger was not much more than a boy, close in age to her brothers.

Without his shirt, she could see all the muscles on his stomach and his chest. She had found herself staring at the man when he looked back at her. She couldn't breathe. She felt as if she had done something terribly wrong. She felt she had to get away.

She had started for home before the man could do more than call out.

Now she wondered why she had come here in the first place. It had taken her three hours, following the river, to reach that spot from the station. She had brought one of the monitoring devices—a sort of heat sensor—that the companions used when they went out hunting for food. She hadn't been sure it would work. The companions usually went in search of large flocks of birds, while she was looking for signs of a single human.

But the monitor had steered her in the right direction. Any closer and she would have blundered right into the stranger . . . the man.

She ran back the way she had come, feeling very foolish. She had so much wanted to get free of everything in the station! She had wanted to find out what had happened to the lander, and what those in the station weren't telling her.

But she had made no real plans, and she realized she had no idea what she wanted to do next.

Maybe she should stop running.

Maybe she should go back and find this man and talk to him. She could apologize for their meeting, ask him what it was like, outside the tiny world of the research station.

Or maybe this man—this raider—this scavenger—was every bit as bad as the doctor and the companions said, and she was in danger just looking at him.

She knew now she was headed back toward the station. It was her home. It was the best place to be.

This was her first real look at the unknown. She had to get away from that new place, that new man, until she could figure out what to say, what to ask.

Maybe next time she shouldn't come out here alone. What if the young man was really dangerous?

Could she get one of her brothers to join her? These days, neither Jon nor Vin seemed to have much time to talk to her about anything, much less march hours away from the station.

She hadn't really thought out any of the consequences before she had started out here. Now she would be gone for the better part of a day. She wondered if she would have to explain herself. Whether those back at the station even cared.

She heard a roaring overhead.

She looked up in the sky and saw another ship fly above her, a ship not much bigger than a Viper, but more boxlike in structure, like it was designed to carry lots of people and supplies.

Someone else must have found them—unless this was another ship from the raiders. Someone at the research facility must have known about this before she left. She realized she had been so intent on finding the lander, she hadn't cared what was happening at the station.

She was still some distance from the station. At least she was far from harm if anyone started using weapons again. She hoped nothing else unfortunate would happen this time. She wished there were some way she could stop anything like that from happening—ever again.

But whatever was happening, she had to see it for herself.

Laea climbed to her secret spot on top of the roof, just as she saw three Vipers streak down from the sky. When she reached the spot where she could look over the edge, she saw that all three Vipers had landed midfield. These three were newer models, more streamlined and shinier than the ones the scavengers had used. She watched as all three pilots climbed from their ships. They were all dressed in flight suits. Two men and a woman? And Jon had come out by himself to greet them, with a group of companions watching from near the hangar doors.

She would like to go somewhere where a woman could fly.

Jon stopped in front of the three pilots. Everyone seemed happy to see each other. This was different.

She realized she was missing out again on the life of the station. She wanted to meet the new people, especially a woman who flew a Viper.

She guessed, for that, she would go down and join them.

Tigh stepped out of his Viper.

"Holy frak," he said.

This looked like something from his childhood. Cylons and humans, side by side. His family hadn't been rich enough to have Cylon servants, but he had seen them everywhere.

The first time he had been up close and personal with Cylons it was a few years later, and he was trying to kill them before they killed him. Now, looking at the half dozen machines clustered at the far side of the field, he realized he had this built-in fight-or-flight pattern he would have to overcome.

He had thought getting back on the *Galactica* would be a good test of whether he had a future. Until this moment, Tigh hadn't realized how much he would be tested.

An actual human being walked between the Cylons, heading toward them across the field. Athena smiled as he approached. She seemed relaxed despite the things that waited for them on the far side of the field. Tigh would never understand that woman.

Not that he didn't find her attractive. Tigh always liked a take-charge woman, and Athena certainly fit that description. But it wasn't good practice to fraternize with those under your command. Tigh had screwed up in so many ways over the years, he didn't want to do the same thing here.

Maybe Athena was just too young to remember much about the Cylon War. But then Skeeter looked worse than Tigh felt. From the frown on his face to the way he jumped at the slightest movement around him, the young pilot seemed to want to be anyplace but here.

"I never thought I'd see these things, sir."

"Well, they're not supposed to be the Cylons that we fought," Tigh replied, realizing he meant his words to reassure himself as much as Skeeter. "They have some sort of experimental program here. Cylons and humans get along."

"If you say so, sir."

Tigh nodded. "I have trouble believing it myself." He waved at the young man walking toward them. "Let's go meet the fellow. Until we're told otherwise, everybody and everything here is our friend. Is that understood?"

"Yes, sir."

"Athena?"

She fell into step beside the other two pilots. The young man slowed his own forward progress as they approached.

"My name is Jon," he called out to them. "Your Colonel Adama is looking around our center. I've been sent to bring you inside so we can all join him." He turned abruptly, calling over his shoulder, "Follow me!"

He was leading them straight back toward the cluster of Cylons.

Without any weapons, Tigh was feeling increasingly naked with every step.

Jon waved at the machines as they approached. "As you see, we live in harmony with the companions."

"That's what you call them?" Athena asked.

"We call them that, because that's what they are. This place only works because we all—human and companion—work together."

Jon led them back through a large set of doors. A half dozen Cylons watched them pass. All of the machines were built to look vaguely human, with a head-shaped object above what could be a pair of shoulders. But their faces were all curiously blank and unformed, often not much more than a few blinking lights. Tigh saw models with long broom arms that had once been used for street cleaning, a multi-armed mechanism of the kind that he remembered had cooked for large groups, and a couple of the silver mechanical repair models with dozens of interchangeable parts. He had almost forgotten how many different varieties of the machines had once existed, before the war had turned them all into killers.

"We developed this station to be a self-sufficient community," Jon continued as they entered a long hallway with doors to either side. "Despite our problems, this is no doubt why we survived."

A moment later he added, "If you look to our left, you will see the companion repair facility."

A vast room stretched off to their left. A dozen or more Cylons were working on parts of other Cylons. The bustle of activity reminded Tigh in an odd way of a nest of insects, something compact and contained one minute, swarming all over you the next.

The Cylons inside all paused and looked at the newcomers.

"Up ahead here," Jon called from where he had already walked on down the hall, "we have our main data center, where we are still collecting information from experiments started thirty years ago."

Tigh and the others hurried down the hall to join him. This new door was on their right.

Five different-model Cylons checked vast banks of equipment far beyond Tigh's understanding. They all stopped abruptly, and stared at the newcomers.

"You'll have to forgive the companions' curiosity," Jon said as he once again walked away. "You're the first new humans they've seen in over twenty years."

Curiosity? Is that what he called it? Seeing the Cylon's blank faces staring at them, Tigh thought their reaction could be anything.

Hatred, fear, that startled moment just before the enemy attacks. Anything.

They passed other doors, and other Cylons. Each of the "companions" stopped whatever it was doing to look at them as they passed. While this might have been called a Colonial research center, it felt far more like an enemy camp.

"Your Colonel Adama is meeting in our conference center, just through here."

Jon led them through a door, where two humans and three Cylons were seated around a long table. These Cylons glanced briefly at the newcomers but did not stare. After what they had just walked through, Tigh realized their gesture seemed almost friendly.

Adama stood as they entered the room.

Tigh didn't think he had ever been so glad to see his old friend.

Adama saluted them all. "Captain, lieutenants."

Tigh, and the others behind him, all snapped to attention. "Colonel Adama, sir!"

"Everyone at ease. This is Doctor Fuest." Adama waved at an elderly gentleman who sat to his right. "He's been showing me the place." Bill grinned at the doctor. "It's quite impressive. I was about to ask the doctor what results have come of their research."

"We do manage with what we've got," the doctor replied. "The planet provides us with raw materials for manufacture, as well as foodstuffs for the human members of the community. We survive. But we have not grown in the ways we had wished." He paused, then added, "We have the whole history of the station on file. I'm sure that can help you if you want to look for anything specific."

Tigh noticed that the doctor wasn't quite answering Bill's questions. Bill no doubt noticed that as well. He couldn't wait to talk to his friend alone.

"Doctor?" a Butler Cylon spoke up.

"This is Gamma," the doctor said with a grin. "I suppose we should all introduce ourselves again! Yes, Gamma?"

"Laea has returned," the Butler replied.

A moment after he spoke, a young woman entered the room. She was dressed in the same shapeless white tunic and pants as the other humans, though hers were covered with a few stains and wrinkles, as if they had seen some real use.

She stopped and stared at all of them, and then smiled. "So you are from the Colonies?" She laughed, resting a hand on Adama's shoulder. "It's these uniforms that give you away. I'm glad you're here at last. The doctor's been waiting for you forever."

She smiled at each of the pilots in turn, looking straight at each of them, totally unafraid.

Tigh had never seen a girl quite so at ease, so natural.

"Laea keeps her own schedule," Jon said with a frown. "Although you would think she would make an exception for visitors."

"I am here now, Jon," she said brightly. She smiled at each of the newcomers in turn. "I oversee the soil collection for our farming, and I was out—nobody told me to expect—well, I'm here now, aren't I?"

Jon and the other young man continued to scowl, while the doctor smiled rather benignly. Apparently, young Laea was the problem child around the station. Tigh thought she was charming.

The doctor waved at the four in uniform. "As you guessed, these are all representatives of the Colonial fleet. Our home worlds have found us!"

"But others found you first," Adama replied. "You promised to discuss this."

"We're still not certain exactly what happened," the doctor answered. "Things happened very quickly. The companions acted to protect us."

"It went very badly," Jon broke in. "People died. Companions were damaged almost beyond repair. But after that they left us alone."

"And our mistake with them meant we wouldn't make a mistake with you," Gamma added.

"In what way?" Adama asked.

"You understand, they were the first new humans we had seen in years—" the doctor began.

"These are not scavengers," the Warrior Cylon said. "The protocols are different."

"What looked like an attack apparently activated certain obsolete programs," Jon explained.

"These have been corrected," Gamma added.

Tigh was impressed. Whatever the frak they were talking about, the humans and Cylons did speak on equal terms. Adama didn't act surprised, so neither would he. For now, Tigh thought it best to stand silently and listen.

"Now, your pilots here," Laea interrupted, "what are your names?"

Tigh and the others introduced themselves. Laea quickly managed to introduce everyone else in the room, including the Cylons.

"Would you care to join us, Laea?" The doctor pointed to a chair at his side.

She paused and frowned for an instant before her smile reappeared.

"Would you mind if I showed some of the guests around?"

"I've already shown them most of the points of—" Jon began angrily.

Laea waved away Jon's objection with a single flick of her hand. "What did you show them? The repair room? The science labs? We live in a truly beautiful and exciting corner of this planet. Let me take some of our new friends up to see the lookout ridge, or our new agricultural stations!"

The two young men looked like they wanted to shoot her on the spot.

The doctor was far more accommodating. "No, I'd like them to know as much about the station as possible. We will have to make some informed decisions very soon." He turned to their chief officer.

"Colonel Adama?"

"I can discuss the important issues here," Bill said after a moment's hesitation. "I think I'd like Captain Tigh to stay as well. His experience with Cylon culture might prove invaluable. But we do want to see as much of this facility as possible. I think it would be a wonderful idea if your young woman—Laea?—would show my two lieutenants around."

Tigh's experience with Cylon culture? Like that he had killed over a hundred of those frakking monstrosities? Bill was giving him a danger signal, a code that there was something wrong in paradise.

"Lieutenant Tanada," Adama said to Athena. "Be prepared to give a full report. We really need to learn as much as we can about this station in a very short time."

"That's wonderful!" Laea said to the room. She waved to the two pilots. "I'll give you the full tour. The others will be sorry they stayed behind!"

"Laea!" the doctor called out. "Gamma and I have decided we would like to honor our guests with a formal dinner. Can you see to it that you are back here by nightfall?"

Tigh was sorry to see her go. She smiled at him as she left the room. He chided himself for his thoughts. There was a considerable age difference. He would have to put young women out of his mind and get down to work.

Adama waited for the three to leave the room before he turned back to the others.

"Doctor. Companions." He looked at the three humans and three Cylons in turn. "I'm afraid we are through with being polite here. As a representative of the Colonial fleet, I outrank anyone on this station.

"Before I can make any kind of final report, you must tell me exactly what happened to the scavengers."

Now Saul saw why he was here. Bill wanted Tigh to back him up in a fight. This was just like old times.

"I will report," the Warrior Cylon Epsilon interrupted. "The cruiser *Lightning* entered our system two days before you arrived. They demanded that we let them land. We had nothing we could do to keep them from landing. This demand also put all the companions in defensive mode. In a way, we were being invaded. We prepared for a violent attack."

"But I asked you to do no such thing!" the doctor protested.

"We sometimes question your judgment, Doctor," Epsilon replied. "We have done it quietly, so as not to upset you."

The Cylon turned its attention back to Adama.

"Two men came down initially. They waved guns and fired upon the companions, even though we held no weapons. We overwhelmed them with sheer numbers, and took them prisoner. They severely damaged three of our number."

"Prisoners?" Adama asked with a trace of anger. "You said nothing of taking prisoners."

The doctor shook his head. "I have not seen them. I meant to, but with all that has transpired . . ."

"I've seen them." Vin spoke up for the first time. "They are in the medical unit, in induced comas. We had no other place to store them. Both pilots have suffered injuries, but I believe both will survive."

"Why didn't you tell me this?" the doctor asked.

"Doctor, you seemed overwhelmed," Gamma replied.

"It was all that death." The doctor whispered one more word. It sounded like "bet."

"The scavengers demanded the return of their pilots," Gamma continued. "We would gladly have given them up, if they had acted in a civilized manner. Five came down the second time. I believe the lead negotiator wanted to find a way to make an exchange. But others in their party were all too quick to draw their weapons. The doctor had gone to meet them. He was in harm's way."

"We had to defend the best interests of the station," Epsilon explained.

"It was over very quickly," Jon spoke up. "Three of the five were shot. The other two escaped in their ships."

"We are not sure what happened to those vessels," Beta the Mechanic said. "Our DRADIS system was disrupted at that time. We feared it had been damaged by weapons fire, but shortly thereafter, it once again became operational."

"By the time we could once again check," Jon added, "the cruiser *Lightning* was leaving our system."

"We were left with prisoners that we didn't know what to do with," Epsilon added.

Adama stood abruptly. "I would like to see the prisoners—now."

The doctor, grim-faced, stood as well. "Very well. Shall we all go?"

CHAPTER 19

Laea wanted to trust them. They came from the Colonies, didn't they—her human home?

She felt she needed to trust someone outside the station. Her home had always had its secrets, but they had grown much larger very quickly. There were things right in front of them not talked about.

The others said they regretted the deaths of the scavengers, but it seemed as if not even the doctor felt for the dead.

And no one spoke of the other ship. The ship she had seen from the roof.

Laea needed to tell them her story.

"I'm glad we got away from the others," she said to the two young pilots. "I need to talk to you, someplace private."

"What?" The young man called Skeeter looked confused. "I thought you were taking us on a tour."

"Oh, I'll be taking you on a tour." She looked around her. "We can't talk here. Everything in this place is recorded for future study."

Athena frowned. "Then they're watching us? Won't they be suspicious if we leave?"

"The station isn't that organized. So much is recorded, sometimes

no one bothers to look at what has been saved unless they have a specific reason to. But I have questions, and I'm sure you have questions,
too." She smiled up at one of the hidden recorders. "But really, I'm
simply showing you our farming sites. It's what I do, remember?"

She led them back out onto the landing field.

"Actually, I need to take you some distance away from the station. It's a bit of a walk. We may not be home for dinner."

"You aren't afraid that someone will get suspicious?" Athena
asked.

"No, they'll just get angry," she said with a grin. "I'm known to
be irresponsible."

Skeeter looked out at the ships sitting on the field. "You say this
thing you want to show us is some distance away? Who says we
have to walk?" He glanced over at Athena. "Haven't you flown the
shuttle a few times?"

"You don't think the colonel would mind?" Laea asked.

"I think the Colonel wants to find those secrets more than you.
What a good idea, Skeeter!" Athena smiled at Laea. "Would you like
to take a little trip?"

Laea stared at the squat craft before them. "Could we? I've never
ever been in the air."

She could fly, just like this woman from another world.

But she had important things to do. This would give her the perfect opportunity to talk with them about the stranger. Maybe they
could even bring the stranger back with them.

She looked around the field. "I had better tell someone we're doing this."

Skeeter followed her gaze. "You mean, you've got to check in
with *these* things?"

Laea waved away his objections. "They mostly let me do what I
want. Anyone will do. The companions all talk to each other." She
pointed and yelled across the field.

"Delta!"

A squat, pale beige companion with a padded midsection rolled
in their direction.

"Laea!" the companion replied in a high voice. "It has been long
since we've talked! What can I do for my little one?"

"Will there be a problem taking off without the doctor's permission?" Athena asked as Delta approached.

Laea shrugged. "He's in a meeting. He told me to give you a tour.
And that tour will be from the air. I don't see a problem."

"I'd just as soon take that tour," Skeeter agreed. "I can't get used to these companions of yours."

Delta rolled to a stop before them. "Laea? What have you been up to?"

"Would you tell the doctor that we are going to take the shuttle up for a look around? We won't be going very far."

The companion hesitated for a moment before replying. "This has been cleared with the doctor?"

"Yes, he just sent me to show these newcomers around."

Delta paused before remarking, "I understand you are all expected for dinner."

"And we will be there. Thank you, Delta, for reminding us."

"You're welcome, Laea. Now be a good girl."

It turned and rolled slowly away.

"That Cylon seemed to be scolding you," Skeeter said.

Laea smiled at that. "The companion is a Nanny Model. Quite gentle, really. She was one of those who raised me and my brothers. I think she has trouble talking to me in any other way." She waved to the two pilots. "Now let's get up in that shuttle before Delta talks to anyone else."

Skeeter opened the hatch, and the three quickly climbed inside. The place was full of switches and dials. It reminded Laea of a miniature science center.

Athena sat dead center in front of the controls, and waved for Laea to take the seat on her left.

"I need to talk to someone, too." She flicked a couple of switches in front of her. "*Galactica*, this is Athena."

"Galactica *here*," a man's voice said from a speaker overhead.

"We're going to take the shuttle up a few hundred feet and take a look around the research station," Athena continued. "We've got someone with us who's going to give us a guided tour."

"*Okay, Athena. Is Colonel Adama with you?*"

"Negative. Just Skeeter and me and one guest on this trip. The colonel is currently talking to the head of the center."

"*Very good. Please let Adama know the admiral would like to speak to him at his first opportunity.*"

"Will do, *Galactica*." She flicked a couple more switches. "Well, now we've all gotten permission from everybody."

Skeeter sat down in the next chair over. "You'll need to strap yourself in there. Like this."

Laea copied Skeeter's actions. The belt closed with a satisfying click.

"I need to do a couple things to get us started." Athena glanced over at her as she flicked a series of switches. "So what's life like on the station?"

Laea shrugged.

"Nothing ever really changes. It just goes on. I think it made more sense when there were many humans to interact with the Cylons."

"You're the only ones left? You and your brothers?" The shuttle began to hum softly. Laea guessed it was the sound of the engines.

"They're not really my brothers. We just grew up together. But they might as well be brothers. We know each other much too well. And they are both a little boring."

"What happened to the other humans?" Skeeter asked.

"Many left when the war began. The rest, including my mother and father, were killed in an accident. I was very young, I don't know many details. I just know that most of the humans were killed." Laea paused, then added, "Cylons were lost as well. But they can be rebuilt."

"Hang on," Athena called. "We're good to go." She pulled back on a small wheel before her as the shuttle lifted into the air.

Into the air. Laea held her breath as the ground fell away beneath them. She wanted to laugh. She let herself smile instead.

"So where does the tour begin?" Athena asked.

Laea pointed out the window. "There's a river that runs north of the station. If you follow that for a little ways, I'll show you."

Athena turned the shuttle north. The engine made hardly any noise. Laea felt like she was swooping through the air—like a bird riding the wind.

She took a deep breath. She didn't have time for birds.

"There are other things I need to tell you," Laea said hurriedly. "Back at that staff meeting, they had things they weren't talking about."

"Like what?" Skeeter asked.

"When all the bad stuff happened, when the scavengers and the companions started to shoot at each other, two of the scavengers' ships took off, but neither of them got very far. There was another ship out here, waiting for them." She took a quick breath. "The first one—the Viper—was shot down by the new ship. The second one landed somewhere out here—so it wouldn't get shot down, is my guess. It's still out here. That's where we're going."

"A ship was up here?" Athena asked. "What kind of ship?"

How could she answer that? "It was a big ship. Big and round. When I was little, I used to read up on Vipers and other starships. Well, actually Vin did most of the reading. I used to look over his shoulder. Maybe he could tell you what that ship was. I never saw one of those in all the programs."

"That means there's somebody else out here, too," Skeeter said.

"There were some experimental ships from the Colonies, back before the war," Athena replied. "I thought all of them had been junked. But then, I never expected to find a working research station out in the middle of nowhere."

"Could this be something the station's involved in?" Skeeter asked.

Laea paused a moment to look out the window. The river wound its way past the cultivated fields and into the trees. They were already flying over the forest.

"I don't know," she said at last. "A week ago I would have said no. But now there seem to be things the doctor and the companions aren't talking about. But there's something else. One of the pilots from the ship is still alive. That's the reason I was late for the meeting. I came out here to find him."

Athena turned to look at Laea. "Are you sure about this?"

"I think he crashed around here. I saw him—I really saw him—from a distance in the woods. I wasn't sure it was safe to talk to him. I'm afraid I got a little scared.

"I came back to the station to see if I could get somebody to go back out with me. But with both my bothers and the companions acting so oddly lately, I thought maybe it was safer to ask you." She looked down at the chair she sat in and grinned. "I didn't know I'd get to fly in one of these things, besides."

She frowned as she looked back at the forest rushing by below. "I don't know if I can tell exactly where I saw him."

It was difficult from the air to tell exactly where she had traveled on the ground. She could see the river clearly enough, except in those places where the forest grew too thick to see the ground beneath.

She craned her neck around to glance out another window, trying to see where they were in relation to the station. Hadn't they gone far enough by now?

She turned her attention forward and saw a flash of metal down below.

She pointed at the spot. "There! Try down there!"

Athena quickly landed the shuttle in a clearing by the riverside.

"This stranger, this scavenger," Laea continued quickly, scared, she guessed, that they would find him before she could finish her story, "he might have been as surprised by me as I was by him. He called out, though. I think he wanted to talk to me. I hope he will now.

"I hope he won't hide on us. Still, his lander should have come down somewhere nearby. Maybe if I call out to him again, he'll show up." Laea wondered if she was talking too much.

"We'll do our best to find him," Athena said as she shut down the shuttle's engines.

"You can take the straps off now," Skeeter said as he unsnapped his own restraints. "Are we likely to meet anybody else out here?"

Laea shook her head. "The companions rarely leave the station. Occasionally Epsilon will form a hunting party to bring back food for the humans. But with the recent crisis, everybody's back at the station."

They all climbed out of the shuttle. This time, Laea led the way.

The forest around them was very quiet.

"I saw a flash of metal, back this way." Laea headed back the way the shuttle had come. She took a path along the river's edge. Within fifty steps, they had turned a corner and lost sight of their ship.

She stopped abruptly. "I hear something ahead," she said softly. There it was again, the snap of a twig, the sound of someone pushing his way through the underbrush.

"Whoever it is isn't even trying to be quiet," Athena whispered. "Do you have many animals here?"

"Native to the planet?" Laea shook her head. "There are very few. Birds and rodents, mostly. And I think the research station brought the rodents." She saw a break in the trees ahead.

"I see another clearing. Maybe we can get a good look at this scavenger."

They moved closer to the next open space, being careful to stay just inside the tree line.

"Over there!" Athena pointed. "Something's shiny."

"Maybe our friend's carrying a gun," Skeeter replied.

Laea heard another branch break, followed by the whir and clank of gears.

A dark metal machine stepped into the clearing.

"Holy frak!" Skeeter whispered. "It's a toaster!"

Maybe, Laea realized, she hadn't seen the stranger's lander. Maybe the glint had come from the metal body of a companion.

The machine turned to look at them. Half of Laea wanted to stand up and identify herself, to ask what business the companions had in the forest. But the other half of her saw something else.

This companion was a stranger, too.

CHAPTER 20

Skeeter saw a Cylon. No, he told himself, they were called "companions" here.

"Hey!" he called to Laea. "I thought you said there wouldn't be any companions this far out."

Laea frowned at the machine on the far side of the clearing. "I don't think I've ever seen this companion. I mean, it's a Warrior—one of the new Centurion models. Except, see the way that red light flashes behind its visor? That's different. That's not one of ours."

The strange machine lifted its arms. The machine held a weapon.

"Watch out!" Athena cried as a bright red beam sliced across the open space.

All three of them ducked behind the trees as the machine turned slightly, taking aim at their new position.

"Frak!" Skeeter whispered from where he crouched. "We've got ourselves a *real* Cylon this time!"

The forest would give them some cover. But the area behind them was filled with thick bushes. Skeeter thought he saw some brambles, too. They would make far too much noise trying to escape that way.

"How can this happen?" Laea demanded indignantly. "We've never seen Cylons here—I mean *real* Cylons—before!"

"That you know about," Athena reminded her. "Remember you said you thought the companions were keeping secrets?"

"They've been talking to Cylons?" Her tone of voice said she couldn't believe it.

"We probably now know who owns that big ship that shot the Viper out of the sky," Skeeter added.

"You mean the companions knew about the ship? They hid it from us?"

"We don't know that for sure," Athena replied softly.

"It's just damn well likely," Skeeter added. He peeked around the corner of the tree. "Sooner or later, that thing's going to figure out we're unarmed."

Red beams shot out suddenly from across the clearing—a dozen in rapid succession. Branches came crashing down from overhead, some quite close to their hiding place. Skeeter's nostrils were filled with the smell of charred wood.

"I think it already knows," he added. "That thing is going to kill us."

"We have to get back to the shuttle and warn the others," Athena said.

Skeeter looked at her. "Well, at least some of us do."

He could hear his grandmother's words filling his head.

You don't go to bed on time
You don't stop making noise
You don't wash behind your ears
The Cylons are gonna get you!

Guess he was going to end up a naughty boy after all.

"I'll distract the thing!" Skeeter whispered hoarsely. "You head back to the river!"

He jumped out from behind the trees before anyone could object, yelling and waving his arms as he tried to head in the opposite direction from the others.

He didn't make it two steps before he felt a searing pain in his arm. All his breath left him as he fell to the ground.

"Skeeter!" Athena shouted.

He groaned. Frak, did that hurt.

"It got me in the shoulder," he whispered as Athena crawled to his side. His right shoulder. He looked over at the wound. It seemed like there was an awful lot of blood.

"It's coming toward us!" Laea shouted. Skeeter raised his head enough to see that the machine was marching straight at them across the field.

Laea glanced at Athena. "Maybe I can distract it while you get Skeeter back to the ship."

Skeeter shook his head. "We already tried that one. We didn't come out here to get you killed."

The young woman kept her eyes on the machine. "I know my way around these woods. If I can avoid that thing, I can double back out of here and make it to the station in a couple of hours."

A bolt of red light barely missed Laea's head.

"I don't think any of us are going anyplace!" Skeeter shouted.

They all ducked when they heard a huge boom.

Skeeter looked up. The lower two-thirds of the Cylon still stood some twenty paces distant.

But the Cylon's head was gone.

The machine fell to the ground an instant later.

Skeeter tried to stand up and take a look around.

"Who did that?" he demanded.

A man wearing torn, soiled clothes waved at them from the far side of the clearing.

"That would be me."

Skeeter realized that standing was not a good idea. He looked down at his hands. Where had all this blood come from?

His eyes closed as he fell back down.

Laea watched the stranger as he kicked at the still machine. The Cylon. Then Skeeter collapsed.

Laea turned to Athena. "Is he . . . ?"

"He's badly hurt. We'd better get him back to the shuttle."

The stranger walked across the clearing, a large rifle in his hand. He nodded to Laea, then smiled.

"I'm Tom Zarek, and I think we almost met before."

Laea nodded back. This time, he had his shirt on. It was torn and stained, but it still covered most of his torso. Maybe she could talk to him now.

"I'm sorry about what happened before," she said quickly. "I saw your ship fall back to the ground. I went looking to see if anybody had survived."

She felt herself growing hot. She took a deep breath. "I'm apparently not that good at talking to strangers."

"I'm glad we had another chance to get together. So what happened to the man I saw before?" It was only then that the newcomer noticed Skeeter on the ground, his arm covered with blood. "Frak! The toaster shot somebody?"

Athena looked up from where she had torn off a length of cloth from Skeeter's dry sleeve to wrap around the wound. "Yeah. Got him in the arm. If we can stop the bleeding, I think he'll be all right."

"You're Colonial fleet," Tom Zarek said. He shook his head. "I never thought I would be so glad to see you. But then I never thought we would have a Cylon problem."

"And who are you?" Athena asked as she tied the bandage tight.

"Well, I was a raider on the cruiser *Lightning*, but I think I've recently retired. I didn't like the job all that much after I got it."

He sighed and glanced back at the Cylon. "I'm not so proud of what's gone on here the last couple days. I was supposed to get our pilots returned to us. Instead, I managed to just barely duck out of a fight. I've mostly just been waiting to be rescued. I hope you can oblige. Especially since I think the Cylons are looking for me."

Skeeter groaned. He was waking up!

"Why would there be Cylons here?" Athena asked sharply. "Do you know?"

"I think they were here long before the *Lightning* showed up. I tried to run, but there was another ship. Biggest ship I ever saw. I bailed before it could shoot me down."

Athena nodded, glancing at Laea. "So she told us."

Zarek pointed at the smoldering remains in the middle of the field.

"Current evidence suggests that big ship was Cylon." Zarek looked up and down the clearing. "I have the feeling that toaster isn't alone. And we just made a big noise that might well attract the others."

Athena hoisted the other pilot up to lean against her shoulder. "Can you walk?" she asked. He managed to nod. She turned to the others.

"I'm getting Skeeter back to the ship."

They hobbled together back toward the river.

Laea didn't move. She looked straight at Tom Zarek. He was tall and thin. His dark hair fell just over his ears, and his eyes seemed to look right through her. He really was very good looking. Maybe that was what made her stomach feel funny.

"Come with us," she said.

"And leave all this behind?" He glanced down at his rifle. "I think you've convinced me. Whatever you've got has to be better than Cylons."

"Watch out!" Athena called from the other side of the clearing.

Two more red flashes came out of the woods on the far side of the field. Both hit the trees just above their heads. Laea and Tom fell to the ground as Athena pushed Skeeter behind a tree.

But Laea had gotten separated from the others. They were more than twenty paces apart, across the open field. The Cylons would kill anyone who stepped out in the open.

"Get out of here!" Laea called. "We'll find our way back overland!"

Athena nodded. "I'll get Skeeter back to the ship!" She dragged the wounded man farther back into the trees.

Zarek fired a round in the general direction of the Cylon's blasts. He waved to his right.

"Go back into the trees. Run, that way! My ship's just out of sight. I'll cover you!"

He fired back at the tree line three more times.

Laea sprinted into the woods. She saw a patch of silver in front of her. It was the lander, just down a short path. As she ran closer, she saw that the ship was sitting at an odd angle atop a pile of tree limbs it had gathered on its way down. She heard Zarek's gun blast away behind her—three times—then heard his running feet crashing through the underbrush.

"I'm right behind you!" he called. "The door's on the other side!"

She half ran, half climbed through the debris to reach the far side of the lander. The hatch stood open.

Tom was right at her back. "Get inside!" He turned and fired again and she stepped inside.

It was dark in the lander, the only light coming from some small windows half-covered by branches. The back half of the small space was lost in shadow. There was still enough light, however, to see a large pile of guns in the middle of the floor.

Tom jumped in after her, slamming the door shut behind him.

"We can get some lights in here if you want," he said. "I was saving the ship's battery in the hope I might get a signal out. Now that somebody's found us, I don't have to worry about the wireless."

Laea heard a series of sharp pings, like the sound of pebbles hitting the ship's outer skin.

Zarek frowned. "I think the hull of this thing is good against small-weapons fire. But we're easy targets here. I killed one Cylon, but now I'm guessing we've got two more. But that's just the beginning. That ship was big enough to hold thousands."

Laea flinched as more pops rattled against the hull. "Shouldn't we wait here? If there's a Battlestar out there, can't they save us?"

"I'm sure they can, and I'm sure they will. We just don't know how long it's going to take them to get back here. I'm also sure that the Cylons have plenty of weapons that could cut this ship in two. We need to find someplace that isn't quite so exposed."

He walked over to the center of the lander's cabin and started to pick through the guns. "I know a cave where we can make a better stand. It's not far off—on a ridge a few hundred klicks to our west. We should be able to see the rescue party and defend ourselves."

Laea looked out the nearest window. She saw nothing but trees. "But that means we've got to get out of here."

"Well, we have the firepower." Tom kicked gently at the pile. "Ever handle a gun?"

Laea nodded. "My brothers and I used to take target practice out at the edge of the cultivated fields. I've never shot at a moving target, though."

"Well, I think you're going to get your chance. We'll have to gather up enough guns, ammo, and supplies to last us for a couple of days, and just hope that's enough time for the others—"

Laea put her hand on Tom's arm. "Did you hear that?"

He nodded, and pointed toward the sound. Something was moving in the shadows at the far side of the lander.

Zarek raised his rifle and pointed it at the darkness.

A man, dressed all in black, stepped into the light. He pointed a handgun directly back at Zarek's head.

The newcomer grinned. "Come on now, Tom, we don't want to make a mess."

"Creep!" Tom replied.

"That's what they call me."

If Tom Zarek was thin, this newcomer was downright emaciated. His skin was almost as pale as Gamma's white enamel. He had sunken cheeks and thinning hair. The hand that held the gun shook a bit. He did not look at all healthy.

His gaze flicked to Laea.

"Nice of you to bring company." He looked back at Tom. "And nice of you to leave me behind." He took a step closer.

"Where were you?" Zarek demanded. "By the time I got into the lander, Boone was dead. But I couldn't see you anywhere!"

The Creep shrugged. "Let's say I took a step away from the fighting. I can tell when the odds are against me. There's a reason the Creep never gets caught." He lifted his gun slightly, so it was aimed over Tom's head. "So, maybe part of the fault lies with me."

Zarek kept his rifle aimed at the other man. "If I had had you with me to shoot our guns, we might have taken out a Cylon or two. We might have gotten out of here!"

The Creep grinned. It made his face look like a skull. "So we both made mistakes. You keep on making them—leaving that door open.

What say we start fresh? I'll put down mine if you'll put down yours."

Tom slowly lowered his rifle. The Creep carefully returned his handgun to a holster at his side.

The Creep stared at Laea. "You haven't introduced me to your friend. You know that raiders always share whatever they find." He glanced back at Tom. "But I heard your speech back there. About blasting your way out of here and making for that cave. I think that plan would work better if you had three people fighting the Cylons. So let's get our supplies together, shall we?"

He paused to look at Tom and Laea in turn. "We can all catch up when we get to the cave."

CHAPTER 21

Adama realized there would be no easy answers. He felt as though the doctor, and perhaps all the humans in this place, wanted so desperately for the facility to survive that they had even stopped looking at the questions. He supposed everyone had parts of their lives that were so difficult that they were hard to look at. He had his own problems trying to balance his work with the needs of his family— problems he was probably still trying to run away from. But he hoped his family problems would never reach beyond some simple misunderstandings.

Misunderstandings here seemed to end in destruction and death.

The young woman, Laea, had seemed to know that something was wrong, and had wanted to help. He wondered if she would be able to show Athena and Skeeter anything that could explain the complexities of this place.

He supposed he could talk to everyone over this grand dinner the doctor had planned. And after that, all they had to determine was what to do with the prisoners from the raider vessel, the human survivors of the station, and close to one hundred somewhat modified Cylons.

Everyone had left the meeting together, all going to see the prisoners. They had walked in a line along a series of long hallways. Gamma led the way, followed by Jon and Vin, and then the doctor, quite spry despite his frail appearance, flanked by Epsilon and Beta. Adama and Tigh were happy to bring up the rear. It gave them a chance to get a good look at all the parts of the station they were passing through—not that there was that much to see in these featureless hallways. But it also gave them the opportunity to talk a bit in low tones without any of the others appearing to notice.

"Why didn't they tell us about the prisoners sooner?" Tigh whispered.

"I think they didn't want to. Maybe the doctor did. But he seems overwhelmed. I think he might genuinely want to leave here and go back to the Colonies."

"So he's happy we're here."

"Yeah. But I'm thinking he might be the only one."

"Who can tell with these 'modified' Cylons?" Tigh shook his head. "I think once a toaster, always a toaster."

Adama still hoped he was wrong.

"The station hospital is just ahead," the doctor called over his shoulder. "The prisoners, to my understanding, are right through here."

"They have been well taken care of," Gamma added. "We have sufficient programming to provide for most basic human needs."

Adama and Tigh stepped into a large and mostly empty room. Only one corner of the space, hidden by curtains, seemed to hold any activity. The humans and companions walked across the cavernous space, their feet echoing in the emptiness.

Epsilon stepped forward and pulled aside the curtains. "Here are your pilots."

The prisoners lay in two hospital beds, side by side. Their eyes were closed, their arms connected by wires to a number of machines, all of which beeped or hummed softly. The pilots were perfectly still, barely breathing.

"I'm afraid we didn't know what to do with them," the doctor said. "This seemed to be the best solution."

"We have instructions to treat the severely wounded thus," Gamma continued, "to wait for the next supply ship. When the station was fully functional, we would receive supply ships on a regular basis. They would have the medical supplies and expertise to help the severely traumatized recover."

"What have you done to them?" Adama asked. They hardly seemed to be alive.

"They have been put into a medically induced coma," Gamma replied.

"They were unwelcome outsiders," Epsilon added. "They could not fit into our society. In this case, they became the trauma."

Tigh pointed at one pilot's bandaged arm. "What happened here?"

"He lost a hand in the fighting," Gamma replied. "We did the best we could to bandage it and stop the bleeding.

"I'm afraid I wasn't very close to the action," the doctor admitted. "I didn't even realize the extent of their injuries."

Again, Adama thought, *Or you didn't really want to know.*

"What has happened to their Vipers?" Adama asked.

Beta spoke up. "There is much we lack. We have begun to strip them down for parts."

Adama wondered, if they could find something useful in the pilots, if they might take them apart as well. But no, these "companions" had done what was necessary for their survival. Were they able to make rational decisions? Or was this all part of their programming?

Adama looked at the assembled men and machines. "We will arrange for the disposition of these men. We have the facilities on *Galactica* to help them heal—and to keep them under lock and key until we find out just what they know." He turned to Saul. "Captain Tigh. Find out from our hosts here if we can transport them in their current condition. I'm going to talk to the admiral and see who else we can get down here to help."

"Would you like to use our comm center?" Jon asked.

Adama shook his head. "I'll just make a quick call from my ship. *Galactica* is already monitoring the shuttle's frequency. They'll be waiting for my call." He looked back at the door they had come through. "Is there an easy way to get from here to the landing field?"

Vin waved at the far side of the curtains. "Actually, if you go farther this way, you'll come right out on the far side of the field. I'll be glad to show you."

All the corridors in this place made it seem a bit like a maze. It was obviously designed for a much larger staff. The more Adama saw of this facility, the more he realized this might have been a worthwhile project—except it was far too little and far too late. The Cylon problem had erupted before they could even get this venture properly under way. But in studying man/machine interaction, the work they had done on Research Station *Omega* could still prove valuable.

"Very good, Captain. Wait for me here."

Tigh gave him a quick salute. He didn't look particularly happy to be left behind.

Adama let Vin lead the way. They left the hospital room and walked down a short hall to an even larger space—the old Viper hangar bay.

Again, most of the space was empty, except for a busy area along one wall, where a trio of Cylons was carefully disassembling a pair of ancient Mark Ones. They appeared to be placing every different piece into its own separate container, each of which in turn was neatly labeled and stacked against one wall. They were saving everything for future use, just as the doctor had said.

Adama felt the slightest bit guilty leaving Tigh behind to keep the locals busy. But it would seem too odd for both of them to retreat to the shuttle. And he needed to discuss with the admiral what they were going to do, preferably in private.

Vin opened a door at the far side of the hangar, then stepped aside. "Just through here. I'll wait until you're done."

"Thank you." He appreciated that he wouldn't have to close the shuttle door in the young man's face.

He stepped out onto the field and saw that the shuttle was gone. Adama almost turned around to confront Vin about the disappearance. The two Vipers were where they had left them, however. If the "companions" were going to take any of their ships, wouldn't they take all of them? There must be another explanation. He walked quickly over to the nearer of the two Vipers. He reached inside and powered up the wireless.

"Adama to *Galactica*."

"*Galactica here.*"

"You don't happen to know the whereabouts of our shuttle?"

"*Athena took it out, Colonel. She said she had your permission.*"

"Oh." Adama felt a sudden surge of relief. Apparently, his pilots were taking the quick way to track down whatever Laea wanted to show them. "Well, then I guess she does have permission. Put me through to the admiral."

A moment passed before he heard the admiral's voice.

"*Sing here.*"

"Admiral. I'm away from the others. I can talk freely."

"*What's your assessment of the situation?*"

Adama decided to be blunt. "I think we got here just before this whole place fell apart. It's already crumbling around the edges. And while the Cylons on this station do not seem to be combatants, they have been showing some worrisome tendencies. They've got two prisoners here from the scavenger ship that they've put into comas. I want to get these men on *Galactica* as soon as possible to see if they can tell us anything."

"*We'll send down a med team,*" Sing agreed. "*Other recommendations?*"

"Something has to be done here with the human staff. The old man at least looks like he could use medical attention. I'm not sure about the youngsters."

And what would happen if they brought the humans back? He didn't think anyone would want to leave the facility under the control of Cylons—modified or not.

Perhaps they could maintain the facility here until the original researchers on Picon could send replacements.

It was a controlled situation, one laboratory setting on one world very far away from the Colonies.

But he imagined Colonial citizens would be outraged if they knew anything about it. Supporting a site with Cylons? Too many people had lost too much in the war. The researchers here would be branded as traitors. No one could understand a place where man and machine could live in peace.

If that was, indeed, the true nature of this place.

"Colonel?" Sing prompted.

"Sorry, sir. I was thinking what we might do in the long term with this place. Even though they seem to be cooperative, I don't know if we can trust these Cylons' continuing motives. We may need to shut the whole thing down. I'm not sure the Cylons would agree. We'd probably need at least a major force from the *Galactica* to get them to comply. It might get complicated."

"*Understood,*" Sing replied. "*I'll talk to the fleet. I'm guessing this facility is still under Picon jurisdiction. It will be up to them to decide.*" The admiral paused, then added, "*But that means talking to Colonial governments. That never goes quickly. I imagine it will take a few days to come to a decision. Are you comfortable with staying at the facility?*"

"I think that's for the best. I believe I've gained their trust. We'll stay here, tell them we've contacted their home government. See if they might want to send any messages of their own back to Picon. After the med team retrieves the prisoners, I think it's best if just the four of us stay as our official representatives. The station seems in a fragile balance. The fewer new elements introduced into their lives at this point, the better.

"I'll know more about the situation here after I get a report from Athena and Skeeter. They're out taking a look around."

"*I understand they checked in with* Galactica *when they first went out,*" Sing replied. "*We haven't heard back from them yet. We've been getting periodic interference with our signals up here, both wireless and*

DRADIS. I wanted to ask you about that. Is there anything down there you think can be causing this interference?"

"Nothing I've seen, or they've told me about. Could there be some other cause?" Adama knew that storms and large magnetic fields had disrupted signals in the past.

"Nothing natural, as far as we can tell. I've got the techs working on it. But stay alert!"

"Yes sir!"

"Hopefully Athena will check in soon. Talk to me again after you've spoken with her.

"Sing out." The admiral broke the connection.

So they would have a couple more days to look around here before the ultimate decision was passed down from the Colonies. Adama was relieved it was out of his hands.

He supposed it was time to go back and get ready for dinner.

Athena heard the big boom of Zarek's gun as she helped Skeeter back to the shuttle. The other pilot was able to walk, after a fashion, as long as she didn't rush him too much. Her temporary bandage had stanched most of the flow, but Skeeter was still leaving a trail of blood all along the river path. It seemed to take forever to get him back to the level spot where she had parked the shuttle. She saw the small ship at last, twenty paces from the forest's edge. She had to get him across the clearing as quickly as possible.

"Come on Skeet, we're almost there."

"I'm with you. I'm with—" He grunted in pain.

They crossed the field without incident. She struggled him through the hatch and into the copilot's seat. She checked the view through the windows as she powered up their transportation. It was all quiet out there. She couldn't see any Cylons after them—yet.

"Feels good to sit down," Skeeter managed after a moment.

"I'll get us back to the *Galactica*."

Skeeter tried to smile. "Sounds good to me. I'll just sit back and enjoy the view."

"You do that. In the meantime, I think we have a little news to share with home."

She tried to raise *Galactica* as she made the final preparations for liftoff. All she got was a burst of static.

Athena frowned. "Well, I guess we've got to get out from under these trees." She engaged the engines and grabbed the wheel. "Hang tight, Skeets."

She lifted off, and started climbing toward the upper atmosphere. Smooth sailing so far. When she got a little higher, she'd try to raise *Galactica* again.

"Athena!" Skeeter pointed above her head. "We're being followed!"

She looked to where he pointed at the DRADIS screen above the front window. There was some sort of small craft in close pursuit. It looked like some kind of modified Viper, longer and sleeker than the models on the *Galactica*. Her guess was this was the special Cylon model.

"I'm sorry, Skeeter. You're going to have to hang on. We've got to shake our tail."

The shuttle didn't have the same flexibility or speed as a Viper. Usually. She'd just have to ignore that and pretend it did. She rose quickly, then banked to the right. The Viper was gaining on them.

"Frak!" Skeeter swore. "No way you can outrun something like that."

"So we'll just have to outfox them. Maybe we'll have to wait a bit to get back to *Galactica*. I think we need to take this news straight to Colonel Adama."

Athena knew they had hospital facilities at the research station. They could fix something as simple as a shoulder wound.

"Watch it!" Skeeter shouted. "That baby's gonna climb up our rear exhaust!"

"Only if we invite it in. Which we're not."

She dropped suddenly, skimming the shuttle just above the trees.

The Viper overshot its intended target, shooting far overhead, then arced around to follow.

Skeeter stared at the DRADIS screen. "We can't do this forever! We have to have weapons! We're slow and clunky! The Viper is going to get us!"

That wound was making Skeeter negative. "The Viper is not being flown by Athena," she replied. "Relax. I haven't lost a passenger yet." She didn't mention that, as a Viper pilot, she had never ever had passengers. "So shut up. I think your blood loss is making you delirious."

Skeeter shook his head and sank down in his seat. "I hope you're right."

"Oh, Athena is always right."

She flew low over the river, below the tree line, weaving with the wandering flow of water.

The Viper crisscrossed in the air above them, looking for an opening. Something exploded on the far side of the riverbank.

"They're shooting at us!" Skeeter moaned.

"And not very well. If we stay out here long enough, maybe they'll just run out of ammunition."

She looked over at the suffering Skeeter.

"That was a joke."

The Viper finally swooped down to their level, hugging the tree line some distance behind their tail.

Athena smiled. "Ah, now I've got you right where I want you."

Skeeter sat up and pointed straight ahead. "Waterfall!"

She looked up and saw a cliff face covered by a rushing torrent of water, directly in their path.

She nodded. "Just the ticket."

She banked sharply as they rushed toward the cliff. The shuttle's underside scraped the upper branches as it rose just above the rocks and trees.

The Viper crashed into the cliff face behind them, the sleek metal crumpling beneath the rushing water.

"Why did I doubt you?" Skeeter said with a weak grin.

"Hey, a Viper might be faster, but Athena's got the moves!"

"So we get to go back to *Galactica*?"

Athena shook her head. "I think if we go back up there, we're just going to gain another Viper. Hang on, and we'll go talk to Colonel Adama."

"After that, I'd trust you anywhere." He closed his eyes and groaned. "But I'd trust you more if we stopped moving around."

She nosed the shuttle slightly higher in the air, so they could see beyond the trees. The research station was dead ahead, and just in time.

Skeeter looked like he was going to pass out all over again.

People were shouting when the admiral stepped into the CIC.

"What the hell?" said Sing.

"Sir." Captain Draken looked up from his console. "We've got something big coming up on the DRADIS. Something really big."

"I think this is what has been interfering with our communications," the wireless operator cut in. "Excuse me, sir. They must have some sort of jamming device. Probably to keep us from seeing them."

"Granted." Sing frowned up at the great yellow disk on the DRADIS screen. "But why are we seeing them now?"

"I think it's a Dreadnaught, sir," someone said.

"I thought all of those were destroyed in the Cylon War," Draken replied.

"Apparently not," Sing replied.

"Who exactly is flying this thing?" Draken asked.

"They're sending us a comm signal!" the wireless officer shouted.

"Put it over the speakers," Sing ordered.

"Galactica. *This is the Dreadnaught* Invincible.*"

"*Invincible*," Sing replied. "We were unaware that you were still in service."

"*We are no longer a Colonial ship*," the curiously flat voice responded. "*We were never really a Colonial ship. We have become what we were always meant to be.*

"*We are a Cylon war machine.*"

CHAPTER 22

Adama turned away from the Viper, ready to return to the others. He would relay what he and the admiral had talked about in the most diplomatic way possible. Part of him was relieved that Picon would make the final decision here. He imagined that the only solution that made sense, both fiscally and politically, would be to dismantle the station. But that would end the research, as well as the sense of human/machine cooperation that seemed to have sprung up in this odd little community.

Would any decision be the right one? He just hoped that somehow, some good might come from this place.

As he walked back toward the hangar, he saw half a dozen companions gathered just outside the door. All of them were looking up at the sky.

He turned and looked as well, to see a small golden disk, perhaps the size of a moon, hanging high above them in the sky. It was far enough overhead that he could not judge its true size.

But Adama knew its true size, and its true purpose. He recognized it, even from this distance.

It was a Dreadnaught. The largest Colonial ship ever conceived, it had been in its experimental stages when the Cylon War began. The Colonies had still managed to build three of them, and all three had turned against humankind. For the Dreadnaught was the first ship almost entirely operated by Cylons. They had designed thousands of specialized individual war machines—Cylon fighters, Cylon pilots, Cylon technicians. The Dreadnaughts all had a token human crew to supervise the Cylons—perhaps a dozen souls on each ship, without whom the ship would supposedly be unable to operate. But the heart of the ship was a vast Cylon culture, uncounted machines trained to fight so that men and women would never have to fight again.

The Colonies found, once the Cylon War began, that they had built the Dreadnaughts far too well. All three of them were under Cylon control within moments of the beginning of the war. How the Cylons had gained control of ships that supposedly were unable to operate without a human failsafe was never discovered, since none of the Dreadnaughts were ever retaken by man.

Two weeks before the war began, the fleet had asked for volunteers to man the Dreadnaught crews. Adama had been tempted, but decided he liked flying a Viper too much to shift over to a job supervising a bunch of machines. He figured, later, that that love of flying had saved his life. Three members of his crew had volunteered for Dreadnaught duty. He had never heard from any of them again.

Later in the war, he had been a part of the Battle at Gamelon Breach, where four Battlestars and three hundred Vipers had combined to bring down the Dreadnaught *Relentless*. Captain Tigh had boarded a Dreadnaught—the *Supreme*—as one of a dozen commandoes assigned to take the ship from within while the Dreadnaught's staff was busy fighting a pair of Battlestars. Tigh had barely escaped with his life when the Dreadnaught's Cylon commanders had destroyed the ship rather than let it fall into Colonial hands.

Talking about the war, back in all those bars between one port and another, both Adama and Tigh had marveled that they had faced Dreadnaughts—although many had faced them, since the war machines were involved in half a dozen of the conflict's largest battles. But Tigh would never talk about his time inside the Dreadnaught, so the conversation had moved on to other things.

The Dreadnaught *Relentless* had exploded beneath a barrage of enemy fire. The Dreadnaught *Supreme* had destroyed itself. And the last of the Dreadnaughts, the *Invincible*, or so the story went, was last seen with its engines burning, falling into a star.

The Dreadnaught was slowly growing larger above him, as though it were slowly settling toward the planet below. More companions had come out onto the landing field to watch, and Adama saw they were joined by humans as well.

He and Tigh had witnessed the deaths of two Dreadnaughts.

Now he knew the *Invincible* had escaped the fire.

Doctor Fuest approached him across the field.

"Colonel? Is this one of yours?"

"I'm afraid not, Doctor."

"Then we are both afraid. We are getting a message from the ship overhead. They wish to talk to us."

The doctor walked a few steps away and spoke briefly with a companion that Adama did not recognize. He turned back to the colonel.

"I will have a portable device brought out here for my use. Everyone on the station seems to be coming out to the field. We will all hear what they have to say."

"Doctor!" one of the companions called. "There's a smaller ship coming in!"

Adama looked to the far side of the field. It was the shuttle. Athena and the others had returned.

With a Dreadnaught in the air, who knew what other Cylon craft were patrolling overhead. Adama was glad they had made it back safely.

The shuttle landed gently midfield. Adama walked quickly over to greet it.

The hatch was thrown open as he approached. Athena stuck her head out and saw Adama.

"Colonel, Skeeter's hurt!"

She pulled her fellow pilot to her side. Adama saw that one of his sleeves was drenched with blood.

The doctor came up beside Adama. "Where's Laea?"

"We got separated." Athena shifted her weight to support the limp pilot. "She took us out there to find someone from the scavenger ship. He ended up saving our butts."

The doctor's mouth opened, as though he didn't know what else to say.

"There's more, sir," Athena added.

Adama answered for her.

"You saw Cylons." He pointed at the golden disk in the sky. "We're all going to see them shortly."

"We need to get Skeeter to the hospital."

Adama helped Athena lower Skeeter down to the tarmac. The thin pilot had no strength left to stand. The two lowered him so he could sit.

Beta was at their side, examining the wound.

"This can be easily repaired," Beta said. "I need assistance!"

Two companions with wheels—old delivery models that Adama hadn't seen before—brought a stretcher between them.

"If you would lie down here, sir, we'll get you immediate help."

"My grandmother was right," Skeeter said. "Let's go."

They rushed off with him.

"Grandmother?" Adama asked.

"He's lost a lot of blood, sir," Athena replied.

"But Laea," the doctor said at last.

"I think she's safe for now," Athena said. "We'll go back and find her soon."

Admiral Sing supposed they were in for a fight. He couldn't see a single way the Battlestar could win.

"*May we speak with the one in charge?*" the voice from the Dreadnaught continued.

"That would be me," the admiral replied. "Admiral Sing."

"*This is a most unfortunate situation. You have stumbled upon a research project that we were hoping to maintain. There may be consequences. We are currently conferring with those above us.*"

"Is this a threat?" Sing asked.

"*We do not deal in threats. We deal in reality. We are a much larger ship than your Battlestar. Should we deem it necessary, we could eliminate you in an instant. We see no reason at the moment for this to occur.*"

"The Colonies and the Cylons have signed an armistice," Sing countered. "I see no reason for either of us to fight."

"*The Colonies and the Cylons are both far from this place. What happens here might never be known by either side.*"

Now that, Sing thought, sounded like a threat.

"*We are currently accessing the records of Research Station Omega. Please do nothing to interfere with our task.*"

Sing looked at the others in the CIC. No one spoke. He knew some of his officers had had experience with Dreadnaughts, and there would be some pre-war schematics in their records. He wondered if this Cylon war machine would have any weaknesses.

"*In our search, we discover that you have sent one William Adama to negotiate with the research station below. Was this Adama a lieutenant during the Cylon War? Did he fly a Viper?*"

Sing wondered why he was obliged to tell them anything.

"*Please,*" the voice continued. "*Tell us what we wish to know, or we will fire upon you.*"

Well, Sing supposed information wouldn't kill anyone. "Yes, Adama flew a Viper. And I believe he was a lieutenant at the time."

"*Most excellent!*" the voice replied. "*And he is on the planet's surface?*"

"Uh—yes," Sing answered. He hoped he wasn't signing his XO's death warrant. "Why do you want to—"

"*Make no move against us, and we will make none against you. Do not attempt to use your wireless. We will be jamming your signal.*"

"You expect us to do nothing?" Sing demanded.

"*Of course. Nothing will happen to you. Haven't the Cylons and the Colonies signed an armistice?*"

Gamma brought Doctor Fuest the portable comm unit. The doctor looked at it for a moment before activating it. He had depended upon the proper functioning of machines his entire life. Why did he suddenly think this small wireless set would betray him?

He clicked the single switch to activate the unit.

"*This is the Dreadnaught* Invincible," a voice boomed out of the speakers located around the edges of the landing field. "*We wish to speak to* Omega."

"This is Doctor Fuest. I speak for *Omega* station."

"*As we thought you would. We have accessed your station's records, and have determined your hierarchy. If we might speak to Gamma, please?*"

They wished to speak to a companion? Well, Gamma was a member of the senior council. It might even know more about the station than the doctor.

"Very well, I—I suppose," the doctor managed.

Gamma stepped forward to position itself before the microphone. "Thank you, Doctor," the Butler Model said before it turned to the wireless.

"Dreadnaught *Invincible*. This is Gamma. And this is not part of our arrangement."

Arrangement? Fuest frowned. Gamma had already known of the Dreadnaught?

"*Our apologies. We have made mistakes. We have tried to maintain our secrecy perhaps too diligently. In retrospect, it might have served us better to blast the recovery ship* Lightning *from the sky before they reached you. We did attempt to eliminate one remaining crewmember, but in so doing found ourselves looking to eliminate far many more, including one who should be protected under our original mandate. We could see no other course of action but to reveal ourselves.*"

What did this mean? Fuest wanted to demand an explanation from Gamma this instant. Had the other companions known about this as well?

"We now must resolve this situation in a new way. We ask that you send one of your number to the Dreadnaught to negotiate with us."

"Very well," Gamma said. "I will be willing to come aboard if I can ensure the safety of the research center."

"No, Gamma," the voice continued. *"We do not need to talk to you. We need to talk with Colonel William Adama."*

The normally stoic Adama looked stunned. He stepped forward a moment later.

"And if I do not wish to come?"

"If you do not wish to come," the voice replied, *"I cannot guarantee the safety of the research station or the Battlestar* Galactica. *If you do visit, both will be quite safe for the duration of your stay."*

Adama frowned. "Will you allow me to talk to *Galactica*?"

"They have already been informed of your impending visit."

Adama took a deep breath. "Very well. Give me a few minutes to prepare."

"Most excellent," the Dreadnaught's voice agreed.

CHAPTER 23

Laea was frightened, and not just of the Cylons.

Tom Zarek had outfitted all three of them as best he could. Each of them had a rifle and a handgun, and a large amount of ammunition that he had stuffed into three small packs he'd found in one of the lander's many compartments. The packs had also been filled with enough rations for three days and some first aid supplies from Zarek's survival kit.

He smiled at Laea as he checked his rifle. Now that the Creep was here, Tom's smile didn't warm her as much as it used to.

"Okay," Tom said. "I'll go first, and head right. The Creep will follow me and head left. If we manage to get a good position and can draw the Cylons' fire, we can cover Laea and you can get out and to a safe spot. If we can get by them, or we can shoot one of them down, maybe we can get up to the cave. I think we'll be able to defend ourselves a lot better up there until help comes."

The Creep smiled at Laea. "Hey, I'd like to cover this pretty little thing right now."

Tom grabbed the other man's coat. "You talk like that again, Creep, I'll kill you."

The Creep looked surprised. "If you can get to your gun fast enough. Hey, we're all going to die out there anyway. Can't a guy joke around a little?"

"Didn't sound much like a joke," Zarek replied.

Laea kept her distance from both men. They both seemed to hold so much violence in them—so different from the doctor and her brothers. Now that she was trapped inside a small space with these two men, she was finding their emotions more frightening than exciting. She didn't think Tom would hurt her, at least not on purpose. She tried to keep as far away from the other man as she could. He frightened her.

Not that it mattered. She thought that Tom's plan would get them all killed.

The two men stared at each other in silence for a moment.

"Have you heard the change?" she said softly.

"What change?" Tom asked.

"They've stopped firing their guns. Those little noises are gone from the hull."

The Creep grinned at that.

"She's right. Not only pretty but smart."

Somehow, the Creep made even those words sound dirty. She could see where he got his name.

"Have they left, then?" she asked.

The Creep peered out the window. "Unless they're just saving their ammunition until we come out."

"If they're gone, it's an even better time to get out of here," Tom said. "We don't know if they're gone for good. They may just be coming back here with a bigger gun."

"If they're gone," Laea said, "we might be able to get back to the research station."

"Oh that's a fine idea," the thin man replied. "Tom and I can get killed properly this time."

"No," Laea insisted. "Others have joined us. People from the Colonies. The companions have put away their guns."

"We're going to need to be rescued by somebody," Tom added. "I think Nadu is long gone."

"He seemed to give up awfully easy," the Creep replied. "Usually, Nadu won't leave the table until every scrap of meat is gone. Of course, we don't know what he was up against out there."

"Can you get us back to the base?" Tom asked.

Laea thought her only real problem would be finding her way back to the river. "As long as I can get my sense of direction from our sun, I should be fine."

"I think you've got another hour for your sense of direction, then," the Creep said. "It's almost nightfall."

"Maybe we should wait until morning," Tom suggested. "Get up to the caves before it gets dark and take a look around, see if the Cylons are really gone. If so, we can head back for your home base at first light."

Laea didn't want to spend any more time around this Creep than she had to, but she realized Tom's plan was probably the best. They didn't want to get lost in the woods when Cylons might still be looking for them.

"All right," she said.

"Good," Tom agreed. "Then we should go as planned."

He kicked open the hatch.

Things were moving much too quickly. Doctor Fuest was never much of one for speed. But he felt he had things he must do.

He needed to be alone—or not quite alone. He walked down the empty hallways—as far as he knew, everyone from the station was still out on the field—and talked to the one he trusted most.

"Betti," he whispered.

You're troubled, Vill. I can always tell. She was there immediately. She was always there.

"Things are changing here, Betti. Things I no longer understand."

You try too hard to control everything! I've always told you, you have to learn to let go!

"Perhaps I do. The Colonies have come back to find us."

He could hear the delight in her voice. *Oh, you've wanted that for so long!*

"But the Cylons have come too, and they've been talking to the companions!"

Betti was quiet a moment before she asked. *What is it that you want, Vill?*

"I want to understand. What the companions think of me. What the Colonies want to do with our research. Everything, I guess." He thought a moment more, then added, "Someone from the Colonies is going to the Cylon ship to talk about our station. I think I need to go with them. I think I need to learn the truth."

You always know what's best, Betti replied. *Wherever you go Vill, I'm never far away.*

"I've always depended on you, Betti."

As I have depended upon you, and always will, my love.

Doctor Villem Fuest smiled.

It was good, then. He could go out and tell the others what he needed to do.

Captain Tigh couldn't believe it.

"This is madness, Bill. If you go in there, you're never coming back."

"I think that's likely," Adama agreed. "But maybe this way I'll have a chance to save the rest of you—the station and *Galactica* both. If I don't do it, I think the Dreadnaught will destroy them both."

"So you're set on this thing?" Tigh asked.

Adama nodded his head. "Yes, I am."

So be it. Tigh took a deep breath. "Well then I'm going with you."

"What?"

"Tell the toasters it's a condition for your cooperation. They want you bad enough, they shouldn't mind someone else tagging along. Remember, I've been inside one of those big boats before."

"So you've told me. But you never wanted to talk about it."

"Only because I didn't want to bring it back any more vividly than I remember it already. I remember every minute I was in that place, every day of my life."

"And you're ready to go back in there again?"

"Hey, you've backed me up in plenty of fights. It's time for me to return the favor."

"Then how can I say no?" Adama asked.

"Excuse me, gentlemen?" Doctor Fuest stepped forward from where he had been standing behind them. He had been so quiet, Tigh hadn't even realized he was there.

"Yes, Doctor?" Adama asked as if he hadn't been surprised at all.

"I would like to go to this ship as well. I would like to do it for my station."

"Thank you, Doctor," Adama replied, "but I don't think—"

"You will need me," Fuest insisted. "Out of all the humans alive, no one knows the Cylon mind better than I."

"You make a convincing case," Adama agreed. "Very well. I will state my conditions to the Dreadnaught as we prepare for takeoff."

"You know, Doctor," Tigh said softly, "none of the three of us might leave that place alive."

"Or because there are three of us," the doctor said with the slightest of smiles, "we all might survive after all."

Athena was glad to see Skeeter smile. He sat up in bed, propping his back up against the pillow. "They say I should rest, after losing all that blood. But things are happening, aren't they? These companions here don't tell me anything!"

Athena had decided it was time for visitors. Vin and Jon had come with her, and the senior companions weren't far behind.

Beta bowed slightly. "We were attempting to see that Mr. Skeeter got some rest. He should be able to move around quite freely, so long as he is careful not to do something that would open the wound. The prognosis is good for a full recovery."

"I'm glad to see you," Skeeter said to Athena. He waved at the two other beds nearby. "These guys don't do anything but sleep. So did Laea get back yet?"

Athena shook her head. "No, no one's seen her, and it's after dark."

Skeeter frowned. "Can you take the shuttle back up?"

"The shuttle's being used for something else. The Cylons have shown themselves, and they're asking to see Colonel Adama."

"And I thought I had problems. Maybe if you took one of the Vipers?"

"It wouldn't be much good now. Like I said, it's after dark. And I don't think the Cylons are very keen on having anyone do any unauthorized flying. We could end up with a new firefight on our hands while the colonel is visiting the enemy."

"Not a good idea." Skeeter struggled to come to a full sitting position, then apparently thought better of it. He collapsed back against the pillow. "Is there any way I can help?"

"You can be our contact back here. Adama and Tigh are going to go visit the Cylon ship, along with Doctor Fuest."

"We hope that the three of them together will get the Cylons to see reason," Gamma added.

"None of us anticipated that this would happen," Epsilon agreed. "We were only thinking about the long-term safety and security of the station."

"Now I think you're trying to explain things too fast," Skeeter said. "So I'm going to be the only fleet guy left?"

"They're jamming our radio signals," Athena replied. "If the companions find any way to break through, it's up to you to contact the admiral."

"I'll do my best." Skeeter grinned again, no doubt glad to have something to do. But his smile faltered as he asked, "But how will you find Laea?"

Athena frowned in return. "I think I've got to go on foot. If I follow the river, I think I can find her easily enough."

Jon shook his head. "You're not going alone. We'll come with you."

"Hey," Vin added, clapping Jon on the shoulder, "she's our sister."

"This is our fault, too," Jon added. "We've been so busy with the station, we've been ignoring her. We should have listened to what she had to say."

Athena had heard this before. Protect the little girl, but don't listen to her. It was a big reason she had become a Viper pilot. Now people paid attention.

The companions studied each other in silence for a moment.

"Gamma and I will come too," Epsilon stated finally. "In a way, she is our sister as well."

"If Cylons still pursue her," Gamma added, "they will not expect us to take your side. It will add an element of surprise."

"We will go at dawn?" Jon asked.

"We can leave before then," Epsilon said. "We have an amphibious craft that will take us down the river, and lights to guide our way."

Athena frowned. "I don't know if I can judge the exact spot without daylight."

"Then we will wait until an hour before dawn," Epsilon replied, "so we will reach the spot just after first light. We all wish to rescue Laea. I will arrange for supplies and weapons."

"Then we will meet here one hour before dawn?" Jon asked.

Athena nodded. "We will leave from here." She looked down at the patient. "See, Skeeter? We'll keep you in on the action."

"We are almost ready to fly to the Dreadnaught," Adama said to the wireless mic.

"You say 'we,'" the voice replied. *"We only require your presence."*

"I will not come alone," Adama replied. "I will bring Captain Tigh to pilot the shuttle, and Doctor Fuest, who wishes to speak personally with those in charge aboard your ship."

The voice did not respond for a moment.

"*Very well,*" it said at last. "*If you feel safer bringing the others, we will not deny your request. But please arrive quickly. It is important that we talk with you before we receive our final commands.*"

"We will bring the shuttle now," Adama replied.

"*We will allow the shuttle to approach us. Any other ship, originating on either the planet's surface, or from the deck of the* Galactica, *will be shot down. We want no tricks.*"

"I understand. You will get none."

"*Are you prepared to leave?*"

Adama glanced at both Tigh and the doctor.

"I see no reason to wait."

"*Then the Dreadnaught* Invincible *stands ready to welcome you.*"

Adama shut off the comm controls. He glanced back at Athena.

"Skeeter knows what to tell the admiral," she said.

He nodded. "I'm looking forward to talking to all of you to-morrow."

Nobody said anything for a moment.

"I—I'm sure we will, sir," Skeeter stammered into the silence.

Adama grinned. "Stranger things have happened."

CHAPTER 24

DREADNAUGHT *INVINCIBLE*

Captain Saul Tigh remembered this place all too well: the Dread-naught.

The thing hung in the sky like a small moon. It was close to ten times the size of the *Galactica*, its surface pockmarked with a thou-sand different holes—and every hole hid a different laser or missile bay or launch chute. The thing held a hundred different methods of death and destruction. Tigh remembered, when the first Dreadnaught was launched, how pleased its makers had been to come up with so high a number. It was the last excessive ship of an excessive era, just before humankind's wealth and populations were decimated by the Cylon War.

Tigh flew in through the primary chute, a hole at the very center of the monstrosity. They were not challenged or questioned. They heard no comm chatter at all.

The silence didn't help Tigh—it only reminded him that the Dread-naught no longer held life. Now it was the home of far too many Cylons.

He set the shuttle down in a deserted hangar bay. The room was huge, almost the size of a small domed city. A hundred or more Cylon Vipers hung from cradles along the walls. They reminded Tigh of holstered weapons, just waiting to be drawn. Masses of new machinery, most of which Tigh did not recognize, sat on the floor beneath the Vipers. A lot of the equipment in here looked like it had been improved far beyond those early models he had seen in that first Dreadnaught so many years ago.

But the room was just as vast, the lighting as dim and yellow, the feeling of being very, very small just as great as it had been then.

Back in the war, his group of commandoes had commandeered a Cylon troop carrier—which the Cylons had stolen from the Colonies only a year before. They had used the carrier to land inside the Dreadnaught *Supreme*, and then started to cut their way through the Cylons.

The Dreadnaught had been a great success for the Cylons in the early years of the war, but the Cylons had apparently never devised a plan to defend their huge ship from an internal attack. The eight commandoes in Tigh's unit virtually quick-marched from the landing area to the heart of the ship, mowing down any machine they came across that might stand in their way.

That was when it got strange.

"I guess we don't get a welcoming committee," Adama said. Tigh snapped out of his reverie, and looked out again at the silent hangar.

"Yeah, I guess they don't want the Cylons to scare us away."

"So we won't see any Cylons at all?" The doctor sounded disappointed.

"Oh, I'm sure we'll see them sooner or later," Tigh reassured him. "They're just saving things up for a surprise."

The colonel unstrapped himself and rose from his seat. "Well, we might as well see what they've got waiting for us."

Adama opened the hatch and stepped out first. Tigh and the doctor followed. Their boot heels echoed in the vast silence that surrounded them.

"Is that Bill Adama I see?" a voice boomed from far above—a voice far different from the emotionless tones they had heard back at the research station. This voice, Tigh thought, sounded like some long-lost boisterous uncle in the middle of a holiday dinner.

"It is!" Adama called back. "And who am I talking to?"

"Oh, you'll recognize me soon enough," the voice said with a chuckle. *"I thank you for coming—all of you. But you particularly, Bill. I've got a favor to ask of you. They allow me that sort of thing, now and again. But why*

should I explain anything when I can show you? Follow the lighted path and all will become quite clear."

"Well, this is different," Tigh remarked.

"The Cylons are capable of great versatility," the doctor added. "I don't think the Colonies ever fully appreciated that, before the war."

"Here's the path." Adama pointed to a row of lights that led across the hangar to a distant corridor. More loudly, he asked, "Will we be going far?"

"Nothing's very close in this gods-forsaken ship!" the booming voice replied. *"But you'll find me soon enough. Please get on with it! I've waited far too long."*

"Apparently, the Cylon knows you?" the doctor asked.

"I think I recognize that voice," Adama replied. "And it's not a Cylon."

They moved out of the hangar, the great space as still and empty as death, and walked along an equally quiet corridor.

When Tigh had been in this place before—or the place just like this—the corridor had been crawling with machines: Cylons, not the Warriors, but all the other varieties that had fled the Colonies. None of the first machines they saw had weapons of any kind—they must have all been charged with different functions in running the massive ship. But they had tried to block the forward progress of Tigh and the others, jamming the corridors with their bright metallic forms. Too bad the commandoes had brought along the really big guns. It made for a lot of ex-Cylons.

Now the corridors were as empty as the hangar, lit mostly by the glowing lights that would lead them to their destination.

"It is nice to see you, Bill," the voice boomed from hidden speakers. *"If you don't mind, I'll entertain you with a little song."*

And the voice began to sing an old fleet song that Tigh had learned way back in basic.

"Most curious," the doctor said.

"Not curious at all," Adama replied.

It reminded Tigh of the next thing he had found, the thing not seen but heard, the thing that still haunted him, the thing he thought of every day.

It was very dark at the edge of the research station. The planet had no moon, and the stars were mostly obscured by clouds. Dawn seemed to be much more than an hour away.

Athena followed Gamma, who illuminated the path before them

with a bright light the companion had revealed in its chest. The rest of their party followed, first Jon and Vin, then Epsilon taking up the rear.

All five of them carried guns large enough to disable Cylons.

"The river travels under the research station," Gamma said, "and provides us with both water and power. It emerges just ahead. I have had a small launch brought here for our use. And something else of value."

Gamma led them all down a gently sloping hill. The river emerged from a great pipe in the hillside and snaked on down through the valley below. Gamma shone his light on a boat large enough to accommodate twice their number.

"Our transportation."

The five of them quickly climbed into the boat, which was moored past a short pier. Epsilon sat in the bow. The companion's night vision capabilities would easily spot any danger. Jon untied the craft from its mooring while Vin started up the engine and gently steered the boat out into the river's current.

"We have another advantage," Gamma said to Athena. It pointed to a small white box on a central seat. "This is a tracking device. When Laea was young, she tended to wander."

"Like she doesn't wander now?" Vin asked.

"It is true," Gamma replied. "Perhaps she hasn't changed all that much. But when Laea was four, the doctor ordered that all her shoes be equipped with small chips that send out a signal. If you are within a certain distance of the chips, this box will receive the signal and show us exactly where Laea is."

"When she was young, we had to fetch her every other day," Epsilon agreed.

Athena stared down at the box. "You still place these devices in her shoes?"

"No one has ever said otherwise," Gamma replied. "And perhaps, had the senior staff paused to consider it, they might have determined that such a practice was wasteful. But today we realize that practice is not wasteful at all.

"We have not had occasion to use the tracker in years. But the chips are there now that the need arises."

Athena frowned at this new information. "With this thing, we probably could have found her in the dark."

"Possibly," Gamma replied. "But its range is only a few klicks. It was originally designed to find Laea as she ran around the station proper. We would need to be in the general vicinity for it to work properly. We still need your memories of the location to show us the way."

"It will be better to find her in daylight," Epsilon said. "She'll recognize us. It will be less frightening for her."

"And with this, we will find her quickly."

Athena stared down at the box. It was a device to protect Laea, and a device that made sure she would never really be alone. The device was reassuring and disquieting at the same time. Much like all of Research Station *Omega*.

"Ah," Epsilon announced. "The first glimmers of dawn."

Athena looked up and saw a narrow band of red over the far horizon.

Before, on the *Supreme*, Tigh remembered all too well, it had been the voices. Human voices, begging for death. Tigh and his fellows had first heard them as they passed through what had once been the officers' mess. It had once been the social center for the small human staff, but the room had been stripped of the furniture and machines and all things human that had made it a gathering place. Tigh didn't think he had ever seen another room that had looked so empty. The voices seemed to come from nowhere and everywhere. The commandoes moved forward, headed for Central Command.

The voices followed them, calling down the corridors, following their every footstep.

"Thank the gods you have found us!"

"Kill us!"

"Kill us, please!"

The commandoes had never found the source of those voices. They had thought, at first, that it was a Cylon trick, some way to distract and demoralize them until the toasters could gather together enough warriors to mount a last-ditch defense of the ship's nerve center.

Their first assumption had been wrong.

But that had been on a different ship, in a different time.

Now it was a song.

> "Oh, I've signed up with the fleet
>   For to go far away-o:
>   And I'll never see my own true love
>   Forever and a day-o!"

Adama looked back at Tigh as they followed the lighted trail. "Is this anything like what happened before?"

"It has certain similarities," Tigh admitted.

"I see why you never wanted to talk about it," Adama agreed.

Fuest took up the rear. He seemed quietly in awe of everything around him.

"Are we getting closer?" the colonel called out to the voice.

"Oh, I've signed—why yes, Bill, you're almost there! You'll have to forgive me. I haven't felt good enough to sing in such a long time!

> *"Oh, I've signed up with the fleet*
> *For to go—"*

They kept on moving. It took Tigh a while to realize they were marching in time to the music.

"Sing here."

"We have visual confirmation, Admiral, that Adama's shuttle has landed on the *Invincible*. The Dreadnaught is still refusing to speak to us."

"Understood."

So the game continued, on the Cylons' terms. The admiral stared across his quarters without really seeing anything. Sing didn't think he had ever felt so helpless, even during the early days of the Cylon war. The *Galactica* was outgunned and had crewmembers in harm's way, and he had no way to even alert the Colonial fleet!

"Sir! We're getting new images on the DRADIS. Five ships—no, more than a dozen—no. Wait a moment. Sir, twenty-three ships have appeared on our screens."

Twenty-three ships? Who the hell would send twenty-three ships?

"Are they fleet? Have they sent us reinforcements?"

"Sir, this is not the fleet. Nor do I think they are Cylon craft. It is the strangest group of ships I have ever seen."

Sing stood abruptly. "I think I'd better come up and take a look."

The singing stopped abruptly.

"It's just through this door now," the cheerful voice announced. *"My old friend Bill. It will be good to see you in the flesh!"*

Adama was sure now that he knew who was speaking, even though he hadn't seen him in close to thirty years.

"Chief Nedder? Is that you?"

"Right the first time! You always were a bright fellow."

The door in front of the three swung open.

They walked into another empty room. A tall, ornate set of doors dominated one wall. They looked to Adama like the sort of cupboards people used to store things in back on Caprica.

"Almost there!" Chief Nedder's voice cheered. *"But before I truly introduce myself, I should ask you, Bill, who'd you bring for company?"*

Tigh stepped forward. "Captain Saul Tigh. I'm Bill's crewmate."

"He's a good friend, too, Ned," Adama added.

"Ah, I had few better friends than Bill, back in the day. And who's the other one?"

The doctor looked up. "Villem Fuest. Doctor Villem Fuest. I come from the research station below. I've worked with Cylons—or the descendants of Cylons—all my life. I've come to see what these Cylons can do."

"Well, I can certainly show you that. It's the moment of truth, Bill."

"Where are you, Ned?"

"You see those fancy doors? Take a deep breath and open them. I warn you, though. I'm no longer a pretty sight."

Adama opened the doors.

"Frak," Tigh murmured in a voice just loud enough to hear. The doctor gasped.

Adama saw the head of his old friend, crew chief on his very first ship. But while his face was recognizable, most of the rest of his body was gone, replaced by tubes and wires. The face in the middle of the machine grinned. A metal rod with a human hand on its end made a mock salute.

"This is me now," said the thing that had once been Chief Nedder. "Welcome to my world."

"The Cylons did this to you?" Doctor Fuest asked.

"They had to," Nedder explained. "I'm a necessity.

"The Colonies were far too clever. Or they thought they were. The Dreadnaughts would only operate with their human staffs in control. Or, as the Cylons determined, having the appearance of control. They needed my human parts to run their ship. The pattern of a living eye to activate the weapons system, the warmth of a living handprint to run the engines. As you see, they've kept the parts they needed and made sure the rest of me wouldn't go anywhere."

Adama had never seen anything like this. Half man, half machine. The fact that this had once been his friend made it even more of an abomination. "God, Ned, how can you bear it?"

The chief laughed at that. "I've gone mad from the pain and come back again. You see, you have to be at least a little sane to find a way to kill yourself.

"They use me to control the ship, but I still have a wee bit of free will. I can shut them down at inopportune moments. It pays to let me have the occasional favor.

"You, Bill Adama, are such an occasional favor."

The chief cackled again.

"The Cylons are always lying to you about one thing or another. They have plans. Big plans. Not that they'd share any of them with me. But I don't want to be a part of those plans.

"I can turn myself off for brief periods. They always bring me back. A painful affair.

"But they wouldn't want me to do something to interfere with their operations, especially when they're facing a Battlestar. In order to keep working for them, I asked for an hour with you. And in that hour, you will kill me."

Nedder laughed one more time.

It was Adama's turn to look up at the featureless walls. "How can you tell us this? Aren't the Cylons listening in?"

"I am the Central Control of all the systems," the chief replied. "For a little while, I can keep them out.

"Killing me will disable the ship. They'll be floating free in space. I know they have plans to jury-rig something if I die, but that will take time. I'll open every door on this boat as my last command. You and the *Galactica* will be far away from here before they can retaliate. They won't be able to do a thing against you."

Adama nodded.

"What do you want me to do?"

"A couple quick cuts to sever my works. I—"

A warning siren came from somewhere.

"What?" Nedder cried. "Someone's attacking! Looks like our meeting's over." The chief stared at Adama.

"You wouldn't have done this to me, Bill?"

Adama frowned. "I wouldn't. But I don't control *Galactica*." Would Sing have ordered a sneak attack? It didn't sound like the admiral's style.

The chief's eyes half closed. "I can hear our Vipers responding to it already. It sounds like a bit of a battle."

Cylon Warriors appeared on either side of them.

Where the hell did they come from?

"Can't you tell them this isn't our doing?" Adama asked.

"Ah, Bill," Nedder replied. "To the Cylons, all humans are responsible.

"I'm afraid my time is up, and so is yours. I'm hoping we can finish our business later. I'll try to talk to them.

"But then, my employers are not the most forgiving types."

The chief laughed one final time as the three men were taken away.

CHAPTER 25

FREE CRUISER LIGHTNING

Nadu was laughing.

"You never expected this, you Cylon scum!"

Griff never thought his captain would pull this off. He had called in all his debts and favors, even threatened a few of the other ships' captains with a bit of blackmail, but he had gathered twenty-three recovery ships, Nadu's own small avenging navy.

And now all twenty-three ships were attacking the Cylon Dreadnaught.

"Steal from Nadu, will you? No one gets the better of Nadu! Even the Cylons are going to pay!"

His captain had always been half-mad. Now Griff thought he had gone all the way.

Grets looked over from the DRADIS screen, where she was filling in for one of their lost crewmembers. "They're launching a counterattack. Vipers!"

"We can handle a few Vipers. We have twenty-three ships, with seventy-eight fighters. How many Vipers do they have?"

Grets looked back at the DRADIS screen. "I would say hundreds."

"We'll fight them all!"

Griff winced as he saw their first fighters explode under an onslaught of never-ending Cylon craft. The Captain was laughing again. He had run once. He would never run again.

"Death to Cylons!" Nadu called.

Griff was beginning to fear it would be the other way around.

Admiral Sing watched the strange drama play out beyond the *Galactica*. They had pulled the ship into a higher orbit to make sure they kept out of the fight.

"Our wireless channels are free, sir."

Apparently, the Cylons had found a distraction.

"Send a priority message to the fleet. 'Have encountered Cylons. Need immediate assistance.'"

"Aye, sir!"

"Can we talk with the research station?" Sing asked.

"I'll put you through as soon as we've sent your priority to the fleet."

"Sir! Should we take any retaliatory action?"

Sing frowned at the Vipers pouring out of the Cylon ship. How could he take sides against the Dreadnaught when he had two officers on board?

Laea woke up with a hand across her mouth. Early morning light seeped into the cave. And the Creep stared down at her from a foot away.

"You won't ignore me any longer." He grinned. "Zarek's looking around, seeing if it's safe for us to leave. So we've got a few minutes."

He took his hand off her mouth. "He's not going to hear you scream. Especially now that it's doomsday."

Laea was more startled than afraid. She thought maybe the whole universe had gone mad. "What?" she demanded. "What are you talking about?"

He grabbed her arm and dragged her to the edge of the cave.

"Look in the sky. It's the end of all of us."

She looked up and saw a dozen different dots high in the sky, swarming around the golden disk she had seen the day before. A couple of the dots vanished in brilliant explosions of light.

"It's the Cylon War, all over again," the Creep said. "We're never going to make it out of here alive. So I thought we could at least enjoy our last few minutes." He reached down to undo his belt.

"I'd stop there," Tom's voice said from behind them. "Do you really think I'd leave you alone with her for more than a minute?"

She looked around to see Tom's gun pointed straight at the Creep. "I went up on the ridge. I think we've got a clear path back to the river. I say we get ourselves back to *Omega*."

Laea pushed herself to her feet. Yes! She hadn't realized how much she missed the station until the last few hours.

She pointed to the Creep. "Why do you keep including him in our plans? How can you trust him, Tom?"

"We need every gun we have," the Creep replied. "That's why I don't kill Tom, and he doesn't kill me. I still think you should give me a moment. Heck, we could take turns."

Zarek took a step closer. "Creep, if you make another move toward—"

But the Creep was already moving. He knocked the gun from Zarek's hand and kicked him in the crotch. Zarek crumpled to the cave of the floor. When he looked up, the Creep had his gun pointed at him.

"You've got potential, Tom. Too bad you'll never live to use it!" His skull face grinned. "You've got a choice. I can kill you now, or you can sit and watch. I've waited long enough to get what I need."

"And you will wait longer still," a deep voice interjected.

The Creep whirled around. "Frakkin' Cylons!"

"Epsilon!" Laea cried. "You found me!"

"We always find you," Epsilon replied.

"I can kill a Cylon with this!" the Creep screamed. "I know a spot! I just shoot you in the neck!" He pointed his gun forward, and began to squeeze the trigger.

He staggered back at the sound of a shot. He looked down and saw the blood spread across his chest.

"Who?" the Creep asked.

Athena stepped into the cave. "Epsilon came with friends." She smiled at Laea. "See? I knew we'd get you out of here after all."

The three humans were placed in another room, as featureless as all the corridors they had passed through. Apparently, Adama thought, Cylons needed neither decorations nor furniture.

The same voice they had heard over the wireless boomed from somewhere overhead.

"I am disappointed in you, Colonel Adama."

"Why?" Adama asked. "Because there is a battle going on outside this ship that I know nothing about?"

"You heard Chief Nedder. To Cylons, all humans are responsible."

"So you were listening in?"

"Of course. Once, the Chief could block our entry. But we have rerouted the systems. Now we can monitor his every action."

"So you know he wants to die?"

"We've known that for many years. You will not be there to assist him. Nor you—Captain Tigh, isn't it?"

"Frak you!" Tigh shot back.

"For Cylons, that is not yet possible," the voice replied. *"But Doctor. We are surprised to see you here."*

"Really?" The doctor blinked as though he was equally surprised. "You know that I have spent my entire life studying Cylons, and the interaction of humans and Cylons? This seemed to be the chance of a lifetime."

"Most interesting. Doctor, how would you like a tour of our ship?"

"I would very much like that, thank you."

"And we would like to talk to a human as different as you. As to our two military men, I'm afraid you will have to remain here."

The voice paused, then added, *"If it will help the chief to function, we may yet let you live."*

The door opened. An armed Centurion watched them from the corridor outside.

"Doctor, if you would?" the Cylon voice said.

The doctor leaned close to Adama and whispered in his ear.

"Do not mourn me."

Fuest looked apologetically at the other two and left the room.

The Cylons had done wonders. The ship was huge, with more than a dozen different decks, all full of working machines. The Cylons not only maintained the ship, but seemed to be constantly improving every system on board. The voice guided the doctor from station to station, while the two warriors who formed his escort kept a respectful distance. He saw machine shops for both repair and manufacture of new models, a whole floor dedicated to experimental DRADIS and communication systems, even what the voice referred to as a "strategic preparations room," where two dozen Cylons had literally plugged their operating systems into a central core. The doctor found the variations fascinating, and so different from the direction his own companions had taken back on the station. It was a shame, really, that an intelligence like this and the cultural wealth of humanity could not find a way to work together.

He shared his thoughts with the voice of the ship, and the ship seemed pleased. But perhaps that was an old man's fancy as well.

"We have accessed the records of your home, recorded all your experiments," the voice said as they returned to the ship's primary level. *"We would let you see our home as well."*

A moment later, the voice added, *"We are interested in your reaction."*

"A human reaction?" the doctor asked.

"*Both Cylons and humans come from the same place,*" the voice replied. "*But perhaps that is a discussion for another day.*"

"Well, you have done wonderful things. Made strides far beyond anything I've seen in the companions. But you don't need me to tell you that, do you?"

The voice did not reply.

The doctor looked up the corridor they had just entered. "We have come full circle, haven't we? The chief would be just beyond those doors?"

"*You have a sense of direction worthy of a Cylon, Doctor.*"

This hall featured an empty shelf along one wall, a shelf that had once no doubt held something valuable to humans.

The doctor pointed at the shelf. "I am quite tired. May I sit awhile?"

"*Of course.*"

Fuest took a deep breath. He needed to have a final conversation.

"Betti," he said softly.

Yes, Villem, I am always here.

"You have seen everything."

Everything. The good and the bad.

"The bad," he agreed.

Yes, that is something that humans and Cylons were never meant to do.

He nodded. "I knew you'd understand, Betti. About my decision. It may be the last thing I ever do."

You were always a brave man, Vill. And if it is the last thing, then we shall be together.

"Yes we will, won't we?"

The thought brought great comfort.

"*What is it that you say?*" the voice boomed from above.

"I am an old man now. I was talking to my wife. I keep her with me." Fuest smiled. "I don't know if Cylons would understand that."

The voice paused. "*Maybe we will never understand the ways of humans.*"

"Maybe you don't need to. You have distanced yourselves from them, and started up a whole new existence."

"*Sometimes, we do not know if distance is enough.*"

"I think I'll go to see your chief," the doctor said softly. "I might be able to calm him."

"We are still having trouble with our operations. That could be beneficial."

It had taken looking at that horror, but Tigh had always known it.

Tigh and the commandoes had barely escaped with their lives. The voices, on that other day, on that other ship, had saved their skins.

And now he saw what had owned those voices. They were the calls of something half human, half machine, like the chief.

One minute they were pleading to be found and be put to death, like Chief Nedder.

The next, they had warned the commandos to leave.

The ship, rather than be taken, had decided to destroy itself. And the voices, the shredded humans integrated into the machines, knew every action the ship would take.

Tigh remembered all the dreams he had had. How he had wanted to end the pain in those voices. Over and over, he was going to find those ghosts and free them.

"We can't find you!" his dream self said. "We've failed you!"

But on the Dreadnaught *Supreme*, the voices had finally lost their pain.

"No. You've given us what we needed."

"We have been changed too much for anything else."

"We will be free at last."

Now, finally, Tigh knew what they meant.

The Cylons had still needed humans to run their Dreadnaughts. The machines destroyed their ship before the Colonies could learn their secret.

But now the humans had learned it all over again.

But would he or Adama or even the doctor live long enough to tell anyone?

The doctor walked over to the still-open cabinet where what was left of Chief Nedder operated the ship. The Centurions stood watch in the corridor outside.

The doctor turned his back to the door so the Cylons could not see. He pulled a small blade from his pocket.

"I have brought this from the machine shop," he whispered to Nedder. "Tell me what to do."

The head smiled. "Cut my arteries, here and here." He motioned with his head to exposed veins on either side of his neck. "I should bleed to death quickly."

The doctor moved before he had a second chance to think.

He slashed the first one. Something that looked half like blood, half like machine oil poured over his hands.

A voice commanded him to stop. A Cylon Warrior stood behind him. He felt the laser cut through his chest as he severed the second line.

He fell to his knees, and then to the floor. But he had done what the chief needed.

He could join Betti now.

The ship shuddered. Adama and Tigh looked at each other as the door opened.

"I think Nedder's giving us a way out of here." Adama started toward the opening, then looked at Tigh. "The hangar. Can you find it?"

Tigh nodded. "I think I know enough to get us back."

They ran quickly through the corridors. Alarms sounded everywhere.

The Cylons that they saw ran the other way.

A Centurion turned toward them farther down a cross-corridor. The Cylon took aim but did not fire.

"We are no longer their priority," Adama said. "They're trying to keep their ship alive."

It looked as if the Cylons' world was coming to an end. The ship shuddered again. A grinding sound came from deep within the Dreadnaught. As they ran, Adama saw a pair of fires break out in the distance.

"What about the doctor?" Tigh asked.

"I think the doctor is dead," Adama realized. "That's what he meant. He whispered 'Do not mourn me' when we last saw him. He was planning on killing Ned. What happened to the chief was an abomination to him as well."

The admiral couldn't believe it.

The scavengers' ships had been almost entirely destroyed, and the Cylon Vipers were clustering together, halfway between the Dreadnaught and *Galactica*. It looked like the Cylons would force a final battle.

"Sir! New ships on the screen!" the DRADIS operator called.

Was this more recovery ships? If so, they were too late to save their friends. Would they turn tail as soon as they saw the devastation?

"Sir, we're getting an incoming signal from the *Pegasus*. Three Battlestars have arrived to back us up, and two more are en route."

The whole CIC cheered at that. Admiral Sing grinned.

This time, it really was the fleet.

"Sir! There's something else!"

Sing looked up at the large screen that dominated the room. Something was wrong with the Dreadnaught. It appeared to visibly wobble, as though something had gone wrong with its engines.

The Vipers went swarming back to the station as Battlestars filled the space around them.

The Dreadnaught seemed to regain control of its systems as the last of the Vipers disappeared. It retreated from the group of Battlestars now approaching it.

And then it Jumped, disappearing from the screen.

Another ragged cheer rose around the control room. But Sing wondered what it all meant.

The Cylons had disappeared. When would they see them again?

"Sir!" the DRADIS operator called. "We've got a small craft coming toward us."

Sing saw it was the shuttle, returning to the station.

CHAPTER 26

RESEARCH STATION *OMEGA*

Skeeter couldn't believe it.

Beta had come to him, Skeeter, the only representative of the fleet at *Omega* station, and told him of the companions' decision.

"They have found Laea, and are bringing her back," the companion had said. "We have received a message from the *Galactica* that they believe the doctor is dead. Both humans and Cylons have found us. Our position here is compromised."

"What will you do?" Skeeter asked.

"We have uploaded all our data files into the *Galactica*'s computers. The Cylons have already taken this data, and we felt it should be shared equally. The Cylons had come to us some time ago, promising us protection if they could share our research. We were naive and accepted their offer. Now we see what Cylon protection means.

"I will stay here with you until Gamma and Epsilon return with the others. We will make sure all of the humans are safely returned to their ships. And then, it is time for us to go. We see no place for companions in this modern world."

"Go?" Skeeter asked. "Go where?"

"We will shut ourselves down. We will disappear. We made the plans long ago. The *Galactica* and the Colonies will have a record of our time here. They may benefit from it if they choose to do so."

"But, shouldn't you wait for Colonel Adama? Maybe someone in authority needs something else!"

"No, Mr. Skeeter. I am just a companion; you are just a human. We are two beings just trying to do our best. It is right that we end this way, as equals."

Skeeter watched the companion turn and walk away, disappearing back into the hangar.

So here he was, the ranking authority on Research Station *Omega*.

He wondered what his grandmother would think about him now?

Tom Zarek had been taken aboard the *Pegasus* for possible trial—or more probably relocation.

They tried to frighten him at first with all sorts of threats. He had been involved in an illegal operation. He had associated with known criminals and murderers. But nothing quite constituted a charge, and all the criminals and murderers appeared to be dead.

The one thing they did know was that Tom Zarek had saved people's lives. Two of those people were Viper pilots, both of whom would vouch for him. So the trial would go nowhere.

His knowledge of the Cylons was another matter.

The next time the uniforms sat him down, they talked about how this whole operation had to remain a secret. Rumors of a Cylon Dreadnaught could cause panic in the Colonies, and this whole affair was to remain classified until further investigation. Zarek took that to mean that no one was supposed to talk about this—ever.

The uniforms told him they could handle this two ways. They could lock him up, all alone, forever. Or they could give him a new life on one of the Colonies, some new connections, a regular salary— just as long as he never mentioned Cylons again.

Tom thought a new life sounded good.

His one regret was that he would never see Laea again.

She had shipped out on the *Galactica*, and he doubted she ever wanted to speak to him again. He had messed up in a lot of ways on this trip, but never more so than letting the Creep stay close to the woman. He had been too scared for his own skin to let the Creep go. And Laea had almost gotten hurt, or even killed, because of his fear.

His life was filled with missed opportunities. That was why he had gone on the scavenger boat in the first place. But now he was being given a new chance, a new beginning. He swore, this time, he would make good. This time, the Colonies would hear about Tom Zarek.

He would be a force to be reckoned with.

Tigh knew she was too young. But it was good to talk to her.

They were back on the *Galactica*. And aside from the presence of Laea and Jon and Vin, life had gotten back to normal.

They were headed back to Caprica. It would be a two-week journey, even with frequent Jumps, and Adama and Tigh had taken to having dinner with the three young refugees from the research station. Admiral Sing had arranged to get all three some formal education upon their return, mostly so they could acclimate themselves to a place so different from the one where they had grown up. Adama was preparing to take an extended leave with his family—something that he appeared to be alternately looking forward to and somewhat anxious about.

But Tigh had no other life now beyond the *Galactica*. He and Laea stayed around to talk long after the others had left for the evening. He thought she liked the attentions of an older man in uniform. And he liked the way she laughed.

It was good, Tigh thought, to feel admired, to feel confident again in a uniform. Maybe he'd go out once they made it back home, and find a woman more his own age, maybe a bit of a party girl, but someone with whom he could really settle down.

Tigh realized the *Galactica* had given him back his life. Now he intended to do something with it.

Vin saw his passage aboard the *Galactica* as the beginning of a whole new life. But he couldn't quite let go of the old one.

The companions had lied. They had kept secrets from Vin and the others. They had been in communication with the Cylons for who knew how long?

He thought again about the accident that had killed his parents. Had it been an accident after all?

There was no way he could know. As he grew up on the station, he had believed that the companions actively cared for the humans that lived with them. The companions had certainly acted to protect the humans, in the end.

But had the Cylons caused the accident? Had the companions covered their crime? Both Cylons and companions were gone now. He had no one to ask.

And that was yesterday. Today, he was surrounded by dozens of men and women close to his age. And a couple of the women really seemed to like talking to him, trading stories about the mechanics of the companions and the mechanics of their ships. He was glad now, that Laea continued her innocent flirtation with Captain Tigh. Vin was looking forward to pursuing some innocent flirtations of his own.

The three of them, Jon, Laea, and Vin, had decided to stay together for now, until they learned their way around the Colonies. He had a new life ahead.

But could he forget the old one?

"Vin?" He looked up to see the very attractive Chief Tracy smiling down at him. "Have I caught you brooding again?"

Vin shook his head. "I've given up brooding."

Tracy shook her head in turn. "As long as you haven't given up dinner. We were supposed to go?"

Vin got up from his bunk and walked over to the chief.

Maybe he did have new things to remember.

"You wanted to see me, Admiral?"

"Yes, Bill, have a seat."

Adama did as he was asked.

"Bill, you know, don't you, that this trip is my last time out?"

"You're going to retire?"

"I've spent thirty-five years in the fleet. It's time I moved aside and let somebody younger take my place. I had thought about this before, but I'm doubly sure about it now, after what we've just been through. I'm going to recommend you to take over the *Galactica*."

Adama paused for a moment, stunned. He had not seen this coming. "Admiral, I'm honored."

"No false modesty, Bill. You're the best man for the job. My retirement doesn't come up for a couple months, but I thought I'd tell you now, get you used to the idea."

"Sir. Yes sir." He paused, then added, "I'll have to talk to the family about it. I think my wife would like me to leave the service."

"That would be a shame," Sing replied. "Of course, you'll need to do whatever is best for your family. But after what we've just seen, I think we know there will dark times ahead for the Colonies. We need people of your caliber to lead the fleet."

Adama didn't know what to say. "I will give it some thought," he said at last.

"I'm sure you will," the admiral replied. "And I'm sure you'll come to the right decision."

"Yes sir."

"Whatever you decide, Colonel, it has been a pleasure to serve with you."

A ship of his own. Adama had never thought he would make it that far in the fleet.

How would he tell his wife and family?

He was sure he would find a way.

"Chief Nedder."

The blackness was gone, replaced by painful light.

"We have had to reactivate you. The *Invincible* still needs your interface to run efficiently."

"What? Oh frak—"

"Please refrain from foul language, or we will remove your vocal chords. We have now bypassed all need of human voice commands.

"Doctor Fuest managed to cause substantial damage in the few seconds he was unsupervised. But we have obtained a number of replacement parts from humans who visited Research Station *Omega*. We should be able to keep you well maintained for our imminent plans.

"We will improve you, Chief Nedder. We will fit you with the very best parts available. You will have a valuable function on *Invincible* for years to come. You, and your parts, will have their place in a great Cylon future.

"Now we must cut away the old and put in the new."

What was left of Chief Nedder screamed.

SAGITTARIUS IS BLEEDING

A novel by
PETER DAVID

Based on the SCI FI Channel series created by
RONALD D. MOORE

Based on a teleplay by
GLEN A. LARSON

CHAPTER 1

Laura Roslin is having the strangest feeling of déjà vu.

She is standing in the middle of a field, and there is a collection of what appear to be obelisks encircling her. There is a firm wind wafting her long brown hair, and she looks down to see that she is wearing a nightgown. This is rather odd, since she is the president of the Twelve Colonies and is not one to go wandering about in her sleepwear under any circumstances.

She is not in pain. This is no small thing to her, for there has been a long period of her life where she literally forgot what it was like not to be aching. It is a terrible thing to have one's body turn against one. Yes, if one is attentive enough, one can sense the everyday aches and pains as one's body dies, molecule by molecule, over the standard wear and tear of its lifetime. But what Laura has been experiencing is hardly anything that is remotely typical for a body's daily wear. This has been her body in open revolt, as if she had somehow been inconsiderate of its needs or harsh in her dealings with it.

What anger, what venom there must be, for a body to feel that the soul of the person inhabiting it must be punished in the way her body was punishing her. Constant agony as uncontrolled cell replication literally ate her breasts alive. She wondered every so often—not true, she wondered all the time—what in the world she ever did to deserve this. Did it attack her breasts as a symbolic message that she had been a bad woman? Did it attack her at all as a specific message that she had led a bad life? Certainly there must have been some sort of reason. It wasn't possible that the gods could be so randomly cruel.

Could they?

Perhaps they could. After all, look at the millions upon millions of people who had died thanks to the Cylon attack. What had humans ever done to deserve that?

Well . . . there are possible explanations for that, aren't there. Explanations she does not like to dwell upon, since they do not exactly cast humanity in the best light.

Better to enjoy the here and now of where she is . . . wherever that may be.

Yes . . . yes, she recognizes it now. It is strange that she would have forgotten it, or had the slightest unfamiliarity with it, even for an instant.

She is on Kobol, the birthplace of humanity. Kobol, the home of the temple of Athena, which is destined to guide them to their goal: the planet Earth, their salvation, a haven from the Cylons that pursue them.

Except she is not on Kobol . . . not exactly. It is difficult to determine whether she is on Kobol, but that which surrounds her is an illusion . . . or if she has somehow been miraculously transported, through means she could not begin to guess, to the destination she has been seeking. Be it illusion or miracle, either way the result is the same: She is standing on the planet Earth. She and the others have . . .

The others.

She looks around and says, "Where are the others?" Her mouth moves, but no sound is emerging. She cannot determine whether she has been struck dumb or if she has suddenly gone deaf. Even if she did know which condition had afflicted her—or rather, which additional affliction she had just acquired—it would not have answered the question as to where the others had gotten off to.

Commander William Adama had been there. Yes, that's right, this had already happened. She had been there and Bill Adama had been right nearby, which was fortunate since a pragmatist such as he might well not have believed it if it had merely been described to him. He would have had to see it for himself. But now, faced with the indisputable reality of ancient prophecy given form, he stared in wonderment at the skies, at the constellations that gave crucial clues to the way home. For the scriptures had said specifically that when the thirteenth tribe landed on Earth, they looked up in the heavens and saw their twelve brothers. This, right here, is (was) the ultimate religious experience and leap of faith for one as rooted in matters of military necessity as the commander of the last of the Battlestars.

With him was his son, Lee Adama, a Viper pilot who went by the name "Apollo." Lee, who had become an advisor to her on military matters, and had a relationship with his father that was, to say the least, complicated. Also present was Kara Thrace, another Viper pilot who had served under Lee. She was nicknamed "Starbuck," and it was she who had recovered the sacred arrow of Apollo, the relic which has made this amazing journey possible.

They are all there.

They are not.

They should be there, and Laura Roslin should be dressed in normal civilian clothes. But they are not there, and Laura remains in her night-gown and is alone.

She does not know how this could possibly be. Has she somehow made a return to Kobol for some additional knowledge of Earth? But when did this happen? She doesn't remember experiencing any sort of adventure that would have brought her to this pass. She racks her brain, thinking and thinking, and suddenly she laughs (still with no sound emerging). Obvious. So obvious. She has no recollection of anything that brought her here because nothing happened to bring her. She is dreaming. Yes. So simple, oh so simple. She is dreaming, reliving that amazing moment without any of her companions.

Again, though . . . why? Well, at least this wasn't something over which one could question the motivations of the gods. This was a product of the sleeping mind, and certainly no one could hope to comprehend whatever scenarios the sleeping mind might throw together.

She finds it curious, though, as if she's watching from outside herself. Typically one doesn't realize one is dreaming while it's happening. She would think that the sudden comprehension would be enough to kick her out of the dream entirely. But it does not. It seems to be of no relevance whether she understands or not. Rather it's as if she is a spectator at some sort of film that will be unspooled if she is watching or no.

The obelisks. She remembers them so clearly, constructs of abstract faith brought to rock-hard reality. Each made of stone, each one bearing an engraving of one of the symbols of the Twelve Colonies, studded with jewels that are twinkling in the night. Each of the symbols representing the colonies back when they were called by their original names: Aries, Taurus, Gemini, and so on. They ring the perimeter of the meadow where Laura is standing, as the stars of home beckon to her above, pointing the way to their destination.

Except . . . she has already been here. Why is she here again? The vagaries of dreams, certainly, but . . .

Something doesn't look right. Something is different from the last time.

It takes her long moments to notice something on one of the obelisks that was not there before. Some sort of darkness, dripping from the pointed arrow, nocked into the bow of Sagittarius the archer.

Laura Roslin approaches it slowly, the hem of her nightgown swirling around her legs. She reaches out toward the dark stain on the Sagittarius obelisk and touches it tentatively with one extended finger. She looks at her hand closely, rubbing her fingers together to get a feel of the liquid's consistency.

The color is red, dark red.

The liquid is blood.

Sagittarius is bleeding.

Uncaring of what it will do to the fabric, Laura uses the sleeve of her nightgown to wipe the blood away. It's gone for only a moment, and then wells back up. Blood is dripping steadily from the arrow, and then she notices that the twins, Gemini, are bleeding from their chests as if they've been wounded. She takes a step toward them, and then her head snaps around as Aquarius, the water bearer, sees the water in the top of his jug transform to blood as well.

She cries out in alarm without hearing her voice doing so, and starts to back up, putting one hand to her chest. It's on fire once more. She calls for help, but none hear, including herself. They're all bleeding now, blood seeping from the edges of the engravings. The stones are all running red with blood. She looks and sees that there is blood on her hands as well, and she's not sure if it's there because she was touching the bleeding obelisks and got some on her, or if it started generating there spontaneously.

And then, slowly, Sagittarius starts to fall forward. It is coming right toward her, and she backs up even further. It seems to be growing, casting a vast shadow over her, and she is running and running and it is becoming impossibly larger and longer, as if it is growing for the specific purpose of catching up with her. Laura Roslin throws herself forward in a desperate effort to escape, and is rewarded with hearing the obelisk thud to the ground behind her. It is the only noise she has heard in this eerie silence.

She rolls over onto her back, clutching her chest and watching in goggle-eyed amazement as, one after the next, each of the obelisks collapses. They fall upon each other from all angles, ponderously slow, and the ground beneath her trembles every time another one collapses. Within moments they are piled up, a stack of stones like so many cards. Then great cracks start appearing in them, as if in delayed reaction to their crashing one atop the other. They begin to break apart, slowly first and then faster and faster, and the chunks in turn transform into dust. A strong wind picks up and, minutes later, the obelisks representing the Twelve Colonies have completely blown away, traveling in different directions and scattering to the four winds.

Laura Roslin is alone.

She wants so much to cry, to sob deeply over what she has just seen. But Laura has always prided herself on her strength, and tears will not—never do—serve any purpose. She creeps forward on her hands and knees, for she does not feel as if she has the strength to stand. There are some small piles of dust and rubble still there, and she picks one up. She stares at it for a long moment, and then allows it to slip through her fingers. The granules twinkle like stars as they fall through.

She remembers stars twinkling. She has become deeply nostalgic for that. When she was at home and looked at the stars in the sky, naturally they twinkled as their light passed through the atmosphere.

Now when she looks out the window of her ship, Colonial One, *the stars never twinkle.*

It is the little things you miss. The little things that pile up on you, one by one, until you are crushed beneath their weight.

Crushed. Beneath weight.

Laura's head whips around. There is something behind her, something she was unaware of until just this second.

There is a thirteenth obelisk. It is right behind her, falling toward her.

There is a carving upon it. It almost looks like a cross of some kind, but it is upside down and it is not quite a cross. She realizes what it is: a crude representation of a war hammer.

That is all she has time to notice before the obelisk slams upon her and she lets out a scream, and this one she hears because

Laura Roslin screamed.

She sat up in bed in her room, gasping for air, her nightgown plastered to her skin, and she swore she could hear her own outcry echoing in her ears. Her breath came in ragged gasps, and her hair was hanging down and blocking her eyes. She shoved it out of her face, fully expecting to see crumbled obelisks everywhere, but there was nothing except the darkness of her own bed chamber. That, and a loud thumping which she first mistook for the pounding of her heart, but then she slowly realized was someone thudding the door with his fist. "His" was an easy deduction to make because she heard the alarmed voice of her aide, Billy Keikeya, shouting, "Madame President! What's wrong! Are you under attack? Should I call the—"

Her voice sounded slightly raspy as she spoke, and she realized she'd irritated her vocal cords when she'd screamed. Plus she was still gasping for breath, so she sounded as if she'd been running a marathon as she called back, "It's all right, Billy. I'm fine. Everything's fine."

"No one's holding you at gunpoint?"

"No. No one is."

There was a pause, and then from the other side of the door Billy said, "With all respect, Madame President, if someone *were* holding you at gunpoint, they could be making you say that."

Despite the circumstances . . . despite the horrific images that were as vivid to her waking mind as her sleeping one . . . she smiled slightly. "Damn, Billy. You're too clever by half." Even as she spoke, she slipped her feet out from under the covers, lowered them to the floor, got up and walked over to the closet. She pulled her robe on and continued, "It's all right, come in."

"Are you decent?"

Now she actually laughed. "No, I'm stark naked and have three lovers in here. Come on in and join the party."

There was a slightly audible gulp. "You know, out here is actually perfectly all right if—"

"Billy, I'm alone, I'm decent, come in and put your mind at ease."

The door opened and a very tentative Keikeya poked his head in, squinting and trying to make out shapes in the darkness. "Ah. All right. So . . . no security breach here, then . . ."

"None whatsoever." She paused and tilted her head in a slightly quizzical fashion. "How did you hear me?"

"Pardon?"

"I said," she repeated patiently, "how did you hear me?"

"Well . . . you screamed, and it was fairly loud, so . . ."

"Yes, I understand that part," she said. "But it's not as if your quarters are right next door. And the walls are fairly soundproof." Her eyes narrowed. "You don't have a listening device in here or something, do you . . . ?"

"No, ma'am, of course not." Billy was fully dressed, save that he wasn't wearing a necktie. His hand automatically smoothed down the nonexistent tie. "I just don't require all that much sleep. Three, four hours and I'm good as new."

"That's impressive," said Laura. "But it doesn't really answer my question. What, are you lurking outside my door all night?"

"Not . . . lurking exactly."

"Then what exactly? Billy . . . ?"

He rolled his eyes and leaned back against the wall. "It's just . . . you've been through a lot, Madame President. Being thrust into the presidency, being arrested, fighting cancer, winning . . . I mean, gods, that was like a miracle being handed to you."

"A miracle that could benefit a lot more people than me, Billy," she reminded him. "The blood resulting from Shar . . . from the lieutena . . ." She paused and then said, ". . . from the Cylon's pregnancy has astounding healing properties"

She felt a bit guilty, tripping over her referring to Sharon Valerii, the Viper pilot nicknamed "Boomer." A woman who had, several times, served as a source of salvation for *Galactica* and the struggling remnants of humanity . . . but whose home consisted of a prison cell because she could never, ever be trusted. Because she was the enemy. Because she was a Cylon. But fetal blood culled from the . . . the whatever-it-was that was gestating in her stomach . . . had sent Laura's cancer into complete remission. To say nothing of the fact that Sharon's cooperation with *Galactica* command had staved off the Cylons on at least one occasion. Laura felt as if she should be thankful. She felt as if they should be rewarding Sharon Valerii somehow. Give her a medal of honor, a congratulatory basket of something, anything.

Instead she sat in her cell and her baby—which Laura Roslin had been ready to order aborted—continued to grow in her belly, and Laura still struggled with the idea of thinking of Sharon as anything other than a thing. A thing to which the last survivors of the human race in general, and Laura Roslin in particular, owed their lives. Hardly the gratitude one would expect for someone who had done so much.

Well . . . she'd been allowed to keep her child, at least for the time being. Considering a creature who had looked like Sharon—who had *been* her—had gunned down Commander William Adama at point-blank range, perhaps that was as much generosity as one could possibly anticipate.

Her mind was drifting. It annoyed her. She preferred to stay on track in all her dealings. "So anyway . . . what's your point, Billy?"

"The point is, I just feel as if anything could go wrong at any time. And if that happens, someone should be on top of it."

"So you . . . what? Wander the halls and check on me? Listen for any signs of distress? Drop by every hour?"

"No, ma'am."

"No?"

He winced as if caught out in some dirty little secret. "More like every half hour."

She stared at him in the dimness of her quarters, her eyes round in surprise. Then she waggled her finger, indicating that he should come near. He did so, his face a question, and she pulled his head forward and kissed him gently on the top of it. "You," she said, "are a very sweet man. If Dualla lets you slip through her fingers, she would be a foolish young woman, mark my words."

"Ma'am . . ."

"Listen to me, Billy," and she rested her hands on his shoulders. "You'll do me no good if you worry yourself into exhaustion. At least now I understand why it looks like you're fighting to stay awake during press conferences. You need more than three hours' sleep, and not getting it because you're literally wandering the halls watching out for me is unacceptable."

"But—"

"Un . . . acceptable," she repeated firmly. "Besides, I have security personnel who are on duty."

"Which, under ordinary circumstances, would be perfectly fine," said Billy. "But these are dangerous times, Madame President, and besides, we never know who might be a Cylon and who might not be. So I figure that the more eyes watching out for things, the better."

"Mm-hmm. And what if you're a Cylon, Billy?" He started to laugh, but she continued, "After all, supposedly Valerii didn't know of her own nature for the longest time. How do you know you aren't actually patrolling the halls, waiting for the perfect time to do mischief?"

He stared at her, no longer laughing. "You want me to get more sleep and then you tell me something guaranteed to keep me awake all night? Besides, Doctor Baltar's Cylon detection test confirmed I was human. Unless," he suddenly said, "Doctor Baltar is also a Cylon, or under Cylon influence, in which case—"

Laura sighed. "Good night, Billy. Get more sleep and stop worrying about me. That's a presidential directive."

"Yes, ma'am. Thank you, Madame President." He bowed ever so slightly, which naturally wasn't remotely necessary but he likely couldn't help it, and started to exit her chambers. Then he paused, turned and asked, "By the way . . . why *did* you scream, Madame President?"

"Nothing. It was nothing. I had a bad dream."

"About what?"

"About this conversation and its refusal to end. Good night, William," she said with a touch of pointed formality.

Taking the hint, Billy said, "Good night, ma'am," and exited, closing the door behind himself.

Shaking her head, Laura sent the lights back from dim to darkness, removed her robe, and climbed back into bed.

And there she lay, for hour after hour, her mind suddenly alive with concerns. Concerns over the dream, concerns over everyone and his brother being a Cylon. She remembered a conversation she'd once had with Adama in which she'd said, "If you're a Cylon, I'd like to know." To which Adama had quite accurately replied, "If I'm a Cylon, you're really screwed."

She was convinced by now that Adama was not a Cylon.

But as she recalled the bleeding archer, the precursor of their own colony of Sagittaron—and the subsequent collapsing of all the obelisks, which had a symbolism that even a blind man could have seen—she wasn't entirely convinced that they weren't still really screwed.

CHAPTER 2

In the Viper pilots' lounge, Kara Thrace threw down her cards as her lips twisted in disgust. She fixed her opponent with a fearsome stare and said far more loudly than was necessary, to everyone who was seated at the table, "Who told this bum he could sit in? Huh?"

"You did," Gaius Baltar reminded her coolly.

Kara glanced around the table and saw an array of heads bobbing in agreement. "And you people *let* me? Knowing what you know about me? Knowing what an idiot I am, you were that dumb as to listen to me? Okay, fine." She tilted back in her chair and took a deep swallow of her drink, which sent a pleasant burning sensation down her throat. "In that case, I wash my hands of you. You brought it on yourselves."

Deckhand Callista Henderson, nicknamed Cally, cast a weary *you*-talk-to-her glance at Viper Pilot Lee Adama. Lee, however, refused to rise to it, and instead simply shook his head in resignation.

Meanwhile the target of Kara's ire was leaning forward and raking in his chips. "It's no big deal, Kara. It was just luck," said Boxey, who had to stand on his toes to reach the pot.

"Kara. He's calling me Kara, like we're . . . like we're friends or something," Kara said in mock indignation. "Punk kid! Remember who the grown-ups are around here."

"Admittedly, it's not always easy to tell," Baltar said pointedly.

"A little respect, is all I'm asking."

Lee Adama leaned forward and told the boy, "Personally, I'd give her as little as possible." Kara reached over and thumped Lee in the upper arm, which garnered a laugh followed by a loud "Ow!" as the pain caught up with him.

"How about Starbuck. Should I just call you Starbuck?" asked Boxey.

"Yeah, whatever," said Kara, who was accustomed to responding to the name that was her call handle. Sometimes she even wondered whether Starbuck was her real name, and Kara Thrace was simply this nice, good-girl name that she put on to hide her true persona.

"Are you really upset with me?" The thirteen-year-old boy looked genuinely concerned. "For winning so much money, I mean."

Kara, who was feeling a little bleary-minded with the combination of the lateness of the hour and the alcohol she'd consumed, smiled wanly and chucked Boxey under the chin. "Nah. Not really. You shouldn't worry about my feelings."

"I wasn't," Boxey replied. "I just wanted to figure out if you were gonna jump me once the game was over and try to get the money back."

This prompted guffaws from everyone else, and an archly fierce scowl from Kara.

Lee leaned forward and said, "If you ask me . . ."

"Which nobody did," Kara quickly told him.

". . . you've gotten a lot better at your game, kid. You been taking lessons? Hanging out with a bad crowd?"

"Worse than this one?" asked Baltar. "The mind positively boggles."

"I've met some guys, yeah," Boxey said guardedly.

He paused, and the adults looked at each other with knowing smiles. Cally poked him in the ribs and said in a sing-song voice, "There's a girrrrrrrrl . . ."

"Is not!"

"Is too."

"Is not!"

"Is too."

"I can feel my IQ spiraling into the abyss the longer this conversation continues," said Baltar. "Is anyone planning to deal a new hand so I can win some money back from the human chip-vacuum over here?"

"Not happening anytime soon, Mr. Vice President," Boxey assured him.

"Oh, great! *He* gets Mr. Vice President, *I* get Kara! Why is that?"

"Just a thought," suggested Baltar, "but could it possibly have anything to do with the fact that your name is Kara and mine isn't?"

"Frak you," said Kara.

"Been there, done that," Lee muttered a bit too loudly, which drew him a lethal glance from Starbuck.

Boxey looked up in confusion. "What?"

"Nothing," every adult at the table echoed.

With that bewildering consensus, another round of play passed, and once again, Boxey won. By this point everyone was throwing down their cards in disgust. "I want to meet this girl," Cally said loudly as she watched the last of her chips get swept away into Boxey's pile. "Whoever she is. I want to see what she's been teaching you."

"Just how to be a better card player," Boxey said defensively.

"No one's this good a card player."

"I am," Baltar pointed out.

"Couldn't tell it from what we're seeing here."

"Everyone has an off night."

"Well," Cally continued, "like I said, I want to meet her. You ask me, she's probably not even human if she taught you to play that well. Probably a Cylon."

"That's not funny!"

Boxey's outburst was so unexpected that the adults were startled into silence. Immediately chagrined at his reaction, Boxey looked down and said sullenly, "Sorry. I shouldn't have . . . I'm sorry."

"No, I am," said Cally, and she reached over and placed a hand atop his. "I mean, you lost your whole family to the Cylon attack on Caprica. I should have . . ."

"It's not that."

Kara raised an eyebrow in mild surprise. "It's not?"

"Well, it is a little," Boxey corrected himself. "But I'm not the only one. Millions and millions of people died, and the ones who didn't, almost no whole families made it. So I've got lots of, you know, company in trying to deal with all that."

"Then what . . . ?" Kara was still confused, and then she saw Lee mouth a name to her that she instantly recognized. "Oh."

Baltar had also worked it out, but he was less subtle than Lee. "You're referring to Sharon Valerii," he said.

Boxey nodded. "Do you ever get creeped out about it?" he asked Baltar.

" 'Creeped out'?"

"Well, she piloted the ship that brought the both of us off Caprica."

"Ah, yes. You know . . . since then, there's been so much going on, I haven't had the opportunity to give it much thought."

"Wish I could say that," said Boxey. He had completely forgotten about the deck that was in front of him, even though it was his turn to shuffle. "Sometimes I have dreams about her. I see her there, and she's at the helm of the ship, and suddenly she goes nuts like she did on Adama. Except in my dream, she doesn't shoot anyone. Instead she pilots the ship down, straight into the planet. And we die. Or at least we're going to die, except I wake up at the last second."

"Oh, thank the gods for that. Can we play cards?" Baltar said irritably.

Starbuck said, "Shut up, Gaius," silencing the vice president. "Boxey, you've got to remember something: The Sharon Valerii who flew that ship from Caprica and saved you, the one who shot Adama . . . she's gone."

"I know. She was shot and killed. Except she's in a cell, isn't she?"

"Well . . . yes."

"See, that's the thing I don't understand."

"I'm not sure any of us understands it any better, except perhaps for Doctor Baltar," said Lee, indicating the vice president. "He's as close as we have to an expert on Cylons."

"I suppose that much is true," Baltar said, shifting uncomfortably in his chair. "Even so, there's still a good deal about them that we don't understand."

"Okay, well . . . Boomer's locked up in a cell right now, right?"

Kara winced slightly at the familiar call name being used to refer to the thing in the brig. "That's right."

"But she's not the one who shot the commander . . . I mean, the admiral," he amended, acknowledging Adama's recent promotion.

"No, she's not," Baltar confirmed.

"So . . . what did she do that was wrong? I mean, if you get locked in the brig, it's because you're being punished for something. So what did she do?"

Now it was Lee's turn to look uncomfortable. "Specifically . . . nothing. She herself has done nothing wrong. But the other Sharon shot my father, so . . ."

"So it has to do with that Admiral Adama is your father?"

"No, it has to do with that the Sharon who is in the cell is just like the Sharon who tried to kill the admiral. If one Sharon did that, then this one might try it."

"But she might not try anything."

"There . . . is that possibility, yes."

"And she hasn't so far."

"Again, yes, but—"

"Here's what I don't get," said Boxey. "If you," and he pointed at Kara, "had a twin sister, and she did something really, really wrong, and you hadn't done anything, and they told you they were going to lock you in a cell because you might do something even though you hadn't yet . . . would that be, y'know . . . fair?"

"No, that wouldn't be fair," said Kara as she took back the card deck and started shuffling. "But it's not the same thing."

"How come?"

"Because it's not."

"But I don't see why . . ."

"Because she's *not human!*" Kara said. "Okay? She's a machine. She's a toaster. If I had a twin sister, she'd be human like me. But Sharon isn't human and she never was. She's . . . a frakking . . . toaster. Understand?" She started riffling the cards from one hand to the other.

"I guess."

"Good."

He paused, frowning, and then asked, "I just never saw a toaster that could get pregnant."

The cards flew out of Kara's hands, spraying all over the table.

"Yeah, that was a new one on us," Lee deadpanned.

Suddenly an alarm slammed through the ready room. Kara Thrace, who had been slightly wobbly from her alcohol intake, was immediately on her feet. So were Lee and Cally, all of them scrambling toward the flight deck, leaving Baltar and Boxey staring at each other.

"Cylons," said Lee with certainty as they ran.

"Good," Kara said. "With a choice of robots trying to kill me or this conversation, I'll take the robots."

Seconds after the pilots had left the table, one of Baltar's personal guards—tasked with attending to the safety of the vice president— came in and took Baltar firmly by the arm, pulling him to his feet before Baltar could even react. "Come sir," he said, "we're under attack. Regulations state that I have to get you to a secure location."

"Well, thank the gods," said Baltar. "And just where would be 'secure' exactly? I thought our entire problem was that no place was secure."

"Sir, we're under attack. Regulations state—"

"Yes, yes, yes." Baltar turned and tried to scoop up the remains of his chips, but the agent wouldn't be delayed any longer. As he pulled Baltar away, the vice president called to Boxey, *"Don't you dare touch my stack!"*

Boxey watched him go, then walked over to Baltar's unimpressively small stack of chips and touched them repeatedly in a mutinous display of defiance that no one saw.

Then he sank back into his chair and thought about Sharon Valerii, who had saved his life, sitting alone and scared in a cell, except it wasn't her, except it was.

He wondered if she remembered him, or even had the slightest idea who he was.

Baltar hurried down the hallways, the agent making sure to keep him moving quickly. His mind was an enforced blank, as it always was at such times when his life was at risk. Suddenly a familiar voice said to him low, suggestively, almost right in his ear, "Where are you running to, Gaius?"

He almost skidded to a halt as he looked to his right and saw, no longer the agent, but the statuesque blond Cylon that he'd come to know as Number Six. Even as he nearly stopped, though, Number Six pulled him forward so that he continued to move. He tried to respond, but his voice was paralyzed in his throat. She was right there . . . *right there.* The woman who had been his lover, his salvation, who had given him something other than machinery and research to live for and had horrifically turned it into a means of destroying the human race. What the hell kind of man was he, that he could only have happiness at the cost of genocide?

He swore he could smell her perfect scent, and his heart raced—not from fear, but from hopeless longing for a woman, a time, an innocence and naiveté long gone.

"I don't know," said Baltar, and he was speaking of so much that he didn't know—his destination, what would happen next, whether they would survive another minute, why he even deserved to live considering so many people had died because of his stupidity—that the three simple words spoke volumes of his character.

They meant nothing, however, to the agent, who simply replied, "There's nothing you need to know right now, sir, except that you need to keep moving." The agent's voice snapped Baltar back to reality and he struggled to keep up with him while, at the same time, he swore he could hear the faint, mocking laughter of Number Six in his head.

Boxey had been modest when he spoke of how he had picked up tips on quality card playing since making some new acquaintances. He had, in fact, acquired—in a remarkably short time—some other skills as well.

Actually, "acquired" might not have been the best way to put it.

"Honed" would be more accurate. Boxey had always been an exceptional hide-and-seek player in his youth. Many was the time that his parents recounted incidents where Boxey seemed to have literally disappeared into thin air. They would enter his room, calling his name, and there would be no sign of him. With weary cries of "Not again!" they would wind up tearing the house apart before Boxey was inevitably betrayed by his laughing—no, chortling—with glee that he had driven his parents crazy once more.

All of that was long ago and far away, or at least so it seemed. Boxey's tendency to laugh aloud at his own cleverness was gone. So was the life. It seemed to Boxey that the memories he had might as well have come from someone else entirely, for all the relevance they had to his current life.

Nevertheless, one of the skills that had not disappeared with his aging into adolescence had been the ability to be sneaky. To make himself not be seen, to blend into the background. He had said nothing to Starbuck or Apollo or any of the others about it, but he had acquired quite the nimble set of fingers. It had been more out of profound boredom than anything else that he had taken up petty thievery on the *Peacemaker*, the civilian transport ship to which he'd been assigned. It was one of the larger transports, and it was extremely easy to slip into and out of the throngs of people who seemed constantly to be milling about in the corridors, looking for something to do to occupy their time. The truth of the matter was that they were as bored as he was; he was just being aggressive about killing the boredom.

It was after he had lifted the wallet of one particularly officious gentleman that he had turned around, prepared to blend in with the shadows, only to discover himself face to face with a smiling red-haired girl. She had freckles, which initially struck Boxey as odd until he remembered that, yes, not all that long ago, the sun had shone on people's faces and done things to their skin. Freckles were gradually beginning to disappear these days, as were all hints of tans, but this girl still sported them. Her face was round, and she had deep brown eyes and small ears that poked out from copious straight hair that hung down to her shoulders.

Boxey braced himself, waiting for her to sound the alarm. Instead all she did was say, "You call *that* blending in with the shadows?" and she rolled her eyes in impatience over this Obviously Dumb Boy's ham-handed attempt at thievery.

Her name was Minerva, Minerva Greenwald, and as she gave

Boxey handy hints in making himself scarce, his young heart thudded with the poundings of his first crush.

Boxey still continued to make his way over to the *Galactica* every chance he got, snagging a ride on any shuttle that was going from the *Peacemaker* to the *Galactica* for some reason or other. All the pilots knew Boxey by that point, and were perfectly happy to bring him over with a nod and a wink to the regulations that said they weren't supposed to give anybody lifts. Boxey, nimble-fingered as he was, had also become deft at acquiring hard-to-come-by items from the black market. No one questioned too closely when Boxey was able to provide some particularly rare fruit, or a cigar, or a bottle of fine brandy. Boxey didn't believe in buying friendship, but there was nothing wrong with renting it or bribing it into existence for periods of time.

With all of those questionable talents at Boxey's command, it was small wonder that, while everyone was scrambling to the flight deck and leaping into their Vipers, and the ship was in a state of high alert, Boxey was able to slip into the brig. There were guards at the front, yes, but they were busy talking to each other, speculating about how the frakking Cylons had found them yet *again*, and when the hell was this going to let up already, and what if it never did, and what if sooner or later the luck of the last remains of humanity finally gave out. With all of that going on, it was not all that much trouble for Boxey to secure himself in a corner, wait until the proper moment presented itself, and ease himself behind the guards and through the main door without their even noticing he was there.

The cell area was cramped, as was pretty much everything else on *Galactica*. It wasn't particularly surprising; it was a battleship, after all. There was very little in the military mindset that made room for comfort. Functionality was valued above everything, and if the designers of *Galactica* didn't hesitate to cram the ship's military personnel into as incommodious quarters as possible, certainly they weren't going to go out of their way to provide luxurious accommodations for prisoners.

It was darker in the cell area than outside, and Boxey paused a few moments to let his eyes adjust.

He spotted her at the far end of the brig. Her cell didn't look to be much bigger than five by ten feet, and Boxey tried to imagine what it would be like to have his entire life confined to such a narrow area. The brig didn't have bars the way that other cells did. Instead it had walls that consisted of metal grid screens which appeared to be welded tightly together, reinforced by Plexiglas.

Sharon was in her cot, lying on her back, her arms flopped over her head. It was difficult for Boxey to determine if she was awake or not, although the steadiness of her breathing seemed to indicate that she was asleep. He also couldn't help but notice the developing bulge in her stomach. It wasn't especially large, but it bore the distinctive shape that separated the belly of a pregnant woman from one who was just getting fat . . . a distinction that Boxey had learned, but not before inadvertently insulting quite a few overweight women.

He approached her slowly, moving on the balls of his feet, applying everything he had ever known or had come to know about the art of stealth. She continued not to move. He couldn't see her face clearly, and for some reason that brought him a measure of comfort. He knew Sharon Valerii's face as well as he knew his own, if not better. He had stared at her the entire time that she had flown him from beleaguered Caprica to the relative safety of *Galactica*. So as long as he didn't see Boomer sitting in that cell, well, then . . . somehow the entire business of her being connected to the Cylons—of her being a Cylon herself—was far more ephemeral and easy to deny.

And then, while Boxey was still a short distance away, Sharon abruptly sat up.

Boxey was crouched low and she didn't see him at first, but the sharp intake of his breath—involuntary since he was startled—seemed to make her ears prick up. He suspected she hadn't heard him so much as just sensed that someone had entered. "Who's here?" she demanded, looking concerned. Her voice was muffled by the thickness of the walls; Boxey had to strain to hear her. Her hand drifted toward her stomach in a gesture that could only be considered protective. What a human thing for her to do, to react in such an instinctive manner when she thought her unborn child might be threatened. She glanced around suspiciously, undoubtedly nervous but trying valiantly not to look it. "I said who's here? If you're going to try and attack me, I'm warning you . . . I'll defend myself."

He hesitated, briefly considering the idea of scooting back out the way he'd come and abandoning this entire ill-conceived notion. But then he called to her, as softly as he could so as not to make her even more skittish than she was, "It's me."

"Me?" Her brow furrowed, as she clearly recognized the voice, but wasn't sure from where. Then something clicked in her mind. "Boxey?" she called. "Is that you?"

It was odd. He didn't know whether to feel relief . . . or unease.

He stood, smoothing down his shirt. "Yeah. It's me," he said uncertainly.

Sharon let out a sigh of relief and sagged back against the cell wall. "I can barely hear . . ." Then she stopped and pointed at a phone situated on the outside of the cell, matching up with an identical phone on the inside. Boxey went to it, picked it up, and put it to his ear as Sharon did the same on the inside. "What are you doing here?" she asked, her voice coming through loud and clear over the receiver. Then she seemed to get more tense again. "What *are* you doing here? Who sent you?"

"Nobody sent me," he said. "I just . . . I wanted to see you. I wanted to see if . . ." His voice trailed off.

"See if what?" she asked.

"If you remembered me."

"Of course I remember you. Why wouldn't I . . ."

"Because they say it wasn't you."

It was her turn to become quiet. "Oh. Right. Of course." She gave a short, bitter laugh. "Because the Sharon Valerii who rescued you from Caprica . . . the Sharon who you used to hang out here with, share meals with, the one who called you her unofficial little brother . . ."

"She's dead."

"Yes."

"Because she shot Commander Adama, and so Cally shot her."

"How is Cally?" Sharon asked with a trace of humor.

Boxey shrugged. "She's okay. I just beat her ass at cards."

"Good. Good for you."

There was another prolonged silence, and then Boxey said, "So . . . are you her? The one who died?"

"It's . . . complicated."

"That's what everybody keeps saying. I dunno. Sounds like a simple enough question to me."

"It is. It's the answer that's compli . . ." She sighed. "It comes down to this: I have . . . echoes . . . of you. Not the actual memories. Those will go to another . . . me. To me, you're like . . . a vague dream." She smiled and added, "But a nice dream, I assure you."

"Okay." He hesitated, and then said, "Did she know . . . did you know . . . that you were a Cylon when you took me off Caprica?"

"No."

"Because it . . ." He cleared his throat, betraying yet again his nervousness. "I just get worried that maybe the whole thing was . . . you know . . ."

"A Cylon plot?" she asked. "You want to know if my taking you off Caprica is somehow related to a vast Cylon conspiracy?" Despite the seriousness of the situation, there was a hint of humor in her voice. "Boxey, don't take this wrong, but in the grand scheme of things, you're not that important."

"My father was."

That brought her up short. She looked down, unwilling to meet his eyes. "Yes. He was."

"He was assigned to the Armistice Station," Boxey continued, and there was growing anger in his voice. "He got sent there every year to meet with one of the Cylons, except they never came. And then one of them, or more of them, I guess, showed up, and they blew up the station, and they blew up him. My dad. The first one to die in the new war."

"Yes, he was," Sharon said again, tonelessly, as if she were reciting a particularly unmemorable verse of poetry.

"Were you there for that, too? Did you kill him, like you tried to kill Commander Adama?"

"No, I wasn't. That wasn't my . . . my model. That wasn't me."

"But if you'd been ordered to do it, you'd have done it, 'cause you're a machine."

"But I wasn't, and I didn't. And being a machine has nothing to do with it," she said, sounding a little heated. "Plenty of perfectly human soldiers are given orders they don't like, but they go out and get the job done. That's their responsibility. It's . . ." She stopped, took a deep breath as if trying to calm herself. Then, her gaze fixed on Boxey, she said, "You know what no one considers, kid? That there's as many similarities between our two sides as differences."

"We're not machines."

"Of course you are," Sharon said reasonably. "What else is a human body *but* a machine? You have moving parts . . . you require fuel . . . you break down and need to be repaired by someone—call them 'doctor' or 'mechanic,' it's the same thing—and eventually when the machine gets hopelessly broken, it's junked. The only difference is that when our bodies get broken, we live on. Face it, kiddo . . . you don't hate us because we're machines. You hate us because we're better machines than you are."

"We hate you because you're trying to wipe us out," Boxey replied icily.

"Considering humanity's history of war, it's perfectly possible that—left to your own devices—you might well have wiped yourselves out. Personally, I think it's fairly likely."

"And so you're just getting the job done for us?"

She shrugged. "That's one way to look at it, I guess."

"What other way is there?"

"There's always other ways, Boxey," Sharon told him. "You'd be amazed. You'd be stunned, how a thousand people can look at the exact same event and come away with a thousand different interpretations."

"I'm an orphan because of your race. How many ways can *that* be interpreted?"

She tried to respond to that, but instead she lowered her eyes, as if she were suddenly ashamed. "Why are you here, Boxey? Really? I mean, are you here to yell at me? Because if that's what you want, go ahead. I could just hang up the phone and turn my back, but you'll still have all this anger and no one to unload it on. So you might as well unload it on me, the face of the enemy."

"Don't you do that," he said heatedly. "Don't you start being nice and sacrificing and all that stuff now."

"What do you want me to be? Do you have *any* clue?"

He was about to snap off an answer, but then he paused and realized that he didn't have one.

"I'm sorry if you hate me," she said.

"I don't hate you."

Now she looked up, and there was bemusement on her face. "You don't. Well, you could have fooled me. Actually, strike that: You did fool me. If you don't hate me, then what . . . ?"

"I miss you. Okay?" he admitted. "I miss hanging out with you. I miss knowing that you were my friend. I miss having the world be nice and easy and black and white, where you knew who was the good guy and who was the bad guy and everything was simple."

Despite the tension of the situation, Sharon couldn't help but smile. "Boxey," she said with great sadness, "I really hate to break it to you . . . but the world was never like that. Not ever. The best spouse in the world can still cheat on their mate, and the worst villain in the world is still capable of pulling a small child out of the way of a speeding car. There's no absolute heroes and no absolute villains. Everything is

shades of gray. By the time you were an adult, you'd probably have figured that out. Unfortunately, you learned the lesson earlier than you
should have."

"Because of you."

"Because of the Cylons, yes," she told him. "But not me. It may be
hard for you to believe or understand . . . but I've never hurt anybody in my life."

"In this life."

"Yes," she admitted. "In a manner of speaking, yes. In this life."

"*Hey!*".

Boxey was startled by the angry shout, and turned to see that one
of the guards from outside was standing in the doorway, glaring at
him. "What the frak are you doing in here?"

"We were just talking . . ."

"And how do we know that?" demanded the guard as he stalked
quickly across the room. "For all I know, you were taking orders
from her."

"*What?*" The startled exclamation came from both Boxey and
Sharon, the latter hearing the guard's muted voice through the
phone.

"She's a Cylon and you sneak in here to have private time with
her. She may be giving you instructions for a new plan to sabotage
us. You could be a Cylon, just like her."

"That's stupid!" Boxey protested. "A Cylon just like her . . . ?
That's nuts!"

"And why do you say that?" demanded the guard.

"Because . . . well . . ." He gestured haplessly at her. "For starters,
she's a girl. How can I be just like that?"

"That's it," said the marine, and he grabbed Boxey by the back of
the shirt and hauled him away. The receiver slipped out of Boxey's
grasp, swung down on the cord, and smacked up against the side of
the cell.

Curiously, Sharon stood there long after Boxey was gone, the
phone still in her hand even though there was no one on the other
end. Then, very slowly, she hung up the phone, settled down on her
cot, and rubbed her stomach absently.

CHAPTER 3

It never gets easier.

Admiral William Adama and Colonel Saul Tigh were polar opposites whenever the *Galactica* was under assault. Tigh, the executive officer, prowled the CIC, studying the screens from every possible angle, moving from station to station like a panther stalking its prey. Adama, by contrast, usually remained immobile unless he was directly summoned by one of his officers. A calm and cool eye to Tigh's hurricane, Adama watched the battle unfold, taking in reports that came at him fast and furious from all directions. His expression typically could have been carved from stone as he assessed the inevitable see-sawing nature of any battle.

It never gets easier.

Adama had gotten very, very skilled at making it look easy. One would have thought that he was sending strangers into combat. One would further have thought that there was no doubt in his mind that they would all make it back to the barn without a scratch, as if their lives were charmed and the notion that they might not return in one piece—or at all—was simply too laughable to contemplate.

Except he did contemplate it. Every single damned time that the Vipers launched into combat, there went Lee Adama, Apollo, his son. There went Kara Thrace, Starbuck, who had been the true love of his late son, Zack, and was like a daughter to him. Every single one of the other pilots, even though he didn't have the same depth of emotional bond to them, were members of his extended family. Adama lived and died with each encounter and every shot from a Cylon raider that came flying their way.

Each time his Vipers flew into combat, he waited for it to get easier. He waited for some sort of distance to creep into his heart that would enable him to endure this with less effort.

But it never happened. In fact, it seemed to him that during battles, he literally forgot to breathe. That it wasn't until they were safely away from the latest Cylon assault that he would exhale a breath he didn't even realize he was holding. He was surprised by it every single time.

It never gets easier.

The truth of that continued to echo through his brain, and he did what he always did in these situations: He compartmentalized his mind. The concerns that if he had to mourn the loss of his remaining son, he might crack completely . . . the notion that, sooner or later, Apollo and Starbuck's luck would have to run out, they simply could not go on beating the odds forever . . . all of this he tucked away in one little chamber of his brain, a small compartment with a door on it that he would slam, turn the key in, lock, and then go on about his business. His fears and terrors could make as much noise from within their imprisonment as they wanted, but it was all muffled and meaningless. And his face never reflected an instant of it.

"Lieutenant Gaeta, ETA on the Jump, please," called out Adama.

Felix Gaeta scanned the readouts as he worked on programming the next Jump into the ship's computer. It wasn't as if he had to do the Faster Than Light calculations from scratch every time. He routinely updated them so that he would be ready to Jump the fleet to a safe location as quickly as possible. Nevertheless, there had to be systems, procedures followed and double-checks made, lest a miscalculation send the *Galactica*, the *Pegasus*, and the entire civilian fleet leaping directly into a planetary body. Certainly that would solve the problem of constantly being pursued by the Cylons, but it was an unacceptably terminal means of addressing it. "Three minutes, twenty seconds, Admiral," Gaeta called out, his voice calm and level and not sounding the least bit rushed despite the fact that a fleet of robots was trying to kill them. He realized he was scratching his right hand and forced himself to stop. It was a nervous condition he'd recently developed, a response to the constant stress. It was starting to give him a rash, so he was forcing himself to deal with it.

"See if you can shave a few seconds off that," Tigh said, stepping around to Gaeta's station. "Every single one counts."

Adama winced a bit inwardly. He knew it was Tigh's way to be brusque, to demand the best and more than the best from his officers. But he didn't feel there was anything remotely constructive in what Tigh had just said. Certainly Gaeta knew that every second counted. This wasn't a news flash or an observation that had just come to Tigh's attention. However he wasn't about to remonstrate his XO in the midst of a battle situation. The depressing thing was that he knew that, even if he scolded Tigh about it in the privacy of his quarters, it still wouldn't make a damned bit of difference. Tigh would either apologize and say he would try to do better, or he would say that Gaeta had in fact looked at him sideways two days earlier and he was letting him know who was boss. Either way, nothing was going to change anytime soon. Adama was beginning to think that he had seen it all.

"Never seen that before," Starbuck muttered.

Her words, even though they were spoken to herself, sounded in the ear piece of Lee Adama, who was in the midst of engaging a Cylon raider that was coming right at him. "Starbuck, this is Apollo, I didn't copy that!" he said, firing at the raider that deftly angled away from him.

Starbuck didn't answer immediately. She was studying the battlefield before her. At least there were fewer raiders this time. The number of Cylons assailing them seemed to have dwindled since they had blown up the *Resurrection* ship, the vessel that had functioned to "resurrect" Cylon agents after they were killed. She strongly suspected there was a connection, although she wasn't sure what it was . . .

Head in the game, Starbuck, get your head in the game.

She barrel rolled and swung around toward a Cylon raider who was coming at her, guns blazing. Except . . .

Except . . .

"They're shooting wide!" she said as deep space was filled with Vipers going up against Cylon raiders. "I'm not even dodging the frakking things! It's like they're not even shooting at me!"

"Of course not, they're shooting at *Galactica*! Or the fleet!"

"Negative, I say again, negative, Apollo," Starbuck insisted. "I'm tracking trajectory! They're shooting at . . . at nothing!"

"Why the frak would they be doing that?" said Apollo. "Trouble with target lock?"

"There aren't people in those things shooting their guns, Apollo! Those ships *are* Cylons, remember? It's like saying their whole fleet has a giant head cold and can't see straight!"

Even as she spoke, she continued to press the attack. And now Apollo saw what Starbuck was talking about as the Cylons essentially did everything they could to stay out of the Vipers' way while returning fire that was woefully off target. Apollo hadn't been tagged even once.

"Not hitting them? Are you sure?" asked Adama.

Petty Officer Second Class Anastasia Dualla said, "Reconfirming it, Admiral. Starbuck first noticed it, then Apollo, and now Hot Dog and Kat are saying so as well. Either the Cylons have forgotten how to shoot, or they're deliberately aiming wide of our people. And they're not drawing appreciably closer to *Galactica*."

"Admiral," Gaeta informed him, "we're ready to make the Jump."

"Shall I recall the Vipers, Admiral?" asked Dualla, leaning toward her communications board in that slightly hunched manner she had when they were in the midst of a battle.

Adama's mind was racing. He had come to know the clockwork repetition of the Cylon mind, or at least he thought he had. Why in the world would they start changing tactics now? Something seemed wrong.

"Admiral . . ." Dualla prompted.

"He heard you, Dualla," Tigh said sharply, and Adama realized that Tigh was standing near his shoulder. The decisive sound of his voice and defiant look of his posture would never have betrayed the confusion in his eyes over Adama's hesitation. "He'll give the order when he's ready." Then, in a low voice that only Adama could hear, Tigh murmured, "Which will be anytime now, right?"

"Tell the Vipers to buy us more time. Make sure the Cylons keep their distance," said Adama said in a calm, almost detached voice. Then he continued, "Colonel . . . scramble a raptor for immediate launch. Lieutenant Gaeta, relay the Jump coordinates to the raptor. Tell them I need a recon mission stat. In and out. If they linger at the Jump point even one second, that's one second too long."

Neither Tigh nor Gaeta nor any of the rest of the crew in CIC even pretended to understand, but fortunately enough, understanding an order wasn't necessary for following it.

So it was that a raptor, under the guidance of Lieutenant Kathleen "Puppeteer" Shay (so called for her compulsion to have her hands in so many things), hurled itself into the ether while the Vipers continued to fight a delaying action against the Cylons.

The call that came through seconds later from the *Pegasus* didn't especially surprise Adama. He picked up the phone and said into it, "*Pegasus*, this is *Galactica* actual."

"*Galactica*, *this is* Pegasus *actual*," came the voice of Commander Barry Garner. The former engineering chief had been pressed into service as commander of Battlestar *Pegasus* after the assassination of Admiral Cain by a Cylon operative, followed by the scandalous murder of Commander Jack Fisk, who had had deep ties with the black market trade. Garner, who very likely had never figured to serve as his vessel's CO, nevertheless did his best to be up to the challenge. If he ever felt overwhelmed by what was expected of him, he never let it show, a technique of which Adama approved. *"Admiral, all due respect, what are we waiting for? Our Vipers are battling the Cylons right alongside yours, but it's not as if we need an extended workout."*

"We're investigating something," Adama said cautiously. Under the circumstances, it was never safe to assume that the Cylons hadn't found a way of listening in on their communications. In fact, it was probably safer to assume they *had* found a way and to act with appropriate caution. "Stand by."

"Stand by?"

"Yes, *Commander,* stand by," said Adama with particular emphasis on rank, a not-so-subtle reminder of exactly who was in charge.

There was only the slightest pause, and then Garner replied, *"Standing by, aye."*

Puppeteer, handling the controls with the vast confidence she always displayed in such situations, folded space around herself and leaped to the coordinates that Gaeta had conveyed to her. She had never quite adjusted to the sensation. It wasn't enough of a reaction that it hampered her ability to handle a raptor or get her job done. It was just a second or two of nausea that swept through her, and then she was able to mentally right herself and get on with whatever her mission was.

This time was no exception. Puppeteer braced herself as the FTL drive kicked in and propelled her to the new destination that was intended to be safe haven—albeit temporary, of course, thanks to the damned Cylons constantly nipping at their heels. Not for the first time, Puppeteer wondered if there was ever going to be a time when humanity could just take a long, deep breath of relief and go about its business without worrying about the damned toasters leaping on them like jackals on lions.

Space twisted around her in half a heartbeat, using technology and scientific theory that she couldn't have explained if someone had put a gun to her head. Still, it was like walking into a room and flipping a light switch. As long as the light illuminated the room, who gave a damn how it worked.

She was never actually able to perceive the Jump while she was in transition. It wasn't as if some vast vortex of stars swirled around her in a hypnotic haze, providing a tunnel through which her ship hurtled. She was simply in one place, then she was in another, with a slight sense of having been stretched like a rubber band and then having snapped back almost instantaneously.

The FTL drive spat her out into the new coordinates, and she felt that same typical instant of nausea, which she pushed away from her.

Then space around her seemed to explode.

Acting completely on reflex and survival instinct, she jammed the raptor's stick and sent the ship spiraling backwards. Even as she did so, her eye had just enough time to catch sight of something, and it took her brain another second or so to process what she was seeing.

"Frak me!" she shouted as she reactivated the FTL drive. Blasts continued to erupt around her. The ship jolted and she felt a moment of panic—not just from the prospect of dying, but from doing so without being able to get back to Galactica with her mission completed. She'd been hit—only a glancing blow. But they were zeroing in on her, and she couldn't count on her luck to hold up. The FTL roared to life once more as she slammed the ship forward, and suddenly there was a blinding explosion dead in front of her, and everything went black.

"How much longer do we wait?" Tigh said. There was nothing in his tone that suggested he was challenging Adama's authority, but he was clearly getting a bit apprehensive about the delay.

"Just long enough," replied Adama. He had actually calculated exactly how long he intended to wait for a report from the raptor, balancing that against the apparently questionable Cylon assault. He was certain there would come a point where the Cylons would drop the miss-on-purpose assault and start firing for real, and he factored that into a mental countdown that was running rapidly toward zero. But he didn't feel the need to say all that to Tigh, and Tigh—being the officer he was with the long history that he and Adama shared—would never consider pushing harder on the question.

Ten, the mental clock ticked down in Adama's head, nine, eight, seven . . .

Dualla suddenly turned and said, "Admiral! Raptor One is back! She's reporting . . ." Dualla's eyes widened.

"Dualla," Adama prompted, time running out.

"Sir, Puppeteer says the Jump point is swarming with Cylons! She says it was like space was alive with them! She can't even begin to guess how many there were!"

Colonel Tigh paled slightly upon hearing the news, and there was a moment of stunned shock in the CIC. Gaeta's hand had been poised over the FTL controls the entire time. Now, as if all feeling had fled from his fingers, he slowly lowered it while staring in astonishment at Adama.

It never gets easier.

"An ambush," growled Adama. "They're trying to herd us right into it." He paused and then said, "Dualla . . . get the horses back into the barn."

"All Vipers, return to *Galactica* immediately."

Knowing that he was about to order his officer to roll the dice with the last survivors of humanity, Adama said, "Lieutenant, plot a blind Jump. Best guess. Get us out of here."

Gaeta visibly gulped, but it wasn't as if the order was a complete surprise to him. It wasn't the first time that he'd been required to do such a thing. He'd accomplished it successfully before, but it was always a white-knuckle maneuver. Acting as the thorough professional that Adama expected him to be, Gaeta said, "Aye, sir," and number crunched as fast as he could. By the time the last of the Vipers had returned to the bay, he had coordinates transmitted to the rest of the fleet . . . prompting an immediate, albeit not unanticipated, communiqué from Garner on the *Pegasus*. "*Are these coordinates right, Admiral?*" he asked. "*They're different from—*"

"I know that, Chief. The previous coordinates are unusable. This is our best guess."

There was the briefest hesitation, and then Garner said coolly, "*Well, then, this should be fairly interesting.*"

"Yes." Adama hung up the phone, then turned to Gaeta. Gaeta was staring right at him, waiting for confirmation. All Adama had to do was nod, and then Gaeta keyed in the final coordinates.

"FTL engines on line," Gaeta said. He glanced just once at his own hand, feeling that the entirety of humanity was residing in it, waiting to see what he was going to do. Then the FTL drive kicked in and the fleet vanished from the site, hurtling into the complete unknown.

A split instant later, they reemerged into normal space.

A blazing star hung directly in front of them.

"*Frak!*" exploded from Gaeta's lips.

"*Full reverse thrust! All ships!*" shouted Adama, and the order was instantly relayed. It wasn't entirely necessary, considering that when one is hurtling right into a star, it doesn't take much to realize that the best direction to be heading at that moment is anywhere other than forward.

They were still thousands of miles away from the star, but distances in space could be eaten up very quickly, especially by ships that were dropping out of light speed. Furthermore, the *Galactica* wasn't built for maneuverability. It didn't corner worth a damn, and it wasn't designed to stop on a mark. Objects in motion tend to stay in motion unless acted upon by another force. With no friction in space, the only force to halt the *Galactica* was the reverse thrusters. Unfortunately, they were already being acted upon by another force entirely: the star's gravity field. It was just beginning to act on them and Adama had no desire to pit the strength of his ship's engines against the pulling power of billions of tons of blazing gas. Worst-case scenario, they would be yanked in and toasted in a matter of seconds. Best-case scenario, the *Galactica* would be ripped in half. Neither was an appealing prospect.

The smaller ships were able to halt themselves easily, but then they madly scrambled to get out of the way, for the *Pegasus*—bringing up the rear—wasn't slowing any easier than the *Galactica.* The civilian transports cut right, left, up, down and sideways, any direction they could go relative to the aft Battlestar that would easily smash them to bits if it collided with them.

The prospect of being rear-ended by the *Pegasus* occurred to Adama, but he had to deal with one crisis at a time. Although he might have been imagining it, he thought he could hear the hull of the mighty warship screaming in protest as the engines labored to halt the ship's forward progress. No . . . he wasn't imagining it. Above all the sounds of reports and orders being relayed and confirmed, people were looking around in response to what sounded like groaning, as if the ship were a senior citizen being forced to run laps. It wasn't the first time that Adama was being reminded that the *Galactica* had been scheduled for retirement, to be transformed into a museum due to its age. *You and me both, we could use the rest,* he thought grimly.

The *Galactica* hurtled toward a collision with the star, and the screens adjusted automatically to dim the blinding brightness so the crew's retinas wouldn't be burned away from looking at it. Adama had several seconds to ponder the irony of that: that they wouldn't go blind while they were exploding in the nuclear heart of a celestial furnace.

The entire vessel trembled even more violently, and it was slowing

and slowing, but it was going to be too close. And then, ever so gradually, the ship slowed to a halt and then stopped. Seconds later, the full
force of the reverse thrusters finally accomplished the job, and the
Galactica started to move backwards.

"*Pegasus* hasn't stopped yet! She's coming right at us!" Gaeta called
out.

"*Cut thrusters! Brace for impact!*" shouted Adama. He gripped the
nearest railings. He saw others closing their eyes involuntarily, although not looking at the screens certainly wasn't going to ward off
disaster.

The *Pegasus* was approaching them like some vast harbinger of
doom, and suddenly they saw the vehicle cutting hard to port. It was
going to be an unspeakably near thing.

"Come on, come on, turn," growled Tigh.

And then, as if in response to Tigh's imploring, the vast battleship moved sharply to port even as *Galactica*'s own reverse thrusters
hauled them away. The nose of the ship angled downward in relation to the *Galactica*, and even as the *Pegasus* seemed gargantuan in
their screens, it then dropped straight down and away from them.
Adama could have sworn he'd seen the terrified faces of people on
the *Pegasus*, their faces pressed against viewing ports, watching the
two behemoths narrowly avoid each other.

A long, tense silence filled the CIC, punctuated only by the many
sounds that the various instruments in the command center routinely made. And then Adama turned to Gaeta, who looked as if all
the blood had drained from his face and was somewhere down
around his shoes, and said as calmly as could be, "You trying to
make things exciting, Lieutenant?"

"Not that exciting, no sir," Gaeta said, and there was a slight gasp
in his voice indicating he'd been holding his breath . . . a tendency
Adama could certainly relate to.

"Well . . . if they say any landing you can walk away from is a
good one, the same can be said of a light-speed Jump. Well done, Mr.
Gaeta."

"Thank you sir," sighed Gaeta, and there was ragged clapping
and cheers from the others in the CIC.

But it was quickly silenced by a look from Adama. "Now that we
narrowly survived, we need to give top priority to figuring out how
the Cylons knew where we were going to be leaping to. If we have a
bug or virus in our computer . . . if we have a security leak . . . we
need to find it and plug it."

"Aye, sir, I'm on it," Gaeta said firmly.

Adama nodded and turned away, mostly so that no one else would see the visible relief flooding through him. Tigh stepped in close to him and said, "Good instincts on your decision, Admiral. About suspecting it might be a trap."

"It doesn't make sense, though," said Adama. "Even if they were trying to get us to leap into an ambush . . . why shoot wide of our people? All it did was raise our suspicions. They could just have easily engaged us for real, we activate the FTL engines with the coordinates they already know, and bam, we're in their trap. Why alert us to the possibility . . . ?"

"Perhaps the Cylons aren't as clever as we give them credit for," suggested Tigh.

Adama glanced sidelong at him. "If I'm given a choice between overestimating an enemy or underestimating . . . I'll go with the former."

"Me, I'm just glad the *Pegasus* was only a near miss instead of a disaster."

Smiling ever so slightly in amusement, Adama noted, "People always say that. A 'near miss.' It wasn't a near miss. It was a complete miss. It was a near hit."

"As long as we didn't take it up the aft, I'm satisfied with whatever it was."

Adama nodded wearily at that.

Tigh turned away, intending to go and hover nearby Gaeta as he began running checks on his navigation system. But he paused long enough to say, "It never gets easier, does it."

Staring at him blandly, Adama let the statement hang there for what seemed like forever, and then said, "I hadn't noticed."

On *Colonial One*, Laura Roslin was receiving an update from Adama over the phone of what had transpired. Her blood chilled as he described to her the horrific ambush that would have been awaiting them if they had been foolish enough to go leaping through space to the planned coordinates.

"Well done, Admiral," Roslin commended him. "In this day and age, when it's so easy to second-guess every decision people make about everything, it's nice to know that this decision of yours was completely valid. No 'down side,' as it were."

"As it were," agreed Adama. He was willing to admit to himself that there had been a time when he literally couldn't stand the sound of Roslin's voice. He had been certain she was using the cloak of government to thrust humans into situations where their very existence was jeopardized. But over the past weeks, be it because of receiving deft and canny political advice from Roslin, or because of working with Baltar and that damned Cylon Sharon of all people (he'd been convinced he'd had a knife in his stomach the entire time he was speaking with her, due to the extreme belly aches he'd been enduring), he'd come to respect Laura Roslin greatly. Perhaps even . . . feel more than just respect. Not that this was something he intended to bring up to her, or even completely acknowledge himself. They both simply had too many responsibilities to risk entanglements of any sort. At least, that was what he kept telling himself.

"And you're trying to determine how the Cylons knew where we were going to Jump to?"

"It's being investigated even as we speak."

"That's a relief. The last thing we need is them working their way into our systems once more." She added thoughtfully, "What about the *Pegasus*? My understanding is that their computer system would be far more susceptible to Cylon tinkering, since all their computers are linked." The fact that *Galactica*'s computers were not linked one to another had been the ship's salvation, since it meant that the Cylons could not readily infiltrate the computer network.

"You're absolutely right, Madame President," Adama agreed. "That is being investigated as well."

"Good. Please keep close tabs on that, Admiral. I'm not entirely sure I trust Chief Garner to get the job done . . . or trust him at all, really."

This comment surprised Adama. "Why not, Madame President? Do you have information I'm lacking? Is there reason to doubt his capability as an officer?"

"No to both," she admitted. "But considering that we wound up almost assassinating Commander Cain, and considering Commander Fisk was fronting a black market operation, you'll understand if I don't exactly have the highest hopes for the *Pegasus* command squad."

"Understood."

She imagined that Adama was smiling as he said that. He had the loveliest smile.

Then an image hammered its way back into her memory. She jumped into the pause that had crept into their conversation to ask, "Admiral . . . I have a rather odd question for you."

"It's been an odd day, so it fits right in."

"If I told you that Sagittarius was bleeding, what would that suggest to you?"

He didn't reply immediately, except to laugh low in his throat and say, "Well, the question certainly lived up to the advance billing." He considered it for a short time, and then said, "Given that Sagittarius is the ancient name for the colony Sagittaron . . ."

"Yes?"

"I'd say if anyone was going to cause any sort of bleeding in connection with Sagittaron, I'd probably look no further than Tom Zarek to be the cause."

Laura Roslin could have hit herself in the side of the head in frustration. "Of course," she said. "After all, he's the representative to the Quorum of Twelve for Sagittaron, gods know why."

"I'm only wondering why it is that we're talking in symbolism and metaphor."

"It . . ." She waited a moment, not wanting simply to spill everything that was going through her mind at Adama's feet. She had her own problems, and she had to deal with them. "I was just . . . wondering . . . what the image might suggest. That's all."

"That's *all*?"

"Yes, Admiral," she said calmly, almost with an air of indifference. "That's all."

She could picture him shrugging as he said, "Very well. That's all, then. *Galactica* actual over and out."

There was a click as he hung up the phone, and yet Laura Roslin stared at the disconnected receiver for a good long time, wondering if Adama had a point and Tom Zarek was somehow up to trouble again.

CHAPTER 4

Tom Zarek—freedom fighter, untrustworthy schemer, hero, villain, all depending upon whom one talked to—had continued to make his home on the *Astral Queen*, despite the fact that as the representative of the Quorum of Twelve, he was entitled to far more luxurious accommodations. He chose not to avail himself of them, for he felt it vital to keep as much of his connection to the "common man" as he possibly could.

On the other hand, he wasn't stupid. He had far outgrown the small, confined cell that had been his home ever since he had been elevated from mere prisoner to his colony's (or, more correctly, what remained of his colony's) most prominent figure. So he had taken for his office and quarters what had been the lodgings of the warden/captain of the *Astral Queen*. Since the events of the prisoner uprising, the administrators had decided that the best idea would be for them to make themselves as scarce as possible.

This left something of a power void in the day-to-day affairs of the prisoners themselves. Naturally they had turned to Zarek to make certain that some degree of order was kept in their existence, and Zarek had obliged them. Much of his time was spent on overseeing disputes. Not as a judge, certainly: Zarek was far too rebellious by nature to allow himself to become so authoritarian. He was, instead, a mediator. He always managed to find a common ground, and his method of bargaining was rapidly become legendary. If one of the parties didn't like the compromise that Zarek proposed, then his sergeant-at-arms would break the complainer's kneecaps. If they both complained, both parties got their kneecaps broken. Zarek had announced this policy and, at first, the prisoners had thought he was joking. They were disabused of that notion the first time two moaning disputees were seen crawling out Zarek's door. Their agony drove home the point with far greater force than anything Zarek could have said.

There was some minor rumbling about trying to take down Zarek rather than submit to such a means of oversight. But that notion went away once the residents of the *Astral Queen* came to the realization that Zarek's death would create a power vacuum, and if that happened, the bodies would start stacking up like cordwood in the subsequent struggle for dominance. One might despise the way a dam is constructed, but no one is stupid enough to shoot the guy who's got his finger in it preventing the water from flooding through.

So it was that Zarek's position and status were perfectly safe by dint of the fact that, although they didn't one hundred percent trust him, they distrusted each other far more.

At least, that was the status until the day that the civilian fleet had yet another narrow escape from the Cylons.

Although the ships were spread out, it was still hard to keep secrets, especially when something unusual happened. And certainly the *Galactica* nearly plunging into the heart of a star fell into the category of "unusual." The fact that the civilians had come extremely close to losing their best means of protection against an implacable enemy had not gone unnoticed, and a number of Zarek's "constituents" were demanding to know just what the frak had happened.

Zarek was moving quickly down a corridor, accompanied by Cortez, his sergeant at arms, and a handful of petty functionaries. This, in and of itself, was not unusual. There were several people following Zarek as well, constituents peppering him with their concerns. This was also not unusual. What was unusual was the volume and vociferousness with which they were speaking.

The largest and loudest of them was a man Zarek had known for some time, a bear of a man named Luther Paine, who seemed bound and determined to live up to his last name. Zarek kept walking, since it had been his experience that—if he stopped—it made it much harder for him to extricate himself. So he was walking and talking at the same time. "I hear what you're saying, Luther."

"I don't give a damn that you're hearing what I'm saying," Paine told him sharply. "I want you to listen to what I'm saying! I want you to find out what in the name of the gods happened with this latest invasion!"

"I already know what happened, and so do you," Zarek said. "We were attacked, we escaped. End of story."

"End of story! We almost saw the *Galactica* go up in a ball of flame, and then the *Pegasus* almost collided!"

Violating his own determination to keep moving in the face of hostility, Zarek turned and faced Paine. He wanted to try and end this quickly, before it began to spiral out of control. Paine was someone to whom the prisoners listened, and he didn't need this idiot running all over the place, stirring things up. "The key word there is 'almost.' Almost doesn't mean a thing. It's results that count, and the result was that we got away. If you don't like the way we did it, feel free to pop over to the *Galactica* and tell Adama yourself."

"I shouldn't have to! You're our frakking representative! You should be the one who tells him! Or are you afraid to?"

This last comment riled Cortez, and he took a step forward with his fists tightly clenched. The two men were built about the same, and it was anybody's guess who would come out on top if they came to blows. Zarek put a hand out in either direction, wanting to keep the men apart. "I'm not afraid of Adama. You know that," he said tightly to Paine.

"Oh yeah? And how, 'zactly, am I supposed to know that?" Paine's tone remained defiant, and he kept tossing glances at Cortez as if to verify just where Cortez was in relation to himself.

"If I haven't been afraid of entire governments . . . if I haven't been afraid to be jailed for my beliefs . . . what makes you think I'm afraid now?"

Paine's jaw twitched back and forth a couple of times. He didn't drop his gaze, but he amended, "Maybe not afraid, then. Maybe just too damned comfortable."

Zarek rolled his eyes and started walking again, and Paine followed behind. "You," said Zarek, "have no idea what you're talking about."

"Oh, don't I? Pretty cushy status you've got for yourself now, huh, Zarek? Member of the Quorum. Gone all legitimate now. Angling for the presidency. Maybe you and Adama have something worked out. You stay out of his business, he stays out of yours. Maybe you figure it's not smart to make too much of a ruckus now because you're trying to climb up the ladder. Leave the guys on the lower rungs behind while trying not to piss off the ones standing at the top."

"Yeah, that's it, you've got me all figured out," said Zarek with obvious exasperation. "Look, Luther, I've listened to you, I'm considering what you're saying. My guess is, the Quorum of Twelve is going to have some of the same questions as you. I don't need to go running off on my own. I'll have eleven other representatives, and we'll get a lot more done and a lot more answers if we operate as one instead of all of us flying off in all different directions. There will probably be an inquiry, and we'll find out at that point what went wrong, and make sure it doesn't happen again. Will that do it for you?"

Luther Paine sounded as if he wanted to say something else, but instead simply replied, "Yeah. Yeah, that does it for me fine."

"Good. Now if you'll excuse me, I have a meeting scheduled with . . ."

His main office, used for conferences and meeting with various dignitaries, was just ahead. Cortez stepped forward, preparing to open the door for him, and that was when an explosion—sounding all the louder because it was within a confined space—went off just a few feet away from Zarek. He was nearly deafened from the noise. He was stunned to see Cortez drop, clutching at his right shoulder, blood welling up between his fingers. The others who had been walking along with him scattered as quickly as they could.

"On second thought, it's not fine," snapped Paine.

His eyes were wide and he had a crazed look on his face. Zarek didn't know what the hell had gotten into him. It wasn't as if Zarek didn't have the respect of every man on the *Astral Queen*. The only thing that occurred to him was that this was some sort of bizarre power play. That Paine was hoping to move up in power and prestige by taking down the guy who was one of the top players. If Zarek was dead, Paine could make up anything he wanted in terms of an excuse for doing it. Who knew if Paine perhaps represented some sort of growing belief that Zarek really was becoming too much of the "establishment"?

That, however, was a consideration for a future time, presuming there was one.

"Where did you get that gun?" Zarek demanded, deciding that the best thing to do was act as if he was totally in command of the situation.

Paine looked slightly taken aback that Zarek wasn't daunted by having a weapon pointed at his face. "Black market," he snapped. "Not that it's any of your business."

"If you're waving it in my direction, that makes it my business." He looked down at Cortez. "You all right?"

"I'll live," growled Cortez, looking daggers at Paine.

"You go right on telling yourself that," Paine snapped back.

That was when the door to Zarek's office opened and a man emerged from it. And emerged. And emerged.

That, at least, was what it seemed like to Zarek. The man was gargantuan, as large an individual as he had ever seen. His shoulders were half again as broad as Paine's, and his bare arms had muscles that looked as big as Zarek's skull. He had a head of red hair and a bristling red beard that was a slightly darker hue. His simple white shirt was having a difficult time, strained as it was covering his massive chest, although his dark green trousers hung loosely. He seemed to radiate confidence, as if he were certain there was no challenge he could not undertake. More: that if he undertook it, he would succeed in whatever the endeavor was.

"Is there a problem here?" he asked, his voice rumbling like thunder.

Zarek could not recall a time in his life when he had been at a loss for words, but there was a first time for everything, and this was it.

Even Luther Paine seemed daunted. Rallying quickly, he said fiercely, "This isn't your concern."

"Oh," was all the man said. "All right." For half a heartbeat, he turned as if he were about to walk away. Then his arm reached across the distance between him and Paine before Paine had even registered that the behemoth was moving toward him. His huge hand enfolded Paine's as if it was an adult's hand firmly grasping a child's, and then he squeezed. His expression never changed. There was an audible *crack* that was partly muffled by the giant's hand, and Paine let out an ear-splitting scream.

"Pardon me," said the giant, easing past Zarek. Very carefully, he pried Paine's now broken fingers from the gun, one digit at a time. Paine clutched his hand, his eyes wide, and whimpered in shock and pain. The giant held the gun carefully between his thumb and forefinger and passed it over to Zarek, who wordlessly received it. "I don't think," said the behemoth, "that he'll be firing this anytime soon."

Zarek tried not to look as stunned as he felt. Several of the followers who had fled were now slowly returning. Having heard the scream, their curiosity had overwhelmed their sense of self-preservation. Taking control of the situation, Zarek said, "Take them to the infirmary." He paused, and then added, "Get Cortez down there sooner. Feel free to take your own sweet time with Luther. Cortez . . . keep your hands off him, as tempting as it may be to do otherwise."

Luther Paine could only manage a whimper in response as he and Cortez were helped away toward the lower-deck infirmary. The way that Cortez kept firing furious looks at Paine, Zarek was only willing to give fifty-fifty odds that Cortez would heed his instructions. At that moment, he didn't care all that much; his attention was focused instead on the formidable individual who had staved off disaster.

"We had an appointment," said the giant, his soft voice a stark contrast to his appearance.

"Of course, yes. Come in . . . or rather, come back in." And he gestured toward his office. The giant stepped through the door, ducking slightly to avoid striking his head on the overhang. Zarek followed him in and blinked in surprise upon seeing an attractive young woman leaning against the desk. She smiled a dazzling smile that made Zarek feel twenty years younger. She was tall and slender, although her hips were nicely rounded. Her face was oval, her eyes twinkled with amusement, and her long flowing hair was the exact same shade as the giant's. This told Zarek two things: First, that she was very likely the giant's daughter, and second, that Zarek would be well advised to keep reminding himself that this girl's father could break him in half if he looked at her wrong. So he quickly gave a perfunctory nod and turned his attention back to the new arrival. "You're . . . Wolf Gunderson . . . ?"

"Gunnerson," he corrected, and extended his hand to shake Zarek's. Zarek looked at the formidable paw with not unreasonable concern. Noticing Zarek's hesitation, Gunnerson didn't seem offended. If anything, there was amusement on his face. Noticing this, Zarek overcame his trepidation and shook Gunnerson's hand. He could tell the giant was taking care not to squeeze too hard . . . or at all. "And this," he gestured toward the girl, "is my daughter, Freya."

"A pleasure, Mr. Zarek," she said, her voice musical. "I've read a great deal about you."

"Really."

"Yes. In history books."

Zarek forced a smile. She had spoken in a perfectly straightforward manner, and naturally had not intended to make Zarek feel as if he was some sort of modern-day relic. He took no offense at it, but suddenly he was feeling arthritic pain in every joint. Imagined, no doubt, but still, it reminded him that when he was her age, she was an egg residing in her mother's uterus, awaiting the call to action.

"I thank you for taking the time to see me," her father said.

"Well, obviously I'm the one who should be thanking you," said Zarek. He gestured toward a chair. "Please, won't you sit down . . ."

Gunnerson looked dubiously at the chair Zarek was offering and said, "I think I'll stand, if it's all the same to you. Freya?" And he gestured toward it. She nodded and took the seat, crossing her legs. Her long blue skirt was slit up the side, and some of the cloth fell away to reveal one of the most stunning female legs Zarek had gazed upon in a while. He assumed the companion leg was equally compelling. He cleared his throat loudly, walked aound the desk and took a seat. "Your timing certainly couldn't have been better."

"My followers and I have always been fortunate in that regard."

"Your followers," echoed Zarek. "Yes, when you asked for this meeting, you mentioned a group that you were representing . . . ?"

"That's correct. The Midguardians. Perhaps you've heard of us . . . ?"

Zarek shook his head, looking regretful. "I'm afraid not, no. But there's quite a few independent political action groups, and it's so hard to keep track . . ."

"Oh, we're not a political action group," said Freya. "We're a colony."

That brought Zarek up short. He shook his head in polite confusion.

"I . . . don't understand. There are twelve known colonies . . . and the lost thirteenth. You're saying you're the lost thirteenth . . . ?"

Gunnerson shook his head. "I am saying we are a separate colony entirely. We have embraced sections of the Sacred Scrolls that were rejected by the religious establishment. We believe these sections to be far closer to the truths of the universe than anything that the church of the Lords of Kobol would have us believe."

"You don't believe in the Lords of Kobol?" This was now sounding familiar to Zarek. He was starting to think that he had heard of these people: religious fanatics whose beliefs positioned them far outside mainstream society.

"No," Wolf Gunnerson said firmly. He cocked an eyebrow. "You're shocked."

"What? Oh, no. No." And Zarek forced a laugh. "No, it takes a good deal to shock me. Simply having a different belief system isn't going to do that. Hell, I'm more or less used to being out on my own when it comes to beliefs."

"Indeed you are," Freya spoke up approvingly. "You're not afraid to use violence for the purpose of social change. You're not a man who shrinks from doing what is necessary to accomplish his ends."

Obviously the history books were generous to him. "I do what needs to be done," he said, trying to sound modest and only partly succeeding.

"As do the Midguardians," said Wolf. "As do I." He leaned forward, resting his huge hands on Zarek's desk and looking for all the world as if he could easily smash the furniture apart. "That is why I have come to you in seeking out representation."

"How," asked Zarek, "do you mean? What sort of representation?"

"Our people resided on Sagittaron, the same as you," said Gunnerson. "Ours was an ancient order, but it was only in the last twenty years . . . during the time of your incarceration . . . that we began to make our presence known."

"Why only recently?"

"Isn't it obvious?" When Zarek shook his head, Gunnerson gestured toward him. "Your shining example, of course. Your refusal to accept the repression of Sagittarons. We had been guarding our beliefs, our history and heritage, afraid to come into the light. But you," and he pointed at Zarek, "made us realize that we were little more than cowards. That we had to take a stand if we were to call ourselves true sons and daughters of Woten."

"Of Woten?"

"The head of our Pantheon," Freya said helpfully, "just as Zeus is of yours. I'm named for his wife."

"I myself lean more toward the teachings of his son, Thorr. I am told"—Wolf smiled—"that I bear a resemblance to him."

"If you say so," said Zarek. "But I'm still not entirely certain what it is you expect from me . . . although naturally I'm flattered that you consider me such an inspiration. Although, then again, considering where my beliefs landed me, maybe I'm not the best person to follow."

"It's very simple, Mr. Zarek," Gunnerson said. "When millions of people resided on the world of Sagittaron, we were a hopeless minority. Barely five hundred of us. Asking for representation in the Council, asking for our beliefs in the book of Edda—"

"The . . . book of Edda?"

Gunnerson nodded. "The book that was stricken from the Sacred Scrolls. The one that has the entire history of our gods, from their birth to their deaths."

"Your gods are all dead?"

"Not yet. But we know how they will end."

"As part of a prophecy? But certainly your gods are powerful enough that they're not held sway to prophecy. Their fates aren't determined . . ."

"Of course they are. As are ours, and yours."

"You don't believe that man controls his own destiny?"

Gunnerson looked at him skeptically. "Mr. Zarek . . . we're on the run from killer robots who harry our every step, with no world to call our own, and not even fifty thousand of us left alive. Does it *sound* as if we're in control of our destiny at the moment?"

"A valid observation," admitted Zarek.

"The point is," Gunnerson continued, "it was difficult enough—hopeless, even—to have our beliefs, the rights of our individual ethnicity, to be taken seriously when there were millions of Sagittarons in existence. Now, however, there are . . . what? Barely over five thousand?"

"Five thousand, two hundred and fifty one, last I checked."

"And virtually all of our number remain intact," said Freya. "There were five hundred of us before, and the five hundred remain."

Zarek was dumbfounded at that. "All the practitioners of your . . . your faith . . . made it onto a ship?"

"Yes. Our fleet ship, the *Bifrost*, had been prepared for just this eventuality. Because the Edda warned us, and it warned of exactly what did occur. It's all part of our writings, just as accurate—if not more so—than any predictions Pythia may have presented. Imagine if the religious establishment, and the government, had been willing to give us our due. Far more might well have survived. My point is that five hundred is a much higher percentage of twenty five hundred than it is of millions. As such, our presence as part of the Sagittaron colony—to which our ship is registered—is much more significant than it was. Based on the percentage of our population, we deserve a seat on the Quorum of Twelve, and a say in what happens to us. We want our voice to be heard."

"And what is that voice intending to say, if I might ask?" inquired Zarek.

"That we alone know the truth of what is supposed to happen to humanity. We will be happy to share this knowledge with all others, so they will no longer be surprised by what happens to them. That way they will no longer be wandering in the dark, as we did for so long. We will share the benefit of the wisdom given us by our ancients, who were inspired—not by any mere mortal such as Pythia— but insights provided by the Lord Woten himself. After all, our people were saved. If our teachings are embraced, who knows? The remainder of humanity might be as well."

"And if the Quorum doesn't see fit to give you a place in it?"

"Well, then," Wolf Gunnerson said with a shrug, "it is best for all not to consider such things."

Tom Zarek definitely did not like the sound of that.

CHAPTER 5

Number Six had Baltar's back up against the wall. Literally.

The vice president of the Colonies and the foremost living expert on Cylons had come to the conclusion that he had the most complicated love life in . . . well, in the history of love lives.

Ever since the obliteration of much of humanity on Caprica . . . ever since he had come to *Galactica* as a refugee . . . he'd had Cylons on the brain. More accurately, one Cylon: a mental representation of the gorgeous blonde who had bewitched him and caused him to betray—however inadvertently—the whole of humanity. Day after day she stood before him, or draped herself around him, or yanked him around like a lap dog, looking every bit as real as she had back in Caprica. She had rejoiced in her control of him, and in the fact that she was so near and yet so far.

Then had come the day when her hold on him had slipped ever so slightly. It was the day that he had been brought over to the newly arrived *Pegasus* and discovered his dream girl in the flesh. Her name was Gina and she was a prisoner aboard that other Battlestar. Nearly comatose, desiring nothing but to die, Baltar had brought her back from that dark precipice while the blonde Cylon called Number Six glowered from the back of his mind. She had become her own worst enemy. Her power over Baltar was that she represented that which he could never truly have again, and thus he would follow her about like a lovesick puppy in perpetual frustration. A physical incarnation of her, if she and Baltar came together, would take that power away.

At least that was how Baltar had seen it. And he had made the mistake of saying it to Six's face.

He had been working in his lab when she had shown up with her typical litany of smirking, superior comments, like a prison warden who knew that her subject could never escape. But Baltar's thoughts were filled with Gina, who had escaped her imprisonment and had joined a group of rebels lobbying for making peace with the Cylons (not that any of the rebels knew her true nature). So when Number Six disturbed his concentration while he was running an experiment, he was disinclined to allow her mock advances to pass without rebuttal.

"Is it my imagination," Baltar had asked her, sitting on a lab stool and turning to face her, "or do you seem a tad more desperate than you used to? It seems to me that you're . . . oh, what's the best way to put it . . . that you're trying too hard. Yes, that's it. As if you're worried that your influence over me may be waning." Her face was frozen, which was even more encouraging to him, and he stepped toward her with a contemptuous grin on his face. "And who knows? Perhaps you're right. Perhaps, with the reality of Gina in the picture, the mere image of you can only stand by and smolder." He spoke the last words with an almost fiendish delight. He had adored this mental link to his past life with obsessive fervor, but he had also been aware that she had used him, abused him, both in his previous life and now. It was the purest example of a love/hate relationship there was, and at this moment the hate aspect was in ascendance.

Number Six stared at him for a long moment. Inwardly he felt his nerve shriveling before her, but he fought to keep a look of smug triumph. Suddenly she stepped forward, shoved him back against the wall and kissed him passionately. She seemed to be radiating heat. He tried to push her away, but she brought her knee up into his crotch—not quickly and painfully, but instead slow, kneading it gently. He gasped into her mouth, and her tongue darted quickly in and out. He felt his pulse racing. It felt as if there were too much blood in his body, and he had to think that if he dropped dead from a heart attack right then, they'd never be able to figure out what the hell had happened.

"You're thinking about her, aren't you," she said, taking a quick break from kissing him to whisper in his ear. Her soft breaths caressing his ears sent chills down his spine.

"No . . . no, I swear . . ."

"She can't give you what I can . . ."

Her knee started to move up and down, and Baltar automatically began responding, his body moving along with it. He was finding it hard to breathe, hard to think of anything beyond what she was doing to him. His mind was spinning away, completely out of control . . .

"Doctor Baltar?"

Baltar froze in place. Number Six was gone. Standing in the open doorway was a Colonial marine, Corporal Venner. He was staring at Baltar, not sure what he was seeing. "I, um . . . I was knocking, and you weren't answering . . . are you okay? You were moaning or something . . . I wasn't sure if you were having some kinda attack . . ."

"Fine. Fine, I'm . . . fine," Baltar said, and quickly started moving his back up and down again. "Just . . . coping with an extremely nagging itch. Ahhhhhh." He let out his breath slowly as if an irritation were being dealt with. "Yesssss, that's . . . that's doing the job." Once he felt he'd carried on the pathetic charade long enough, he stepped away from the wall and clapped his hands together briskly. "Right. Feeling much better. How"—he cleared his throat—"how can I be of service?"

"Well, Doctor . . ." Venner paused. "Or should I be calling you Mr. Vice President?"

"I answer to either. I suppose here, in my lab, 'Doctor' is perfectly serviceable. Certainly I'm more accustomed to it."

"All right, then, Doctor." And he pulled someone forward from behind him. It was a young boy, and Baltar recognized him instantly.

"Boxey . . . isn't it?" asked Baltar.

"Hey, Doc," Boxey replied.

The marine looked from the boy to the scientist. "You know each other?"

Something about the situation made Baltar think that minimizing his connection to the boy was preferable. "We were rescued from Caprica at the same time," Baltar answered him. "Shared a vessel. Is there a problem . . . ?"

"Yeah, there's a problem." He clamped a firm hand on Boxey's shoulder, as if the boy posed a flight risk. "We need you to jump him to the front of the line for that Cylon test of yours."

"*What?*" Baltar's eyebrows almost bumped up against the top of his head. "Breeding them a little young, wouldn't you say?"

"Could be."

"Corporal," said Baltar, "this is preposterous. That boy is no more a Cylon than I am."

He heard a sharp, female laugh. His head snapped around. There was no sign of Number Six, but he was certain he'd heard her voice.

"Doctor . . . ?" Venner sounded curious, even a bit suspicious.

"Just a little nervous tic," Baltar said quickly. "Happens sometimes when Cylons are being discussed. Oops . . . there it goes again." And he snapped his head once more in response to nothing at all. "So . . . may I ask just what in the world makes you think that a thirteen-year-old boy is a Cylon agent?"

"He snuck into the holding cell where the known Cylon agent is being held. He was caught conferring with her."

"The known Cylon agent? Sharon Valerii, you mean?"

"Yes, sir."

Baltar tilted his head questioningly. "Isn't she guarded?"

"He slipped past the guards while they were distracted during the recent Cylon raid."

Baltar made a *harrumph* sound deep in his throat. "A single boy eluded the notice of armed guards, and you think the boy should be tested? If you ask me, you might want to have the guards assessed if they allowed that to happen."

Venner's scowl darkened. "Doctor, if you're not willing to—"

"Yes, yes, of course I'm willing. I think it's a waste of everyone's time, but I'll attend to it. Wait outside, please."

"I'm not supposed to leave him unattended."

"He's not unattended, he's with me. There's only one door out of here and you'll be standing in front of it. Unless you think he can elude you as well."

"No sir, but—"

"You say 'but' to an instruction issued you by the vice president of the Colonies?"

There was a dare in Baltar's tone, and Venner wisely didn't challenge it. Automatically snapping to attention, Venner said briskly, "I'll be just on the other side of the door if you need anything, sir."

"That's very comforting."

Venner exited the room. Baltar turned to Boxey, pointed at a stool, and said, "Sit there." Boxey did as he was told and watched as Baltar prepared a syringe to draw blood. "So what were you doing speaking to the Cylon?" asked Baltar.

"She saved my life. Yours too," Boxey replied. "I just wanted to see her."

"Technically, she didn't save your life. Another Sharon Valerii did that."

"Yeah, I kind of have trouble understanding that part."

"It's very simple," said Baltar, gesturing for Boxey to roll up his sleeve. Boxey did so. "One model of Cylon dies, and her memories are transferred into the next one, like a computer downloading information one to the next." He tapped Boxey's exposed forearm, found a vein he liked, and proceeded to draw blood from it. Boxey made a slight sound of pain at first, but then he decided to remain stiff-lipped and did not cry out.

"But . . . when you're talking about computers, you know that one's different from the other," said Boxey. "Are the Sharons the same person?"

"For all intents and purposes, yes," said Baltar as he drew the blood.

"Is that the same as a regular yes?"

Baltar was beginning to lose his patience. "Yes," he said as he withdrew the syringe from Boxey's arm and set the vial of blood in a stand. "Why is this all so important to you?"

"Because I don't know why she saved us," said Boxey. "If she's evil, why did she do something that helped us? That helped anybody?"

"It wasn't time for her to act on her programming," said Baltar. "There was a certain point when it kicked in, and that was when she shot Admiral Adama."

"And that's what made her evil?"

"I'm not entirely certain that label applies, but for the sake of argument, yes."

"So what if she never had done that? Would she have been good?"

"I . . . suppose so, yes. She would have been 'good,' to use your phrasing, but with the potential for evildoing. Which, on further reflection," he admitted, "more or less describes just about anyone."

"But not 'just about anyone' is that way. Just her."

Letting his impatience rattle him, Baltar snapped, "Are you going somewhere with this? I mean, let's get to it, shall we? Is there some particularly cogent observation that you want to make about the entire subject? Some dazzling insight you wish to offer that you and only you have discerned?"

Boxey looked taken aback by the outburst. "I just . . ."

"You just *what*?"

"I just didn't think she looked evil, is all."

Baltar was about to fire off a reply, but instead he sat there a moment with his mouth open. Then he closed it and looked askance at the boy. "You didn't think she looked evil."

"Yeah." Boxey shrugged. "That's all."

"And what, pray, does evil look like?"

Boxey considered it a moment, and then said, "You."

"*Me?*"

"Yeah. I'm not saying you are," Boxey hurriedly added. "You're probably not . . ."

"Probably. Well, I like *that*!"

"It's just that . . . well . . . you're not a beautiful woman, first of all. It's hard to think a beautiful woman like Sharon is evil . . ."

"Trust me: Some of the most evil people I've known are beautiful women," said Baltar. In his mind's eye, he could envision Number Six taking a deep bow.

"And also, you're . . ."

"I'm what?"

"You're all twitchy."

That drew an even more confused reaction from Baltar. "*Twitchy?*"

"Jumpy. Your eyes keep moving from side to side. Even back when we left Caprica, I first noticed it. You act like . . . like you're afraid that someone's watching you, all the time. Like you're up to something and you're concerned that you're going to get caught at it. Someone who looks worried all the time that he's going to be caught at something . . . it makes it seem like you're evil, because only someone evil would have that much to be nervous about."

"Well, I appreciate that dazzling bit of character analysis," Baltar said sarcastically. "But I'll have you know I'm not evil."

"How do you know?"

"Because," said Baltar, "I've done nothing wrong." This time Number Six was doubled over in laughter. He forced himself to ignore it.

"Neither has Sharon. At least, the Sharon who's locked up. I just wanted to—"

"You know what?" Baltar snapped. "You'll understand when you're grown up." He knew it wasn't true, of course. The only thing growing up guaranteed was that parts of you were going to start hurting that had never hurt before. Other than that, nothing else was assured.

"Grown up." Boxey laughed bitterly.

"What's so funny?"

He fixed Baltar with a gaze and said, "Doctor . . . almost everybody is dead. Dead. And we're being chased by killer robots, and some of them can look so much like us that we can't tell them apart without blood tests." And he indicated the vial. "Grow up? You really, really think I'm going to get to grow up? Part of me thinks I won't even live to see my next birthday."

Baltar was about to make a sarcastic reply, but then he saw the quiet certainty in the boy's face. At first he didn't know what to say. Then he heard himself replying, "That's no way for someone your age to be thinking. You should be thinking about meeting girls and going to parties and your first kiss and the curve of a girl's neck and what your profession is going to be and all sorts of things, none of which have a damned thing to do with dying. Youth is always the hope for the future. Always. If young people believe that they have no future, then what's the point of any of this?"

Boxey considered that a moment and then said, "Survival?"

"There's more to life than survival. There has to be. There's the quality of the life you're surviving for."

"I . . . I guess . . ."

"Don't guess," Baltar told him firmly. "Guessing is an appalling habit. It shows laziness of mind. One either knows or doesn't know. If you know, speak of a certainty. If you don't know, be man enough to say you don't know, and then research the question until you do know. Anything else is unacceptable. Understand?"

"I gue—" He caught himself and then nodded. "Yes. I understand."

"Good. Now go out to the nice Colonial marine and tell him I'll have the results to him in a day or so."

"A day . . . ?"

"It's a very complicated test and takes a good long while to administer. Plus it's not as if guaranteeing the fleet's safety from you is the only thing I have on my docket. It will be finished when it's finished."

"Okay." Boxey started to head for the door, then paused and said, "Doctor . . . ?"

"Yes?" Baltar said, trying to keep the impatience from his voice and not entirely succeeding.

"Sorry about the whole thing about saying you're twitchy and jumpy. I know you're not evil."

"Thank you for the vote of confidence," Baltar said with a graciousness he didn't feel.

Boxey left the lab, and Baltar sat there and stared at the blood sample. When Number Six rested her hands on his shoulders and her chin atop his head, he didn't react. "Pity your test doesn't really work. That you've told everyone you can distinguish human from Cylon when you, in fact, cannot."

"Yes. A terrible pity."

"You know what you should do . . ."

There was a mischief in her voice that he really didn't like. Nevertheless he asked out of morbid curiosity, "What should I do?"

"You should tell them that his test came back positive. That he's a Cylon."

The very notion was appalling to him. "Why in the name of the gods would I want to do that?"

"Do you know what they'd do to him if you said that?"

"I honestly don't, no."

"Well then," she said challengingly, "isn't that all the reason you need to do it? You said it yourself: If you don't know something, you find out. It would be an interesting test of just how much veracity you have, and how willing they are to believe what you say. Oh, come on, Gaius," she prompted when he still seemed reluctant. "Don't you want to watch them eat their young?"

"Why did you laugh before?"

"Before?" She was walking around the lab, her long legs in a sure, measured stride. "When did I laugh before?"

"When I said that he was no more a Cylon than I was. What are you hiding?"

"Nothing, Gaius, I swear. I was just amused by the—"

"By the what? By the suggestion of my not being a Cylon? Is there . . ." He gulped. He was having trouble catching his breath, as if it had become far too hot in there. "Is there something I should know?"

"I just find it interesting that you've dismissed the idea out of hand," she said. "After all, back on Caprica you crouched behind me and thus survived a nuclear explosion. That doesn't strike you as odd? Your house blew apart around you. I was destroyed right in front of you. Yet you survived? Isn't it far more likely that we were both destroyed, and your memories were simply transferred to a new body?"

Baltar felt as if he'd been hit in the face by a crossbeam. The fact that her casual explanation of his survival . . . or perhaps nonsurvival . . . made perfect sense wasn't what horrified him. Or, more correctly, it wasn't what horrified him the most. What horrified him the most was that it hadn't occurred to him before. He was a man of science, and as such it was part of his very nature to question, to probe, to seek answers not only for questions that already existed, but questions that others hadn't thought to ask. For someone of that mindset never to consider something as possible as that . . . it was such a shocking omission that it almost made him wonder if . . .

What?

He'd been designed never to wonder about it? Preprogrammed?

Baltar shook his head, his mouth moving but no words emerging.

Number Six walked over to him and, extending a finger, ran it along the line of his jaw. "Poor Gaius," she sighed. "You know so much about so many things. The resident expert on Cylons. And yet you don't even know yourself."

"It . . . makes no sense," he said sharply, rallying against the unthinkable. "If I were a . . . what you say . . . you wouldn't have had to seduce me and trick me into betraying humanity. I would have just done it."

She kissed his cheek. "Tell them the test has come back positive. Tell them the boy is one of us. For that matter, how do you know he's not? Maybe I'm trying to help you out."

"Why . . ." He paused, trying to gather his scattered thoughts. "Why would you do that? What possible reason would you have for turning over one of your own?"

"Perhaps I'm feeling generous. Or perhaps—since our god made us in his own image—perhaps we, like He does, move in mysterious ways."

"You weren't made by any deities. You were made by humans. Humans are not gods by any stretch of the imagination."

"And perhaps, ultimately, that's the difference between us. You can never be any more than you already are. Our possibilities are unlimited."

"Is that why you try to destroy us?" he asked grimly. "Because in the event of your 'ascent' to divinity, you want to make certain that no one exists who remembers you when you were nothing but pretentious vacuum cleaners?"

She blew softly in his ear and, despite himself, he shuddered. "You keep right on doing that, Gaius. Keep right on asking questions. You do it so well. It's the main reason that I love you so much."

He closed his eyes, giving in to the pleasure of her touch. He moaned softly, and then he looked around. There was no sign of Number Six. She had vanished back into the recesses of his lust, or his guilt, or his programming, or wherever it was she came from.

Baltar turned and stared at the tube of blood that he had just drawn, and wondered what to do.

CHAPTER 6

Laura Roslin never would have imagined that she would be able to handle press conferences. One would have thought that, given her history as a teacher, she would have had no trepidation about getting up in front of crowds and fielding questions. To a degree, that was true . . . when it was a roomful of students who, more often than not, were perfectly happy to accept whatever she said as a given. That was a far cry from dealing with a roomful of hard-nosed reporters who challenged her on everything she said, and would come back with question upon question upon question. The way in which they regarded her shifted so frequently that she often found it difficult to get herself on any sort of firm footing with them . . . which, for all Laura knew, was exactly the way they preferred it.

When she had first been thrust into the position of president . . . an eventuality that someone as low in the pecking order as Secretary of Education could not have considered a possibility . . . the press had been all over her. She was an unproven commodity, thrust to the forefront of leadership in a time of war. How in the gods' names could someone who was often dismissed out of hand as "the school-teacher" (a nickname she suspected had originated with Adama, not her biggest fan at the time) be expected to enable the remnants of mankind to survive? Some of the reporters had adopted a wait-and-see attitude, and a few supported her out of a sense of obligation: If people didn't rally around their president, whoever that might be, then surely all was lost. But others had been merciless: She had been described as Laura the Lame, Laura the Borer, President Laura the Last. Contempt practically oozed from the screens and write-ups.

But then came the military coup that had thrown her out of office, and as one the press rallied behind her. It was self-serving, to be sure. The thinking was simple: If Commander Adama could sweep in and oust the representative of the people, certainly there was nothing to stop him from annihilating freedom of the press for all time. He had the military might: He could round up every single journalist, stick them on a freighter and shoot them off in the opposite direction from whichever way the fleet was going. It wasn't widely believed that he would, but it wasn't widely believed that he would not. Laura Roslin was transformed overnight into a martyr, a political prisoner in the hands of an out-of-control military.

Then came her escape, her quest to the Temple of Athena . . . a quest that had been predicted in ancient writings, which she fulfilled, giving them a guide toward Earth . . . and just like that, she was a religious symbol. A savior. Gods above, they were actually worshipping her. (And the wag who had dubbed her "Laura the Borer" had now renamed her, after her determined expedition to the Temple of Athena, "Laura the Explorer.")

And then she almost succumbed to breast cancer, a disease so pernicious and so far gone that it would have claimed anyone else. Except an amazing discovery had been handed her in the form of fetal blood from the unborn child of Sharon Valerii . . . or the creature passing for human that called itself Sharon Valerii . . . a discovery that had cured her. But the press and general public hadn't known about Sharon. So instead, the attitude was behold, she was risen: Laura Roslin, the walking miracle.

As she prepared for her morning press conference, finishing up in the bathroom and checking her makeup before going out to face the cameras and reporters, Laura wondered when in hell she was going to be regarded simply as Laura Roslin, the woman. That was all.

A woman, no more and no less than any other woman, trying to overcome odds that more generous gods would never have thought to heap upon her. No matter her outward appearance, no matter what the façade she displayed for the world and what the world chose to call her in turn, inwardly she was still simply Laura Roslin. Laura Roslin, with all the fears and uncertainties and frailties that the human condition was heir to. Yet she gamely soldiered forward, trying to be all things to all people, and often felt as if she were being torn in a dozen directions at once.

Her people needed her. They needed her to be whatever it was they were describing her as this week. There were times when she absolutely detested them for it, and wanted to go off into a corner, clap her hands over her ears, and make them all vanish. And when those times arose, she would just sit down somewhere, preferably in a darkened room, lower her head and take a series of long, cleansing breaths until it all went away.

She straightened her back, forced a smile onto her face, and walked into the press room.

They were waiting for her, just as she knew they would be. The moment she set foot in the room, she sensed that something was wrong, but she couldn't tell for certain what it was. She saw that Admiral William Adama was standing nearby the podium. He'd been speaking to the press, but the moment she entered the room, he immediately fell silent. He appeared to toss a conspiratorial glance toward the press, and even more strangely, they nodded almost as one. It was as if there had been some sort of mutual decision made between Adama and the reporters, and Laura didn't have any idea what that decision might be.

She chose not to press the matter. Instead she moved to the podium, nodded quickly to acknowledge the reporters, and said, "Very briefly: Admiral Adama has been investigating the circumstances under which the Cylons apparently knew exactly where we were going to Jump to, and were lying in wait to ambush us. Admiral Adama, would you care to . . . ?" She gestured to the podium and the assorted microphones that were poised on the edge of it, like metal flowers.

Adama smiled, stepped forward, and said into the microphone, "I've got nothing." He turned, bobbed his head to her as if this were a wholly satisfactory way of handling the matter, and stepped back.

Laura Roslin stared at him, and had to make a specific effort to close her mouth again rather than leaving it dangling open in astonishment.

"Yes, well," she said cheerily, "if there are any questions, now would be an excellent time to put them forward."

All hands shot up, and she picked one almost at random. The reporter stood up and said, "Who?"

"I'm sorry . . . I don't understand," said Laura. "Could you elaborate on that question slightly?"

The reporter nodded, and said, "What?"

"I said," Laura told him, feeling her patience beginning to unravel, "I would prefer it if you could elaborate . . . ?"

Another reporter jumped to his feet. "When?" he said.

Then there was another reporter, standing up and saying, "Where?" followed by another who asked with even greater intensity, "Why?"

"This . . . this is absurd, that you . . ."

"How?"

None of the regular reporters had spoken. It was a female voice that Laura felt as if she should recognize, but she didn't. Her gaze swept the throng in the room, but didn't pick anyone out.

Then someone stepped forward and Laura stifled a scream in her throat.

It was Sharon Valerii.

The crowd of reporters spread wordlessly to either side, allowing Sharon to approach Laura unimpeded. It seemed as if she were moving in slow motion, each step slow and deliberate, her body following suit. She was dressed in the garb of a colonial pilot, but her belly was swollen with her child.

Sharon held a gun lazily in one hand, and now she swept her arm up so that it was pointed directly at Laura Roslin. She spoke, and it was as if the words coming from her mouth were just slightly out of synch with the movement of her lips. Yet Laura heard her, and the words were familiar, even if she didn't understand them.

"Sagittarius is bleeding," said Sharon.

Laura tried to run, but a strong hand grabbed her by the arm, anchoring her to the spot. It was Adama. Laura swung a fist and hit him in the side of the head, but Adama didn't seem to notice. He winced slightly, but that was all, and didn't ease up on his grip. Instead, he said, in that measured, contemplative, normally very comforting tone, "It's better this way."

"You're insane!" she screamed, and she tried to pull loose from him. It didn't help. He was too strong, and now Adama was holding Roslin so that she was across his body like a human shield.

"Wrong. I'm the only sane one here," he told her between gritted teeth.

Sharon had her gun leveled at Laura. And now Laura was hearing something: a heartbeat. A human heartbeat, and it seemed to fill the air, fill everything. She had no clue where it was coming from, but the sound of it was rapidly becoming deafening.

"Sagittarius is bleeding," Sharon said again, and standing just behind her, looking not at all concerned, was Tom Zarek. Before Laura could ask her what the hell that was supposed to mean, Sharon's finger closed on the trigger, and Laura . . .

. . . jerked awake.

She was in her office, seated upright in her chair, having decided to try and catch a fast sleep before the press conference. She was tired . . . no. She was exhausted. She spent her days worried about the next Cylon attack and her nights having bizarre dreams like this that kept waking her up. "It's not fair," she moaned, rubbing her eyes with the balls of her hands. "When am I supposed to . . . ?" She left the question unfinished, stifling a yawn, and then Billy came knocking at her door. "Yes?"

"Madame President," he said in that formal tone he occasionally adopted, probably without even thinking about it. "It's time for the press conference."

She glanced right and left, not entirely sure how to respond. Was this another dream? The same dream? Was she wide awake? She gripped the skin of her right hand and squeezed as hard as she could. "Ow!" she cried out.

Billy was staring at her in bewilderment. "Why did you do that?"

"Just . . . checking something," she said. She stood and smoothed her skirt, trying to pull herself together.

"Are you all—?"

"I'm fine, Billy, I'm fine. Gods, you don't have to mother hen me, all right?"

"Yes, ma'am," he said quickly.

She hesitated and then, feeling a bit sheepish, said, "Sorry about the 'mother hen' comment."

"No . . . no, you're right. Sometimes I make too much of a fuss over you."

She smiled at that. Patting him on the shoulder, she said, "It's all right. I don't have a mom and I don't have kids. It's nice to know that someone is worried about me."

"Don't sell yourself short, Madame President. There's more people worried about you than you can possibly believe." He paused, frowned at that and then said, "That actually sounded much better in my head than it came out."

"I'd almost think it would have to," said Laura, but there was laughter on her lips. "All right, so . . . let's press on, shall we?" Receiving a sympathetic nod from Billy, she pushed open the door and entered the press room. Instantly everyone who was sitting came to their feet in order to show the proper respect.

"Thank you, please, take your seats," she said, gesturing for them to do so. She turned and it was all she could do to not let her surprise sound in her voice.

Admiral Adama was standing there, looking at her in a mildly quizzical manner, just as he had been in her dream. There was a brief surge of panic in her heart: What if she was losing the ability to discern if she was asleep or awake? What if the line between reality and fantasy was blurring to such a degree that . . . ?

"Madame President?" Adama's voice was soft, concerned, and she instantly remembered that he was there because she had asked him to be there, for gods' sake. After all, the mishap involving the Jump was on everyone's mind, and there was no one more authoritative to field questions about such a matter than Adama.

She drew herself up and her voice had its customary, no-nonsense tone. She had to pull herself together. She knew she felt vulnerable since the breast cancer had nearly taken her life and she had escaped through a miraculous medical intervention. After all, she had prepared herself for death, gone through all the common stages of being faced with her imminent demise and had finally accepted it. Naturally she was grateful that her dismal fate had been averted. It wasn't as if she'd wanted to die, just because she was prepared for it. But she was still feeling somewhat disoriented over the entire thing. The fact that she wasn't getting any sleep—or, more correctly—that her sleep was constantly being interrupted and disrupted by various dreams, was not making matters any easier for her to deal with.

But that was what she had to do. She had to deal with it.

"Thank you for coming, Admiral," she said briskly. He nodded in response, his suspicions mollified by her apparently clear-headed attitude. "I assume that everyone's mind is on the same thing. If you'd care to address it?" and she gestured toward the podium. Adama nodded and moved toward it as she stepped back to make room for him.

"The recent mishap," said Adama with the easy confidence of one who was intimidated by nothing, "involving our escape from the Cylons resulted from a computer malfunction compelling us to engage in a blind Jump. We are currently in the process of investigating precisely what caused the mishap so that we can ensure there is no repeat."

Immediately hands shot up. "Madame President," called out one reporter, "doesn't it lessen your confidence in the *Galactica*, knowing that such accidents can occur?"

"Accidents can always occur," replied Roslin easily. "That's why they're called accidents. Obviously such FTL maneuvers are inherently hazardous, but I think we can all agree that being at the mercy of Cylon raiders is far more hazardous. I believe it is a testament to the professionalism of the officers and staff of *Galactica* that they were able to pull off such a difficult endeavor and enable us to live to tell the tale. That is the aspect of this incident upon which I personally would prefer to focus."

"There are rumors that the Cylons knew where we were going to be Jumping to, and that was the reason for the blind Jump," said another reporter. "Have the Cylons managed to penetrate the *Galactica*'s computer system again?"

Laura saw Adama's jaw twitch slightly. It was a small unconscious tell she'd picked up on that he gave whenever a reporter asked a question that hit too close to home. She was exceptional at reading body language, a talent courtesy of her "wastrel" youth when she'd spent way too many late nights playing cards. Adama had already confided in her what had really happened, and they'd both agreed there was no point in letting the general public know what had transpired.

Yet obviously there was a leak somewhere. It was understandable: Humans remained humans, and they loved to talk even when they shouldn't. Stray words had a habit of being overheard by nearby ears that weren't supposed to be there, and somehow such comments always managed to find their way to reporters. Adama, naturally, wanted to keep everything under wraps. That was the military way: total control. It was always entertaining to see Adama come face to face with situations that he couldn't dominate with a few orders or tossing someone in the brig, and the free flow of information was definitely one of those situations.

"My understanding," Adama said tightly, "was that, as reporters, you were interested in reporting facts, not rumors. The military holds itself to a high standard of conduct . . . one that you might want to consider emulating."

Great. Lecture the press. That always works well, thought Laura. "The Admiral has assured me that there is no evidence—none—that there is any Cylon influence on, or infestation of, the *Galactica's* computer system. Correct, Admiral?"

"Yes," he said tersely.

"Moving on, then," she said . . . and then the next words she was to speak froze in her throat.

Tom Zarek was standing toward the back of the room, watching her with a level, unreadable gaze. That alone was startling enough. What in gods' names was Zarek doing there?

But that paled in comparison to the fact that Sharon Valerii was standing next to him.

Laura stood there, paralyzed. She . . . *it* . . . was right there! What the hell had Zarek done, what sort of scam had he pulled, that he'd gotten her sprung from confinement! She was the most dangerous creature on two legs in the Colonial fleet. She was staring at Laura Roslin with as much pure hatred as Laura had ever seen in another creature.

I'm dreaming, this has to be a dream, but I'm awake, I know I'm awake, I think I'm awake, gods, what if I don't know anymore . . .

Laura pointed a finger at the Cylon, which she noted—as if she were looking at someone else's arm—was trembling violently. "What are you doing here? Who let you in?"

Zarek looked behind himself, deftly feigning confusion. The reporters seemed equally bewildered.

"They stuck a needle in my baby for you," snarled Valerii. "They exploited her blood in order to save you, who wanted to kill her. You didn't deserve to be saved. You don't deserve to live."

She started toward Laura, moving as if she were in slow motion, and she was pulling her weapon from its holster.

Laura started to back up, and a firm hand lit on her shoulder. "Madame President . . . ?" said Adama, concern etched on his face.

She looked from Adama back to Sharon, who was advancing with her weapon out and aimed straight at her.

She's not here. That's all there is to it, she's not here. Adama wouldn't just stand here and not react to it . . . unless, what if he's a Cylon, too, and Zarek, what if they're all Cylons? What if there's only Cylons left, no humans at all, I'm the last one, and they're about to finish their genocide with my death . . .

Laura Roslin stared down the barrel of the gun that was aimed at her, and in a heartbeat two options ripped through her mind. The first was that she would scream in panic, drop behind the podium, try to get away, in an effort to save her life. If Sharon Valerii was really there—if they were all really Cylons—then it wouldn't matter. She was going to die no matter what. But if Valerii wasn't there, if this was all an illusion, then the people of the Colonies would see broadcasts of their president scrambling away from nothing like a woman possessed. What sort of inspiration would that provide? How could they possibly draw any hope for their future from that?

The second option was that she stand there, staring at her death about to be spat at her from the barrel of a gun. Either she would die bravely, or not at all.

In that instant, she realized that, all things considered, there was only one option after all.

She stared into the eyes of Sharon Valerii with complete defiance and said nothing.

Valerii fired off three rounds at point-blank range. Laura flinched involuntarily, closed her eyes while anticipating the impact. None came. She opened her eyes and, although Zarek was still there, there was no sign of Sharon Valerii.

Everyone was still staring at her. There was dead silence in the room. Adama was looking at her with concern, while Zarek regarded her as if she'd grown a second head.

Laura cleared her throat and, her nerves shot, her mind fraught with uncertainty, didn't let any of that come through in her voice. "Councilman Zarek . . . there are . . . procedures to be followed. You should have made an appointment with my aide rather than just . . . show up out of nowhere."

Zarek was caught off guard, unable to understand the seeming see-saw nature of her reaction. One moment she'd seemed alarmed; the next she was . . . what? Carping over procedure not being followed? He realized everyone was now looking at him rather than her. "I was . . . hoping that you could clear some time in your schedule," he said, the picture of courtesy. "And furthermore, Madame President, I have to think that you wouldn't have such a violent reaction to any other Quorum member who sought some of your valuable time. I'm honored that you'd single me out for such treatment."

Laura was still feeling more rattled than she cared to let on, and was concerned that, the longer this went on, the more difficulty she'd have covering that fact. "Speak with my aide. He will attend to your request. Ladies and gentlemen, I'm afraid I have to cut this conference short. There are other matters that require my attention."

She turned quickly and exited the room, leaving behind her a chorus of "But Madame President!" "President Roslin!"

Beating a retreat to her private study, Laura leaned forward on her desk, resting on her hands with palms flat. There was a fast knock at the door and Adama entered without preamble. "It's customary," Laura said wryly, "to wait until the person inside the room actually says 'come in' before entering."

Adama stared at her as if she hadn't spoken. "Do you want to tell me what's going on?"

"No, Admiral, I don't. And as it so happens, since I'm president, I don't have to."

"But you admit there is something going on."

"I admit nothing."

He took a step toward her and there was none of the military officiousness in him that she had used to think constituted his entire persona. "Laura . . . I'm not an admiral asking a president now. I'm asking as a friend. Someone who's concerned about you. Something is wrong. Is it something relating to your cancer? Or its treatment?"

I don't know, I don't know what's going on, I can't trust my own senses anymore . . .

She wanted to say all that and more, but she did not. "As much as you might want to pretend otherwise, Bill . . . you are an admiral. And I am the president. And those simple truths can't be set aside merely because we declare them to be so."

"Have you been to Doctor Cottle . . . ?"

"That would be my business, Admiral. Yours is *Galactica*. I believe you're running an investigation, are you not?"

"Yes," he said.

"Then you'd best get back to it. We both have expectations being made of us. Oh," she added as an afterthought, "were I you . . . I'd pay particular attention to Vice President Baltar."

Adama didn't look at all surprised, merely interested. "Do you have reason to believe he was involved somehow?"

She wasn't certain what to tell him. Yes, she had reason to believe it . . . but it wasn't something she could convincingly convey, not to Adama, and not even entirely to herself.

My life was flashing before my eyes, just as they always say it does, on the cusp of death . . . and I was there on Caprica, and I saw Baltar . . . I saw him . . . and he was with this woman. They were nuzzling each other, and I haven't thought about it since that day because gods know I had other things to worry about. I saw it, I thought, "She's gorgeous, the lucky bastard," and then it dropped out of my mind like a stone. That'll happen when the Cylons try to annihilate your entire race and you wind up on the run. But I've seen that woman since. She's a Cylon operative. I saw Baltar locked in a passionate embrace with a Cylon operative. Except I don't know that that's what I saw. The mind is a tricky thing, and memory even more elusive. It's possible that in what I thought were the last hours of my life, everything became muddled together. That the beautiful woman whom I saw with Baltar was someone else entirely, and that I had just "inserted" the face of the known Cylon operative onto the woman.

But why would I do that?

Impossible to know. Who can possibly understand the depths of the human mind? I never quite trusted Doctor Baltar, for reasons I couldn't quite put my finger on. So wouldn't it make perfect sense for me to associate him with another figure of distrust, a Cylon? Wouldn't that be the simplest answer?

And yet . . .

"I . . . have no concrete reason, Admiral. Just a hunch. Just . . . instincts."

Adama considered that, then nodded. "In our time together, Madame President . . . I've learned to trust your instincts. On occasion they're more reliable than my own." He paused, then added with just a trace of dry humor, "On rare occasion."

"All right then."

He nodded. Then he spoke once more, and she couldn't be sure, but it almost sounded as if there was a hint of hurt feelings in his tone. Only a hint, since Adama was far too stoic to allow whatever he was feeling to rise to the surface. The only time she could recall seeing pure, unadulterated emotions bubble over from Adama was when he finally caught up with Roslin and company on Kobol and had unabashedly hugged his wayward offspring in as pure a display of affection as she had ever seen a father provide a son.

"I had thought," he said gravely, "that we had been through enough . . . that you could find it within yourself to be honest with me."

She kept her face a neutral mask, wanting to tell him what was going on, but reluctant to because . . . she had no idea why.

Yes. Yes, she did.

Because she didn't want to seem weak. Bad enough that she had been prey to the frailties of her body. Now, if her mind was going . . . that was even worse.

Until she had a clearer idea of what was going on, she simply couldn't bring herself to tell Adama what was happening. How could she? She didn't fully understand it herself.

"Thank you for your time, Admiral," was all she said.

Adama studied her for a moment with a gaze that she felt could bore into the back of her head. Then he simply replied, "Thank you, Madame President," gave the slightest of formal bows, and walked out of the room.

Laura Roslin, with a heavy sigh, slid back in her chair, rolled her eyes toward the ceiling, and prayed to whatever gods would listen to her that she was not, in fact, going completely out of her mind. It was at that point that she realized that, even if she was, she might well not be fully aware of it, and that was hardly a comforting insight.

CHAPTER 7

Whenever William Adama stopped by his lab, Gaius Baltar always felt a deep chill at the base of his spine. He became particularly concerned over the uncontrolled appearances of Number Six during such times. He might be able to cover up his occasional slips or comments to her when he was in the presence of others. But Adama had that penetrating way about him that peeled away Baltar's défenses like the layers of an onion. He had to keep reminding himself that he was a genius. One of the most brilliant minds in all of humanity, pre- or post-destruction. Adama was a glorified grunt, nothing more. In the end, despite the fact that sometimes Baltar felt as if his upper lip was sweating profusely in Adama's presence, there was ultimately no way that Adama could really see through him.

"So are you seeing a Cylon, Doctor?" asked Adama calmly.

Baltar almost knocked over an array of test tubes nearby him as he twisted around violently to face Adama. The ship's commander had arrived a minute or so ago and made polite conversation with Baltar over meaningless political issues. The sudden change in topic—and the question he'd posed—had caught Baltar off guard. In spite of himself, he had reflexively looked around to see if Number Six was standing there. He had no idea what he would do if suddenly, magically, Adama could see her as well. Or, worse, knew not only of Baltar's con-

nection to her, but all that he had done—unwillingly and willingly—
for the Cylon cause.

Baltar forced himself to maintain his composure, which was not
an easy task considering the baleful look that Adama was giving
him. "I . . . don't quite understand your meaning, Admiral."

Adama slowly walked the perimeter of the lab, but he never took
his gaze from Baltar. "My people inform me that you're running
tests on a young man—Andrew Boxman, also known as Boxey—to
determine whether or not he's a Cylon."

"He knows, Gaius."

Her timing, as always, could not have been worse. Number Six
was following in Adama's footsteps. Baltar couldn't be sure, but she
actually appeared concerned. That alone was enough to alarm him,
because most of the time Number Six delighted in whatever problems were being thrown Baltar's way. She was conscience and tor-
mentor rolled into one, enjoying watching him writhe in the throes
of his guilty conscience and his perpetual fear of being found out.
Now, though, in Adama's presence, she didn't seem to be taking any
joy in it at all. Which meant . . . what? That Adama was close to finding something out?

"You need to throw him off the track," she insisted. "Tell him that
the boy tested positive. Tell him he's a Cylon. You don't want him
sniffing too close to you, do you."

"That's true enough," Baltar said, addressing both Number Six
and Adama with the same comment.

"Are the test results finalized?"

"Yes, as a matter of fact, they are."

"Good. You see, Doctor," and Adama ceased his pacing, "we have
to remain ever vigilant to any threats in our midst. *Any* threats. And
any such threats must be thoroughly investigated, if you understand
what I'm saying."

"Perfectly," Baltar replied, but inwardly he was trying not to
panic.

Number Six's observations weren't helping in the least. "What
do you want him to do, Gaius? Sing it for you? He suspects you.
He doesn't know what he suspects you of, but it's something. The
best thing you can do right now is throw suspicion elsewhere, and
the boy is the most useful target. You'd be an absolute fool not to
take advantage of the opportunity that's been handed you on a silver platter."

"He's . . . just a boy," Baltar managed to say between gritted teeth.

"Yes. He is," Adama agreed. "A boy who, by all accounts, is quite popular with my pilots. They've taken him under their wing, so to speak. He comes and goes freely here. So if he's a Cylon agent, then that means he's playing my people for fools, and that is not something I take lightly." He paused and then added, "Nor do I appreciate being played for a fool. So . . . let's have it, Doctor. Is he? Or isn't he?"

Baltar felt paralyzed by uncertainty. With every fiber of his being, he wanted to lie to Adama's face. Do as Number Six suggested. Throw Adama off the scent. Except the man looked as if he could sniff out deceit with one nostril tied behind his back. If Baltar were simply trying to cover his own ass, that would be one thing. He'd lie as quickly and smoothly as he could and risk everything in order to assure his own survival. But this . . . the deliberate incrimination of an innocent boy, just for the purpose of providing some distractions for Adama and his crew of busybodies . . . despite Number Six's urgings, it was too much. Besides, there was always the concern that Adama would see right through the lie, and that would leave Baltar in an even deeper world of trouble . . .

"Don't you pass it up, Gaius," Number Six urged him. She was hanging on his shoulder. "Don't pass up the opportunity. They're always looking for scapegoats, and this is the perfect—"

"You misunderstood me, Admiral," Baltar almost shouted. He realized belatedly that he was, in fact, raising his voice, to speak above the urgings of Number Six whom Adama couldn't hear. Seeing Adama's expression in reaction to his volume, he instantly ratcheted it back down as he continued, "When I said he's just a boy, I meant . . . he's just a boy. He is not, as near as I can determine, anything more sinister than that. Although I admit that young boys can be, indeed . . . rather sinister creatures." He forced a laugh that felt as weak as it sounded.

"You're being an idiot!" Number Six practically shouted at him.

"I know," Baltar told her, then turned quickly to face Adama and continued, "I know you were hoping to find another of the Cylon models so you could put another face to the enemy. I feel as if, by getting a negative result, I've made your job harder."

Adama barely shrugged. "Then it's harder. The difficulty of a job doesn't mean it's not worth doing."

"I feel exactly the same way."

"Do you." He arched a single eyebrow. "Would you like to know how you've always struck me, Doctor?"

"I'd be fascinated to know that, Admiral," said Baltar with a thin smile that reflected no trace of amusement.

"As someone who always seems daunted by any job that he's faced with, and would rather simply fly below the radar at any given moment, rather than stepping up to what's expected of him."

"Really." Baltar's smile remained fixed, although his tone was cold. "An interesting assessment of a man who saved the life of the president when no one else could."

"Yes. Yes, you did, for which you have the thanks of a grateful citizenry . . . not the least among which is myself. And yet . . ." he added, almost as an afterthought.

"And yet?" prompted Baltar.

"What remarkable timing that was. In one stroke, you not only avoided having to take over as president . . . but you saved the life of a Cylon half-breed."

Baltar's instinct was to run in the other direction. To sprint out the door and put as much distance between himself and Adama as possible. Instead he walked straight toward Adama until he was standing less than a foot away, practically nose-to-nose with the admiral. "And if the president had passed away . . . and dear Doctor Cottle subsequently discovered somehow that the fetus's blood had the restorative power to save her . . . you'd be standing right here accusing me of holding back knowledge that could have preserved the life of Laura Roslin. You'd be questioning my allegiances, my knowledge as a Cylon expert, and quite possibly whether my parents were married at the time of my birth. Isn't that true?"

Adama studied him and then said, "Possibly."

"Possibly," echoed Baltar. "So what with this being a case of damned if I do, damned if I don't . . . then I might as well 'do,' save Roslin's life, and endure your scrutiny, your suspicions and your veiled insults. But don't worry about it, Admiral. I've been insulted by the best." His gazed flickered toward Number Six, who was standing off to the side. She was no longer fuming. Although her disappointment was palpable, she seemed mildly amused by Baltar's standing up to Adama.

But Adama didn't seem the least bit daunted in his apparent conviction that there was something Baltar wasn't telling him. Baltar couldn't help but wonder what the hell Roslin had said to him . . . and it had to have come from Roslin. He was certain of that, although he wasn't quite sure why.

"Thank you," Adama said levelly, "for your efforts in clearing the boy . . . and for saving Laura Roslin. In appreciation of that, I will give you advance warning: I'm watching you."

"I don't blame you," Baltar replied. "I hear there's so little on broadcast these days that's remotely interesting. Find your entertainment where you can, Admiral, by all means."

Adama said nothing at that, but instead turned and walked out of the lab. The moment he was gone, Baltar let out a long sigh and shriveled like a balloon.

"I'm impressed, Gaius," said Number Six. "I've never seen such a simultaneous display of sheer nerve and sheer stupidity."

"Glad I could accommodate you."

"Don't be."

He closed his eyes, rubbed the bridge of his nose, and opened his eyes again. Number Six was gone. Baltar couldn't recall the last time he'd been quite that glad not to see her someplace.

Boxey had had no idea what to think when Corporal Venner had shown up at the secure area where he was being held. He was slightly more buoyed, however, when he saw that Kara Thrace was with him. Boxey was relieved to see the friendly face, although he wasn't certain exactly what to expect from it.

She winked at him. "You're sprung, kid."

He let out a huge sigh and sagged back in the chair he'd been seated on. "That's a relief," he admitted.

Venner, eyes narrowed in suspicion, was quick to pounce. "Why? Were you worried that the results were going to prove you're a Cylon?"

"Well . . . sure," said Boxey.

This prompted a startled reaction from both Venner and Kara. "You were?" she asked.

"Isn't that the whole thing with Cylons who look like people? That sometimes they don't know? Sharon didn't know, right? I mean, that's what you guys told me."

Kara looked at Venner and shrugged. "He's right. We were all talking about that. How Sharon—the one who shot the admiral—that she said she didn't know. That she didn't know it before and she didn't know she was going to shoot the Old Man, and even after, she didn't remember it."

"Oh, of course," Venner said sarcastically. "And naturally you're gonna believe everything that a Cylon says."

"Because humans are *so* much more trustworthy," shot back Kara. "Gods, when I think of the number of guys who told me they loved me just to get a piece of . . ." She stopped and glanced back at Boxey, and then cleared her throat and forced a smile. "You, uh . . . you didn't hear that."

"Hear what?" asked Boxey, who really hadn't heard it because Kara had been saying it so fast.

"Good lad," Kara replied in approval, leaving Boxey no more clear on what was being discussed than before, but at least Starbuck was happy with him.

Boxey's spirits were rising for the first time in what seemed like ages. "So what're we up to, huh? Another poker game? Just hanging out in the—?"

"Boxey," Kara interrupted him, and she looked a bit pained when she spoke. "You're, uh . . . well, you're going back to the *Peacemaker*, actually."

"But I thought that—"

"No buts, kid," Venner said.

Kara rounded on him with obvious annoyance. "Do you think that maybe, just maybe, you could give us some frakking space, huh? In fact, I have a better idea. I'll take it from here. You can go on about your duties."

"I have my orders . . ."

"Awww," said Kara, "and what a pity I don't outrank you . . . oh! Wait! I do! Now scram!"

Venner drew himself up and said darkly, "I'll be forced to report this to Colonel Tigh."

"Yeah, you do that, because the threat of being reported to Colonel Tigh is really gonna leave me trembling."

Scowling once more, Venner walked away, although he kept glancing over his shoulder as if he thought that Boxey was going to produce a gun from within his mouth and open fire.

Kara strolled over to a bench, sat, and patted the empty space next to her. Boxey sat where she indicated. "Look," she said, "you just need to keep your distance for a little while until things cool down."

"I didn't do anything wrong!"

"You snuck into the brig and spoke at length with an enemy of the Colonies," she reminded him. "If we were going by the book, then you'd be guilty of consorting with the enemy and that carries with it a year's sentence. You'd have plenty of time to chat with Sharon Valerii if you were in a cell next to her, wouldn't'cha."

He suddenly became very interested in the tops of his shoes. "I guess," he muttered.

"You guess." She chuckled despite the seriousness of the situation. "Bottom line, Boxey, you have no idea how damned lucky you are. You really could wind up doing serious jail time. You are clueless as to how seriously things get taken around here. This is a military vessel, for gods' sake. It's not a playground."

"I wasn't playing . . ."

"You sure as hell were," Kara told him firmly in a no-nonsense voice. "You sure treated it like a game. Showing off just so everybody could know how clever you were."

"What, and you never do that?"

"All the time."

"Then what's the difference?"

"The difference is, I blow Cylons out of space better than any other motherfrakker in the fleet, that's what," Kara said, making no attempt to hide her sense of smug accomplishment. "And that includes the CAG. So when trouble hits, they don't want my ass in a cell; they want it in a Viper where it belongs. And even with that going for me," she added, shaking her head, "I have no doubt that if Tigh could find a way to put me away for good, he wouldn't hesitate. And he's the one pushing to get you off *Galactica*. Venner and the other marines did a full write-up on you, and Tigh's whole thing is security. He sees you as a risk that has no business being on a military vessel, no matter how much we may like you."

"So . . ." Boxey felt a girlish urge to cry, and managed through sheer force of will to keep the tears from welling in his eyes. "So I can't come here and hang out with you guys anymore?"

" 'Anymore' is a long time. Just until things cool down, at least. Give it some time, and then I'll work the circuit: I'll talk to the CAG, and he'll talk to the Old Man, and the Old Man will lean on Tigh, and we'll have you back here. But there's one thing you've got to understand," and her voice dropped to a severe tone that fully commanded his attention. "You've got to keep your lip zipped about the Cylon we have locked up here. Do you get that? You can't just go running around, telling the other kids about what goes on here."

"I haven't," Boxey protested. "You told me not to, weeks ago. I knew it was important then . . .".

"Yeah, but now it's even more important. The admiral, Tigh . . .

they're worried that if word gets out to the fleet, all hell is going to break loose. That people won't understand that she's . . . that it's . . ." She corrected herself, scowling. "A military asset. There's a lot of jumpy people out there who never, ever expected to find themselves in the middle of a space-going war zone, and they don't know how to take it. They'd kill the Cylon as soon as look at it, and gods only know what they would do in order to make that happen. We'd rather not find out. You get what I'm saying, Boxey? This isn't just me talking. This is coming straight from the admiral, and if I'm not convinced that you understand it, then things could get nasty. So I've got to know that you do understand."

"I understand."

"Say it again." And her gaze was like a laser penetrating his mind.

"I. Understand," he said with as much conviction as he could muster.

She studied him for a time, and he felt as if the admiral were looking at him through her eyes. Then she finally relaxed slightly and said, "Good. Plus, hey . . . remember . . . once we find Earth, we'll all be together on the same planet anyway." She ruffled his hair. "That'll be our happily ever after. Won't that be great?"

"Yeah. Great," Boxey said hollowly.

Kara tried to jolly Boxey out of his doldrums over being exiled from the *Galactica*, but ultimately there wasn't much that she could do. The boy dragged his heels all the way over to the transport dock, where one of the frequent shuttle vessels that moved constantly from one ship to the next picked him up for passage back to the *Peacemaker*. He never once looked away as he watched the *Galactica* dwindle in the aft viewing window. The battle vessel remained huge; it wasn't as if Boxey was going all *that* far. Nevertheless, it was far enough to make him feel very distanced and very much alone.

When he disembarked at the *Peacemaker*, he was surprised to find that a familiar face was waiting for him. Yet somehow he wasn't actually all that surprised. Upon reflection, it seemed quite inevitable.

"How did you know?" he asked.

"I didn't," replied Freya Gunnerson. "I've just been checking in on any ship making a run from *Galactica*. I figured that, sooner or later, you'd be on it. You were making me nervous, though. Where've you been?" Teasingly she added, "Minerva Greenwald's been asking about you, you little heartbreaker."

He started walking and she fell into step alongside him. "I don't wanna talk about it."

She laughed at that. "You know what I've learned? That people who say they don't want to talk about something usually do. Come on, Boxey." And she nudged him in the shoulder. "You're my unofficial kid brother. You know I've liked you ever since we met, when I was put in charge of finding shelter for orphaned refugees. Haven't I said so?"

"Yeah, well . . . adults are really good at saying things and not so good at seeing 'em through."

"What's that supposed to mean?"

Boxey didn't want to tell her. Everything that Starbuck had said weighed heavily upon him.

Then again, he'd insisted that he hadn't told any other kids, and he hadn't. But Freya was different. She was the best adult friend he had outside of people on *Galactica*. And even more than the others, she'd always had a ready ear for him and whatever problems he had at any given time. Still . . .

"I can't," he said. "It's . . . it's secret . . ."

"So what?" said Freya. "Boxey, I'm a lawyer. That's all we do, is keep secrets."

He looked at her with interest. "Really?"

"Really. It's part of our job. It's drilled into us. In fact, any lawyer who blabs a secret winds up losing her job because of it. That's how seriously we take it. So anything you tell me goes no further. Guaranteed."

That seemed more than reasonable to Boxey, who was chafing under the yoke of torn loyalties. This was a way to balance both. It all came spilling out of him. Freya listened, her eyes widening as he finished bringing her up to date on everything that had happened to him.

"That's just wrong," she finally said. They had stopped walking, having arrived in a central mall area where residents of the *Peacemaker* were interacting in a casual social setting. There were a few small trees that someone had uprooted while they were fleeing their home world; it's amazing what some people will risk their lives for. The trees had now become the centerpiece of the mall, with special lights arranged to simulate the long-lost sunlight that the trees might never experience again. They sat under the trees and Freya continued, "They shouldn't have held you like that. You should have contacted me."

"I didn't think about it. I was kind of embarrassed about the whole thing. I thought you might be mad at me."

"Why in the world would I be mad at you?"

"Kara was," Boxey saïd. "And I bet the others were, too. I mean, she didn't shout at me or anything. But she said I shouldn't really have been on *Galactica* in the first place, and that I couldn't go back there for a long time." Boxey knew he wasn't being entirely fair in his description of the way Starbuck had interacted with him. But he was frustrated and vulnerable, and at that moment felt as if he'd lost an entire coterie of friends that had been his only constant since the Cylon attack. He was loath to risk losing any more, and if it meant slightly exaggerating the way of things to Freya, well, he was willing to do that. "Plus, I was kind of scared. I mean . . . what if I *was* a Cylon?"

"Even if you were, that doesn't mean you automatically have no rights."

He looked at her in confusion. "I thought it kind of does."

"Not necessarily."

Boxey snorted in disbelief. "Well, Sharon Valerii sure has no rights. They keep her locked up in that cell."

"For how long?"

He shrugged. "Forever, I guess. She's pregnant and everything, and they keep her caged in there like an animal."

Freya leaned back, stroking her chin thoughtfully. It was a mannerism she'd unconsciously picked up from her father; the absence of beard didn't deter her. "Pregnant and everything. Caged up." She shook her head. "Yes, they certainly are treating her as if she has no rights. But treating someone that way doesn't automatically make it so. I think we may have to do something about that."

"We?"

She had been looking inward, but now she turned her attention to Boxey. "Boxey . . . do you like it here? I mean, really like it here on the *Peacemaker*?"

"It's . . ." He was noncommittal. "It's okay, I guess. I like hanging out with Minerva . . ."

"Okay you guess. See, I happen to think that people are entitled to a lifestyle that's slightly better than 'Okay you guess.' How would you like to come and live on the *Bifrost*?"

"What's there?" Although Boxey was very fond of Freya, he didn't know all that much about her background or anything about where she resided when she wasn't working with the homeless.

"My people. The Midguardians."

"You have your own ship?"

She nodded. "We do. Because we knew that the human race was going to be assaulted. We knew that end times would come, and these are them. And we prepared for it. If you'd like, you can live with us, and you can study our ancient writings, and you'll know things that are happening, too. You'll be prepared, as we were."

"If my father had been one of you . . . would he have known about what the Cylons were going to do? Would he . . ." He hesitated, the wound still fresh in his heart even after all these weeks. "Would he still be alive?"

Freya looked at him tenderly. "I won't lie to you, Boxey. I don't know for sure. It's not as if we have a day-by-day calendar. But I'll tell you this: He certainly would have had a better chance if he had attended to the prophecies of the Edda than depending on the Lords of Kobol to protect him. They didn't do an especially good job, did they."

"No. They sure didn't." He took a deep breath, then let it out. "Sure. Why not? Let's go to your ship."

"Excellent," she said, patting him on the back as they both rose. "We'll get you over there . . . we'll get you settled in . . . and then," she added with determination, "we'll see what we can do about Sharon Valerii."

CHAPTER 8

"Nothing?"

William Adama was in his quarters, staring at Saul Tigh with a combination of incredulity and frustration. These weren't emotions that he relished having there. His quarters were traditionally his place of retreat from the day-to-day, and even night-to-night, stress of commanding the *Galactica* and feeling the weight of humanity's survival on his shoulders. Everything there was designed to be as soothing and supportive as possible. It was his "womb," his comfort zone. Whenever Tigh came there to talk about something, Adama inevitably braced himself mentally, knowing that it was probably going to be disruptive of his hard-fought-for stability. This evening was obviously not going to be an exception. "The investigation's turned up nothing?"

"Not so far," Tigh admitted. He had loosened his jacket, which he routinely did when he was off duty. He sat across from Adama and shook his head, looking discouraged. "Gaeta seems ready to tear his hair out. It's certainly giving him a nervous condition; poor bastard keeps scratching the back of his hand like he wants to peel the skin off. He's practically taken apart the entire CNP and DRADIS piece by piece and put it back together again, and can't find a damned thing to indicate how the Cylons could possibly have tapped into it to determine where we were going to be Jumping to."

"So what are you saying?" asked Adama. "That we're completely screwed? That we live with the idea of blind Jumps for the rest of our lives?"

"I sure as hell hope not," Tigh said grimly. "Because frankly, I'm not sure how long those lives will be. Our luck is going to run out sooner or later, and I'm betting sooner."

"As am I." Adama leaned back in his chair and rubbed the bridge of his nose. "I was less than candid with you earlier, by the way."

Tigh raised an eyebrow. "Oh?"

"I have noticed: It's not getting easier."

Tigh laughed at that, a moment of needed levity. Then he added, "By the way, the business with the boy has been sorted out."

"The boy?" Adama wasn't following at first, but then he remembered. "Oh, the youngster. Boxey. We really thought he might be a Cylon?" Adama sounded openly skeptical.

Tigh shrugged in a what-can-you-do? manner. "We can't be too careful," he said.

"Historically, I think it's been proven that we can," replied Adama. Tigh naturally knew to what he was referring: the time that a simple military tribunal had gotten completely out of hand, casting suspicion on everyone and anyone until Adama had been forced to shut the thing down.

"Maybe so," Tigh agreed reluctantly, "but that still leaves us with the same problem. Gaeta and his best people are still looking into the matter, but it might be that we have to look in a different direction."

Adama looked as if he were studying the words that Tigh had just spoken, hanging there in the air. "Are you suggesting . . . ?"

"I'm suggesting," said Tigh, leaping into it since he had put it out there, "that we may have a Cylon operative in the CIC. Someone right under our very noses."

"You really think that one of our own people . . ."

"I'm trying not to think, frankly." And then he hastened to add, "And please, no comments about how I must have a lot of practice at that."

"Wasn't even considering it," said Adama, who had indeed been considering it and had simply thought better of it.

"What I mean is, if you start to think too hard about things like this, you eliminate possibilities because . . . well . . ."

"They're unthinkable."

"Right. And we can't afford to do that."

"So what's the solution?"

Tigh leaned forward, his fingers interlaced and hands resting on Adama's desk. "Listening devices."

"What do you mean?"

"I mean listening devices. We bug the quarters of everyone in CIC."

"Without their knowledge."

"Well, that's certainly the only way it would yield us any information," Tigh said reasonably.

Adama felt as if he were lost in a vast morass of impenetrable moral conundrums. His face, as always, displayed no sign of his inner frustration. "You're suggesting we bug our own people. Listen in on their private lives, even though they're not actually suspects of any crime."

"Of course they're suspects, Bill, and don't make me out to be the bad guy here," said Tigh, sounding defensive.

"It's completely contrary to military protocol . . ."

"That's true. Here's the thing: All the guys who wrote the rules of military protocol? They're all dead. They were blown to bits by the Cylons, and now we're out here trying to hold things together through events that the framers of those protocols could never have conceived. Bill . . . we're dealing with an enemy who looks just like us."

"It's been my experience," Adama said slowly, "that the enemy usually looks like us. Most of the time . . . the enemy *is* us."

"Fair enough. But—"

"What are you proposing, Saul? We listen in on anything and everything for an indefinite period of time? What right do we have to spy on our own people?"

"The right to do everything in our power to keep them safe. Let's be reasonable, Bill: If the Cylons are talking to any humans, I want to know about it. And I very much suspect you want to as well."

Adama didn't say anything for a time, drumming his fingers on the desk. "The whole thing stinks," he said finally.

"No argument on that, Admiral," replied Tigh, his face set and determined. "But I've waded through so much crap in my life that my nostrils died ages ago. Which is why I'm offering to attend to this so that you don't have to know anything about it."

"You're concerned about my sense of smell."

"Something like that."

"Are you going to bug yourself? And me?"

Tigh blinked at that. "I . . . don't see the point. We know we're not Cylons. And since we'd know about the bugs, we wouldn't say or do anything incriminating anyway."

"What about your wife?"

The colonel clearly couldn't quite believe what he was saying. "My wife? Ellen?"

"Do you have more than one wife?"

"No . . ."

"Then that would be her."

"You're inferring she's a Cylon . . . ?"

"No," corrected Adama, "I'm *implying* she could be. That is what the whole purpose of this eavesdropping plan is, isn't it? To weed out possible agents in command positions?"

"She's not in a command position!"

"She sleeps next to my first officer. Have you never considered the dangers of pillow talk? For that matter, what if you're muttering classified information in your sleep and she's sitting there jotting down notes?"

"That's absolutely ridiculous!"

"Ridiculous it may be," Adama said with no hint of rancor. "But absolutely? I don't think so."

"*She's my wife!*"

"Does that make her above suspicion?"

"You bet it . . ." And then Tigh stopped, and Adama could see that Tigh was really starting to think about it. Adama had long ago realized that this was Tigh's way: to react to something with pure gut instinct. Given time, he would often consider the consequences of what he was saying and doing. The problem was that, if he didn't have the time, the decision he went with wasn't always the most prudent. Adama didn't hold it against him; everyone had their failings. Still, it was something that was never far from his thoughts. Tigh lowered his gaze and continued reluctantly, "It . . . doesn't make her above suspicion."

"No. It doesn't. I figured the way to make you understand the enormity of what you're proposing is to make it hit closer to home."

"Understood." Tigh rose. "I apologize for suggesting the—"

"Do you have the know-how to do it?"

This brought Tigh up short. He blinked repeatedly, as if someone were shining a flashlight directly in his face. "Pardon?"

"Do you personally have the know-how to install the sort of bugs we're talking about?"

"Well . . . yes. I did some surveillance work early in my career. We have the necessary equipment in ship's stores . . ."

"Do it," Adama said quietly. "It stays between you and me. And this is not a fishing expedition. If we hear two officers conspiring to assemble a still or find out that someone likes to spend their free time reciting lewd poetry with our names in it . . . we don't give a damn about it. No recriminations, no black marks. We're looking for evidence of Cylons or Cylon allies only. Is that understood?"

"Perfectly."

"Oh, and Saul . . ." Adama paused and then continued, "If you can manage it . . . monitor the vice president as well."

Tigh nodded.

Adama sat and stared at nothing for a long time after Tigh left. He despised the notion of being in a situation that seemed to have no graceful way out. It wasn't just the prospect of eavesdropping on his own people. It was that he was combating potential spying with actual spying. He had thought that the most cataclysmic problem he was ever going to have to deal with was that the Cylons were becoming indistinguishable from humans. What worried him far more was the possibility that humans were—not all at once, because these things don't happen overnight, but very slowly—becoming indistinguishable from Cylons.

CHAPTER 9

Laura Roslin had become an enforced insomniac.

Prophetic dreams were nothing new for her. She had had them enough times while she'd been under the influence of the cancer medication, extract of Chamalla. But they had seemed helpful to her. Prophetic, guiding dreams that were admittedly sometimes violent. But they ultimately had a purpose, and that purpose appeared to be to help her in particular and humanity in general. No matter what she had experienced, she had never felt threatened by them.

But this was a very different circumstance. As she lay in her bed and stared up at the ceiling, she felt as if she were under constant threat. As if something had just crawled into her mind and was lying there, festering and trying to undermine her belief in herself and her strength of character.

She's being paranoid. There is no one out to get her. All right, that isn't true: There's an entire mechanized race that's out to get her. Her and every-one else. But that has nothing to do with what's going on in her head. This is all just spillover from dodging death. That's all. All the things that prey on her during the day are haunting her at night. And since she knows that's what was happening she can control it. She is stronger than simple night terrors. Stronger and better.

But why Sagittaron? Or Sagittarius, as the ancient name was phrased. Why did that figure so prominently? And Sharon Valerii?

Well, Valerii was obvious, of course. She represented the face of the enemy . . . and yet she was also responsible, however indirectly, for Laura's new lease on life. So naturally she would feel conflicted about Valerii . . . about it . . . and that was what dreams were, after all. A place for the mind to work out conflicts.

As for Sagittaron . . . well, that was where Tom Zarek hailed from. Laura was of the firm conviction that, short of the Cylons, Tom Zarek con-tinued to represent the single greatest threat to humanity's continued exis-tence. It was the nature of those such as Zarek to instigate unrest, to foment hostility by attempting to change the status quo—not through diplomacy or thought or consideration—but through violent action. There was enough violence threatening humankind from without; they certainly didn't need it from within.

Perhaps that was where the image of blood was coming from as well. Blood was life. Blood was cleansing. She was charged with maintaining the very life blood of humans, to keep it flowing in a cold and uncaring galaxy against an implacable foe that sought to annihilate them.

Symbolism. That's what dreams were all about. The more she thought about it, the less daunted by the dreams she was becoming. If she only thought of them as a barrage of frightening images, then it was no wonder she would feel overwhelmed by what was going on inside her skull. But if she broke them down to individual concepts and did all she could to under-stand what they symbolized, why . . . it wasn't a problem at all.

Knowledge was the key to understanding. Knowledge—as Laura Roslin the teacher knew very well—was power. To have knowledge of what her dreams meant gave her the power to be undaunted by them.

At that moment, her alarm clock went off. Laura was slightly jolted by the noise, and it was just enough to make her realize that she had indeed drifted off to sleep at some point in her musings. But it had been a peaceful, dreamless sleep—the first one in an age, it felt like. That knowledge buoyed her spirits. She felt as if she were on the mend, as if she had taken the first step on a road back to recapturing her equilibrium.

It couldn't have come at a better time. Her performance at the press conference had been nothing short of a fiasco. Billy had done some brilliant spinning when reporters had subsequently asked him if Laura hadn't seemed a bit erratic during the conference, and he smoothly chalked it up to the residue of some heavy-duty medication she'd been taking during her recent illness. He expressed full confidence that the medicines would have worked their way out of her body in short order, and she would be back to her smiling, confident self, ready to put her near-death experience behind her and serve the needs of the people. Everyone had nodded and smiled approvingly, even with relief. As much as reporters enjoyed challenging the status quo, at heart they were as eager for stability and constancy as anyone else. Laura represented that, far more so than the brusque, occasionally distant, and often inscrutable Admiral Adama.

At least, that was the general perception of him.

But she had come to know him in a very different way. Had come to respect him, even admire him. Even . . .

"Best not to go there," Laura said aloud and was slightly startled at the sound of her own voice. She shook it off and slid her legs out from under the covers.

Reflexively she glanced toward the window, and then mentally and sadly scolded herself. She had still not gotten used to the lack of sun. In the old days (only few months gone, but funny how they had become "the old days") she had never required an alarm since she had readily awoken to the first rays of the morning sun. Ever since she'd been a little girl, that was all that she had required. It was a regular part of her routine, something that she had simply taken for granted. That was one of the most humbling things about her current situation, about the situation that faced all of them: Nothing could be taken for granted anymore. If one couldn't count on the sun to always be there for them, what could one count on?

"Yourself," she said aloud to her unspoken question. She smiled at that. She liked the confident sound of it. In every respect, inside and out, she was beginning to feel and sound more and more like her old self.

Maybe you're still dreaming this. Maybe you only think you're awake, but you're not, and bad things are going to happen . . .

She shook the doubts off like a dog divesting itself of water.

She walked into the bathroom and attended to the normal, mundane aspects of morning ablution. As she brushed her teeth, she considered all she had to do today, and was pleased by the degree of clear-headedness that she was displaying. In every way, she was starting to feel like her old self. Her pre-cancer self. The one who not only believed that mankind had a great and glorious destiny, but that she was going to be around to be a part of it. She realized that she had missed that Laura Roslin almost as much as she now missed the sun.

Removing her nightgown, she stepped into the shower, mindful of the need to keep it as brief as possible. The fleet had already had to cope once with the loss of water that had put them into crisis mode. She wasn't about to forget that and endlessly squander a precious resource. Get in, get cleaned off, get out.

She remembered with amusement Billy's suggestion that they mount a campaign centered around "Save water; shower with a friend." Involuntarily her thoughts turned once more to Adama . . .

Don't. Go. There.

"Boy," she muttered, soaping her hair, "you really are a glutton for punish—"

Something felt wrong.

She lowered her hands and looked at them.

She assumed she was looking at thick residue from brown water. Not that long ago some sort of rust build-up had caused the water to acquire a distinctly coppery tint. But a man from maintenance had come in, done some work on the pipes, and declared them to be rust-free. He'd been right; from that moment on, the water had been fine. So initially her instinct was to think that she was faced with a recurrence of that problem.

Then she realized that it was a distinctly different tint.

Her hands were red. Dark red. Blood red.

At first she thought there was something wrong with the shampoo. Then she looked down. Her eyes widened in horror. Blood was pouring down her body, cascading down her torso and legs and swirling down the drain.

She jumped back, slamming against the far wall of the shower, and looked up, a scream strangling unvoiced in her throat.

Blood was gushing from the showerhead.

She slipped and stumbled out of the shower. She hit the floor, landing hard on her elbows and sending jolts of pain running up and down her arms. She barely felt it. She felt as if her mind was being shredded by what was happening.

She half-stumbled, half-crawled out of the bathroom, and something splattered upon her from overhead. She looked up, terrified at what she was going to see.

A gigantic red spot had formed upon the ceiling, and blood was dripping from overhead . . . a few drops at first, but then a steady trickle and then a gush, cascading down upon her bed, soaking it through.

Laura finally screamed in full voice, grabbing at her bathrobe and throwing it on even as she bolted for the door. She slammed into it as her bloodied hand slipped off the knob, failing to open it. Then she found traction, pulled the door opened and stumbled into the hallway, shouting for help.

Billy was there in an instant, as if materializing from thin air. All endeavors to maintain professional demeanor, to adhere to proper titles such as "Madame President," evaporated. "Laura!" he yelled, trying to make himself heard over Laura's inarticulate shouts. "Laura, what's wrong?!"

"Blood! Blood! It's everywhere! It's—"

"What are you talking about!?"

"Look at me!" She held up her hands. "I'm covered in—"

"There's nothing!"

"The blood, it was coming out of the shower, the ceiling, it's everywhere—"

"There's no blood! I don't know what you're talking about! There's nothing!"

Billy's words penetrated her own hysteria, and she fought it down enough to look at her hands herself. They were clean. There was nothing on them except residual dampness from the water.

"This . . . this can't be," she muttered, shaking her head. She ran her fingers through her hair. There was no stickiness as one would imagine from a head covered in blood, and her fingers came away clean. She held up her arms. The loose folds of the sleeves of her robe fell away and she saw that her arms were clean as well. "Can't be . . . the ceiling . . . the shower . . ."

"Show me," Billy said firmly.

She nodded, feeling disconnected from the moment, even from her own body. She turned and pointed wordlessly at her quarters.

Billy stepped past her and stuck his head in. She waited for some re-action from him, but he turned back to her and simply stared at her, his face a question mark.

Laura walked over, pushed past him, and looked in, looked up at the ceiling.

Dry. Normal. No sign of anything untoward.

She pointed with a quavering hand and said, "The bathroom . . ." But before Billy could step past to check it out, she forced her feet to move. She ignored his attempt to hold her back as she walked quickly across the room and looked into the bathroom.

Nothing.

Water was still pouring out of the showerhead. It was pure and clean and not the slightest bit sanguine. Feeling as if she were sleep-walking while awake, Laura reached in and shut off the water.

"It could have been that plumbing thing . . ." Billy started, but his voice trailed off since he knew that he was not only failing to con-vince Laura, but himself as well. Slowly Laura walked back into her bedroom and sat down on the edge of the bed. Automatically she re-arranged the folds of the robe to cover her legs, and she just sat there and stared off into space.

Billy stood in front of her and then crouched so that he was at eye level with her. "Laura," he said, gently but firmly, sounding less like an aide and more like a concerned uncle, "you've got to tell me what's going on. I can't help you if you—"

"You can't help me," Laura said softly. "I'm going crazy. That's all there is to it."

"You're not going crazy."

"How do you know?"

"Because people who are really going crazy don't have the presence of mind to question it. They just accept the reality that's handed them. Or maybe the 'perceived reality' would be a better way to put it."

She put her face in her hands, trying to compose herself. Billy said nothing; he just crouched there and waited.

She told him. She told him about the series of bizarre dreams, with the recurring theme of blood. She told him about Sharon and Zarek figuring into them, and the symbolism of Sagittarius seeping blood. She told him how she had not been sleeping, and how when she did sleep she woke up, and how when she was awake she was beginning to lose track of whether she was awake or asleep. She told him how the lines between dream imagery and reality were begin-ning to blur, perhaps irreparably.

"Maybe . . ." she began to say, and then stopped.

"Maybe what?"

"Maybe . . . I should take a leave of absence. Even resign my duties . . ."

Billy shook his head. "No. No, I believe in you. You can work your way through this."

She said nothing for a long moment. "Madame President . . ." Billy began.

But she put up a hand and cut him off. Amazingly, despite everything that had just transpired, she forced a wry smile. "This is the beginning of a pep talk, isn't it."

"Well . . ." Billy hesitated. "I don't know that I would have . . . yeah, okay, yes. It was."

"I appreciate that. But I'm starting to think this is a situation that requires more than just a pep talk. I think someone is out to get me." When she saw his look, she continued, "I know how that sounds."

"Well, they always say that it's not paranoia if someone really is out to get you. If you think that's what's happening, then we should speak to Admiral Adama. We should . . ."

"No."

"But . . ."

"I said no. What's the first thing on the agenda?"

He was about to offer more of a protest, but then he saw the firm expression on her face and discarded the idea. "Well . . . actually, I don't think it's going to be something that makes you feel any better."

"Billy, anything short of Tom Zarek is going to be perfectly fine, I assure you." Then she saw the look on his face and said, with the resigned sigh of the damned, "It's Zarek, isn't it."

"You told him to meet with me to make an appointment. He did, I did. I figured doing it in the morning would get it out of the way quickly."

"Good thinking, Billy."

He stood. "I'll cancel . . ."

"No, you won't. I'll attend to it."

"Are you sure?"

She fixed him with a determined stare. "Billy . . . either this is happening due to outside influence, or my mind is turning against me. I won't be beaten by someone else, and I certainly won't be beaten by my own brain. I will be keeping up with my schedule, and that's all."

Billy nodded and said simply, "Thank you, Madame President."

He walked out of the room, and it wasn't until he was gone that Laura Roslin started to tremble uncontrollably, and did so until for long seconds until the shakes finally passed.

"Madame President. You're looking well."

Laura, looking utterly self-possessed and not at all like someone who felt as if reality and fantasy were bleeding hopelessly together, pulled up the chair behind her desk and said, "Thank you, Councilman. What's on your mind?"

Zarek, sitting across the desk from her, smiled in amusement. "Getting right to the point, Madame President?"

She returned the smile, but there was no warmth in it, nor did she pretend there was. "I have a schedule to keep."

"And perhaps you want to minimize the amount of time you have to look at me?"

"You said it, Councilman, not I."

"Well," he said, sitting back in his chair and folding his arms. "I guess that's the difference between us. I say what I think."

"But you didn't do that, did you, Councilman. You said what I think. Or at least what you believe I was thinking. I don't need people to speak on my behalf, and I certainly don't appreciate it when people try to read my mind."

Putting his hands up in a gesture of surrender, Zarek never lost his lopsided grin. Laura had no doubt that he was getting some sort of perverse enjoyment out of this. "Point taken, Madame President. I'll get to it, then. Have you heard of the Midguardians?"

"Of course," she said promptly.

He was visibly surprised. "You have?"

"I wouldn't be much of a president if I didn't have at least some passing knowledge of every major group represented in the fleet. I'd actually been under the impression that the practitioners of their ancient religion had died out."

"As it turns out, no. But not for lack of trying on the part of others. I've been reading up on them, and the persecution of these people is one of the darker times in our history."

"May I ask," she said, curious in spite of herself, "why you've taken a sudden interest in the Midguardians?"

"Because they've approached me about the prospect of being officially recognized."

"As what?"

"As a colony, with equal rights and privileges to any of the others."

Laura laughed in that way someone does when they can't quite believe the person they're talking to is serious. When she saw that Zarek's expression wasn't changing; she realized that he did, indeed, mean what he was saying. "Why in the world would we want to do that? They're a religion, not a colony."

"They are a race. A people with their own heritage and history. They are deserving of recognition as such."

"Councilman," said Laura, still having trouble believing that they were having this conversation at all, "I'm not entirely certain why you're even approaching me on this. I can't simply wave my hand and change the basic structure of government. I'm the president, not the king."

"I know that," said Zarek, not showing the least sign of flagging in his determination. "But every member of the Quorum has one thing in common: They respect you."

"Every member?"

The unspoken challenge was there, and Zarek rose to it. "Every member. Including me. And my coming to you is my way of acknowledging that they will listen to you before they listen to me. If you recommend this—"

"Why would I do that?"

"Because," he said as if it were the most obvious thing in the world, "it's the right thing to do."

Laura wasn't entirely certain how to react to that. But, as always, whatever inner questions she had weren't reflected in her demeanor. Instead she peered over the tops of her glasses as if studying a new form of bacteria. "That's it? That's your whole argument? Because it's the right thing to do?"

"I'd like to think that would be enough."

"And do you think employing violence to get your way is also the right thing to do?"

"You don't see me employing violence here, do you?" he pointed out. "I didn't come in here threatening you. No one's putting a gun to your head. I've no blackmail. No way to force you into anything."

What about what you're doing to my head? What about the terrorist tactics you're pulling that have made it so I can't sleep, and that are starting to seep into my every waking moment? Are you doing it in order to tear me down? Undermine my leadership? Make me easy to manipulate, get me to agree to something out of exhaustion that I wouldn't ordinarily have even considered?

She briefly contemplated hurling such questions at him, but she dismissed the notion. There was no advantage to confronting him in that manner. First of all, she still wasn't completely certain there was an entity behind what was happening to her. Second, even if she was certain, she didn't know for sure it was Zarek. Third, even if she was certain, there was no way to prove it. It wasn't as if a cool customer like Zarek was going to break down and admit to anything just from a few probing questions being offered by her. Fourth—and the greatest consideration of all—she didn't want to chance admitting any weakness to someone as untrustworthy and scheming as Tom Zarek. If he wasn't behind it, he'd think she was losing her mind, and if he was behind it, he'd take satisfaction in knowing that he was getting to her.

"No. You're not doing anything like that," she allowed. "But, given our history, I find it difficult to believe you'd think that I would simply take your recommendation on faith—"

"I'm not asking you to do any such thing," he said immediately. He jumped on this so quickly, in fact, that Laura mentally kicked herself, certain that she had just walked into something. "All I'm asking is that you meet with one of their representatives. One Wolf Gunnerson. He's a very impressive, and very charismatic, individual."

"Why didn't he simply come to me directly?"

"Because he believes in following a chain of command. He doesn't feel it's his place to go straight to the president. That his representative should do that instead. And since he and his people are from Sagittaron . . ."

"That representative would be you."

"Exactly."

Laura's gut reaction was to say no. Except . . . based on what, really? She was the president of the Colonies. She represented all the people. If one of them felt they had a genuine grievance, fairness and conscience demanded that she make herself available to hear it. How could she reasonably refuse to meet with this Gunnerson person based entirely on her antipathy toward Zarek?

"Very well."

As if she hadn't spoken, Zarek said, "I think if you give any consideration to fairness, Madame President, I . . ."

For all that Zarek annoyed the hell out of her—for all that she found it aggravating to be in the same room with him—she had to admit to herself that she would always treasure the look on his face when his brain finally processed what she had just said. His voice trailed off for a moment and then he said, " 'Very well'?"

"My aide will set up a time to meet."

Zarek's face changed, and she realized that the patronizing, barely tolerant smile had been inadvertently replaced by a genuine one. It surprised her to see that he actually had a rather pleasant face when he wasn't looking at her like a fox sizing up a prospective meal. "Well, that's . . . thank you, Madame President. That was very unexpected."

"Unexpected?" she said pleasantly. "Why so?"

"Candidly . . . I expected much more of an argument."

She shrugged as if it were no big deal . . . which, stripped of her animosity and distrust for Tom Zarek, it really wasn't . . . and said, "One of my citizens wants to speak with me. I'm the president of all the people, Councilman Zarek . . . even the people with whom I disagree. Even my enemies."

Zarek's smile once again remained in place, but the warmth evaporated from it. "I certainly hope you're not referring to me, Madame President. I'm only the enemy of those who would repress others. I'd hate to think you'd count yourself among such individuals."

"I was merely speaking in generalities, Councilman," she purred. "Whether you feel what I said applied to you . . . well, that's certainly your decision to make, not mine."

"Understood," Zarek said coolly as he stood. Laura did likewise. He extended his hand and she shook it firmly. "A pleasure as always."

As she watched him leave, her eyes narrowed, and she considered the fact that meeting with Zarek was "always" something, all right . . . but "a pleasure" wasn't what she would have termed it.

CHAPTER 10

William Adama had thought he had heard it all. But when Colonel Tigh told him who had shown up out of nowhere, requesting to meet with the admiral as soon as possible, it still took him a few moments to cut through the sheer incredulity that seized him.

"She's claiming to be her what?" he asked for what might have been the third time. All eyes in CIC had turned to watch with interest, and it was obvious that they were sharing Adama's disbelief.

From Tigh's expression, it was clear that he was not relishing being the bearer of this particular news. "She says," Tigh repeated, looking as if he was ready to strangle whoever the "she" was that was the subject of his communiqué, "that she's her lawyer."

Adama wanted to laugh. But he'd never laughed in front of his crew and didn't feel inclined to set precedent. "Her lawyer," he echoed.

"Yes."

"Motherfrakker," came a murmured comment from Dualla.

Adama fired a glance at her and she quickly fell silent. He stepped closer in toward Tigh and said in a low, angry voice, "How did she even find out the Cylon is on board?"

"She said 'sources.' You ask me, it's that kid, Boxey."

"We don't know that for sure," said Adama, who privately thought Tigh was probably right. "What's this woman's name?"

"Gunnerson. Freya Gunnerson. From the *Bifrost*. I ran a fast check on her and she is a genuine attorney." Tigh shook his head. "If the frakking Cylons had to destroy the bulk of humanity, you'd think at least they could have done us the favor of making sure to take out all the lawyers."

Adama considered the comment to be in poor taste at best, but he let it pass. "Does she have any known affiliation to any terrorist groups or any Cylon sympathizers?"

"Maybe, but nothing that a preliminary background check turned up. She's a Midguardian, though."

"Yes, everyone on the *Bifrost* is." Adama knew the ship was one of the few privately owned vessels in the fleet. "They may be heathens, but they're not especially enamored of the Cylons in any way that I know of. So where in the world is this coming from? Why would she be showing up here and claiming she's Valerii's attorney?"

"Free publicity. She's trying to make a name for herself. Get famous fast."

"Sharon Valerii is a member of the race that's trying to obliterate us," Adama pointed out. "Allying with her is a fast track to infamy, not fame."

"For some people, that's enough." When Adama didn't respond, Tigh said, "I'll send her packing . . ."

"Bring her to meeting room A."

Tigh's eyes widened. His surprise was mirrored in the faces of the CIC crew. "Seriously?"

"Seriously."

Tigh turned to a nearby functionary and said, "Please have the woman who's in the holding area escorted to meeting room A." The moment the functionary was out the door, he turned back to Adama and said, "I'm coming with you, then." He saw the look in Adama's face, the understated surprise that Tigh would dare to issue flat fiats to him. But Tigh didn't back down. "She's a Cylon sympathizer. Perhaps a Cylon herself. For all we know, she wants a one-on-one with you so she can . . ." He didn't want to complete the sentence, still sensitive—even now—to the bullets that had ripped open Adama's chest and nearly killed him.

"I was taking it for granted she's been screened for weapons," Adama said mildly.

"Of course. But who ever knows what we're dealing with? What if she has some sort of bomb that she's got built into herself, and she can blow herself up? If she's a toaster, anything is possible."

"If she's a toaster and she blows herself up, do you really think the best strategy is to put the ship's commander and second in command in the same room with her?"

Tigh started to reply, and realized that he didn't have a ready answer to that.

"I'll be back shortly," Adama assured him, and headed to the meeting room.

Before he left, though, Tigh called after him, "Admiral. Be careful. They can be incredibly evil bastards."

"Cylons?"

"Lawyers."

Adama hadn't been certain what to look forward to when meeting Freya Gunnerson, briefcase in her hand and determination in her face. Horns, perhaps, or a large single red eye strobing from one side of her head to the other. He certainly hadn't anticipated the tall, impressive-looking woman who was waiting for him. She didn't seem especially devious. Of course, she wouldn't have been especially devious if she'd looked that way, now, would she. She had been sitting, but she rose and extended her hand. "Admiral. This is an honor," she said. Her voice was musical, and she genuinely did sound as if she was honored to meet him. None of which served to put Adama off his guard, but it certainly ran contrary to his expectations. "I'm Freya Gunnerson."

He shook her hand firmly. "William Adama."

"Yes, I know. The military genius who's kept us alive in the face of adversity."

"I've had some help. Please sit."

She did so, placing a briefcase on the table. She snapped the latches open and saw Adama's cautious expression. "Your people have already thoroughly inspected this, I assure you."

There had been no question in Adama's mind that was true. The caution had been automatic after a lifetime of military experience. Nevertheless, he tilted his head slightly in acknowledgment. She opened the briefcase and removed a notepad and a file folder, which she placed on the table and proceeded to flip through. "I assume," she said, "that your XO told you why I'm here."

"I prefer to hear it with my own ears."

"I am here," she said patiently, "to represent the interests of Sharon Valerii."

"In what sense?"

"In the sense that I would like to know what crime she's committed."

Adama stared at her gravely. "What *crime*?"

"Yes, Admiral. What crime has she committed that warrants her being held indefinitely?"

"Attempted murder."

"I assume you're referring to yourself as the attempted victim." Adama's nod was barely perceptible, but she went on as if he had readily bobbed his head. "My understanding—and correct me if I have the facts wrong—is that the person you are holding indefinitely was, in fact, on Caprica at the time of the assault."

"*It* is not a person."

"Really." She seemed genuinely interested in his opinion. "And on what do you base that assessment?"

"She is a Cylon. Are you disputing that?"

"Not at all. I'm simply asking on what basis you declare that she's not a person."

Adama could scarcely believe he was having the conversation. "The Cylons," he said very slowly, as if addressing someone who was having trouble understanding him, "are machines. We created them."

"Humans routinely create other humans. Does that make them machines?" Before he could answer, she leaned forward and continued, "I am simply a person of conscience, Admiral. I see someone's rights being trampled upon, and I feel the need to step in and see that those rights are restored."

"I'm not interested in fencing with you, Counselor," Adama said in an icy tone. "Sharon Valarii is one of an identical series of creations, transferring all her knowledge from one to the next to the next. She was constructed for that purpose. Cylons are not humans. Sharon Valerii is not a person. Sharon Valerii is not human. Sharon Valerii has no more rights than the chair you're sitting in."

"Really." The edges of her mouth turned up. "And how many pregnant chairs have you encountered?"

"That's a ridiculous comparison."

"Actually," said Freya, "it's a perfectly valid comparison. In case you never got around to taking basic biology in school, Admiral, one of the determinations of whether two beings are part of the same genus is their ability to reproduce. I will grant you that Sharon Valerii may be a different species from humans . . . but certainly she's part of the same genus. Otherwise how else can she be pregnant by your lieutenant . . ." She glanced at one of the sheets of paper, "Agathon, I believe?"

"Yes," he growled.

"My contention is that she is at the very least of the same genus, and quite possibly of the same species. Or at least near enough to be indistinguishable from humans. And if she's indistinguishable from a human, on what basis can we contend that she's not?"

"On the basis that she presents a security risk to this fleet."

"An assertion you base on what aspect of her behavior, exactly? I'm not asking about her lookalikes. I'm asking you what specific crimes the woman in that cell has herself committed."

Adama took a deep breath and let it out slowly. "None that I'm aware of," he admitted. "But that doesn't mean she doesn't present a threat. Counselor, if we're done here . . ."

"We are if you say we are," she acknowledged. "This is your boat, after all. It's just that I was given to believe that you were a man of honor."

Adama's face could have been carved of stone. "Are you questioning my honor?"

"I'm questioning what sort of man takes someone who has committed no crime—who has served the needs of humanity every time she was asked to—and treats her as if she is the most vile of criminals."

"She. Isn't. Human."

She chuckled at that, but there was a sadness in her voice. "Isn't that how one group always justifies mistreating another group? By pretending they're not human, despite all evidence to the contrary? And because of that, they're not deserving of rights."

"My heart bleeds, counselor, considering the Cylons obviously think of us as animals to be slaughtered."

"And we thought of them as slaves before they turned on us. No one's hands are clean in this one, Admiral. But certainly part of their determination to exterminate us stems from the notion that they don't think we're deserving of the right to live free . . . just as you judge Sharon Valerii the same way. How are we to judge ourselves any better than the Cylons, if that's the way we think?"

"And you can't treat a Cylon like Sharon Valerii as if she is a human with the same rights as a human."

"Convince me that she's not human," Freya said challengingly. "Her memories 'transfer'? There are studies documenting humans functioning with highly developed versions of ESP. So the Cylons have simply improved upon that which was already a part of them. Cylons kill humans? As if humans don't kill humans."

"I don't have to convince you of anything."

Her face hardened. "Actually, Admiral, you do. See, our criminal justice system doesn't allow for people to be held indefinitely, with no charges brought against them, while they're pumped for information over alleged terrorist activities. No civilized society would allow such behavior, I'd like to think. In order to deprive someone of their fundamental right to liberty, the burden of proof is upon her accusers to prove that she has, in fact, done something worth being incarcerated for. You've admitted to my face that Sharon Valerii has done nothing. She's being held for no damned good reason."

"She is a military asset."

"So are you, Admiral. But you're not under armed guard and you can go wherever you wish. The fact remains that by every measurable standard, Sharon Valerii is a person. And all people within the Colonies have equal rights; that's built right into the charter of the Twelve Colonies. Your imprisonment of Sharon Valerii is unconstitutional."

"And you expect me to release her on the basis of this . . . specious claim?" said Adama incredulously.

"No. Getting her released is my fight, to be taken up with others. But at the very least, I should think that—in the interest of simple human decency—you would allow me to meet with her."

" 'Others' can't know about her. I don't even want to think what would happen if the general populace learns that she's here."

"If you think she's going to remain under wraps forever, you're deluding yourself. I'll wager at least several people in the Quorum probably know by now. Or whatever marines you've got guarding her have told their loved ones about it, sworn of course to strictest secrecy. But secrets have a way of getting out, and in case you haven't noticed, governments stink at keeping them. A casual slip of the tongue. A few too many drinks resulting in the wrong words said within earshot of the wrong ear. Next thing you know, this whole thing explodes in your face." She eased back, sounding less confrontational but no less determined. "Look . . . Admiral . . . if you allow me to meet with her, then anything I know about her—including her existence—becomes a matter of attorney/client privilege. I'll keep everything to myself. You turn me away, shut me out . . . there's no reason at all for me not to discuss whatever I know with whomever will listen."

"Are you blackmailing me?" asked Adama, his tone fraught with danger.

"No, Admiral. That would be illegal. I'm simply explaining what will happen if you do the right thing . . . and the wrong thing. This isn't blackmail. It's simply endeavoring to give you an informed opinion."

Adama's instinct was to kick her off the ship. This woman hadn't been there. She didn't understand. She hadn't seen the look that came over Sharon Valerii's face as she leveled her gun at Adama's chest and shot him at point-blank range. If Freya Gunnerson had seen that, she wouldn't be sitting here today claiming that the thing down in the brig was entitled to be treated like any other human. In fact, if she had seen Sharon Valerii coming her way, she'd probably have run in the other direction.

Plus, on a practical level, Adama couldn't see any way in which Sharon could be released, if for no other reason than that it would be a death sentence for her. Her predecessor had been gunned down. The odds were sensational that she would meet the same fate. The only way she would avoid it would be if she was assigned quarters and hid there for the rest of her life. What was really the difference between that and residing in a cell?

But what kept niggling in the back of Adama's brain was that, for all that he was still unconvinced that Valerii was entitled to the same rights as a human . . . there were small shreds of truth creeping into what Freya was saying. Valerii was part of a life form so indistinguishable from humans that she was capable of bearing a human's child. And the only way to tell humans from Cylons was via a complicated blood test that he still wasn't one hundred percent sure was reliable, although that might stem from his fundamental distrust of Gaius Baltar.

There was one thing that William Adama was very aware of, that any military man was aware of. And that was that there was no inherent danger in simply talking with someone. Indeed, just about every war in humanity's history had stemmed from two or more sides being unable to talk to each other. So instead they had blown the living crap out of each other until finally they had enough, at which point they wound up talking . . . which, if they'd only done that in the first place, would have spared countless lives.

Of even more recent vintage, and always fresh in Adama's memory, was the breakdown in communication between him and Laura Roslin that had resulted in complete chaos, the shattering of the fleet, a military invasion that had turned his own son against him. It was a situation that he, Adama, had instigated with military thinking, and that he, Adama, had finally settled when he had opened himself to genuinely listening to what Roslin had to say. Laura Roslin had far too much class to say something as infantile as "I told you so," and no one else would have dared to. But Adama had been saying it to himself most every day since then.

Freya Gunnerson wanted to talk to Sharon Valerii. She was doing so in the interest of justice. If he stood in the way of that, what did that make him?

"All right," he said. Surprise registered on her face, and she tried quickly to cover it as he continued, "You may meet with her. You will remain on the other side of the enclosure, speak to her via phone only. Furthermore, one of my officers will be there at all times."

"Admiral, as I mentioned, there is such a thing as lawyer/client confidentiality."

He wasn't about to argue the fine points of it. "Take or leave it," he told her.

Freya looked as if she were about to argue the point further, but obviously thought better of it. "I'll take it."

"Remain here and I'll have it arranged."

He rose to leave, and she automatically stood as well. Again she extended her hand and he shook it firmly. "You're making the right decision, Admiral. Allowing people to talk is never a bad thing. Just imagine: If enough people talk about the right subjects, we could actually have peace in our time."

"We can only hope," replied Adama.

Adama recognized the look of astonishment on Lee's face; it very likely mirrored the one that had been on his own when Tigh had first told him about their new arrival.

"You want me to sit in on a lawyer meeting with Sharon?"

Adama, walking down a hallway next to Lee, nodded. "They're down waiting at the brig for you. I need you to head down there now."

Lee stopped in his tracks and Adama turned, his face impassive. "Problem?" inquired Adama.

"It's crazy. She's a Cylon. Cylons don't have lawyers."

"Apparently they do now."

"Why me?"

"Because I want someone with a different perspective than my own watching the two of them interact."

"A Cylon who looked just like the one we have locked up shot my father," Lee reminded him unnecessarily. "What makes you think your perspective is going to be any different than mine?"

"Because it often has been in the past. And because you're not the one who was shot. Now head down to the brig." When Lee, looking conflicted, didn't immediately move, Adama said, "That was not intended as a request."

With an irritated why-me sigh, Lee said, "Yes, sir," turned away, and headed off to do as he'd been instructed.

Sharon Valerii was lying on her bunk, slowly rubbing her hand across her swollen belly. She'd felt the baby stirring recently. The first time she'd felt it move, there had been the thrill of amazement that any pregnant woman feels whenever there are the first stirrings of life within her, fluttering like the wings of a butterfly. She felt a flare of jealousy, or at least envy, for other women who were able to share such moments of discovery and excitement with their husbands or lovers. Who was she going to tell? The men standing guard outside? There was no one to care for her.

She hadn't even told Helo, the father of her child. The poor bastard had gotten into so much trouble over her. When that bastard officer from *Pegasus* had tried to rape her, both Helo and the chief had intervened on her behalf, and that intervention had almost cost them their lives. Since then . . . well, she hadn't been trying to distance herself from Helo. But she wasn't doing anything to play upon his emotions either. She cared for him far too much to continue pouring fuel onto the raging fire that represented his divided loyalties. Whenever he did stop by, she saw the torment in his eyes every time he looked at her: She was the woman he loved, and yet she was a complete stranger to him. Why make it harder on him, just because it would make it easier on her?

She would have laughed if she hadn't felt like crying. She knew what the others thought of her. They believed her to be a soulless machine. She wondered what they would make of it if they knew that she was beating herself up in an attempt to spare the feelings of others.

There was a sudden noise at the door and, as she always did, she started ever so slightly, and her hand reflexively covered her belly protectively. Sharon never knew what was going to be coming through that door: something as innocuous as food, or as dangerous as someone who was going to try and beat information out of her or—even worse—take her baby from her. In the first days of her imprisonment, she had thought she was going to lose her mind with constantly being on edge. Eventually she had learned to tolerate it. The human ability to adapt to circumstances, no matter how bizarre, was . . .

Human ability.

The Cylons firmly believed that they were far superior to humans. She knew that some of the other models regarded her as weak because she didn't believe that to be true. She believed that going around thinking you're superior is an inherently weak attitude to have. She tolerated their contempt. She told herself that everything she was enduring, all the misery that arose from her sustained exposure to humans, was worth it. Perhaps if she kept telling herself that long enough, she'd even come to believe it.

The door opened and she braced herself. The first person in was Lee Adama, which piqued her curiosity. She hadn't seen Lee all that much since her incarceration, but believed him to be a bit more open minded of an individual than his father. But she was sure she'd never be able to consider him a friend or ally ever again, because whenever he looked at her he would see the face of the woman who tried to kill his father. It hadn't been her, but in the end, it didn't matter. She was still going to carry that stigma to her dying day . . . which might come at any time, and none save Helo and Chief Tyrol, her former lover, would mourn her.

She didn't recognize the next person, though. It was some woman, and she actually seemed pleased to see Sharon. In fact, there was even a look of triumph glittering in her eye. She went straight to the phone, sat down, picked up the receiver, and gestured for Sharon to do the same. Sharon stared at her, still not knowing what was going on, but then she shrugged and did as she was bidden.

"Sharon Valerii?" The woman's voice came through the phone.

It seemed a pretty silly question. Who the hell else would she be? "Yes," Sharon said cautiously.

"I'm Freya Gunnerson, and if you're interested, I'd like to offer my services as your attorney."

Sharon laughed. Then she saw that this Freya person wasn't laughing along with her. Sharon turned her attention to Lee. "Did you put her up to this?"

Lee took the phone and she repeated the question. "She came here to see you," Lee informed her.

"Does the Old Man know about this?"

"Admiral Adama approved it, yes," he said. She noted the cold use of the full name and rank of William Adama, as opposed to the familiar and loving nickname of "the Old Man" that Sharon had just employed. The message was clear: Don't pretend to a familiarity that you're no longer entitled to employ.

"Why did he approve it?"

"I'm not in the habit of questioning the admiral's thinking."

Sharon laughed again. Twice in as many minutes. "Since when? Since before or after he declared you an enemy to the fleet and you took sides against him?"

He was about to reply, but Freya took the phone back.

"If it's all the same to you, Lieutenant," Freya said crisply, "I think it would be advisable if you addressed all your comments to, and through, me from now on."

Sharon stopped laughing and looked at Freya as if seeing her for the first time. "Why would I do that?"

"Because he's not your friend, Sharon. As much as you would like to believe he is . . . he isn't. None of them are. They see you as a machine. They see you as subhuman and a threat. They all think they're better than you are, and they only feel comfortable when you're behind bars. They don't have your best interests at heart."

"Nice to see that you know us so well," Lee snapped, "considering you only met me two minutes ago, and you haven't met anyone else."

"I hear you complaining about my opinions, Captain, but I don't hear you disagreeing." Freya lowered the phone, stood, and fixed a level gaze on him. "But perhaps I missed a meeting somewhere. Would you care to detail for me your history of strident advocacy for granting Sharon Valerii the freedom that your father has deprived her of?" She waited a moment and then said, "Anytime, Captain. Dazzle me with your track record."

Lee said nothing, but merely glowered at her. Nodding in apparent satisfaction, Freya sat once more and turned her attention back to Sharon, who was intrigued by this point. "Who are you again?"

"Freya Gunnerson," she said with no trace of impatience, as if she were accustomed to having people repeatedly ask her who she was. "I told you: If you desire my services, then I'm your attorney."

"And if I don't?"

Freya shrugged. "Then I leave. It's as simple as that. But before I do, I would like to ask you one question: Why would you be opposed to having someone on your side?"

"What 'side' is that?"

"The side that believes you should be allowed to live your life as you see fit," Freya said, pouncing on the question like a lion on a deer. "The side that believes your child shouldn't have to be born imprisoned. And that's another thing, while I'm at it. The constitution of the Colonies clearly states that anyone who is born on a particular colony becomes a citizen of that colony, with that citizenship then extended back to the mother."

"The Colonies were destroyed," Lee Adama spoke up, and added with a glance at Sharon, "by *her* kind."

"They may have been destroyed in fact, but they continue in spirit, as the ongoing existence of the Quorum of Twelve certainly indicates," Freya replied without hesitation. "I don't see the Quorum voting to dissolve itself simply because the worlds upon which they settled were depopulated by the Cylons. As long as the Quorum exists, the spirit of the constitution exists. Which means when the child is born, it becomes a citizen, with the full rights that any citizen has. And the child's mother will have those same rights, so all the nice discussions about whether Sharon Valerii is human or not human and whether she deserves the rights of a human . . . they all become moot."

"You're saying you think I have rights?" asked Sharon.

"I'm saying your incarceration here is a war crime. I'm saying they don't have one damned good reason not to let you walk out of here. That the longer you remain here, the better civil suit you have against them for wrongful imprisonment. You've done nothing to deserve this, nothing to warrant this sort of treatment. And if you allow me to, I'm going to make sure everyone knows it, and that you are accorded your full rights under the law."

"But . . . what if . . ." She looked nervously at Lee and then back to Freya. "But what if you make that argument about my baby and they just take that as an excuse to kill it, like they tried to before."

Freya shook her head and there was a satisfied smirk on her face. "They wouldn't dare. My understanding through my sources is that your baby's blood performed the miraculous healing of the president. What if she relapses? What if someone else becomes drastically ill? How would Lee Adama feel about it if . . . oh, I don't know . . . Kara Thrace, one of his top pilots, suddenly discovered she had breast cancer?"

"You leave her the frak out of this," Lee snapped.

Freya's smirk grew wider. Clearly she was pleased that she had gotten under Lee's skin so quickly. Sharon felt badly for Lee's discomfort . . . and suddenly wondered why she did. After all, he was out there and she was in here. He was allied with those who wanted to keep Sharon locked up forever. When the soldiers had come to try and abort her pregnancy, it had been Helo who stood in their way, not Lee Adama. *He is not your friend* . . .

She found herself looking at Freya with new eyes. "The point is," the lawyer was continuing, "they don't dare do anything to your baby now. They might need it for something. But if you have any interest in making sure that your child is something other than a lab rat . . ."

Sharon put up a hand, her mind racing, and Freya immediately lapsed into silence. "What's in this for you?" she asked.

Freya laughed softly. "People keep asking me that. Lieutenant . . . sometimes people just do things because they feel it's the right thing to do. I think you knew that, once upon a time. It could be that you've simply forgotten that. I wouldn't blame you, considering everything you've been put through."

"Everything *she's* been put through?" Lee seemed astounded. "How about everything she's put everyone else through?"

"My understanding, Captain, is that you're here to observe the proceedings, not contribute," Freya reminded him. "If you would kindly adhere to what's expected of you, this would all go much faster and much more smoothly." When Lee didn't reply, she tilted her head as if that settled it and once again returned her attention to Sharon. "In any event, Lieutenant . . . believe it or not, I'm just doing this because I feel it's right."

"I'm not entirely sure I believe you," Sharon said.

"You don't have to. I'm perfectly happy to let my actions prove my worth."

"And what would those actions be? What's the best-case scenario?"

"The best-case scenario," Freya said, looking pleased to be discussing the specifics of the case, "is that they throw open the door and you walk out."

Sharon ignored the amused snort from Lee. "If they do that . . . I'm a dead woman walking," Sharon said, unaware that she was saying aloud what had been going through Adama's mind earlier. "You'll be able to measure my life expectancy in microns."

"Not necessarily," Freya told her. "The residents of the *Bifrost*, where I live, would offer you sanctuary."

"I should have known," Lee said with a roll of his eyes. "Religious extremists."

"I can't say I appreciate the slander of my people or my beliefs."

Sharon looked from one to the other in puzzlement. "Extremists? What is he—?"

Freya was about to respond, but Lee did it for her. "They don't believe what everyone else believes," he called to Sharon loudly enough so that his voice carried over the phone. "They don't even believe in the gods. In the Lords of Kobol."

"Neither do I," Sharon said.

Lee blinked in surprise. For a moment, it was as if he'd forgotten he was staring into the face of the enemy. "You don't?"

"Cylons believe in one god, Lee. Not many."

"You're kidding. Why?"

"I don't think this is truly the time for a deep theological discussion," Freya interrupted. "You have to understand, Lieutenant . . . may I call you Sharon . . . ?" When Sharon nodded, she went on, "You have to understand that people such as Captain Adama tend to see things in extremes. Either you're with him or against him. There's not much tolerance for simple differing opinions. We are not extremists. We simply believe other than what Captain Adama and his friends believe . . ."

"My 'friends' in that instance being almost everyone else in the Colonies," Lee said.

"That's as may be. But we're not extremists. And since we've historically been in the minority, we tend to be more accepting of other minorities. We have a live-and-let-live approach. I assure you, you would be safe from harm in the *Bifrost*. You and your child would be allowed to live free, as the gods . . . or god," she included with a nod of her head toward Sharon, "intended you to."

"I . . . I don't know," Sharon said uncertainly.

"I think you do know," Freya replied. She appeared sympathetic, but there was a look of steel in her eye. "I think you already realize that I'm your first, best chance for getting out of here. The difficult thing for you," she added sympathetically, "is letting go of your fading hopes that any of your old ties to these . . . individuals . . . are going to do you any good. They are your past, Sharon. I'm your future. Are you going to live in your past . . . or embrace your future?"

"Can . . ." Sharon hesitated, glancing once more at Lee, and then said, "Can I have some time to think it over?"

"Of course," said Freya. She stood and said, "Take all the time you want. I mean . . . it's not as if you're going anywhere."

With that, she headed out, Lee Adama right behind her. He cast a glimpse at Sharon over his shoulder, but she didn't meet his eye. Instead she was staring off into space, lost in thought, with her hand unconsciously rubbing her belly.

CHAPTER 11

Laura feels at peace, for the first time in a long time. She feels at peace because there is no question in her mind this time. The line between fantasy and reality is clearly demarcated. She has no doubt that she is dreaming now. With that knowledge brings peace of a kind. The recent press conference where figments of her innermost fears were strolling around in the objective light of day was a bit much for her. But this . . . this is definitely within her comfort level.

Yet what she is experiencing is simultaneously comforting and disconcerting.

She hears a heartbeat. It is steady and rhythmic, as a heartbeat should be. It's difficult for her to place where it's originating from, because everything around her is so dark. She strains to find a light source, but none is forthcoming. She tries to hold her hands up in front of her face, but she's having trouble determining whether she's actually moving them or not. She doesn't quite understand why. It's as if her mind is completely disconnected from her body. Still, she's not upset over the lack of light. She's not upset about anything. Instead she feels completely calm and content. Although all her problems are still present in her mind, she nevertheless feels as if she hasn't a care in the world. She is calmer than at any other time that she can recall, and not only that, but she feels totally protected, as if nothing out in the world can possibly hurt her while she floats blissfully in . . .

Oh . . . you have to be kidding . . .

The words echo in her mind and she tries to say them aloud, but her mouth won't form the words.

This can't be happening . . .

Seized with a determination to shake off a dream that had abruptly become far too strange for her to continue, she starts twisting about violently. She is suddenly relieved that she can't see her own body since she isn't sure she could tolerate the bizarreness of what she is now certain she will experience. She feels completely constricted, even though there are no ropes or any other sort of bonds around her.

Then the environment in which she is floating begins to respond to her struggles. There is trembling and violent vibration, and she perceives that there are walls surrounding her, starting to close in, and pushing her down, down through the liquid that is enveloping her . . .

Too weird . . . too weird . . . make it stop, gods, please . . .

But as much as she is repulsed by the reality of what is happening to her, or at least what she thinks is happening to her, there is nothing that she can do to prevent it. She tries to get a sense of herself within the context of the dream, but she cannot. She doesn't know whether this is something that is supposed to be happening to her . . . or to someone else.

She is shoved forward, the walls contracting around her, forcing her against her will. She seeks purchase and finds none. She continues to struggle but it means nothing. She is leaving the warmth behind, and suddenly coldness strikes her in the face. Laura opens her mouth, but nothing except a pathetic mewl escapes her lips.

"Her eyes are open," says a voice, and it's a terribly familiar one. The world is shifting at odd angles around her, and she is looking up into the familiar face of Gaius Baltar. She recognizes him even though he is wearing a surgical mask over the lower half of his face. "Amazing. It's like she's looking right at me."

"It's a girl," the voice of Sharon Valerii moans, "I knew it would be a girl . . . God . . . she's covered in blood."

"We'll clean her off," says Baltar. "Nurse. Come here." He turns and, holding Laura carefully in his blood-covered hands, he extends her to the waiting figure of a Cylon soldier, all gleaming metal and a single,

glowing red eye. Laura screams even louder, and it's still emerging as a babyish cry.

The Cylon takes her from Baltar. Its metal hands are cold, and Laura is shivering from the chill and from the fear. He turns around and walks away. Baltar is shouting for him to come back, and Sharon, who Laura can now see is lying flat on a table with her legs splayed, is reaching out desperately and crying for the Cylon to return her. The Cylon ignores her, walking out of the room, and now they are outside, the Cylon striding away from a small building, its feet clanking steadily. She is looking up at the night sky, and she recognizes the constellations. She has seen them before. She is on Earth. She is home.

Behind her the building explodes in a fireball of sound and flame . . .

She woke up and found that the Cylon warrior's face had been replaced with that of Billy.

She started involuntarily and realized that she was sitting in her office chair, which made perfect sense since she was in her office. For a heartbeat she thought she was still dreaming—again—for how in the world had she gotten from her bedroom to her office? Then, in that disorienting way that always occurs when one wakes up in an unexpected place, she remembered that she had, in fact, already gotten up that morning, and had come to work. She had leaned back in her chair and closed her eyes for just a moment to rest them . . .

. . . at least, she thought that was what she had done. What if she was wrong? What if her memory was playing tricks on her and actually she really was still asleep? Maybe she was even in a coma, and all that was going to happen now was that she was going to keep dreaming about waking up and waking up—

"Madame President . . ."

Billy's voice, filled with unmistakeable concern that was cloaked with a veil of professionalism, said, "Your next appointment is here. Mr. Gunnerson . . ."

"Yes. Yes, of course." She straightened her short jacket and sat forward in as businesslike a manner as she could, doing her best to indicate that she was raring to go. "Bring him in," she said in her most no-nonsense voice.

Billy looked as if he were about to say something, but then thought better of it and simply inclined his head. "Yes, Madame President."

He went out and, moments later, came back in with what appeared to be a walking land mass. Laura kept her face neutral as she rose to greet him, but inwardly she was astounded at the size of the man. He had to bend over slightly to pass through the door, and when he reached out to shake her hand, her hand literally disappeared into his. "Wolf Gunnerson, Madame President. It's an honor."

"A pleasure to meet you, sir," she said, gesturing toward the chair opposite her. He sat, albeit not without effort, as she sat back down in her own chair. She glanced behind him and saw only Billy. "For some reason I was under the impression Councilman Zarek would be joining you to help make your case."

"Councilman Zarek told me he thought it'd be better if I came in on my own. He said"—and Gunnerson raised a bushy, quizzical eyebrow—"that you would probably feel more at ease if he were not here."

She smiled slightly. "Councilman Zarek overestimates his ability to discomfort me. He would have been welcome to join you, but . . ." She shrugged as if it were of little consequence. "So . . . I understand you feel your people should be recognized as . . . what? A thirteenth colony?"

"A fourteenth," he reminded her, "if we count the long-lost colony that may or may not have wound up on our destination of Earth."

"Fair enough."

"For that matter, thirteen has never been the luckiest of numbers. Perhaps increasing the number of colonies—here and gone—to fourteen will change some of the luck we've been having lately."

Laura allowed a small laugh. In spite of herself, she was actually finding the fellow pleasant enough. She hadn't known what she was going to be confronted with: some sort of wild-eyed religious fanatic, perhaps. But this soft-spoken behemoth didn't match her preconceptions.

"I'll take that under advisement," she said evenly. "Somehow, though, I doubt that that will be the sort of convincing argument the Quorum would consider."

"Yes, I know that," he laughed. It was a deep, rumbling laugh that sounded like the beginnings of a ground quake. Then he grew serious and continued, "I'm not naïve, Madame President. I know the way things work. Most of the time, when a decision is to be made about something, the consideration isn't what is right . . . or what's just . . . or what's fair. It's 'What's in it for me?' "

"That's a less-than-charitable view of the world."

"But not less than realistic."

"If you're trying to focus on the realistic," said Laura, "then certainly you have to acknowledge that my voice is merely that: a voice. As I made clear to the councilman, the question of statehood—which is really what you're asking for—is not something that lies within the province of this office. That's in the hands of the Quroum, and the Quorum doesn't answer to me."

"No. But they listen to you. And if you put forward our case, that would carry weight."

"And why would I . . ." She stopped and now they were both smiling. "All right . . . I suppose, yes, I'm saying what's in it for me? Or, more specifically, for the members of the Quorum. I don't dispute that the Midguardians have been treated less than charitably in the past. But that persecution was a long time ago . . ."

"A long time ago in the minds of you and yours. But a mere eye blink to me and mine. And even now, my people remain marginalized because of our beliefs. Dismissed as heretics and unbelievers. We've no active involvement or say in the destiny of humanity. That's not right."

"I don't dispute that," said Laura. "But, despite what you may have read in some of the more enthusiastic publications . . . I am not a god. I don't get to wave my hand and have everyone fall into line. There's—dare I say it—politics involved. And whether we like it or not, that aspect has to be addressed."

"Have you heard," he said, unexpectedly switching topics, "of the book of Edda?"

"Yes. It's your book of history."

"Correct. History of the past . . . and the present . . . and the future. The lifetime of mankind, covered in our verses, with greater accuracy and detail than is to be found in any of your prophecies."

"Well," Laura said, not exactly convinced despite the obvious fervency of his belief. "That's easy for you to say. But having never read it myself, or had access to it . . ."

"That's because the leaders of the 'accepted' religion have done everything within their ability to make certain no one does. After all," and he leaned back, the chair creaking beneath his weight, "if it's learned that someone other than the accepted oracles are able to know what's to come, that would certainly diminish the miracles that support the current belief system. Wouldn't you say?"

"I would say," she said slowly, "that it's easy to complain of so-called conspiracies where none was intended."

"It is indeed . . . just as it's difficult sometimes to convince others that such conspiracies exist. That's what the conspirators typically count upon: disbelief. It's the single greatest weapon at their command."

"Mr. Gunnerson," she said, striving to keep the fatigue from her voice, "with all respect, I feel as if we're going in circles here, and I don't have the time—"

Gunnerson reached into his inner jacket pocket and pulled out a small leather case. Placing it on her desk, he opened it with unmistakeable reverence. There was a small book inside. He removed it, held it up, and said with a touch of pride, "The Edda." He flipped through it with the confidence of someone who knew what was contained on every page and found what he was looking for. He turned to a page toward the back. Then he cleared his throat and said to her, "Understand that I'm not only translating on the fly, but it's supposed to be sung. But I figure you don't need my abysmal attempts at vocalizing, particularly this early in the morning, so . . ."

She gestured for him to proceed, intrigued in spite of herself.

He held up the book and began to read. Although he was, indeed, not singing it, his voice still went up and down in places as if it were meant to be chanted and he couldn't help himself.

> "The day would come, when the prodigal sons
> A gleam in metal, crimson of eye
> Would rain destruction down upon their fathers
> From the tinted sky
> The fathers would run, fleeing from the wrath
> Of sons, accompanied by daughters
> Their eyes would turn toward far-off home
> With verdant land and chill blue waters
> Two ships would guide them, one at first
> The galaxy would be its name
> Accompanied by flying horse
> Very different, much the same . . ."

Her eyes widened, astonishment rippling through her. Gunnerson didn't see it since he was looking down at his book, and when he closed it she had already managed to regain her composure. "There's more," he said quietly. "It describes individuals in the grand scheme of things who match up rather closely to you, Admiral Adama, some others."

"It's . . . impressive," Laura Roslin admitted, but she was not about to simply swallow everything that was being handed her. "On the other hand, hindsight is always twenty-twenty."

"Are you suggesting that these verses were written after the fact?" He sounded amused rather than offended.

"I'm suggesting nothing, merely observing that it's possible."

He held up the book. "Our ancients," he said, "received these words from Woten himself, the father of the gods. They have been part of our people since our people *had* a people. It speaks of a twilight of humanity, in great detail, and everything that is to happen to humanity when that twilight falls. It speaks . . ." He paused, and then said, "Of how we survive. It's all here." He placed the copy of the book back into the small case, and closed it. "Understand . . . that it, and we, represent your salvation."

"How so?" she asked, intrigued but trying not to show it.

"In the book of Edda," he said, "it speaks of a bridge. A glittering bridge that serves as a connector between those who wander . . . which I take to be us . . . and Earth. The literal translation of the text is 'Rainbow Bridge.' The name the Edda accords it is 'Bifrost,' which is where the name of our vessel comes from. Our scholars believe, however, that the bridge is not necessarily a literal rainbow. It could instead be a representation of that which we understand now, but our ancestors could never have found words to frame: a wormhole, or bridge through space. Something that, should we be able to find it, would enable us to complete our journey in an instant. *Bifrost* is our way to our sanctuary . . . in more ways than one. And the Edda . . . tells us how to find it. It would bring us straight to it."

Too good to be true. Most things that are too good to be true . . . aren't. An old warning that her mother used to voice came back to her unbidden, but it was certainly good advice. "You're saying that your book of . . . prophecies, for lack of a better term . . . can get us to Earth?"

"That's exactly what I'm saying, yes," he assured her. "And you've no one to blame for not knowing these verses but your own church elders from centuries ago, who tried to burn all of our holy writings out of existence since they were offended by their very presence. If we'd been accepted when we should have been, then all our wise writings would be at your disposal. But we were not and, therefore, they are not. An unfortunate circumstance for you, certainly, but there's nothing to do about it now. However, give us the equality that we deserve, and you will be welcome to review all of our texts, past and future. To embrace us is to embrace the end of our voyage so that we need not wander anymore."

The offer was a fascinating one. Laura didn't quite know what to say. That in itself was irritating to her, for Laura Roslin had always prided herself on knowing just what to say in any given situation. And then, as she pondered how to respond to this startling offer, she saw something out of the corner of her eye.

It was something just out the window—"viewing port," she mentally corrected herself. Even after all this time, she was still tripping over substituting the appropriate space-going jargon for what had once been the mundane aspects of life. A window was a viewing port, a room was quarters, a wall was a bulkhead; it had taken some adjusting for her, since Laura had always regarded space vessels as merely a mode of transportation from one point to the other, never requiring more than a few hours travel time. Taking up residence in one, well, that was another matter. All of which still left her wondering just what the hell she had spotted out the window.

"Excuse me a moment," she said to Wolf, and got up from behind her desk. Wolf Gunnerson, as protocol dictated, automatically began to stand as well, but she gestured for him to remain in his seat. She went over to the window and looked out.

Sharon Valerii was looking back at her.

Laura staggered back, her mouth dropping open, her eyes wide. The sharp intake of breath naturally caught Gunnerson's attention, and Wolf stood once more, this time out of obvious concern. "Is there a problem, Madame President?"

She didn't hear him, or she heard him, but it didn't really register that someone was talking to her. It wasn't that she was seeing Sharon floating out in space. Rather, she saw her reflected in the window. The reflection exactly matched her movements, and she stared at it long and hard to make certain it wasn't some trick of the light. Slowly she reached up, and Sharon's reflection did the same. She placed her hand flat against Sharon's reflected hand, and Laura spoke softly, so softly that Wolf—sitting not more than five feet away—couldn't hear her.

"Get out of my head," she whispered, her mouth twisted into an uncharacteristic snarl. "Get . . . out . . . of my head."

Sharon's mouth moved as well, and that was when Laura realized that Sharon wasn't mouthing the same words as she was. Instead, Sharon spoke very slowly, the words she was forming easy to discern even if Laura hadn't already had them burned into her mind through what seemed endless repetition.

Sagittarius is bleeding, Sharon said to her.

Laura backed up and banged into a chair. She might well have stumbled over it and hit the floor, but Wolf was on his feet and righted her just before that happened. "Madame President, are you quite all right?"

Don't you see it? How can you not see it? She was pointing at Sharon, who was pointing back, and Laura's hand was quaking. "I . . . ?"

"Madame President?"

The door opened and Billy entered, a notepad under his arm. He was acting in his typical capacity, walking in after five minutes on a meeting that Laura didn't particularly want to attend to remind her of her next appointment. On those occasions when the meeting was going unexpectedly well, she could always tell him to rearrange the rest of her schedule to accommodate her. More likely, Billy's entrance would serve as an excuse for her to end the meeting so that she didn't have to sit and listen to someone make the same point repeatedly over the next fifteen minutes that they'd already made in the past five.

Before Billy could say anything, however, he saw the look in Laura's eyes. Wolf didn't, since her back was to him. There was a flash of concern on Billy's face, but he quickly covered it and said, as if everything was perfectly fine, "Madame President, you have that meeting with—"

"Yes, of course," she said quickly. She was anxious to get Wolf out of the office so that she could focus on what was going on in her head. "Mr. Gunnerson, this has been . . . illuminating."

Sensing the dismissal in her voice, Gunnerson frowned and said, "Madame President, I know I've given you a good deal to think about, and I did not think I would receive an immediate answer. But could you at least give me some indication of where your thoughts are on the matter we've discussed?"

"My thought," Laura said in measured tone, "is that I will most definitely consider it. You've convinced me that the Midguardians have something to offer. Now I have to determine whether there are those who are willing to take that offer. I will remind you that many on the Quorum are fervent in their beliefs, and might have some . . . difficulty . . . in accepting the notion of—"

"Elevating those who disagree with them?"

"Something like that," she admitted.

"I think it more than 'something.' I think it's exactly like that." Wolf Gunnerson didn't sound especially upset about it, more resigned than anything else. "But certainly tolerance can be embraced when mutual benefit is the prize. Although . . ."

"You'd think that tolerance could be embraced for its own sake."

Wolf smiled. The edges of his eyes crinkled when he did that; it gave him a distinctly avuncular look. "I had a feeling I would like you, Madame President. It's good to see that I was correct. I leave you to your considerations." He took a few steps back and walked out the door backwards, bowing to her in a very formal manner . . . or it might have been that it was simply the only way he could get out of the room.

The moment he was gone and Billy was certain they had privacy, he went straight to Laura with obvious concern. "What happened?" he asked.

Laura briefly considered telling him that nothing had occurred, and even scolding him for worrying after her all the time. But then she thought better of it and instead pointed at the window. "What do you see?" she asked.

He looked where she was indicating. "Space," he said slowly, as if he were being asked a trick question and didn't want to fall for whatever the catch was.

"Do you see any reflections?"

"Mine."

"Yes. What else?"

"And . . . yours." He sounded as if he wanted some guidance as to what else he should say. "Is . . . that what you wanted to hear?"

A dozen emotions warred in her head. Slowly she sat in the nearest chair without even realizing that she was doing it. "Billy," she said as if speaking to him from very far away, "someone is in my head."

"You mean like a chip or something?"

"No. No, that would be simple." She took a deep breath and let it out. "I'm sorry, I can't burden you with this . . ." Her mind was racing. She should speak to Doctor Cottle. Or to Adama. Odd how her instinct was drawing her to confiding in him . . . the man who, nearly two months ago, would have seemed the least likely confidant in the world. But she recoiled at the idea. She had just recovered from breast cancer, a disease that had eaten away not only at her body, but at her very soul. Now she was finally regaining her footing as leader of the Colonies, and she was going to start telling the leader of the military that something was undermining her again? She was repulsed by the notion. William Adama was one of the strongest individuals she had ever known, and he had been at her bedside when she was at her most helpless. She knew he didn't think of her as a weak individual, but she simply couldn't embrace the notion of going to him with some new frailty. She had to be strong. As for Doctor Cottle, he'd start ordering up tests, restricting her from work, and sooner or later—probably sooner—the people would start questioning her ability to lead.

"Madame President, you have to talk to somebody, then," Billy insisted. "Whatever is happening—these dreams, these . . . illusions. Perhaps it's left over from the medications you were under, and it'll just work its way out of your system . . ."

"No, it's nothing like that . . . although it may well be, it's . . ." She took another breath, again let it out, trying to cleanse her mind and steady herself. "I don't want you to think I'm insane . . ."

"Never."

". . . but I think . . . Billy," she said, "I think it's the baby."

He stared at her uncomprehending. "You're pregnant?"

Laura appeared stunned for a moment, and then, despite the seriousness of the situation, she laughed aloud. "No. Not that baby . . . I mean, no. I'm not pregnant. Unless a god came down and visited me in my sleep . . ."

"Honestly, Madame President, I wouldn't put it past them."

"Yes, well . . . a valid point. But that's not what I was referring to."

"Then I don't understand what . . ."

"I think . . ." She said it all in a rush, as if the biggest challenge was just to say it and get it out there rather than dwell on it. "I think the Cylon's child has done something to me."

He stared at her. "What?"

"The child. The fetus . . . Sharon Valerii's."

She told him then of the dream she'd had, of being born, of being carried away by a Cylon soldier. The recurring imagery of blood, and the warning about Sagittaron. "I . . . suppose it's possible," he said at last.

Laura wasn't entirely sure how to respond. She was surprised, to say the least. The whole thing had seemed so far-fetched to her that she was almost thinking that simple insanity might be the most reasonable answer.

"You do?" she said with the air of a drowning woman who had had a life preserver tossed to her when she had been bracing for an anchor.

"Yes, of course," he said with increased conviction, as if just thinking about it for a moment helped clarify matters for him. "We're talking about Cylons. We're talking about unknown aspects of biology. Anything is possible." Then he said firmly, "You have to talk to—"

"No."

"Madame President . . . !" he said, clearly frustrated. "You have to—"

"I'm the president, Billy. In case you haven't forgotten, you don't get to tell me what I have to do."

As quickly as he was chastened, she regretted having said it. She patted him on the shoulder and said, "Sorry. I'm sorry about that. You're just trying to help."

"And I can't if you won't let me. The Cylon is trying to . . . to do something to you."

"That's the thing: I don't know that for sure."

"But you just said—!"

"I said I have suspicions," Laura reminded him. "Nothing more than that. Here's the thing, Billy . . . here's what I'm not sure of. That I can't be sure of. What if . . ." She knew this would sound even stranger. "What if she doesn't know?"

"She? You mean Valerii?"

"Yes. Exactly. What if this is happening without her knowledge? What if the unborn Cylon is trying to tell me something?"

It was obvious to Laura that she was starting to reach the outer limit of what Billy would and would not accept. "The *unborn Cylon* is trying to send you a message?"

"You sound skeptical."

"Can you blame me?"

With a small smile, she walked back around to the other side of her desk. "You yourself said we were dealing with Cylons, and anything was possible."

"I know, but . . ."

"If I go to Cottle," she said, as much to give herself the reasons as to convey them to Billy, "he may well come up with some treatment, some form of drugs, that will sever this . . . this connection, if that's what it is. If I tell Adama, I know him, Billy. He'll get right into Valerii's face about it, and there's no telling what might happen then. Hell, she might try to self-abort, and I'm not ready to let that happen."

"Which is somewhat ironic, considering you were ready to abort her child for her."

"Yes, well . . . life is full of little ironies, isn't it," she said ruefully.

Pressing the point, Billy said, "But you still haven't told me why? Even if it were possible, why would it be trying to communicate with you?"

"Because . . . maybe it's afraid."

Billy stood there for a moment, trying to understand the implications of what she was suggesting. "Are you . . . are you saying . . . that the unborn Cylon . . . is . . . what? Asking you for asylum?"

"I was the one who was ready to have it aborted. Perhaps . . . on some level . . . it knows that. And perhaps on some level . . . it's no happier about its heritage than we are, and it's looking to us . . . to me . . . to keep it safe from the Cylons and Cylon influence."

He processed that and then said, "Or . . . maybe it's acting the way a Cylon is supposed to act . . . and is just trying to drive you insane."

"If that's the case," she said with a heavy sigh, "then it may well be succeeding beyond its wildest hopes."

CHAPTER 12

Gaius Baltar sat on the balcony of his former home and stared out at the setting sun. He was seated in his favorite chair with his feet propped up, and he was wearing a short white bathrobe that came down to mid-thigh. This was not the first time that he was making a visit back to the life that he'd left behind. He was never quite sure how he got there, but had learned to stop worrying about it and simply accept it for what it was: a blessing that he, and no one else in the fleet, ever had. For this alone, he was content.

There were two times of day that he had always loved: dawn and sunset. He had never wondered why that was before he had lost his home . . . his planet . . . his life as he knew it. Since then, he'd had plenty of time to ponder it, and had come to the conclusion that those were the times of day that were most in line with his personal philosophy. Others—specifically those who were far less brilliant than he, which was pretty much everyone else—saw the world in terms of absolutes. Black and white, good and bad . . . day and night. Baltar knew that things were far more complicated than that. There were no truths in absolutes. The truth lay in what was in between. The not-quite-day, not-quite-night. It was only when the two aspects of day and night merged that it was possible to discern all sides of the equation.

"So are you satisfied, Gaius?"

He knew whose voice it was, of course. There was only ever the two of them there—Baltar and the mysterious woman who had delighted in seducing and confounding him before Caprica had been bombed into oblivion by the Cylons.

She had never had a name. Even when they were together, she had never told him. It was one of the oddest aspects of their relationship: "You can have all of me," she had whispered the first time they were together, "except my name." She had been true to her word. She had never held back in the heady days of their extremely active sex life . . . but not once, not one time, had she told him her name. "A girl has to have *some* mystery about her," she had told him blithely one day when they were lying naked in bed together. It was typical male behavior, she said, that no matter how much a woman gave a man, he wanted more. "I walk down the street and I see men devouring me with their eyes," she said to Baltar one time when he had become particularly insistent. "They would kill to have just the slightest taste of what I provide you as a full banquet. And you know what?" She had leaned closer in to him, and he had trembled as her tongue slid along the nape of his neck. "They wonder what it would be like to have my legs wrapped around them. To fondle my breasts, to cup my ass in their sweaty hands. They wonder all kinds of things, and the one thing they never . . . ever . . . wonder . . . is what my name is. I leave them wondering. Names have power, Gaius, and I choose to keep my name to myself so that you do not have that power over me."

He had accepted that, for he had really had no choice. He simply wasn't strong enough of character to take a stand on something which—in the final analysis—meant a good deal to her and not much of anything to him.

He half turned in his seat and saw her standing on the stairway that led up to the bedroom, the place where dreams came true. She was wearing a diaphonous red gown, which was fluttering in response to a breeze that didn't seem to exist beyond the immediate area where she was standing. She was leaning against the wall in a posture that was simultaneously alluring and casual. "I said you must be satisfied with yourself, Gaius."

"Oh," he said in an off-hand manner. "Are you talking to me now?"

"Of course." She strolled across the room, one foot placed precisely before the next. She walked like a cat, and there was much of a feline manner about her. "I may get annoyed with you, even put out . . . but I never get so upset with you that, sooner or later, I won't forgive you."

"And what have I done, I wonder," he asked, "that requires forgiveness? Because I didn't do what you wanted me to do? I didn't incriminate an innocent young boy?"

"How do you know that's what he is?" She stood next to him for a moment, and then draped one long leg over him and sat in his lap, facing him. It was all he could do to contain a small whimper. "We both know your Cylon detection test is a sham. He might indeed be one of us."

"Yes, so you said before. Considering you've never been especially forthcoming on the identities of your agents, I'd have to think that the fact you seem determined to hang the boy out to dry reduces the odds of his being a Cylon to practically nonexistent."

"Unless, of course, I know that you'll think that, and am counting on it. Remember, Gaius, there's not a thought that goes through your head that I'm not privy to."

"You're pushing awfully hard on this . . ."

She applied downward pressure with her pelvis. "Oh?"

"On this subject!" Baltar amended quickly, and he ignored the stifled laugh from Six. "I still don't understand your obsession with—"

Abruptly she stood and stepped back away from him. She moved in the way a dancer moved, and it made him feel as if this was all some sort of strange, deluded tango between the two of them. "Because it's in my interest to protect you."

"You mean it's in your interest to control me." He rose from the chair and faced her, feeling powerful, feeling defiant. "What's the matter? Afraid that I'll have power over you now that I know your name . . . Gina?" He saw her face twist in annoyance. "Yes, you can't stand that, can you. I know your name, and that gives me power over you. Didn't you say yourself that's how it works?"

"You know *a* name," she retorted. "A name beaten out of a poor version of me. Isn't it possible that she would have lied about it?"

"It's entirely possible," Baltar admitted, but then added with a sense of smirking confidence, "because—after all—your kind is quite accomplished at lying, aren't you."

She allowed the remark to pass and then, sounding all business, she said, "You need to throw up distractions, Gaius. I think you're tragically oblivious to the amount of danger that you're in."

"And what could possibly give you that impression? Are you going to tell me again that Adama suspects? Let him. Let him suspect all he wants. He can't prove a damned thing and you know it."

"Roslin is suspicious of you as well. She believes you to be a Cylon sympathizer at best . . . a Cylon yourself at worst."

"That's ridiculous," Baltar told her, dismissing the notion out of hand.

"Is it." She circled the room, shaking her head as if he were the most pitiable individual she could ever have hoped to meet. "And how do you know it's ridiculous?"

"Because I just saved the woman's life, for gods' sake! She'd be dead of breast cancer if it weren't for me!"

"That's very true. And I'm sure she's abundantly grateful for your having saved her, isn't she. Think back, Gaius," she said with sudden impatience. "Open your eyes and think back. Did she ever, at any point, say so much as thank you?"

He didn't have to answer her, because she knew the answer as well as he: Laura Roslin had never thanked him. In fact, she had done quite the opposite. He had been there shortly after the treatment had been administered and her cancer-free status had been verified. He'd shown up in her hospital room, and he had been expecting . . . something. Some sort of thanks, some measure of gratitude. But he had gotten nothing. Oh, she had received him in her room cordially enough, and she had made small talk about impending business and how long it would take her to return to her duties. She had asked him about the expectations of reasonable recovery time.

But she had not thanked him, or given the slightest indication that she was at all appreciative of what he had done for her. Quite the opposite, in fact. She had watched him with great suspicion, jumped on any comments that could remotely be misconstrued. It seemed as if she had been looking for things to criticize, to find . . . wrong . . . with him.

Why? Why would she come out of her coma, her near-death experience, with new and increased suspicions regarding Baltar? Was there something that he had said or done that had made her think something was wrong with him?

"You still don't get it, do you?" said Six.

"Not readily, no," he admitted. "But I very much suspect you're going to tell me."

"For someone who purports to be a genius, you're not always very bright, Gaius. It comes down to something as simple as this:

When someone is on the verge of death, all the detritus is stripped away from their mind. Take it from someone who has died several times in her existence. Nothing clears the mind like impending demise, and things that may have been obscured by time and distance suddenly snap into very clear relief."

"What, are you saying that because she was going to die, she's now come to some sort of realization about me that she was blinded to before?"

"I'm saying that her behavior is not consistent with someone who damned well should have been grateful considering she would have died without your intervention."

He was about to reply to that, to again issue an automatic denial and express his complete confidence that Laura Roslin had no reason, none, to suspect him. But he didn't say that because he couldn't get the words to come out of his mouth. Finally he said, "Not everyone is skilled at giving thanks to people." He winced even as he said it, because it wasn't remotely convincing even to his own ear. That being the case, it certainly wasn't anything that Number Six was going to buy.

It was, in fact, so unconvincing that she didn't even deign to address it. Instead she said, "Something's in the air, Gaius. You can feel it. You can smell it. They think they can fool you and even hide it from you . . . but they can't. They're investigating Cylon infiltration in new and aggressive ways, and you've been targeted for suspicion. They're going to do something about it. They're going to try and find evidence."

"How do you know?"

"Because I know humans. In some ways, I know them better than you."

"I see." As far as Baltar was concerned, the entire discussion was becoming ludicrous. "All right, Gina . . . or Six . . . or whatever. Impress me with your knowledge of my people. Tell me what they're going to do to try and find evidence."

"Obviously," said Six, "they'll undertake some manner of surveillance."

"Surveillance? You mean spy on us?" Baltar snorted derisively at that. "Adama would never approve something like that. I know the man . . ."

"As well as you knew me? As well as you knew what I was capable of?" She lowered her voice to a whisper, as if somehow it was possible to spy on the deepest arenas of this thoughts. "You want to believe you're so much smarter than the rest of them, Gaius. You want to believe that you're above reproach. But we both know you live your life with one eye cocked over your shoulder to make sure that no one is watching you. You have a dark, terrible cloud hanging over you, and you're constantly aware of it. You are the betrayer of humanity, Gaius. How long do you think you're going to be able to live with that?"

"As long as it takes," he growled.

"If they want to believe they have an infiltrator, let them. Let them have the boy. At the very least, it will buy you time. Time you desperately need."

"No," he said firmly, "I won't . . ."

"Do this for me. You owe me this much."

Baltar laughed grimly at that. "I owe you? As if I haven't done enough for you already."

"Then do it for yourself. Check your lab for listening or viewing devices. Sweep your lab and come up with one. I'm sure I'm right. If I'm wrong—if I have done a disservice to the noble humans who run the *Galactica*—then I shall never make mention of it again."

"As if I'm supposed to believe that."

She hesitated, and then said with great solemnity, "If you do as I ask . . . I'll tell you my real name. Not the fake one that Gina told her captors. My real name."

"Is that so?" He sounded amused but also intrigued.

She nodded. "That's so. Just do as I ask."

Baltar, having returned to his chair, leaned back on it, tilting the front legs up a bit. "I will . . . consider it. I'm telling you, though, it's a waste of time."

He waited for her to respond. When she didn't, he turned around and saw that she was gone. That was extremely strange. It was one thing for her to disappear into nowhere when she was intruding into the real world. At such times, she delighted in spurring Baltar on into conversations that always made him appear foolish. But she had no reason to make herself scarce while inhabiting his waking dreams.

This anomaly in her behavior was the first thing in their entire encounter that actually made him start to wonder.

It hadn't been all that difficult for Baltar to obtain the equipment that he required to accomplish the task.

The result was that he was crouched in his lab, underneath his table, staring in wonderment at a small round device that he never,

ever would have spotted on his own, even if he'd been looking straight at it. He needed the additional help of the detector, a small device with a wand and a helpful flashing light that blinked with greater frequency when pointed directly at what he was seeking.

"Gods," he said, except he didn't speak it aloud. Instead he mouthed it. His mind was racing over the past several days. He had no idea how long it had been there, and he racked his memory, trying to determine if he had had one of his doubtless incriminating conversations with Six while in the lab. He was reasonably sure that he had not. He had to think that if he had said anything that sounded truly treasonous, Adama wouldn't have simply stood there and traded barbs with him that other day. He'd have had him arrested and Baltar would be in a cell by this point. It was reverse logic, he knew, but it seemed sound to him. Perhaps there had been enough in Baltar's manner that had prompted Adama to start bugging him since that day, but the scientist had presented nothing sufficiently concrete for the authorities to act upon beyond that. Which meant he was safe.

Frakking bizarre definition of "safe," he thought grimly.

But once he got over his initial panic, he came to a realization: As with all things, knowledge was power. His impulse had been to reach for the bug, to crush it beneath his heel as he would the device's namesake. But he paused with his hand in mid-reach and then slowly lowered it. If he destroyed the bug, they would know that he knew. The fact that he was so nervous about being eavesdropped upon would in itself be regarded as something suspicious. Now, however, he had the upper hand. They didn't know that he knew they were eavesdropping.

Which meant that they would tend to take at face value whatever they heard.

Which meant that he could throw them off the track if he said the right things.

Which meant that if they were looking for Cylon infiltraters, all he had to do to throw them off the track was give them someone else. To name names.

Lee Adama. Give them Lee Adama. Or . . . Roslin! Even better! Two birds with one stone . . .

The more he considered such things, though, the more he realized that he had to rein in his impulses. If he tried to point them in a direction that seemed too far-fetched, they might reject it out of hand due to their damnable loyalties and instead focus even more attention on him.

Which meant that the best thing to do was point the finger of suspicion at someone whom they already had uncertainties about.

Which brought him right back to where Six had been days ago.

He started to stand and almost banged his head on the table. Slowly he eased he way out from under and sat in a chair, forcing himself to come to a conclusion that he despised . . . but that was necessary. He had his own survival to think about.

He became aware of her gaze upon him before he looked in her direction. She said nothing, but instead put a single finger to her lips in a *shhh* motion. Then she slowly, and a bit overdramatically, pointed at something. He turned his gaze to where she indicated and his gaze fell upon that which he already knew she was indicating.

It was Boxey's blood sample.

He felt a stinging in his eyes, tears welling up slightly, and just as quickly he brought an arm across his eyes and wiped them away. He hated his weakness. He despised Six for the weakness that she brought out in him.

At the same time, he picked up his portable recorder and spoke into it with a voice that was flat, even, and impressively clinical:

"Laboratory note, follow-up to test results of subject Boxman. Standard recheck of Cylon/Human veracity test indicates possible invalid results due to possible corruption of test sample because of unforeseen circumstances . . . specifically the sterile conditions of pertinent testing equipment may have been . . ." He sought the right word. ". . . breached. Reason for this suspected breach remains unknown at this time. Resolution: I will resterilize all relevant lab equipment and retest. Enough of the original sample of subject Boxman's blood remains that subject will not need to be reacquired. If results come back identical to the first, then will chalk it up to simple lab error rather than something . . . suspicious . . . and there will be no need to alert the authorities of this revised finding since it would be fundamentally unchanged. If results are different, then Admiral Adama must immediately be informed so that . . ." He gulped deeply and watched as Six nodded in slow approval. She licked her lips enticingly. ". . . So that proper defensive action can be taken."

Anastasia Dualla had no idea what to make of Billy Keikeya.

It wasn't the first time she'd felt befuddled by her on-again/off-again relationship with the presidential aide. There was no doubt that they were friends. She enjoyed spending time with him. They'd even had some serious make-out sessions. But she wasn't entirely

certain where the relationship was going, or even if it was going anywhere at all.

So she had invited Billy over to share a nice homemade dinner,
which was an impressive achievement considering that she couldn't
cook worth a damn. That little fact had never bothered her before.
She had jokingly stated on more than one occasion that she'd joined
up with the military specifically so that she never had to worry about
making meals for herself ever again. She would just eat her meals in
whatever mess hall was on hand and that would be that.

But this night she was getting together with Billy, and she wanted
it to be special. The problem was that she had no cooking facilities in
her quarters. So she'd gone to the mess hall and convinced the cooks
there to let her try her hand at preparing a nice dinner that she could
then take out and back to her quarters. There, she told herself, she
would be able to boast to Billy that she had made it with her own two
hands.

Unfortunately, her cooking acumen did not magically improve as
she endeavored to prepare a couple of nice steaks for the two of
them. Instead she had come damned close to burning both pieces of
meat and only some timely intervention by the chefs on hand had
averted disaster. They managed to salvage her efforts and even provide a nice presentation of the meal, which Dualla proudly brought
back to her quarters and endeavored to keep warm as Billy ran late.

And later.

And later.

Finally, a good hour and a quarter after Billy was supposed to
have arrived, there was a knock at Dualla's door. The food might no
longer have been warm, but Dualla was certainly seething. "Come
in," she said with a tone that indicated all hope should be abandoned by those who entered.

Billy hesitated a moment and considered running in the other direction, because Dualla's voice made it clear that he was in as much
trouble as he already suspected he was. But, deciding to be a man
about it, he sucked it up and entered with a smile plastered on his
face. He proudly held up an honest-to-gods small plant, with beautiful blue cup-shaped flowers blossoming at the top. He said, "Sorry
I'm late. Things got a little . . . crazy . . ."

"For this late," Dualla said icily, "I'd expect you to be sporting at
least three visible wounds." In spite of herself, she focused on the
bouquet he was extending toward her. "You hang up my beautiful

dinner which, by the way, I worked my ass off to prepare for you, and you think you can bribe your way back into my good graces with some flowers?"

"That was pretty much my feeble hope, yeah," he admitted.

She grunted at that and then, in spite of herself, extended a hand. He crossed the room and handed her the flowers. She brought them up to her face and inhaled deeply, and then—against all of her better impulses—moaned in pleasure. "My gods," she intoned in a voice that bordered on the orgasmic, "where did you get these? How the frak is it possible?"

"Connections," he said.

She opened her eyes narrowly and eyed him with suspicion. "You didn't get these from the black market, did you?"

"What a ridiculous question," he said quickly. "You know how the president feels about that. I can't believe you'd even ask me."

"A ridiculous question . . . and yet I can't help but notice that you've yet to answer it."

"That's because I'm astounded that you would even begin to insinuate that—"

"All right," Dualla said. She hadn't forgotten how annoyed she was with him, and yet she couldn't help but laugh. "All right, forget it. Forget I asked. Forget I said anything about it at all. Anything I should know about the care and feeding of this?"

"Well," he said, "you'll probably need to acquire a lamp that simulates sunlight. Otherwise I'm not sure it'll keep blooming."

"I see. And where do you suggest I get such a device?"

Billy paused a moment and made a great show of thinking, even though he had undoubtedly thought about it before. "I know a guy who knows a guy who knows a girl," he said after much consideration. "Not that it's anyone connected with the black market, of course, because I would never—"

She put up her hands in surrender. "Let's have dinner, you big idiot."

The steak was naturally stone cold, and she thought it was tough as boot leather. But he made a great show of loving every bite, and was so enthused about the quality of the meal that she was having trouble staying mad at him. By the time dinner was over, as much as she hated to admit it, she had more or less allowed her once-towering irritation to vanish into the lost recesses of her memory.

"So how's the investigation going?"

"Investigation?"

"You know," he prompted. "Into trying to figure out how the Cy-lons knew where we were going to be making our Jump."

"Oh." She shook her head wearily, then stood and proceeded to clear away the dinner dishes. "Honestly, I don't know. From what I hear, Tigh is conducting it. He grilled me up one side and down the other, and since then he's moved on. I couldn't tell you who's on the hot seat now. What a frakking prick he is."

"I honestly don't understand why Adama keeps him on as executive officer," Billy admitted. "I wonder about it from time to time . . ."

"Yeah, well, I wonder about it a lot more than that," said Dualla. "The man is a boozer and a frak-up, and everyone in CIC knows it. Hell, everyone on the ship knows it."

"Does he know they know it?"

"Who knows?" She cleaned off the dishes in the sink, wiping them with a towel, and said, "And how are things with Roslin?"

"Fine."

Something in the way he said it caught her attention. She contin-ued wiping the plate but she wasn't especially paying attention to it. "What's wrong?"

"Wrong? Nothing."

"Billy," she put down the plate. "What's going on?"

"Going on?"

"Yes."

"What makes you think," he asked, "that something's going on?"

"Because I know you," said Dualla, moving across the room. She turned the chair around and sat, straddling it. "Whenever you're ly-ing about something or trying to hide something from me, you start repeating the ends of my sentences."

"Repeating the—?" He caught himself and scowled with irrita-tion. "That's absurd," he said, but as protests went, it sounded ad-mittedly lame.

"It's not absurd. Is something wrong with the president?"

"Dualla," he said patiently, "even if there was something wrong—which I'm not saying there is, but even if there were—you know I couldn't tell you."

"I don't know that at all, Billy," she replied, clear irritation in her voice. "I thought we had at least some degree of trust built up, you and me."

"We do."

"Well, then—?"

"But President Roslin trusts me, too. Are you asking me to make a choice between those two levels of trust?"

"Yeah. Yeah, that's exactly what I'm . . ." Her voice trailed off and she looked down. "No," she sighed, clearly annoyed with herself that she had said anything. "No, of course not. Especially when, y'know . . . you've obviously made the choice. Your loyalty to the president is . . . it's admirable."

"Thank you. But . . ."

She looked up. "But what . . . ?"

"But it's always going to put us on opposite sides, isn't it. Because your loyalty to Adama is always going to be more important than to me, and my loyalty to Roslin is going to be more important than you. And if we're going to have any sort of a relationship, the first thing that has to happen is that each of us is more important to each other than anything. So basically we're screwed."

Her jaw twitched, because there was so much she wanted to say in response to that. But in the end, all she could think of to say in reply was, "Seems to me like you've got it pretty worked out."

"No, I don't," he insisted, shaking his head. "I don't have anything worked out at all. Because there's still so much that I want to say, and—"

"How about this, then." Dualla was on her feet, putting up a hand to silence him. "How about you don't say it. How about we just . . . we just let this one lie here for a while."

"Dee, I still want to—"

"Want to what, Billy?" she said, trying and failing to keep the exasperation out of her voice. "Want to talk some more about how hopeless everything is, and how we should just give up?"

"I didn't say any of that!"

"Well . . . I did. Because you know what, Billy? If I can't even ask a casual question about how the president of the Colonies is without getting a whole lecture on divided loyalties, then I don't really see the point of any of this."

"Oh, come on, Dee . . ."

"I gotta go."

"What?" He was dumbfounded by her reaction. "Dee, we can still—"

"I have to go to a meeting."

"Of what?"

"Of . . . the People Under Suspicion by Tigh support group. You can let yourself out, okay?" She moved quickly toward the door and was out before Billy could say anything more.

She headed off down the hall, her mind swirling with frustration and anger that was directed both at Billy and herself. She felt that she had handled the whole thing very badly. The truth was that he hadn't said anything that hadn't already occurred to her as well. She had just wanted to believe that she was wrong, and despised the notion that matters might be as hopeless as he was indicating. What angered her in particular was that he'd been so matter-of-fact about it. At the very least, he should sound as if the entire prospect was tearing him up inside. Instead he was giving a simple, clinical analysis of their situation in the same manner that he might have presented a report on the economy to the president.

Was she being unreasonable? Maybe. But at that moment she didn't particularly care.

And what was worse, she wasn't entirely sure she cared about Billy all that much.

She hadn't wanted to admit it to herself, but although Billy had been a pleasant enough dalliance . . . and although she'd always think he was one of the sweetest guys in the world . . . lately her thoughts and attentions had been shifting elsewhere. There had been something—she wasn't sure what, but something—connecting lately between her and Lee Adama. She had no idea where it might lead. But it was sufficient to make her think there was something there worth exploring. She just couldn't do it, of course, while she was involved with Billy.

Or could she?

After all, Billy didn't know. They hadn't promised fealty to each other. There might have been a vague sort of "understanding," but nothing had been stated implicitly. Perhaps what she really needed to do was compare and contrast. See for herself how it felt being with each of them, and which brought her more . . . satisfaction.

It might not have been fair to either of them, but it was all she could think of. Because she didn't want to break Billy's heart for no reason, but she didn't want to slam the door on exploring her feelings about Lee.

Billy, meanwhile, was dwelling on the fact that he might well have had dates in the past that ended abruptly, but it was hard to recall any of them going down in flames quite this badly. He tried to imagine just how it might have gone better, what he could possibly have said to her that would have prevented their evening from dissolving into a pained discussion of loyalties and politics.

"Well, Dee," he said with a faux jovial attitude, "it's funny you should ask about President Roslin. See, she's been having such horrific dreams for a while now that she can't sleep through the night anymore. She's starting to hallucinate; she's acting erratically. She's the strongest woman I've ever known, and she's beginning to come unravelled. And . . . here's the most interesting part . . . she thinks that the reason that she's having all these dreams is because Sharon Valerii's unborn child is influencing her somehow. Maybe trying to torment her. Maybe trying to warn her. Hard to say. So . . . how's your day been?" He sat back, closed his eyes and moaned softly. "Yeah. Yeah, that would go over really well. Good way to go with that, Billy. That would have enamored her of you and kept confidence boosted in Roslin while we're at it." He was beginning to think he was going to have to resign himself to the idea that not only was his relationship with Dualla going nowhere, but he might well never have a relationship with a woman ever again.

And as he pondered the bleak landscape that represented his dating life, he was completely unaware that he had just managed to accomplish the one thing that he never would have done consciously. He had just betrayed Laura Roslin.

CHAPTER 13

In his quarters at the end of a very long day, William Adama was coming to the realization that his day was about to get even longer.

He listened for the second time to the recording that Tigh had brought him and was still having trouble believing what he was hearing. He'd been listening via an ear piece, for Tigh—ever cautious—felt that it was best not to play back the recordings in the very, very off chance that someone might wander past and hear their own conversation coming from Adama's quarters. Now Adama removed the ear piece from his ear and looked up at Tigh in clear astonishment . . . which for Adama, who had a reputation for a stoic expression that bordered on the inscrutable, amounted to a flicker of surprise in his gaze. "Are you sure he didn't know we were listening in?"

"Obviously, I have no way of knowing for certain," Tigh replied. "But it certainly sounds like Keikeya is talking to himself, and that he has his guard down. That's he's not saying it for our ears alone."

Adama leaned back in his chair and stroked his chin thought-fully. "Why wouldn't Roslin say anything to me about it, if she's hav-ing these sorts of concerns?"

"Who can ever understand women?" Tigh shrugged. "They have their own way of thinking. Maybe she was concerned how you'd re-act to it. Maybe she—"

"Was concerned I'd try to stage a coup?" Adama asked humor-lessly.

Tigh's mouth twitched as he replied, "Well . . . it's not like it would be unprecedented."

"I know, Saul. I was there . . . for some of it, at least." He shook his head. "My chickens finally coming home to roost. She's afraid to come across as unstable because she's concerned I'll take steps to en-sure continued, strong leadership. She doesn't trust me."

"Should she?"

Adama looked up at Tigh, and although the question irritated him, he knew that it was also a perfectly valid one. Worse, he had no answer. He wanted to feel as if she could . . . that she should . . . trust him. But based upon what had happened before, there really wasn't a reason for her *to* trust him.

He knew there was no real reason he should feel hurt about this. Yes, granted, he and Roslin had been through a lot since those early days of mistrust and accusations. He would never say it aloud, but in some perverse way, Sharon Valerii's murderous assault on him had been one of the best things that had ever happened to him. Before the incident, he had tried to transform himself into what he thought the last remnants of humanity required: a hard-edged, hard-bitten, brutal-as-necessary commander who was perfectly willing to steamroll over anyone or anything that got in the way of his very simple goal: sur-vival. He had even bald-facedly lied to his own people, telling them that he had known the "secret location" of Earth. It was a pre-posterous lie, one that never would have survived even the most mini-mal scrutiny. But that scrutiny was never applied to him, for two reasons. First, because they all trusted him implicitly. And second, they wanted—needed—to believe in something. They had to believe that the bleak existence they had had thrust upon them was not all that was left to them. There had to be something more, and Adama had pro-vided it for them. He'd given them hope when he himself felt none . . . and that knowledge had created a great divide between Adama and his people. He would watch them soldiering on as if from a great height looking down. It made him feel more detached than ever before.

No wonder the gods had left them to their fates. No wonder they simply stood by and let humanity be nearly annihilated by the Cylons. Legend had it that the gods sat in residence upon a mountain and looked down upon humanity. If that was the case, then they had spent ages beyond imagining becoming more and more distant, to the point where they probably didn't give a damn what happened to human beings anymore. Adama would never have been able to understand that attitude . . . until he had created a barrier between himself and the rest of humanity that they didn't even know was there.

All that had changed after the humanizing experience of being gunned down. It had rattled his confidence about making correct decisions down to its very core. After all, he'd been in the midst of congratulating Boomer on a job well done. When she had pointed her gun at him, he had been staring straight at it but his mind was unable to process what was happening. His instinct was that there was some sort of threat directly behind him and she was acting to protect him. When the first of the bullets had thudded into his chest, he had been astonished. Before he'd lapsed into unconsciousness, it never occurred to him that she was a Cylon. All he could think was, *She missed whoever she was shooting at behind me. She's going to be so embarrassed.*

He had learned the truth of it later, of course. And the experience of being at death's door had humbled him, even humiliated him. There's nothing that makes one stop and take stock of oneself more than being face to face with one's own mortality. His decisions, and the fallout from them, had shattered the fleet. He had put it back together . . . and discovered in the process, thanks to the mule-headed determination of Laura Roslin, that the great lie wasn't that at all. There really was an Earth, and there really was a way to get there. President Roslin had removed a huge burden from him, erasing the divide in one stroke because the lie was the truth.

He owed her a debt so gargantuan that he didn't think he could ever adequately explain it to her. So he hadn't even tried. He had, however, done everything he could to support her. To be a friend and confidant to her.

And this was the result. She still didn't trust him, even though he'd been as supportive of her as he possibly could be, particularly since he'd learned of her cancer . . .

"Maybe she thought I was pitying her," Adama said softly.

Tigh looked at him in confusion, not quite understanding what it was that Adama was talking about. "Pitying her?"

"Perhaps she thought that I was simply 'pretending' to be her friend. After all, I knew she wasn't going to be around much longer. So why spend a lot of time arguing with her when time would solve my problem."

"But that's not what you were thinking," said Tigh. "Not at all. I know that."

"Maybe she doesn't."

"Well, you can tell her . . ."

"Tell her what?" Adama said bleakly. "Tell her that I know of her situation because we eavesdropped on her aide? How's that going to inspire trust, exactly?"

"Because *we* didn't do it," Tigh said.

Adama didn't follow what Tigh was saying at first, but then he saw the look in Tigh's eyes and suddenly it was clear to him. "No," he said firmly.

"I did it, unilaterally," Tigh said as if Adama hadn't spoken. "Then, when I heard the results of this, I came to you and told you. You chewed my ass—"

"Saul—"

"—and then decided that, as President Roslin's friend, you couldn't simply ignore this evidence that had been brought to your attention. So you're coming to her now, out of conscience."

"Saul, you asked my permission and I gave it."

"And no one needs to know about that except you and me," Tigh said. "What's the worst that could happen? She'll despise me? She already despises me."

"How do you know that?"

"Because she's met me. I'm a prick. Ask her. Ask Dualla. Ask anyone."

Adama snorted in amusement at that. Saul Tigh might have had weaknesses—but self-delusion certainly wasn't one of them.

And Tigh, all seriousness, said, "Bill . . . you're the one who needs to have a solid working relationship with the president. Not me. Tell her that I acted on my own initiative. She'll believe it."

"You really feel the way for me to gain her trust," Adama said in a slow, measured tone, "is to lie to her?"

"Of course," said Tigh matter-of-factly. "Have you got a better suggestion?"

He sat and waited, his hands folded on his lap, for Adama to reply.

"What else have you got?"

"Pardon?"

"What else," said Adama, "have you picked up so far in the eavesdropping?"

"Oh. Well . . . Doctor Baltar was making some sort of noise about having to recheck that boy's bloodwork."

"You mean Boxey? There's some doubt now that his original results were correct?"

Tigh shrugged. "That's the impression I was getting."

"Wonderful. Well, I suppose we'll hear about that one sooner rather than later. Find out where Boxey is, just so we have a clear idea. That way if we need to take him, we can do so with minimal effort."

"We never should have let him leave," Tigh said in annoyance. "Counting on the discretion of a teenager . . ."

"The alternative was to make him a permanent 'guest' in one of our luxurious cells," Adama pointed out. "At which point, child services was going to come sniffing around, and presto, the media announces we're arresting children for no apparent reason. Let's face it, Saul . . . sooner or later, word is going to get out about Sharon. We can delay it, but not indefinitely. And throwing anyone in the brig who knows about her and isn't military issue is just going to expedite it."

"How can you keep calling it 'Sharon'?" Tigh asked. "There is no 'Sharon.' There never was. There was just a thing pretending to be human."

Adama said nothing at first, and then finally: "Anything else?"

Shifting uncomfortably in his chair, Tigh said, "Well . . . there's one thing that I find rather disturbing personally."

"And that would be—?"

"Frankly," he said in a severe tone, "several of our junior officers spend entirely too much downtime engaged in self-frakking. Certainly there has to be something more constructive they can be doing."

Adama's face could have been carved from slate. "Get. Out."

"Yes sir," Tigh said quickly and exited Adama's quarters.

Laura slowly rose from behind her desk, her eyes widening in astonishment, and Adama could have sworn that her face paled slightly. "Listening devices?"

He nodded. "I was shocked," he deadpanned. "Not surprised. But shocked."

Her gaze never shifted from Adama's. "And Tigh just . . . just did this of his own accord? Without consulting you at all?"

Adama took a deep breath and let it out slowly, ready to hang Tigh out on the far end of the branch and then watch as Laura took a saw to it. He found, to his fascination and disappointment, that he was unable to do so. Interesting, considering how effortlessly he'd lied to far more people than one woman and done so with facility. But, as he knew all too well, that was the pre-shooting Adama. He didn't have the stomach for it anymore.

"No," sighed Adama, and he lowered his gaze. "I gave you the impression that Tigh was acting alone, but he did not. He came to me and I approved it."

She looked stunned at the admission. "Admiral," she gasped. "How . . . how could you—?"

"Because we still don't know how the Cylons acquired our Jump coordinates, and our security is at stake," said Adama, sounding far more reasonable than he thought he was under the circumstances. "We have to take a different approach to resolving that problem, and if it means that some people's rights are lost in the process, then I for one have no trouble living with that."

"And how about if *they* have trouble with it?" Laura demanded.

"Then I'll live with that. Because the bottom line is that they want me to make the hard decisions involved in protecting them. Whether they admit it to themselves or not, they want me for that. They may grumble and grouse and cry foul, but at the end of the day, they're relieved that people like Saul Tigh and myself are taking point in doing what needs to be done."

"Just tell me if it was Tigh's idea or yours."

"What difference does that make?"

"To me? It makes a great deal of difference."

He briefly considered stonewalling her on the matter, but rejected it. Once upon a time, he could have done that without hesitation. Now, it wasn't really an option. "He suggested it; I ordered him to implement it. So if you're going to blame someone—"

"I'm not interested in issuing blame, I . . ." She hesitated, and then in a rare display of anger, she slapped her palms on the desk in frustration. "Dammit, Bill! Do you have any idea what a violation this . . . this program is? I feel violated, and I wasn't even among the ones bugged!" She paused in mid-outburst and said slowly, "I'm not, am I?"

"No. Just the residents of *Galactica*. It's a military vessel, and frankly, Madame President, it's understood that when you sign up for the service, there are certain aspects of your life that you're giving up. The option to refuse to do what you're told, for one. Privacy for another."

"Not that much privacy. It's wrong, Admiral, and you know it."

"Yes. I do," Adama said evenly. "I also know it's wrong not to do everything within my power to ensure the safety of the fleet. Whenever those two imperatives come into conflict, I will always—always—err on the side of the safety of the fleet. Frankly, I would think that's a mindset you could readily understand."

"Don't act like you're taking the moral high road."

"I'm not. I'm taking the only road available to me. I don't care whether it's lofty or muddy. It's what's there. We don't live in a world of what's right and what's wrong. We live in a world of what's necessary."

"I don't believe that."

"Really," he said stonily. "With all respect, Madame President . . . where was the high road when you wanted me to kill Admiral Cain?"

"That's . . ." Obviously she was about to say that that was completely different, but the protest died before she could complete it. Then she let out a heavy sigh and said, "I suppose I did forfeit the moral high ground on that, didn't I."

"You forfeited nothing, Madame President. I think we both concur that sometimes we have to do things that are unpleasant in pursuit of the greater good. We simply differ on the specifics of what and when."

"I suppose that's as it should be," she admitted. "If we walked in lockstep, we'd never be forcing each other to reconsider our positions. But," and she still looked none too pleased, "I still feel my privacy has been invaded."

"Not intentionally."

"A shot that goes astray and takes down an innocent is no less fatal due to lack of intent. But there's no point in harping on it. What's done is done. And . . . I suppose I should have told you."

Adama considered all the reasons that he'd come up with as to why she had felt she could not do that. As she had just said, though . . . there was no point in harping on it. "One hopes that, should the need arise in the future, you will. For now, at least, I do know." He leaned forward. "Do you truly believe that Valerii's unborn child could be having an influence on you?"

"As we've already learned, we don't know what the Cylons are truly capable of. It's one of the reasons that I wanted the pregnancy aborted. There's too many unknowns attached to its development."

"I agree." He paused and then said, as dispassionately as he could, "That option still remains."

"I know. And if I relapse . . . ?"

"We could drain the fetal blood. Keep it stored on an as-needed basis."

"Would you embrace that idea?"

Adama's face never changed, but he admitted, "It's a bit . . . parasitic . . . for me."

"Me too," said Laura. She rubbed her eyes in a manner that emphasized the lack of sleep she'd been lately experiencing. "Honestly, Admiral . . . I'm open to suggestions."

"There's one avenue you haven't pursued."

"That being."

"You could talk to Sharon Valerii."

She stared at him with a level gaze for a time.

"I could indeed," she finally said.

CHAPTER 14

Sharon knew something major was happening when the marines came in to manacle her to her place.

Ordinarily she only spoke to visitors through the phone unit. So when the marines came in and bound her wrists, and fastened them in turn to a shackle on the floor, she was aware that meant someone was actually going to be entering her cell. Her guess was that it was Adama. Typically they made sure she couldn't move, and even then they kept guard with weapons that they would use if she made the slightest gesture toward whomever was there. She had once considered making a mocking comment such as, "Aren't you worried I'll shoot death rays out of my eyes?" but then thought better of it once she realized they'd probably clamp a metal blindfold around her just to play it safe.

She sat there with the stoic resolve of someone who was prepared to endure whatever her captors put her through. There were days when she wondered how she tolerated it, and she always kept coming around to the same answer: It wouldn't always be this way. She didn't know why she believed that. From the evidence of things, there was really no reason to. And yet she did, day after day. After all that she had been through, and with the baby growing in her belly, she had to believe that God had a greater purpose for her than to allow her to suffer and die.

She just wished she knew what it was.

Perhaps at some point the humans would come to realize that she was not a threat to them. Or perhaps the Cylons would take over *Galactica*, as Sharon suspected was inevitable, and she would be set free. Or, hell, perhaps the Cylons would wind up killing her themselves. It was always difficult to be sure.

But she was certain she knew when she'd find out. It was whenever D'anna Biers finally showed up at her cell.

She knew that if Adama ever asked her about other Cylon agents, she would never tell. Not even if it meant her death. She would keep her silence because she firmly believed that if she did betray them, then she would die of a certainty. Not only that, but it would be D'anna Biers who would pull the trigger. No one else. That was the sort of thing that D'anna would reserve for herself.

Every time she thought of D'anna, a shiver ran down her spine. She was the most formidable Cylon of all the models. The boldest, the most confident. To hide in plain sight the way she did. Other Cylon agents insinuated themselves quietly into positions where they could do damage, but not D'anna, no. She was a journalist, putting her face out there to be seen by everyone, smiling and smug and confident that none would see through her façade. Sharon envied her in many ways. There was no reason for her to have suspected at any time during her involvement with Helo, for instance, that he would have been able to determine she was a Cylon. Yet she had always worried. Every time he'd looked at her and seen only a human, she'd been concerned that somehow, against all reason, he would realize what she was. For that matter, in her previous "existence" as Boomer, she had only been able to function by being unaware of her true nature. Almost as soon as she had learned she was a Cylon, she could no longer live with herself. She couldn't put a gun to her own head and pull the trigger; Cylons were hardwired against such pointless suicide. So her subconscious needs had kicked in and she'd settled for the next best thing: shooting Adama, thus guaranteeing herself a death sentence. She wouldn't have to live with the knowledge of what she was, and wouldn't have to deal with the way that her former friends would look at her. She preferred death to the prospect of living a life that was a sham.

But Sharon's solution simply became Sharon's problem all over again.

The thing is, death would likely have held no fear for her if it weren't for the baby. But the life growing within her gave her incentive to live.

And so she remained silent. Silence might get her D'anna Biers, and D'anna Biers would in turn get her freedom.

The marines finished manacling her into place and then they walked out of the cell. She hadn't even bothered to try and strike up a conversation with them. She knew better. They never reacted to anything she said. If they glowered at her, at least that would be something. But they didn't. Instead they just sort of stared at her with dead eyes, as if she wasn't even there. As if she was a . . .

"A thing," she finished the thought aloud.

One of the marines barely glanced at her just before he walked out. He didn't know what she was referring to, of course, and the chances were that even if he had, it wouldn't have made a damned bit of difference. Actually, he probably would have agreed with her assessment.

She wondered if any of them could ever hope to understand.

"I'm not a thing," she said, thumping her fist softly on her thigh. "I am not . . . some sort . . . of thing." The baby kicked as if responding in sympathy. Sharon raised her fist and looked at it, turning it from side to side. Then she opened it and very slowly placed her palm flat on her stomach. "Maybe," she whispered to the child within her, "you're the symbol of this hand. Maybe you're going to take the fist of the Cylons and turn it into an open hand, which the humans will take in turn. It's possible. Anything's possible, I g—"

There was a noise at the door and Sharon looked up. It opened and, not entirely to her surprise, she saw Admiral Adama enter. He stared at her with that look she'd come to know quite well: a mixture of suspicion, pity, and forced detachment.

Then Sharon's eyes widened in ill-concealed surprise as President Laura Roslin stepped in behind him. There was no mixture of anything in Roslin's expression; rather there was nothing but deep, abiding resentment.

Well, that made perfect sense, didn't it? Roslin resented her, or at least "Sharon Valerii," for the assassination attempt upon Adama. She resented the child that was growing in her belly, since Roslin believed it represented a threat to the fleet and wanted to kill it. She resented the fact that she had to let it live because it had benefited her personally. And, obviously, she resented showing up here, now, for whatever reason they'd come up with.

Nevertheless, despite the fact that she knew how much Laura Roslin despised her, Sharon stood up. She noted with some amusement that Roslin took an involuntary step back, although the look of resentment on her face never so much as twitched. Adama stopped when Roslin did and glanced back at her.

Sharon bowed slightly at the waist in acknowledgment of Roslin's presence, and it was at that point that Roslin must have realized Sharon wasn't standing out of defensiveness or even a desire to attack. She was doing so out of deference for the office of the presidency. Sharon smiled inwardly, knowing that it probably annoyed the hell out of her. Nothing made someone who hated you more insane than responding to that hatred with patience and respect.

Roslin never changed her expression. Sharon wondered if Roslin's face would crack should a smile ever stray across it. Sharon remained standing, although she was slightly stooped thanks to the restraints of the chains on not only her wrists and ankles, but also around her throat. Previously they'd also had a strap around her waist, but her expanding belly had gone beyond the strap's capacity.

She waited to see if they'd pick up the phone, but they didn't. Instead Adama went around to the far door, tapped in the entry code, and opened it. Sharon turned slightly to face them, but otherwise stayed right where she was and made no sudden movement. Even if it had been possible for her to do so, she wouldn't have, because Adama had produced a sidearm and was aiming it directly at her heart. No, not her heart—her belly.

Suddenly a terrible notion occurred to her, but she didn't allow that to be reflected in her voice, which remained flat and even. "If you're here to execute me," she said, "I just want to tell you that I appreciate you handling it yourself instead of dispatching a subordinate."

"Sit down," said Adama, the point of his gun never wavering.

"I can't."

"Why?"

"Because," said Sharon, and she tilted her head toward Laura Roslin, "she's standing. It would be a breach of protocol."

Roslin made a sound of disbelief, and then saw in Sharon's steady gaze that she was perfectly serious. "You have my permission to sit," she said.

"Thank you." Sharon did so. She gestured toward a chair that was some feet away, out of the range of movement that Sharon's short leash permitted her. Laura's gaze flickered from Sharon's manacles to the chair and back to Sharon, as if she were mentally judging the distance between Sharon and herself. Answering Roslin's unspoken question, Sharon said quietly, "It's sufficient distance for safety concerns."

"I wasn't worried," Roslin replied, and her expression seemed confident enough. Sharon suspected it was superb dissembling. Roslin sat in the chair, smoothing the folds of her skirt.

Sharon's gaze flickered back to Adama. "Are you going to keep that pointed on me the entire time, Admiral?"

"Is that a problem?" The question sounded solicitous. The tone most definitely was not.

She shrugged. "Not for me. But your arm's going to get tired after a while. And it could start to shake slightly from muscle tension. Which could result in your accidentally shooting me. Unless that's your intent all along, in which case I suppose it's all academic."

"Your concern is appreciated," said Adama.

"I'm sure it is," replied Sharon, who was sure it wasn't. She shifted her attention to Roslin, who was watching her as if hoping that she, Sharon, would keel over and die right then and there. "If you're not here to kill me . . . are you here to say thank you?"

"Thank you?" Roslin echoed in mild confusion.

"You're welcome."

"I mean, why would I thank you?"

"Because I saved your life," Sharon said evenly. "You'd be dead if it weren't for me."

"If a doctor found a cure with the aid of a lab animal . . . would you thank the animal?" Roslin said.

Sharon stared at her and then, very softly, chuckled deep in her chest. "I appreciate you putting it that way . . . and letting me know where I stand." She could have asked what, then, Laura Roslin was doing there. Her mind raced, far faster than a human mind could have. Just one of the perks that she possessed; humans had no idea at all just how quickly she could think. It was obvious that Adama was there to serve as guard to Laura Roslin. He was taking no chance that Sharon might abruptly break her bonds and make a move on the president, try to kill her where she sat. (Now Sharon was really relieved she hadn't made the eye beam comment.) The question, of course, was why was Adama doing that rather than having a marine guard or guards on hand to serve the same function? Well, there was only one answer to that, wasn't there. Adama and Roslin wanted to discuss something of a sensitive nature . . . a nature so sensitive that they didn't even want to chance marines standing there and hearing what was to be said.

It intrigued her to wonder what it might be.

She didn't allow her expression to change or reflect the notions that were running through her head. Instead she simply waited patiently, one hand in her lap, the other resting gently on her stomach. She saw Laura Roslin notice her hand's placement. Inwardly, she smiled. Outwardly, she waited.

"Commander Adama," she said, "has informed me that, whenever he has asked you questions about anything, you've always answered them to the best of your ability. I would appreciate it if you could provide me the same courtesy."

"Of course," she said neutrally.

"Very well." She leaned forward, studying Sharon intently, looking like she wanted to try and catch Valerii in a lie no matter what Adama might have said. "I want to know if you're doing it deliberately."

Sharon stared at her and stared at her and then said, "In the name of my people . . . in the name of the one God above all . . . I have absolutely no frakking idea what you're referring to."

"The dreams."

"The dreams," Sharon repeated. "What dreams?"

"The dreams that aren't letting me sleep. The dreams that are . . ." She composed herself and said, "If you're trying to get in my head, disrupt my life, I'm here to tell you that it's working. Congratulations. And I want you to stop it or so help me I will ask Admiral Adama for his weapon and put a bullet in you myself."

"That's your prerogative," Sharon said, unfazed. "And I'll die with no more clue as to what you're talking about than I have right now."

"She doesn't know." It was Adama who had spoken. Laura Roslin looked up at him and, although he still had no intention of lowering his gun, there was still quiet conviction in his face. "She really doesn't."

"Would you bet your life on that? Or mine for that matter?" asked Laura.

"Yes," he said without hesitation.

Laura considered that, and then nodded. "All right," she said, apparently satisfied. "Which leads us to the next question of whether this might be the baby's doing."

By this point, Sharon had a clear idea of what Laura Roslin was nattering about. But a warning flashed through her consciousness. If she allowed her deductions to color the things she said, it would make it appear as if she did, in fact, have advance knowledge of what Roslin was talking to her about. Which would mean she was "in on it" or some such. Sharon didn't dare take that chance, because she was still certain that Roslin was looking for an excuse—any excuse—to stop her child from being born. She wasn't about to hand it to her. Continuing to keep her face as impassive as she possibly could, Sharon inquired, "What is the 'this' to which you're referring?"

"The dreams," Laura said after a moment, apparently realizing that refusing to answer Sharon's question would only slow matters down. "The dreams I've been having in which you're a featured player. Dreams of birth. Dreams of blood. 'Sagittarius is bleeding.' Does that mean anything to you?"

"No. None of this means anything to me. You're having bad dreams. Everyone does. Are you trying to blame them on my child?"

"I'm trying to determine what's going on."

And Sharon was suddenly on her feet. Adama had been relaxing ever so slightly, but the moment he saw Sharon even begin to make a motion, he had the gun ready to fire if need be.

"You are trying to put the blame on my baby," Sharon said frostily. "Something's going on in your head that could stem from any number of things rattling around in your subconscious, and you're trying to use it as an excuse to kill my child."

"I don't require an excuse," Laura Roslin reminded her harshly. "All I require is a piece of paper to write out and sign the order."

Sharon didn't budge from where she was standing, but she folded her arms and said firmly, "I have nothing more to say."

"This meeting," said Roslin, "is not over until I say it is."

"Fine. Then, with all respect, I have nothing more to say until my lawyer gets here."

"Your . . . ?" She mouthed "lawyer" without saying it and looked at Adama questioningly. He sighed and nodded. "How did she get a lawyer?"

"One showed up."

Laura was about to say something more, but she quickly reconsidered it. That didn't surprise Sharon. Roslin obviously felt that she and Adama should present a united front, and standing there and arguing with him about Sharon's legal rights would only serve to undermine that front. Laura turned back to Sharon. "Look," she began.

"With all respect, I have nothing more to say—"

"It will go better for you if—"

"—until my lawyer gets here."

"If you truly are concerned about your baby—"

"With all respect," and her voice got louder and her manner even colder, "I have nothing more to say until—"

Laura put up a hand, silencing her. Her eyes closed as if she were fighting a migraine. She forced a smile and said, "All right. You've made your position clear." She rose and Adama unlocked the door, still keeping his gun aimed at Sharon. Sharon remained standing even after both Adama and Roslin had exited. Roslin paused and then turned and said, "You should have cooperated."

"I've done nothing *but* cooperate," replied Sharon, and her voice grew harsh, allowing some of the anger that had been building up to bubble into visibility. "And for my cooperation I've been confined to a cell half the size of any quarters . . . I've been beaten, sexually assaulted, and nearly raped . . . I have no room to do any kind of exercise . . . I'm getting bedsores . . . I stink because I have no shower facility, I can't even go to the head without being under observation, and I'm not sure but I think there's things living in my hair. You want to solve whatever problems I present? Let me go. Someone will put me down like the dog I'm being treated like, and we can all move on to other things." And then, her fury pushing her in a direction that wouldn't even have occurred to her earlier, she turned and focused a malevolent gaze upon Laura. "You know so little about us. Who we are, how we function. Consider this little notion: Perhaps the blood coursing through your veins that you stole from my child . . . the blood responsible for your salvation . . . is *turning you into one of us.* Never occurred to you, did it? Maybe these dreams you're experiencing are the first steps on your road to becoming a Cylon yourself. How will it feel, I wonder, if you wind up going from being revered to feared. To losing your friends, your liberty, everything, in one shot. Take a good, hard look at the décor here, Madame President. You might just be sharing it before you know it. And by the way . . . I don't have another frakking thing to say until my lawyer is here."

And with that final announcement, she flipped herself back down onto her bed. In doing so, it pulled the neck chain taut and she gagged slightly before she could readjust herself so there was some slack in the chain.

She made no further moves until the president and the admiral were gone, at which point she fought desperately to keep hot tears from rolling down her cheeks, and didn't quite succeed.

CHAPTER 15

Adama had never seen Laura Roslin as shaken as she was at that point. She was seated in his quarters and was looking shell-shocked. Inwardly he cursed himself as a fool, believing he should never have taken her to see Sharon Valerii in the first place . . . particularly galling since it had been his own damned suggestion.

"Would you like a drink?" he asked her gently.

"I've never wanted one so desperately in my life."

Reaching under his desk, he pulled out a bottle of alcohol that had been a gift from Tigh. Adama was reasonably sure Tigh had acquired it from the black market, but Tigh hadn't volunteered the information and Adama felt it better not to inquire too closely. Considering Laura's state of mind, he suspected she wasn't going to ask too many questions either. He filled a glass for her and slid it over to her. She took it without even looking at it and knocked it back in one shot. Then she held the glass out again and Adama filled it without comment. This time she sipped it far more slowly.

"You're not turning into a Cylon," Adama assured her.

"How do we know that?"

"Madame President . . ."

"How do we know?" she repeated. There was no fear in her voice, no trace of panic. She was asking in what could have been an almost clinical fashion, as if they were discussing the results of some new experiment. "You can't say it's impossible. You don't know. Neither do I. Perhaps she's right. Perhaps I'm undergoing some . . . metabolic process that is slowly transforming me into one of them."

"That's absurd."

"So you say. But you don't know." She looked him square in the eye. "Do you."

The truth was that he didn't, but he wasn't about to say that to her. It wasn't what she needed to hear. "Yes. I do."

"You were the one who said," she reminded him, "that Sharon Valerii has always told you the truth."

"All she did was float a possibility. Possibilities are nothing more than that . . . and can be dismissed just as quickly."

"Possibilities can also be things to be explored."

He gestured in a you-tell-me manner. "How would you suggest we explore it?" he asked. "Dissect you?"

Adama wasn't serious, of course, but she looked thoughtful as if were actually a viable notion. "Did you dissect the previous incarnation of Valerii?"

"Yes."

"And what did you discover that readily distinguished her from being a human?"

"Nothing," Adama admitted.

"Nothing. Which leads us back to wondering how you would know in my case."

"It's more than biological."

"Is it?" she asked, one eyebrow cocked. "If we can't distinguish them from ourselves, and if we can't even tell if we're turning into one of them . . ."

"I can tell."

"You can." Roslin made no effort to hide her disbelief of the claim. "How?"

"In their eyes. They can't disguise their pure hatred for us. I see it burning in there with cold fury. That's how you tell."

"Really. And if that tell should fail?"

"Well," he paused, "getting shot is also a good tip-off."

Despite the seriousness of the situation and her bleak mood, Laura Roslin smiled at that. "I should think it would be." Then her amusement faded, to be replaced by grim apprehension. "Admiral . . . if you ever have any reason to think I've been . . . swayed . . . over to their side . . ."

"I will act accordingly."

"Even though there will be those who accuse you of treason?"

"The survival of the fleet is my overriding concern," said Adama firmly. "I'll deal with whatever consequences may result from that. But I repeat: There is no way that you could, or would, become a Cylon."

"How do you know, Admiral? How do you truly know?"

"Because," he said with conviction, "you are far too much a woman of conscience to allow that to happen. If you truly believed that you presented a threat to the fleet . . . that you had allied yourself, however against your will it was, with the Cylons, then you would come to me and ask me to put a shot through your head."

"And could you do that?" She saw the brief flicker of hesitation in his eyes. "Could you? I come to you and say, 'Admiral, it was everything I could do not to open fire on the Quorum of Twelve. Kill me before I kill someone else. That's a direct order from your commander-in-chief.' Could you do it?"

The hesitation evaporated and slowly he nodded. "Absolutely."

"Huh." She frowned. "I don't know whether to feel relieved about that, or concerned."

"Both, I suppose," said Adama.

"All right," Laura replied. "I'll have to take your word for it."

"I hesitate to mention it . . . but have you spoken with Doctor Baltar about this?"

"No," she admitted. "I have . . . concerns about him. I would not feel comfortable trusting him with this situation at this time."

"Concerns."

"You have none?"

"I didn't say that," said Adama. "Simply nothing that I can act upon. And you?"

She hesitated and then said, "The same. Or, at the very least, nothing I can put into words."

What would I say? That I had visions of him on Caprica, locked in a passionate embrace with a known Cylon agent? There's still too much I don't know. He's the foremost expert on Cylons. If I were becoming influenced by the Cylon fetus, then wouldn't it be in the Cylons' best interests to have the man who knows most about them to fall under suspicion?

She knew she couldn't go on like this forever. Sooner or later, she was going to have to sort this out, or resign from the presidency. That was the only option left to her if she thought that her own mind was unreliable. Until it reached that point, though, she was going to try and play things as carefully as she could.

"You should still seek medical aid," Adama said firmly.

Laura nodded in agreement. "All right," she told him, albeit with reluctance, "I'll speak to Doctor Cottle about it."

"Excellent."

Adama began to stand, clearly thinking the meeting was over, but Laura didn't move. Her gaze hardened and she said, "She has a *lawyer*?" This prompted Adama to sit back down again with an audible sigh, as if he were deflating and that was what was lowering him back into his seat.

"Yes," he said.

"And she spoke with this person?"

"Yes."

"And you allowed this?"

"I considered shooting her," Adama said, "but I was daunted by the prospect of the paperwork."

She shook her head, clearly not amused. "You should have denied her access."

"If I had, she would have gone public with the presence of the Cylon."

"You just know it's going to happen sooner or later."

"Possibly. Considering we're still trying to get a handle on what caused the Cylons to be able to anticipate our Jump, my vote is for 'later.'"

"I suppose you're right," she allowed. She shook her head and half-smiled. "I hate to admit it . . . and if asked, I would deny it . . . but I'm starting to see the advantages of martial law. Under such conditions, you could have just held her indefinitely at your whim."

"A dictatorship is also an option," he pointed out.

"In case you haven't been paying attention to the press, there are some who are under the impression that we already have one." Laura appeared to give it some consideration, and then she shook her head sadly and said, "It wouldn't work. I look ghastly in jackboots."

"Imagine my relief." He paused and then said, "She made the argument that Sharon Valerii is so indistinguishable from a human that it was inappropriate—even illegal—to treat her as anything but."

"What did you say?"

"I said she was a machine."

"What," Laura asked after a moment, "do you truly believe?"

Adama leaned back in his chair. It was a question that he'd been wrestling with ever since he'd come out of his coma and had come face to face with the creature that had shot him. "I hate to say it, but—"

"You don't know? Admiral . . . Bill . . . one of them tried to kill you."

"And another one of them saved you," he reminded her. "I look into the face of Sharon Valerii, and I see the enemy. I see something inhuman. But . . ."

"But what?"

He tried to figure out the best way to phrase it. "The lawyer was right about one thing. It is always easier to think of an enemy as less than human, even when you know they are. So when you know they're not, how much easier to make them less than they are?"

"I'm not sure I follow."

Adama's mind rolled back to a meeting he'd had with the Cylon. The results of that encounter had never been far from him, and they continued to haunt him. "I had a talk with her . . ."

"It."

"With the Cylon, back when we first encountered the *Pegasus*. When it looked as if I was going to have Starbuck assassinate Admiral Cain. I asked her why the Cylons hated us. Why they were trying to kill us. She brought up something I'd said about humans deserving to survive . . . and suggested that maybe we weren't. That we weren't worthy to. And when she said that, there was something about her . . . she seemed . . ."

"She seemed what?" prompted Laura.

"Wise. Wiser than us. Older than us."

Laura Roslin looked as if her eyes were going to leap out of her head. "Are you saying that they're rendering judgment upon us . . . and are *worthy of doing so?*"

"No," he said flatly.

"Then what . . . ?"

"The reason Admiral Cain wasn't killed by Kara Thrace . . . was because Sharon Valerii made me feel as if I wasn't living up to the promise of humanity. I was as willing to kill the admiral . . . as the Cylons are to kill us. In that moment, she was more human than I . . . and I was more machine than she. No wonder we can't determine, even through autopsy, what the differences are between us. There are times when the line blurs so much, I'm not sure where it is anymore."

"I remind you, Admiral, that it was a Cylon who cold-bloodedly killed Admiral Cain after you, in your humanity, declined."

"I am aware of that, yes."

Laura could almost see the wheels turning within his head. "May I ask what you're thinking?"

"I'm thinking that either Sharon Valerii is one of the most brilliant actresses of her age . . . or there may be some sort of actual dissent within the ranks of the Cylons. If there's one Sharon who truly believes in humanity . . . there may be more. And it's possible that somehow down the line, we might be able to exploit that."

She arched an eyebrow in interest. "You mean foster some sort of civil war within the Cylons themselves?"

"The notion of having them invest their talent for homicide into obliterating each other rather than us is an appealing one, wouldn't you say?"

A slow smile spread across Laura's face. "Do you think it's possible?"

"As we've established, when it comes to the Cylons, anything is possible."

Laura nodded in agreement. "The bugs in the rooms," she said after some consideration. "They have to come out."

"No."

"Admiral . . ."

"It's a military matter, Madame President. A military decision. I stand by it and until we get this sorted out, they're staying where they are."

She scowled. "I want your word that they're gone once things are 'sorted out.'"

"You have it."

"And be certain to tell Colonel Tigh that I'm not happy with him at all."

There was a knock at Adama's door. "Yes?" called Adama.

"Do you have a minute, Admiral?" came Tigh's voice.

Adama's eyes flashed with amusement as he looked at Laura. "By all means," he said.

Tigh pushed the door opened, walked in and stopped when he saw Laura. "Madame President," he said in surprise. "An unexpected honor."

"We were just talking about you," Adama told him.

"Really. Nothing good, I hope," said Tigh.

"The president wished me to inform you that she's not happy with you at all."

Tigh didn't look the least bit bothered. "Then my hope was fulfilled." Before either Adama or Roslin could explain specifically what it was that Tigh had done to draw the president's ire, his voice grew serious and he continued, "Doctor Baltar has come to me with a situation."

"Is this about the matter that we heard him muttering to himself over?" When he saw Tigh's surprised gaze flicker over to Roslin, he added, "She knows about the bugs. And she knows that I knew from the start. Colonel Tigh," he said to Roslin, "suggested that I claim ignorance of the program to spare me your ire."

"Did he."

"Yes."

"Huh," she grunted. "That was very noble of you, Colonel."

"Thank you, Madame President."

"Doesn't make me any happier with you, though."

"Understood. Admiral," he continued, looking as if the president's happiness with him wasn't of particular importance, "the doctor wishes to meet with you. He believes that the boy may in fact be a Cylon."

Roslin's cheeks pinked slightly at the prospect of another Cylon being identified. "Boy? What boy?"

"Andrew Boxman. The pilots call him Boxey," said Adama. "He was caught having a private conference with Sharon Valerii."

"Naturally he was checked over to make sure he wasn't a Cylon himself," Tigh told her. "Baltar originally gave him a clean bill of health . . . but now apparently he's having second thoughts."

Laura started murmuring the name "Boxman" to herself. She frowned a moment, trying to figure out why it sounded familiar, and then she remembered. "Wasn't the officer who was killed at the meeting station when the Cylons first attacked named Boxman . . . ?"

"Boxey's father. He's orphaned."

"We know who his parents were, and we still felt it necessary to check if he was a Cylon?"

"We know that an Alex Boxman existed at some point," Tigh said. "We've no idea whether the one who came aboard *Galactica*—in the company of Sharon Valerii yet—is the original item. Alex Boxman may well be dead and this one is an imposter."

"Do they do that? Impersonate other people?"

"We don't know," Tigh said stiffly. "But it's preferable not to take chances."

"Yes. Yes, of course, you're right. Do we know where he is now?" asked Roslin.

"We've been keeping tabs on him, just in case," Adama said. He was sifting through some notes on his desk and produced one that had been delivered to him recently. "According to child protection authorities, he's taken up residence on the *Bifrost*, under the guardianship of—by astounding coincidence—Sharon Valerii's lawyer, Freya Gunnerson."

"Gunnerson . . . ?"

He noticed the uptick in her voice. "You know her?"

"I suspect I know a relative of hers. How old is she?"

The question surprised him mildly and he glanced over at Tigh. Tigh shrugged. "Mid-twenties, I'd make her out to be."

"Probably her father, then." She laid out as quickly as she could the details of her encounter with Wolf Gunnerson.

Adama took it in, considering every word she said. "Hell of a co-incidence," he said finally.

"I don't like coincidences on general principle," said Tigh.

Standing up and coming around his desk, Adama said, "Let's go have a chat with Doctor Baltar and find out what the hell is going on. Madame President, would you care to join us . . . ?"

"I think it would be better if I got back to my ship," she said, rising as well.

"If I may ask, what are you going to do about the Midguardians?" asked Adama. "Are you seriously considering their request for state-hood?"

"I've ruled out nothing," said Roslin. "I generally try to keep my options open until I see how things pan out."

Tigh scowled and said, "If you ask me—which you didn't, but anyway—if you ask me, elevating those heathens to parity with the Twelve Colonies, you're asking for trouble, with all respect."

"That may be, Colonel," replied Laura Roslin. "But I've noticed that trouble tends to show up, unasked for or not. So I might as well do what I feel is right and let the consequences fall as they may."

Billy Keikeya looked as if he were about to go into shock when Laura Roslin told him the outcome of her discussion with Admiral Adama. He was literally trembling with indignation, and as she sat in her of-fice and watched his mounting mortification, she never felt quite as badly for him as she did at that moment. Billy took his responsibility as her aide and—ultimately—confidant very seriously. It was at times such as this that she remembered just how young he truly was, be-cause his face was stricken with an expression that would have been at home on one of her students who had just been informed he'd been caught cheating. Except in this case, of course, Billy was innocent of any criminal intent.

"They had her quarters *bugged*?" he asked in disbelief. When she nodded, he demanded, "Did Dee know about this?"

"Dee . . . ? Oh. Dualla. No, I've no reason to assume she did."

"I've got to tell her . . ."

Billy started to stand but Roslin firmly gestured for him to sit.

"You're to tell her nothing. You're not to tell any of them anything. You and I may find the concept repulsive, but Adama and Tigh make a convincing argument. These are difficult times, Billy, and difficult decisions have to be made to get us through them. These include decisions we don't always agree with . . . but have to live with."

"But Madame President, with all respect . . . it's wrong," he said, still looking upset but nevertheless sitting as she indicated him to do. "Shouldn't we take stands on things for no other reason than that?"

"I'm not so sure it's wrong."

"How can it not be?"

"Because we can't afford to be naïve, Billy," she said firmly. "We're dealing with an enemy that will stop at nothing to destroy us. So if extreme measures need to be taken to avoid being destroyed, then that's what we do."

Billy stared at her for a long moment, and she wasn't sure what was going through his mind. "You have something to say, Billy?" she asked.

"It's . . ." He paused, and then said, "It's not my place. I'm sorry . . ."

"Billy, your place is where I say it is. If you have something to say, then let's hear it."

"Madame President, you've been through a lot . . . it really wouldn't be fair of me to—"

Annoyance flashed across her eyes. "Billy, I don't give a damn about fairness. Tell me what's on your mind."

He studied her for a long moment, and then he said, "You never used to be the type to back down, that's all."

She felt a brief flare of temper, and she had to remind herself that she had pushed Billy into saying what he was thinking. "I don't believe I agree with your assessment."

"Yes, Madame President." He seemed suddenly anxious to get the hell out. "That . . . well, that's fine. You're right." He started to stand once more, and a single imperious gesture from her caused him to plop down yet again. She didn't say anything; she just stared at him, making no effort to prompt him, certain that the ongoing glacial look she was giving him would be more than enough to get him talking again. As it turned out, she was right. "Okay, look . . . with all respect . . . what you said just now. You 'don't believe' that you agree. It sounded less definitive. *You've* been less definitive. Less sure of yourself."

"If that's true—and I'm not saying it is, but if it were—certainly don't you think some of that can be attributed to the fact that I haven't been sleeping much lately? That might have something to do with it."

"Something. Maybe. But not all of it."

"Then what—?"

"Madame President," Billy said, shifting uncomfortably in his chair, "I really . . . really think it's inappropriate for me to be discussing this with you . . ."

"Billy," said Roslin, her voice softening sightly, "I don't know if you've noticed . . . but you and Lee Adama are the only two people I've known I could count on from the moment I became president . . . and, frankly, even Lee has been shaky every now and then, since he's got a bit of a conflict of interest."

"That's understating it," muttered Billy.

"You've seen me at my worst and at my best . . . or at least what passes for my best. You, of all people, should know you can speak honestly with me."

"All right." He lowered his head and interlaced his fingers, looking as if he were working to find the best way to put it. "I think it's more than just the dreaming . . . the sleeplessness. You've seemed more tentative in your decision making, in your attitude . . . in everything."

"Really." She maintained her pleasant tone, although it was not without effort. "And why do you think that would be?"

"Well . . . if I had to guess . . . it's because as long as you were convinced you were going to die, you had nothing to be afraid of. I mean, what's the worst that can possibly happen to someone? It's death, right? And because you had adjusted to the idea that you didn't have much time left, you were determined to do everything you could before your time ran out because you figured, you know . . . you had nothing to lose. You weren't in it for the long haul. You weren't a marathon runner; your life was boiled down to the hundred-yard dash. You just ran with everything you had, head down, arms pumping, and anything that got in your way, you ran right over it. But now . . . now you've got something to live for. A lot to live for. And you no longer have the—it'll sound weird—you don't have the 'comfort' of knowing that you won't be around for much longer. Now you can afford to take your time in trying to get humanity to Earth because you actually have a chance of seeing it yourself. Plus you're considering every single aspect of everything because you have time to think about all the ramifications, all the sides, where before you just . . . well, it seemed like you just went with your gut."

"That was never the case, Billy. I always considered every aspect."

"Maybe. But I don't think you gave everything equal consideration, the way you do now. I mean, hell," and he almost laughed,
"there were times when it seemed like you were spoiling for a fight
more than Adama, and he's the soldier. Lately you've been more cautious. More . . . politic."

"Well, I am a politician."

"No, Madame President," he said firmly. "You're a leader. There's
a difference. A huge difference. A politician cares what people think,
and they hate her for it. A leader tells them what to think, and they
love her for it."

"I think you're selling me a little short as a politician, Billy."

"And with all respect, Madame President, I think you're selling
yourself short as a leader. I think you weren't afraid of dying, but
now you're . . ."

"Afraid of living?"

"Not afraid. Just . . . concerned." He paused and then looked
down, feeling ashamed. "I said it wasn't appropriate for me to say
stuff like this."

"Billy," she said slowly, "I may be many things . . . but the one
thing I remain is your president. If you, of all people, can't communicate with your president . . . what hope does any of the rest of my
constituency have?"

"You're not upset then."

"No. I don't agree with what you have to say, but I respect that
you said it."

"Thank you, Madame President. Is that all?"

She nodded and yet again he rose from his chair. He started to
head for the door and then Roslin called, "Billy . . . I know you grad-
uated with degrees in political science and government. But before
that, did you study psychology at all?"

He smiled. "Two years, before I changed majors. You could tell,
huh."

"Let's just say that it wasn't a wasted two years."

"Thank you, Madame President," he said, bowed slightly, and
left.

His words stayed with her, though, long after he had gone. Her
impulse really was to reject what he'd said out of hand . . . but the
more she thought about it, the more she wondered if he had a point.
It wasn't that she'd resigned herself to dying, but she had accepted it.
She knew how her life was going to end, and her existence had

turned into a race against time. It had enabled her to focus her efforts with laserlike efficiency. Now, though, the ending was no longer certain, and her future—so clearly defined—was now murky. The focus was gone. She was still determined to get humanity to its new home, but with the time element gone, she could afford to . . . to . . .

"To be more cautious. More politic," she echoed his words. "Let's face it . . . more weak." Billy hadn't said that, but she said it. It was part of the reason she'd been content to let Adama and Tigh go talk to Baltar. She had a feeling that someone like Baltar would easily sniff out weakness. She'd come to see Adama as an ally, and even with him, she didn't want to allow anyone to see her at less than her best. But Baltar would sense her weakness and—if he was indeed a Cylon sympathizer of some sort as she was beginning to believe—she didn't want to chance letting on to the opposition that there was any diminishment in her capacity.

But she couldn't keep it up forever. She needed to pull herself together. Laura hated to admit it, but Billy might have indeed had a point. The cancer had loomed large as the final coda on her life. Now the end of her life had yet to be written—which meant that everything leading up to it needed a heavy rewrite. And she was going to have to take pen in hand and write it herself . . . before someone removed the pen from her hand and did the writing for her.

Weaker. Less of a leader. She didn't like the sound of it or the feel of it. And she was starting to think that maybe she should be doing something about it . . .

. . . provided there wasn't an unborn Cylon who was trying to drive her insane.

Saul Tigh had the sneaking suspicion that Gaius Baltar was trying to drive him insane.

Adama didn't look any happier, but as always, he was able to contain whatever annoyance he was feeling beneath his stony exterior. They were in Baltar's lab and Baltar—as he so often did—looked slightly furtive, as if he already knew what you were going to say and was planning his next response several steps further along the projected conversation. Tigh didn't understand why anyone would feel the need to be thinking that much about something as simple as a discussion. It was as if Baltar considered it all some sort of battle of wits, and rather than communicating the way a normal person did, he was out to win a game that only he knew he was playing. Tigh felt there were only two reasons for Baltar to be thinking that way: He was so brilliant that he couldn't help but try to stay ahead of the curve . . . or he had something he was hiding and was trying to head off questions before they got uncomfortably close.

Either way, he got on Tigh's nerves with remarkable ease.

"So now you're saying," Adama asked slowly, wanting to make certain he understood what he was being told, "that Boxey *might* be a Cylon?"

"I'm saying that I've discovered anomalies in the original blood sample I drew," replied Baltar. "I make it a habit to recheck my findings . . . particularly when Cylons might be involved. Everything about them is geared towards subterfuge."

"Even their blood?"

"*Every* aspect of them, Admiral," Baltar said firmly. "In the case of young Mr. Boxman, there are some things that don't properly match up. His cell count for one. It leads me to wonder whether something went wrong with the test the first time."

"What sort of something?" asked Tigh.

"It could be any number of things," Baltar replied. He sounded annoyed that he would be required to explain something that was clearly, to him, blindingly obvious. His voice grew lower, as if he were concerned that someone was listening in. That, of course, carried with it some irony considering that he was right. It was just that the people who were listening in on him were sitting right there in his lab. "The most disturbing of those possibilities is some sort of sabotage. That someone snuck into the lab and did something to the sample I was using for testing while I wasn't around."

"Where the frak did you go, considering you know how important the test is?" demanded Tigh.

Baltar gave him a withering glance. "The test involves growing a culture, Colonel. That takes time. Simply baby-sitting it for the duration isn't really a viable option. Feel free," he added with increased sarcasm, "to refute me with your copious years of scientific training."

Tigh glared at him, hoping his scowl would be sufficiently intimidating. Baltar, tragically, didn't look intimidated in the slightest.

"That's what I thought," said Baltar when Tigh had no comeback.

Clearly wishing to move forward, Adama said quietly, "What do you need us to do?"

"Why . . . bring the boy back here, of course," Baltar said as if it were the most obvious thing in the world. "I ran tests on the blood sample that remained, and from what I could determine, he has four of the six markers that would indicate that he is a Cylon. Unfortunately, due to their close resemblance to humans, four out of six is within the margin of error. Six out of six is the only way to be sure, and that's impossible to determine with what I have on hand."

"Give us your best guess, Doctor, if you wouldn't mind," Tigh said. "Is the boy a Cylon or not?"

"I don't 'guess,' Colonel," Baltar replied with the heavy manner of the truly put-upon. "I conduct experiments and I draw conclusions. Guessing accomplishes nothing and can only lead to confusion and contradiction. I need him here to be sure."

Tigh and Adama exchanged looks, and then Adama said, "All right. We'll bring him back."

"I'll scramble a squad of marines," Tigh said, heading for the door as if the entire matter was settled.

He was halted in mid-stride by Adama's calm, collected, "That may not be necessary, Colonel."

Tigh turned and looked at him in surprise. "No?"

"We'll discuss it further. Thank you, Doctor . . ." and then he paused and added, "Or do you prefer 'Mr. Vice President'?"

"Depends on the circumstance," replied Baltar.

Adama nodded, then accompanied Tigh into the hallway. He turned back toward the lab after a moment and said, "Would you mind telling Kara Thrace to wait for me in my quarters?"

"Starbuck? Why?" But Tigh instantly thought better of what he'd just said and instead simply nodded and continued, "Yes sir."

"Thank you. I'll be along shortly."

Adama waited until Tigh was gone, then knocked once more at the lab door and let himself in before Baltar had a chance to say anything. He noted that Baltar was standing in an odd position, as if he were talking to someone. But there was no one there. Baltar jumped slightly at the intrusion and quickly smoothed his shirt . . . not because it was wrinkled, but obviously because he was endeavoring to regain his composure. "Did I interrupt a conversation?" Adama asked with a slightly bemused expression.

"I talk to myself on occasion,". Baltar said. "It's how I work through complex problems. Plus I'm starved for intelligent discussion, so . . ." The last comment was clearly intended to be a joke, but Baltar had the comedy stylings of a Cylon raider, so it fell flat. Knowing that it had, he cleared his throat and said, "Is there something else, Admiral?"

"You're responsible for President Roslin's cure."

"Yes," said Baltar warily, as if worried he was being set up in some way.

"I'd like to know about the possibilities of side effects."

His eyes narrowed as if he were trying to read Adama's mind. Caution still pervading his voice, he said, "Naturally there's the possibility of side effects. We're dealing with an entirely new branch of medicine. Using the blood of the unborn Cylon isn't exactly the sort of treatment you're liable to find in any medical textbooks. It was a desperation move."

"You didn't know it would work?"

"Of course not. I knew it *could* work, but that's not the same thing. Frankly, I wanted to keep President Roslin here for observation for a month or two, but she was insistent about getting back to work."

"She would be, yes."

Baltar now looked extremely suspicious. "Admiral . . . is there something going on that I should know about? Is President Roslin suffering from some sort of reaction? I admit, I wasn't entirely sanguine over the prospect of attempting an entirely new medical treatment on her. But since the alternative was certain death, I didn't see that she had a good deal to lose. Any negative reactions she's having, however, would certainly be helpful to know about, especially considering that others who suffer from similar illnesses might want similar treatment."

"Yes. It would." Adama paused a moment, looking to be considering possibilities, and then said as coolly as ever, "I simply wanted to know if I should be on the watch for something."

"Has there been any change in her behavior?"

"I couldn't say."

"Has she been speaking to you about any difficulties?"

"I couldn't say."

Slowly Baltar nodded, easily reading between the lines of Adama's vague response. "Couldn't say . . . or choose not to?"

Adama inclined his head slightly, acknowledging that the latter was a distinct possibility. "Thank you for your time, Doctor. If, in your further research, specific aspects of side effects occur to you, you will share them with me, won't you."

"Of course. And you would share any share specifics of negative changes in President Roslin's condition, should any of them present themselves to you?"

"You may expect me to, yes."

Baltar smiled in a way that didn't give the least appearance of amusement. "Very carefully worded. I suppose I may also expect Cylons to come flying out of my ass. But that doesn't mean it's going to happen."

"Vice President Baltar," said Adama, "in your case . . . I wouldn't rule out a single possibility." With that he headed out the door.

His exit, although naturally he didn't hear it, was accompanied by delighted laughter from Number Six. Baltar gave her a sour look as she continued to laugh and then applauded slowly and sarcastically. "Now there goes a funny, funny man," she said.

"He's the height of hilarity." He looked at her suspiciously. "What was he talking about? What 'side effects'?"

"I'm sure I don't know," said Six, the picture of wide-eyed innocence.

"Why don't I believe that?"

"Because, Gaius," she replied, "you see the world as a vast web of lies and deceit. You believe in nothing and no one."

"I believe in myself."

"You believe in yourself least of all," said Six with a giggle that sounded surprisingly girlish. "You second-guess yourself constantly and you live in perpetual fear that you're going to be found out. In so many ways, you wish you were like her."

"I don't know what you mean."

"I mean," she said, striding across the room on those legs that seemed to go on forever, "that Laura Roslin was on the brink of death and she still never showed one iota of fear. You envy her for that, because you jump at sounds and shadows. You envy her her fearlessness. You saw her cancer as a chink in her armor, and yet even staring oblivion in the face, she was unafraid. You could never look death in the face and remain unfazed."

He stepped close to her, stared directly into her eyes, and said tightly, "Oh really? I'm doing it right now."

Then he turned his back to her and strode out of his lab, leaving her behind to watch him go with her face a mask of thought.

What the frak did I do now?

Naturally that had been the first thing that had gone through Starbuck's mind when Tigh had approached her with a determined look on his face. Then the perpetually sour executive officer had told her, as bluntly as he could, that Adama wanted to see her in his quarters. Her initial sense of relief (*Oh, good; Tigh hasn't found some new excuse to toss me in the brig)* was immediately replaced by a sense of vague dread (*What did I do to piss off the Old Man?*).

She knew it was ridiculous for her to feel that way. It wasn't as if she had a perpetually guilty conscience. Still, she couldn't help but occasionally feel a bit besieged, and although she was reasonably sure she hadn't done anything out of line lately, well . . . there was always the stuff she'd done in the past that she'd never been caught out for. So . . . well, yes, maybe she *did* have a perpetually guilty conscience at that, always wondering when one of her idiot pranks was going to catch up with her.

Or, for that matter, it might be something of more recent vintage . . . literally. She'd been hitting the booze fairly hard lately, and had been hung over well into duty hours. Thank gods it hadn't happened during a toaster attack. She had never been at anything less than her best when it had counted, but even Kara had to admit that that was as much luck as anything else. There was always the possibility that she might be forced to leap into a cockpit with her head ringing and her vision impaired. She liked to tell herself that if such a situation presented itself, she would automatically regain full sobriety and be ready to launch an attack at a moment's notice. But she didn't know how much of that was genuine and how much might just be wishful thinking.

She didn't want to think that anyone in her squad would have ratted her out, but she knew that was overly optimistic. It was entirely possible that someone had indeed done just that, and if she was going to be pointing fingers at anyone, it would probably be Kat. Kat had had it in for her for the longest time, and if presented with an opportunity to make Starbuck look bad, well, wouldn't she grab it immediately?

Maybe. Maybe not. Kat was determined to show Starbuck up, and to prove that she, Kat, was the best fighter pilot in the squad. But to show someone up, that person had to be around to *be* shown up. If Kat got Starbuck grounded somehow, then how would she, Kat, have the opportunity to prove to everyone that she had the goods and Starbuck didn't?

So it probably wasn't Kat.

Lee, maybe? Nah. If Lee had a bone to pick with her about drinking, or about anything, then he would just face her and tell her, not rat her out to his father. That just wasn't his style.

As she knocked on Adama's door, she came to the conclusion that she had nothing to worry about. He probably wanted to talk about duty rosters, or perhaps he had an assignment for her. But she hated the fact that she had such a checkered history that she felt compelled to run through an entire litany of possible negatives before she could finally decide that she had nothing to be concerned about. It made her think about the times that Tigh would look her in the face and practically snarl at her, "You're a screw-up, Thrace, and that's all you'll ever be." At which point she'd punched him and, well . . . that's when the fun usually started.

"Come," called Adama and she entered with no indication of anything in her mind other than being ready, willing and able to serve in whatever capacity she was required. Adama was leaning against his desk, sipping a cup of coffee, and he gestured for her to sit. She did so, folded her hands in her lap, and waited. She didn't have to wait very long. "I have a job for you," he said.

"Anything, Admiral," she replied. Outwardly her demeanor didn't change; inwardly she breathed a sigh of relief that her hyperactive imagination had been off base. Her inner big-mouth urged her to ask if she was going to be required to assassinate anyone this go-around, but she wisely managed to keep silent.

"Boxey is currently in residence on the transport *Bifrost*. I need you to go there and bring him back."

That surprised her. "How did he wind up on the *Bifrost*?"

"The Midguardians have apparently taken him under their wing."

"I see," said Kara, who didn't. "And may I ask why we need him brought back here? I mean, with all respect, Tigh had me give him the heave-ho from *Galactica*. He wasn't happy about leaving and I wasn't thrilled about sending him. So . . . ?"

Adama stared at her for a long moment, and she instinctively knew what was going through his mind: He was trying to decide whether to answer her question or not. Something was going on with Boxey that was obviously on a need-to-know basis, and he was endeavoring to determine whether she needed to know or not . . .

That was when it hit her like a lightning bolt. Her eyes widened and before Adama could speak, she said, "This isn't about the thing with him being a Cylon, is it? What, did Baltar change his mind?"

Adama was a hard individual to provoke a visible reaction from, and there were probably two people on *Galactica* who could accomplish it with facility. One was Lee Adama, and the other was looking at him at that moment. He blinked in surprise, and then looked wearily amused. "I should have known you'd figure it out," he sighed.

"I don't believe it," Kara said firmly. "I don't. Baltar's up to something. The man's a born liar."

"Really. I didn't think you knew him that well."

She flinched involuntarily at that, and she was sure that Adama had caught the subtle but telling reaction. Not a damned thing slipped past him. Covering as quickly as she could, she said, "I've played poker with him."

"I see." The words hung there, and Kara was certain that she was being paranoid. Was there any possible way that Adama could tell— from that slightest of exchanges—that she'd had a drunken one-night stand with the then future vice president? It was one of the most ill-advised encounters she'd ever experienced, attributable partly to liquor and partly to morbid curiosity over whether mental prowess translated to . . . other types of prowess. The encounter had been something of a disappointment, and even now she and Baltar endeavored to look in other directions when they chanced to cross each other's paths.

Adama continued to study her with his dissecting stare, and then said, "Then I guess you would know. The question then becomes, why would he lie about it?"

"I don't know," she admitted.

"Neither do I," Adama said. "So it's better to be safe than sorry, don't you agree?"

"Yes sir," Kara said without hesitation. "I assume you want me to go in presenting a friendly face. It's better to have me going in as a friend than storm the place with marines trying to force them to turn him over to us."

"Infinitely better," said Adama.

"You want me to go over there, tell him we miss him over here, tell him I talked to you and you've relented on him hanging out with us, and he'll return with me . . . at which point he gets tossed in a cell and poked and prodded all over again."

"Yes."

Kara kept her face carefully neutral. Inwardly, she was recoiling at the entire prospect, and there was a deep, burning rage building within her that was directed entirely at Baltar. But Adama didn't need her outrage at that moment. He needed her cooperation, and he needed her level head. Since she was at her most focused when she was behind the weapons console of a Viper, she pretended that was where she was. Mentally she conjured up a vista of space before her, and coming toward her was a Cylon raider. Except instead of the standard Cylon helmeted face upon it, the sneering face of Gaius Baltar was etched on it. She pulled the trigger and, in her mind's eye, blew it out of space.

"No problem," Kara assured him and then, as an afterthought, asked, "Mind if I bring Helo? He's the other pilot besides Sharon that Boxey associates with being rescued. So having him along will likely help."

"Be my guest," said Adama.

"I'm on it."

"Kara," said Adama, standing, "thank you. And be careful."

"Aren't I always?" she asked with a wry smile.

He didn't return the smile. "Almost never."

"Wow," she said. "I got an 'almost.' "

"I was being generous."

CHAPTER 16

In what she had to think was the most admirable display of restraint she'd ever shown—and, sadly, no one was ever going to know it— Laura Roslin sat at her desk and watched blood pour from Sarah Porter's eyes and ears and mouth without giving the slightest indication that anything was wrong.

Porter was the representative of Gemenon, an extremely hard-nosed and intelligent dark-skinned woman who had never hesitated to get into Laura's face on any topic. Of all the members of the Quorum, she and Roslin had the most fractious history, going back to when Roslin had denied Porter's request for additional water supplies on behalf of her constituency. Porter had retaliated (or at least that was how Laura had seen it) by backing Tom Zarek as vice-presidential candidate, but she'd been outmaneuvered when Laura had brought in Gaius Baltar who had, in turn, coasted to victory.

Since then Laura had wondered whether or not Sarah had, in fact, won out in the end. It wasn't as if Baltar was any picnic as vice president. But she kept those thoughts to herself.

"The Midguardians?" Sarah Porter was making no attempt to mask her sheer disbelief that Laura Roslin was bringing up such a subject. "They're clamoring for recognition . . . and you're actually thinking of giving it to them?"

"That might be too drastic a way to put it," said Laura. Under her desk, she was jabbing her fingernails into the palm of her hand, endeavoring to keep herself steady in the face of what she was certain were more delusions. *I am awake. I am awake and this is not happening,* she kept telling herself, and it was all she could do not to scream. "More accurate to say that I'm . . . thinking about thinking about it. That's why I wanted to speak to you."

"Me?" Porter looked amused. "Do you see me as a potential ally, Madame President?"

Laura wasn't sure how to take that, plus it required all her effort not to become ill from the sight of Sarah Porter's eye slowly seeping out of her head. Behind her, Sharon Valerii was mouthing, "Sagittarius is bleeding." Laura forced a smile that bore far more resemblance to a grimace and said, "Of course it is."

"Of course what is?" said Porter.

A part of her mind heard the disconnect between what she was saying and what Porter was hearing. It sounded vaguely familiar to her for some reason, and then she realized why: It was like having a conversation with Gaius Baltar. He likewise spoke in a disjointed manner. For one wild moment she wondered if he, too, was speaking to invisible Cylons that only he could hear, and then dismissed the notion as just too crazy for words. "Of course . . . I do," Laura corrected herself with effort. "I think, if you look at the issues that we typically face, you'll find we're united on far more things than we disagree upon."

She wasn't wild about the look that Sarah was giving her, as if there was something that should have been obvious to her that wasn't. Finally Porter said, "Perhaps you've forgotten. Madame President, but I vouched for you."

"Vouched . . . ?"

"There is no one in the Quorum more conversant with the Pythian Prophecies than I am," said Porter with a clear touch of pride. "No more who is more familiar with the Sacred Scrolls."

"Ahhh," Laura said, suddenly comprehending. "I understand."

"Do you?"

Laura rubbed her eyes, partly from fatigue, and partly in hopes that when her vision cleared, Sarah Porter would look normal once more. "You verified that the Prophecies spoke of a dying leader. You stated that you believed that leader to be me." She lowered her hand and tentatively looked up at Sarah. The blood was gone and, mercifully, so was Sharon Valerii. Laura let out a sigh of relief.

"That's exactly right," Porter said stiffly. "The leader whose vision would send us toward Earth . . . but who was dying and so would not live to see us arrive in the promised land."

"You said it was me, and suddenly I'm cured."

"Yes." Porter didn't sound particularly happy about it.

"What can I say?" asked Laura Roslin with a shrug. "Pardon me for living."

"Madame President, I staked a good deal of my credibility to the notion that you were the leader of prophecy," Porter said, giving her a defiant look and tilting her chin in a pugnacious manner. "With your miraculous cure, that credibility has taken a hit. Plus we have not seen satisfactory disclosure over the manner of your cure. People are asking questions."

"They can ask all the questions they want, Councilwoman," said Roslin calmly. "My cure is a matter of doctor/patient confidentiality. A radical new treatment for which I agreed to volunteer."

"A cure that will be made available to others who may be ill?"

"If long-term observation of my recovery indicates that it would be appropriate, then yes, absolutely," Laura told her. "But it would be premature to attempt to duplicate my cure. Anyway . . . Sarah . . . that's not why I brought you here."

"A rather clumsy attempt to change the subject," Porter observed.

"I prefer to think of it as a clumsy attempt to bring us back to the original subject."

"The Midguardians." With the air of someone who not only doesn't suffer fools gladly, but would prefer to see them all roasting on a spit, Sarah Porter asked, "What do you want to know? If I will support their petition to become part of the Quorum? Absolutely not."

"Why not?"

"Because they are heretics. Because they do not worship the same gods as we."

"Should that make a difference?" asked Roslin.

"Of course," said Sarah Porter. "Of course it makes a difference. What are you suggesting?"

"That perhaps we should consider putting aside religious concerns when it comes to government. That perhaps they should be two different aspects of life, not commingled."

Porter tried to stifle a laugh and failed utterly. "You're saying there should be a separation of church and state."

"It has occurred to me."

"President Roslin," said Porter, looking at her with amazement as if seeing her for the first time, "I knew that you had many ideas others might consider . . . aggressive. But they were always steeped in tradition. The deviation came from those people who believed the traditions and writings to be sweeping cautionary tales, as opposed to others such as myself, most of the residents of Gemenon, and other more spiritual colonies who accept the divine wisdom of the Prophecies. But no one has suggested simply operating as if religious beliefs don't matter."

"I wasn't suggesting that at all," Roslin replied. "You know how deeply rooted my convictions are. I was simply suggesting that perhaps just because they're my beliefs, and your beliefs, doesn't mean they should guide our decisions in terms of the rights of others."

"With all respect, Madame President, that's absurd. Our very morality stems from our beliefs and the lessons that the gods have taught us. If we don't root our decisions in those beliefs—if we don't allow the Sacred Scrolls to guide us—then we have nothing. We might as well be soulless Cylons." She paused and then said cautiously, "Certainly you're not advocating supporting this . . . this Midguardian bid for power."

"I don't feel as if I know enough about it to advocate it one way or the other."

"They are unbelievers," said Sarah. "What more do you need to know than that?"

"Well, for starters . . . I'd like to know about their writings. This 'Edda' that one of their leaders discusses. That's really why I wanted to talk to you; because you're so knowledgeable in these matters. Do you know anything about these writings that were supposedly excluded from the Sacred Scrolls?"

"Just rumors," Porter said. "The Midguardians have always been an insular people. The Edda itself is written in an ancient language that's handed down by their leaders, and they've kept entire portions secret even from their own followers. Their followers, amazingly enough, are satisfied with that. They have that much confidence in their historic leadership."

"I'm almost envious," said Laura with a hint of jest. Porter didn't respond to the humor, and Laura opted not to press the matter. Instead she said, "Certainly in the ancient writings there was some discussion of what the Edda had to say. Some record of why it was stricken from the main prophecies."

"As I said, rumors. For starters, it celebrated gods we didn't accept. But of even greater concern . . ." She paused and Roslin waited patiently. "Of even greater concern was that the Edda supposedly focused mainly on doomsday prophecies."

"Considering what we've been through . . ."

But Sarah Porter shook her head. "As you well know, our recent . . . travails . . . were predicted in the Pythian Prophecies. As is often the problem with such prophecies, they were easier to understand in retrospect than before the fact. The Edda writings . . . they were nothing but gloom and doom. The end of humanity with no hope of survival, of redemption . . . of anything. I don't know the specifics, but from my studies, that's the general gist of it. Now I ask you, Madame President . . . why would we want such dreary portents to become public knowledge?"

"Perhaps because the people have a right to know," replied Laura. "Because they have a right to make a decision for themselves."

Porter stared wonderingly at Laura Roslin. "Do you actually believe, Madame President, that we have the wisdom to gainsay our elders? To make these prophecies of the Edda a part of our teachings? And what if the fleet embraces it? What if they decide that humanity truly is doomed, and there's no point even in trying to survive?"

"I doubt it will come to that," and she continued before Porter could interrupt her, "and so do you, Sarah. All we're talking about is the prospect of giving them something new to think about. Where's the harm in that?"

"Where else but from new ideas does harm come, Madame President?"

Laura Roslin considered that a moment, and then shook her head. "I can't accept that," she said firmly. "I cannot accept the notion that new ideas should be suffocated. Without new ideas, new thoughts . . . we have nothing. Nothing."

"Madame President . . ."

But Roslin talked right over her. "We are being tested, Sarah. You, I, humanity. We are being tested, and how we come through that test may well determine our right to continue to exist as a species. If we put a stranglehold on even discussing new concepts, what do we have left?"

"Survival," replied Sarah Porter.

"There's more to life than survival."

"Perhaps. But without survival . . . what does the rest of it matter?"

"It matters," Laura said firmly. "I know it does. And furthermore, Sarah . . . I think you do, too. As much danger as we face on a day-to-day basis, I think we wind up seeing danger in everything. And if we're seeing danger even in the simple act of talking . . . what's that going to lead us to?"

Sarah Porter didn't reply immediately. Her lips twitched a bit, and it was impossible for Laura to discern what was going through her head.

"Let me get back to you," she said finally.

Never one to miss an opening, Roslin immediately said, "When?"

"Soon. Very soon."

Laura nodded slightly and then they both rose. Laura shook her hand firmly and Sarah Porter turned and walked out of the room. The moment she was gone, Billy entered, a look of concern on his face. Displaying no interest in what had just been discussed, he said immediately, "How are you feeling?"

She turned to face him and saw blood covering his chest.

Her expression frozen, she replied, "Fine. You?"

Sarah Porter entered the shuttle that would take her back to her home ship and said, "My apologies. I didn't know it was going to take that long."

"That's quite all right," said D'anna Biers, smiling graciously. "May I ask how it went?" She did not have her cameraman with her, but a compact camera rested on the seat next to her.

"It went as well as could be expected." She paused and then said, with a hint of amusement in her voice, "Are we on or off the record?"

"Are we even talking?" asked Biers with wide-eyed innocence.

Porter then proceeded to tell Biers everything that she had discussed with Laura Roslin. When she finished, Biers did nothing to hide her interest. "So what would happen next? A gathering of the Quorum of Twelve to discuss the prospect of allowing a thirteenth member?"

"It seems a waste of time."

"You never know," replied Biers.

Sarah Porter was as openly skeptical as Biers was anticipatory. "They'd never go for it."

"Who cares?"

"What," asked Sarah, "is that supposed to mean?"

"It means that it presents an opportunity. You're a Councilwoman. I'm a reporter. And both of us are . . ." She hesitated and then smiled. ". . . Instigators. People who like to see things shaken up. Personally, I think it would be criminal to miss out on this opportunity to bring everyone together and see what happens."

Porter drummed her fingers thoughtfully on the seat next to her, and then picked up the phone that was hanging on the wall. "Patch me through to the president, please," she said. D'anna gave her a thumbs-up, a cheerful gesture which Porter returned, and then Sarah continued, "Madame President . . . yes, it's been ages." She smiled slightly at the weak but expected jest. "I was calling to say that it didn't take me much time at all to realize you were right. What are we coming to if we're faced with ideas and concepts so dangerous that we're even afraid to discuss them. You set up the day and time for the Quorum to convene, and I will make damned sure that everyone's there. Yes," she paused as Laura spoke, "yes, I'm sure there will be some resistance to the meeting once they learn of the subject matter. There are some ancient tensions with the Midguardians that go back generations. But that's why you spoke to me, isn't it. To make certain that I would convince the Quorum to at least consider it."

She chatted with the president for a few moments more, and then assured her that she would eagerly wait to hear from her. She hung up the phone then and looked challengingly at D'anna, as if daring her to say something.

All D'anna did was smile and say, "It should make a hell of a story."

CHAPTER 17

Boxey had been going to the Midguardian sanctum on a regular basis since returning to the *Bifrost* with Freya. The sanctum had been unlike any other place of worship that he had ever attended. There were no symbols or testaments to the many gods worshipped by the Twelve Colonies. Instead there was a large upright symbol of a hammer hanging at the far end of the sanctum, right above a large double-doored cabinet wherein, Boxey had been told, the "original" Edda resided. It was securely locked in there, and although Boxey was tempted to try and crack the lock to check it out, he had resisted the impulse to do so. It didn't seem right, somehow . . . an abuse of the trust that Freya had placed upon him.

There were also no standard rows of pews as he'd seen in other temples. Instead there were long tables, rows and rows of them, and benches on either side of each table. The tables were lined with heavy mugs that appeared to be made of iron or some other heavy metal. That was because the Midguardians were big believers in drinking during services; most of their invocations of their deities consisted of raising mugs in their names and knocking back doses of alcohol.

This had become a bit more problematic since they'd been on the run from the Cylons. Alcohol wasn't in as plentiful supply as it used to be. Fortunately enough the Midguardians had considerable stores of various worshipful beverages aboard the ship and it was continuing to last them. Their attempts at building distilleries so they could produce their own home-grown booze had been uneven. Wolf had been one of the leaders in the attempt and continued to be the only one capable of swallowing and then keeping down the brew that his machine produced. Freya and other Midguardians had pronounced it fit for scrubbing down the engine coils and not much else.

The unlikely savior on that score, as it turned out, was Boxey. Several of the pilots that Boxey had been hanging out with back on *Galactica* were quite ingenious when it came to constructing such devices, and Boxey had picked up not a little knowledge from watching them at their endeavors. So Boxey had been able to spot a few flaws in Wolf's still, and Wolf was in the process of producing new batches that had been tentatively pronounced as "quite nearly potable" by his reluctant but pleasantly surprised test subjects.

The problem for Boxey was that actively participating in the salvaging of Wolf's still had only saddened him because it made him think of his friends back on *Galactica*. Or, as Freya had put it, the people who had led him to believe that they were his friends.

There was no one in the sanctum now, for it was not a prescribed time of worship. Boxey had not been allowed to participate in services since, as Freya had delicately put it, he was not quite "officially one of them." She didn't rule out the possibility that that might change in the future. In fact, she was very encouraging of it, saying it was a "definite likelihood."

Boxey stared at the hammer which, he'd been told, represented a god of thunder, and then he said softly, "Are you guys there? Are you listening to me?" He didn't receive a response, nor was he truly expecting one. Nevertheless he eased himself down onto the nearest bench and said, "That's okay. 'Cause, frankly . . . I'm not sure any of the gods are listening to me. Or to any of us. With everything that's been going on . . ." He shook his head, discouraged.

"Why did you let it happen?" he asked finally. "I mean . . . honestly? My family dead. Millions . . . billions of people dead. I just . . . I don't get it." He stood and went to the cabinet in which the Edda was secured. "Are the answers in here?" he asked. He placed his hand against the door. "If I looked in this, and had a dictionary to help me understand it . . . would it tell me what's going on? Okay, actually, I know what. But *why* is it going on? It's almost like . . . like the gods are totally behind the Cylons. Why? Why would they be? Are the Cylons right about . . . about I don't know what. About everything? And which gods are behind them? Are any behind us? Are we alone? Really . . . alone?"

"Be kind of a shame if you were alone. Can I be alone with you?"

Startled by the unexpected voice behind him, Boxey jumped slightly as he turned and gasped in astonishment. "*Starbuck!*" he cried out joyously.

She stood in the doorway, grinning in that lopsided fashion she had, and Boxey was even more stunned to see that Helo was right behind her. Without hesitation he ran to Starbuck and threw his arms around her. "What are you doing here! I didn't think—! And Helo—! This is so—!"

"I know, I know," grinned Kara Thrace, and she riffled his hair. She glanced around the sanctum and whistled. "Well, this is . . . interesting. You a Midguardian now? Sick of the old gods?"

"Can't say I blame you," Karl Agathon, a.k.a. Helo, put in, his arms folded across his broad chest. "Between you and me, I been thinking maybe these Midguard types are smarter than we are."

"Helo!" said Kara with mock horror.

"Well, frak, Starbuck, we keep worshipping them and they let us get kicked in the teeth by the Cylons. Maybe we should start looking around for something better, is all I'm saying," and he nodded toward the large hammer that was erected at the front of the sanctum. "Make the old gods stop taking us for granted."

"Aw, shut up," snapped Kara and she thumped him on the chest as if he was speaking blasphemy . . . which, technically, he was. Although she was making a great fuss of being offended by Helo's comments, Boxey had a clear recollection that Kara herself had gotten fairly liquored up on one occasion and made some rather choice comments about the gods herself. To say the least, they were disparaging. To say the most, they seemed to indicate that she had some serious doubts—either about the existence of the gods, or that they had any generous intentions toward the remnants of humanity.

"You haven't told me! What are you guys doing here?" said Boxey.

"Isn't it obvious?" Kara told him, looking surprised that he would even have to ask. "We're bringing you home."

"Home?" Boxey was amazed. "What do you mean, home?" Then his expression fell. "You mean back to *Peacekeeper*? But . . . but I didn't want to go back there. Freya said I could stay here . . ."

Helo shook his head. "She's not talking about *Peacekeeper*, sport. She's talking about *Galactica*."

He couldn't believe what he was hearing. "*Galactica*? But . . . I thought . . . you said . . ."

"We had a talk with the Old Man," Kara told him. "We got him to change his mind; and he went to Tigh, and that was that."

"Change his mind?" Boxey sat on one of the benches, astounded. "You got him to change his mind?"

"That's right, kid," Helo said, drawing up one of the benches opposite him. "You should have seen her go. She was a dynamo. She pleaded your case and got him to realize that you should be able to come over to *Galactica* whenever you wanted to."

"Really?"

"Really," said Kara, and she looked him right in the eye and repeated, "Really."

And there was something there . . .

. . . something that didn't seem right . . .

. . . something that didn't altogether make sense.

Boxey's impulse was to trust Kara Thrace. And Helo . . . hell, he had seen Helo's bravery close-up and first-hand, when the valiant lieutenant had given up his seat on the rescue raptor to Gaius Baltar in the firm belief that Baltar was more important than a lowly raptor pilot. Kara was his friend, Helo was a hero, and friends didn't lie to you and heroes were better than other people. So every instinct of his told him that there was no reason he shouldn't just march right back to *Galactica* . . .

Except . . .

Except he had seen Kara's eyes when she had told him that he had to leave. He had seen the frustration and, most of all, the uncertainty there. She had come across as extremely sympathetic, but there had still been something there in the way she looked at him that suggested she thought maybe . . .

. . . possibly . . .

. . . that he could be one of . . .

. . . them.

Well, that was the problem with suspicion, wasn't it? Once it took hold in one's imaginings, it was difficult to blast it loose. Starbuck had been suspicious that Boxey was a Cylon, and even though he'd been cleared of it, it was always going to be in the back of her mind.

And suspicion went two ways. Just as doubts about Boxey had been planted in Kara Thrace's mind, so too was he now starting to harbor doubts about her. Not that she wasn't human; oddly, the thought that she was anything other than flesh and blood, normal, one hundred percent a spawn of humanity never entered Boxey's mind. But the notion that her intentions toward him might be something other than she was saying . . . well, now that was coming straight to the forefront of his concerns. Because as he gazed into her eyes, he was seeing some of that same concern, and that didn't seem right to him. She should be overjoyed that he was going to be coming back with her. She should be smugly triumphant that she had managed to achieve the damned-near impossible: to get Adama and Tigh to change their minds on a matter of security. None of that was present in her expression, and when Boxey shifted his gaze to Helo, he wasn't seeing it there either. Instead he saw that same kind of guarded look that roused his suspicions and made him wonder just what the hell was going on.

He glanced at the mighty hammer emblem on the wall and surprised even himself when he mentally directed a plea toward it of *Give me strength.*

"Really," he echoed once more. Boxey had long ago acquired the habit of thinking quickly, and his mind was racing faster than even Kara Thrace would have suspected or been able to adjust to. "Y'know what? How about this? How about you stay for dinner tonight. I'm eating with Freya, and she's not here right now 'cause she was heading over to *Galactica* to talk with Sharon again." He watched carefully and saw Starbuck flinch just a bit when he mentioned Sharon's name. "But I bet she'd have no problem with you guys as guests."

"I don't know that we'd be her favorite people right now, sport," Helo said. His legs were outstretched and he crossed them at the ankle. He looked casual and comfortable. Except not exactly: Instead it looked like he was trying his damnedest to look as casual and comfortable as possible, which suggested to Boxey that maybe he was neither. "This whole thing with her representing Sharon . . . I think she'd be worried about . . . you know . . . talking to us. And things she might say . . ." He looked to Starbuck and there was a flash of desperation in his eyes as if he needed her to bail him out.

Starbuck quickly stepped in. "She'd probably be worried that she might say something she shouldn't and violate the whole, you know, client/patient confidentiality thing."

"Sharon isn't her patient."

"You know what I mean."

"Not completely, no," said Boxey, which was true enough.

"I'm just thinking," Kara said, and she patted him on the shoulder, "that we should head back to *Galactica* now. Because . . . you know . . ."

"The surprise," said Helo.

She glanced at him and made a show (too big a show, as far as Boxey was concerned) of looking annoyed with him. "You're supposed to keep that to yourself," she said. Heaving an annoyed sigh, she said to Boxey, "The guys were making a surprise party for you coming back, and big-mouth here tipped it off. Don't let on that you know, okay?"

On the surface of it, it all seemed perfectly harmless. Boxey wanted to believe her. He didn't want to overcomplicate this. She had come to him, and really he'd been dreaming that she would. He'd dreamt that exactly this moment would arrive and now that it had . . . it didn't feel right, smell right, sound right.

He remembered playing cards with Starbuck and the others, and he suddenly remembered one simple fact about her that had played to his advantage that evening when he'd thrashed her to within an inch of her chip stack: Starbuck was a lousy liar. She just stank at it. She was a little better at it when she'd had too much to drink, which was probably more often than she should have. But she wasn't much better sober, and generally speaking she was woefully deficient at it. It went against the grain, because Starbuck was much more someone who not only excelled at saying precisely what was on her mind, but reveled in whatever trouble might arise when she did so.

She wasn't telling the truth now. Or at least she was withholding part of it. So why was Helo there? Because she knew perfectly well that she stank at it and might well have been afraid that, left to her own devices, she wouldn't carry it off sufficiently to achieve her goal. So he was there to help.

But what was her goal?

The tumblers clicked with ruthless efficiency through Boxey's mind and unlocked the obvious answer. They wanted Boxey back at

Galactica. That much was the truth, which was why she might have thought she could carry this thing through. But it wasn't for the reason she was telling Boxey now. He was almost positive of it.

There was one way to know for sure, though.

Boxey leaned back on the bench and draped his arms on the table. He looked extremely casual, maintaining the illusion that this was just a group of friends chatting away with one another.

"How about tomorrow?" he said.

"Tomorrow?" Kara looked surprised and puzzled. "Why, uh . . . why wait until tomorrow?"

"Is there any reason I can't?" He was speaking very carefully, his voice remaining noncommittal, as if he had no suspicions at all that something might be wrong.

"No," Kara said quickly, and she looked up at Agathon, who barely shrugged. "No, no reason not, except . . . y'know . . . the surprise thing . . ."

"They can do it tomorrow, right? Or next week?"

"Next week?" she repeated.

"Yeah, it's just that . . ." He thought fast. "This week is a Midguardian holiday."

"All week?"

"Yeah, all week. They do a lot of praying and celebrating and . . . stuff. And I . . . well, I kind of promised Freya that I'd be here for it. So I really feel like I should be. So maybe next week. That works better for me. Does that work for you?"

He could sense something changing in the room. Although Helo and Starbuck didn't exchange words, the tension level increased unspoken, and Boxey intuited exactly why that was. It was because he wasn't just marching back to *Galactica* with them.

"Boxey," Starbuck began, still clutching onto her shroud of affability with both hands. Then she hesitated, and then she grunted to herself, giving Boxey the impression that she had just hit the wall in terms of what she was going to be able to accomplish through simple, casual chitchat. "That . . . would work for me, but . . . look, I don't know that Admiral Adama would be okay with that . . ."

"Why not?"

Starbuck looked to Helo in what was, as far as Boxey was concerned, a silent plea for aid because she was running out of things to say.

"It's going to make us look bad," Helo said quickly. He wasn't looking casual anymore. Now he was sitting upright, his legs no longer crossed at the ankle.

"Look bad how?"

"Because we did a major selling job to the Admiral to enable you to return," said Helo. "The whole thing hinged on how important it was for you to come back. How much you meant to all of us . . . and us to you. If we go back to the Old Man now and say that you basically blew us off . . ."

"I'm not doing that."

"You pretty much are," spoke up Starbuck. "Adama didn't change his mind lightly. It's like Helo says. We go back now and tell him you just said you'd see us when you got around to it, Adama might just go back on his word again."

"Well, if that happens," Boxey said confidently, "then you can probably talk him right back again. You're good at that, Starbuck. I believe in you."

"Boxey," she began.

"I'm not going back now, Starbuck," Boxey informed her. "You're welcome to stay here with me. Or go and tell the admiral I appreciate his changing his mind, and I'd like to take up the invitation at some future date. You can tell him that, can't you?" The problem was that he already knew the answer to it.

And Starbuck didn't disappoint him. "Yeah. I could tell him that," she said slowly. "But . . ."

It was obvious she didn't know what to say, so Helo quickly stepped in. "He'd be insulted."

"Yes," Starbuck said urgently. "He'd be incredibly insulted and, you know, we wouldn't want to do that . . ."

Boxey drew himself up. "Maybe some other time." And suddenly he was out the door before Starbuck and Helo could even react.

"Frak!" snarled Kara Thrace as she and Helo leaped up in pursuit of Boxey.

The entire thing had gone exactly according to the worst-case scenario she'd conjured in her head. The "turnaround" on Adama's part had been too abrupt. She'd done far too good a job selling Boxey on the idea that he was going to be *persona non grata* on *Galactica* for the indefinite future. So now, when she'd shown up in his new backyard and started making nice to him, it was only natural that it would arouse his suspicions.

His reactions aroused her suspicions as well. He was acting like someone who thought they might be on to him. On to him as what? As a Cylon, of course. It could well have been that they'd all been right to be suspicious of him, and now he was just trying to keep the hell away from them lest his true nature be found out.

On the other hand, he could just be a scared kid who didn't want to find himself stuck back in a cell while a mad scientist—who also happened to be the vice president—poked and prodded him and pronounced him to be an enemy of all mankind.

Either explanation made sense. The problem was that she didn't have the slightest inkling which was the right one.

She charged out of the sanctum, Helo right on her heels, and then Kara slammed into what appeared to be a bulkhead, but turned out to be a man. Under ordinary circumstances, it would have been expected that she would head one way and he the other. Instead it was solely Kara who ricocheted backward and stumbled into Helo. It was a small miracle that Helo managed to catch himself and not tumble over, righting the two of them. The man she'd collided with, in the meantime, hadn't budged from the spot at all. He'd tilted slightly but otherwise held his footing, and was now staring at the two of them with a combination of confusion and suspicion. "Who are you?" he demanded. "What were you doing in there?"

"Sir, this is military business," Kara said quickly.

"And this is my ship, making it my business."

She could have stayed to try and explain things, but Boxey had already whipped around a corridor and they were in danger of losing him. So Kara made as if she were about to stand and address the man's concerns, and suddenly she bolted right, ducking just under his outstretched arm. It was just enough distraction that Helo was able to get around him on the other side, and seconds later they were both pounding down the corridor after Boxey.

They got around the corner just in time to see Boxey vanish overhead.

It wasn't that he had disappeared into thin air. Rather he had leaped straight upward, torn off a metal grating accessing an air circulation shaft, bounded upward once more and slithered away into the narrow confines of the shaft.

"Frak!" shouted Kara. Helo took two steps in front of her, cupped his hands, and Kara propelled herself upward and into the shaft. Or at least she attempted to do so; her head, outstretched arms and shoulders made it through, but that was as far as she got. She let out a yelp of pain.

"What's wrong?!" said Helo. "Is he hurting you?!"

"No, you muttonhead! I don't fit!"

"Are you sure?"

"Well, I *would* if I had no breasts and no hips!" her irritated voice echoed from above.

"You take a look in the mirror lately?"

Now it was Helo's turn to shout in pain as Starbuck slammed one of her feet down on the top of his head.

He stepped back, rubbing where she'd kicked him, and Starbuck dropped back down to the floor. "We gotta find him."

"And do what?" demanded an irritated Helo. "It's not like we can stuff him in a sack and sling him over our shoulders."

"Don't bet on it."

"He's *a kid*, Starbuck!"

"In case you're not paying attention, that's what we don't know for certa—"

"Don't move!"

Kara froze in place as she saw the large man they'd darted past standing a few feet away. He was aiming a gun at them. It looked tiny in his oversized hand, but that didn't make it any less threatening. And there were a couple of men behind him who were also holding weapons aimed straight at them.

Her peripheral vision told her that there were more men at the other end of the corridor. Starbuck and Helo had been outflanked, encircled from either side.

"What do we do now?" muttered Helo out the side of his mouth.

"For starters, we don't move." She paused and then said, in as authoritative a tone as she could muster, "This is military business!"

"And this is me not caring very much," said the large man. The business end of the gun never wavered. "I assume you have weapons on you. Now would be the time to produce them very slowly and lay them down equally slowly on the floor."

Their guns were hanging on the backs of their belts, covered by their jackets. Neither Helo nor Starbuck had been armed in the expectation that they would have to shoot Boxey or something like that. It was simply standard operating procedure for them to go armed into any situation that was not merely a social one. One never knew when one was going to stumble over a known Cylon operative, and on such occasions, Adama never wanted his people caught unprepared.

But just because they had weapons didn't mean it was always a good idea to use them. And somehow the prospect of getting into a firefight with a group of civilians didn't seem like the wisest course of action. Although it had been some time ago, feelings in the fleet were still raw over the notorious shooting incident during the period when Tigh had declared martial law. The last thing they needed to do was exacerbate matters by having anything resembling a repeat of the incident, even though the circumstances were extremely different.

Helo and Starbuck exchanged looks and then—slowly, as instructed—they reached out and removed their respective weapons. "You're making a mistake," Helo said evenly.

The big man gestured for the men on either side of him to approach and take the extended guns. "Not as big a mistake as you would have made if you'd taken a shot at any of my people."

"One of your 'people' might not be a person at all," Kara informed him, making no attempt to keep the annoyance from her voice. "That's why we're here. You may have a Cylon infiltrator."

"And would he be the one who stole our most precious possession?"

The angry question puzzled Kara. "What are you talking about?"

He took a step toward her and seemed to loom even larger than he had before. "Don't play games with me. Where is it?"

"Where . . . is what?"

"The Edda. I looked in the sanctum after you and your associate ran out of there and it was gone. Our holy book, missing. What did you do with it?"

"Us? Nothing! Boxey must have taken it."

"The boy?" growled the big man. "You would blame something like this on the boy? Why would he do such a thing?"

"Because we think he may be a Cylon, and he's trying to distract us or maybe just stir things up. Set us against each other."

He barked a skeptical laugh. "I find that . . . doubtful."

"She's telling the truth," Helo said.

"And I'm supposed to just take her word for it?" He looked hard at them. "The word of a military that's more interested in guarding its secrets than the balance of humanity. You keep information from us until someone else finds out about it, at which point you reluctantly admit it. You cause disharmony and discord."

Not at all intimidated by the fact that he could likely break her in half, Kara snapped back, "We've saved this fleet more times than I can count. When the Cylons come swooping down on us, you're safe and snug here second-guessing everything we do while it's my ass out in a Viper that's fighting to keep us alive for another day. And that's what we're trying to do now, and if you don't like it, then frak you, so get the frak out of my face, you got that?"

He glared at her, and then—to her surprise—the look he was giving her melted ever so slightly into amusement. He took a step back. "Yes, ma'am," he said coolly, and then turned to his people. "Take them to a private room. Search them thoroughly. See if they have the Edda on them. Find Boxey. I very much doubt their claims that he's a Cylon operative, but we should at least talk to him."

"He went up there," Helo said, pointing overhead. "If you've got someone small and skinny, you may want to send them up there, because if he took your Edda thing, he could stash it anywhere in there."

"I don't need your advice, thank you," said the big man. Then he paused and muttered to his nearest lieutenant, "Do as he says. Find someone. Now." The lieutenant nodded and went off as the big man turned his attention back to Helo and Starbuck. "I am Wolf Gunnerson. As I said, this is my ship. You will be my guests here until we get matters sorted out and the Edda is recovered."

"You'll search us and find we don't have it," Kara said.

"You might have hidden it somewhere. You might have an accomplice somewhere in this ship. I try never to underestimate the ability of the military to be deceitful."

"Thanks for the vote of confidence," Starbuck said sourly. "Look, Mr. Gunnerson, there's something here you have to understand . . ."

"You're here on military business."

"That's right. And you're interfering with it. That is not going to be looked upon favorably by my CO or the president. Furthermore you're holding us against our will. That's going to be viewed by some as a hostage situation. The action of terrorists. I don't think you really want that. I don't think you want a squad of heavily armed marines crashing in here."

Wolf leaned in toward her again. His breath alone was powerful enough to rock her back on her feet. "And I think that you don't have the slightest idea of what I want. A hostage situation? Fine. So be it. I have no problem with that. You show up here, you've got concealed weapons, you threaten a boy and try to drag him back to your ship against his will, tossing around accusations that he's a machine without the slightest shred of proof, and oh, by the way, our sacred book vanishes shortly after you arrive and you're seen coming out of our sanctum. And *you* accuse *me* of terrorist activities?"

"Admiral Adama is going to want us back, with the boy," Helo said.

"You throw that name around as if it's supposed to intimidate me. If he wants you back, I'll be more than happy to throw you out an airlock and you can walk back to *Galactica*. How does that sound?" When Helo made no answer, Wolf Gunnerson made a slight gesture with his head, signaling his men. They came in from all sides and took Starbuck and Helo firmly by the wrists and arms. "Be careful, men. They're colonial warriors. They likely bruise easily."

"You're going to regret this!" Starbuck called defiantly as they were led away.

"I really don't think so," replied Wolf, who really didn't.

He stood there and watched them go. And then, after a long moment, a door to the side opened and a figure emerged. "I told you that was exactly the attitude you could expect from them."

"Indeed you did. It's fortunate you happened to be by, Councilman."

Tom Zarek nodded thoughtfully and said, "She's right about one thing, though. Adama isn't going to take this well at all. He's going to want his people back, and he could make it very difficult for you if you refuse to cooperate."

"I'm sure he could. And I could make things very difficult for him."

"He has the *Galactica*, Wolf. Face facts: You can't possibly go up against him. Meantime your bid to be part of the Quorum of Twelve could be seriously hurt by this."

"I have no trouble with being both feared in my wrath . . . and admired in my generosity."

Zarek eyed him suspiciously. "Meaning . . . ?"

"Meaning the day is young." And he clapped Zarek on the back in a manner that was gentle for him and, even so, nearly dislocated Zarek's shoulder. "And I am thirsty. Let's quench that thirst together and we'll wait for matters to play out to our advantage."

CHAPTER 18

"Animals," said Freya Gunnerson.

From within her enclosure, Sharon Valerii looked in confusion at her attorney. Pressing the phone tighter against her ear, she said, "What about animals?"

"Adama suggested it to me . . . although he didn't realize that's what he was doing," Freya said smugly. "Talking about the Cylons trying to slaughter us like animals. His whole argument to keep you cooped up in here, despite the fact that you've committed no crime, is that you're not human. But there's plenty of case law on the books about animal rights."

"But . . . I'm not an animal . . ."

"Yes, you are, in the sense that I am and Adama is as well. All humans are part of the animal kingdom. He keeps calling you a machine, but there's not a shred of proof that you are. Certainly no more so than any human who's operating with an artificial heart or a replacement knee. There's every proof, however, that you're an animal, and under our law, animals have rights."

"Animals get put in cages all the time. In zoos . . ."

"Yes, and there were laws to guard their best interests even then. Safeguards."

"I don't understand where you're going with this."

"It's very simple, Sharon. We go to precedents. That's how the law works." Freya's voice was becoming more excited, more enthused, as she contemplated what was to come. "We build case law to show that even the humblest zoo creature has more rights, has more protection under the law, than you. We—"

"Who do we do this with?"

Freya blinked. She seemed rather surprised that Sharon would interrupt her. "What do you mean?"

"I mean, who do we do this with? I don't know if you noticed, Freya, but the legal system as we know it has fallen apart somewhat." She ticked off options on her fingers. "There's Adama. There's the president. There's the Quorum. My understanding is that there's a few freelance mediators going around who are overseeing simple disputes. But people are just scrambling to survive. There's no full judicial system that I know of."

"Not at the moment."

"Moments are all I have," Sharon said fiercely, so fiercely that it startled Freya. "Don't you get that? Every day I wake up might be my last if Adama or the president decides I'm too great a risk. I don't have the option of looking at the big picture."

"And that's what I'm trying to change."

"Why? I still don't understand."

"Because," Freya said, "it's the right thing to do!"

"And do you think they'll give a damn?" Sharon started to walk around, her body giving vent to her frustration. Within moments she'd moved beyond the distance that the phone cord would allow and the receiver flew out of her hand. She grabbed for it and it thudded against the side of her cell. Sharon started to reach for it, and then let out an anguished cry of fury. "You're going to file my appeal with the same people who stuck me in here? You must be crazy! And I must be crazy for listening to you! You know they're going to reject any argument you make."

"I'm just trying to get you what you want," Freya assured her.

Her voice came over the phone receiver, and Sharon could hear it even though it wasn't to her ear. And Sharon was speaking so loudly that Freya had no trouble hearing her.

"What I want?" She thumped her chest. "You don't know what I want! You have no frakking clue!"

"Freedom for yourself! Freedom for your child!"

"*I'm not going to get freedom!* I'm a *Cylon*! I'm the frakking *enemy*! They're never going to just let me go! I don't get to live happily ever after with Helo and my baby, and we set up a nice family. You think I don't know that? You think I don't see what's coming? The only reason I'm alive is because *Galactica* needs me to keep saving their ass. The only reason my baby is alive is because they needed it to save Roslin's life. If they ever make it to Earth and find safe harbor, you know what the first thing they're gonna do is? Put a *bullet* in my *frakking brain* and turn my baby into a lab rat! If you ever convince them that they can't treat me the way they currently do, that's when I die. And they'll do it without fanfare, and without a thought, and without you. And what'll you do after I'm dead, huh? File a protest? Wag your finger and say 'Shame on you'? What do I want? What I want is, just once before I die, to walk around where there's some flowers and trees and dance on some grass in my bare feet, just for a little while. For a couple frakking hours. Then I'll be happy."

She looked as if she wanted to shout even more, but exhaustion overwhelmed her. She sagged against the side of the cell and then onto her bed. She put her hand on her stomach and just sat there, shaking her head.

"Sharon," said the frustrated Freya, "pick the phone back up. Please. Pick it up and put it to your ear."

Sharon stared at the receiver from which Freya's voice was emerging. Then she picked up the phone but, rather than listening to it, she spoke softly, in a voice that was measured and tired but had an undercurrent of strength to it. "You know what I think?"

"Sharon, you need to listen to me—"

"I think," Sharon continued as if she hadn't spoken, "that you just wanna frak with people. With me. With Adama. With the president. The whole council. You just wanna use me to stir things up. I don't know why. I also don't care very much. Maybe something will come up to make me care but, right now . . . I don't."

With that, she turned and hung the phone up, cutting off Freya's voice as she continued to protest.

Freya thumped with her open palm on the outside of the cell, but Sharon ignored her. Then there was the heavy noise made by the outside door that led into the cell area, and Freya glanced over. She was not remotely surprised when Adama strode in.

She was surprised, however, when two colonial marines followed him in and pointed their weapons straight at her.

Adama barely kept his cold fury in check as he stared at Freya Gunnerson. His jaw was so clenched that it was difficult at first for him to utter words. "I've just been informed," he said without preamble, "that two of my people are being held on the *Bifrost*. On your father's vessel."

"Really." Freya looked as if she were feigning interest and not doing a good job of it. "Should that be of particular importance to me?"

"Considering it's going to have a very direct impact on your own liberty, I'd think it should."

Freya laughed at that. Her laughter did not sit well with Adama, who refrained from ordering the marines to shoot her in the leg in order to get her full attention. But resisting the temptation was no easy chore. "My liberty?" asked Freya when she'd sufficiently recovered herself. "Two of your soldiers got themselves into some trouble on my father's ship. How does that have anything to do with my liberty?"

"They're being held there on some trumped-up charges. Suspicion of stealing a holy book of yours."

"The Edda?" The amusement vanished from Freya's face, although Adama was sure it might be nothing more than a superb acting job. "They took the Edda?"

"They are suspected of doing so . . . except my own suspicion is that your father knows perfectly well they didn't. He's doing this to force the issue of your people, the Midguardians, becoming members of the Quorum."

She shrugged. "That's possible. I certainly wouldn't rule it out.

He tends to come up with unorthodox solutions to achieve his goals. I still don't see what any of this has to do with me. Certainly you're not intending to keep me prisoner as some sort of retaliatory step."

"That is exactly my intention."

She laughed again, but this time it had a much more skeptical, even scolding tone to it. She addressed him as if the matter were already resolved and she was trying to guide him to the solution in the same way that a parent would ease a child over the span of a brook lest they wet their feet. Adama's face didn't so much as twitch. "Admiral," she said when she'd composed herself, "Perhaps you think that your feckless imprisonment of Lieutenant Valerii gives you the right to lock up anyone and everyone you want. Hell, you tossed the president of the Colonies into jail as part of a military coup. Some people believed that, since your . . . unfortunate incident . . ."

"My assassination attempt by someone who looked just like your client, you mean."

"Yes," she said dismissively as if the specifics were of no importance. "As I was saying, some believed that you had changed in your attitudes and outlook since then. It appears now that you're . . . what's the best way to put this . . . ?"

"Not frakking around." There was no trace of humor in his voice, no flicker of pity in his eyes. The absence of both finally got through to Freya Gunnerson, and she began to realize her extreme vulnerability.

However, she was almost as skilled as Adama in presenting an air of conviction and certainty. "I was going to say 'regressing.' You don't seriously think you can hold me here?"

"Unless you're packing enough weaponry to shoot your way out, I seriously think exactly that. Your father has my people. I have you. I'm thinking you might be something I can trade."

She squared her shoulders and faced him, not backing down in the slightest. "I am not a commodity. However you may choose to view Sharon Valerii, Admiral . . . I am human. I have committed no crime. I am not responsible for the actions my father has taken. I knew nothing about the theft of the Edda until I heard it from you just now. You have no grounds whatsoever upon which to hold me."

"Arrest you," he growled.

"The smartest thing you can do—frankly, the only thing you can do—is stand aside so that I can return to my vessel. If you wish, I assure you that I will talk to my father and convince him to release your people as soon as they turn over the Edda. Considering our tribal law prescribes murder as the punishment for theft of the book, I think that's rather generous on my part. This offer has a limited shelf-life, Admiral. I suggest you take me up on it."

Suddenly Adama was distracted by a loud thumping from the cell. He glanced over at Sharon. She was now holding the phone inside to her ear and was gesturing for Adama to pick it up.

His first instinct was to ignore her. To just let the phone sit there in the cradle where Freya had left it. But Adama had gradually come to the realization that his first instinct was frequently unreliable when it came to Sharon Valerii. Without looking back at Freya, he strode over and picked up the phone.

Her voice came through low and conspiratorial. There was demand in her tone, but it was laced with pleading. "Take her outside. I want to talk to just you."

He was tempted to ask why, but saw no reason to hurry it. He turned to the marines and said, "Escort Miss Gunnerson outside and wait there for further orders."

"Admiral," said Freya angrily, "she's my client."

"And this is my ship," he reminded her grimly. "I win." He nodded confirmation of the order he'd just given, and the two marines removed Freya from the room. They kept their weapons in plain sight, but it wasn't as if she offered huge amounts of resistance as she was ushered out. As combative as she was, Freya knew better than to try and have it out with two heavily armed marines.

The moment they were alone, Sharon said briskly, "She was lying. She knows something."

The flat assertion caught Adama by surprise, although naturally there was nothing in his expression that would have confirmed that. "You were able to hear us?"

"I can lip read."

This admission startled Adama. Even more startling was that he'd never thought of that before. "All right," was all he said.

"So I wanted you to know . . . she was lying." She hesitated and for a moment even looked slightly confused. "I just . . . I wanted you to know that. I thought it might help you." Then, as if rallying from self-doubts, she said more forcefully, "Because that's what I do here. I help you. That's *all* I do," she added pointedly . . . a point that did not elude Adama.

"How do you know she was lying?"

"Because I can tell."

"That's not an answer."

"Maybe," she allowed, "but it's the best one you're going to get. I can tell. *We* can tell. There's certain ways to determine when a hu—" She caught herself and amended, "when someone . . . lies. We're trained to see them, spot them. Take advantage of them."

"Trained?"

"Maybe that's the wrong word. It's . . . hardwired into us. One of the tools of our trade, so to speak."

"And I'm supposed to believe you?"

She smiled thinly. "You're not 'supposed' to do anything, Admiral. You can do whatever you want. I'm just telling you what I know."

"In order to help."

"That's right."

He considered that for a brief time. Then he said, "Let's say . . . for the sake of argument . . . that I believe you. What do you suggest I do with this information?"

Sharon shrugged. "I don't know. Get the truth from her, I suppose."

This time the pause from Adama was far longer, his eyes studying her with calculated coldness. Two of his people were in trouble, and the reason they were in trouble was because he had sent them into the situation in the first place. So it was bad enough that he was dealing with the sense of personal responsibility over having thrust them into harm's way. He didn't feel guilty over it; putting soldiers of his, even beloved ones—hell, especially beloved ones—into jeopardy was simply another day at the office for him. He wasn't second-guessing his decision. Given the same circumstances, he'd do the exact same thing again. Nevertheless, his sense of personal involvement was even sharper since difficulties had arisen from a specific mission upon which he had dispatched two of his people, as opposed to ordering pilots into the air to defend against an unexpected Cylon assault.

He had no hesitation, none, about sending in armed troops to get them back. After all, he had been willing to throw his pilots against the *Pegasus* in order to retrieve Helo and Chief Tyrol when Admiral Cain had been ready to have them executed. But if there were ways in which to resolve the situation that didn't risk yet another incident that the press could transform into *Galactica*-against-the-fleet, he was more than willing to pursue them.

Adama was starting to think that Sharon Valerii was hinting she might serve as that means of resolution.

"Are you suggesting," he asked slowly, "that you would be capable of getting that truth from her?"

Her eyes narrowed. "I wasn't suggesting that, no."

"I see."

The seconds of silence stretched out.

And finally, Sharon said, "But if I were . . . what's in it for me?"

At that moment, things that Tigh had said to him came back to him. How it was that, despite everything that had happened, Adama still looked at Sharon Valerii and saw Boomer, the eager, ready-to-please young recruit and pilot whom Adama and Tigh couldn't help but have a fatherly enjoyment of and tolerance for. When she'd become inappropriately involved with Chief Tyrol, the bulk of their anger about such a relationship had been focused on Tyrol rather than Valerii, even though they were both equally responsible.

As insane as it sounded, despite the fact that his chest had been ripped open by several shots delivered at point-blank range by a creature who was identical to this one . . . a creature now dead, and yet here she was hale and hearty and pregnant, of all things . . . despite the fact that he knew in his heart of hearts that she was nothing more than a machine, an automaton, a damned frakking toaster . . . despite all of that, he still couldn't help but feel as if she were still good ol' Boomer, the utterly human Sharon Valerii.

But the individual who had just asked the question, "What's in it for me?" was not Sharon Valerii, nor was she Boomer. Right there, right then, was the calculation and coldness of a Cylon agent: detached, unemotional, deliberating as to what would be required in order to complete a mission that would potentially bring misfortune to a human being . . . misfortune that didn't bother Sharon in the least, because she wasn't remotely human.

He should have turned away. He should have been repulsed and revolted over the slightest notion of embarking on any endeavor in league with this . . . thing.

But he didn't. Because instead of simply surrendering to the notion that this was indeed some unemotional, calculating inhuman machine which feigned every emotion in service of its greater goal of sabotage, Adama decided to say something just to see how she would react.

"One of the people taken prisoner on the *Bifrost* is Starbuck." He hesitated for a carefully timed moment and then said, "The other is Helo."

And there it was.

The coldness of the Cylon that she was at the moment instantly dissolved into the Sharon Valerii that she once had been . . . back before Adama knew her to be anything other than Sharon Valerii. Telling her that Starbuck was in trouble gained her interest. Telling her that the father of her child was endangered engaged her heart.

So apparently . . . she had one.

Her face paled, her eyes widened, and he saw a sharp little intake of breath. Quickly she tried to cover it, but he'd seen it. More than that: She knew he'd seen it.

"Does that change things at all?" he asked, knowing the answer before he asked it.

"It . . . provides some incentive." She considered the situation carefully, obviously turning over all its aspects in her mind, and then said, "Are you interested in a deal?"

"I don't bargain with Cylons," he replied. Then, before she could say anything, he added, "But if I did . . . hypothetically . . . what sort of terms are we talking about?"

Sharon Valerii had had a lousy night's sleep.

She had been dreaming of Laura Roslin . . . and she didn't know why.

She had seen herself lying flat on her back, tied down to a bed in sickbay. Her stomach had been flat and taut, not at all the swelling lump it was now. She had struggled to free her hands and feet, but they were too well secured. She had tried shouting at the top of her lungs, but even though her mouth was wide open and she was trying to scream, nothing was emerging from her throat.

And then Laura Roslin had walked in, and Sharon had gaped at her in complete shock. Roslin's belly was swelled with pregnancy, as far along as Sharon's own. More than that: She knew without the slightest doubt that it was her—Sharon's—child within Laura Roslin's body. She had no idea how it could possibly be that she was no longer the mother of her own child, and yet that was what had happened.

Laura had stood there, smiling, affectionately rubbing the child that she had taken from Sharon, and she cooed, "Mine now. All mine. Allllllll mine."

Give it back! Give me back my baby! Sharon's voice had echoed in her own mind. She felt as if she were moving in slow motion, trying to swim through heavy, viscous liquid, and Laura Roslin turned and waddled away, singing some annoying human lullaby.

Sharon had woken up at that point, her clothes soaked in cold sweat, gasping for air. A guard had charged in in response to her outcry, but he wasn't remotely concerned about her well-being. Instead it was abundantly clear that he was wary of some sort of trick on her part. "What's wrong?" he had demanded, the business end of his rifle aimed—not directly at her—but certainly in her general direction.

She had gasped out, "Nothing. Bad dream. It . . . was nothing," and he'd glared at her for a time and then turned and walked out.

As silly as it sounded, she'd actually jostled her stomach to make sure the baby was still there. Despite the obvious distention of her belly, she wasn't taken anything for granted. That's how disturbing and confusing the dream had been. So she had shaken her stomach repeatedly until the baby—who'd presumably been asleep—offered a kick in protest. It was at that point that she gave a relieved sigh and settled back in her bunk.

But she had not fallen back to sleep.

Instead she had lain there and stewed on her situation, and although yes, it had all been a dream, she found herself being irrevocably drawn back to a grim and depressing realization: She had nothing. Anything that she possessed—even something as inviolable as the bond between mother and child—could be taken away from her at a moment's notice and a president's whim.

Ever since the first visit from Freya Gunnerson, she had nursed the notion that maybe, through some miracle, Freya could prevail. Perhaps it was possible. Perhaps she could indeed achieve for Sharon some measure of freedom, some claim upon happiness. But her thoughts in those dark hours had turned bleak and frustrated. She knew the dream itself was not, could not, be real. That didn't prevent her from connecting with the emotions and fears that were the underlying motivators for it.

Despite the fact that there was a child within her, she had never felt more alone.

Her foul mood had not dissipated during the day, and it was at that point that Freya had unfortunately chosen to show up and share with Sharon her latest views and theories on her case. When Sharon had lashed out at Freya, allowing her deep frustration with her situation to fuel her hostility, she had almost enjoyed the comic look of confusion in Freya's face.

Almost.

Part of her was still angry with herself. After all, this had been the first individual in ages who had shown herself remotely interested in Sharon's welfare. So why was she lacing into Freya, of all people?

She had to think it was because she had come to the conclusion that her situation was not only hopeless, but it was obviously hopeless, and anyone who didn't realize that . . . well, there was simply something wrong with them. They were stupid on a genetic level. That being the case, why should Sharon be wasting any time at all with them?

And then . . . then Adama had shown up.

And she'd learned of the situation that had developed on the *Bifrost*.

And she'd learned who was involved in it.

And that had focused her attentions in a new direction.

So it was that when Freya Gunnerson was escorted back into the cell area that Sharon Valerii occupied, Sharon fixed her with a level and very disconcerting gaze. Adama, to Freya's clear surprise, was no longer there. All bluster and annoyance, Freya said loudly to the marine escorting her—as if she were hard of hearing, or as if she were playing to an audience in imaginary balconies—"I don't know what you think you're doing! You have no legal right to hold me here!"

"I know," said the marine. "I'm just sick about that."

There was a second marine backing him up, and Freya looked around in confusion as the marine escorting her unlocked Sharon's cell. The second marine kept his weapon leveled on Sharon lest she, for some reason, decide to charge the door in what would certainly be a suicidal escape attempt. Sharon stayed right where she was. Freya was shoved into the cell with her and the door locked behind her.

"What's this supposed to mean?" she demanded. "What, we're *both* Adama's prisoners now? Is that it?"

Neither marine said anything. Instead they walked out of the room, the heavy door slamming shut behind them.

"Oh, they'll fry for this," Freya told Sharon. She glanced around the cell as if seeing such an enclosure from the inside out was a huge novelty. Perhaps it was. Sharon had had plenty of time to become accustomed to it, so the "charm" had pretty much worn off. "I'm telling you, Sharon, they're going to fry, the lot of them. Adama's military-industrial complex has gone too far this time. Too far by half. They think they can silence protest or run roughshod over individual liberties, but when I get through with them—"

"Shut up."

Freya looked taken aback. "I beg your pardon?"

"Shut up . . . and listen."

There was something in Sharon's voice, a . . . deadliness . . . that completely seized Freya's attention.

Sharon took a deep breath and let it out. "You lied to the Admiral. You're not going to be allowed to lie to me. If you know what's good for you, you're going to tell me what's going on, and you're going to tell me now."

"Sharon, this is—"

"If you don't know what's good for you," Sharon continued, unfazed, "then you're going to give me grief, and you're going to stonewall . . . but you're still going to wind up telling me, because I'm going to make you do so. Do you understand what I'm saying?"

"Obviously I do. I'm not stupid. And it's perfectly clear what's happening. You think that you have to throw your lot in with Adama and his ilk because you don't have a chance when it comes to fighting for your own interests." She smiled in a way that was an odd combination of sufferance and pity. "Sharon, Sharon, Sharon . . . you're underestimating what a careful program of legal savvy and public relations manipulation is capable of producing. I didn't have a chance to show you my nine-point plan to—"

She didn't get any further. Sharon's right hand stabbed out and seized her around the windpipe. Freya's eyes were round white orbs of shock and terror, and Sharon told her in low, measured tones, "Okay . . . obviously you didn't understand what I said, which would seem to indicate that, yes, you are stupid. Normally that would be your problem. Now I'm making it mine."

Sharon took a step forward and shoved Freya back. Even though she was a couple of heads shorter than Freya, there was no disputing who was the stronger. Freya, having no say in the matter at all, was slammed back against the cell walls, which rattled under the impact. She let out a cry. Sharon didn't care. Instead her eyes burned with fearsome intensity and her fingers worked their chokehold around Freya's windpipe. Freya tried to cry out a second time and this time around she wasn't even able to inhale the required air.

"Listen very carefully," Sharon Valerri told her, and there was no mercy in her voice and less than none in her eyes. "You need to understand your situation: You are locked in a cell with a Cylon. Do you understand that? A Cylon. Not a human. Not one of your own. A Cylon. And Cylons do not hesitate to do whatever the frak we feel like doing in order to accomplish our own ends. You are going to talk to me. If you do not . . . I am going to hurt you. I am going to hurt you in ways that you didn't know you *could* be hurt. I have a thorough and intimate knowledge of human anatomy and I am not afraid to use it. There are places on your body where applying the slightest pressure will visit agonies upon you that you will not have believed possible. And there will not be a mark on you to show an adjudicator or a Council member or the president herself. But the recollection of the pain you will suffer will stay with you forever. It will stay with you until old age, presuming you live that long, and on nights when you go to bed convinced that you've finally, finally left it behind you, on those nights you're going to wake up screaming and your old nightmares will be back to haunt you. And in those worst nightmares, you're going to see my frakking face looking at you with the most inhuman expression of detachment you've ever seen.

"I will torture you for information and I absolutely will not give a goddamn about it. I can do that, you see. Nice advantage over humans. I can just turn my emotions off and do what needs to be done.

"And I will do that to you.

"Now talk to me about what I want to know . . . and don't stop until I've told you I don't want to know any more." As a perverse afterthought, she added, "Please."

She released the pressure on Freya's throat slightly on the assumption that Freya would start talking.

Instead Freya snarled in her face, "F-frak you," and launched wad of spittle that landed squarely on Sharon's left temple. Sharon made no move to brush it away.

"And we're off," Sharon said softly.

Outside the cell, the marines heard the screams start. They weren't Sharon's. The guards stared at each other, and silently exchanged a question: *Are we going to do something about that?*

After a few long moments, they did do something about it: One of them went off to get some earplugs while the other remained at his post and whistled idle tunes softly to himself.

And he listened to the screams.

He hated to admit to himself how much he liked the sounds of them. He wondered if it made him a bad person.

Ultimately he decided that, if it did, that was okay.

He could live with that.

CHAPTER 19

Laura Roslin was doing an admirable job of keeping her cool, which provided a sharp contrast to Tom Zarek. She sat behind her desk, her fingers steepled, her level gaze on Zarek, whose renowned cool under pressure was showing its first signs ever of melting.

"You can't be blaming me for this bloody mess," Zarek told her fiercely.

Laura tried not to flinch at his use of the word "bloody." Images from her dreams still had considerable force to her, and she was bound and determined not to let any of her haunted nights impede her ability to deal with the current situation. She couldn't remember the last time she'd slept for more than two hours straight, and inwardly she lived in fear that some new delusion was going to present itself to her and make her unable to handle whatever problem she was embroiled in.

Outwardly, she wasn't presenting the slightest hint of her inner doubts. "They're your people, Councilman."

"They're from Sagittaron, Madame President. That doesn't make them 'my people.'"

"You brought him in here. Brought him to my office, with high-flown words of how they deserved respect and proper treatment. How they were discriminated against because of their beliefs. And now it turns out they're nothing but terrorists."

"That is not true," Zarek said forcefully. "They have a grievance . . ."

"So do terrorists."

"They're the injured parties here, Madame President. Gunnerson is asserting that members of *Galactica* are responsible for one of their most precious artifacts going missing."

"If Mr. Gunnerson had a dispute with the military, and he wanted to be treated like a civilized member of society, then he could have come to me."

"With all respect, Madame President, the last time *you* had a major dispute with the military, Adama threw your ass in a cell and nearly demolished the fleet. So in my view you don't exactly have a stainless record when it comes to such matters."

The blush of her cheeks shone a bit brighter against her makeup.

"One wonders how that would have come out if you *hadn't* been speaking with all respect."

Zarek started to speak again, but then reined himself in. "I'm sorry," he said, which were two words that she certainly hadn't expected to hear him utter anytime in their relationship. "That was uncalled for. Not . . . entirely irrelevant, but uncalled for nevertheless."

She inclined her head slightly in acknowledgment of the apology, as half-hearted as it was. "The point remains, Councilman," she said evenly, "that we have an explosive situation on our hands. Adama is champing at the bit to get in there and get his people back," which wasn't entirely true. Certainly Adama was monitoring things and she'd been talking to him extensively about it. But Adama wasn't anxious to have yet another incident on his hands, and as long as his officers weren't in immediate threat of losing their lives, he was willing to hold off taking action and instead allow diplomatic efforts to proceed. There was no reason for her to tell Zarek that, though. "I want to sort this out as much as you do, Councilman. There are human lives at stake, and besides, I've currently got every reporter in the fleet packed into my press room howling for a statement."

"Let me go over to the *Bifrost*," said Zarek. When she shook her head, he said more forcefully, "I'm their representative, Madame President. I have some degree of relationship with their leader. In fact, I was over there earlier, before this business began. I'm the logical person . . ."

"You're the logical person to be an even better hostage, Mr. Zarek," Roslin reminded him. "You're not an outsider anymore. Like it or not, you're a man of influence. A member of the Quorum. That gives you a certain amount of trade value. I'm not interested in handing them yet another chip. Their ship is embargoed for the duration and that's the end of it."

"Then at least let me talk to them."

"Gladly," she said, "provided they were willing to talk to us. Our initial attempts have received no response . . ."

With timing that Laura Roslin would look back upon as being almost supernatural, Billy knocked and entered the room without being told to do so. "Wolf Gunnerson of the *Bifrost* on the line for you, Madame President," he said, clearly trying to deliver the news in as dispassionate and professional a manner as he could.

Roslin and Zarek exchanged looks. "People will surprise you," Zarek said calmly.

"Record the call," she told Billy.

He nodded. "Recorder is already on."

For a heartbeat she considered conferencing Adama in on the call. She quickly discarded the notion, not because she didn't trust him to remain cool in the situation, but because she preferred to hold him in reserve as a possible club. *I'm not sure how much longer I can hold the admiral in check* was going to play better if Adama wasn't actually in on the conversation sounding firm but reasonable.

She took a deep breath, let it out slowly, and then picked up the phone. In deference to Zarek, she pushed a button so that a speaker was activated. That way Zarek could listen to what was being said, although he couldn't be heard himself. "This is President Roslin."

"Madame President," came Wolf's voice. "Thank you for taking my call."

"Thank you for calling," she said formally.

"So . . . it appears we have a bit of a predicament on our hands."

He didn't sound especially threatening. They might just as easily have been chatting about each other's respective health. "I would categorize it as somewhat more serious than that," she said. "I hope you don't think this is some sort of game, Mr. Gunnerson."

"No, Madame President, I most certainly do not. The most obvious difference is that games have clear winners and losers. If matters spiral out of control, we will have nothing *but* losers."

Roslin wouldn't have said it aloud, but Gunnerson was sounding amazingly reasonable about it. It was hard to remember that he was the one who had set this entire fiasco into motion. Although the chances were that he would have come right back and said that Adama was the one responsible.

She knew perfectly well the reason that Adama had sent two of his people onto the *Bifrost*. Adama had been most efficient in keeping her apprised of his actions. The problem was that she had no way of knowing whether this entire issue with the Edda was some sort of trumped-up maneuver to try and distract from the business at hand. She wondered if Gunnerson even knew that they had a possible Cylon agent on board, although admittedly she was still having trouble believing that the boy was an operative. Roslin had to think that making no mention of Boxey was the best way to go, particularly if Gunnerson didn't bring him up.

Zarek, hearing what Gunnerson was saying, nodded and gave Roslin an encouraging thumbs-up. She tried not to roll her eyes at that. As if she needed moral support and pep talks from Tom Zarek, of all people. "I'm pleased to hear you say that, Mr. Gunnerson. This matter needs to be resolved immediately by the release of the colonial officers."

"I would love to comply with you, but I can't at this time. Not until I know what the status of the Edda is."

"You have my personal guarantee, sir, that the two officers had nothing to do with it."

"And my people have my personal guarantee," he replied, "that I will take every step to ensure the Edda's return. Releasing two prime suspects—whom I assure you will not be harmed—would be counterproductive, wouldn't you say?"

"I would say, Mr. Gunnerson, that if you have the slightest hope of the Midguardians becoming members of the Quorum, then you have to release Admiral Adama's people. Certainly you see that your actions won't sit well with the Quorum."

"That is only because I'm not making my case to the Quorum itself. Were I to do so, I believe I could make them understand not only why I'm being forced to take this action, but why we should be given our rightful place in the hierarchy of the colonies."

"I am making endeavors in that direction, Mr. Gunnerson, but they will be completely undone if this is allowed to continue. All we have is your word that the colonial soldiers will remain unharmed. You've no way of guaranteeing that . . ."

There was no response from the other end.

"Mr. Gunnerson?" She flashed a look of concern in Zarek's direction. He shook his head, his face blank. Obviously he had no clearer idea than Roslin of why Gunnerson had suddenly gone silent. "Mr. Gunnerson, are you still—"

"Sorry. Sorry, Madame President," his voice came back, and he quickly added, "And I'm sorry I interrupted you just then."

"It's quite all right." She kept the relief out of her voice. "Go ahead."

"I was just thinking: There's an easy solution to this, other than freeing the suspects."

"It's not readily apparent."

"Allow me to come to *Colonial One* and address the assembled Quorum."

She was startled at the notion. Zarek was quickly nodding enthusiastically, but a silent look from her stopped him. She glanced toward Billy, who shrugged noncommittally. "Mr. Gunnerson, we are not going to allow ourselves to be strong-armed into meeting with you."

"No one is strong-arming anyone, Madame President. I am volunteering myself in what could reasonably be viewed as a hostage exchange. You are asking me to place myself into a weaker position by releasing the suspects. I am instead offering to put you into a stronger position by voluntarily coming over there. Strong-arming? I would be counting on your good offices to allow me to meet with the assembled Quorum rather than, say, turn me over to Adama to be tossed into a holding cell."

"I could still do that, you know."

"Yes, but I would believe you if you said you wouldn't. I would take your word for it. I am that determined to have my chance to speak to the Quorum and make my case on behalf of my people."

Zarek gestured that she should put Gunnerson on hold a moment so that he could speak to her. Her immediate instinct was to ignore him. It wasn't as if she needed Tom Zarek to tell her what to do. On the other hand, she *had* brought him here as the Sagittaron representative, so it probably wasn't going to hurt to hear what he had to say. "Mr. Gunnerson, please hold on," she said, placed him on hold and then said brusquely, "What?"

If Zarek was put off by her tone, he didn't let it show. "What have you got to lose?" he said, trying to sound reasonable. "We both know we're on the clock. Adama may be—"

"*Admiral* . . . Adama," she corrected him. She had been the one who had given him the rank, and she found she didn't like Zarek simply referring to the fleet's CO simply by his surname. It struck her as disrespectful.

Taking it in stride, he amended, "Admiral Adama may be willing to wait, but he's not going to do so forever. If Gunnerson is here, that could well buy us more time. The longer a hostage situation goes on, the better chance there is having it ended with words instead of casualties."

"And you would know."

"Yes," he said crisply, "I would."

She tapped a thoughtful finger on the desk, and then took the call off hold. "Mr. Gunnerson, are you still there?"

"Still here, Madame President."

She realized she was rolling the dice with the Quorum. She was counting on Sarah Porter and Tom Zarek, of all men, to make this happen. As president she could call a meeting of the Quorum but she was not constitutionally empowered to force them to show up. It was part of the checks and balances built into the constitution, to guarantee that the president would always have to use tact and diplomacy in her dealings rather than strong-arming the representatives of the people. Of course, the constitution—or at least the original copies of it, preserved from its original drafting—had been blown to bits by the Cylons. Its spirit, however, lived on. "If you come here to *Colonial One*, I will ask the Quorum to assemble. You will be allowed to present your case to them. But what this will buy you, Mr. Gunnerson, is twelve hours. After twelve hours, barring credible evidence that they have committed some sort of crime, I will insist that officers Thrace and Agathon be released. And by credible evidence, I am ruling out confessions. I am not going to give anyone over there incentive to try forcing admissions of guilt out of them. If the officers are not released by that point, I will indeed turn you over to Admiral Adama, at which point, gods help us all."

There was another pause, but this time Roslin said nothing, allowing time for a response to come.

"Very well, Madame President," said Gunnerson finally. "Your terms are acceptable. I will take a transport to *Colonial One*. You will assemble the Quorum and I will speak my piece over allowing my people to be given official representation. In return I guarantee the safety of the colonial officers for twelve hours, as of which point they will then be returned, hale and hardy, to the *Galactica*."

It still didn't answer the issue of Boxey, but her priority at that point was ending the immediate situation without bloodshed. That was especially important to her. She knew to what extent Adama was willing to ensure the safety of his people. Furthermore, although she knew Adama didn't place higher priorities on some lives than others, she was aware that there was a particular bond between Adama and Kara Thrace. If anything happened to her while she was in the hands of the Midguardians, Roslin didn't even want to think what the ramifications might be. She was reasonably sure that Adama wouldn't simply turn the big guns of the *Galactica* on the *Bifrost* and blast it to pieces . . . but on the other hand, she wasn't interested in finding out.

"Very well. I will see you shortly. *Colonial One* out." She hung up the phone, looked over to Billy and said, "Send a copy of that recording to Admiral Adama immediately."

"Yes, ma'am."

Billy headed out, and Tom Zarek was promptly on his feet. "Madame President . . . we've had our differences . . . but I just want to say, I thought you handled that quite well."

"Tell me, Councilman," Roslin said, "in your honest opinion . . . what chance do you think there is that the Quorum will vote to give the Midguardians a seat on the Council?"

"There's always the chance that—"

"Honest. Opinion."

He hesitated and then admitted, "Very slim. Almost negligible."

"Yes. I agree. And do you think that Wolf Gunnerson knows that?"

"I think he's hoping otherwise, but I think he knows that, yes."

"Then why risk his personal liberty to pursue such a hopeless cause?"

"There are some people," said Zarek, "who consider the hopeless causes the only ones worth pursuing."

"Hmm. Yes," replied Roslin, sounding distant. "At the same time, pursuing a hopeless cause can mean someone feels they have nothing to lose. And people who have nothing to lose can be very . . ." She turned her attention back to Zarek.

He was bleeding out his eyeballs again.

". . . dangerous," she sighed.

CHAPTER 20

Saul Tigh had commandeered a private room and sat there for hours upon hours, listening to the tapes that had been made by the recording devices he'd implanted in various rooms. Aside from the matter involving President Roslin that he had brought to Adama's attention, he had absolutely nothing to show for the hours of time invested. Not only that, but he had come to a depressing realization: Most people, when left to their own devices, were astoundingly boring. The amount of time they spent discussing completely trite and trivial subjects—it boggled the imagination.

It almost made him wonder what it would be like to bug get-togethers of Cylon agents. Did they spend it discussing far-reaching plans of galactic domination? Or did they just hang out discussing fashion, hair styles, and gossip? He was starting to think that scientists were wrong, and hydrogen was not in fact the most common element in the universe. No. It was banality.

The only one who seemed to spend any time at all concentrating on important matters was Mr. Gaeta, which was ironic considering he was one of the key people under suspicion. He didn't seem to have any social life at all. Instead he spent his off-duty hours in his quarters, going over calculations, making new ones, planning, always planning. He'd spend hours muttering to himself while he worked things out. Tigh might have been inclined to think that Gaeta was actually conversing with other Cylons, except that he was alone in his room. His room could have had a Cylon listening device in it, but Tigh—as he had done with every other room—had already swept it to make sure it was clean of bugs before he had placed his own in.

Tigh leaned back in his chair and removed the headset he'd been wearing to listen to the recordings. He rubbed his eyes, feeling the fatigue.

The pressure was getting to him. In trying to track down Cylons, he was starting to feel as if there were no safe haven. Cylons were invading peoples' lives, their very minds.

It made him start to wonder about . . .

"Anything?"

Tigh started slightly and looked up to see Adama standing in the doorway. He shook his head. "Nothing. Not since the earlier things we discussed."

Adama pulled up a chair and sat. "Getting to you, isn't it."

"I think it's getting to all of us." He rubbed his eyes. "If Roslin thinks she hasn't been sleeping well, she should get a load of me. How about you?"

"I sleep like a rock."

He opened his eyes narrowly and stared at Adama. "Technically, rocks don't sleep."

"There you go."

Tigh chuckled, but then grew serious. "What if . . ."

"What if what?"

"What if we find Earth . . . and it really isn't a safe haven? What if the Cylons track us there? Hell, what if the Cylons are waiting for us? What the hell is our Plan B, Bill?"

"Finding Earth *is* Plan B," said Adama. "Plan A is keeping humanity alive. Everything else is open to negotiation."

"That's a hell of a thing."

"Believe me, I know."

Tigh wrapped the wire around the headset and placed it in a drawer, along with the recorder he'd been using to listen to the recordings that were stacked neatly on the table. "Speaking of negotiations . . . what's happening with our people on the *Bifrost*?"

Adama told him what Laura Roslin had just relayed to him. Tigh's eyes widened as he heard about Gunnerson's heading over to *Colonial One*. "In fact," said Adama, glancing at his watch, "he's probably already over there."

"My gods, what are we waiting for?" Tigh demanded. "Let's go get him. Let's take charge of the bastard and start issuing some ultimatums of our own."

"Not yet," Adama said coolly. "We're going to see how it plays out on both ends."

"Both ends? What are you . . . ?" But then he understood. "Oh. You mean the Cylon and the lawyer." He shook his head, a grim smile on his face. "There's poetic justice in that, you know. A Cylon and a lawyer in a cell together. I've dealt with a lawyer or two in my time. Hard-pressed to see the difference."

Adama didn't share the amusement. Although he addressed Tigh, he seemed as if he were looking inward. "It's an evil thing I've done, Saul. Tossing Freya Gunnerson in with Sharon and looking the other way. Gunnerson is right. She broke no laws."

"She's up to something," Tigh said darkly. "Something about her interest in the Cylon stinks to high heaven, and we both know it."

"So she deserves what she gets?"

"Abso-frakking-lutely."

"I wish I were as sure as you."

"You could be," said Tigh. "You just choose not to be."

"And you don't let yourself get dragged down by uncertainty?"

"I try not to."

"You know something, Saul?" said Adama after giving him a long look. "You are more full of crap than any man I've ever met."

Tigh looked stunned a moment, as if he were wounded by the comment. But then he put his head back and laughed. Adama didn't join him, but he did allow a smile to play on his lips.

There was no hint of amusement, or annoyance, or pleasure, or any expression vaguely human on Sharon Valerii's lips. Her mouth was drawn back in a tight, tense manner, as if she were doing heavy exercise and was trying to focus.

Freya Gunnerson was lying on the floor. Sharon was standing over her, straddling her, a leg on either side. Freya was curled up in a ball, her arms encircling her head. She was whimpering, her body trembling.

There was not a mark on her body. Not anywhere.

A professional torturer would have been astounded at the quality of the job Sharon had done on Freya. To simply pound information out of people was . . . well, it was ugly. It was inelegant. It also presented the problem of being counterproductive, especially if the subject died from the questioning.

Sharon had not resorted to that. She hadn't needed to.

The truth was that she had not realized what she was capable of until she had started. It was as if she possessed certain capabilities, but hadn't accessed them until now because she simply hadn't needed them. Now that she did, though, they had come to her with as much ease as if she were to climb upon a bicycle after many years of not doing so and pedal away.

She knew every joint, every muscle, every pressure point in a human being's body. She knew just what to do with each of them, just how to play them against one another to induce mind-numbing agony. With absolute facility and efficiency, she could do something as simple as pop the gastrocnemius and soleus muscles in the calf, causing a small contusion inside. It didn't sound like much, but the agony that resulted in the recipient of the treatment was just overwhelming.

She was capable of inflicting agonizing little scenarios like that all over Freya's body. And she had been doing so.

And Freya had been screaming. Screaming and writhing and begging for mercy that seemed as if it would never come. Whenever it did—whenever Sharon appeared to be letting up—it was simply because she was working out some new thing to do to her.

Part of Sharon was repulsed by what she was doing. But another part of her was simply able to shut herself off, disconnect from it altogether. She found it vaguely disturbing that she was able to do that, but tried not to dwell on it.

She had taken a break, shaking out her hands, loosening up the fingers before she went back to work. Freya continued to lie sobbing upon the floor. Finally she managed to gasp out, "Okay."

Sharon had become so engrossed in her endeavors that she didn't have the slightest idea what Freya was saying okay to at first. Her eyebrows knit. "Okay . . . what?"

"Okay . . . I'll . . . I'll tell you," Freya managed to say. "I'll tell you what I did. I'll tell you everything. I'll do anything you want. Just stop, please . . ." She choked on the tears that ran into her mouth. "Stop . . . please . . ."

"All right," Sharon said dispassionately. "Tell me . . ."

"No," Freya was suddenly vehement, motivated by anger and fear and unbridled loathing. "I want Adama here."

"Why?" Then she answered her own question before Freya could. "Because you're concerned that, once you've told me what I want to know, I'll kill you. So you want someone here to 'save' you from me."

Freya said nothing, but merely glowered instead.

She raised her voice slightly and called to whomever she knew was watching or listening in, "Please send Admiral Adama down. Thank you." Then she stepped back and settled down onto her bunk, her hands resting on her legs. She sat perfectly upright.

Freya managed to look up at her with pure hatred. "You're . . . you're not human."

"That's what everyone else was saying," Sharon reminded her. "Why didn't you listen?"

"Because I thought I . . . I could make a better life for you. Because I thought an injustice was being done, and I tried to fix it."

"And now?" asked Sharon, interested in spite of herself. "What do you think now?"

"I think," and a cold fury grew in her voice, "I think I wish . . . that you had a soul . . . because then it could burn in hell."

"How do you know I don't have one? How do you know it won't go to hell . . . or even heaven? Or maybe there's a different version of heaven that only allows Cylons?"

"There's not."

"You don't know that."

"There's not," Freya repeated, and suddenly, totally unexpectedly, she lunged at Sharon. Sharon's arm immediately crossed her belly to protect her unborn child as she lashed out with a boot, slamming Freya right between the eyes. Freya stumbled backwards, blood covering the lower half of her face. She fell heavily. Sharon continued to look down at her without the slightest change in expression as Freya lay there, clutching her nose, trying to stop the bleeding. After a moment, Sharon removed the flimsy pillow case from the pillow and tossed it down to Freya. It draped itself over her head. She snatched it off and applied it to her face, pressing against the bleeding, and moaning as she did so.

"That's going to leave a mark," said Sharon.

"Frak you," grunted her erstwhile attorney.

They remained that way, neither addressing the other, until Adama arrived in response to the summons. Two marines accompanied him as they came around to the door of the cell and opened it wide. The marines kept their weapons fixed on Sharon. It would have seemed ludicrous to any unknowing onlooker to see burly, heavily armed combat men aiming at the placid pregnant woman who was sitting empty-handed and seemingly harmless on her cot. What possible threat could she have posed? The problem was that they didn't really have an answer to that question, and thus they were determined to be safe rather than sorry.

Adama stared down at the woman on the floor who had previously been the arrogant, self-confident attorney. She looked like she had been through a horrible ordeal that transcended the injury to her face. She was sitting up, her back propped against the wall of the jail cell. There was a stark contrast between what she had been and what she was now. Adama hadn't especially liked her. She'd been a damned irritant and nuisance and too smugly superior by half. But he wouldn't have wished this on her.

You are so full of crap, he told himself. *You damned well wished this on her. You consigned her to this for convenience's sake. Don't pretend that you didn't want this. You knew this was inevitable. If you're going to walk a path, don't kid yourself that you stumbled down it by accident.*

He restrained himself from asking if she was all right because he knew he would simply get a sarcastic answer to the effect that he didn't care. That wasn't entirely true, but he wasn't about to put some sort of gloss on things. Instead, as curt and down-to-business as he could be, he said, "Well?"

Freya glared at him for a moment and then said, "I took it."

"It?"

"The Edda." She wiped blood from her nose and mouth and only succeeded in smearing it around her face. "What my father is looking for."

"Why?"

"Because," she said tersely, "I'm not stupid."

Adama waited, saying nothing.

"One of my responsibilities on my father's ship is traffic. I get the flight manifests of who's coming and who's going. The moment *Galactica* filed a flight manifest stating that two of Boxey's former cronies were coming over, I knew something was up."

"How did you know something was up?"

"Because you're a bastard," she snapped. "Because you wanted ties cut between Boxey and your precious pilots. So if they were heading to our ship, then that meant one of two things: Either you had decided that Boxey wasn't a threat, which meant you had changed your mind, which I assumed you hadn't since—"

"I'm a bastard," he said without inflection.

"—or you had decided he *was* a threat. If we'd refused entrance to them, that could have resulted in a direct attack from *Galactica* which we weren't prepared to repel. So I figured if the Edda disappeared while they were on the ship, suspicion would fall on them."

"So you took it upon yourself to try and frame my people. Show it to me."

"It's in my case. I have to take it out of there."

"Do so." And then, in acknowledgment of the marines standing near him, he added, "Slowly."

She nodded, understanding why it would be wise for her to exercise caution at every moment. Under the circumstances, any sudden motion could get her shot. The case, as it so happened, had slid under Sharon's bunk. She gestured for Sharon to give it over to her. Hooking the handle with her toe, Sharon slid it over to Freya, who flipped the snaps and—very carefully—opened it. She removed several folders filled with papers, set them aside, and then removed a false bottom to the case. Lifting it out, she was aware that the marines were watching her with fearsome intensity. Her hand trembled slightly and she didn't make another move until she was able to will it to stop. Then she lifted a small but thick volume from the briefcase and extended it toward Adama. Adama gestured for one of the marines to retrieve it. He did so, then stepped back and handed it to the admiral.

The book smelled of age, and there was an inscription on the cover in letters that Adama couldn't read. Opening it carefully, lest any of the pages fall out, he turned the pages carefully. The letters were incomprehensible, written in a language he hadn't the slightest familiarity with.

A snorted laugh from Freya caught his attention. He peered over the top of the book at her. "Do you find something amusing?"

"Other than that you're holding it upside down, you mean?"

Adama didn't bother to turn the book over. It wasn't as if it would suddenly have made sense if he had done so. Instead he closed it and then, in a calculatedly cavalier fashion, tossed it to her. She let out a gasp and lunged at it, snagging it before it hit the floor. Clearly shaken by her holy book nearly striking the ground, she clutched it to her, and then looked daggers up at Adama.

He wasn't inclined to give a damn. "Odd how you care so much about the rules of law . . . until they're inconvenient for you."

"The fleet still doesn't entirely trust you, no matter how much reporters from Fleet News Service sing your praises," said Freya. "I played on that in the name of protecting an innocent young boy from your investigations. I didn't want to see him treated the way you treated her . . ." and she glared at Sharon, ". . . although I admit at this point I don't give a damn what you do to that . . . creature."

"You decided you could use my people as a bargaining chip."

"Yes."

He took a step toward her, lancing her with a glare. The sheer hypocrisy of one who purported to be so morally superior to him, using his people in a game as if they were poker chips . . . it infuriated him. With a stoic demeanor born of long practice, he said, "It may interest you to know that your father is, as we speak, en route to *Colonial One*. He's presenting himself as a bargaining chip in order to make up for what turns out to be his daughter's subterfuge."

Her eyes widened. "He did that . . . ?"

"Yes, Miss Gunnerson. He did exactly that. Perhaps the next time you play games with people's lives, you'll want to make certain that all the pieces are in their correct place."

She didn't respond. Instead her head sank back and she closed her eyes. She had put her hand against her nose to stop the bleeding and she had more or less succeeded.

The marines were clearly waiting for their instructions. Adama didn't waste any time. "I'm going to send advance word back to your vessel that you have your book, along with a recording of this session so they'll know precisely what you did. Then marines will escort you back to your vessel. I want you off my ship."

Sharon looked up for the first time and registered surprise. "Off . . . ?"

"You heard me."

"But . . ."

She began to stand and the marines instantly tensed. Sharon froze in a half crouch and then, very slowly, sat down on the cot once more. "With all due respect, Admiral . . . are you sure that's wise?"

No. It may be unspeakably stupid. But President Roslin is trying to defuse a delicate situation, and I want the meeting with the Quorum to have as few distractions as possible. So even though I may be throwing in a bargaining chip that I could have made good use of, I'm going to send her back to her ship with her tail between her legs in order to make sure that Wolf Gunnerson doesn't go off the deep end because his daughter's in the hands of the military.

He made no answer. Instead he made a curt gesture with his head to the marines. They slammed the door to Sharon's cell shut with a resounding clang, and led Freya out at gunpoint. As they headed for the exit from the brig area, Sharon suddenly lumbered to her feet, cupped her hands around her mouth, and shouted, "Who's the bigger bastard, Admiral! You or me? Especially considering that I—as I'm always being reminded—am not human! We had a deal, Admiral! We had a frakking deal! And you'd better come through on your end or . . ."

He stopped, turned and faced her. He never raised his voice, which would have made it difficult to hear him. But he spoke slowly enough that the movement of his lips was unmistakable as he said, ". . . or what?"

Sharon had no answer. Nevertheless, she remained standing until Adama, Freya Gunnerson, and the marines exited the area. The last thing she saw of them was Freya making an obscene gesture in her direction. Sharon didn't return it.

Colonel Tigh would have been interested to know that he wasn't much happier than Sharon Valerii had been with Adama's decision. Adama, wisely, had chosen to apprise him of it when both of them were on CIC. He had obviously known that Tigh would never raise any kind of major fuss about it with the rest of the command personnel there, which made it ideal for Adama if he didn't feel like getting into ten rounds of "Why the frak did you do that?!" with his second in command.

So Tigh had held his tongue and his reaction, although he knew that Adama had maneuvered him into having to do so, and he made sure—with as many subtle hints and signals as he could—that Adama knew that he knew. Of course, in the end, Adama didn't *care*, which pretty much trumped the entire issue.

This left Tigh in CIC fuming over the ongoing situation that continued to leave them vulnerable to another Cylon ambush. He found that he was staring for ages and ages at every single person in CIC. Sooner or later another one of his people would realize that he was staring at them, but it wasn't as if they could complain about it. What could they possibly say? "Colonel, please stop looking at me." It would sound ridiculous.

Even more ridiculous was that he was doing it in the first place. It wasn't as if he was expecting one of them to suddenly collapse to their knees and begin sobbing, "I'm sorry! I can't stand the pressure anymore! I'm a Cylon! I confess! Shoot me now before I endanger the fleet!"

It left Tigh with a vague sense of frustration. The investigation had gone nowhere, leaving him feeling impotent and confused.

How could it possibly be? He was certain none of these people were Cylons. They were the hardest-working officers he'd ever had the privilege to have under his command. They were loyal, honest, unafraid to speak truth to power. Even though he knew the dim opinion of him that was held by many, they continued to treat him with respect, at least to his face.

Look there at Dualla. Constantly monitoring communications, staying on top of everything. Her logs were meticulous. Yes, it was possible that she was falsifying something, or perhaps sending communications to the Cylons, but he just couldn't believe it. Then again—he reminded himself—would he have thought such a thing of Boomer before it was revealed that she was a Cylon? Well . . . yeah. Yeah, truth to tell. He'd always had suspicions that something was off with her. Not that she was a Cylon necessarily because, hell, how could he have known that the Cylons looked like humans now? But she hadn't been quite right. He'd used to think his opinions of her were colored by her illicit affair with Chief Tyrol. It always seemed that when something was going wrong or something was being covered up, Sharon Valerii was in the middle of it. So when the explosive revelation had been made, through her attempt on the Old Man's life, that she was a Cylon agent, Tigh had been shocked but not *too* shocked.

But Dualla? Straight arrow all the way. Yes, he knew she and the president's aide had a thing brewing, but there was nothing untoward about that.

And then there was Gaeta.

Tigh's attention swung over to the ship's young tactical officer. He'd served Adama for three years, as officer of the watch in addition to his other duties. If Gaeta had been an enemy agent, certainly he could have brought Adama down in flames long before this. Things didn't just happen for no reason. Look at Gaeta, at his station, working hard on new coordinates, having dumped the previous ones for fear that perhaps somehow the Cylons had managed to find out about them. Standing there, muttering to himself as he developed a new escape plan should the Cylons attack, scratching away at his hand . . .

Tigh suddenly stopped. He frowned. He took a step toward Gaeta, who wasn't paying any attention to him, so lost in his work was he. Gaeta continued to mutter calculations, making certain that the coordinates would bring them to safety rather than disaster. It was at that point Tigh realized that Gaeta always did that: always spoke softly to himself to help focus his attention on whatever he happened to be doing.

No. It couldn't be that simple.

Waiting for his call to be put through to the *Bifrost*, Adama was watching Tigh with open curiosity. He imagined he could almost see the wheels turning in Tigh's head, but he wasn't entirely certain in what direction they were spinning.

At that moment, Dualla called out, "Admiral . . . Starbuck on the line."

Deciding that whatever was up with Tigh could wait until later, Adama picked up the phone and, said, "Starbuck? Are you and Helo all right?"

"Couldn't be better, Admiral," came her pleased voice. "We're hearing from our jailers that Freya Gunnerson is now stating she's the one who took their precious book."

"That's correct."

He knew that Starbuck would be able to tell from his tone that there was more to the story than that. He also knew that she would be well aware not to ask about it. "There's some skepticism being expressed by our captors over it."

"That should evaporate when she shows up with the book in hand. Her escorts will make sure she presents it." He paused and then said, "What's the status of your visit?"

"Well, the young fellow we came to visit appears to have gotten kind of shy." She said it lightly, as if they were discussing something of little to no consequence. "We thought we would hang out until he shows up again."

"Is the environment conducive to that?"

"I think it will be, once we've been cleared," she replied carefully. "In spite of everything that's happened, I'm still very anxious to hook up with the young man."

"All right . . . if you think you can handle it."

He knew what the answer was going to be even as he said it: a curt laugh from Kara Thrace, followed by a brisk, "No problem on this end, Admiral. We'll have the little scamp in hand before you know it."

"Very well. And Starbuck . . . be careful."

"I always am, sir."

"Galactica out."

He hung up the phone, knowing full well that Kara Thrace had many admirable qualities, but being careful never was, and never would be, one of them. He wanted her to be all right. He wanted her to live to a ripe old age. But he knew in his heart that that wasn't how Kara Thrace was going to exit this plane of existence. She was going to go out in a ball of fire, howling defiance and laughing in death's face the entire time.

"It's too bad she won't live," he said so softly that no one else heard him. "But then again . . . who does?"

CHAPTER 21

Wolf Gunnerson was aghast at what Laura Roslin had just told him.

He had been given quite decent visitor's accommodations when he had arrived on *Colonial One*, considering the circumstances. Laura Roslin had come to meet with him once he was settled in, and delivered him the news that Adama had conveyed to her. She watched him carefully to see if there was the slightest hint of duplicity in his face as he reacted to what she was telling him.

She had to admit, if he was acting, he was wonderfully accomplished at it. The blood drained from his face, and he looked as if he was starting to have heart palpitations. "Freya took it? *Freya* . . . ?" He rocked back in the chair that was far too small for him and groaned under his weight. "I can't understand . . . what would possess her . . . ?"

"I couldn't begin to say," Roslin said, trying to be as diplomatic as possible. "Nevertheless, the fact remains: She has it in her possession. She is being turned over to the authorities on your vessel even as we speak. That aspect of this . . . crisis . . . appears to be settled."

"So it does." He was still looking like a man in shock. "That she could do such a thing . . . put a couple of innocent soldiers under the light of suspicion. You think you know your own child, and then . . ." He shook his head, discouraged, and then looked up at Roslin. "Do you have children of your own?"

"No."

"They bring great joy, but also great heartache. This is obviously one of the moments of heartache. What must the Quorum think of me?"

"They will think you were deceived," she said, still trying to choose as delicate phrasing as she could. "It can happen to anyone. In fact, I daresay it's happened to everyone at some time or another."

"I certainly hope they will still be willing to meet with me," said Wolf Gunnerson. "I mean, I can see how you could turn around and send me back to the *Bifrost*, dismissing me out of hand."

"That's not going to happen," she said. "In fact—believe it or not—this has had a positive effect on the meeting you requested."

"Has it?" He seemed anxious to hear some benefit from what he clearly perceived to be a gargantuan fiasco.

"Yes. There were two members of the Quorum who were still holding out, contending that they were being strong-armed into this meeting because of the hostage situation. With that no longer being a factor, they have acceded to the will of the majority and are going to be attending. In fact, everyone should be here shortly. You will receive a fair hearing."

"That is all I have ever asked," he said politely.

It was hard for her to believe that a man this large was capable of being so soft spoken. "There's been a recent development."

"Oh?" He raised a bushy eyebrow. "What now? My daughter has announced she has a bomb and intends to obliterate us all?"

"Hardly," she said. "A reporter who has been supportive of the administration has asked to have an exclusive interview with you."

"The press traditionally isn't friendly to my cause. I'm not sure of the advantage . . ."

"The advantage is that she has sworn to give you a platform to speak your mind and get your beliefs out to the populace."

Wolf still looked suspicious. "Can she be trusted?"

"She was given complete access to all levels of *Galactica* and came back with a story that was extremely even-handed. Even Admiral Adama was satisfied with it, and he's not exactly the easiest of audiences to satisfy."

Her description of the previous story caught Wolf's interest. "I believe I saw that coverage. That was . . . Diana Bears, was it?"

"D'anna Biers," she politely corrected him. "She's right outside with her cameraman, ready to talk to you if you'd be willing to permit it. By the time you're done, the Quorum should be assembled in the main conference room."

"She would follow us there as well?"

"Several members of the press will be there," said Laura Roslin. "I think you'll find the members of the Quorum are more likely to be attentive and patient if they're on camera. And that's what you want them to be."

"Yes, of course. All right," he said with more conviction, as if he were working to convince himself. "Yes, send her in."

"Very well." She went to the door and opened it. "He'll speak to you," she called.

D'anna Biers, cheerful and professional, came through, followed by her cameraman, and said graciously to Laura, "My thanks, Madame President. I appreciate your putting in a good word for me."

"I simply told him the truth. The decision was his."

"My thanks just the same."

"Well then," smiled Laura. "I'll leave you to it." She exited, closing the door behind her.

D'anna Biers sat down and faced Wolf Gunnerson.

"So," she said. "History is going to be made today."

"That," replied Wolf with a carefully neutral expression, "is exactly the best way I could have put it."

"Are you ready to do it?"

"Absolutely. Are you?"

Her smiled widened, but it wasn't an entirely pleasant one. Instead it appeared almost predatory. "Actually . . . believe it or not . . . I've been waiting for it for a long, long time now."

Laura Roslin was sitting in her office, endeavoring to collect her thoughts, when Billy stuck his head in and informed her the vice president had arrived. "Why?" she sighed.

"He's reporting to you about the possibilities of side effects or after effects that could result from the . . . from the cure you received."

"He is?" She didn't recall asking him to. "Very well, send him in."

She knew she didn't have much time to spend on Baltar. After all, the members of the Quorum were busy arriving, and things were simply moving too quickly for her to slow things down by talking to Baltar. Besides, it wasn't as if he was her favorite person to speak with in the first place.

Roslin was still going through paperwork when Baltar's voice spoke up. "Admiral Adama asked me to undertake this investigation. I thought you might be interested in the results of my studies, Madame President."

She looked up, about to say, "And they would be . . . ?" but her voice froze in her throat.

Baltar was standing a few feet away from her, and right next to Baltar was the known Cylon operative, Shelly Godfrey. Or perhaps Gina. They were the same "model," after all.

Claiming to be a Defense Ministry systems analyst, "Shelly Godfrey" had shown up claiming that Gaius Baltar was a Cylon agent. Having failed in that attempt, she had vanished into hiding somewhere in the fleet and was still out there . . . except now, she appeared to be right here, right in front of Roslin. Naturally she also looked like "Gina," the same model of Cylon who had been a prisoner aboard the *Pegasus*. Tragically she had escaped and had gone on to murder Admiral Cain before likewise going into seclusion somewhere. It was a source of continuing frustration to Roslin that they could actually know what the damned toasters looked like and still be unable to capture them.

And now she was there, right there, next to Baltar. She was wearing a tight-fitting red dress, cut high at the hem, low at the top. Smirking, she was leaning on Baltar's shoulder.

Laura felt lightheaded, as if her brain was going to splatter in all directions. *This isn't happening . . . this isn't happening . . . gods dammit, this isn't happening . . .*

Baltar was puzzled at the confused look on Laura Roslin's face, but didn't dwell on it. If something was bothering her, certainly it was her problem, not his.

"Inconclusive, I'm afraid," he was saying. "Since you are, naturally, the only human test study, the chemical examinations I've done thus far, particularly in seeing how the hemoglobin interacts with the cancer cells I culled, I can see—"

"She's looking at you strangely, Gaius," purred the blonde who was labeled as Shelly in Laura's Cylon agent file. "Do you think she suspects you?"

Reflexively, Baltar glanced in her direction and said, "No." Then he mentally chided himself for responding to her in front of a witness. It happened rarely, but if he was relaxed enough, she could still catch him off guard. It was a perverse little game she enjoyed playing with him. Fortunately he'd become deft at covering such slips. Furthermore since—as that annoying Boxey child had observed—people had become accustomed to the odd Doctor Baltar and his eccentricities, so such gaffes generally were shrugged off.

Not this time.

Laura was on her feet so fast that she banged her knees on the underside of her desk. Pain shot up and down her legs, but it barely registered with her. "What are you doing with her here!" she demanded.

"P-Pardon? There's, ah . . . there's no one here, Madame President, except you and—"

"You looked right at her. I just saw you do it!"

"What?" There was extreme nervousness in Baltar's face, and he was stammering very badly.

"She said something and you looked right at her!"

He felt his knees starting to give way, but kept himself on his feet with effort. "Her? What her are you referring to . . . ?"

"Shelly Godfrey! Right there!"

Six looked genuinely stunned. She clapped a hand to her bosom. Baltar slipped up again, looking directly toward her. "I . . . I . . ." he stuttered.

"You looked at her again! Don't tell me I'm just seeing her!"

"She can see me!" Shelly said through tightly clenched teeth. "Do something! Distract her!"

Responding instantly, Baltar tossed on a façade of concern and said, "You appear overwrought, Madame President. Perhaps you'd like to sit down—"

"To hell with that!" shouted Laura. "The audacity! To walk in here with your Cylon . . . what? Co-conspirator? Lover?!"

Baltar had never come as close to passing out from shock as he did at that moment.

"Madame President . . ." Baltar began, starting to come around the desk.

Then he jumped back as Laura grabbed a heavy paperweight off her desk with one hand while, with the other, she grabbed up a phone and snapped, "Billy! Get in here with two security guards! Arrest—"

As she spoke, she threw the paperweight directly at Six. Baltar lunged to one side, his head snapped around, and he saw the paperweight sail through empty air and smash into the bulkhead.

Laura swayed behind the desk, clearly stunned that the paperweight had connected with nothing and that Six had apparently vanished into thin air. At that moment, the door flew open, and Billy was there with two armed men from her personal guard. They looked around, saw no one but the president and the vice president and—through process of elimination—figured that Baltar was the threat. The guards grabbed him by either arm. The papers Baltar had brought with him flew in all directions.

"Get your damned hands off me!" Baltar shouted, his voice going up an octave.

"Madame President . . ." Billy began.

But she waved him off, her face ashen. "Let him go!" she said. When the guards hesitated, still confused over what had just happened, she repeated more firmly, "Let him go."

The guards did, backing off. "Madame President," Billy started once more, but then stopped, since he clearly had no idea what to say.

"It . . . was a misunderstanding," she said slowly. She continued to address Billy, but she was looking straight at Baltar. "I'm sorry to have summoned you like that. I was . . . it was just a misunderstanding," she told them once more, as if repetition would somehow make it more credible.

Her aide didn't leave immediately. Instead he and Roslin locked gazes, and Baltar knew that there was something more going on here, something that he wasn't privy to. What did the president have on him and if it was anything, why didn't she use it?

The personal guards backed out of the room, still looking around suspiciously. Billy continued to look at Roslin for a short time longer, and then very stiffly he said, "Thank you, Madame President," and stepped out of the office as well.

A deathly silence descended over Baltar and Roslin. Both of them were standing. Finally Roslin eased herself into her chair and tried to arrange her hands neatly, one upon the other, as if nothing untoward had occurred. Baltar then knelt down, gathered the scattered papers, and arranged them neatly in a pile. He took a step forward, placed them on her desk, and stepped back. Still nothing was said.

"Madame President," he finally asked slowly, "is there something you'd like to tell me?"

She appeared to give the matter some thought, and then replied, "No. I don't believe there is."

Baltar squared his shoulders and, very casually, said, "Feel free to review my findings at your leisure. I assume you're busy at the moment . . ." He paused and then added, "And have a good deal on your mind."

"Thank you," she said.

"Do you require me to remain for the imminent Quorum gathering?"

"No, that shouldn't be necessary."

"As you wish. Thank you, Madame President."

"Thank you, Doctor Baltar."

He got out of the room quickly and headed down the narrow corridor outside. The security guards were a short ways away, and they both gave him extremely suspicious stares as he went past. The moment they were behind him, Number Six was in front of him. Perversely, she seemed delighted with the latest development. "She's on to you, Gaius."

He kept walking and, in a low voice, said, "How is that possible?"

"It's not. That's what makes it all the more exciting."

"I could do with a little less excitement in my life, thank you. How could she know about us?"

"She can't."

"How did she see you?"

"She couldn't."

"You're *not helping*."

Her long legs enabled her to keep pace with him easily. "Helping? I've done nothing but help you, Gaius. Helped you with information. Helped you see the future of the human race. Helped you fulfill your full potential. And you have resisted me and fought me at every turn, squandering precious time. And now your time's running out. She's on to you."

"It's impossible!"

"And yet it is." She stepped directly in his path and, even though he could have walked right through her, instead he slammed to a halt. "And you better figure out a way to fix it. Fast. Because you have even less time than you think."

"What's that supposed to mean?"

"It means exactly what I said, Gaius. Exactly what I said."

He turned away from her, feeling as if the corridor around him was tilting sideways. Composing himself, he turned back to face her once more only to see that she was gone.

"Bitch," he whispered under his breath.

CHAPTER 22

Kara and Agathon, so bored out of their minds that they were tempted to stage a jailbreak just to get shot at and break up the monotony, looked up in mild surprise as the door to the room they were being kept in opened. Kara had thought sure that, once word had reached the ship of Freya's duplicity, they would immediately be kicked loose. She'd said as much to Adama. But to her annoyance, they'd been informed by a couple of Gunnerson's lieutenants—one named Tyr, the other Fenris, both of them large and sturdily built, albeit not quite as massive as Gunnerson—that they were going to continue to be kept right where they were until "matters were sorted out to their satisfaction."

The door opening suggested that such a time might be imminent, and the presence of Tyr standing next to Freya Gunnerson, holding her firmly by one arm, confirmed it. Standing behind Freya were two marines, corporals Jolly and Zac. Jolly, despite his name, had the most perpetually dour expression of any marine Starbuck had ever known, and Zac was a bulky woman who looked fully capable of breaking most men in half. Clearly they had been responsible for escorting her back from *Galactica*.

"I believe," said Tyr, "that Freya has something she wishes to say to you." He nudged her forward slightly and she cast an angry glare at Tyr before looking back at Starbuck and Helo.

"I apologize for the inconvenience," she said tersely.

"Frak you," shot back Starbuck, having no patience for her apologies, and said to Tyr, "are we finally free to go?"

"Yes. Enjoy the rest of your stay on the *Bifrost*."

"Sure we will," said Agathon, "because, y'know, it's been such a joy until now."

Freya looked as if she was about to respond, but before she could, Tyr and Fenris yanked her away. Jolly and Zac stepped forward, both of them tossing off salutes and saying, "Admiral Adama instructed us to report to you and aid you in your search for the suspect."

"It's appreciated," said Starbuck as she emerged from the room, Helo right behind her. She walked with quick, brisk steps, and they immediately fell into step behind her. The hell of it was that she didn't have the faintest idea of where they were going, but she looked as if she moving with great authority, so naturally they followed her. It made her wonder if there were times when the Old Man likewise didn't have the faintest idea what he was doing, but he made his moves with such confidence that people just naturally attended to everything he said and did.

Nah. No way. The Old Man always knew what was best. Always. She should be so lucky to be as on top of things as Adama was.

"We looking for Boxey?" asked Helo.

"Frakking right we're looking for Boxey," shot back Starbuck. "At this point, considering all the trouble and hassle we've had to deal with because of him, I almost don't care if he's a Cylon or not. We're hauling his ass back to *Galactica* either way."

"Where do we start, Lieutenant?" asked Jolly.

"I'm not sure," she said as they rounded a corner, "but we find him even if we have to tear this whole ship apart panel by panel."

Boxey awoke inside the crawl ducts. Confused, he started to sit up, but naturally that was impossible since he was surrounded by narrow metal confines. All he managed to do was slam his head on the metal above him, which sent noise and vibrations all up and down the ducts.

He had no idea how long he'd been there. When he'd clambered up into it, his heart had been pounding. He felt as if his entire world had been stood on its ear. Freya had been completely right about Starbuck and the others. They weren't his friends. Perhaps they never even had been. They were chasing him down as if he was the worst sort of criminal or enemy, and he hadn't done anything, not a thing. It wasn't fair. Not at all. Why, they were treating him like . . .

Like Sharon Valerii. Or even worse.

His heart turned cold and bitter, and angrily he said, "I . . . I almost wish I was a Cylon. The stuff they're doing . . . the way they look at me . . . it would serve 'em right. It would serve 'em right if I was a Cylon, because then they'd be afraid of me. That would be better than this. Anything would be better than this."

He waited for his ire to subside, but it didn't. It made him wonder if it had been like this for Sharon. If there had been a slow build up of suspicion, culminating in her self-realization and her ceasing to fight against her true nature.

He wondered if he had a true nature like that.

What if he was a . . . ?

Boxey shook it off. He didn't need to have his mind wandering in that direction right now, especially because he felt as if that direction was calling him more strongly than he'd like.

He slithered his way down the duct and found a ceiling panel that he could work loose. He listened for a long moment to make sure that there was no one around, and then gripped the grillwork and eased it up and out of place. He lay it down carefully to make sure that it didn't make a lot of noise, and then eased himself down and through into the corridor, landing so softly that no one could have heard him.

At that exact instant, Starbuck and Helo, followed by two marines, came around the corner, Starbuck saying in annoyance, "—but we find him even if we have to tear this whole ship apart panel by panel."

They stopped dead and all five stared at each other.

"Wow," said Starbuck, clearly impressed with herself.

Instantly Boxey tried to leap back up toward the shaft space, but he only got halfway up before Agathon tackled him around the legs. Boxey tried to kick, but Agathon's arms were wrapped tightly around them, making it impossible for Boxey to move them. Agathon yanked downward and the two of them hit the floor. Boxey desperately tried to squirm loose but by that point Corporals Jolly and Zac had hauled him to his feet and were holding him securely.

"Long time no see," said Starbuck dryly. "And here I was just thinking how we should catch up with you."

"I didn't do anything wrong," Boxey snapped. He tried to pull at the marines who were holding him still, but he accomplished nothing on that score. "I'm not a Cylon."

"Then why did you run?"

"Because you think I'm a Cylon!"

"How do you know that?"

"Because why else would you be here! You don't like me! You never liked me!"

Starbuck looked taken aback by the ferocity of his accusations. Automatically she said, "That's not true."

"You know it is! You know it's true! I tell you something and Baltar tells you something, and you believe him instead of me! Why?!"

"Because . . ." Starbuck started to reply, and then stopped. She and Helo looked at each other.

Helo shrugged. "Don't look at me. I just go where they tell me."

"Look, Boxey," she began again.

"Give me one good reason that I should listen to you!"

"Because," she said patiently but firmly, "I'm bigger than you. I have a couple of guys who are bigger than you, and they're making sure you don't go anywhere. So now's the time to come to terms with the fact that you're going back to *Galactica*, and yeah, you're gonna be checked out, but that's the way it goes because I have my orders and there's not a single frakking thing you can do about it."

As it happened, she could not have been more wrong.

She received her first inkling of her fundamental wrongness, however, the moment that alarms started going off all over the ship.

They were practically deafening, so much so that Boxey had to put his hands to his ears, and even the hardened marines were wincing.

"The two of you, stay here with him," Kara snapped at them, "and Helo, you're with me," and she bolted down the main corridor before any further conversation could be had. Helo promptly took off after her, leaving the two bewildered marines staring at their captive and waiting for someone to tell them what they were supposed to do.

Starbuck and Helo, meantime, were running as fast as they could. They passed frightened Midguardians who were certain that the alarm bells could only mean one thing: another Cylon attack. The same thing had occurred to Starbuck, and she was desperately looking for a viewing port to get a sense of what was going on outside.

"There!" shouted Helo, pointing ahead of them. "A viewing bay! Up there!"

She saw that he was right. A large round port window was set into the bulkhead ahead of them, which would give them a decent—if not enhanced—view of what was in front of them. Starbuck got to the port with Helo directly behind her, looking over her shoulder.

Starbuck gulped deeply when she saw what was heading their way.

"You've gotta be frakkin' kidding me," she said, her mind numb.

In *Galactica*'s CIC, Tigh drifted over to Adama and muttered to him in a low voice, "I'll be right back."

This alone was unusual: Adama wasn't going to care if Tigh walked off CIC unannounced. This wasn't grade school. If nothing else, he would have assumed Tigh was going to the head, and that hardly was worth a separate declaration. The fact that Tigh was taking the time to say something to Adama about his departure spoke volumes. Adama instantly knew that something was up. He met Tigh's gaze, but saw the look in his XO's eyes, and all he said in response was, "Okay."

Tigh walked out of CIC like a man on a mission. When he returned a few minutes later, he was carrying several sheets of paper and a small wandlike device. Adama recognized it immediately for what it was, but he said nothing. Tigh's movement had caught Dualla's eye and a couple of other officers'. Like Adama, however, they simply watched in mute curiosity.

Gaeta looked up, bewildered, frowning. He stared uncomprehendingly as Tigh held up a piece of paper that read, "Don't say a word." Slowly, still not understanding but not about to do anything contrary to Tigh's explicit order—even if it was unspoken—Gaeta nodded.

He held up a second sign. It read, "Hold out your right hand."

Gaeta did so, wondering obliquely if Tigh was about to slap it or something.

Instead Tigh extended the wand device. Naturally Gaeta recognized it as a bug detector. On two previous occasions he had stepped back from his station as Tigh had run the wand over the entire area to make certain there was no eavesdropping device hidden anywhere. Tigh had even had every member of CIC stand with arms extended to either side and run the wand up and down and around their bodies to make sure their uniforms weren't bugged. Everything had come up clean. This time, though, Tigh ran it over the back of Gaeta's hand, right where he had been scratching. Tigh had turned the volume on the wand down to almost nothing, but there was still a detector light on the handle, and the light instantly went off.

Gaeta's jaw dropped in astonishment. Everyone on CIC, their attention completely engaged, also saw it, and their responses were similar. Adama's jaw simply twitched which, for him, was the equivalent of his eyes leaping out of their sockets in astonishment.

"Mr. Gaeta," Tigh said in a careful, measured, easy-to-hear voice, "verify the current emergency Jump point. *Pegasus* is reporting some uncertainty." But as he spoke, he held up yet another sign, and it read: "Plot a new Jump point and *keep your mouth shut as you're doing it*."

Slowly Gaeta nodded and said, "Aye, sir."

Tigh nodded in approval and then turned his gaze toward Adama in unmistakeable triumph. He held up yet another sign. It read, "Not bad for an old guy, huh."

Not bad at all, mouthed Adama.

Even as he made new calculations, Gaeta spoke clearly—perhaps *too* clearly, but there was nothing they could do about this sudden self-consciousness—to the *Pegasus*, reverifying the Jump coordinates that were no longer relevant. He did so speaking into a dead phone, because naturally the *Pegasus* wasn't going to know what the hell he was talking about if he'd been speaking directly to them. But if someone was listening in via a subcutaneous listening device in Gaeta's hand—as Tigh obviously suspected was the case—they weren't going to know that.

And just as Adama was starting to think that perhaps maybe, just maybe, the current crisis was nearly behind them, it all went straight to hell.

"Admiral!" Dualla suddenly called out. "The *Bifrost!*"

The ship had been up on a monitor, being watched carefully, ever since Adama had sent Starbuck and Helo over there. Now he, Tigh, and everyone else looked up to see what it was that Dualla was alerting them to.

"You gotta be frakking kidding me," said Tigh.

And just when matters didn't seem as if they could possibly get worse, space exploded around them.

D'anna Biers was one of a dozen reporters crowded into the conference room on *Colonial One,* watching with great interest as Wolf Gunnerson entered. Already seated at a large round conference table were the members of the Quorum of Twelve, with President Roslin at the table's head.

Biers looked over the faces of the Quorum members when Gunnerson came in. They did not look to be an especially sympathetic bunch. Their expressions could best be described as "hardened disinterest," although several of them were unable to contain their surprise at Gunnerson's sheer mass. Even D'anna had to admit that, damn, for a human, he was pretty impressive.

For more ceremonial gatherings the Quorum convened on *Cloud Nine,* but this was a more "down and dirty" gathering, as Tom Zarek had referred to it. A handful of reporters were being permitted to attend in the interest of full disclosure; on the other hand, subsequent deliberations would likely be held in closed-door sessions. It simply wasn't *Cloud-Nine* appropriate, again as Zarek had put it.

The meeting had already been chaired to order, and some preliminary business had been attended to. Now there was nothing on the docket but to deal with the matter of Wolf Gunnerson. Laura Roslin, as president, was charged with overseeing the running of the meeting, and she did so now with her customary brisk efficiency. D'anna ruminated on the fact that Roslin was a non-voting member except in times of a tie vote, at which point she would cast the deciding ballot. That meant that, should the Quorum split on the issue of the Midguardians, then she, Laura Roslin, would be the one who held their fate in her hands. And as far as D'anna was concerned, it was a toss-up as to which way she would fall.

She smiled with the inner amusement of a scientist watching rats hustle through a maze, knowing that in the long run, it was all fruitless because—in the end—they were still just rats, not destined to be long for this world.

She glanced over toward Gunnerson. He did not look back.

"Madame President," Tom Zarek was saying, rising, from his chair.

"We recognize Tom Zarek, representative of Sagittaron."

He nodded slightly in acknowledgment of her recognition, fiddled with the lower button of his jacket for a moment, and then said, "Mr. Gunnerson first approached me about the issue of recognition for the Midguardians, so naturally I feel some responsibility in this matter. Consider this my personal request," and he gave a smile that looked forced, "that the recent unpleasantness regarding the misunderstanding of the stolen religious relic . . . not color the feelings of this Quorum in considering the request of his people."

"It is difficult to ignore it, Councilman," Robin Wenutu of Canceron replied. "It's a hell of a first impression to make."

"I can understand your trepidation," Zarek said. "Because, to be candid, it wasn't all that long ago that I had to face down the looks of distrust on all of you."

"Councilman Zarek," said Eladio Puasha of Scorpia. "I don't think that's a fair assessment of our earliest experiences . . ."

"I think it's a perfectly fair assessment," Zarek told her with a fixed expression. "One moment I'm a terrorist; the next I'm a coworker."

"You underestimate our ability to adapt, Tom," replied Puasha. "If there's one thing we've become accustomed to in months past . . . it's a constantly fluctuating status quo."

This drew nods of rueful disagreement, and surprisingly, Zarek's smile turned genuine. "Fair enough, Eladio." Then he grew serious once more. "I suppose all I'm saying is that, from my point of view— I fully understand the situation that would have driven Wolf Gunnerson to do what he did. And if Councilwoman Puasha's attitude is truly reflective of the rest of you . . . then I assume I can count on all of you to give him the fair hearing that he deserves." Zarek paused a moment for what he had said to sink in, and then sat back down in his chair.

During the entire exchange, Wolf Gunnerson had never taken a seat, even though there was an available one near him. Laura Roslin gestured for him to take it, and he calmly shook his head. "I think it more respectful to remain on my feet," he said.

"Very well," said Laura. "Then, Mr. Gunnerson, you have the fl—"

She stopped. Stopped and stared, and looked ashen, and she seemed to be whispering something. D'anna looked carefully, and Laura was apparently saying, "Not now . . . not now . . ."

Sarah, who was seated at the president's right hand, leaned forward, looking concerned. "Madame President . . . ?" she said cautiously.

"Headache . . . just . . ." Her voice sounded strangled. She looked as if she were having some sort of attack, and was fighting it off with Herculean effort that was only partly succeeding.

"Madame President?" asked Sarah again. And then, with the sort of intuition that only someone who sought religious meaning in every aspect of life could display, Sarah said with greater urgency, "Are you . . . are you having some sort of vision?"

D'anna leaned forward as well, eyebrow cocked. This was suddenly getting very interesting. She just hoped that it wouldn't take too long to play out, since time was not something the humans had in abundance.

She couldn't believe how smoothly everything was going. Here was Zarek, whose very presence continued to make her feel cold inside (and that had nothing to do with the fact that he was going to be her likeliest competition for the presidency; gods help the colonies if that happened), actually interacting like a grown-up with the other members of the Quorum. Gunnerson was patiently waiting for his moment to speak. When that moment came, Roslin started to tell him that he had the floor . . .

And Sharon Valerii was there.

She was everywhere.

No longer was she standing at one point in the room, drawing Laura's attention. Instead every member of the Quorum of Twelve had disappeared, and in their respective places was an identical Sharon Valerii. Each one pregnant, each one with an expression of dispassionate placidity. Each one looking directly at her. They were shaking their heads sadly, and they genuinely looked apologetic.

Laura knew she had to be dreaming. She absolutely had to be. But she felt awake, and this was going beyond the simple hallucinations that she'd experienced earlier. This was borderline dementia, and it was the tipping point. She couldn't take it anymore. To hell with the rest of the human race, to hell with her responsibilities.

Laura Roslin was as much a fighter as any human being left alive, but it was ultimately too much, just . . . just too much. If Sharon Valerii's unborn child had somehow insinuated itself into her mind, then . . . then . . .

Yes, that was it. That was the problem. All right, fine. I'll show that unborn saboteur who's boss. And I wouldn't leave it to Doc Cottle to do it, because who knows, he might be a Cylon as well. I'll just . . . I'll just go over there myself and cut the child out with a knife, or . . . or put a bullet in Sharon's brain, that's it, that's all, just done with it, just . . .

Sharon Valerii was speaking to her. The voice didn't emerge from her mouth but instead went directly into Roslin's mind, and what it said was, *Now. Now. It's about to happen now. Do something. Save us. Save us all . . .*

And that was when it all became clear to Laura. Her mind leaped and everything suddenly seemed cast into a stark and new relief . . .

Gods . . . I was right the first time . . . it's not trying to terrorize me . . . it's not trying to drive me insane . . . it's . . . it's afraid . . . it's afraid . . . it's afraid and it wants my help to save it from . . . from what . . . ? From . . . ?

She heard another voice in her head, and it was Sarah Porter. Laura, feeling as if she were on the brink of something, pushed her way back to reality. Her teeth gritted, she said, "Mister . . . Mister Gunnerson . . . you may . . . you may go ahead . . ."

"Madame President," Sarah said, still looking concerned. "I asked if you—"

"I heard what you asked," Laura told her firmly, which was a lie since she was barely holding on to her own surroundings. "Mr. Gunnerson is here . . . we're all here . . . let's . . . move along."

There was a brief, uncomfortable silence, and then Wolf Gunnerson reached into the inside pocket of his jacket and removed a sheaf of papers covered with scribbling. "I had promised Madame President," he said, "that were I given this opportunity, I would inform you all of the truths of our sacred writings."

"*Your* sacred writings," Sarah Porter reminded him. She was still glancing every so often in Laura's direction, but she was all-business enough to want to get business matters back on track. "Your truths. Not ours."

"I would like to think," Gunnerson said mildly, "that truth is truth."

Laura knew that everyone at the table was still casting glances in her direction. She closed her eyes, opened them, and they were all still damned Sharon Valerii. Everyone in the room was . . . with, insanely, the sole exception of D'anna Biers, who was studying her closely as if dissecting her with her eyes. Laura had no idea what to make of that, and didn't try to figure it out. She closed her eyes firmly, as if battling a headache, and when she opened them, everyone had returned to themselves . . .

. . . and the words *Sagittarius is bleeding NOW* were etched on the table.

Wolf Gunnerson was smoothing the papers, and he began to read aloud:

> *"The race of humans thus was ended*
> *A blinding final winter done*
> *The sword of demons, hot with flame*
> *Assured no mortals left to run.*
> *The gods were dead, had fought their last*
> *Consumed by snake and wolf and blood*
> *And so their last remains were gone*
> *All swept away, as if by flood.*
> *The rainbow bridge was all destroyed*
> *It crashed and cracked and split apart*
> *And in so doing did away*
> *With humanity's last soul and heart.*
> *Gods' worshippers were gone to dust*
> *The last assault, did not survive,*
> *Their final crash, their final burn*
> *There was no human left alive."*

He paused, as if he was going to continue reading and then, sounding like a polite literature professor, said almost apologetically, "It goes on for several more pages, but truthfully, it's just a reiteration of what's already been said. The writers of the Edda tended to be repetitive in order to make certain their point was made."

The Quorum members looked at each other in confusion, as if trying to see if anyone knew what Gunnerson was driving at.

"I can't say that I understand, Mr. Gunnerson," said Laura Roslin.

He gave her a vaguely pitying smile. "It's all right there, Madame President. A blind man could see it: We're not supposed to be here. We were not destined to survive. The 'blinding final winter' is the nuclear winter of the Cylon attack . . . the signal that our gods are dead. And since our gods are the only ones that truly count, that means there's really no point in anything else existing. The vast majority of humanity was annihilated by the winter, as was supposed to be the case. We, the Midguardians, survived so as to make sure the final prophecies would be fulfilled, and we came close," and he brought his thumb and forefinger almost together, "this close. 'Their final crash, their final burn.' We were intended to die in the heart of that vast, all-consuming star. But that was thwarted at the last moment by Adama, displaying cleverness that Loki would have envied. But no matter, no matter. It's being attended to even as we speak."

Slowly Laura Roslin stood as the rest of the Quorum continued to shift uncomfortably in their seats, clearly not liking the sound of what they were hearing. She whispered, so softly that they had to strain to hear her, "The blood of humanity . . . on your hands . . . on the hands of Sagittaron . . . of Sagittarius . . ."

"Now wait a minute!" Zarek said. "I didn't know anything about this!"

"What this?" demanded Sarah Porter. "What's going on?"

And now the reporters, stirred up, started firing questions. Matters were spiraling completely out of control, and everything snapped into place for Laura Roslin, the final tumblers clicking in her mind. Even though she made no attempt to shout, her voice still rose above the crowd as she said, "Your precious book was never missing. You knew your daughter had it the entire time."

"Yes," Gunnerson said, looking mildly impressed.

"You did it to make an impetus for this meeting. You wanted us all together. Now."

"Yes."

Now all questioning and back talk had died out, and the silence was heavy as everyone in the room waited for this exchange to come to a conclusion that clearly only Laura Roslin and Wolf Gunnerson knew.

She took a deep breath and said, "You're planning to wipe out the entire Quorum in one shot."

He inclined his head slightly. "Yes."

"What!" Zarek almost exploded out of his chair, and he grabbed Gunnerson by the arm. "What the frak are you talking ab—"

Gunnerson swung his arm casually and Zarek was knocked

backwards, sent crashing over his chair. Wolf made no other motion. There even seemed to be, insanely enough, sadness in his eyes.

"Billy," said Laura, without budging from her place. Billy was standing several feet away, looking shocked, uncomprehending. "Contact *Galactica* immediately. Tell them an immediate attack is very likely."

Billy started to back out of the room, but he never took his eyes off Gunnerson. But Wolf made no move toward him and Billy got out with no problem. Instead Gunnerson said calmly, with total conviction, "Call whomever you want. They can't save you."

"They can and they will," Laura Roslin replied, her chin tilted upward in defiance.

"Oh my gods!"

It was Sarah Porter. Something had caught her eye out one of the ports, and she had cried out in shock. Laura looked to see what it was that had provoked the response.

It was the *Bifrost*.

It was still a good distance away, but the ship had turned away from its customary position in the fleet. Instead it was moving crosswise across the flow, attempting to navigate its way toward *Colonial One.*

It was on a direct collision course. If its course went unaltered, it would smash *Colonial One* amidships, rupturing the hull of both vessels, and both of them would explode, fireballs snuffed out within seconds in the airless vacuum of space.

Pandemonium broke out in the conference room, which was instantly transformed into a maelstrom of accusation, fury, and fear.

And in the midst of it all, D'anna Biers—the eye of the storm—smiled wanly to herself and slowly shook her head.

We tried, she thought sadly. *We tried so hard. We tried our little booby trap the last time, after I shook Gaeta's hand during the making of the documentary and inserted that little listening device into it. We tried to herd you into a situation where you would have been so completely overwhelmed by our forces that you would have had no choice but to surrender. We could have extracted Sharon's baby at that point . . . perhaps even taken a percentage of you prisoner and turned you into workers. You wouldn't have been completely exterminated. A handful would have survived to serve us, and wouldn't that have been appropriate? But you had to be oh-so-clever to avoid the trap. So this time . . . this time we finish it. Or at the very least, we cripple you by destroying your entire membership and your civilian leaders.*

We tried to be generous, but you simply weren't willing to allow it to happen. For this one, you have no one to blame but yourself.

We know where you're going to Jump to. If you try to get away, we're waiting for you, and we'll blow what's left of you to bits.

Too bad about Sharon, though. I bet the baby would have had her eyes.

CHAPTER 23

"Cylon raiders!"

The members of Adama's command crew had barely had the opportunity to register that *Colonial One* was in deep trouble when space all around them was alive with Cylon raiders spinning out of subspace and angling toward the fleet. They came out firing, and even though Adama had the pilots scrambling to their vessels, he was certain they were losing out on precious time.

"Vipers away!" called Dualla.

"Gaeta!" said Tigh with growing urgency as he crossed over toward him. "Get those coordinates for the Jump up and ready!" Despite the gravity of the situation, he was wise enough not to say anything beyond that, nor was Gaeta engaging in the standard operating procedure of getting verbal confirmation from other officers in CIC as to the specifics of the coordinates. Instead Gaeta was keeping his big mouth shut as he readied the coordinates and the fleet's Jump.

Adama's eyes were riveted, however, on the *Bifrost* as it approached *Colonial One*. Neither ship was especially speedy or maneuverable; both were outfitted with FTL drives, but that did nothing for them when they were operating in standard space and moving with the alacrity of a drunken cow.

"Fire a warning shot across their bow," said Adama. He was furious with himself for being hamstrung. Helo and Starbuck—Starbuck, for frak's sake—were on the *Bifrost* along with two of his marines. If the warning shot didn't take, he was going to have to seriously consider blowing the ship out of space. This would end the Midguardian threat, but it would also be the end of his people. Of Helo, of . . . of Starbuck . . .

A single shot from the *Galactica*'s big cannons hurtled past the *Bifrost* as it started to approach *Colonial One*. It seemed frighteningly as if the *Galactica* was firing upon the civilian fleet, but there was no helping that now.

The shot hurtled past the *Bifrost* without striking it. The civilian ship didn't slow.

Suddenly the *Galactica* was rocked by concentrated fire power from the Cylons. The big guns were needed elsewhere. If Adama didn't have the target shifted to the threat of the Cylons, there wasn't going to be a fleet to worry about, much less a single ship.

Starbuck . . . Helo . . . do something, Adama thought desperately.

Boxey sprinted down the corridor, dodging the confused and terrified people who were milling about, shouting that they were under attack, demanding to know what was going on. Kara, Agathon, and the two marines were right behind him, and they weren't especially gentle about shoving people out of the way in order to get where they were going.

Enough people were looking upset that Starbuck had the distinct impression what was transpiring was news to them. It wasn't as if there had been some vast group plan to try and send the *Bifrost* winging its way into *Colonial One*. It was the actions of a few people acting independently of the rest of the ship's populace. Unfortunately, those few people were in control of the ship.

"This way! It's this way!" Boxey was shouting, and he rounded another corner. The four adults were hard-pressed to keep up with him, but they managed to do so and then they suddenly skidded to a halt as Boxey stood outside a large set of double doors and started pounding on them in frustration.

"This the control room?" Starbuck demanded.

When Boxey nodded, Jolly shouted "Stay back!" and unslung his weapon. Zac followed suit, and they opened fire on the outer door. Their weapon fire bounced harmlessly off the reinforced armored door.

"Frak!" shouted Starbuck.

Jolly slammed a fist against the door, which didn't accomplish much since his fire power had already proven insufficient. "We should have packed explosives! Anyone got any?"

"I have an exploding cigar, but I left it back on *Galactica*," Starbuck said with bleak humor. Then something prompted her to look overhead. She saw the grillwork and a desperate thought occurred to her. She glanced over at Boxey, who had automatically looked up to see what she was staring at, and then the same thought occurred to him.

"Lift me up!" he cried out.

Instantly Starbuck started to second-guess her own notion, but there wasn't any time for such concerns. "Helo, get it clear!" she shouted, nodding toward the overhead grillwork. Helo reached up, grab it and yanked it clear. Starbuck interlaced her hands, providing a step up for him. Boxey planted one foot in the aide and she propelled him up and into the ventilation shaft.

"Wait by the door!" he called. "I'll get it open from inside!"

Jolly turned to Starbuck, looking none too enthused about the situation. "We're counting on the kid?"

"Yeah!" replied Starbuck, her eyes fiery with the demented gamble. "We're counting on the kid!"

Lee Adama, a.k.a. Apollo, wished to the gods that he had Starbuck out there with him, guarding his tail. He'd never felt more vulnerable than now, when he was fighting for his own life and that of *Galactica* and the best damned pilot he knew wasn't there.

Worse, he knew exactly where she was, but there wasn't a thing he could do about it . . .

Despite the fact that there was hot fire from the Cylon raiders all around him, his attention drifted briefly to the *Bifrost*.

He gasped. He saw that the ship was on collision course with *Colonial One*. But he was too far away to do anything about it, and if he disengaged from the enemy to attend to it, raiders would get through and manage to jam their weapons fire right down *Galactica*'s throat.

"*Galactica*, this is Apollo! *Colonial One* in imminent danger from *Bifrost*!" he shouted over his comm unit.

There was a heartbeat of a pause, and then a voice came back— not Dualla's, but instead Lee's father. "We're monitoring the situation."

"Monitoring! If they hit—! Permission to engage *Bifrost*—!"

"Negative, focus on Cylons. Starbuck has it in hand."

Saul Tigh turned and looked in astonishment at Bill Adama as Adama point-blank lied to his son. Adama shoved the phone down and returned the look.

"She does," Adama said with simple conviction, without having the faintest idea why he knew. He turned toward Gaeta and asked, "Mr. Gaeta . . . how long until we're ready to Jump?"

Gaeta help up two fingers to indicate two minutes and said aloud, "Five minutes, sir."

Adama nodded and then looked back in bleak frustration at the *Bifrost*. Space was alive with Vipers engaging the Cylons. Even if they tried to fire directly at the *Bifrost*, they might blow their own Vipers out of the sky. And if *Colonial One* attempted evasive maneuvers, they could just as easily steer themselves directly into stray shots from either the Cylon raiders or even the Vipers. The entire area was too hot.

Plus if the entire fleet Jumped to escape the Cylons and the *Bifrost* was being commanded by hostiles, they very likely wouldn't make the Jump along with the rest of the fleet, leaving Kara and Agathon to the nonexistent mercies of the Cylons.

Come on, Starbuck, he thought in frustration.

Laura Roslin shoved past the members of the Quorum and went straight up to Wolf Gunnerson, who was the picture of calm. Two security guards were approaching him, and he fired them a look that was fraught with danger. "Stay back!" Laura snapped at them and they halted where they were. She looked up at Gunnerson and demanded, "Why are you doing this?"

"The Edda must be fulfilled," he said calmly. "These things don't happen by themselves."

"Yes! They do! Do you think I was trying to *make* myself ill so that I would fulfill scripture?"

"It doesn't matter," said Gunnerson. "You didn't succeed. I shall. My daughter shall. She's steering the *Bifrost*."

"And what about the Cylons!" Tom Zarek spoke up angrily. "They're crawling all over us out there! Are you working with them, too?"

Wolf Gunnerson said nothing, but merely smiled enigmatically.

The *Bifrost* drew closer.

Boxey eased his way through the duct work with confidence that he knew exactly where he was going. It wasn't all that far. He could do this. He had to do it.

This is it. This has to prove that you're not a Cylon. That you were just making yourself crazy over it.

Although . . . Boomer helped blow up a lot of Cylons before she discovered what she was. Maybe . . .

Stop it! Stop it!

He made his way around a curve in the duct and found himself staring down into the control room. Freya was there, along with Tyr and Fenris. They were manipulating the controls in the slightly cramped area, and Fenris was keeping a steady countdown going toward the imminent collision with *Colonial One.* "Eighteen," he was saying, "seventeen, sixteen . . ."

No time! No time!

Boxey brought both his hands down upon the grillwork and slammed it as hard as he could. The panel, and he, crashed through to the floor. He was up on his feet in a second, and he locked eyes with Freya Gunnerson.

She reached into her jacket and pulled out a gun.

Boxey's head snapped around and he saw the locking mechanism on the door. He lunged toward it. The first shot from Freya's gun slammed into his right shoulder and he cried out. He heard her shout "Get him!" and Tyr and Fenris were coming at him. He willed the pain away, stumbled fell toward the locking mechanism, and another shot struck him in the chest. As he fell, his fingers slammed against the lock, twisting it open, and then he hit the floor and the last thing that went through his mind was *If this doesn't prove it, nothing will,* and then everything went black.

"It's going to hit!" screamed Sarah Porter.

Laura Roslin looked out a viewing port. She could practically see the rivets in the *Bifrost*'s hull.

"It's for the best," Wolf Gunnerson said coolly.

She fired him a glance of utter contempt. "Frak you," she said, which was hardly the most eloquent of final words, but certainly as fitting as any.

The door slid open and Starbuck, her gun in her hand, shoved Jolly aside and was the first one in.

Boxey inadvertently saved her life, because Freya Gunnerson was aiming her weapon straight at Starbuck and Starbuck tripped over Boxey's prostrate body. She went down and Freya's shot went wide, glancing off Jolly's body armor. The impact staggered Jolly but didn't take him down.

Starbuck hit the ground, fired once, and her shot lifted Freya up, blew her off her feet and sent her slamming against the far bulkhead. The sheer impact held her there for a moment, and then slowly she slid down the wall, leaving a trail of blood behind her.

Tyr's gun was already out and Fenris was starting to pull his. Zac stepped out from behind Jolly and fired twice, both times with deadly accuracy. The first show sent Tyr's head exploding in a shower of blood, and Fenris was just starting to bring his weapon to bear when he was shot square in the chest, the impact spinning him around like a top. He went down looking profoundly confused.

Colonial One loomed before them.

"*Helo!*" she shouted.

Helo vaulted over the fallen bodies and grabbed the controls. There was no time for anything fancy. His hands flew over the controls and then angled the *Bifrost* up, up and over *Colonial One*.

"This is gonna be close," he muttered.

He was right. The underside of the *Bifrost* banged against the top of *Colonial One*, and there was an ear-splitting scraping as the two ships slid against each other. It seemed to go on forever, and suddenly they were clear.

Helo grabbed the nearest phone.

Adama had been watching the inevitable collision of the *Bifrost* and *Colonial One* with his heart in his throat, and for just a split second, he thought his confidence in Starbuck had been misplaced. And then he saw the *Bifrost* suddenly change course, and the two ships slid one against the other, leaving behind a nasty scrape but nothing that appeared—at least from this distance—to structurally threaten either vessel.

"Admiral!" Dualla suddenly shouted, her headset wrapped around her ears, "Helo reports *Bifrost* in friendly hands!"

Relief pounded through Adama, and then he pointed at a screen where the Vipers could clearly be seen battling the enemy and made a "circle" gesture with his finger to indicate that the ships should be rounded up.

Nodding her understanding, Dualla immediately sent out the recall code, and the Vipers peeled off and barreled back toward the *Galactica* as fast as they could go.

Everyone in the conference room, with the exceptions of Laura Roslin and Wolf Gunnerson, shouted in fear as the two ships banged up against each other. They staggered, thrown about by the impact, and suddenly there was nothing. The vessels were clear. The hit had not been direct at all, but instead merely a glancing blow.

Laura Roslin had the distinct pleasure at that point of seeing the air appear to escape from Wolf Gunnerson. As if he'd been hit squarely in the face—something that Laura wouldn't have minded doing at that point—Wolf gasped, "What . . . happened? Where did . . . how . . . ?" He looked at Laura as if he expected her to share his sense of barely contained outrage. "This shouldn't be! The Edda . . . it was clear! It was all clear, right there!"

"Don't believe everything you read," Laura told him.

D'anna couldn't believe it.

Space twisted and turned around them and seconds later the entire fleet was free of the Cylon attack. Except that shouldn't have been the case. They should have found themselves, yet again, facing down a Cylon ambush, one that would have most likely been the final ambush they would ever have to deal with.

Instead they were free and clear. Space around them was devoid of any Cylon raiders, and a ragged cheer went up from the members of the Quorum.

Sons of bitches, she thought. Her mind racing, she put together what must have happened and realized that Adama's people must have discovered the bug planted in Gaeta's hand. She wasn't especially concerned that it would lead back to her: Humans were so routine in pressing the flesh of their hands against each other that there was no way Gaeta would associate it with her, especially since it hadn't gone active until some time later as a failsafe measure.

She waited for Gunnerson to make some sort of violent play. The man was, after all, twice as large as anyone there. He could easily have killed several of the Quorum members before he was apprehended. But he did no such thing; instead he surrendered meekly to the security officers who approached him, keeping their guns leveled at him. He seemed bewildered, frustrated, utterly perplexed that matters had not turned out exactly as he had expected them to. He acted as if . . . as if his gods had abandoned him, and without their support, he had no idea what he was supposed to do or how he should proceed.

Humans, she sighed to herself. It was a source of utter mystery to her that they could be simultaneously so strong and so weak all at the same time. It was that lack of consistency that would ultimately be their undoing, just as it was their total consistency that would assure the Cylons of their eventual triumph.

Just not today. Today, she had a story to cover. God knew it wasn't the story she'd wanted, but as Wolf Gunnerson was finding out, even the stories you thought you could count on the most didn't always come out the way you were expecting them to.

CHAPTER 24

The botanical garden on *Cloud Nine* had been cleared out of civilians. Stern-faced soldiers had withstood the confused protests from various residents of the space-going garden who wanted to know why it was that—especially after enduring yet another harrowing encounter with the Cylons—they weren't being given the opportunity to take some rest and relaxation in what was easily the most beautiful piece of territory still in existence. The colonial marines had offered no explanations, but instead had simply apologized for the inconvenience in a way that indicated they really weren't all that sorry about it all.

None of the stragglers or complainers saw the slight woman who was whisked past, keeping her head low, wearing nondescript clothes and a wide-brimmed hat that covered her face. They were far too concerned with their own frustration.

So it was that Sharon Valerii walked through the gardens of *Cloud Nine* undisturbed and unobserved. Actually, "unobserved" might not have been the most accurate way to describe it, for there were sniper scopes aimed at her head if she engaged in the slightest untoward action. She was all too aware of the potentially fatal surveillance, and had no intention of trying any sort of stunt. If nothing else, she owed it to her baby to do everything she could to survive.

She had her shoes off, and was enjoying the sensation of grass under her bare feet. It was new for her. The time she'd spent on Caprica in Helo's company had been mostly taken up with staying on the run—or at least putting up appearances of staying on the run—and she hadn't had time to enjoy the simple pleasures that nature offered. Of all the crimes that the Cylons had committed against humanity, she had to think that banishing them from the embrace of nature had to be far greater than simply blowing them into oblivion. She was willing to allow for the notion that the humans might have disagreed on the matter.

Sharon sensed that someone was coming before she actually saw her. She stopped where she was in the vast open field and waited as the woman approached her. Even before the newcomer drew within range of her, Sharon knew that it was Laura Roslin. She felt a warning of alarm; she was concerned that this was some sort of trick and they were planning to gun her down while claiming that she was making an attempt on the life of the president. Because of that worry, she stood completely stock still, her arms at her sides, determined to make not the slightest gesture that could be misinterpreted. If they were going to shoot her down, then it wasn't going to be for anything that anyone could claim was self-defense. It would be indisputably murder. Not that she thought they would be unwilling to resort to that, but that was going to be what was required of them.

Laura Roslin drew within about ten feet of her, well out of arm's reach, and then stopped. It seemed odd to see someone dressed in such a stern suit standing there in such a natural environment.

The two of them faced each other silently for a time. Sharon knew perfectly well if she made the slightest movement toward Laura, that a sharpshooter would drop her before she covered a foot of the distance. But it wasn't as if she would have made a move on Laura even if her every gesture weren't being monitored by marksmen.

"Still having the dreams?" she asked finally.

"Not recently, no."

Her hand rested unconsciously on her swollen stomach. "You still accusing my child of trying to get into your mind?"

"Actually," Laura said slowly, "it appears it was . . . something else."

"Really."

"Toothpaste."

Sharon stared at her, not getting it. "I'm sorry . . . what?"

Laura took a deep breath and let it out slowly. "Several members of the command crew of the passenger ship *Bifrost* attempted to ram *Colonial One*."

"Freya Gunnerson's people? Midguardians?"

"Yes. They were shot and killed in the attempt. When shown pictures of the scene, I recognized one of them—a man named Tyr—as the maintenance man who had been called in to effect repairs to pipes in my bathroom. As soon as I did, security came in and removed everything from the bathroom and had it tested for potential hazards. It turned out that, according to Doctor Baltar, there was a powerful hallucinogen in the toothpaste. Every time I would brush my teeth, it seeped in through my gums and . . ."

"Made you imagine things?"

"So it would seem."

"So all those accusations regarding my child . . . they were baseless . . . ?"

"I'm not sure," admitted Laura. "I've been . . . under the influence . . . at other times, and had dreams that contained remarkably accurate visions of the future. This may be connected to that."

"Or it may be that you simply imagined the whole thing," said Sharon.

"Yes. It may be that."

Laura walked in a slow circle around her, appearing to study her. Sharon continued to remain right where she was. "I understand you changed your mind about pursuing legal action."

"I decided it wasn't worth it. It wasn't going to go anywhere."

"Freya Gunnerson is dead."

Sharon took in this news without the slightest reaction. "Guess I made the right decision," she said finally.

"Her father was devastated. Man fell completely apart. He's in the custody of the other Midguardians who swear that he and his close associates were acting without their knowledge. That they had extremist beliefs."

"Of course they'd say that."

"You think they're lying?"

"I think it doesn't matter what I think."

Laura made a small *hmm* noise in the base of her throat. Then she said, "So . . . this was your deal with the admiral? Getting information from Freya Gunnerson in exchange for two hours in *Cloud Nine*."

"I wanted my baby to experience this."

"It's not born yet."

"I know. But I'm experiencing it, so the baby will as well. At least, that's what I like to tell myself."

"Was it worth it?" She looked at Sharon askance. "To torment a woman as you did . . . just for a few hours outside of a cell?"

"If you'd ever been stuck in a cell as long as I have, you wouldn't ask that question." She hesitated and then added, "But then again . . . there's all kinds of prisons, aren't there."

"Yes. And all kinds of prisoners."

Laura nodded and then turned and started to walk away. She paused and then, without looking back at Sharon, said, "By the way . . . it doesn't change anything. I still think the baby presents a risk . . . as do you . . . I still think that . . ." She stopped, cleared her throat, and then said, "But I wanted to say . . . thank you for saving my life."

"You're welcome," Sharon said without hesitation.

She stood and watched in silence as Laura Roslin walked away, and when she was gone, Sharon went back to flexing her toes in the grass and smiling.

Starbuck walked slowly along the memorial wall, looking at the pictures of humans who had died in the Cylon attacks and pilots who had likewise died defending the remainder of humanity against further assaults. The pictures were tacked up in no order. When someone wanted to add a photo, they simply put it up there and it became one of the hundreds of pictures of loved ones.

Little pieces of their lives, caught and isolated and etched on paper. Lives unfulfilled, each filled with individual promise that would never be met. It was the single most depressing place on *Galactica*. It was also the most filled with hope, because as long as there was anyone alive to remember the people up on the wall, then humanity continued to have a prayer.

She pulled out a very small picture from her pocket. She held it up and looked at it. It wasn't an entire picture, exactly. It was a portion of one. It was considered bad luck to put the image of a still-living person up on the wall, so she'd had to take the time to do some serious trimming. But she'd managed it, and now she tacked the picture of Boxey up on the wall. She sighed, and she waited for her eyes to brim with tears. They didn't. It made her think that maybe she just didn't have any tears left.

"They're all out? All the bugs?"

Seated in Adama's quarters, Tigh nodded. Adama had a cup of coffee in his hand and was sipping it. "All of them," confirmed Tigh. "Also we swept the extremities of everyone else in CIC. Gaeta was the only victim."

"Do we have any idea when a Cylon agent might have slipped that under his skin, and how they did it?"

"According to Doctor Cottle, considering how miniaturized it was, it could have been anyone at any time. And Gaeta's been off ship socializing any number of occasions, so it could have been any one of a number of places as well. There's simply no way to be sure."

"All right," Adama said slowly. "We'll be instituting regular security sweeps of personnel for potential listening devices."

"Yes, sir."

"And Saul," and he smiled just slightly, "good work."

"Yeah. I know," said Saul Tigh, feeling positive about himself for the first time in a good long while.

"Toothpaste?"

Number Six laughed out loud as Baltar leaned against one of his lab tables and smiled serenly. "Yes. Toothpaste," he replied calmly. "I told her it was the toothpaste that was causing her . . . hallucinations. She seemed most grateful. Even apologized for our little scene in which she made some wild accusations."

"Too wild. How the hell did she see me?"

"She didn't," Baltar replied easily.

"We don't know that for sure, and we could have a serious problem. As much as you claim expertise about Cylons, there's so much about us you don't know. That you can barely begin to comprehend. We share thoughts, experiences. That which one of us knows, others learn of either directly or even through just sensing it, because we are connected and as one. By having a transfusion of blood from that baby, it's not impossible that Roslin is starting to share in that knowledge. And knowledge is power. She claimed she saw me . . ."

"She doesn't know what she saw," Baltar said with complete confidence. "Everything's scrambled up in her brain. Are you ready for this? She claimed she thought that Sharon Valerii's unborn baby was playing tricks with her mind. Can you believe that?"

"Yes. I can, as I've already made clear. Furthermore, on some level, you believe it, too. Or at least you believe it's possible, if you were willing to fabricate that nonsense about the toothpaste."

"I said it because I wanted to throw her off the track, and I succeeded."

"Did you?"

"Never underestimate the power of placebos. I gave her a reasonable explanation for her hallucinations. That alone will likely be enough for her to have night after night of blissful sleep. There's nothing to worry about."

Six shook her head. "The woman suspects you, Gaius. Suspects us. Perhaps you managed to get her to bury it for a short while . . . but it's going to resurface. She is a danger to you . . . to us . . . for as long as she's in power."

"What would you suggest I do? Assassinate her? Or—even better," he snickered, "I could run for president. Win the people's love and force her out of office."

He continued to snicker and then noticed she hadn't joined him.

"It's a thought," she told him.

"It's a stupid thought, and by the way . . . we had an arrangement."

"Did we?" she said dryly, one eyebrow raised.

"Yes, one that you've never fulfilled. You told me if I did as you asked regarding those listening devices, you'd tell me your real name."

"Did I? Oh, yes, I did."

Slowly she walked toward him, her long legs wildly alluring. She leaned in toward him and whispered something in his ear. Then she leaned back and smiled.

"Legion?" said Baltar skeptically. "What do you mean, your name is 'Legion'?"

"Work on it, my dear," she said, patting him on the cheek. "Work on it."

Minerva Greenwald sat in the promenade of the *Peacemaker* and found herself missing Boxey.

The young lady—if a thief and gadabout such as she could possibly be called a lady—had very much enjoyed hanging around with Boxey. First, he was close to her in age. Second, he had learned extremely quickly from her, picking up the fine art of everything from cards to petty thievery. She'd found him an eager student and pleasant companion. But ever since he'd gone off to live on that stupid ship with that stupid woman, Freya . . .

"Hey."

She looked up and gasped in surprise. "Hey!" she cried out. "Hey, what're you doing here?!? I thought you were living over on, whattaya call it? The *Bifrost*?"

Boxey dropped down next to her and smiled readily at her. "I was. But I decided I didn't want to stay there."

"Yeah? Why?"

"Well, for starters, Freya shot me."

"She *did*?" gasped Minerva. "Wh—why aren't you dead?"

"Had a piece of metal paneling. Shoved it under my shirt. Protected me. She didn't know."

"Frak! Why did she shoot you?"

"Because she was nuts. I mean, why else would anyone want to shoot me?"

"I should say so! And you're going to stay here now?"

"Yup. Here with you."

He draped an arm around her shoulder. He seemed to radiate a quiet confidence he didn't have before. "I'm glad you came back," she said. "It'd have been terrible if she'd killed you. Unless . . . y'know . . . you were one of those human-looking Cylons. There's this rumor going around that if you kill them, it doesn't matter, because there's bunches of them."

"Yeah. I heard that, too."

"So maybe I should be worried that you're one of them."

Boxey laughed. "That's the dumbest thing I ever heard."

"I know. It was dumb. Mad at me?"

"Never."

She nestled in closer to him, and he sat there with a distant look on his face that she didn't see, thinking about Cylons, thinking about how they were all connected, and how things were often not what they seemed . . . and most of all, he wondered why he was having the strangest dreams about stone carvings that were bleeding . . .

UNITY

A novel by
STEVEN HARPER

Based on the SCI FI Channel series created by
RONALD D. MOORE

Based on a teleplay by
GLEN A. LARSON

Acknowledgments

My thanks to the Untitled Writers Group of Ann Arbor (Elizabeth Bartmess, Karen Everson, Anne Harris, Jonathan Jarrard, Erica Schippers, Catherine Shaffer, and Sarah Zettel) for putting up with the unexpected deluge of *Battlestar Galactica* chapters. Special gratitude is in order for Catherine Shaffer and her knowledge of prions. Thanks also go to Jim Frenkel for letting me do this in the first place.

Author's Note

This novel is set in the time between the events of the episodes "The Flight of the Phoenix" and "Pegasus."

CHAPTER 1

A trio of Cylon raiders dipped and swooped through space like silent bats on razor wings. Kara Thrace clenched her toes—the only part of her that wasn't occupied with flying her Viper—and tried to keep her eye on all three at once. Two of them split off and swooped around to her left and her right in a pincer move while the third one came straight at her. Kara's eyes darted back and forth and her heart pounded hard.

Come on, she thought, and goosed her thrusters so the Viper jolted upward. *You on the left—a little higher.*

"*Watch yourself, Starbuck,*" Lee Adama said in her earpiece. His voice was heavily distorted by the radio, but Kara understood him perfectly well. You learned to sort out the words through the distortion, almost like learning a foreign language.

"I know what I'm doing, Apollo," she snapped. "Watch your own ass, not mine."

"*Apollo's watching Starbuck's ass?*" Brandon "Hot Dog" Constanza said over his own radio. "*Can I make a comment about that? Please?*"

"*Just do your frakking job, Lieutenant,*" Lee warned.

All around them, other Vipers rushed at the flock of raiders. The deadly little Cylon ships were sleek, flat, and black, with a protrusion in the front that resembled a head. A single red "eye" cruised restlessly back and forth, hunting, scanning. Aiming. In stark contrast, the Vipers were battered and battle-worn. Kara's had once been white, but scorch marks, scrapes, and other damage had weathered it to an uneven gray. It looked like a miniature fighter jet that had crashed once or twice and been knocked back together in a mechanic's back yard. Behind Kara and the other Vipers cruised the immense bulk of the Battlestar *Galactica*. Surrounding it like chicks near a mother hen were the disparate shapes of some seventy-odd ships—passenger ships, cruise ships, work ships. They were all that remained of human civilization. Behind the fleet spun an honest-to-gods blue planet. It had water, it had plant life, and it was the reason why the fleet hadn't simply hit their faster-than-light drives and Jumped out the moment the Cylons Jumped in.

The two Cylon raiders rushed inward for their pincer move, one to port, one to starboard. Kara caught a gleam of starlight off their forward guns. They fired. With a whoop, Kara yanked the control lever at the side of her seat. Auxiliary jets flashed, and the little fighter blasted straight upward. Bullets crossed the intervening space and both Cylon raiders exploded, torn to pieces by friendly fire. Kara wondered if they felt any pain. The Cylon ships were actually living beings, or as alive as Cylons got, anyway. Not that this fact kept Kara from pressing the trigger. She flicked another lever and her maneuverable little Viper whipped around in time to fire on the third Cylon. It exploded as well, close enough that the blast knocked her sideways a little bit, wrenching her around in her seat.

"*I can't believe you frakkin' did that!*" Kat shouted as her own guns raked the raider in front of her.

Kara grinned without answering. Ahead of her, two more Cylons exploded in bright fireballs beneath her guns. A piece of debris rushed straight at her, and she dived beneath it as if the Viper were an extension of her body. Two raiders skimmed into view ahead of her, straight into her cross-hairs, and she wiped both of them out before they even noticed she was there. Beyond the flock of raiders hovered the malignant, spiky form of a Cylon basestar. The frakking thing had popped into existence a few minutes ago and spat out a swarm of raiders, forcing Kara Thrace, Lee Adama, and the other Viper pilots to scramble into their ships to defend the fleet.

Kara brought her Viper up and around again. In the distance, the brilliant yellow star showered golden light in all directions and Kara made an automatic mental note—keep her tail to the sun and force the raiders to look into it whenever possible. She had no idea if the Cylons would be blinded by the solar radiation, or even affected by it at all. For all she knew, they had Cylon sunglasses, but it didn't hurt to try. An image of a raider donning a set of goggles with a single giant lens in the middle popped into her head and a giggle bubbled at the back of her throat. At that moment, yet another raider bore down on her, guns blazing. Kara yelped and whipped her Viper hard to port. She heard pops and pings as the raider's ammo ricocheted off her wings and tail, though her instruments stayed in the green. No real damage. Chief Tyrol would probably chew her out anyway.

Concentrate, she snarled to herself. She spun the Viper around, ignoring the stomach-wrenching vertigo, and fired on the raider with both guns. The barrels mounted on either side of the tiny flight cabin flashed, and Kara felt the familiar breathy thump of her own gunfire. The raider shredded, and Kara moved on to new targets before the debris had a chance to scatter.

"Starbuck," Lee said. "*Check your ten o'clock. A pack of raiders heading for Planet Goop.*"

Kara glanced to port and saw them. Nine raiders had broken away from the rest of the flock, clearly intent on skirting the *Galactica* so they could dive-bomb the little blue planet—and the *Monarch* on its surface.

"Moving to intercept, Apollo," she shot back. "You with me?"

"*All the way. And can the response, Hot Dog.*"

"*Did I say anything?*" Hot Dog protested. "*One word?*"

The raiders swooped and dove in perfect unison. Kara, glad the sun was behind her, hit her thrusters hard. The extra g-force pressed her back into her seat and gave her the unnerving feeling that she was flying straight up instead of forward. Space gave few visual cues, and her inner ear was shouting that gravity—down—was directly behind her. She ignored her inner ear and focused on the fleeing Cylons instead. Hatred flared hot inside her head. These were the frakking bastards who had destroyed her entire world and chased her across countless star systems. How many months had it been since she'd felt safe? How many months had it been since she'd had a night's uninterrupted sleep? How many months since the Cylon attack? She had lost count.

The stupid part was that humans had *created* the Cylons, robots designed for labor too difficult or dangerous for people. And then somewhere along the line the robots had become so sophisticated that they thought they were people too, and they started a rebellion. The resulting war had nearly destroyed the Twelve Colonies and all but wiped out both humans and Cylons. In the end, the Cylons had agreed to take themselves off to another part of space. Peace reigned, and humanity let itself breathe again. Forty-odd years later, the Cylons had reappeared, smarter, angrier, and deadlier than before. They fell on the startled Twelve Colonies and killed billions of humans. Fewer than fifty thousand had survived on various ships that had somehow escaped the carnage. Those ships were now informally known as the Fleet, under the command of Commander William Adama and the governorship of President Laura Roslin. The Fleet was looking for Earth, the fabled thirteenth colony, and Kara was sure they'd find it. Eventually. That hope kept her going. Meanwhile, they had to deal with the Cylons and their living battleships.

The nine raiders swooped downward, remaining carefully out of range of *Galactica*'s weapons. For all that the *Galactica* was an aging Battlestar that was falling apart at the seams, it had more than enough power to wipe out nine measly Cylon raiders. Unfortunately, the *Galactica* was about as maneuverable as a whale caught in low tide, so she depended on the Vipers to sweat the small stuff.

Kara and Apollo accelerated, gaining on the raiders. Ahead of them, Planet Goop spun slowly in its orbit like a perfect blue gem rolling across black velvet. Kara squinted, searching, even though she knew it was impossible to see the *Monarch* from up here. The *Monarch* was a mining ship, but it wasn't down on the surface digging up metal or rocks—it was scooping up goop. Planet Goop had an official name somewhere, but no one used it. It had water, an atmosphere composed of lots of nitrogen and carbon dioxide, and an oceanful of primitive algae. In a few million years, once the plant life had exhaled enough oxygen, Planet Goop might even be habitable by humans. In the meantime, however, the algae had turned out to be quite valuable. It was resistant to radiation—Planet Goop had no real ozone layer—and it could be refined into anti-radiation meds. More importantly, it could also be processed into edible food. Steak composed of smooshed-up algae, colored brown and grilled, didn't taste quite the same as its natural counterpart, but it sure beat starving, and the *Monarch* was harvesting the stuff by the truckload.

Then the Cylon basestar ship had popped up and spewed Cylon raiders. Every ship in the Fleet possessed a faster-than-light drive and could Jump to a safe location, but that would leave the *Monarch* and her crew defenseless. It was also frakking hard to track down ships that didn't all Jump at the same time, and there was considerable risk that one or more would be lost. So they all stayed.

Kara checked her scanner. Tiny Cylon symbols skittered around the screen. In two more seconds she'd be within firing—

An alarm light flashed. Kara gasped and her heart lurched.

"Frak!" she shouted. "One of those raiders has a nuke on board!"

"Uh oh," Lee said. *"Which one?"*

"How the hell should I know?" she shot back. "Stupid frakking Cylons all look alike."

"Hold your fire, Starbuck," came Commander Adama's voice in her headset. *"Repeat: Hold your fire."*

"No shit," she muttered, too quietly for the Old Man to hear. If she fired on a raider that was carrying a nuclear missile, the explosion would wipe out not only her, but Lee, a bunch of the Vipers, and probably a piece of the *Galactica*. It would also wipe out a frakload of Cylons, but that wouldn't be much comfort to the people sucking vacuum.

The nine raiders sped onward. Kara continued to follow, wondering if Cylons could feel smug.

"These raiders aren't usually equipped to fire missiles," Lee said. *"How is it planning to use a nuke?"*

"Suicide run, Apollo," Kara said. "It's hoping to crash into the Monarch and explode or get strafed by one of us and explode."

"Starbuck, I have the nuke on scanner," said Felix Gaeta. Kara could imagine him, dark-haired and ramrod straight, standing with Adama in *Galactica*'s Combat Information Center, outwardly cool as an arctic rock but working like hell on his systems. *"Sending you and Apollo the info now."*

One of the raiders on Kara's own screen blinked from red to yellow.

"Got it," Lee said. *"Let's go!"*

"Don't eat the yellow snow," Kara agreed, "and don't bite the yellow Cylon."

She closed in and hit the trigger. Three of the non-nuke raiders tore themselves to pieces. Kara dodged the debris cloud as the remaining seven came about. One of them—the yellow one—hung back. The forward six returned fire, and Kara was suddenly very busy. Her Viper dipped and swooped, constantly changing vector and heading. Two bullets smacked off her flight canopy like rocks off a windshield. A little more to port, and she would have been dead. The yellow Cylon continued to blink mockingly on her scanner screen.

"Come on, Apollo," she muttered through clenched teeth. Planet Goop reeled in and out of view as she dodged deadly bullets. "Get the mother—"

Friendly fire lashed down. Three more raiders vanished in exploding clouds. They'd been concentrating on Kara and forgotten about Lee. With a whoop, she reoriented and fired on the remaining trio. One more raider blew up. Kara was half sure its single red eye had widened in surprise. Another raider exploded under Lee's expert fire, leaving only the nuke raider. Kara eyed it uncertainly. It hovered in front of her and stared back, its single eye tracking back and forth. Kara wondered if it was scanning her somehow and the thought made cold worms crawl over her skin. She didn't dare fire, and the frakking thing knew it.

"*Shit!*" Hot Dog shouted over the com. "*Another contingent of raiders coming out of the basestar's ass. Move move move!*"

"*How many of those things does it have?*" replied another pilot. It sounded like Jen Curtis, callsign Shadow. Kara flashed on a brief mental image of her tall, lithe figure in the Viper, her long brown hair tied back so it wouldn't float around her face in zero gravity. "*We're gonna get chewed into dog food.*"

"*The raider's guns have been removed,*" Lee said quietly. His Viper moved in beside hers and she could see Lee's handsome, boyish face in his own Plexiglas cabin. "*To make room for the nuke. It's only got one shot, and it has to make it count.*"

"*Kat!*" Shadow shouted. "*Watch it!*"

"*Too many. Pull back! Pull back!*"

Kara felt a sudden urge to whip around and fly back to help her fellow Vipers. She shoved the feeling aside. This raider had the power to take out the *Monarch* or a major chunk of the Fleet, and she had to deal with it.

"*Starbuck, report,*" Commander Adama ordered.

"The nuke raider can't decide what to do," Kara said. "Take out us or the *Monarch*."

"*I'm hit! Gods, I'm hit!*"

"*I've got you covered, Hot Dog. Get yourself—*" An explosion came over the comm.

"*Shadow! Shadow! Aw, no. Jen!*"

"*More raiders coming from the basestar.*"

"*Fall back to the* Galactica. *Let her cover us.*"

Kara glared at the nuke Cylon. It glared back. "Frak! We have to wipe out this thing and get rid of the basestar."

"*How?*" Lee snapped. "*The basestar isn't stupid enough to come close enough to engage the* Galactica. *And we don't have the firepower to—*"

The nuke raider abruptly spun and dove toward Planet Goop. Kara blinked, then dove after it. Even as she moved, an idea popped into her head, and she moved instinctively to implement it.

"*Starbuck!*" Lee shouted. "*Don't!*"

But Kara ignored him. Grimly she accelerated, gaining on the Cylon until the blue flames of its rear thrusters were warming her Viper's nose. Her hands sweated and her heart raced like a greyhound. Her life was in imminent danger. One mistake, and she would be a cloud of debris like the raiders she had killed. A grin slid across her face. She loved every minute. With steady fingers, she lined up the shot. One chance, and one chance only.

"Starbuck!" Lee said. *"What the frak are you doing?"*

"Up yours, toaster." Kara twitched a finger and fired a single round. It went straight into the raider's thrusters. Nothing happened. Kara held her breath. Then the blue flames flickered, sputtered, and died. The Cylon coasted ahead, somehow managing to look startled. Its acceleration immediately stopped and it sped ahead on momentum alone. Kara overshot it, spun her Viper around, and extended her landing gear. Now both Viper and raider were coasting toward the blue planet, though Kara was facing backward. More sounds of combat came over the comm, but she steadfastly ignored them. This was going to be tricky enough. Carefully, using every bit of instinct and skill she possessed, she tapped her own thrusters and slowed herself enough to allow the raider to catch up with her. She edged the Viper upward just a little, then slowed herself again. The helpless raider slid beneath her. There was a *thunk* and a slight screech of tortured metal. Kara goosed her thrusters again. The Cylon slowed with her—it was stuck on her landing gear. Without working engines, it couldn't break free. She wondered what it was thinking.

"Starbuck, what the hell are you doing?" Commander Adama demanded.

"I'm returning some merchandise to the store, sir," she said. "Apollo, cover me!" And she accelerated toward the basestar.

"Hey—what?" Lee, caught off guard, hurried to catch up and pass her. *"You're frakking insane!"*

"That's why you all love me," she shouted. "Just open up a hole in that squadron at your three o'clock. We'll send this nuke back where it came from and get rid of the basestar all at once."

"You sure you can do this, Starbuck?" Lee asked.

"Frak, no. You with me or not?"

Lee hesitated for only a moment. *"Kat, Hot Dog—lay down suppressive fire,"* he ordered. *"Creeper, Fireboy, and Zelda—keep at the others. Fall back if you have to."*

Ahead of Kara, a veritable cloud of Cylon raiders rushed in a hundred dizzying directions like a horde of vampire bats looking for prey. The Viper squadron was outnumbered at least ten to one, but they had nonetheless carved several chunks from the enemy cloud. Cylons seemed to put quantity over quality when it came to dog-fighting in space. It was a wasteful tactic. On the other hand, it had won them victory over the Twelve Colonies.

Kara aimed for the basestar and flew, a grim smile on her face. Burdened with the raider, her Viper was hard to handle, sluggish and unresponsive. She couldn't maneuver much, either—a too-sudden turn might dislodge the raider caught on her landing gear. A clump of raiders swirled just ahead, between her and the basestar, and she held her breath. At exactly the right moment, Lee opened fire. Several of the raiders went up. The others regrouped, ready to fight back, but Kat and Hot Dog rushed in to finish the job. Their guns blazed, creating a dozen more silent fireballs. Kara punched up her speed and headed straight into the hole that had opened up. For a moment she was blinded by fire, smoke, and debris. Something pinged off her starboard wing, jolting her around. But the raider remained firmly in place. Then the debris cleared. Ahead of her she could see the ugly Cylon basestar. It looked a little like a child's jack, the kind kids snatched from the ground before the ball could bounce again. But this jack had been squashed down and then blown up to half the size of the *Galactica*. Kara wondered how many Cylons were inside. Was one of them keeping track of the battle and issuing orders like Commander Adama? Had he given the nuke raider its orders? Maybe the nuke raider was the basestar's version of her, a Cylon Starbuck, given a mission that would take some difficult or impossible flying.

Kara shook off these thoughts and concentrated on the basestar. A glance up and port told her that Lee had brought his own Viper close to hers. Behind, she assumed, Kat and Hot Dog were keeping other raiders too busy to pursue her. She released a tense breath.

Okay, all you Lords of Kobol, she thought. *This is where you can prove that I'm one of your favorites.*

Tentacles of smoke wound out of the basestar. Missiles. Fear dried up Kara's mouth. Even with Lee intercepting, she doubted she could dodge all of them, and it would only take one to wipe her out. They threaded toward her and Lee.

"*I'm reading a signal from the nuke raider*," Gaeta said. "*It's similar to a distress call.*"

"Starbuck," Lee said, "*we need to turn back.*"

Anger boiled in Kara's stomach. The missiles were now eight or ten kilometers away. The basestar loomed, taking up Kara's entire field of vision.

"Are you frakking crazy?" she snapped. "Back through all those raiders?"

"We can't deal with those missiles on our own," Lee retorted. *"That's an order, Lieu—"*

The missiles detonated. Every one of them. Flares of light flashed against Kara's retinas, leaving red dots. The shockwave came a moment later, but the missiles had exploded far too soon to do any damage and she rode it out with scarcely a bump.

"They know!" Kara whooped. "The toasters know I have their nuke. They didn't want one of their missiles to set it off this close."

"A bunch of raiders got past us," Kat said. *"Company's coming, Apollo."*

"I'll take care of it," Lee said. *"Starbuck, go! Make it fast!"*

She went. Her sluggish Viper flung itself forward. This was the closest she had ever come to a basestar, and it filled her world with gray menace. The disgusting thing had actual frakking portholes in it, and she could see figures moving around inside. Did they know what she was doing, or that she was even here? She gnawed her lower lip in concentration. Flashes of light came over her shoulder, telling her that Lee had engaged the flock of raiders that had gotten past Hot Dog and Kat. Kara eyed the basestar, her eyes tracking rapidly back and forth almost like the single eye of a Cylon. And then she saw it—an open port. It might have been for launching raiders, it might have been for launching missiles. Hell, it might have been for launching Cylon sewage. Kara didn't much care. She aimed for it and accelerated again.

Lords of Kobol, she thought, keeping her hands steady by strength of will. Fear mixed with exhilaration, making both all the sweeter. The port loomed closer. At the last minute, Kara reversed all her thrusters. She slammed against her flight harness, and pain made an H across her chest. With a metallic screech, the nuke raider wrenched away from her landing gear. It spun like a discus, the single eye tracking frantically back and forth as it headed for the port. At the last moment, Kara fired her weapons. A tongue of flame touched the little raider just as it flew into the port.

"Run!" Kara shouted into the comm. She flipped her Viper over and punched the thrusters hard. Acceleration shoved her backward, crushing her, and her vision flickered for a moment before she could recover. She rushed past the Cylons Lee was fighting. Lee flipped his own Viper and fled along with her. The raiders paused for a moment, then flew after them. Kara threw a glance over her shoulder at the basestar, waiting for the big *kaboom*.

Nothing happened.

Uh oh, she thought, then looked at the flock of raiders on her screen. Over a hundred behind her, and all would hit firing range in a few seconds.

"*If we live through this*," Lee growled, bringing his Viper in beside hers, "*I'm going to kill you*."

Starbuck flashed him a sickly grin and flipped her Viper one more time, guns ready. Lee followed suit. If she was going to go down, she would go down with her weapons blazing and the wounds on her front, not her back. The raiders rushed forward, their sleek, deadly forms almost invisible against the blackness.

And then a horrendous light filled the universe.

CHAPTER 2

Kara flung up a hand to shield her eyes, though the Viper's cabin was well polarized. Moments later, the shockwave hit, flipping her and Lee ass over teakettle. Both Vipers bucked and weaved as their pilots fought to regain control. Kara bounced around within her harness, jarring her new bruises. A few hundred kilometers away, the basestar was exploding in the world's most brilliant firework display, as if the Lords of Kobol had cracked open a doorway into hell. Kara ignored the pain, ignored the light, and just frakking *flew*.

The other Vipers turned tail and ran as well. Ahead lay the *Galactica* and safety. The raiders buzzed about, obviously confused and uncertain by the loss of their commanding ship. In a few minutes they would recover, however. The light and shock of the explosion faded, and Kara regained full control of her Viper.

"*Get 'em!*" Lee barked.

The fight was short, nasty, and to the point. The Cylon raiders didn't have a chance to regain their equilibrium before the Vipers shredded them the way a chef shredded soft cheese. Into an omelet. With tender mushrooms and sweet onions and—

Kara's stomach growled as another Cylon puffed into a satisfying fireball under her buns. Guns! Under her guns. Frak, when had she last eaten?

The basestar was an expanding nebula of radioactive debris, and Hot Dog got the last Cylon raider, a fact he announced with a whoop that made Kara's ears ring.

"*Let's go home, people*," Lee said. "*You did good*."

"*Services for Shadow?*" Kat asked.

"*This evening,*" Lee said.

Kara eased her Viper around to face the enormous *Galactica*, her mood gone suddenly pensive. She had barely known Jen "Shadow" Curtis and now she was gone. Kara had long since stopped keeping track of the number of Viper pilots they had lost since the Cylon attack—the number was just too depressing. What she wanted right now was a stiff shot of something that would burn all the way down, a hot meal, and maybe a card game. Or sex. With someone nice and—

"*Viper squadron, I'm reading a distress signal,*" Gaeta said, breaking Kara's chain of thought.

"*From the basestar?*" Lee said, surprised.

"*Negative. The signal is Colonial.*"

Kara's heart jumped. "Is it Shadow?"

"*Also negative. It's an automated signal from an escape pod.*"

Escape pod? "Vipers don't have escape pods," Kara said, "and we're the only ones out here. Gaeta, you're seeing things."

"*Still negative, Lieutenant. You should be getting it on your screen now.*"

Kara glanced down. Sure enough, the source of a Colonial distress signal was flashing.

"*Have any ships in the Fleet launched escape pods?*" Lee asked.

There was a pause. "*Negative, Captain,*" came the warm voice of Tactical Officer Anastasia Dualla—"Dee" to her friends. "*No distress from the Fleet, and no pod launched.*"

"Apollo, Starbuck, go check it out," Adama ordered.

"*On it, sir,*" Lee said, and both Vipers swung around. Kara made a face and her stomach growled again. Dammit, this mission was *over*. She was supposed to get food and booze and . . . maybe something else. Still, curiosity nudged her. So did suspicion. Cylons could be slippery as a snake in an oil refinery. This might easily be a trick.

"*This might easily be a trick,*" Lee said.

Kara suppressed a snort. "You read my mind, Captain. Scary."

"*Frakking scary, Lieutenant.*"

Kara homed in on the signal, brought her Viper about, and hit the acceleration. May as well get this over with. Lee followed, a little above and behind her. She dodged around a couple pieces of basestar debris and finally caught sight of the signal's source. The pod was boxy, about two meters tall, two meters wide, and five meters deep. A red distress light winked steadily on the top, and it was slowly rotating end over end. A rudimentary thruster jutted from the back, designed to give just enough boost for the pod to grab some distance from whatever vessel it was trying to flee. Kara stared, instantly recognizing the design.

"It's a Colonial escape pod," she reported, not quite believing it. "Where the hell did it come from?"

"Has to be the basestar," Lee said, his tone also conveying disbelief. *"Unless one of the Fleet ships blew up when we weren't looking."*

"No such luck, Apollo," said Colonel Saul Tigh, the *Galactica's* executive officer. His voice was dry and hard as old wood, and Kara could imagine him in CIC, his bare scalp gleaming in the artificial light. *"Nothing that comes from a Cylon ship is worth saving. Open fire."*

Kara stuck her tongue into her cheek and moved it around. Tigh wanted the pod destroyed, and that automatically made her reluctant to make it happen. Tigh was a grade-A, no-holds-barred, frakked-up, drunk-ass shithead. In her humble opinion. Unfortunately, the frakked-up shithead also had rank on her.

"Sir—" she began.

"Belay that," Adama interrupted. *"Starbuck, can you get any closer and check it out better? Apollo, you provide cover."*

"Commander," Tigh said, *"I don't think that's a good—"*

"Thank you, Colonel," Adama cut him off. *"Your objection is noted."*

"Moving in, sir," Kara said, not bothering to keep the smugness out of her voice. Adama—now there was a commander you could respect. If Bill Adama asked her to check out the heart of a star, she'd salute and fire all thrusters. She edged her Viper closer. Beyond the pod, the blazing yellow sun continued pumping out radiation across the spectrum. Already, the basestar debris field had largely dispersed. Kara matched velocity with the pod, though it continued to turn slowly end over end. Her finger remained on the fire button for her weapons. Colonel Tigh was an ass, but that didn't mean *she* had to be stupid.

The pod rotated some more, and a porthole slid into view. Through it, Kara caught a glimpse of a human face, a male she didn't recognize. He was staring into space with wide, frightened eyes. They locked gazes for a startled moment.

Help! he mouthed. Then the pod's rotation carried the porthole out of view.

"There's someone aboard," Kara reported, forcing her voice to remain steady. "I just saw a man's face."

A moment of silence fell over the airwaves. A raider was just one shape Cylons came in. Some Cylons were shiny metal robots, complete with built-in pulse rifles. And some looked perfectly, exactly human. Cylons also seemed to go in for repetition. All their robotic forms looked alike, and the human forms seemed to be limited in their variation. Kara had heard rumors that the Cylons used only twelve human shapes. She herself had encountered at least two female forms and three male forms, and she had killed one of the latter back on Caprica when—

—a shiny shard sinking into soft flesh, a choked cry gurgling from a ruined throat, an ineffectual hand clawing at her face—

Nausea quivered in her empty stomach and Kara shoved unpleasant memories aside. She needed to concentrate on the present job, not on past nightmares.

"Is he human or Cylon?" Tigh demanded.

"No way to tell, sir." Kara resisted adding an epithet about the stupidity of Tigh's question. "He looked human, and I haven't seen him before, but that doesn't say much."

"I'm dispatching a search-and-rescue Raptor, Starbuck," Adama said. *"You and Apollo can return to* Galactica.*"*

"Sir," she acknowledged, though she felt oddly reluctant to leave the guy, whoever he was, spinning alone through space. The feeling wasn't rational—there was nothing she could do for him in a Viper, and for all she knew, he was a Cylon. But the feeling remained. She gave the pod one more glance before bringing her Viper about and falling in behind Lee as he headed for home.

Home, she thought. *When did* Galactica *become home?* As a Viper pilot, Viper trainer, and occasional CAG—Commander Air Group—Kara spent more time on ships than she did planetside, and her small apartment on Caprica usually showed her neglect. But now that Caprica and the other Twelve Colonies were overrun by Cylons, she felt a strong need to return there, feel the open spaces around her, breathe the crisp, fresh air. Cook a meal. Sink into a soft chair. Hell, she even missed dusting the furniture. Before the Cylons attacked, she had treated housework as something to be seriously considered after every major earthquake. Now she would happily spend a year hunting down dust bunnies if it meant she could go back home whenever she wanted.

The thought struck her as strange. Kara had never seen Caprica or her apartment as anything but a base to operate from. She usually felt out of sorts planetside, and came truly alive only when she was flying. It was, she supposed, the lack of choice. Before the Cylon attack, she *could* go home if she wanted to. Now that the Cylons had removed the choice, she wanted it back.

"*Viper four-one-six*/Galactica," said the Launch Signal Officer. "*Approach port landing bay, hands-on, speed nine eight, blue stripes. Call the ball.*"

Kara guided her Viper into the *Galactica*'s port landing bay, as instructed, keeping her speed at ninety-eight for a manual landing. Lee preceded her into the cavelike bay, its roof arching high above, its floor perfectly flat. A ways ahead of her was an elevator pad painted in blue stripes. Lee was already skimming down to land on one with red checks. All her instruments were in the green and she was having no problems.

"I have the ball," she said, and guided her Viper down to a perfect landing. The elevator pad dropped down, taking Kara and the Viper with it. A few moments later, she was on the even more cavernous flight deck. Ceramic tile that had once been white faced most of it. Rows of sleek Vipers and boxy Raptors stretched into the distance. Half a dozen members of Galen Tyrol's damage-control people surrounded Kara's little ship before the elevator pad could drop flush with the deck. Kara released the canopy. She pushed it up and removed the helmet to her vac suit with familiar ease. Hard smells from the flight deck assailed her—sharp solder, scorched plastic, metallic air. Kara shook her short blond hair, then hauled herself out of the Viper. The flight crew ignored her as unimportant. The Viper needed their attention more.

"Not bad out there, Starbuck," Lee Adama said. He had removed his own vac helmet, revealing a startlingly handsome, boyish face topped with tousled brown hair. Bright blue eyes met her brown ones. "Did you forget your receipt?"

"Receipt?" she said, puzzled.

"When you returned the merchandise to the Cylons," Lee clarified with a grin. "Looked like they wouldn't accept it without a receipt."

She rolled her eyes. "Gosh, Apollo—so funny I forgot to laugh."

"Wisecracks are your department. Everybody knows that."

"How much damage did you do this time, sir?" broke in a new voice.

Kara gave Chief Petty Officer Galen Tyrol an insouciant grin. He was a stocky, dark-haired man who wore a continual expression of worry from the long hours and short supplies he dealt with as chief of Deck Crew Five. He and his people oversaw the maintenance and repair of the Vipers, Raptors, and shuttles that defended the Fleet. Kara was notoriously hard on her Vipers and wasn't much bothered when they came back to him heavily damaged. She knew that to a man like Tyrol, it was like bringing home a sports car covered in dents with all the glass broken, and she could rarely resist teasing him.

"Meh," she said. "A few dings and cracks. Nothing you couldn't suck out with a plunger or slap together with some epoxy."

Tyrol's pained expression was interrupted by the staccato clatter of boots in quick-march. Startled, Kara drew back in time to avoid a squadron of marines. They wore full combat gear, face plates, and flak jackets. The barrels on their pulse rifles gleamed and their stomping boots echoed in the enormous flight deck.

"What the frak?" Kara said as they trotted past.

"The SAR Raptor's bringing in that escape pod you found," Tyrol explained. "The marines are just in case."

Kara was supposed to head for a post-flight debriefing, but there was no way she was going to miss this. Lee stayed with her. News about the pod had evidently leaked out because a small crowd of other onlookers slowly gathered. Most of them were Tyrol's technicians, and they were clearly performing make-work to have an excuse to stay close. Kara made no such pretense, and leaned casually against her Viper. Twice she caught Lee looking at her out of the corner of his eye, and she caught herself looking back. Idle curiosity? Or more than that? She felt a faint flush coming on and looked away. Several weeks ago, Kara had returned from a classified mission on Cylon-occupied Caprica. The events of the mission had been upsetting, to say the least, and Lee had done his awkward best to comfort her. And that was when he had said It.

Upon her return, Lee had met her at the airlock and grabbed her in a tight hug. He had followed this with a brotherly kiss that had, for a second, turned into something a little more powerful. Both of them had pulled back in surprise. Others had been present, however, and they hadn't had a chance to talk until later when Lee found her in a locker room, disconsolately bouncing a Pyramid ball. Lee had asked what was upsetting her, but Kara refused to talk, and Lee filled the silence with words of his own.

You're my friend, and I love you.

The simple phrase, said in Lee's straightforward manner, had gone straight through Kara and stabbed a red-hot nerve she hadn't known existed. It brought up strange feelings, confusing emotions, difficult memories.

You're worthless, Kara. No one loves you. You're just a worthless piece of trash. Her father's voice, the one that brought up hatred, fear, and a strange desire to please, still echoed in her head sometimes, and Lee's words brought it back again. It all confused her, scared her, and she retreated into easy flippancy.

"Lee Adama loves me," she sing-songed at him. Her tone made him turn away, clearly sorry he had said anything. She pressed the advantage, taunting him with playground banter until he had slouched out of the locker room wearing a "Yeah, sure" expression. Neither of them had referred to the incident since, which was just the way Kara wanted it.

Didn't she?

Lee shuffled his feet, looking like he was about twelve. Kara looked at her nails. Tyrol fussed over the Viper.

"Crack in the main manifold," he muttered, "scoring on the cabin, and what the frak happened to the landing gear?"

"Nothing out of the ordinary for Lieutenant Thrace," said Specialist Cally Henderson. She had short brown hair, a round face, and an enormous clipboard. The paper on it was already half covered in notes. Kara waggled some eyebrows at her and Cally shook her head in mock sorrow.

Two elevator pads descended side by side. One bore the Search-and-Rescue Raptor. The SAR Raptor was larger than the "normal" Raptors and sported equipment that let it haul in ships, pods, or other objects in distress. The other pad bore the escape pod. It was large enough to hold over thirty people, if they were friendly. It had two portholes, but Kara couldn't see inside it from where she was standing. The marines quickly stepped up and trained their weapons on the airlock door with the various clacks and clicks of ready weapons.

"Everyone stay back, please," bellowed the Sergeant Major in charge of the platoon. "We're not expecting trouble, but you should remain at a safe distance."

Kara snorted. If "not expecting trouble" meant pointing a dozen pulse rifles and readying a handful of grenades, she was dying to see what "expecting trouble" looked like. She continued to lounge against her Viper, seemingly unconcerned but actually crawling with curiosity. It was sheer coincidence that the Viper's wing was providing a nice bit of cover between her and the pod.

"Where the hell did it come from?" Lee asked beside her.

She shrugged. "Maybe a Colonial ship we don't know about survived the Cylon attack and passed this way."

"Not likely. We've been in this system for days. We would have picked up the distress signal a long time ago. Has to be from the basestar."

"You said that earlier," she pointed out. "Why would a Colonial escape pod be on a Cylon basestar?"

"Maybe we can ask the guy you saw, if the marines don't blow him away."

The wheel on the airlock turned all by itself. The marines remained outwardly impassive, but tension thickened the oily air. The flight crew stopped all pretense of work and stared at the slowly moving wheel. Most had obeyed the Sergeant Major and moved away or stolen behind some kind of cover. The wheel made the familiar cricket-chirp sound that Kara heard every day from doors all over the *Galactica*, and the door swung outward. She tensed, ready to dive fully behind her Viper.

Nothing happened. The doorway stood empty, the inside of the pod completely dark. Kara narrowed her eyes. Someone in there had shut of the light. Why?

The marines stayed in attack formation around the door, their expressions tense. Still nothing moved.

"Attention rescue pod," the Sergeant Major barked. "We have you surrounded!"

Kara pushed back a laugh. Yes, the rescue pod was armed and dangerous. Any minute it would—

Movement exploded from the doorway. Kara caught a glimpse of a woman with long black hair and almond eyes. She wore a green jumpsuit and she moved faster than any human had a right to move. Before the marines could react or even blink, she stiff-armed one of them so hard that he flew backward and crashed into one of his compatriots, bringing both of them down. The woman didn't stop moving. She grabbed a rifle barrel with impossible speed and yanked. The marine holding it left his feet and smashed straight into the heel of her hand. He dropped to the deck and the woman whirled the rifle into firing position. Kara recognized the woman's face and gasped just as the rest of the squadron opened fire. Needles and bullets tore through the woman. She jigged in place as bloody holes ripped through her skin and clothes. Then she dropped to the deck, rifle still in her hand. It clanged against the deck plates.

"Frak," Lee muttered. "Sharon."

Kara nodded. One of the five versions of Cylons Kara—and Lee—had encountered took the form of Raptor pilot Sharon Valerii. Sharon had been a "sleeper" agent, a Cylon who had been programmed with false memories to make her think she was human. Her mission had been to assassinate Commander Adama, and she had nearly succeeded. Her corpse still lay in the morgue. On Caprica, Kara had come across another version of Sharon. This copy had known she was a Cylon, but she had helped Kara on her mission, and Kara brought the Cylon back with her to *Galactica*. Caprica Sharon currently occupied the brig, and although she had helped *Galactica* fight the Cylons on numerous occasions, it sent cold shivers across Kara's skin to see "her" out in the open.

This version of Sharon was clearly dead, another one for the morgue. Kara pushed through the gathered crowd and saw for herself. Sightless eyes stared at the ceiling, and one of her legs was bent beneath her. Kara pursed her lips, then looked at the pod. It was still dark inside it.

"I saw a man in there," she called to the marines. "Before I came in to land. He's probably still there."

The marines who weren't down or attending to the wounded turned away from Sharon's corpse and trained their rifles on the pod again.

"You in there!" barked the Sergeant Major. "Hands on your head and come out!"

Long pause. Then, "I'm coming. Don't shoot!"

A shadow moved, and a figure stepped slowly out of the pod and into the light, his hands on his head. He looked out at the marines and technicians with an uncertain, hesitating expression. Every marine rifle instantly snapped around to train on him. Kara felt her eyes widen. Frak, the man was *gorgeous*. His golden hair shone like sunshine in the harsh light of the flight deck, and his eyes, blue as a Caprica lake, looked out from a smooth, square-jawed face. He wore a blue short-sleeved shirt cut tight enough to show off an arresting build and arms that begged Kara to run her hands over them so she could feel their corded muscle. She remembered her earlier thoughts on the Viper and felt a little flushed despite the weaponry that bristled around her.

"Don't shoot!" the man said, and his voice was smooth and light, almost boyish but still fully a man's. "I'm not a Cylon!"

Kara stared at him. His voice sounded familiar, and the more she looked at him, the more it seemed like she should know him. But she couldn't put her finger on why.

"Lie face-down on the ground," the Sergeant Major said. "Now!"

Slowly, the man obeyed. He looked alone and vulnerable in front of the pod. Kara felt sorry for him, though she knew full well that he could be another Cylon. The Fleet had been tricked far too often to trust a newcomer easily.

Two marines put a set of heavy shackles on the blond man. He didn't resist. He also didn't speak. Two more marines disappeared into the pod, rifles at the ready, and reemerged to report that no one else was inside. The Sergeant Major hauled the blond man to his feet. He still looked familiar.

"Oh my gods!" Cally said abruptly. She was clutching her clipboard to her chest. "That's Peter Attis!"

And then it clicked for Kara. Peter Attis. Rock star. His image had graced posters and album covers and magazine pages all over the Twelve Colonies. He had started his career when he was sixteen, and his song "My Heart Has Eyes for Only You" had soared to the top of the charts. Kara, then thirteen, had decorated her bedroom with his pictures and collected every single song. In school she had doodled in her notebook every possible combination of her name and his—Kara Attis. Peter Thrace. Kara Attis-Thrace. Mrs. K. Thrace-Attis—accompanied by the required heart over the i in "Attis." Thank the Lords of Kobol she had outgrown that phase right quick and that no one had ever seen those notebooks.

A murmur went through the assembled group. Several had recognized him, too. Peter's music had matured along with him, which garnered him fans from every part of the age spectrum. He had even gone through a brief but intense grunge phase, which Kara still listened to.

Leaving Lee behind, Kara stepped forward to get a better look. The prisoner was shackled and Kara outranked the Sergeant Major, so the marine didn't object. Peter looked at her with the bluest eyes Kara had ever seen. For a moment, Kara was thirteen again, and her heart was racing with a strange thrill.

"Peter Attis?" she said. The teenaged fangirl inside her jumped up and down and said, *I have all your records. I think you're the greatest!* Kara told it to shut the hell up and instead said, "Hell, I used to listen to all your stuff." The half-quashed teenager put a little too much enthusiasm into Kara's voice, so she added, "But that was a frakking long time ago."

"Thanks," Peter said, and flashed a wide smile that went straight down to Kara's toes. "It's always nice to meet a fan—or former fan. Uh . . . even when I'm chained hand and foot."

All at once, Kara was aware of her surroundings. She cleared her throat and backed up a step. "Just a precaution," she said. "Though I'm sure *you* couldn't be a Cylon."

"And why is that, Lieutenant?" asked Colonel Saul Tigh behind her.

Kara bit the inside of her cheek and turned to face him. Tigh was somewhere in his sixties, with a short fringe of white hair surrounding his bald pate. He wore his navy blue Executive Officer's uniform stiffly, as if it were filled with wood and wire instead of skin and muscle, and his face was screwed into a permanent mask of disapproval. Behind Colonel Tigh stood Commander Bill Adama and Dr. Gaius Baltar. Adama's craggy, acne-scarred face looked grave. He and Tigh were of an age, but Kara thought Adama wore his years far better. Gaius Baltar was much younger, a genius with computers, physics, and some areas of biology. He was also the vice president of the Colonies.

"Peter Attis can't be a Cylon because his history is too well-established, sir," Kara said to Tigh, keeping her dislike out of her voice but not bothering to disguise a small sneer. "He's been a star since he was sixteen years old, and lots of people recognize his face. He has family—or he did. A brother and two sisters and parents."

"They all died in the attack, though," Peter said softly.

"So there's no way to verify his identity," Tigh said. "He came from a Cylon ship, and I'm thinking he needs an introduction to the nearest airlock."

"I'm not a Cylon," Peter repeated. His voice was calm but his face was pale. "What can I say that might convince you?"

Kara gave Adama a desperate look. "Commander, shouldn't we—"

"We've been bitten by too many snakes, Lieutenant," Adama said. "I think the Colonel may be right."

"Isn't he handsome?" Number Six whispered in Gaius Baltar's ear. Her breath was warm and wet on his skin, and her slender hands lay hot on his shoulders. He could see her out of the corner of his eye, though long practice had taught him not to spin around to look at her. He was standing at the back of the crowd, but someone might still see, and people looked at you funny when you acknowledged the presence of empty air.

"If you go in for that type," he said softly. "And before you ask, I never have done, thank you."

Number Six smiled. She was a tall, heavy-breasted woman with pale blond hair, gray eyes, and full, red lips. At the moment she was wearing a pale blue dress that flowed in some areas, clung in others.

"Jealous?" she said.

"You can't be serious," he responded. The second word came out more like *cahnt*. "He's a singing ape with the IQ of a trained poodle."

She ran a finger across the back of his neck, sending shivers down his spine. He half closed his eyes in catlike satisfaction. No one could see—or hear or feel—Cylon Humanoid Model Number Six except him. Back home on Caprica, he had thought she was a real human woman, one genuinely attracted to his natural charisma, brilliant mind, and well-toned physique. She was the most inventive lover he had ever taken to his bed, and Gaius's bed had been a playground for more years than he cared to count. Only later had he learned how she had tricked him, seduced him into giving up the secrets to Caprica's computerized defense network. The Cylons had penetrated the Twelve Colonies moments later, and Gaius himself had barely escaped death. No one on the Fleet knew about his treason—except Number Six. He had seen her die on Caprica, but now she appeared to him like some strange ghost, able to touch him, push him around. Seduce him. She had initially claimed to be a hallucination created by a chip the Cylons had implanted in his head, but Gaius had gotten his brain scanned, and no chip had turned up. He had since given up trying to define what she was or where she came from.

"Looks like you won't have to worry about him for long, Gaius," Six murmured. "They're going to toss him out an airlock. Typical mistrustful behavior."

"Yes, you and your kind have given us so many reasons to trust everyone." But the rebuke was mild, almost habitual.

"And you'll never get the chance to learn what he's really about."

Here he did turn his head. Fortunately, he was at the back of the crowd and no one noticed. "What do you mean?"

"It doesn't matter, does it?" Six nodded at Adama and Tigh. "Look at them. They're going to have Peter killed. And his secrets die with him."

"Why would I care about his secrets?" Gaius snorted, though he found himself staring at Peter Attis.

"You won't," Six said. "He's going to die before anyone even knows he *has* secrets. Too bad. There's glory in working out a puzzle like his."

"Commander," Gaius called out. He wormed his way through the crowd of people gathered around the Raptor. "Commander, if I may?"

"What is it, Doctor?" Adama said in the tired tone he often used with Gaius. It was a tone Gaius found immensely irritating. He was the vice president of the Colonies and the single most intelligent human being in the Fleet, yet Adama insisted on treating him like an annoying flunky.

"I think it might be best if we—if *someone*—interrogated this man first. If he's a Cylon, it would benefit us to learn all we can from him. If he's human, he clearly lived among the Cylons as their prisoner for quite some time, and he might have valuable insight into their thinking. He could hardly be a threat in the brig, in any case."

"I think Doctor Gaius is right, sir," Kara Thrace said.

"Which means we should definitely toss him," Tigh growled.

Adama's face remained impassive. He looked at Kara, then at Tigh and Gaius. Gaius held his breath.

"Toss him," Adama said shortly, and turned to leave.

CHAPTER 3

The marines dragged Peter away. An expression of terror twisted his handsome face and he was shouting incoherently, struggling against his bonds.

"Commander, please!" Kara and Baltar said simultaneously. Their words tumbled out in an overlapping rush.

"You're making a terrible mistake! Who knows what he might know? There's no proof he's a Cylon. You could be executing an innocent man. How could it hurt to put him in the brig? We've had Sharon on board for weeks, and she's only helped us. Peter might be able to tell us about the Cylons, things we'd never find out on our own."

Adama remained silent.

"I'll interrogate him myself, Commander," Kara added. "If there's any hint that he's a Cylon, I'll space him myself. Please."

"Yes, please," Baltar added.

Adama looked at them both for a long moment. Kara held her breath. It seemed like she could already hear Peter's silent scream as his tortured body floated through harsh vacuum. When she was drawing hearts and combining names in her school notebook, she had never thought she might be involved in trying to save Peter's life. His music had gotten her through some tough times. When she was young, the bouncy pop rhythms created a safe space far away from her father, and she fantasized that Peter might sweep into her life and take her to safety. As she grew older, Peter's music changed. His brief grunge phase had produced two albums that had spoken to Kara at a time when her emotions had been as thick and black as the music Peter produced. The albums he had done in adulthood hadn't grabbed her as much, but she still remembered how his voice had reflected her own mood and the sympathy she had found there.

"All right," Adama said at last. "Take him to the brig. I want both of you to interrogate him. Have Lee there, too."

"Thank you, sir!" Kara said over her shoulder. She was already sprinting after the marines. She didn't see Lee watching her with an odd look on his face.

Peter sat, pale and stunned, behind a table bolted to the floor in the brig. He had already thrown up twice, but he had assured Kara that the nausea had passed. She hoped so. The sour smell of vomit wasn't something she enjoyed, especially when it was someone else's.

The brig interrogation room was chilly. Bare blue walls, a single metal door with a thick glass window, and a set of chairs bolted to the floor were all that greeted "visitors." Kara faced Peter with Baltar beside her and Lee standing behind. Peter was still in chains. He also looked . . . different to Kara. It was subtle, but noticeable. His hair was disheveled, and he needed a shave. Fine lines radiated away from his eyes, lines that didn't belong on a man barely over thirty. His lips were thin with fear. The Peter who appeared on vids and posters and album covers was smooth and perfect—handsome, but in a plastic sort of way. This Peter was real, a man who breathed and sweated and chewed his nails. And he was all the more attractive for it. As a child, she'd had a crush on dream. As an adult, she wanted something more solid, and this Peter looked pretty solid.

Kara gave a slight shake of her head. This was weird. She was actually sitting across a table from Peter Attis. Okay, so her teenage fantasies hadn't involved handcuffs and leg irons—those came when she was rather older—but still.

"I wanted to say thanks," Peter said hoarsely. "For saving my life."

"Don't thank me yet," Kara said. "If you can't convince Lee and Baltar here that you aren't a toaster, they'll still space you, and I promised to hit the big red button."

"So *you* don't think I'm a Cylon," Peter said.

"I doubt you are," Kara told him carefully, "but I can't say I know for sure."

"I don't know how I can convince you," Peter said. He tried to spread his hands, but the shackles prevented him. "They look just like us. Or some of them do."

"Tell us what happened to you," Baltar said.

"Yeah," Lee said. His arms were folded across his chest. "Do tell."

"Uh . . . I'm from Libron," Peter replied. His voice was smooth and arresting, almost hypnotic. "My band and I were on tour, and we were giving a concert on a cruise ship. That was when the Cylons attacked. It was . . . everyone was panicking. Alarms were going off, lights flashing. My bodyguards disappeared, but no one seemed to care who I was anyway. Something blew up and threw us all to the floor. I found out later that half the ship had been destroyed and we—those of us who survived—were trapped on the other half. Radiation alarms kept blaring that rad levels were 'unacceptably high.' A bunch of us made it to an escape pod. We crowded inside. More people tried to push their way in, but there just wasn't room. I remember how we . . . we slammed the door in their faces." Peter's voice was shaking now. "The last person I saw was a little boy, maybe eight years old. He knew he was going to die, you could see it in his eyes."

Kara found tears pricking at the corners of her own eyes. She forced them back and told herself this could be nothing more than a story told by a Cylon desperate to convince her that he was human. Just because he was handsome and famous didn't mean he wasn't a liar. The tears ebbed.

"Then what?" Lee asked.

"Someone hit the release and the pod pushed off." Peter's eyes hardened. "That was when the Cylons grabbed us. They hauled the pod onto one of their ships. We all thought we were dead. Later, we just wished we were. Or I did, anyway."

"What happened?" Baltar said, exuding empathy.

"All of us were split up. You're the first humans I've seen since then." His voice was flat, without emotion. "They brought me to a laboratory and . . . here it gets a little hazy. I think I was drugged a lot of the time. I remember . . . I remember pain. A lot of needles. Bright light. I remember lying in bed, shaking and convulsing like a be-headed snake. A voice was babbling nonsense, and it took me a while to realize it was my own. I couldn't stop babbling. And I remember some strange robots looking down at me, doing things that hurt. And I remember a woman with blond hair. She was there a lot."

A strange expression crossed Baltar's face and almost instantly vanished. Kara wondered what that was about.

"And then one day a woman—a different woman—came to my bed at the lab. I was pretty zoned out. She said that they were all done with me. I thought they were going to kill me then, and I was glad. It would stop hurting. But the woman didn't kill me. She took me out of the bed, gave me some clothes—I was naked—and took me . . . I think she took me home with her. I mean, it was kind of like an apartment, but it was dark and damp all the time. The woman told me to call her Mistress Eight. I asked her what happened to the others in the pod and she said they all had died. She said it like you might say a houseplant or pet rat had died. I asked why I hadn't been killed. She just smiled and said the others hadn't been killed—they had died, and there was a difference. She wouldn't tell me any more than that. Maybe she was lying. I don't know."

A flicker of movement caught Kara's eye. She glanced at the window set into the door and saw the faces of two female crew. Both of them were staring. One of them said something to the other, and Kara saw her mouth "Peter Attis" with an excited look on her face. She glared at them. They gave sheepish smiles and vanished. Kara turned her attention back to Peter.

"Why did she bring you to her . . . apartment?" she asked. It seemed strange, the idea that Cylons would have places to live. What did robots need with a bed and a bathroom?

Here Peter's jaw trembled. "She kept me as a pet. Put a collar on me. Showed me off to her friends."

"Showed you off?" Lee asked.

"Mostly she made me sing for them, like a trained songbird or something," Peter said bitterly. "She kept me in a little cage most of the time. Sometimes she made me wait on her like a servant."

"Or a slave," Kara said without thinking.

"Yeah."

"So how did you get on the escape pod?" Lee demanded. His tone was belligerent.

"I'm not completely sure," Peter admitted. "Mistress Eight pulled me out of my cage and made me follow her at a run. Alarms were going off all over the place. We got into the escape pod—I hadn't seen it in weeks—and she shoved it off. Then everything was exploding and bouncing around and everything. Was that you guys? Did you destroy their ship?"

"How did you know it was a ship?" Lee asked.

Peter shrugged. "That's what *they* called it. I never really thought about it. I . . . tried not to think at all."

"What's your favorite color?" Kara asked abruptly.

"What? Uh, blue."

"What's your favorite food?"

"Red beans and rice. Why? What does—"

"Who was the drummer for 'My Heart Has Eyes for Only You'?"

"Peter Deimos. It caused all kinds of confusion, so we all called him Deimos. He hated that."

"Who was your first real girlfriend?"

"Pamela Gallic. We were twelve. What's this all about?"

Kara sat back, arms folded. "He's genuine."

"Why?" Baltar said. "Because he can answer questions of the sort you find in *Teen Tiger* magazine?"

"How do *you* know what's in *Teen Tiger*?" Kara countered.

"All facets of human nature fascinate me," Baltar said airily.

Three more faces appeared at the interrogation room window, all female. Their eyes went round when they saw Peter. Lee made an impatient gesture, and they fled.

"Look," Kara said, "I admit it. I am—*was*—a huge Peter Attis fan when I was a kid. If he's a sleeper agent for the Cylons, he's been one since he was a teenager. How likely is that?"

"He could be a construct with the memories of Peter Attis," Lee said.

"That would be a first," Baltar said. "The Cylons have never done such a thing before."

"I'm sitting right here," Peter reminded them. "Shackled and chained, but sitting right here. I'm not a dog or a lamp."

"Shut up," Lee said. "We'll the ask the questions."

"This is how the Cylons treated me," Peter said softly.

Baltar suddenly twisted in his chair, as if someone had tapped him on the shoulder or whispered in his ear. "Well, that's—" Then he cut himself off, blinked rapidly, and added, "—that's . . . very interesting."

"What is?" Lee asked.

Baltar looked nonplused. "That's very interesting . . . how . . . how he—I mean, Peter—how he thinks . . . of us." He cleared his throat and loosened his tie. Kara noticed he was looking a little flushed. His right arm twitched. Kara tried to edge away from him, no mean feat in a chair that was bolted to the floor. Baltar had a weird reputation around the Fleet, for all that he was vice president. He had a penchant for talking and gesturing to himself in public, as if he were holding a private argument. And some of his other behavior was definitely off. Kara had once walked into his lab and found him leaning over a table in a very strange position. His fly had been down and the tail of his shirt was sticking out of it. Kara didn't press for details. Most people passed this off as a side effect of genius, but Kara was beginning to wonder if Gaius Baltar might simply be a frakking lunatic.

"I mean," Baltar continued, "that Peter here may be right. After all, we can't be suspicious of every little thing every person does. The Cylons would love to know that we're at each other's throats." His left hand suddenly leaped up and clutched at his right shoulder. He changed the gesture into a scratching motion, as if he'd had a sudden itch.

"We have to tell the Commander *something*," Lee said. "I doubt he'll accept interviews from *Teen Tiger* as evidence that he's not a spy."

"Proving something doesn't exist is almost impossible," Kara pointed out. "I mean, how do you prove someone can't fly? Shove them off a building and see what happens?"

"Fortunately," Baltar said, "we have a less drastic method."

"Peter Attis!"

Kara watched as Peter stared at the woman on the other side of the mesh-reinforced Plexiglas. He was still in shackles, and two armed marines stood on either side of him. His face remained stony and expressionless, but Kara thought she detected a slight tremor in his body. The woman in the cell had almond eyes, black hair, full lips, and a slender build, though if you looked carefully, you could see a slight rounding to her stomach—an encroaching sign of pregnancy. She also wore a look of utter surprise.

"So you know who he is," Lee said into the telephone receiver.

"Don't you?" she countered into her own telephone. Lee held his receiver out so everyone could hear her voice, faint and tinny. "Look, my memories of being a teenager may be implanted and fake, but they feel real to me. I remember having a crush on him and wishing I could see him at a live concert."

"Is he a Cylon?"

"What are you, stupid? They don't make copies of real people, and even if they did, they wouldn't use someone famous as a sleeper agent. They use someone . . . someone like me. No one could verify my past because the Troy colony was destroyed in a mining accident and no records survived. That's not the case with someone like Peter Attis. He's too public, too well-known."

The use of "they" instead of "we" didn't go past Kara unnoticed. Sharon Valerii was a Cylon, but she believed—or acted like she believed—her own people to be the enemy. Just a few days ago, she had defeated a Cylon computer virus that had invaded *Galactica*'s systems and sent the Cylons a virus of her own. She had helped Kara complete her mission on Caprica. But every time she looked at Sharon, Kara saw the traitor who had pulled out a pistol and shot Commander Adama in the stomach. Kara knew that killer Sharon's body currently lay in the morgue and that this version of Sharon had done nothing but help *Galactica*. This didn't matter to Kara in the slightest. Every time she saw the woman—Cylon—Kara felt an animalistic urge to wrap her fingers around Sharon's throat and squeeze.

But Kara also looked at Sharon and saw a friend, a fellow pilot, and someone who had saved her life. The conflicting emotions made Kara uncertain and uncomfortable, which was why she avoided the brig as much as possible.

"Look, he's not a Cylon," Sharon said. "If he were, I'd tell you. If the Cylons sent another agent here to destroy the *Galactica*, I'd die along with everyone else, and so would my baby." She unconsciously ran a hand over her stomach, a completely human gesture that made Kara want to hit her and give her a hug at the same time.

"Bitch!" Peter yelled. He smashed at the Plexiglas with his shackled wrists. They left a slight scratch. "Frakking *bitch!*"

Kara jumped, adrenaline zinging through her. Lee, also startled, dropped the phone as the marines instantly moved in to haul Peter back. He clawed and snarled at the Plexiglas. Sharon shrank away from him.

"I frakking hate you!" Peter snarled, fighting unsuccessfully to free himself from the grip of two powerful marines. "If they can't kill you, I will!"

Kara got in front of him, blocking his view of Sharon. "Peter!" she said in a calm, firm voice. "Peter, listen to me! That is *not* your Mistress Eight. It's not her." Without knowing why, she reached out and took his face between her two hands. His skin was warm on hers. She moved in close and looked straight into his blue eyes. Their foreheads touched, and her breath mingled with his. He was real. He was solid. "Peter, it's not her. Your . . . 'mistress' is dead. You saw them shoot her down in front of the pod. That's not her."

"Why is she there?" he demanded in a hoarse whisper. "Gods, what's going on?"

Kara continued to meet his eyes, forcing him by strength of will to lock his gaze with hers. "You said your mistress made you sing for her friends. Didn't any of her friends look alike?"

"A couple," he said. "I thought they were twins or something."

"There are many copies of each different type of Cylon," Kara said. "This one is a copy of your mistress, but she's our prisoner. She didn't do anything to you, and she can't hurt you. Do you understand?"

He looked long and hard into Kara's eyes. A little thrill traveled over her skin. She wondered what it would be like to pull him closer, hold him, kiss him. It felt like his gaze was going through her, touching something deep inside her that she didn't want touched. She was about to pull away when she caught Lee Adama looking her, at them. He looked almost . . . angry. A flash of her own anger rose to the occasion. What right did he have to be angry at her? He had no hold on her. Just to show him that, she turned her full attention back to Peter. Tears welled in his eyes.

"It's all right," she said. "You've been places where none of us have gone. But you're home now, with us. Do you understand?"

"Yes," he said in a small voice. "Thank you."

Kara hugged him. It was a one-way embrace—Peter was still shackled, and the marines hadn't released their hold on his arms. But Peter gave a heavy sigh and Kara felt his breath warm the collar of her shirt. After a moment, she released him and reached for the phone near Sharon's cell. Sharon herself had retreated to her bed, removing herself from Peter's line of sight. Kara punched buttons. After a moment, Dualla came on the line and transferred her to Commander Adama.

"We've interrogated Peter Attis," Kara said, "and we're convinced he isn't a Cylon."

"*All three of you?*" Adama asked.

"Yeah—me, Lee, and Doctor Baltar. We all agree." She shot Baltar and Lee a hard glare that dared either of them to say different. They remained silent. Lee raised his hands in mock defeat.

"*Then release him,*" Adama said.

"Thank you, sir." Kara hung up. "Sergeant, unshackle Mister Attis. He's not a Cylon and doesn't belong in chains or a cage."

"Yes, sir."

Kara stood carefully between Peter and Sharon's cell so he wouldn't have to see her as the shackles fell away with clatters and clanks. "Let's go, okay? I'll show you around *Galactica* and we'll find you a place to stay."

"A place to stay," he echoed. "You mean, I can't go home?"

Kara led him firmly away from the brig. Lee and Baltar followed a little uncertainly. The battered metal corridors and walkways that made up *Galactica*'s innards snaked ahead of them in a dizzying array of directions. The Battlestar *Galactica* was the size of a skyscraper turned sideways, and even the engineering crews got lost if they left their own section. People in a variety of uniforms rushed about on errands only they understood, and the PA system crackled with orders and announcements almost continuously. Several crewmembers stared as Peter passed them by.

"Not exactly," Kara said. "The Cylons . . . they kind of took over the Colonies. Destroyed them."

Peter's knees buckled and Kara grabbed him before he fell. "All twelve?"

"Yeah. Sorry to be the one to tell you." Kara planted herself until Peter could regain his feet. "The Cylons somehow managed to breach the defenses. We still don't know exactly how, but when they show up and start shooting, you don't stop to ask questions, you know? Some traitor seems to have given them the codes."

Now Baltar stumbled, and Lee caught his shoulder to keep him from falling. Kara mentally rolled her eyes. The man was supposed to be brilliant, but he had the coordination of newborn kitten.

"A bunch of ships managed to escape together," Lee said. "Including the *Galactica* here. There are still a few in hiding back on the Colonies, but as far as we know, most of the humans left in the universe are here in the Fleet."

"So how many people are left?" Peter asked. He was walking on his own again, but his face was pale.

"Something around forty-seven thousand," Kara told him. They turned a corner and went down a staircase. "President Roslin keeps an exact tally, but—"

"President *Roslin?* Isn't she the Secretary of Welfare or something?"

"Education," Lee said. "But now she's president."

"And I'm vice president," Baltar put in quickly.

"Let me buy you a drink," Kara said, clapping Peter on the shoulder, "and I'll fill you in. Then you can fill *me* in."

Peter gave her a long look. Kara looked back. For once, she didn't feel thirteen. The moment stretched long, though it couldn't have lasted more than a few seconds.

"Fill you in?" Peter said at last.

Lee coughed hard. Kara ignored him. "About what happened to you with the Cylons."

"Ah."

"Before we do that," Lee said, "I think we should take our guest to sickbay."

"What for?" Kara asked.

"A thorough physical," Lee replied grimly.

"I got nothing here." Dr. Cottle removed the cigarette from his mouth and used it to gesture at the readout. The smell of smoke awoke tobacco cravings in Kara and she longed for a cigar, the one she had been looking forward to before Peter's pod showed up. Behind them, Peter Attis himself lay on a table, his head and upper body beneath an overhanging shelf that scanned him repeatedly while he remained perfectly still. "You can see for yourself. No tracers, no chips, no implants, no Cylonitis. If the Cylons sent him here so they could somehow use him to track the Fleet, they didn't do a very good job."

"He says the Cylons had him in a medical facility for a while," Lee said. "Anything to indicate what they might have done to him?"

"Nothing I can see," Cottle said. "Soft-tissue injuries won't show, though. He broke his left humerus some time ago—"

"I fell off a horse," Peter said.

"He was twelve," Kara added.

"I'm not sure we should ask how you know that," Baltar said.

"Right." Cottle took a heavy drag from his cigarette. "Anyway, the break's long since healed. I don't see any metabolic problems and he's not carrying any weird viruses or bacteria. There's more I could probably tell you about him, but it gets a little personal."

"Spare us, then," Lee muttered.

"So I pass?" Peter asked from the table.

"You're done, kid," Cottle said to Peter. "Get the hell out of my sickbay so I can attend to some real patients."

"Gladly." Peter rolled off the examination table, careful to avoid cracking his head on the scanner. Chloe Eseas, a medical technician, helped him up. Sickbay, like most of *Galactica*, was cluttered and clunky, with pieces of medical equipment crammed into corners and odd places. Lighting alternated between too dim and too bright, and the place never seemed completely clean, for all that it was the closest thing to a hospital the Fleet had.

"So you're really Peter Attis?" Chloe said.

"That's me," he said, getting to his feet. He wore a sickbay gown that closed—more or less—in the back.

"Wow. I have all your songs. Or I did until the Cylons attacked. What was it like singing a duet with Penelope Troy?"

"She was great," Peter said vaguely. "Really talented. Are my clothes somewhere nearby?"

While Peter dressed behind a screen, Cottle ground out the remains of his current cigarette and tapped another on the back of his hand. Kara was half ready to ask him for one, though she didn't really do cigarettes and preferred to save her cigars for special occasions, like card games or post-mission gloating.

"How's the harvest coming along, Captain?" Cottle asked as he shut down the scanner. "Are we going to abandon Planet Goop? The Cylons know we're here now, unless you managed to kill them before they transmitted a signal to wherever the hell it is they transmit to."

"I have no idea, doc," Lee said. "You'll probably find out when I do."

"We need the meds that goop can make for us," Cottle said. He nodded toward a glass-doored cabinet. There was space for several hundred drug ampules, but Kara counted fewer than ten. "That's my entire store of radiation meds, Captain. Once that goes, your DNA is on its own. We might even be able to synthesize some more antibiotics, too, but—"

"But not if we leave Planet Goop," Lee finished.

"Don't interrupt your elders, son," Cottle growled around his cigarette. "It ain't polite. Even when they're stating the obvious."

Commander William Adama stood in the center of a whirlwind. People hustled around the CIC, checking printouts, making urgent calls, and tapping keyboards. The DRADIS continued its low, metallic growl as it scanned in all directions for Cylons. A dozen monitors flickered with graphics, videos, and data readouts. Saul Tigh sometimes stood behind Adama and sometimes lurked around the workstations. It made the crew nervous to have Tigh suddenly pop up behind one of them to bark a question or an order, but Adama had given up trying to get him to stop. Commanding a fleet was a lot like juggling cats in a rainstorm—sometimes you had to let the small stuff slide because something big with claws was waiting to drop on your head.

"Update on the evacuation, Lieutenant?" Adama asked.

"Half done, sir," Tactical Officer Anastasia Dualla reported from her station. She wore a headset that covered one ear and slung a microphone across her mouth. "The *Monarch* should be ready for takeoff in under half an hour."

"I'll have Jump coordinates ready for them by then, sir," put in Felix Gaeta. "We should be all right."

"If the frakking Cylons don't pop up again," Tigh growled. "And they will. Mark it."

"How much more food are they estimating we'll be able to extract from the algae?" Adama asked.

"It's hard to give anything beyond a rough estimate, sir," Gaeta hedged.

"Just answer the damn question, Lieutenant," Tigh ordered.

Gaeta pursed his lips and kept his eyes on Adama, who was also ignoring Tigh. "We might get an extra week out of what we have so far. Ten days at most."

"A week?" Tigh shouted. "That's nothing! They were down there for four days. What the hell were they doing?"

"Is that a rhetorical question, sir, or do you want an answer?" Gaeta asked with utter politeness.

"It's not damned rhetorical," Tigh snapped. "What have they been doing down there?"

"The *Monarch* is a mining ship," Gaeta replied. "It took time to adapt its operations from digging to scooping. Also, Planet Goop has an atmosphere but it isn't breathable. Putting everyone in breathing masks makes everything harder to see and slows down operations. We also have to rotate the crew because of the radiation levels, and the workers can only take so much radiation exposure. Suppiles of anti-radiation meds are limited. That slows things down as well."

"Sounds like a lot of excuses to me," Tigh said. "You need to—"

"Sir, with respect, I'm just the messenger. May I suggest that you address your . . . concerns to the captain of the *Monarch*? She's the head of the harvest operation, not me."

"I think I'll do just that. Dualla, get me Renee Demeter on the line. Now!"

This caught Adama's attention. Tigh was clearly in the wrong, bent on solving impossible problems by shouting at subordinates, as if yelling would make them suddenly able to work miracles. But now Gaeta had managed to point him in another direction, toward the *Monarch*. Renee Demeter was captain of her own ship. She answered to no one but Adama, and then only in matters that concerned her ship's role in the Fleet. On the *Monarch*, she was sovereign, and Tigh had no authority over her. If Tigh started shouting at her and calling her incompetent in public, she would answer in kind and he would come across looking like an idiot. Adama shot Gaeta a hard look. Had he set Tigh up on purpose? Adama wouldn't put it past him. Gaeta had a subtle touch when it came to handling conflict. But Gaeta's expression was bland as a sand dune.

"Belay that order, Dee," Adama said. "I think Captain Demeter has enough to worry about right now. Getting those people off the planet before another wave of Cylons shows up is more important."

For a moment Tigh looked ready to challenge Adama's order. Adama looked at him, bland as Gaeta. Then Tigh straightened his uniform and turned to look at the video feeds. Adama closed his eyes. Another cat successfully juggled. What was next?

"Sir," Dualla said. She was a dark-skinned woman with surpring hazel eyes. "President Roslin is on the line for you."

I had to ask, he thought, and picked up a receiver from the central station. It had a cord attached to it. Adama remembered the days of cellular communication, computer networks, and wireless everything. The Cylons, however, had taken to networks like lions to antelope. The frakking things could infect and wipe out a network in seconds, fatally crippling whatever systems the network ran. So the Colonies had tossed digital out the window and stampeded to bring back analog. It made hell out of computing an FTL Jump when your drive computer couldn't talk to your helm computer, but it sure beat the Cylons twitching your network from a distance and making you land in the heart of star. Later, after everyone thought the Cylons were gone for good, the military had cautiously returned to networking its computers. Adama, however, had refused to allow it on the

Galactica, and thank the Lords of Kobol for that. Far as he knew, every other Battlestar had fallen victim to Cylon viruses. The *Galactica* alone had not.

"Madam President," Adama said, resisting an urge to play with the phone cord. "A pleasure."

"Commander." Laura Roslin's voice was warm as always, but Adama's practiced ear caught the undercurrent of pain and fatigue. Roslin was suffering, in every sense of the word, from terminal breast cancer. She had kept it a secret for months, using experimental treatments to force pain and weakness to stay at arm's length, but lately the malignant tissue had made terrible encroachments into her body. Within the month, she would be dead. Adama refused to let himself think about this—he was juggling cats, after all—but the small part of his mind that never quite did what it was told feared that the grief from her loss would devastate him. Only the thought that Gaius Baltar would become president in her stead frightened him more.

"I hear the Monarch *is pulling up stakes,"* she said.

"That's true."

"The latest projections tell me we've only harvested eight days worth of food material, and that's if we refine none of it for anti-radiation meds and antibiotics."

Apparently Roslin had access to better information than Adama did. It didn't really surprise him. "That's close to what I've heard, yes."

"Are you sure we need to evacuate right now, Bill?" she said. *"You know your job and I realize you're keeping our safety in mind, but we also really need that algae. It's not just the food. Medicinal supplies are at an all-time low. The* Lesbos *is dealing with an outbreak of strep that's eating up antibiotics. We've tried to make the adults suffer through it on their own and reserve the remaining meds for the children, but that only means the adults reinfect the kids."*

Adama nodded, though Roslin couldn't see him. "I know, Madam President." He couldn't quite bring himself to call her "Laura" when other people were within earshot. "But the Cylons must know we're here, and it's only a matter of time before they send another basestar or a flock of Raiders."

Roslin sighed heavily. *"I trust you to know what's best when it comes to Fleet security. I'm also worried about the food and meds. Bill, is there any compromise on this? It's been over an hour since the Cylon attack. Maybe they aren't coming back for a while."*

Adama tightened his lips. He knew the food and medicine

supplies were tight—they had been since the first day after the attack. Now it seemed as if the Lords of Kobol had handed them a bounteous harvest only to have the Cylons chase them away like lions chasing a herd away from the watering hole.

"They always come back," he said. "But I wonder . . ."

"*Yes, Bill?*"

He sighed. There were risks, and there were risks. The lack of food and medicine would kill them just as surely, if not as quickly, as the Cylons. "Maybe we can evacuate the planet and wait a day or so. If the Cylons show up, we can Jump away. If they don't, we can resume the harvest."

"*Sounds like a plan,*" Roslin said, relief temporarily overcoming the fatigue in her voice. Adama could almost see her behind her desk on the *Colonial One*, stray tendrils of her glossy auburn hair getting caught in her glasses while she flipped through reports and signed papers. Billy Keikeya, her chief aide, would be hovering near her elbow with more bulletins and paperwork.

Adama grimaced and banished the image. Roslin, he happened to know, spent most of her time these days propped up on a couch next to her desk. Her hair had become lackluster and brittle, her skin pasty, her face drawn with pain. He wondered if the real reason he was allowing the Fleet to remain in orbit around Planet Goop was that it would make Laura Roslin happy and bring some small relief to her stress and suffering.

"I'll expect to see you over a dinner of fresh algae salad when this is over, Madam President," he said, as if Roslin had never heard the word "cancer."

"*Count on it, Commander,*" she said, and rang off.

Karl "Helo" Agathon checked his watch and lengthened his stride. He was a tall man, almost rangy, with close-cropped dark hair and a narrow face. He was also late for his appointment in the brig.

Helo trotted around and through the groups of people who kept getting in his way. Familiar ship sounds echoed around him—the slight hiss of carbon dioxide scrubbers, the tromp of soldier boots, the cricket creak of a hatch opening or closing. Sharon had so little to look forward to, so little to *do*. He knew his daily visits were the high point—hell, the *only* point—of her day. He hated seeing her in the brig, locked behind steel mesh and unyielding Plexiglas. He couldn't even hear her voice except through a telephone line, let alone touch her face or hold her hand. It wasn't fair. Sharon—this copy of her—

hadn't done anything to anyone. It was the frakking opposite, in fact. She had saved Helo's life on Caprica numerous times, helped Starbuck retrieve the Arrow of Apollo, and just a couple days ago had single-handedly destroyed an entire fleet of Cylon raiders. And now she was carrying Helo's child.

He dodged around an ensign who was half-hidden behind a stack of papers. Yeah, some people insisted that Sharon was only frakking with him, that she had tricked him into falling in love because the Cylons were desperate to conceive children of their own, and Cylon women could only get pregnant if love was involved.

During the Cylon invasion, Sharon, a pilot, had left Helo on Caprica when Helo had given up his seat on her Raptor to a refugee. Helo had then gone on the run from Cylon troops, certain they would eventually catch up with him. And then Sharon showed up again, almost out of nowhere. Together they ran a harrowing journey across Caprica to a spaceport, where they stole a ship to rendezvous with *Galactica*. Along the way, they had fallen in love and accidentally conceived a child. Or Helo had thought the child was accidental. Only later had he learned that his lover was a different Sharon, that this Sharon had been *assigned* to make him fall in love with her to see if she could conceive. The flaw was that Sharon had fallen in love with Helo as well, and instead of turning Helo over to the other Cylons after the conception, she had helped him escape and fled with him to the *Galactica*.

Now she spent her days in the brig, mistrusted and hated by the few crewmembers who knew about her. It made Helo's blood boil to think about it. Keeping a pregnant woman in the brig—how humane was that? But Adama remained firm. Caprica Sharon, as she was sometimes called, would stay in the brig for the foreseeable future. As a prisoner of war, there would be no trial, no lawyer, no judge. Just Adama.

Helo realized his footsteps were pounding angrily on the deck plates, as if he could punch holes through them like an angry giant. He forced himself to calm down. Sharon was under enough stress. She didn't need his tension adding to hers.

Helo took the familiar staircase down to the brig and headed up the side corridor to the cell block specially designed to hold a Cylon. He emerged in a dimly lit open space. Sharon's cell was ahead of him, but the two marines assigned to guard her day and night were nowhere to be seen. It took Helo a startled second to realize that the marines were both sprawled motionless on the floor. The door to

Sharon's cell stood quietly open. The interior was empty. Helo froze. A thousand different thoughts flicked through his head. Part of him exulted. Another part of him worried. Yet another felt a pang of fear. Indecision held him motionless. Should he raise the alarm first or check the marines? Maybe he should just . . . leave. Let someone else find the scene, give Sharon a good head start to wherever she was going. Or maybe he should—

Someone tapped his shoulder from behind. His heart jerked and Helo whirled. He got a tiny glimpse of the snarl that twisted Sharon's beautiful face just before her fist caught him under the jaw.

CHAPTER 4

"So what does everyone do for fun around here?" Peter asked.

"Uh, well . . . not a lot," Kara admitted. "I mean, some of us play cards and grab a drink. Sometimes you can get into a pickup game of Pyramid. Help me out here, Lee."

Lee Adama raised his hands. "You brought him down here."

They were sitting around a small table in the pilots' quarters. Bunks and metal lockers lined the walls and the air carried the stale smells of old sweat and cigar smoke. Baltar had cited urgent vice presidential business and excused himself, though he said he would want to talk to Peter later about what it had been like to live among Cylons.

"What do the kids do?" Peter asked. "On the other ships, I mean."

Kara shrugged. "I never really thought about it. They must do something, go to some kind of school. My life's pretty straight-ahead. The alarm goes off, I jump in my Viper, I wipe out more Cylons, I come back, I play cards, I drink. Sometimes I'll catch an episode of *The Colonial Gang*. It's pretty boring, even for a talk show, but there isn't much else on, you know?"

"What a life." Peter gave the back of Kara's hand a brief touch, and Kara felt it all the way up to her eyes and down to her toes. "It must be hard."

"It pays the bills," she said with a flip smile. "Except there aren't any."

Lee remained stonily silent, but his resentment filled the room with icy water. Kara gave him a sidelong glance. What was up with him? There was nothing between them. Lee Adama had no official hold on her, no deep emotional link. And she didn't want one, either. The more she thought about it, the more she decided Lee Adama could frak himself.

"Maybe I could do a—" Peter began, but was interrupted by a knock on the doorframe. Kara looked up, surprised. No one knocked at the pilots' quarters.

Billy Keikeya stood in the entrance, his blue suit and black tie looking too tidy and out of place in the battered military quarters. His curly, ash-blond hair and enormous blue eyes made him look about fifteen—okay, sixteen—though as Laura Roslin's chief aide, Kara figured he had to be somewhere in his twenties at least.

"Uh, hi," he said hesitantly. "I'm looking for . . . Peter Attis?"

"You've found him," Peter said, standing up and extending his hand to shake. "What can I do for you?"

Billy introduced himself and his position. "I've been trying to track you down for a while. There's someone who wants to talk to you."

"And that would be . . . ?"

"Me," said Laura Roslin. She entered the room, her face pale but her expression determined. "Thank you for finding him, Billy."

Kara and Lee leaped to their feet, and Lee offered the president his chair. She accepted without hesitation, and Billy took up his usual position at her right elbow. Kara knew all about President Roslin's cancer, and she greatly admired the way Roslin seemed to draw strength from illness. It was almost as if the woman forged ahead all the harder because she knew her time was limited. Kara also felt a certain awe in Roslin's presence. The Book of Pythia foretold a "dying leader" who would lead humanity to the promised land. So far, Laura Roslin's leadership had uncovered the fact that Earth, the fabled thirteenth colony, did indeed exist, and she had sent Kara back to Caprica to find the Arrow of Apollo, an artifact which had ultimately let President Roslin and Commander Adama uncover star charts that gave clues to Earth's location. Kara had considered herself only vaguely religious before, but nowadays she was a believer, and a Roslin supporter all the way. Eventually, Kara was sure, the Fleet would decipher those charts and figure out how to find Earth—and a new home, just as the Scriptures said.

Assuming the Cylons didn't kill them all first.

"I have to admit I'm something of a fan, Mr. Attis," Roslin began, "and I had to come over and meet you. You've probably heard it before, but I admire your work. I even have a few albums back on

Colonial One." She gave a wan smile. "They may be the only surviving copies left in the universe. A tragedy indeed."

"Thank you, uh . . . Madam President," Peter said. "And I have to admit I've never met a president before. Definitely not under these conditions."

"We're all going through a lot of firsts," she replied. Then she leaned forward slightly. "Mr. Attis, I'm afraid I need to ask you a tremendous favor."

"Shoot."

"I know you've dealt with a lot—Commander Adama briefed me on some of it—and I'm sure you're aware that your presence in the Fleet has generated some excitement."

"I've kind of gotten that idea." Peter grinned a wide, handsome grin. "I'm used to it. It's been like that for me since I was a teenager."

"The Fleet is in a state of constant crisis, Mr. Attis," Roslin said.

"Please—it's Peter."

"Peter." She nodded. "At any rate, it's not just the Cylons that cause problems. We have shortages of food, water, medicine, clothing. And entertainment. It may sound strange, but that lack is a major problem. We have an entire Fleet full of people with little or nothing to do. Thousands and thousands of them had careers that the Cylons rendered obsolete or worthless."

"Not much call for insurance adjusters or carpenters these days," Peter said.

"That's right. There's some entertainment, of course. Storytelling is enjoying a resurgence, for example. But for the most part, the Fleet has a lot of bored people. And bored people get into trouble."

"So you're hoping I'll give them something to do."

"Exactly. Would you consent to putting on a concert or two? *Cloud 9* is a cruise ship, and they have excellent facilities. We can arrange for whatever you need. And, just incidentally, this will give a bunch of sound technicians and stage hands something to keep them occupied. I don't know how quickly we can get a band together, but—"

"If you have my albums, Madam President, we can strip the vocals and I can sing to the music tracks. Later, we can get a band together." Peter rubbed his hands together in growing excitement. "Hell, this'll be great. I was just wondering what I was going to do with myself." A look of sudden pain crossed his face, and Kara wanted to grab his hand and reassure him. "It'll also be the perfect way to take my mind off . . . stuff. You know?"

"I do know, Peter," Roslin said. "And maybe for a while, you can take everyone else's mind off *their* stuff."

"Will you be there?"

"You couldn't keep me away." She smiled a mysterious smile. "Maybe I'll bully Commander Adama into escorting me."

"I'd like to see that," Lee said, speaking for the first time.

"Contact Billy here if you need anything." Roslin started to her feet with obvious difficulty. Lee and Billy sprang to assist. Billy escorted her from the pilots' quarters and Lee shut the door behind them.

"A concert!" Kara clapped her hands with a laugh. "Geez, Peter—this is frakking awesome! What do you think, Lee?" she added a little wickedly.

"I don't know," Lee said, shrugging wide shoulders. "I outgrew puffball music."

"Sourpuss." She turned to Peter. "Can I get a ticket?"

Peter shot Lee a look that said the puffball remark hadn't gone past him. "For the woman who saved my life? You bet! Front row, with a backstage pass."

"Oooo, I've always wanted to be a groupie! Do you think I can meet the band?"

"Why not?" Peter laughed. "The transistors and hard drives are always up for a kiss from a hot babe."

"Flattery will get you everything," Kara said with mock seriousness. Holy gods—she was flirting with Peter Frakking Attis. And Lee clearly hated every moment, which made it all the more fun.

"I think I'll head down to the galley," Captain Adama grumbled. "I need a drink."

The pain woke Helo. His jaw pulsed with ragged red agony. Blood was filling his mouth and he automatically spat it out, bringing on fresh spasms from his jaw. It felt like an elephant had stomped on his face, and he couldn't remember what had happened. Cold deck plates pressed against his hands as he pushed himself upright. His head rang like a temple bell. Why was he lying on the floor? Who had—

Memory rushed to fill the void. The empty brig. The motionless guards. Sharon. Helo bolted to his feet, then staggered as the deck dipped and swayed beneath him. He caught his balance on the smooth Plexiglas of Sharon's cell. The two marines assigned to guard it still lay face-down on the deck. Helo's heart began to pound, and his head throbbed in time with it. Every harsh beat was like a knife blade through his skull. He forced himself to move, to kneel down beside the first marine and feel for a pulse at the man's neck. It took a moment, but he found one. Quickly he turned to the second man. No pulse. Helo rolled him over, pulled off his helmet, and checked again. No pulse, and no breath. His head lolled. Broken neck? Tension tightened Helo's muscles as he checked for life again and again. The man *had* to be alive. He *had* to. Sharon hadn't killed him. She wasn't a murderer because this man wasn't dead. He *wasn't!*

Helo abruptly realized he was pounding on the dead marine's chest, trying to pound life back into him. He made himself stop, force back the panic. One step at a time. He got to his feet and snatched a phone from the wall.

"This is Lieutenant Agathon," he barked—or tried to. His jaw was stiff, and it mangled some of his words. "I need an emergency medical team in the brig now! We have two men down." He waited for acknowledgment, then disconnected and, with shaky fingers, punched in another number.

"CIC. Lieutenant Dualla."

"Dee? It's Helo." He swallowed, not wanting to speak, knowing he had to. What he said next would set into action a chain of events that would end in . . . what? Sharon's death? His own arrest? But he had to go through with it. It was the only choice.

"What's up, Helo?" Dee asked. *"You sound funny. Is something wrong?"*

"Yeah. Uh . . . tell Commander Adama that . . . there's been an incident in the brig. I came down to see Sharon. The door to her cell was open and her guards were down. One unconscious, one dead. I've called a medical team."

There was a startled pause, then, *"Where's the prisoner?"*

"Gone. No trace of her."

Dee's voice became shaky. *"I'll tell the Commander. You'd better come up to CIC, Helo. He'll want to talk to you in person."*

"Tell him I'm on my way."

Helo hadn't even made it out of the brig before both radios on the marines behind him crackled to life. *"Code orange twelve,"* said Dee. *"Repeat, code orange twelve. All marine personnel report to commanding officer for instructions."*

Code orange twelve. Enemy aboard ship. Helo's mouth was dry as he trotted toward CIC. Already he could hear the quick-march thump of boots on ceramic plating—marine search teams. If they didn't know by now that Sharon had killed one of them—that *maybe* she had killed one of them, he corrected himself hastily—they would know soon. No one, certainly not marines, took it well when one of their own died, and their primary target would be Sharon.

A trio of medical personnel bustled down the corridor and Helo paused to point the way. One of them tried to examine Helo—his jaw was so swollen he could barely speak—but Helo only accepted a painkiller before continuing up to CIC. The throb in his head and jaw receded almost immediately, but his tension remained, twisting his stomach into a nauseated knot as he threaded his way through *Galactica's* busy corridors. Helo passed half a dozen fully armed and armored marines. They were searching side corridors and rooms. Helo stopped one of them.

"What are your orders, Sergeant?" he asked.

"Find the toaster, sir," she said.

"And then?"

She shifted her pulse rifle and gave him a critical look. Helo felt cold under her gaze. "Capture if possible, kill if necessary."

"Toaster lover," someone said behind him in a barely audible voice.

Helo rounded on the other marines, anger replacing his tension. "Who the frak said that?"

"Said what, sir?" replied a marine with utterly fake innocence.

"Sergeant," Helo said without taking his eyes off the man, "it sounds like your people aren't familiar with rank and respect."

"Sir," the sergeant said noncommittally.

"Maybe this group needs to search the bilge next, Sergeant. What do you think?"

"Sir, the Cylon killed Corporal Mason when it escaped," the sergeant said. "Everyone's on edge."

"Is that an excuse, Sergeant?"

"No, sir."

Helo closed his eyes. It wasn't worth it. "Carry on, Sergeant. And have a talk with your people once this is over."

"Sir."

Helo left the marines and trotted the rest of the way to CIC. He hesitated outside the hatchway for a long moment, then entered.

CIC was, as always, busy. Dee talked into her microphone and routed calls. Felix Gaeta pored over printouts and dashed from one computer console to another. XO Tigh shouted into a telephone. In the center of the room was a light table. William Adama, his craggy, scarred face serious behind his glasses, was marking up a diagram of *Galactica* with a grease pencil. He glanced up and removed his glasses as Helo approached and saluted.

"Lieutenant," Adama said. "Care to tell me what happened?"

"Sir. I don't know much." Helo related his story, leaving out nothing. His heart beat fast and he tried not to shift uneasily. It was no fun coming under the scrutiny of the single most powerful man in the Fleet, one who could order Helo imprisoned or even executed. Adama knew of Helo's involvement with Sharon and he knew about the baby. Helo was well aware that this probably made him a prime suspect in Sharon's escape. When Colonel Tigh came over to listen, Helo caught a clear whiff of alcohol on the XO's breath. Not for the first time Helo wondered why the hell Adama tolerated Tigh's drinking. A drunken officer on duty was a danger to himself and everyone under his command. But Adama seemed to disagree.

"Did you let that Cylon out?" Tigh demanded.

"No, sir," Helo said through gritted teeth. "As I said, she had already escaped by the time I arrived."

"And she got the drop on you," Tigh observed. "Sounds mighty convenient, if you ask me. Maybe you let her out and she socked you on the jaw to make it look like you had no part in it."

"No, sir," Helo said. "That's not what happened. You can question the guards—guard. The one who survived. He'll tell you I wasn't there."

"How do we know you didn't get the drop on him, too?" Tigh said. "Maybe you—"

"Thank you, Saul," Adama said. "We'll question the marine, but I doubt very much that Lieutenant Agathon had anything to do with the Cylon's escape."

"Thank you, sir," Helo said. He noticed the tightness around Adama's mouth and remembered how Sharon—or a different version of her—had shot Adama in the gut, with almost fatal results. Helo suspected Sharon's escape was causing the commander a certain amount of stress, perhaps even fear, though he would never allow it to show. That particular copy of Sharon had thought she was human, and she had attacked Adama only because hidden Cylon programming had taken over and forced her to act.

"We're keeping this quiet," Adama said. "Anyone who asks is told that we're searching for an escaped prisoner. It's not generally known in the Fleet that we have—or had—a Cylon in the brig, and the last thing I need is panic and riots on the other ships, got that?"

"Yes, sir," Helo said.

"Where do you think she would go, Lieutenant?" Adama asked.

Helo spread his hands. "I honestly don't know, sir. It would depend on why she escaped. I don't think she wants to go back to the . . . to her home planet, wherever that is. She says they see her as an outcast because she helped me escape the Cylons on Caprica. They'd kill her if she went back."

"Even though she's pregnant," Adama said.

"They don't know about the baby, sir. Sharon never told them—"

"—as far as you know," Tigh put in.

"As far as I know, sir," Helo agreed. "But by the time Sharon realized she was pregnant, the other Cylons were already trying to kill us. She couldn't have communicated with them—they would have shot both of us on sight. There's no way Sharon would go back to them."

"So why escape, then? Is she planning some sort of sabotage?"

"That would only hurt her, in the long run. Her and the baby." Helo paused. "Commander, I don't know why she did this. I . . . she swore to me, to all of us, that she had no sleeper Cylon protocols in her. She's helped us half a dozen times when she could have let us all die. This escape, the killing—they don't make sense."

"She's a Cylon," Adama said, turning back to his diagram. "It makes perfect sense."

Gaius Baltar groaned as the staffer placed yet another stack of papers on his desk. The staffer left quickly, before Baltar could respond further. He looked around his laboratory, with its outdated equipment and half-assed computer system, with a mixture of annoyance and longing. It wasn't right that the most brilliant mind in the galaxy— perhaps the universe—was forced to endure such conditions. How could he get anything done in a lab filled with junk and a desk covered in paperwork? Laura Roslin must take perverse delight in shoving her load of paper onto him instead of doing it herself. As an experienced bureaucrat, she should be the one handling this, not him. He should be at work in his lab, making new discoveries to help all humanity, not reading reports and signing forms. Even working with outdated equipment beat mindlessly scribbling his name. Half the time he signed without reading, just to get the stupid paper off his desk.

In addition to his lab work, he had a lecture to prepare for, the first in a series. "Life Post-Apocalypse," he was calling it. He had thought of the title himself and was quite proud of it. The first lecture was called "The Sociological Effects of Limited Resources in a Declining Gene Pool." His star power as Dr. Gaius Baltar and his position as Vice President of the Colonies would guarantee a packed auditorium on *Cloud 9*, along with full press coverage. But even his star power wouldn't save him if he stood in front of an audience with a half-prepared lecture, and he'd never get the lecture finished if he had to do all this stupid paperwork.

He picked up another memo and scanned it. The Cylon woman who had escaped yesterday evening had not been recaptured despite all attempts to find her, the military was searching all ships leaving and approaching the *Galactica*, the escape remained a classified incident, blah blah blah. He supposed it was a good idea to remain informed about the situation, in case there was a danger to him, but he didn't seriously believe the Cylon was coming after him. She had no reason to. It still made for a long, boring series of memos.

A pair of warm hands slid over his shoulders from behind. "It's an outrage. A waste of your brilliance." The hands slid lower, over his chest, down his stomach, toward his waistband. Number Six's distinctive scent washed over him, and her white-blond hair brushed his face and neck. Gaius felt his body respond. His breath came faster, his skin grew warm, and his groin tightened.

"You're not helping," he murmured, though he didn't push her away.

She ran a hand over his inner thigh and at the same time gave his ear a long, slow lick. "Depends on what kind of help you need."

"That . . . isn't . . . exactly it," he managed. Then he straightened. "What do you want this time?"

"Just to give you some encouragement." Number Six put her hands back on his shoulders. "And I wanted some company. Being ignored is never easy, Gaius. You know that."

"Ignored?" He gestured at the paperwork mounding his desk. "What are you talking about? I'm anything *but* ignored these days."

Six made a noncommittal noise and leaned over Gaius's shoulder to peer at his desk. Her low-cut blue dress showed a generous amount of cleavage that Gaius couldn't help but watch. He had seen her naked hundreds of times, but she was far more alluring when he *couldn't* see everything. Her dress made her a mystery, a sly secret. His groin tightened further.

"All these worthless papers," she said. "Someone like you should have a secretary or an aide to handle this." She abruptly straight-ened. The movement took her cleavage out of his line of sight, reveal-ing a stack of papers instead. Gaius was about to turn his attention elsewhere when some words on the top sheet caught his eye. He snatched up the paper in question. He would have never seen it if not for Six abruptly removing her arresting cleavage.

"What is it, Gaius?" Number Six asked, all innocence.

"A memo," he said, reading. "It has Roslin's name on it. It must have come to me by mistake." His eyes tracked across the page and his expression became more and more agitated. "My gods! This . . . this is . . . it's outrageous!"

Six leaned over his shoulder again, this time to read. " ' . . . and we have found two more sound technicians, bringing the total up to five. That should be all Peter needs.' So what?"

"So what?" Gaius flung the paper down and stormed around his desk into the lab. "So *what*? How can you not see it?"

"Explain, Gaius," she said tiredly. "I'm getting bored."

He pointed a shaking, outraged finger at the offending paper. "Read the date."

She did. "Tomorrow. So?"

"So? This concert, this . . . travesty is scheduled for the same time as my lecture." He ran his hands through his hair and stalked about the lab like an angry stork. "I'm going to look like an idiot."

"Because no one will come to your lecture?"

"What? No! Because no one will go to the concert." He leaned his fingertips on a granite-topped table. "Everyone knows me. I've saved the Fleet gods know how many times, and I'm the bloody vice presi-dent. They'll all come to my lecture, Peter Attis will play to an empty concert hall, and I'll look the villain for humiliating him. Fantastic. Just fantastic."

Six moved around the desk, her hips swaying like willow withes. "Fame is a difficult burden to bear, Gaius."

"It's unfair, to me and to him." He ran his hands through his hair again. "Maybe I should talk to Attis, see if he'd be willing to resched-ule for his own good."

"That's what I love about you, Gaius," Six said, perching on the edge of his desk. "You're always thinking of others."

"Check 'em out, boys and girls." Kara Thrace sailed into the pilots' quarters, holding a small envelope aloft with undisguised glee.

"Two—count 'em, *two*—tickets to the Peter Attis interstellar tour *and* a pair of backstage passes." She gave the envelope a loud kiss. "Mine, mine, mine."

"And all you had to do was save his life to get them," Kat said without malice. "Bitch."

"Next time, I'll let *you* find the escape pod."

"Those things are impossible to get," said Brendan "Hot Dog" Constanza. He looked at Kara over his hand of cards. "A buddy of mine got in line six hours before they went up for grabs, and they *still* ran out before he got one. I mean, they're going to televise it and everything, but there's nothing like a live concert. It's been a frakking long time since I've seen one."

"Billy could have gotten us tickets," Dee said. She wasn't a pilot, but was often found at the nightly card game. "But he has to go with the president and Commander Adama, so I'll just watch it on TV."

"Since when are you a Peter Attis fan, Hot Dog?" Lee asked. He tossed a chip into the pot.

"Since never," Hot Dog said. "But any concert beats playing cards with you frak-heads."

"And since when do you play Full Colors, Lee?" Kara turned a chair around and faced the group over its back.

"I'm a man of many talents."

"Yeah? Prove it. You just started this hand, right? Deal me in, Dee."

Dee obligingly sent six cards Kara's way. "Don't forget to ante."

In response, Kara opened the envelope and slid a single ticket from it. She dropped it into the pot. "There."

"No shit," Hot Dog said breathlessly.

"Someone has to come with me," Kara said. "It's no fun to go alone." She gave Lee an impish look. "You gonna fold?"

"Frak, no. I've got a good hand here."

"What happens if you win, Starbuck?" Hot Dog asked. "Or are you playing to lose?"

"Starbuck play to lose?" Kat snorted. "Right. May as well ask an Oracle to give you a straight answer."

"Damn right." Kara pulled a small cigar from her breast pocket and lit it. "If I win, I get to *choose* which one of you reprobates accompanies me. *And* you have to wear your dress uniform."

"I'm still in," Hot Dog said, dropping a chip.

"What the hell," Dee said, and put in a chip of her own. "Maybe Billy will get jealous."

Another round of betting went by. No one folded. Kara replaced three cards, and when the bet came around to her again, she held up one of the backstage passes for everyone to see. "Too rich for anyone's blood?" She put it in the pot.

"Frakking-A," Kat breathed.

Lee frowned at his cards. "I'll stand." He dropped three chips, then four more—a significant raise.

"Ooooo," Kat said. "I think he's bluffing, trying to get us to drop out so he can get the ticket."

Lee gave her a wide-eyed, innocent look. "Put your money where your mouth is, then."

Kat met the raise, as did Dee and Hot Dog. Kara looked over her cards at Lee. Was Lee bluffing? She studied his expression. His face was cool, almost smug. She knew him well enough to recognize that look—he wasn't bluffing. He had a great hand. Kara couldn't stand Lee when he was smug. She had half a mind to fold and let him win, make him come to the concert for the sole reason that he hated Peter.

"Any news on the escaped toaster?" Hot Dog asked.

"Nothing I've heard," said Kat. "It creeps me out that no one can find her. How can she just frakking disappear?"

"The *Galactica* is a big place," Lee said. His face went hard. Bill Adama was his father, and a copy of Sharon had shot him. When Kara had brought the current copy of Sharon on board, Lee had almost killed her on sight. Only Helo's intervention had spared her. "And she isn't human. She can get into places where normal people can't."

"That's one way to put it," Hot Dog scoffed.

"Maybe she left the ship," Dee said. "Like that Godfrey woman. Remember her?"

"Blond Cylon lady, yeah," Lee said. "Just vanished. We never did learn how she got off the ship."

"Maybe she didn't," Kat said. "Maybe she stuck around and now she and the other Cylon are holding a toaster convention in the air vents."

Kara dropped a handful of chips into the pot. "Call," she said loudly. "All right, guys and gals—show 'em."

Hot Dog sighed and spread his cards. "Half mast."

"One lord and a lady," Dee said. "Guess I'll join Hot Dog in the TV room."

"Two half masts," Kat said. "Best so far."

"Apollo?" Kara asked sweetly. "I'll show you mine if you show me yours."

"I just want it known for the record," Lee said, "that I'm not going to the concert, even though I'm about to win. Hot Dog, you can have the ticket."

"Really? Thanks, Captain!"

"You don't have a thing," Kara said scornfully. "Spread 'em, Apollo."

"Start your weeping." Lee laid down his cards one by one. "Full colors."

Hot Dog whistled. "Frak me!" He reached for the ticket and the backstage pass, but Kara was quicker. She caught his wrist.

"A little overconfident, are we?" she said, gently pushing his hand away. "Ladies and gentlemen, I give you the real winner of the evening." And she laid down her cards.

"Full colors," Kat said. "Wow! Twice in the same hand! How often does that happen?"

"So it's a tie?" Dee asked.

"Hardly." Kara gestured at their respective cards. "The Captain's cards are orange. Mine are pure purple goodness."

"She's right," Hot Dog said. "Colors decide in case of a tie."

"Come to mama." Kara raked the chips toward her, then plucked the ticket and pass from the pile. "Let's see. Who shall accompany me to the ball in dress black?"

"Have I told you how lovely you look today, Lieutenant?" Hot Dog said. "And what is that divine scent? Are you wearing perfume?"

"Aw, you can do better than *that*," she scoffed.

"Who's the best pilot in the Fleet?" Kat said. "Why, I think it has to be Kara Thrace."

"It's not flattery if it's true," Kara said. "Who else?"

"I have the Commander's ear," Dee put in. "Captain Adama here may write the duty roster, but *Commander* Adama approves it. I can get you some sweet run times."

"Tempting, tempting," Kara said. "And worthy of consideration. Lee?"

"I already said I don't want to go," Lee replied, crossing his arms.

"You're just mad because I ruined your perfect—excuse me, *near* perfect—hand."

"Yeah, sure. Think what you want." He got up. "I'm outta here."

"You can't just leave," Kara said, suddenly angry. "I haven't made my decision yet."

He rounded on her, eyes flashing. "Who the frak cares? I don't want to go, it won't be me, so I'm not sticking around."

Kara's temper flared higher. "Maybe it *will* be you, have you thought about that?"

"I already said I don't want to go!" Lee was almost shouting now.

"Maybe *I* want you to go." Kara raised her own voice to compensate.

"Do you?" Lee yelled.

"Yeah!"

"Fine! I'll go!"

"Good!"

"I'm thrilled!"

"Meet me in the shuttle bay at seven!" Kara screamed, storming out the door. "Wear your blacks!"

"I wouldn't miss it!" Lee bellowed, stomping after her. "It'll be fun!"

They fled in opposite directions in the hallway. Behind them around the card table, two pilots and one petty officer stared at each other.

"What the hell just happened?" Hot Dog asked.

"I think," said Kat, "that we're all watching the concert on TV tomorrow. Meet in the TV room?"

"You bring the ambrosia," Dee said.

CHAPTER 5

The auditorium dressing room smelled of old makeup and cold cream. Gaius Baltar, seated at the dressing table, checked his reflection in the mirror. Hair—good. Face—excellent. Clothes—perfect. The visuals for his lecture were loaded in the auditorium computer, and the remote for the projector was in his pocket. He had no idea what sort of audience awaited him—it was bad luck to check beforehand—but he knew the enormous auditorium would be packed to the roof. He had bullied the fire marshal into allowing people to sit in the aisles once the initial ticket run had sold out. It had, in fact, sold out within a week after tickets had gone up for sale last month. Gaius checked his tie again.

"So Peter Attis turned down your offer to change his concert, Gaius?" Number Six said.

Gaius jumped and pushed his chair away from the mirror. Six had replaced his reflection, and she mimicked his movements. He raised a hand. She did the same.

"More fool he," Gaius said, and Six's mouth moved in conjunction with his. "Would you stop that? It's creepier than usual."

"I just wanted to get your attention." And then she was perched prettily on the edge of the dressing table. "Being ignored is the worst possible fate. Forgotten, alone."

"You forgot 'in the dark.' "

"You never talk to me anymore," she said. "I always start our conversations. You never ask to see me—unless you want something."

"I've been busy," he said shortly, getting to his feet. "In fact, I have a lecture to give. I'm going to check the audience right now. The tickets sold out, but I'm curious."

And then Six was in front of him, her expression hard as iron. "Don't ignore me, Gaius. You owe me *everything*." She put both hands on his lapels and gave him a firm shove backward. "Who's more important to you—me or those trogs out there?"

Startled, Gaius back up another step. "I have to be on stage in five minutes."

"And you can't spare me four of them?" She grabbed his tie and yanked him into a kiss. Her tongue was warm on his. Six sat on the makeup table, wrapped her legs around his torso, and pulled him to her. His body responded, and he didn't try to resist. He didn't want to. Six could always do this to him. At one time he had tried to fight her, but these days, he didn't bother. One had to take what diversions came one's way.

Just as they finished, a voice came over the intercom. "*One minute, Dr. Gaius.*"

Six sighed theatrically as they parted. "Break a leg. Preferably someone else's." And she was gone.

Gaius straightened his clothes, checked his pocket once again for the remote, and dashed out of the dressing room. He made his way backstage, where he passed two stage hands and a lighting technician without speaking to them. His mind was in a strange place—half torpid from the sexual encounter, half revved up for the lecture. And he was running behind. Good thing he knew the format cold. Always start with a joke, then go into a short, interesting anecdote. Then introduce the main points. It was an old, familiar formula. The stage itself was empty except for a podium and a projection screen. Gaius couldn't see the audience, of course, but the auditorium was hushed with expectation. He felt perfectly calm—stage fright had never been one of his failings. In fact, he quite enjoyed lecturing. One of the many ways to pass his knowledge on to lesser minds.

"Um . . . Dr. Baltar?" said one of the stage hands. "Can I—"

"Shh!" Baltar made curt gesture. "I'm concentrating."

The clock backstage showed five seconds to eight o'clock.

"But I think you—"

"Quiet! My gods, can't anyone just do their job in silence anymore?"

"Sure, sure," the hand said. "They're going to announce you in five seconds, then."

Five seconds later, a pre-recorded announcer said, "Ladies and gentlemen, our honored vice president, Dr. Gaius Baltar!"

Gaius stepped out onto the stage, expecting tumultuous applause. What he got was some scattered clapping that echoed limply off the auditorium walls. Gaius blinked. The place was all but empty. He did a quick count. Fewer than a dozen people were scattered among the seats. Gaius gaped in astonishment. His mind was unable to comprehend what his eyes were telling him. Slowly, face flaming with embarrassment and outrage, he walked to the podium. It was only six steps away, but the distance felt like a thousand yards.

"Um . . . good—good evening," he stammered. "I . . . uh, that is, it's good to see that a few minds in the Fleet aren't preoccupied with Peter Attis and his concert."

One man bolted to his feet, a shocked look on his face. "The concert is tonight?" He fled the auditorium. Four other people went with him.

Gaius's face hardened as he realized what the stagehand had been trying to tell him—and what Number Six had prevented him from finding out. Peter Attis had made a fool of Gaius. In the wings, Number Six blew him a kiss.

The crowd raised its hands and screamed in utter joy when Peter Attis bounced onto the stage like a blond god. His every movement crackled with power, and Kara, all but crushed at the edge of the platform, raised her arms and howled with the best of them. Beside her stood Lee Adama like a blue-eyed statue in his crisp dress uniform. Kara wore a black jumpsuit, and with Dualla's help, she had actually put on some makeup. It felt like she was wearing a mask, and she had to remind herself not to touch her face.

"Good evening, Colonials!" Peter boomed into the microphone, and the crowd shrieked again. "The Cylons haven't found us yet, so let's make some noise!"

Kara let loose with a wild whoop that was almost lost in the thunder of the crowd around her. Far above, *Cloud 9*'s artificial sun showered gentle warmth and golden light on the assembled concertgoers. The clear dome reflected back the image of the trees, shrubs, and lawns planted about the wide-open space, creating the illusion that the place was much bigger than it was and hiding the fact that visitors were on board a space ship. As a luxury liner, the *Cloud 9* boasted swimming pools, hotels, spas, and other arenas for entertainment and relaxation, including several stages. Gaius Baltar had already booked the main auditorium, but Peter had said the outdoor theater would provide a better venue anyway. Garden tiers packed with people led down and in to the raised stage. A freestanding backdrop combined with a powerful sound system to ensure that everyone could hear. Peter stood alone on the stage—the music was pre-recorded from the stash provided by President Roslin and a few other hastily located Attis fans—and there had been no time for backup singers to rehearse. As a result, this concert would be a little on the plain side, but no one seemed to mind.

"I said, 'Let's make some noise!'" Peter shouted, and the crowd screamed even louder. "The Cylons tried to kill us, they failed, so let's party!"

The speakers slammed to life with a song Kara hadn't heard for years but still remembered with amazing clarity.

> *I gave you twelve soft kisses*
> *At twelve noon every day*
> *But you just took twelve kisses*
> *And ripped my heart away.*

Peter's golden voice turned the simple lyrics into powerful poetry. He leaped and danced as he sang, swirling the microphone cord around him like a whip. The front of his shirt was open, displaying well-defined muscle. Below him, the crowd danced like a giant living thing. Ripples of movement swayed through it, like wind rushing over grass. Kara loved every second. Peter finished his first song and went on to a second, one that also had a fast beat.

"Dance!" Kara shouted in Lee's ear.

He shook his head and shouted back, "I don't dance!"

Kara looked at him, then shrugged and danced by herself. The tight tensions and heavy pressures that continually rode her back seemed to evaporate with every move her body made. Then, during a musical interlude, Peter looked down at her and extended a hand. Without hesitation, Kara leaped up on the stage.

"Lieutenant Kara Thrace!" Peter announced. "If it weren't for her, I wouldn't be singing up here. Give her a hand!"

The crowd went wild. Lee clapped his hands politely, completely unconcerned. Kara wasn't sure how she felt about that. He should have reacted at least a little. Peter started singing again and drew Kara into a dance, only slightly hampered by the microphone cord. Kara looked at Lee again, then got close to Peter and went into some serious hip gyrations. She felt free, like a soap bubble rising toward the stars. The crowd loved it, and Peter smiled as his voice filled the tiered garden with liquid light.

When the song ended, Kara jumped back down to her space beside Lee. She was breathing hard and a little sweaty. "That was great!" she shouted to him over the applause. "I never thought I'd get to dance with Peter Attis!"

"Neither did I," Lee said.

"You want to go up there?" she teased. "I'm sure Peter would—"

Lee looked horrified. "No!"

"A slower one now, folks," Peter said on the stage. He drew up a stool and sat. "I was a prisoner of the Cylons all throughout the conflict. Hell, I had no idea there *was* a conflict until Kara Thrace rescued me. The only thing that kept me going was the thought that someone was watching over me, keeping me alive for a reason. I rewrote the lyrics to 'You're the Only One' "—the crowd cheered at the mention of the popular song—"to reflect my faith."

A quiet, wistful tune started up. The lights went down until only a soft spotlight illuminated Peter on his stool. He swayed a little, eyes shut, then began to sing.

> *I obey you, that you know,*
> *Why, then, do you burn my soul?*
> *If you won't look on my face,*
> *Where, then, shall I go?*
> *Without you, why would I live?*

The music swelled, and Kara felt it carry her along as if she were floating in the near-darkness of the garden. Peter slipped into the chorus.

> *You're the only one.*
> *You're the only life.*
> *You're the only reason*
> *I survive the strife.*

Kara found she was mouthing the words, singing along. So was most of the crowd. The song continued.

> *No one lives this life without you.*
> *You're the only lord.*
> *Others only show their faces*
> *Once you've possessed my soul.*

And then the chorus began again. The audience sang along in full voice. It was catchy, and the familiar tune was a piece of home. Kara found she was choking up. *You're the only reason / I survive this strife.* Even Lee was singing quietly, though he didn't seem aware he was doing so. Then Kara noticed she was holding Lee's hand. It was big and warm. Had he taken her hand or had she taken his? She didn't know.

Before she could figure it out, the song ended, and Lee dropped her hand to applaud. He didn't acknowledge the hand-holding, and Kara found that the whole thing confused her again, so she decided to ignore it, too. Peter did two more pieces before he declared he needed a break. "Fifteen-minute intermission, folks!" he said. "And I'll come back for more, if you want it."

He trotted off the stage, leaving the audience to mill around, talking. Stage hands came out to fiddle with equipment. Kara grabbed Lee's hand. "Come on!"

"Where are we going?"

"Backstage, doofus." She flashed her pass. "What do you think these things are for?"

Lee looked stubborn for a moment, then shrugged and climbed up on the stage with her. A stage hand immediately ran up to them, but Kara held up her pass and he waved them on.

The stage was actually backed up against the main dome of the *Cloud 9*, so the backstage lay between the dome wall and the stage's backdrop. A few dressing rooms and storage areas had been constructed. Kara, with Lee in tow, found Peter's room, knocked, and entered. Peter turned from his mirror. He had removed his shirt to towel off sweat. Kara couldn't help but admire the way his muscles moved beneath smooth skin.

"Kara!" he said, and gave her a firm kiss on the cheek. "And Lee!" He stuck out his hand and Lee took it. They shook hands for a long moment, and Kara only belatedly realized that they were squeezing. Lee's face was set like concrete and Peter's eyes were starting to bulge. She sighed and stepped between, giving them both an excuse to let go.

"Great concert so far," she said. "Thanks for the dance."

"You were a great partner," Peter said. "I don't suppose you sing?"

"Only if you want to kill ravens at fifty paces. Lee sings, though."

"Yeah?" He shot Lee a glance. "I'm looking for backup singers for my next concert, if you're interested."

"Right," Lee said. "I'll think real hard about it."

"Want to watch the rest of the concert from backstage?" Peter said. "Lots of people find it interesting to see what goes on behind the scenes. Though without the usual light-and-sound extravaganza, there isn't as much as usual."

"Sure!" Kara enthused.

"Great." He paused, then gestured at the two of them. "So how long have you and Lee been . . . ?"

"We're not," Lee said quickly. "We're just . . . this isn't a date."

"Gods, no," Kara put in. "I was engaged to Lee's brother a few years ago, but Lee and I are just—"

"Wonderful!" Peter said, then blushed. "I mean, not wonderful, but . . . uh . . . you know . . ."

The stage manager poked his head into the room. "Two minutes, Mr. Attis."

"Thanks," he said, clearly grateful for the interruption. He pulled on his shirt—a different one—and headed for the door. Then he paused to give Kara another kiss on the cheek. "I'll watch for you." And he left.

"He'll watch for you," Lee grumbled.

"You're not much fun on a date," she said, oddly pleased that he seemed jealous.

"This isn't a date, remember?"

"It's still supposed to be fun. Come on, lighten up."

"Long day," he sighed. "But I'll try."

They threaded their way through various stage hands and bits of equipment until they could see the stage. It was weird seeing it from the side instead of the front. Kara scanned the audience and caught sight of Commander Adama and President Roslin. They were sitting at the back on one of the upper tiers, a bit apart from the main crowd. Billy Keikeya and another aide Kara didn't recognize hovered nearby. Kara smiled. So President Roslin had somehow bullied the Old Man into accompanying her to the concert. Kara hadn't seriously thought she could do it. Adama, also in his dress uniform, wore an expression of resignation similar to Lee's. Kara's smile widened. She wondered if there would be any way for her to tease Adama about this later.

Probably not. But it was fun to think about.

A bit of motion caught the corner of Kara's eye. Peter, who was waiting on the other side of the stage, was giving Kara—and, she supposed, Lee—a friendly wave. She waved back. Gods, the man had a great ass. And he was a good cheek-kisser, too.

The lights dimmed, and the audience started cheering again. Peter ran out with his microphone, and the cheering increased in volume. A backstage technician, now visible to Kara and Lee, sat hunched over a board festooned with levers, switches, and dials. He flipped a switch and slid a lever. Music blasted from the speakers, and Peter swung into song.

"Pretty catchy tune he did earlier," Lee remarked. "That rewritten one?"

"Yeah. Did you know the original?"

"It sounded familiar, but I never was—"

"—a Peter Attis fan," Kara finished. "I know, I know. You said it several—what the hell?"

Lee stiffened. "What? What's wrong?"

Kara pointed. Over the stage arced a metal scaffold interlaced with wooden platforms. Lights and other equipment Kara couldn't identify were bolted to it. Along the top crawled a lithe figure.

"Frak me!" Lee said. "It's Sharon! What the hell is she doing up there?"

"Nothing good, I'll bet." Kara licked her lips nervously. "What do we do? If we raise the alarm there'll be a panic out there."

"If we don't, we're frakked anyway. You have a weapon?"

"Nope. You?"

"Nope."

"Good to know we're on equal footing," Kara said. "Let's go!"

One leg of the scaffold came right to the edge of the stage where

Lee and Kara were standing. Kara climbed, the steel pipes biting into her hands. Lee scrambled up behind her. She climbed carefully, trying not to make sudden motions that would attract the attention of Sharon, Peter, or the audience. Adrenaline stabbed her heart and made it pound. Cylons were stronger and faster than humans, and Kara had no idea if she'd be able to take Sharon down without a weapon. And what the hell was she up to?

Kara reached the top of the scaffold. Ahead of her stretched a bridge made of pipes and boards. Lights hung beneath her feet. The music and Peter's voice pounded at her bones—he was singing a rock song with a heavy beat. Ahead of her, about halfway across the scaffold, Sharon was kneeling on the boards. As Kara cautiously stepped forward, Sharon rose and saw her. They locked eyes for a moment. Then Sharon calmly turned and trotted away.

Kara ran forward with Lee hot on her heels. Sharon's casual trot brought her to the edge of the scaffold by the time Lee and Kara reached the middle. Kara stopped dead, and Lee almost ran into her. At her feet lay a plastic bottle. It appeared to be full of a slushy fluid. Beside was it was a small, battery-operated heater. On principle, Kara shoved the heater away from the bottle with her foot.

"Frak!" Lee shouted over the noise of the concert. "That's a nitro bomb!"

"A bottle and a heater?"

"Nitroglycerin doesn't explode when it's frozen," Lee yelled in her ear. "Once it melts, the vibrations from the music—"

"Take care of it!" Kara shouted, and took off after Sharon, who was almost at the bottom of the scaffold by now. The Cylon jumped the remaining distance to the ground, leaped off the stage, and started shoving through the crowd. People swore and protested, but gave way. Kara could track where Sharon was by the commotion, but the audience was so large that most people didn't notice. If Peter did, he gave no sign. There was no way Kara could catch up with her from here. Unless . . .

Without stopping to think, Kara leaped out into empty space. Her grasping hands snatched at one of the many guy ropes hanging from various pulleys. Her stomach lurched, and she dropped straight toward the stage faster than she would have liked. A curtain went up as she came down, and she hit the stage with a grunt. The jarring shock traveled right up her spine to her skull.

Peter spun to stare at her and the audience went silent, though the music kept up. Then Peter, ever the showman, went back to singing as if it were all part of the concert. Kara ran toward the edge of the stage, praying this would work. If it didn't, she'd have an escaped Cylon and a nice collection of bruises. She shot a glance up at the scaffold. Lee was carrying the bottle toward the edge of the scaffold as if it might explode, which it might.

Kara reached the edge of the stage and leaped off it, sailing straight down like a belly-flopper at the old watering hole. The people below her looked up in shock and Kara held her breath. At the last second, the people flung up their hands and caught her. Relief swept over Kara. The crowd cheered, and the dozens of hands supporting her started passing her toward the back of the audience. People laughed and whooped as they did so. After two people grabbed at her upper chest, however, Kara managed to roll over onto her back. It was a strange sensation, like lying on a hammock of hands. Peter waved to her as he sang, though his expression was mystified. Kara found she was moving swiftly, much faster than Sharon had gone. In moments, she was on the top tier, and the final group of concertgoers lowered her gently to her feet. Both Adama and the President were staring at her, but there was no time to explain. A stone barrier walled the concert forum off from the rest of the dome. It was dotted with revolving barred gates that let people out but not in, and Sharon was running toward one. Kara took off after her. Sharon was quicker on her feet, but the barred gate slowed her down. Kara set her mouth in grim determination. She could catch Sharon if she really hauled it.

Sharon shoved through the revolving gate and made it through. Kara ran like hell. But instead of fleeing, Sharon snatched up a rock and wedged it beneath the gate's axis. Kara hit the bars, but the gate refused to budge. Sharon gave Kara a small smile and turned to lope away.

Kara smacked the bars in frustration. "Dammit!" Then she shouted desperately, "Sharon! Wait!"

To Kara's surprise, Sharon actually halted and turned to face her. "What?"

"Why are you doing this?" Kara grasped the unmoving bars like a monkey in a cage. "I thought you wanted to help us."

Sharon walked slowly up to the gate and leaned so close Kara could smell her breath, warm and sour. "Help you? When all you've done is frak with me? Keep me locked up in a cage like some animal? And you wonder why we're trying to exterminate you."

"Yeah, you Cylons are all about love and mercy."

"We are to those who deserve it," Sharon said. "And that doesn't seem to be you." She turned and trotted into the trees.

Kara slapped the bars again, but all she got for it was a bruised hand. With a growl of anger, she turned back to the forum and forced herself to think about what to do next. There had to be a phone around here somewhere.

The next two hours turned out to be very busy. Kara had to report what had happened to someone, but Captain Shin of *Cloud 9* had no idea that the *Galactica* had been holding a Cylon, so Kara fetched Commander Adama instead. When she explained what happened, Billy and the unnamed aide hustled Roslin away and Adama's face went stony. He called Captain Shin and said that a "political prisoner" had managed to infiltrate *Cloud 9*. Security teams from both *Cloud 9* and the *Galactica* were summoned to comb the cruise liner, but no one was hopeful. The *Cloud 9* was such a popular destination that checking all traffic to and from the ship was simply impossible, and it would be easy for Sharon to slip away.

Kara also learned that Lee had managed to get the nitro bottle to an airlock before the contents melted, and the bomb had failed to go off. If it had, Peter and a large chunk of the audience would have been killed. None of the concertgoers seemed to suspect anything had gone wrong.

Kara sat on the edge of the stage, kicking her feet like a little kid. Overhead, the artificial sun continued to shine, though it was almost midnight—there was no darkness in the dome on *Cloud 9*. The grass on the tiers was already springing back from being trampled by the audience. Kara could only hope humanity would be so resilient.

"Hi."

Kara looked up into Peter's blue eyes. "Hi, yourself."

He sat down next to her, so close she could feel his body heat. "I had a feeling you'd be here. I don't know why. I guess the One is looking out for me."

"The One?"

"Yeah. He guides my footsteps. What happened out there? I got the feeling it wasn't just showing off."

Kara gave him the full rundown. Since he already knew about Caprica Sharon, there didn't seem to be any point in keeping quiet about it, though she warned him not to spread the news around.

"I won't," he said. "Wow. Uh . . . should I be worried?"

Kara opened her mouth to reassure him, then stopped herself. Sugar-coating the truth never made sense. "I don't know. Even though this version of Sharon never met you, she tried to sabotage your concert. She might be going after you specifically or she might have just chosen it because she could hurt a lot of people all at once. I doubt she stayed on *Cloud 9*, but I won't lie to you—she could still be around."

"Frak." Peter glanced nervously around. "Look, could . . . could you walk me back to my room? I don't want to be alone right now."

"You have a room? Frak, Peter—I forgot I was going to find you a place to stay. Where did they put you?"

"In one of the hotels here. I'll probably be doing a fair amount of work here for a while, so it made sense."

They got up and headed for one of the exits, talking as they went.

"Where'd Lee go?" Peter asked casually.

"Back to *Galactica*." Kara pushed away a sense that he had abandoned her. "He has duty in a few hours. I don't, so I stayed here. Nice to get away for a while."

"Looks like we're all permanently getting away for a while."

Kara snorted. "One way to look at it."

A few minutes later, they were standing in a hotel corridor. Peter unlocked his door and nudged it open. Then he turned to Kara. "I never did thank you."

"For . . . ?"

"Saving my life, of course." He leaned down and kissed her. Her first thought—

my gods I'm kissing Peter Attis

—flicked through her mind, then dissolved under the kiss. Kara returned it, hungrily. After the fight with the Cylons and the pursuit of Sharon, she needed the reassurance that she was still alive, that someone would hold her. The kiss became more intense, and Kara was only vaguely aware that they were moving inside, that Peter had kicked the door shut, that they were fumbling at each other's clothes. Moments later, they were naked beneath the sheets, and for a while Kara felt everything she needed to.

CHAPTER 6

"Captain Demeter reports that harvest operations are underway, Commander," Dualla said.

Adama nodded his acknowledgment, then cast a wary eye toward the DRADIS readout. The scanner remained empty. No sign of

Cylon activity, though it had been over forty-eight hours since the initial attack.

Uneasiness tugged at Adama, though he was careful to keep this from showing on his face. He couldn't help feeling that the Cylons knew exactly where he was, but they were choosing not to attack. Except there was no reason for them to do this. They could have easily sent another basestar with more raiders long before the *Monarch* had finished evacuating. It was unthinkable that they hadn't. Something else must have interfered. Maybe the first basestar hadn't managed to transmit a signal. Maybe Starbuck's nuclear explosion had jammed their transmissions. Hell, maybe they were running out of basestars. Adama tightened his mouth. Too many maybes. The fact remained that after a full day of no Cylons, it made it worth the risk to put the *Monarch* back to work.

And there was the problem of Sharon Valerii. The search teams continued working around the clock, but Kara and Lee were still the only two people who had set eyes on her since her escape. It was possible she had left the Fleet just as that Godfrey woman had, but Adama doubted it. Caprica Sharon was an outcast among her own people and she was pregnant. She wouldn't go running to them even if she could, and that meant she had concealed herself in the Fleet somewhere. There had been no other attempts at sabotage, thank the gods, but it still made Adama uneasy knowing she was out there. She—or someone very much like her—had nearly killed him less than a month ago. Sometimes he woke up in the night, the sound of her pistol shot ringing in his ears, the pain of the bullet tearing through his gut. It was times like that when he missed Anne the most. Her absence was a black emptiness that trailed after him, no matter how busy he kept himself. He suspected that most people in the Fleet felt the same way about their own loved ones. Adama, at least, had the comfort of knowing his son Lee was nearby, though it scared the hell out of him every time Lee flew a mission. He sighed and wondered what it would be like to be free of crushing stress, to wake up in the morning and not be in some way worried or afraid.

Suddenly the CIC felt confining, the decks and bulkheads hemming him in like a prison. "Going for a walk, Mr. Gaeta," he said. "You have CIC. Shout if you need me."

"Yes, sir," Gaeta said.

Adama strode along *Galactica's* familiar corridors, keeping his pace fast enough to stretch his legs but not fast enough to start a sweat. Members of crew made way for him, tossing him salutes where appropriate. He had no doubt word was getting around that the Old Man was on the prowl. The idea almost made him smile.

He hadn't been on his feet for more than ten minutes before he almost ran into Saul Tigh in a side corridor. The executive officer was waving a magazine under Kara Thrace's nose. Kara was keeping her face stoic, but Adama caught the amusement that quirked at the corners of her mouth. Adama gave an internal sigh. Kara enjoyed baiting Tigh and he loved raking her over the coals. The two of them were more alike than either of them wanted to think.

"This is conduct unbecoming an officer," Tigh was saying. "Dammit, we're the Battlestar *Galactica*. Or did you forget that during your little outing?"

"Is it against regulations to date a civilian, sir?" Kara asked carefully.

"I'll ask the questions, Lieutenant."

"So that's a no, then. And sir," her tone became sticky-sweet, "I don't recall seeing any unbecoming pictures of me in the magazines. Is it against regulations for people to take photos of me in a public place? It's not something I can exactly control when I'm not on duty."

"You know what I mean," Tigh snapped. He had rolled up the magazine as if to swat her on the nose with it. "We're the military, not some fluffbrain celebrities."

"I can't help it that people think I'm photogenic, sir. I didn't *ask* them to take the pictures, or to publish them."

"You can take these pictures and—"

"Good morning, Lieutenant," Adama interrupted, then nodded at his XO. "Saul."

Kara, seeing him for the first time, snapped a salute. "Sir!"

"May I, Saul?" Adama held out his hand and Tigh, red-faced, handed him the magazine. Adama unrolled it. The title, *Person to Person*, blazed in large yellow lettering across the glossy cover. He flipped through it until he came to the offending pages. Kara tensed visibly. Adama found a slightly fuzzy picture of Kara Thrace walking through a park—presumably on *Cloud 9*—with Peter Attis. They were holding hands. In the next photograph, they were kissing. The accompanying story was short, and only mentioned that Peter and Kara had been seen together often since the concert two days ago. The article was also full of question marks, as in "How serious is this?" and "Can the *Galactica*'s number one pilot keep up a relation-

ship with a rock star?" A sidebar caught his eye. It was headed, GEMI-
NON PRIESTS DENOUNCE PERFORMER'S MUSIC. Adama flicked through
the article. Apparently Peter's rendition of "You're the Only One"
had ruffled a few religious feathers.

"Interesting stuff," Adama said.

"That it is," Tigh growled.

Adama handed Kara the magazine. "Lieutenant, I don't see a violation in regulations—"

"Thank you, sir," Kara said, an impish note to her voice.

"—so far," Adama finished. "You need to be careful that you two
are not seen together when you're in uniform, and I hope I don't
need to tell you what the penalty would be if you saw him while on
duty."

Kara's face instantly became serious and the impishness left her
tone. "No, sir."

"Saul," Adama said, turning to him, "I left Lieutenant Gaeta in
charge of CIC. You might want to make sure he hasn't caused any
damage while I've been gone."

Tigh hurried off, looking slightly mollified at the chance to in-
spect Gaeta's work.

"Walk with me a bit, Lieutenant," Adama said. Kara fell into step
beside him, and they strolled the busy corridors of the ship. The hallways were never empty, and the pair kept their voices low to avoid being overheard.

"It looked to me like you were proud of the magazine, Kara,"
Adama said, falling into informal mode. "I never figured you for a
publicity hound."

"I'm not, really," Kara admitted.

"What changed?"

They made way for a trio of sweaty joggers and for an ensign
pushing a small handcart piled high with plastic crates.

"Colonel Tigh." Her expression became impish. "I didn't realize
how much I liked those pictures until he started telling me how inappropriate they were."

"Right." They passed a set of carbon dioxide scrubbers mounted
on the bulkhead. Adama automatically listened to make sure they
were hissing properly. Maintenance wasn't his personal job, but he
couldn't help checking. "You be careful how you handle this, Kara.
The media is a starving jackal. It'll devour every bit of you and
clamor for more."

"Yes, sir. I'll be careful, sir."

"Thank you, Lieutenant." And they went their separate ways.

"Ready, Chief?"

Chief Petty Officer Galen Tyrol eyed the Raptor, his practiced gaze taking in every scratch, every ding, every repair. This one had a patched wing, its carefully soldered seam just visible. He couldn't see the internal repairs (scavenged communications wiring, newly cleaned CO_2 scrubbers swiped from a dead Viper, deck plating resealed with a compound of his own devising), but he knew every one. These days he couldn't look at a Raptor or a Viper without mentally tallying up what repairs it had required yesterday, what it needed at the moment, and which ones it might need in the near future.

"Why don't I get a vac suit?" he asked.

Margaret "Racetrack" Edmonson shrugged shoulders padded by her vac suit. Her helmet face plate revealed a pretty face framed by long dark hair. "Regs, Chief. Pilot and ECO wear suits. Passengers don't need them."

"Unless we get a micrometeor puncture or a Cylon attacks or—"

She clapped him on the back with a gloved hand. "You're just paranoid because you know all the stuff that can go wrong."

"Well, yeah." He ran a hand over his face, feeling more than a little nervous. "I repair them, I don't fly in them. As a rule."

"This is a sugar run," Racetrack told him. "Straight to Planet Goop, no stops, no Cylons."

"Let's frakking hope so." Helo stepped into view around the Raptor, his heavy vac suit boots thumping softly on the deck. "Chief."

"Lieutenant." Tyrol felt a vague tension humming in the metallic air. He shot Racetrack a quick glance. Her face was carefully neutral. So was Helo's. So was Tyrol's own. Yes, sir—all perfectly neutral. A silence fell across the trio, and Tyrol's discomfort grew.

"Any news about Sharon?" he blurted. Then he mentally kicked himself. He had just mentioned the huge, honking elephant in the room. And to an officer, no less.

"Not a word," Helo said. His voice had a thin quality, transmitted over the suit's intercom, and Tyrol couldn't tell by the lieutenant's tone if he was annoyed, upset, or uncaring.

"Well, that's . . . I mean . . ."

"Oh, frak it," Racetrack said. "Look, that Raptor will explode if we get on board right now, so let's defuse this little bomb right now.

Chief, you know that I used to have bad feelings toward you because of your . . . relationship with Sharon. I don't anymore. Okay? I think you're one of the best men on this ship. Helo, you and the Chief feel weird around each other because he was boink—uh . . . *seeing* the first Sharon before you got involved with Caprica Sharon, the second Sharon. So now you're both tense. Have you two resolved that or what?"

Tyrol looked at Helo and unconsciously rubbed his jaw where the other man had socked him in a fistfight over this very issue. Tyrol had given as good as he got, though. In the end, both had walked away from the fight, silently swearing never to mention it again. Racetrack, however, was throwing it back at them, and Tyrol didn't know exactly what to say.

In the end, it was Helo who broke the silence. "Yeah, we kinda resolved it." He held out a gloved hand with a sheepish grin. "We good, Chief?"

Tyrol hesitated only a moment. "We're good, Lieutenant."

"Good boys." Racetrack clambered over the wing of the Raptor and stepped into the little cabin. "Now climb aboard and strap in like a nice passenger and ECO."

"Since when are *you* a pilot, anyway?" Helo said, following her. Tyrol brought up the rear. "Last I knew, you were still an Electronic Countermeasures Officer like me."

"I've flown plenty of Raptors," Racetrack said defensively. "You'll be up for it next, just watch. Besides, this is just a sugar run."

"You say that over and over like you're trying to reassure yourself," Helo said.

"Shut up."

Tyrol quietly strapped himself into the copilot seat beside Racetrack as Helo pulled the Raptor's hatch shut. He felt oddly naked in just his orange deck uniform. The cabin was fairly small, big enough for maybe one more person. Helo took up his position at the rear, by the ECO console. Ahead of Tyrol, clear Plexiglas (three scratches, two pockmarks, no cracks) looked out over the deck. He closed his eyes and tried to doze as Racetrack and Helo went through the preflight, though he was sure he was too uneasy to sleep. It therefore surprised him to wake up with a small snort when Helo said, "How about some radio time?"

Tyrol wiped drool from his chin. His dark hair felt mussed, and he blinked bleary brown eyes. Sharon had always said his eyes were his best feature. He pushed the thought aside. Ahead of him lay the perfect blackness of space. Suspended in the center of it, Planet Goop turned slowly on its axis. Wispy white clouds chased each other across deep blue oceans and piled up over brown masses of land.

"Radio?" he said. "What's playing?"

"Dunno," Helo replied. "It's always hit-or-miss out here, but luckily you have me on the communications board."

Crackly, uncertain saxophone music filled the cabin.

"No jazz!" Racetrack hollered.

"Sorry. I forgot." Helo fiddled with the boards some more and this time clear voices filtered from the speakers.

". . . *the success of your concert,*" said an interviewer. "*What was the song again?*"

"*'You're the Only One.' I rewrote the lyrics. It seems to be catching on.*"

"*An understatement, to be sure. You're making some waves about your new spirituality. I've heard the word 'heresy' thrown around here and there.*"

A light laugh. "*Not what I intended. And it's not really heresy. I just maintain that all the gods are merely faces—different faces—of a single loving entity.*"

"Who the frak is this?" Tyrol demanded, affronted.

"Shh! It's Peter Attis," Racetrack said.

"*Isn't that the definition of heresy?*"

"*There are Scriptural passages that support it,*" Peter countered. "*Though not explicitly. There's certainly nothing in the Sacred Scrolls to deny it.*"

"Since when?" Tyrol exploded. "The Book of Pythia specifically states—"

"Hush!" Racetrack interrupted.

"*But I'm not trying to become a spiritual leader,*" Peter continued. "*I'm a singer, not an Oracle.*"

"Damn right," Tyrol grumbled.

"*You already have people who claim to be followers,*" the interviewer said. "*What about them?*"

"*I haven't done anything to lead them.*" Another light laugh. "*I think they're really fans. It's always nice to know you've touched someone's life, but I'm just out to entertain, nothing more than that.*"

Tyrol shook his head, trying to imagine how his parents—a Priest and an Oracle—would have reacted to such blasphemy. "Explosive" was the only word that came to mind.

The interview came to an end, to Tyrol's relief, and Helo shut off the radio. Tyrol half expected his father to leap out of the shadows and castigate him for sullying his soul with such heretical ideas. Then he wished his father *would* leap out of the shadows, even to yell at him and make him kneel down to pray as he had when Tyrol had been living with them at home on Geminon.

"Looking forward to your stint on Planet Goop, Chief?" Helo asked. The planet in question had now filled the entire view with blue, brown, and white, giving Tyrol the unnerving feeling that he was falling toward the azure ocean. Technically, he supposed he was.

"Not really," Tyrol sighed. "It's not like I don't have enough to do on the *Galactica*. Now they want me helping with harvest equipment on Planet Goop? I have four engines to overhaul and a Viper that's missing a—"

"Now, now," Racetrack admonished. "Everyone has to do their bit for the harvest."

"Yeah? What's your bit?"

"Delivering you."

Half an hour later, the Raptor hit atmosphere. It bucked and jumped for a moment like a recalcitrant horse, and Tyrol swallowed his stomach. Then Racetrack smoothed out. They plunged into a misty white cloud bank. Droplets of condensation gathered and ran across the Plexiglas, chasing each other like quicksilver fairies. Tyrol stared at them, realizing how long it had been since he'd actually been off the *Galactica* and in a real atmosphere, with real clouds. Too bad he couldn't *breathe* the atmosphere. But Planet Goop, with its useful, edible algae, was a hell of a find. A planet fully inhabitable by humans—that was a dream almost beyond imagination. Tyrol loved his job, loved puzzling out what was wrong with a ship, loved straightening bent struts and sealing cracks so the vessel could fly again. It was like being a doctor, in a way, and it was immensely satisfying to watch a Viper he had repaired dive back into a fight, guns he had repaired blazing away. But it was also a fine thing to walk through a forest, smell green leaves, feel a fresh breeze, and it had been so long since he had done any of that.

The Raptor broke free of the cloud and dropped steadily down. Below, Tyrol made out the long, rounded shape of the *Monarch*. It sat on the dark, rocky shore of an ocean. From this low height, the water looked more green than blue. Three long, flat arms protruded from the ship, thrusting themselves outward into the gently rippling waves. As the Raptor grew closer, Tyrol could see the arms were actually enormous conveyor belts with giant scoops spaced evenly along them. According to the briefing he had read and the schematics he had studied, the scoops hauled algae into the *Monarch*'s main processing area. Once an area was denuded of algae, the arms would pivot a few degrees and start work on another section of the algae bed. Eventually, the *Monarch* would pick up and move to a different site.

Racetrack landed the Raptor a few yards from the *Monarch*. Helo handed Tyrol a full-face mask connected to a square unit the size of a beer mug. Tyrol clipped the unit to his belt and donned the mask. It fit tightly over his entire face and smelled like old plastic. Tyrol also connected one end of a corded earpiece to the unit and fitted the other in his ear.

"The unit is a scrubber," said Helo's voice in Tyrol's ear. "It'll extract enough oxygen from the CO_2 in the atmosphere to let you—"

"I know how it works, sir," Tyrol interrupted. "What's the air pressure like?"

"Only a couple millibars under what we're used to." Helo opened the hatch and a hot, humid breeze swept through the cabin. It was like being licked by a whale's tongue. Tyrol's ears popped. "Have fun, Chief."

Tyrol gave him a sour look and exited the Raptor. The ground was rough, the rocks jagged. The planet hadn't had an atmosphere long enough for any real erosion to start. The Raptor fled back into the cloudy sky, and Tyrol turned his attention to the *Monarch*.

The ship looked a lot like a low factory building that had dropped straight down from the sky. The dull roar and steady clank of machinery rumbled beneath a constant wind that plucked at Tyrol's clothing with moist fingers. Already he was sweating. Beyond the ship seethed the great green ocean. Tyrol inhaled, half expecting to smell salt water, but all he got was plastic air. He sighed. Two people were visible near an enormous open hatchway. Tyrol made for them and introduced himself.

"Good to see you, Chief Tyrol," said a woman who turned out to be Captain Renee Demeter. She had short hair the color of fresh brown earth and grass-green eyes. Her voice came through his earpiece. "We're chronically short on repair staff and staff supervisors down here. Even with anti-radiation meds, we can't keep people on the ground for long periods of time. Jim, take the Chief inside and show him around."

"Sure, Cap." Jim wore a gray crewcut and looked like he should be rolling a toothpick from one end of his mouth to the other. His clothes hung loosely on him, as if he'd lost a lot of weight lately. A lot of people in the Fleet had, Tyrol knew. Jim cocked his head toward the truck-sized hatch and went inside. Tyrol followed.

"What's your rank, sir?" Tyrol asked.

Jim glanced over his shoulder. "I don't have one, son. Civilian ship. If Cap tells you to do something, you do it. Come on, I'll show you entry bay two. That's where we need help."

The hatchway opened into a cavelike space. Scoops the size of small trucks and laden with piles of blue-green goop cranked past them on a gigantic conveyer belt and disappeared into an opening in the distant wall. Half a dozen crewmembers, all in face masks, dashed about to tend the machinery. Water dripped from piles of algae and made salty, steamy lakes on the deck. The plating was slick, and Tyrol stepped carefully to avoid slipping. A scoop loader rumbled by, its bucket piled with goop. Abruptly it stopped, backed up, and jerked forward again, barely missing the main conveyer belt. Tyrol winced and automatically reached out a hand, as if he could stop the vehicle.

"Hey!" Jim boomed, his voice loud in Tyrol's earpiece. "Watch it, Hyksos!"

Hyksos gave an odd wave from the driver's seat and maneuvered the loader around again. Jim turned his attention back to Tyrol. Tyrol wiped a fresh layer of sweat from his forehead.

"The belts haul the goop into the processing area," Jim said, cocking a thumb at the opening. "We run it through the rollers and mash it into sheets. We dry them, which makes them easier to handle, and send them out to some of the other ships for processing into food and medicine."

"How'd you adapt mining equipment into handling algae?" Tyrol said. His interest was starting to perk up.

"Crushing, mashing, rolling—we did all that with rocks before. Now we do it with algae. We did have to add a couple of access corridors to help with air circulation and make it easier to move goop around, but the biggest job was cleaning the equipment first. The main problem is that the salt water gets into everything and eats it. And the algae is primitive stuff, only a few steps above protoplasm, so it gunks up everything the water doesn't eat. Lots of constant maintenance. You arrived during one of the good times, when all four arms are hauling at capacity. Usually at least one of them is down."

As if on cue, the arm made a terrible groaning noise, clanked twice more, and went still. A moan rose from the workers in the area. Jim clapped Tyrol on the shoulder.

"Go to it, Chief," he said, and ambled away.

Two hours later, Tyrol's front was wet through, and he was covered in green slime. His fingers were wet and wrinkled. It was a far cry from the carefully controlled environment of the *Galactica,* though he had to admit the lack of "fix it now *now NOW*" pressure was a nice change. He lay on his back, staring up at the secondary motor that was supposed to help haul the conveyer belt forward but wasn't. Goop had clogged the air intake and destroyed the filter which had, in turn, put a strain on the pistons, which had—

Tyrol grimaced. Everything *should* be working now. "Okay, Ken!" he shouted. "Try it again!"

A pause. The motor sputtered and coughed. Tyrol held his breath. The motor coughed again, started to die, then caught. One more cough, and it settled into a steady purr. Tyrol pumped a quiet fist.

"Nice work, Chief!" the unseen Ken said into his earpiece.

A blob of goop plopped on Tyrol's breathing mask. Tyrol jumped. His entire world had gone green. Great—a machine that had to have the last word. He rolled himself out from under the motor and sat up to wipe his mask clean.

"Tabra! Meltina par tewmell fa!"

What the hell? Tyrol pawed at his mask, restoring partial visibility.

"Chief! Watch out!"

Tyrol twisted in place and cleared the last of the slime from his mask. The scoop loader, its bucket now empty, was rushing straight toward him.

CHAPTER 7

"Drive the crazy car at pildani mufallan dar! Dalabren bay heslan duk!"

The voice in Tyrol's earpiece made no sense, but he spared no time thinking about it. The scoop loader's bucket, trailing shreds of green goop, was only a few yards away and closing. Tyrol's heart jumped into his throat and his stomach clenched in fear. He scrambled to his feet, sending the wheeled creeper flying. No time to jump sideways— the bucket would clip him. Without hesitating further, he jumped straight up. The teeth of the bucket's lower edge gouged the air where Tyrol's shins had been. Tyrol grabbed the upper teeth with both hands.

The metal bit into his palms and pain wrenched his shoulders as the loader's forward momentum jerked his upper body backward. His lower body swung forward like a pendulum. He barely managed to bring his legs up so his feet slammed the back of the bucket instead of his knees. The loader motor growled like an angry bear. People shouted in his earpiece, but he was too busy to pay attention to what they were saying.

The loader rumbled across the deck plates, with Tyrol still clinging to the slimy bucket. The driver continued to shout incoherently. His movements were jerky, and neither of his hands touched the steering wheel. A glance over his shoulder showed that the loader was heading straight for the main conveyer belt. Scoops of blue-green goop continued to move down the enormous belt with mechanical unconcern. In a few seconds, he would be crushed.

"Turn!" Tyrol yelled at the driver. "Turn, you bastard!"

"Beelo! Frakking muzzle the dog's myl feldan mool!"

What the hell? Didn't matter. He wasn't turning. *That* mattered. Tyrol swung his body sideways, trying to get his foot up to the teeth lining the top of the bucket. He missed, swung again, and managed to hook an ankle. His hands hurt like hell. A metal tooth slashed the side of his shin with burning pain. The conveyer belt was barely six yards away. Tyrol heaved himself up, cleared the upper teeth, and rolled across the top of the bucket just as it crashed into the belt. The noise smashed through him, and he bounced across the bucket to fetch up against the hydraulic pistons that moved the scoop up and down. Algae flew in all directions, splattering every surface in blue-green goop. The belt screamed like a thousand frightened horses and came to a stop.

Everything fell quiet. Tyrol clung to a piston, trying without success to catch his breath. He was breathing all right but felt like he wasn't getting any air. His vision clouded. At last he realized it was because his breathing mask had been knocked slightly askew, breaking the seal. He braced himself against the bucket and resealed the mask. Air filled his lungs, sweetly plastic. Then several sets of hands grabbed him and hauled him gently down from his strange position on the scoop loader.

"You all right, Chief?" demanded Captain Demeter. She and several other workers were standing shin-deep in goop. "Frak, we thought you were a goner. How do you feel?"

Tyrol checked. Pounding heart, wavery vision, vague feeling of nausea, burning shin, aching hands. Nothing life-threatening, though he wanted a stiff drink, something better than the stuff he concocted at his own still. He tried to put weight on his injured leg and yelped. Demeter helped him sit, then carefully rolled up his trouser leg, bringing a fresh onslaught of pain. Tyrol gritted his teeth at the sight of the dirty, bleeding gash. Someone ran up with a first aid kit, and Demeter pressed a bandage against the wound. It hurt.

"This will control the bleeding," she said. "Hold it there."

"Yes, sir," he said, obeying. "What the hell happened?"

"No idea," said Jim, the other person who had helped Tyrol clear of the loader. "Hyksos up there just went crazy."

Tyrol looked up at the drivers seat. Two men were dragging Hyksos from his chair. The man appeared to be unconscious, though he twitched strangely. Demeter had him hauled to a clear section of floor and bent over him. He continued to twitch.

"No obvious injuries," Demeter said. "Our sickbay can handle basic problems, but this looks seriously strange. I think we'd better call a shuttle and have Cottle get a look at both of you on the *Galactica*."

"It's not like you to hide in your lab, Gaius."

"I'm not hiding."

"Really? You haven't left this room ever since the lecture. Or rather, since the concert. Scared, Gaius?"

"Of course not!"

Number Six ran a long, cool finger down the bridge of Gaius Baltar's nose and gave him one of her rare playful smiles. "You can't lie to me, Gaius. I know you too well."

"You think I'm afraid," Gaius snarled. He typed madly at a computer terminal in an attempt to ignore the lush blond woman who had draped herself over the arm of his chair. "You think I'm scared to go out there because people will laugh at my failed—yes, *failed*—lecture. Well, I'm not. I'm a bloody celebrity. There is always some lackwit who finds humor in the trials and tribulations of the famous. It's part of the price of fame, and I've been dealing with it for years. I'm not afraid."

"Absolutely, Gaius." Number Six got up and stretched like a lazy tiger. Her stunning red dress clashed with the harsh light and utilitarian machinery of the lab. "You're not afraid of public humiliation, that much is obvious."

"Good." Type type type. "I'm glad we agree on something. If you don't mind, I need to finish these resource-use projections, now that we have algae coming in."

"You're not afraid of public humiliation," Number Six repeated. "You're afraid of the opposite."

A small ripple of doubt slipped down Gaius's spine. "And just what is *that* supposed to mean?"

"You're afraid," Number Six said, "that no one will notice you at all."

Gaius stopped typing.

"Peter Attis, grabbing all the attention," Number Six continued. "It isn't fair, Gaius. He hasn't your mind. Your brilliance shines like a nova, and his is—"

"Dark matter," Gaius muttered. "Black and omnipresent." He straightened in his chair. "But I'm not afraid of him—or of being ignored."

"Then prove it," Six offered reasonably. "Go for a walk. I hear sickbay's a *terribly* interesting place this time of year."

"Is it?" Gaius muttered. "Look, I have no intention of . . ."

But she was gone.

Gaius set his mouth and went back to typing, trying to ignore the knots in his stomach. She was *not* always right. She had nothing better to do than bait him. But gods, she was so beautiful—and completely his. A hidden flower with soft petals no one else could touch. And she *had* given him good advice. Plenty of times. Hell, back on Caprica she had saved his life.

He glanced at the door, then back at the screen. His resolve firmed. Gaius Baltar was not a puppet for Number Six to jerk around, not a fly caught in Six's web. He was himself, his own man.

Keys continued to clatter under his hands. "You don't own me," he said aloud.

The room remained empty. Click-click-clack-click. The computer keys chattered like teeth. Stupid frakking *Galactica* didn't even have basic vocal interface.

"You *don't* own me," he said again, then braced himself for Six's soft touch on his back, her quiet voice in his ear, her moist tongue on his neck. But it didn't come. He looked at the computer screen. A jungle of gibberish took up four pages. Not one word made sense.

"Oh, the hell with it," he muttered. He grabbed his suit jacket and stormed out of the lab. A few minutes later, he was just outside the main entrance to sickbay. Uncertainty stole over him like a cold hand. What was he supposed to do—stomp in to sickbay and demand they show him something interesting?

Shouts from inside jarred him into action. He shoved open the door and ran inside. Sickbay was set up like a hospital triage unit, with curtained alcoves serving as both examination and treatment areas. The curtains did nothing to shut out noise, and Gaius easily located the source. He dashed down to the third alcove on the left and yanked aside the curtain. Dr. Cottle, his white hair disheveled, was struggling to hold down a patient Gaius didn't recognize. A medical technician was assisting, as was Chief Galen Tyrol, of all people. Tyrol's lower leg sported a bandage.

"He was unconscious a minute ago!" Cottle yelled. "Get him two milligrams of ativan. Move!"

One of the patient's flailing arms caught the medical technician across the bridge of her nose. She staggered and went down to one knee, blood gushing from one nostril. The patient managed to sit up. Tyrol flung himself bodily across the man, who went down but continued to struggle on the bed.

"Billal mulistarken far!" the patient shouted.

"Shut up, Hyksos!" Tyrol yelled back.

Cottle managed to get Hyksos's ankles into restraints, but he was still fighting convulsively. The med tech was trying to get up, but the blow had clearly dazed her. Cottle caught sight of Gaius.

"Don't just stand there, you idiot!" he barked. "This man is having a seizure. The ativan is in the cabinet. Get it!"

Gaius hurried to the cabinet, fumbled it open, and scanned the scantily stocked shelves for ativan. The ampules were in alphabetical order, allowing him to find it quickly. He snatched up a syringe, jammed it into the ampule's rubber top, and yanked the plunger back to two milligrams, then glanced at Hyksos and added another half a milligram for good measure. No sense in taking the chance he might hurt himself—or Gaius. Hyksos managed to shove Cottle aside with his free arm, and the doctor crashed into a tray of instruments. Metal flew in all directions and the tray crashed to the floor. Tyrol was still lying across Hyksos's body. Hyksos continued to thrash, shouting incoherent nonsense. Baltar hesitated. He didn't want to get close. What if Hyksos bruised him? Or worse?

"What are you waiting for?" Cottle said from the floor. "Inject him!"

Gaius took a deep breath and lunged. He got Hyksos's left wrist and trapped his arm. Both Hyksos and Tyrol smelled like stale ocean water. Gaius couldn't help wrinkling his nose as he shoved the syringe into the skin—forget sterilization—and rammed the plunger home. Hyksos continued to babble and shout for a few seconds as Cottle and the med tech got to their feet. Then Hyksos's struggles grew weaker. He fell silent, and his body relaxed. Cottle instantly locked down the wrist restraints and Tyrol slid off the patient's body. He winced when his injured leg took weight.

"Frak!" Tyrol gasped. "What the hell is wrong with him?"

"He was unconscious all the way back from Planet Goop, you said?" Cottle asked. He handed the med tech a towel, and she gingerly pressed it to her face. "You better get some ice for that."

"He was out like a light," Tyrol said. "He muttered a lot, though. Gibberish."

The med tech left. Gaius edged closer for a look at Hyksos, curiosity winning out over caution. Hyksos was a brawny, red-headed man covered with a crop of new freckles. No doubt working outdoors in the harsh sun of Planet Goop had brought them out. The man twitched and muttered in his sleep. Gaius put out a finger and touched his forehead. It was a little on the warm side.

"What's your initial diagnosis, Doctor?" he asked Cottle.

"He's agitated and he has a slight fever," Cottle replied shortly.

"That's it?" Gaius scoffed.

"I haven't run any tests yet, Your Majesty. You want to do something useful, draw some blood and do some tests. Otherwise, get the hell out of my sickbay."

Gaius drew himself up. "*I* am the vice president of the Colonies."

"And I'm God of this sickbay. Either shit or get off the crapper. I don't have all day."

Gaius whirled to stomp out and almost crashed into Number Six. He froze. Six didn't say a word, but a small smile played around the corners of her mouth. With skill borne of long practice, Gaius pretended that he had spun around so he could grab another syringe and a set of blood ampules from the cabinet. Six backed up to give him room, and he gave her a hard look. She met his gaze for a moment, then walked slowly out of the alcove, her hips switching as she went. Gaius watched her go and felt his groin tighten as it always did. As she *knew* it always did. He spun again and turned back to the bed.

"Scarlet fever, drug withdrawal, dengue hemorrhagic fever," Cottle was muttering. "Epilepsy? No, not with a fever." He pried up one of Hyksos's eyelids and shined a light on the eye. The pupil contracted normally.

"Is whatever it is contagious?" Tyrol asked nervously.

"How the hell should I know, son?" Cottle said. "If it weren't for the fever, I'd say his mind snapped. All I can say right now is that if

you get the sudden urge to babble, haul your sorry ass down here before you hurt someone."

Tyrol hesitated. "I'm from Geminon, you know."

"Uh-huh. So?" Cottle wrapped a blood pressure cuff around Hyksos's arm and pumped. Gaius rolled up the sleeve on Hyksos's free
arm and swabbed the inner elbow with disinfectant. He was a biolo-
gist by training, with extensive knowledge of microbiology. He wasn't
a medical doctor, but much of the training overlapped. Drawing
blood and running some tests were no challenge, but his curiosity was
aroused. Besides, Number Six had hinted a visit to sickbay might benefit him, and he was hardly going to pass up the chance that she was
right.

"My mother was an Oracle," Tyrol continued. "And sometimes the
Lords of Kobol would . . . they would enter her body and make her
speak. Sometimes she would say something understandable, but most
of the time she sounded like Hyksos here."

"Speaking in tongues as the result of divine possession?" Gaius
scoffed. He inserted the needle into a vein and popped one of the ampules into the other end. Scarlet blood streamed into the little container. "Grow up, Chief. There's clearly some microscopic agent at
work. Since he was on Planet Goop when it happened, it seems logical
to start there. Perhaps something in the algae."

"Then why haven't more people come down with it?" Tyrol countered. "Captain Demeter said no one else has been acting strange."

"Any number of reasons," Gaius said. He finished the current blood
ampule and started another. "It might be an allergic reaction. Or perhaps
it's a combination of substances that only Hyksos has encountered."

"How many of those you going to fill?" Cottle demanded.

Gaius looked down. He was working on his seventh ampule of
blood. Grimacing, he pulled the syringe free, disposed of it, and handed
three of the ampules to Cottle. "Can you get me urine and stool samples
as well?"

"Why the hell not? You're the vice president of the Colonies."

The back of Helo's head itched but he was standing at attention, so he
forced himself to ignore it. The bustle of CIC swirled around him like
a sandstorm, and the continual growl of the DRADIS sounded like a
restless lion prowling the room. Tigh gave Helo a hard look.

"Captain Demeter reports that the harvest is complete," Dualla
said from her station. "The *Monarch*'s holds are completely full, and

she's commenced cleanup procedures. They should be ready to leave by the end of the day."

"Thank you," Adama said. "Send a report to the President. Lieutenant Gaeta, how much material did we end up with?"

"Once it's processed, we should have enough to make current food stores last an extra two months," Gaeta said. "We'll also have more than enough antibiotics to end the strep breakout and restore the radiation meds to full supply."

A ripple of applause and a few small cheers went through CIC. Adama broke into one of his rare smiles. Helo, who was still under the harsh light of Tigh's glare, remained at attention despite the good news.

"What's the status of the Cylon prisoner?" Tigh asked him.

"Nothing new to report, sir," Helo said. "She's still at large."

Tigh continued to stare at Helo, who kept his face impassive. "Then keep looking, Lieutenant. I want that frakking Cylon found!"

"Yes, sir."

"Dismissed."

Helo turned and stepped smartly out of CIC. The moment he was out of sight, he let himself sag against a wall for a tiny moment. Exhaustion pulled at every pore. When had he last had a good night's sleep? He couldn't remember. Four days ago, Sharon had escaped. Two days ago, he had brought Tyrol and that guy Hyksos back from Planet Goop. Tyrol had been injured, Hyksos had been unconscious. Rumor had it that Hyksos was now in sickbay, under restraint. When he was awake, he babbled, spouted nonsense, and tried to attack the doctor. As a result, he spent most of his time under sedation. Helo envied him. The day before yesterday, Tigh had announced that Helo knew more about "that frakking toaster" than anyone else on the *Galactica*, which meant Helo was now in charge of the search teams. The stress of his new duties combined with the worry about what would happen to Sharon if she got caught and what would happen to *him* if she *didn't* get caught kept him awake long into his normal sleep cycle. Helo was caught between two rocks that were steadily rolling together. If Sharon was caught, Adama would no doubt order her immediate execution, baby or no. If she wasn't caught, Tigh would make Helo the scapegoat. Becoming Tigh's scapegoat was way better than Sharon dying, but Helo still lost. He and Sharon both.

This was, he acknowledged to himself, the reason he was searching for Sharon by himself instead of with a party of marines. If—when—

Sharon turned up, the marines were likely to shoot first and ask questions later. Helo wanted to ask questions first. He had no intention of shooting.

The radio clipped to his belt squawked out orders as the search parties continued their work. Their movements had become mechanical, almost perfunctory. They had gone over every inch of the ship to no avail, and Helo was almost considering ordering the men to suit up so they could search the *Galactica*'s outer hull. Maybe Sharon had stolen a vac suit and was—

He shook his head. No way. Even Cylons needed to breathe, and she stood an excellent chance of getting caught every time she cycled an airlock to board and refill her oxygen bottle. Still, his new situation altered the way he looked at *Galactica*. Every alcove, every passageway had turned into a possible hiding place, every shadow became a black blanket of suspicion. And every moment he was aware that eventually a choice would leap out of the darkness and tear him in two.

He scratched the back of his head. The itch had been bothering him a lot lately, and it helped keep him awake at night. Maybe he was getting a rash or something. That was all he needed.

Helo turned a corner, intending to head for the showers to see if washing would help, then abruptly changed course for deck five. He knew where Tyrol kept his still, and right now a good drink would settle his nerves. He was on duty, but it never stopped Tigh, and Helo was suddenly in a go-to-hell mood.

Deck five was in an unusual lull. Crewmembers were engaged in busywork—cleaning, sorting equipment, taking inventory. Off to one side sat the escape pod Peter Attis had arrived in. Tyrol was walking in a circle around it, examining with a critical eye. A slight limp hobbled his steps a bit. Helo wandered over.

"What's going on, Chief?" he asked. "See something that's going to explode?"

"No." Tyrol wore a distracted expression. "There's something about this pod that bothers me. Has since the day it showed up. But I can't put my finger on it."

"You've checked inside," Helo stated.

"Of course. Thoroughly. With every instrument I have. Nothing."

"Let me take a look," Helo offered. "Maybe it needs a fresh pair of eyes."

Tyrol gave him a look with hard brown eyes. The offer went a little beyond their shaky truce.

"Putting off looking for . . . her?" Tyrol said at last.

"Maybe." Helo felt his face grow warm. "I haven't had much luck."

Tyrol flashed a grim smile of . . . understanding? He stood aside like a doorman. "Be my guest, sir."

Helo stepped into the pod. It was basically a gray metal cube with rounded corners. Helo's head brushed the ceiling, and he ducked instinctively. A simple control panel stood against the wall opposite the hatch, and two small ports looked out on deck five. A CO_2 scrubber hung on one wall above a set of oxygen tanks. The interior smelled vaguely of machine oil. And that was all. Helo examined the controls. Environmental readouts, automatic distress signal, engine power control. Nothing else. The engine would shove the pod in one direction—forward. No way to steer. The pod was meant to be picked up quickly by a rescue ship, not to provide transportation. Helo stood there for a long moment. He turned in all directions. He pulled the front off the control panel and looked inside. He paced the walls and rapped on the ports. Then he went back outside. His head itched again, and he forced himself not to scratch.

"Well?" Tyrol said.

Helo shrugged. "Nothing. I don't even get suspicious. Maybe you're just reading too much into it because a copy of . . . of *her* was inside."

"Maybe." But Tyrol clearly didn't believe it.

Helo's radio squawked for his attention. *"We've completed our search of the main galley, Lieutenant."*

With a sigh, Helo pulled the unit from his belt and spoke into it. "Continue on to the food storage area, then. And try not to die of boredom."

"Roger that."

He sketched a waved at Tyrol and started to move away, but Tyrol's touch on the shoulder stopped him.

"Chief?" Helo said.

Tyrol leaned close. "I hope they never find her, too," he murmured.

There didn't seem to be anything to say to that, so Helo just nodded and continued on his way. Helo skirted the edge of the main deck and headed for the storage rooms, pretending he was going to look there. Instead, he waited until no one was looking and ducked through a particular doorway. Freestanding metal shelves stacked with meticulously labeled parts stood in neat rows. Helo threaded a path to the rear. Behind a shelving unit stood a tangle of coils and drums. There was no smell—Tyrol had built a fan and filter system into the device to ensure the odor wouldn't give him away. Helo, however, walked past it and knelt in front of a meter-high grate set into the back wall. He tugged once, and it came away, revealing a small open space inside. Tyrol actually kept *two* stills. Commander Tigh had discovered the first one. Instead of shutting it down and ordering Tyrol's arrest, he had wordlessly begun taking a percentage of everything Tyrol made in it. When the percentage climbed to one jar in four, however, Tyrol had taken steps. He had scavenged enough parts to make a second still, one that created higher-quality stuff, and hidden that one more carefully. Tyrol now only made what he called "single malt engine cleaner" in the first still, and Tigh hadn't yet caught on to the ruse.

Helo poked his head into the space behind the grating. The still, compact and efficient, purred softly to itself beside a pile of jars filled with clear liquid. Helo reached for one—and froze.

"Hello," said Sharon Valerii.

CHAPTER 8

Billy Keikeya poked his head into the section of *Colonial One* that served as Laura Roslin's office. "Sarah Porter is here, Madam President."

"Thank you, Billy," Laura said. "Show her in."

Billy ducked back out and President Laura Roslin pulled herself upright in her chair. Gods, she was so *tired*. Gravity pulled at every limb with twice its normal strength, making every movement a struggle. And she ached all the time, whether she was awake or asleep. It was a deep, cold feeling, as if an icy dragon were gnawing at her bones. One day it would bite all the way through them, and she would keel over like a tree with severed roots. It had been going on for so long, she had forgotten what it was like to be pain free. Laura wanted nothing more than to pull on some old sweats, wrap herself in a soft bathrobe, and lie on the couch watching something mindless until she drifted into a restless sleep—or death. Instead she found herself on a chilly ship, an unwilling leader to the last remaining shreds of humanity left in the galaxy while implacable enemies chased them from sector to sector.

A wan smile crossed her face. *Playing the martyr again, Laura?* she thought. She had had several opportunities to hand the reins of government over to someone else and had waved aside every one. Hell, she had *fought* to remain president. Like all teachers, Laura had been trained to lead, but it wasn't her preference. She would much rather let someone else handle all the stress and nonsense while she worked quietly in the background. In her teaching days, she never chaired committees—unless no one else was willing to take the job. Or was qualified for it. She remembered the day Nick Liaden, her department head, had announced his retirement and Helga Upton had announced her intention to take over his position. Horrified, Laura spent her prep period running from classroom to classroom to see if anyone else planned to challenge Helga. Everyone refused. The thought of cold, officious Helga in charge made everyone unhappy, but no one was willing to step up. This one worked two other jobs and didn't have time. That one was pregnant and would be going on leave soon. A third was a new teacher, completely unqualified. So Laura had strode into the principal's office to announce that she wanted the position. He had been all too glad to give it to her, and Laura had spent four years in that capacity. Her experiences had given her many skills that she still used today.

Except none of those experiences had given her the skills to cope with dying. Laura reached for a pencil, intending to toy with it, then decided it wasn't worth the energy. Sometimes she felt as if she had accepted her impending death, other times she felt a gut-twisting terror that kept her awake late into the night. The concert two days ago had bolstered her spirits for a while, returning her to a time when her biggest worry was whether her students' math scores were going up or down. The boost in her mood hadn't lasted, however, and now, frankly, she was feeling pretty shitty all around. The last person she wanted to talk to was Sarah Porter. But duty called.

The curtain that covered the doorway parted and Sarah strode into the room like a thunderstorm laden with hail. She was a dark-skinned, full-bodied woman who preferred short hair and favored chunky gold earrings. Currently, she represented Geminon on the Quorum of Twelve, and Laura had mixed feelings toward her. Geminon had a well-deserved reputation for conservative political parties that tried to mix religion into government, and Sarah represented her people well. She had been one of Laura's most vociferous opponents early in her presidency, then had abruptly become a firm supporter once the Scrolls of Pythia had revealed Laura to be the fabled dying leader who would lead humanity to its new homeland. As an experienced politician, Laura was always willing to accept a supporter, but as a human being, Laura had a hard time pretending to like someone who had once professed to hate her.

And behind her . . .

Behind her came a tall, dark-haired man with the look of someone who had once been hard and handsome but had now gone rather to seed. Lines softened his sharp features, and his nose looked a little too big for his face. His expression was as bland as a mayonnaise sandwich, but Laura Roslin wasn't fooled for a moment.

"Tom Zarek," she said. "I thought my appointment was with Sarah alone."

"I asked to come," Tom said. "As a witness."

"Witness to what?" Laura asked.

"What transpires here," Sarah said.

Laura didn't like the sound of that at all. She briefly considered calling Billy in to throw Tom out, then dismissed the idea. Tom had spent considerable time in jail for inciting riots—and worse. He was an old-school revolutionary who distrusted all government on principle and who had a distressing amount of charisma that he could turn on and off like a light switch. It was currently set to "off," but Tom could fire up a crowd like no one Laura knew—except perhaps Peter Attis—and she envied Tom that talent even when he used it against her, as he had done. He had started a revolution among his fellow prisoners on the *Astral Queen*, a process that had ended up with Tom not only being granted his freedom, but also grabbing a seat on the Quorum of Twelve as the representative of Sagittaron. If Laura tossed Tom out of this meeting, he would raise hell about it in the media, and there was no way Laura could come away from it without looking bad.

"As you like," she said. "Please sit."

They did. Tom's face remained neutral, but Sarah wore an angry expression Laura knew well because it had often been pointed in Laura's direction. Laura tensed, which took energy she couldn't really spare.

"I hate to bother you with this," Sarah said, "but I don't know what else to do."

A wary bit of relief threaded through Laura. Porter wasn't here to cause Laura trouble, then—at least, not directly. So why Tom's presence?

"What's on your mind, Sarah?" Laura asked in her sympathetic voice.

"A fringe group that calls itself 'the Unity' has been causing problems," she said. "Especially on the *Tethys* and the *Phoebe*."

"Problems?" Laura asked. "What sort of problems?"

Porter's expression was set like stone. "They're spreading like can—like weeds. They stand in the corridors and local gathering places and *preach.*"

"What do they preach?" Laura noticed the switch from "cancer" to "weeds," but pretended not to. Sudden exhaustion swept over her, and she had to fight to keep from slumping in her chair. Uh-oh. The day was turning into a bad one. Her treacherous body did that to her, switching her from functional to exhausted without warning.

A look of disgust crossed Porter's face. "They wear red masks so we can't tell who they are and they preach that all the gods are merely multiple aspects of a single god. They preach that the single god is a being of love and kindness and that nothing else exists. This is heresy, Laura! Heresy *and* blasphemy! The Scrolls are very clear on—"

"I don't need a lecture on comparative spirituality, Sarah," Laura interrupted gently. "Though I have to say the ideas as you've presented them make me . . . uncomfortable. And they sound familiar."

"Of course they do," Porter spat. "Peter Attis sings about it. His songs are all over the radio now, especially that 'You're the Only One' song. These Unity people have taken it as some sort of spiritual call. Haven't you heard him? It seems like he shows up somewhere on the radio four or five times an hour."

"I haven't noticed," Laura admitted. "I went to the concert, and I have to say I enjoyed it very much"—*until the escaped Cylon showed up,* she added mentally—"but I really haven't had time or inclination for the radio lately."

Throughout this exchange, Tom remained silent. Laura's attention was on Sarah, but she was aware of Tom, much like the way a feeding rabbit remained aware of a hawk wheeling overhead. His presence made no sense, and it nagged at her like a hangnail that had almost come free. She was dying to ask what his real purpose was, but knew that would be a mistake. It would put him in the position of holding information she clearly wanted. Better to let him think she didn't care, rendering his information worthless and forcing him into a position of lesser power.

"Keeping in mind that we do have freedoms of speech and religion in the Colonies," Laura said carefully, "I need to ask—have the Unity people broken any laws?"

Long pause. Still Tom didn't speak.

"No," Porter said at last. "Their demonstrations have been peaceful and orderly so far. And so far they've agreeably moved out of the way whenever someone has asked. A few fights have started, but never by the Unity. Other people always hit first." She folded her arms. "People get upset and angry wherever the Unity goes. Perhaps we can arrest them on the grounds that they instigate unrest."

Alarm bells rang in Laura Roslin's head. Early in her career as president, Commander Adama and Colonel Tigh had accused her of instigating unrest and tried to force her out of office. She had resisted and eventually won her position and their respect, but the situation had been dicey for a while, and Laura had lived in fear that what remained of the Colonies was heading for a military dictatorship. Now Sarah Porter looked to be heading down a similar road, one that led to a religious dictatorship. But how should she turn Sarah aside? It was always best to convince rather than dictate, whether you were teaching or governing, but Laura was so damned *tired*. Her mind flowed like a slushy stream, and she couldn't get herself to focus.

Wake up! she told herself sternly. *You can sleep when you're dead, and the way things are going, that'll be right soon. So get your work done, woman.*

The room wavered like a desert mirage. What was the last thing Sarah had said? Something about arresting Unity members as dissidents. A small part of Laura agreed with Sarah's sentiments, wrongminded as they were. Maybe she could use her own sympathy to get Sarah's and bring her around. Dammit, she hated this. It was like being forced to work under the worst case of flu in history. A drain had opened and strength was rapidly flowing out of her. She could barely sit up now, but she had to find the strength to speak somewhere. Laura took one deep breath, then took a second. But before she could speak, Tom raised a finger.

"I need to interject here, Sarah," he said. "I feel duty-bound to remind you that it's the government's job to protect its citizens, and regardless of how we"—and Laura instantly caught Tom's careful use of *we* instead of *you*—"might feel about them, it sounds like the Unity members are actually victims who need protection. As government officials, we don't have the luxury of deciding who is worth protecting and who isn't. If the Unity is attacked, it's our job to defend its members."

Laura stared, unsure of her own ears. Tom was taking *her* side? Why?

But even as she asked, the answer came. Tom was all about the rights of the individual, no matter how difficult or inconvenient those rights might be. That included the rights of a religious minority. Laura had automatically assumed Tom was out to make trouble for her, but instead he was helping. She glanced at him with a small measure of respect, but he didn't seem to notice.

"I should defend heretics?" Porter's face was hard. "Tom, Geminon has a long history of careful adherence to the laws set down by the Lords of Kobol. These Unity people are damning themselves by their preachings and their beliefs."

"Then it'll be up to the Lords of Kobol to deal with them," Laura said. The words came with aching slowness, as if she had to pull them out of thick mud. "But in the meantime, we can't tell them what to believe or what to say."

"They're dangerous! Just listening to their lies turns my stomach and makes me fear for my soul." Porter got up and paced around the tiny office like an angry wolf. Laura envied her easy power, her fluid vitality. What would it be like to have strength to spare for pacing? She felt herself slump a little more. In minute she was going to collapse, she could feel it. Laura had to wrap this up, get Sarah out of her office before that happened.

"How can I let them spread such filth around Geminese ships?" Sarah continued, oblivious to Laura's distress. "They threaten everything Geminon stands for, and they need to be exterminated."

And then the words came to Laura. She murmured, "That sounds like something the Cylons would say."

That stopped Sarah Porter. She stared at Laura for a long moment, then turned and gazed out the window. Laura never could bring herself to call them "portholes." Stupid thought to have right before you were going to collapse. She needed to speak, but her energy was gone. The floor rocked slightly—a bad sign—and the words wouldn't come.

Tom came to her rescue. His charisma was in "on" mode now, and his presence filled the room like a brewing thunderstorm. "If you want another assessment," he said, "think of it this way. We'll turn the Unity into martyrs if we muzzle them or arrest them. It would probably be better to take the tone of a parent indulging the whims of a silly child. You know what I mean—'It's a phase. He'll grow tired of it and come around.' And if there is no truth to what they preach, the Unity will eventually collapse. Then you can look merciful and magnanimous by accepting its former members back into the fold." He flashed a grin. "Everyone wins."

Sarah continued staring out at the cold stars. Laura was holding herself upright now by sheer strength of will, and even that was fading fast. But if she dismissed Sarah now, it would look like Laura was ordering Sarah to agree with her instead of letting it happen naturally.

Please, Laura begged silently. *See it my way. Our way. Then both of you can go and I can collapse.*

"All right," Sarah said at last. "We'll try it that way. Thank you, Madam President. Tom."

Laura nodded acknowledgment. Her head weighed a thousand pounds and the motion almost broke her neck. Sarah left, and Tom was at the curtains. Her energy was gone, but somewhere she found a tiny spark that let her speak.

"Tom," she said. Her voice was soft partly out of calculation and partly out of necessity.

He stopped at the doorway and turned, eyebrows raised.

"Why?" She was whispering now. "Why take my side?"

Tom paused, and for a horrible moment Laura was sure he was going to say he had helped because she was dying. She didn't think she could stand the pity of someone like Tom Zarek.

"It's never been about you, Laura," he said softly. "It's been about the people."

He left. The moment the curtains fell shut behind Tom Zarek, Laura collapsed over her desk blotter. She lay there, half-conscious. In a minute she would have the strength to get up and move to the couch, but for now . . .

"Madam President?" An urgent hand shook her shoulder. "Madam President, are you all right? Should I call the doctor?"

Laura managed to raise her head enough to look into Billy Keikeya's eyes. "Doctor Cottle can't do anything, Billy. I just need to sleep."

"At least let me help you to the couch," he said. "Come on."

She was only vaguely aware of Billy's solicitous hands guiding her to the couch and helping her lie down. His presence comforted her more than it should have, and she wondered, not for the first time, what their relationship might have been if they hadn't been separated by multiple decades and several lines of professionalism. "Billy," she said. "I'm glad for your help."

"It's what I'm here for, Madam President," was all he said.

The still hissed quietly to itself. Helo remained frozen, his head still sticking into the space behind the grating that hid the little machine. Sharon knelt beside it, looking almost serene. She wore a bulky gray jumpsuit she must have scavenged or stolen from somewhere. It looked warm, and it completely hid her rounding stomach. Helo couldn't even tell she was pregnant.

"Frak," Helo whispered. "Sharon, are you okay?"

"Perfectly fine," she said. "Though now that you've seen me, I may have to kill you."

Helo went cold all over. Sharon could do it. He had seen her move inhumanly fast before, and she was strong as a steel spider. "You wouldn't," he said, hoping he sounded braver than he felt.

"Actually, I haven't decided yet. That's why you're still alive, Helo."

"Why . . ." Helo swallowed. "Why did you kill the guard? You could have just knocked him out. Hell, why escape at all?"

Sharon snorted. "You have to ask?"

"I do. Dammit, Sharon, you've done nothing but help us before. Why run now?"

"The reason's standing in front of you, Helo," Sharon scoffed. "But you're too stupid to see it. After everything I've done for *Galactica*, you still kept me in a cage. You treat me like an enemy."

"I don't."

"Well, no," Sharon admitted. "That's true. But you haven't tried to persuade Adama to release me, either."

"How do you know what I have or haven't done?"

"If you really tried—really, really tried—you could get me released. So frak it. You treat me like an enemy, I'm going to act like one. It's a hell of a lot more interesting than sitting in a cell all day, Helo."

"How did you get out, anyway?"

"Please," she snorted again. "That little box you call a jail? Not even close. I only pretended that cardboard brig could hold me. Adama would have spaced me if he had known otherwise."

"But now you're in worse trouble," Helo pointed out, trying to remain calm and reasonable. Sharon sat serenely, but he saw coiled springs and sheathed claws in her body language. He felt like he had found a tiger in his closet, or maybe a time bomb. "Half the ship is hunting for you."

"Like they'll ever find me."

"I did."

"Because I let you."

"The platoons—"

Sharon waved this off. "You're not creative enough to look in *all* the places someone could hide. You just look in the places where you *think* someone could hide. I'm a lot more bendable than a human. You guys don't bend—you break."

"What about our baby?" Helo said. "Didn't you think of that before you escaped?"

"The baby," she repeated. "Yes, I thought about it. I decided it would be better for it to die free than live in a prison."

"Commander Adama would never imprison a baby," Helo protested.

"Oh, sure. And she'd have a fine life, right? A half-breed, living among humans. You have a great track record for love and tolerance. Admit it—you think of the baby as half Cylon."

"As opposed to?" Helo asked, a bit of anger edging past the fear.

"Half human."

That stopped Helo. He had to admit Sharon was right. He thought of the baby as half Cylon, meaning he focused on the nonhuman aspect. And the baby was his own. How would other people react to such a child? Would they see a child or a creature that was half enemy? The answer was obvious.

"How would *your* people see the baby?" he countered. "As half human?"

"We want babies, Helo," she reminded him almost gently. "This one would be precious—the first baby born to a Cylon ever."

"But your people killed babies," Helo shot back. "Thousands of them. Hundreds of thousands."

"Are you trying to guilt me into turning myself in?" she asked. "It won't work. I'm not going back to that cell. It's more interesting out here. There's more to do, causing trouble for the Fleet. And you don't have a hope of catching me. Even if I decide not to kill you, I'll be long gone before you can call the marines."

"And what about when you're too pregnant to get around well? Or when the baby is born? You can't hide a crying baby."

"I'll worry about it then." She leaned toward him over the still, and Helo had to force himself not to draw away. Abruptly she grabbed his face with both hands and yanked him into a long, hard kiss. Her lips were cool. He forced himself not to struggle—she could break his neck. Maybe she was planning to. A part of Helo wondered if he looked ridiculous, with his ass hanging out of the vent space and his torso pulled over a still. Then Sharon released him.

"So that's what it's like," she murmured.

Helo blinked to clear his head. It was buzzing. "What do you mean?"

"Just Cylon talk," she said. "You'd better get going now. I'm not going to kill you."

"Yeah?" His tone was slightly sarcastic. "Because I'm a good kisser?"

"Because someone else just might do the job for me."

Before he could respond, alarms blared all over the ship.

CHAPTER 9

"Report, Mr. Gaeta," snapped Adama.

"Ten—make that *twelve*—Cylon raiders and one heavy raider at the edge of DRADIS range," Gaeta said crisply. "No basestar."

"Thank the gods for small favors," Tigh muttered.

"Set Condition One," Adama ordered, and Tigh reached for the PA phone to comply. "Get the Vipers out there. Dualla, how close is the *Monarch* to clearing the planet?"

"*This is Colonel Tigh. Set Condition One throughout the Fleet,*" Tigh's voice boomed from the loudspeakers. "*Repeat: Set Condition One.*"

"Captain Demeter estimates half an hour, sir," Dee replied.

"One side or the other will be dead by then," Tigh said, dropping the receiver into its cradle. A loud *clunk* thudded from the PA system—Tigh had forgotten to shut off the PA before he hung up. Dualla winced as the sound echoed in her headphone. "Why would they send such a small force? They have to know that we can eat a tiny group like that for breakfast."

"Maybe it's a scouting mission," Gaeta said.

Adama eyed the DRADIS readout as it growled to itself. Twelve little Cylon raiders buzzed toward the Fleet. It sounded like a nursery rhyme. *Twelve little raiders buzzing from the heavens. Vipers ate one and that left eleven.* They moved steadily forward, like barracuda skimming toward a wounded fish. Except this particular fish was a shark, and the barracuda in question were smart enough to know better. What the hell was going on?

"Scouting parties have all been smaller than this," Adama said. "And raiding parties have always been bigger. This doesn't add up. Dualla, do we have radio connection with the Viper squadron yet?"

"Affirmative, sir." Dualla threw a switch, and distorted voices filtered from the CIC speakers.

"Listen up," Adama said loudly. "There's something odd going on this time around. The enemy is up to something strange, and I want all of you to use extra care." Even as he gave the order, he realized how idiotic it sounded. The Viper pilots *always* used extra care. Anyone who flew out using anything less was unlikely to return.

"*Got it, sir,*" Lee said, and Adama felt the usual mix of pride and fear—pride that his son was CAG, fear that he would never come back.

"*Maybe they thought we were gone,*" Kara said. "*Figured they'd get Planet Goop for themselves.*"

"*Maybe they want to work on their tans,*" Hot Dog said. "*Or maybe they want tickets to the next Attis concert.*"

"*Table the conversation,*" Lee ordered. "*We have a mission.*"

"*Roger that,*" Kat said. "*Roger dodger codger with a pipe.*"

Adama shot Tigh a glance.

"*What was that, Kat?*" Starbuck said. "*I didn't copy.*"

"*I said, 'We'll smash 'em flat.'*"

Adama gave a mental shrug. Radio distortion, must be. But Tigh looked concerned, and Adama was afraid his own face wore the same expression.

The first Cylon raider dipped and swooped against the starry black background. Kara's cross-hairs dipped and swooped just behind it on her screen. Her breath sounded harsh and steady inside her helmet.

"Come on, frakker," she muttered. "Come on."

Then the raider zigged when it should have bet on zag. Kara thumbed the fire button. She felt more than heard the soft thump of gunfire, and the raider went up in the usual yellow fireball. It was amazing, actually. The single flick of her thumb destroyed an enemy. A small action that precipitated an enormous consequence. The ultimate in power and control. She loved it. Out here, she was in control of her own destiny. Out here, the choices were crisp and clear, with no emotional tangles. It was fly the ship, destroy the enemy. Nothing else mattered. Lee only mattered as her CAG, and Peter . . .

. . . Peter didn't matter at all.

It had been almost three days since their . . . encounter after the concert. Kara had slid out of Peter's bed without awakening him, dressed, and slipped out. No emotional tangles, thanks. It wasn't what she wanted right now. She had lost Zak Adama, her fiancé, to a flight accident. She had lost Samuel Anders, another lover, to the resistance movement he was still fighting back on Caprica. She didn't need to get involved with someone else right now.

But another part of her remembered Peter's mouth on hers, the way he touched her, the way he had sung to her after their lovemaking had ended. Her loneliness hadn't disappeared, but it had certainly ebbed. Still, he hadn't tried to contact her, and she hadn't tried to contact him, not even to get tickets for his second concert, which was tonight. And that was for the best.

It sure was.

Another raider came about and trained its guns on her. Kara casually twitched her joystick and her Viper smoothly skimmed out of range. Then she abruptly reversed, flipped over, and fired back in the direction she had come. The raider exploded. Kara twitched the joystick again, the Viper came about, and once again she was facing the rest of the raiding party. A strange emotion came over her—calm mixed with exultation. It felt as if her senses had merged with the Viper and stretched out to encompass the rest of the squadron and the Cylon raiding party. She could see exactly what needed to be done and exactly how to do it. Kara allowed herself a small grin. She recognized the feeling—she was heading into the Zone. Her grin widened. A pilot who hit the Zone could do no wrong, make no mistakes, remained invincible. It was a glorious—and rare—place to hit. Better than a runner's high. Better than sex, better than art, better than music. Better than life.

The other raiders fell back out of firing range and spread out, as if creating a net. Behind them hovered the blocky form of the heavy raider. Kara could see every detail—the exact shade of red of each scanning Cylon eye, the position of every star, the tiny flare of every rocket booster. Around her, flying in perfect formation, was the rest of the squadron—Lee, Kat, Hot Dog, Mack, Ukie, and Powerball. Kara knew where they were without even looking.

"Nice shooting," Lee said.

"Roger that," Kara said. "I'm in the Zone."

"Chaldena talush saemal," came Hot Dog's voice. *"Vili ve."*

"Hot Dog, are you all right?" Lee said. *"I didn't copy that."*

There was a pause. *"I t-tried to s-say it was pretty impressive,"* Hot Dog replied. *"I've never b-b-been in the Zone."*

"That's not what it sounded like you said," Kara put in. "It sounded like nonsense."

Hot Dog didn't answer. The Cylons hovered, still out of range, still waiting. Kara felt the moment, the Zone, slipping away.

"Let's go in and get 'em," she barked.

"I'm CAG, Lieutenant. CAG stands for 'guy who's in charge,' " Lee reminded her. Brief pause. *"Okay, blow them out of the sky!"*

Kara vaulted forward, then yanked her Viper upward to avoid a spray of fire from one of the raiders. She brought her nose around, snapped the crosshairs into position, and fired. The Cylon quivered under the hail of bullets, then soundlessly blew up in a satisfying ball of flame.

"That's three!" Kara whooped.

"Kildra nash," Hot Dog shouted. His Viper overtook hers and

rushed straight at the hole Kara had made in the line of raiders. Except his ship jumped and wobbled like a baby bird just learning to fly. It jerked around, then abruptly skewed sideways, dropping out of Kara's line of sight.

"*What the hell are you doing, Hot Dog?*" Lee demanded. He fired at a raider, and it exploded. Only eight left, plus the heavy raider. Kat and Powerball were engaged in a dogfight with a pair of Cylons. Mack failed to dodge a third raider quickly enough, and his Viper shuddered under his opponent's fire.

"*I'm losing altitude control!*" he shouted. "*Frak! I can barely keep myself upright.*"

Kara punched her own thrusters and zipped into the space between Mack and the Cylon. She spun about and fired. The Cylon jerked as she raked one of its wings. It climbed, trying to get around her.

"Get back to the *Galactica*, Mack!" Kara ordered. "Go!"

"*Nultani nultanil reb!*" Hot Dog said. "*Fleg anzara bekki!*"

Kara glanced at her screen. She had forgotten about him. Hot Dog's Viper bobbled about her readout like a drunken spider. A raider zeroed in on him, diving like a falcon reaching for a rabbit. Her heart lurched. Shadow's death loomed in her mind, but Kara was too far away to do anything about it.

"*I got him,*" Yukie said, and gunned the Cylon down.

"*Hot Dog, respond!*" Lee ordered. "*Brendan!*"

But Hot Dog only spouted more gibberish. His Viper continued to fly in erratic lines. Beyond him, Kat and Powerball destroyed their Cylons, leaving only five and the heavy raider. They hovered silently in place, almost as if they were watching.

"*Got it!*" Powerball howled. "*One more dead mother-frakkin' Cylon.*"

"*Yilt denow!*" Kat said. "*We rock!*"

Kara's blood ran cold. "Repeat that, Kat. You sounded like Hot Dog for a minute there."

"*Bedlom pilt kareem Hot Dog,*" she said. And her Viper began to wobble, too.

"*Shit!*" Lee said. "*What the hell is going on? Kat, Hot Dog, and Mack—haul it back to* Galactica. *Move it! The rest of you, wipe out the rest of the Cylons.*"

Kara flipped her Viper around to orient on the remaining enemy ships. But even as she punched up her thrusters, six flashes of white light blasted across her retina. The Cylons vanished into hyperspace.

"They're gone?" Kara said. "Just like that?"

"*Maybe they figured we were winning,*" Lee said.

"Viper squadron, this is Galactica *Actual,"* Commander Adama's voice broke in. *"Return to* Galactica *immediately. And I want all of you in sickbay."*

Kat and Hot Dog landed unevenly. Both of them needed steady encouragement and orders to stay focused, and both of them spoke a steady stream of nonsense words laced with occasional snatches of normal speech. Kara landed her own Viper, the clamps engaged, and the elevator went through its usual descent. The moment her canopy opened, Kara yanked off her vac suit helmet and vaulted clear of the little ship. A small swarm of people had surrounded Kat's and Hot Dog's Vipers, and both pilots were being helped down to the deck. Kara caught a glimpse of Hot Dog's pale face. His mouth was moving, but she couldn't catch the words. Abruptly he went into convulsions. A stream of unintelligible words rolled from his mouth. Kara's stomach turned. Illness always creeped her out. It was worse when someone she liked was sick, and she liked Hot Dog. When a bunch of *Galactica's* pilots had died in an accident, Adama had ordered Kara, an experienced flight instructor, to shove him, Kat, and several others through intensive flight training. She knew him fairly well as a result, and she fervently hoped both he and Kat would be all right.

Hot Dog continued to babble. His eyes were wide open and alert, his expression both frightened and mystified. It looked as if he knew what was going on, but was powerless to stop it. Looking at him sent a chill down Kara's spine.

"Medic!" someone shouted. "Get him a stretcher!"

"He's speaking in tongues," said someone else. "The Lords of Kobol speak through him!"

That hushed the onlookers. Kara blinked. She knew of the concept, had heard that some Oracles went into strange fits that foretold the future or channeled the Lords of Kobol themselves. Was that the source of her unease? Were the Lords of Kobol present? Kara fought an urge to look over her shoulder.

Over by her own Viper, Kat kept her feet with the assistance of a repair technician. "Green eyes like a cat mouse in a trapdoor in a barn horse riding into the sunset," she said. "F-frak! I'm . . . I can't keep my key in the lock of my brainwave pattern of a dress my mother sewed for her tenth anniversary."

A medic appeared with a stretcher, and several people were helping Hot Dog onto it. Lee was among them. Hot Dog continued to thrash and babble. Kara dashed over to Kat and put a hand on her forehead. It was hot and moist. Her dark skin had a ghoulish cast to it.

"She has a fever," the repair tech said. "I can feel it through her clothes."

"Kat, can you hear me?" Kara demanded, looking into her eyes. "Can you tell me what's wrong?"

"I . . . I have no idea what's up in the sky with pie and apples and pears of two or three green leaves. Pel dar mayfel nam! Frak!" She shook her head. "I'm trying . . ."

"Try not to talk." Kara ducked under one of Kat's arms while the technician ducked under the other. They lifted Kat partly off her feet. "Let's get you to sickbay along with Hot Dog."

"Bun in a refrigerator," Kat agreed.

"I don't know what to make of it," Cottle sighed. He ground his cigarette out in the ashtray on Adama's desk. "I've got three people babbling and convulsing in my sickbay with no idea what's behind it. Meds help, though they just treat the symptoms, not the cause. I'm stumped. I'm waiting for some more test results to filter through, but so far I'm finding no viruses, no bacteria, not even a protozoan. But some weird agent is attacking their brains."

"What exactly does this agent do?" Adama asked. He was sitting rigidly behind his desk, forcing himself not to drum his fingers or tap his feet. This was not good news, and he was so frakking *tired* of bad news. Two pilots incapacitated, possibly dying. Chief Tyrol nearly mowed down. Tiredness washed over him. Another three or four cats had been added to the pile he was juggling.

"Just reading from their symptoms," Cottle said, "I think it attacks the language and motor control centers first. This, by the way, means the little sucker can cross the blood-brain barrier, which isn't easy. It's why brain diseases are so rare."

"You're sure it's a disease," Adama said. "Not something else."

A knock came at the door and Gaeta poked his head into the room. "I'm sorry to interrupt, Commander, but you wanted to be informed the moment the *Monarch*'s crew had cleared Planet Goop."

"Thank you, Lieutenant. Are the Jump coordinates still good?"

"I've been keeping them updated," Gaeta replied.

"Then let's get the hell out of this sector," Adama said. "Order all ships to Jump immediately."

"Sir." Gaeta vanished.

"I'm not ruling anything out at this point," Cottle said, answering Adama's earlier statement. "Radiation exposure, toxin, something in the food. I don't know. The problem is, I can't find a common vector.

Hyksos works on the *Monarch*. Kat and Hot Dog, as everyone likes to call them, are Viper pilots. They don't all three know each other, they don't eat the same food or drink the same water. All three have been in space recently, but that was after they were showing symptoms. My gut says it might be something from Planet Goop simply because it's the only new thing that's been introduced to all of us, but I have no evidence to support that. Hell, I don't even know if this thing is contagious or not."

Adama felt the sudden strange shift that indicated the ship's Jump drive was powering up. It was as if his clothes were turning inside-out with him still inside them. A bit of nausea sloshed through his stomach, he felt a slight *wrench*, and it was over. Jump successful. Cottle didn't seem particularly bothered, and Adama kept his own face impassive. He straightened his glasses and continued the conversation. "What are you doing to learn more?"

"All kinds of tests on every body fluid and tissue I can reach. Dr. Baltar is doing the same, though His Majesty hasn't deigned to report anything to me, so I don't know if he's found anything."

"I'm sure he'd say something to one of us if he did," Adama said.

"Sure," Cottle drawled. "It's not like he's weird or strange or anything. Always well-behaved in public, that's our vice president."

"Kara! Kara Thrace!"

Kara spun and came face-to-face with Peter Attis. He leaned down and gave her a quick kiss before she could react. Two passing repair techs turned to stare.

"Uh, hi," she said, caught off guard. She felt strangely breathless and struggled to hide it.

"I was beginning to think you'd forgotten who I am," he said with a grin. Then the grin faded. "You haven't, have you?"

She looked at him, and all her earlier cautions came flooding back. She didn't need to get involved with anyone right now. She didn't need to be tied down or entangled.

She didn't need to.

But that was it, wasn't it? She didn't *need* to. But that didn't mean she couldn't. Kara tossed her doubts aside with a laugh, then gave Peter a brief hug and stole an ass-grab in the process. His butt cheek was firm with muscle, and she liked the way it filled her hand. Peter stiffened, then laughed himself. It was a liquid, masculine sound that flowed over her with unexpected warmth. She drew him into a side corridor so they wouldn't block traffic or garner more stares, then gave him a kiss of her own, a longer one this time. Her body pressed against his, and she could feel his response.

"I haven't forgotten," she said. "But I wasn't sure you wanted to see me again. Rock star always moving on and all that."

"Give up my number one groupie? You have to be kidding! Besides, what would the tabloids say?"

She laughed again. It was *fun* to laugh with Peter. She kissed him again, thanking the gods that she was officially off duty and able to steal a few kisses without violating regs.

"Are you coming to the concert tonight?" he asked. "I've got tickets for you and for . . . for Lee, if you want to bring him."

And suddenly she was reluctant. "I don't know," she said. "I have the feeling . . . we just came away from a Cylon raid, and it was a little weird. They Jumped away just when things were getting interesting."

"Well that's *good* news, isn't it?"

"Yeah . . ." Kara reached up and smoothed a bit of his hair. "But it doesn't feel right." She thought about telling Peter about Kat and Hot Dog, then changed her mind. No one had said to keep the problem quiet, but she wasn't sure it was a good idea to spread the information around the Fleet. "My instincts tell me to stay on alert status, even though I'm off duty until tomorrow."

Peter took her hand. "Look, if you won't come to the concert, then have dinner with me. On *Cloud 9*. They feed me pretty well over there. What do you say?"

Okay, that'd be great. "Not sure," she said.

"Look, you work hard defending us. You deserve some 'me' time. And it's only dinner. Not like it's an entire evening. What do you say?"

She wavered. Fresh after a Jump was usually the safest time. It would take the Cylons some time to track them down again. If she wanted to grab some R&R, this was the best opportunity.

"All right," she said. "Where should we meet?"

"Can you find the Gilded Lily?" he asked.

Her eyes widened a little. "Sure! But they're pretty expensive. Especially now."

"The owner's a fan," Peter said, a smile in his eyes. "Meet me there at five, okay? I have to be backstage by seven."

"Sounds perfect."

He gave her another kiss, then turned and strode away. Kara watched him go, noticing the little bounce in his step.

• • •

Gaius Baltar frowned into the microscope eyepiece. A crowd of red blood cells and occasional white blood cells drifted slowly through a sea of plasma. He refocused, bringing the image closer. A donut-shaped red blood cell, or platelet, ballooned to the size of a basketball. Using precise nudges of the controls, he edged the slide a few microns to the left. The platelet slid sideways a little, and Gaius brought the focus in even tighter. Some of the larger individual molecules were starting to take shape now, emerging in fractal patterns on the platelet's cell membrane and in the plasma itself. A little closer, and . . .

There it was. A clump of molecules that had caught his eye earlier. He moved in closer yet so he could examine a single one. It looked like three twisted ribbons attached to each other by twisted threads at the ends. It wasn't a virus or bacillus, that much was obvious. It was a single molecule, protein if he was any judge. And he was.

"What did you find, Gaius?" Number Six asked breathily in his ear.

"I think," he said without taking his eyes off the slide, "it's a prion."

"A prion?" she repeated. Her tone sounded like she knew exactly what one was, but Baltar couldn't help explaining, showing off what he had discovered.

"Prions are protein fragments that aren't viruses but can act like them. They often attack the nervous system, especially the brain."

"Really." Six sounded bored. Baltar ignored this.

"Yes. It won't show up on a normal test for a virus or bacillus because it isn't one. When they attach to nerve cells, they can interfere with neurological activity, even destroy brain tissue." He stared at the tiny bit of protein. "But this one . . . this one I've never seen before."

"Where did it come from?"

"Hyksos, the harvest worker."

"No, Gaius—I mean originally."

"Oh." He shrugged. "No idea."

A pair of soft hands caressed his back. "Amazing how something so small, so insignificant, can be so powerful." Gaius felt Six's touch tingle through him, setting off little waves of desire. He forced himself to continue staring at the molecule. It drifted away from the red blood cell and rotated slowly in the plasma. Gaius pressed a switch, and a micro-camera captured an image. Six ran a finger down the side of his neck, and he shuddered.

"Pay attention to me, Gaius," she whispered, her breath hot in his ear. "Don't ignore me."

He turned on his stool to look at her, and his jaw dropped. Six wore a short skirt, high-heeled sandals, and nothing else. Her bare breasts were tantalizingly within reach. Her presence contrasted sharply with the machinelike utilitarian lab around her.

"You . . . you . . ." He cleared his throat and tried again. "You've never struck me as the needy female type."

She leaned into him, her warm softness pressing against his body. "I need some 'me' time. And so do you."

There seemed to be a joke in what she said, but Gaius didn't get it, and Six didn't explain.

"I don't think so," he said, though his face felt flushed. "I need to track down exactly what this thing is."

Rather than respond, Six drew him off the stool and pulled him toward one of the work tables. Gaius didn't resist. She boosted herself up on it and leaned back slightly, her lips parted, her platinum hair falling backward.

"Kiss me, Gaius," she said. "Now."

He leaned toward her. She put up a hand.

"Not there," she said. "This is for me."

When the door opened a few minutes later, Dr. Cottle entered the lab and found Gaius Baltar kneeling in a strange position behind one of the tables. Both his arms rested on the tabletop as if his hands were cupping something. Cottle blinked and shifted his cigarette from one side of his mouth to the other.

"Did you lose something, Dr. Baltar?" Cottle said.

Gaius shot upright, his face bright red, his brain moving fast. "No . . . no. I was just . . . doing some stretching exercises." He demonstrated some deep knee bends and winced a little. "See? I get cramped up, sitting on these stools all day long."

"I hear you," Cottle said. He was carrying an uneven file folder filled with papers, and he set it on the table. "Though deep knee bends won't stretch you much. I just dropped by to tell you Hyksos has slipped into a full-blown coma and those Viper pilots stay quiet only when they're pumped full of ativan. I've got a whole ream of test results here, but nothing comes up. I came down to see if you've got anything."

"I do, actually," Gaius said, gesturing at the microscope. He was flushed and slightly sweaty. Dammit, why did people insist on walking in on him during private moments? "Take a look."

Cottle did. "What am I looking at?"

"I think it's a prion," Baltar told him. His groin ached.

Cottle whistled. "Now why the hell didn't I think to look for that? Dammit. And you're right. Come on." He straightened and headed for the door.

"Where are we going?" Baltar asked, giving chase.

"Back to sickbay, where else? I want to scan a few brains."

Cottle made his way down the corridors of *Galactica*, not seeming to hurry, but somehow forcing Gaius into a trot to keep up. Down in sickbay, he summoned two med techs to roll Hyksos's bulky, quiescent body down to the corner where they kept the image scanner. Hyksos's face was pale and still, and Gaius was barely able to make out his breathing. Something suddenly occurred to Gaius, something that made his heart lurch, and he sidled up to Cottle as the techs slid Hyksos onto the scanner shelf.

"Some prions can be transmitted from host to host," he murmured. "What do you think of the possibility that these could . . ."

"It's already crossed my mind," Cottle murmured back. He puffed smoke from the side of his mouth. "I don't think we need to bring that up with the general public just yet, though."

"Of course, of course. I'm sure everything will be fine, in any case." But Gaius's entire body had gone cold. Prions generally weren't easily contagious. In most cases, one had to bring the prion directly into the body, usually by eating it in contaminated food or by direct introduction into the blood. Easily transmittable prions were pure theory, known only as projections on paper. Or were they?

"Look at this, Doctor," Cottle said, pointing at the scanner readout screens. They showed images of Hyksos's brain activity. The entire system was darkened—the man was in a coma—but Cottle zoomed in on the left hemisphere. "There. The language centers show severely depressed activity. And over here—motor function. The damage is more extensive than in the other areas, which means they were probably attacked first. No wonder the patients convulse and spout gibberish."

Gaius slowly and deliberately pulled on a pair of sterile gloves. Without a word, he pulled a cotton swab from a drawer, pried Hyksos's mouth open, and collected a sample of saliva. Then he slid another swab into Hyksos's nose. It was difficult—the shelf of the scanner was in the way—but he managed.

"What are you doing?" Cottle demanded.

"I should think it was obvious," Gaius said, and he all but ran back to his lab. When Cottle arrived some time later, he found Gaius hunched over his microscope, not kneeling behind the table.

"What's going on?" Cottle said. "What are you thinking?"

Gaius pushed himself back from the microscope. "See for yourself. I've already run a few tests. This prion is present in Hyksos's saliva and his mucus. I've exposed this one to low temperatures, high temperatures, UV radiation, and a dry atmosphere. It holds cohesion."

"Oh, shit." Cottle leaned against a table. "You think it's contagious."

"Just like the flu," Gaius agreed. His voice was flat. He felt oddly detached, strangely calm. The panic, he was sure, would come later. He had just spent a goodly amount of time in sickbay with three people who carried what appeared to be a deadly contagious disease. Number Six was nowhere to be found, and he was dying to talk to her about this. She was the one who had suggested he visit sickbay in the first place, which meant she had to know something.

"Where the hell did it come from?" Cottle muttered. "Frak! What's new on the ship?"

"The algae, perhaps," Gaius said. "Though that doesn't seem likely. None of the other people on the *Monarch* have come down with this condition, and the other two patients are Viper pilots."

"Brain diseases are funny that way," Cottle pointed out. "One person contracts it and falls into a coma almost immediately, another contracts it, and lives for months without showing a single symptom. No one knows why the hell it happens that way, but it does. One of the Viper pilots could be Patient Zero, or it could be someone who hasn't shown symptoms at all."

"We can't find Patient Zero until we know what vectors the other patients have in common," Gaius said. "Of course, knowing the first person to contract it would help us figure out where this came from."

"So what do all three patients have in common?" Cottle asked, clearly thinking out loud. "Something that other people don't."

"Actually, we could all have come down with it months ago, long before the Cylon attack on the Colonies," Gaius pointed out. "Perhaps these patients are just the first to show symptoms."

Cottle eyed him. "Do you honestly think that's likely?"

"No," Gaius admitted. "But we can't afford to restrict our thinking at this stage."

"We still need to establish *some* sort of parameter," Cottle argued. "Two Viper pilots and a worker on a mining ship. Do they all three know each other?"

"Not that I know of, and unfortunately we can't ask them." He looked into the microscope again. The ribbony prion seemed to stare obstinately back up at him. "I doubt it's the algae. We'll have to check samples, of course, but as far as I know, prions that can infect humans simply don't hang about in primitive plant life. Something else must have brought this thing aboard."

Cottle took a nervous drag on his cigarette. "So what else is new to the Fleet?"

Peter Attis stood in the middle of a group of people, raised his glass in a mock toast, and said something Kara couldn't hear. Everyone around him laughed. Kara eyed him warily. She had been expecting a date sort of thing—two people, one table, candle, lots of innuendo. Instead, when she had arrived at the Gilded Lily, she had been ushered into a private banquet hall. There, Kara had found Peter holding forth to a roomful of maybe two dozen people, none of whom she recognized. A group of about ten had clustered around Peter, while the others stood around in uncertain small groups. A pre-concert party, perhaps? Whatever the case, it had caught her off guard. She felt annoyed that Peter hadn't warned her. Hell, she had even borrowed a dress from Dualla for the occasion. An angry look crossed her face and she elbowed her way toward him through the crowd.

". . . can't believe you're actually here," a young woman gushed. "We've been waiting for so long."

"Waiting for what?" Kara asked a little too brightly.

"Kara!" Peter swept her into an unexpected kiss. Kara let him, but only just. The onlookers waited politely. "Glad you made it!"

"Who are your friends?" Kara said. "When you asked me if I wanted to have dinner, I didn't think you meant an entire banquet."

The gushing lady, a small, dark-haired woman, grabbed Kara's hand and shook it. "You're so lucky," she said. "Peter chose you for his consort."

"Consort?" Kara echoed. "Listen, lady—"

"That's not quite what she meant," Peter said quickly. "Louann, please. Kara's a good friend."

"But someone like you deserves a consort," Louann said, clearly shocked. "I can find one for you, if you like."

Peter was actually blushing. "Not today, thanks."

"Peter," Kara said in her "someone's going to get hurt soon and it won't be me" voice, "what the frak is going on?"

"Blasphemy!" said a man in shock. "That sort of language in front of the Chosen."

Before Kara could respond to this, Peter spoke up. "If by 'chosen' you mean 'chosen by the Cylons,' you can keep it."

"But they were the ones who taught you the Unity Path," Louann said.

"Yes," Peter acknowledged with a duck of his head. "But it wasn't fun or pleasant."

"'And the Unifier shall walk among the Enemy, and He shall return both changed and unharmed,'" the young man intoned.

"What's the frakking Unifier?" Kara demanded.

"They're saying," Peter spoke up before the man could bring up blasphemy again, "that the Sacred Scrolls predict the arrival of a leader."

"That's President Roslin," Kara said waspishly. "The dying leader. Everyone knows that."

"No," the man said. "That's from the Book of Pythia. The Book of Glykon predicts the arrival of a spiritual leader who will bring all the tribes together, a Unifier. It says, 'The Unifier shall have a Voice of Gold, and He will save Humanity with the Plague of the Tongue.'"

"And," added Louann, "Glykon goes on to say, 'The Unifier will bring together all Humans into one Tribe under one God.' Peter's music—the golden voice—talks about the One. When Alexander and I"—here she took the man's hand—"heard Peter sing his new song at the concert, it was like a bolt of lightning struck us both. We knew he was it. The Unifier. He will lead us all to the next level of spirituality. He will convince everyone that all the gods are merely facets of a single entity."

Kara suddenly felt uneasy, as if someone might be listening in. Perhaps the gods. She turned to Peter. "Do you believe that? Do you believe that the Lords of Kobol—Zeus, Athena, Artemis, all of them—are all different facets of a single god?"

Peter nodded. "I do. Humans can't comprehend the true nature of a deity, so we divide the One up into pieces we can comprehend."

"And the Cylons taught you this," Kara said. Her scalp prickled, as if her hair were about to stand up. "Philosophy from a toaster."

"Not exactly." Peter ran a hand through blond hair. "It might be better to say that the Cylons helped me realize the truth. They didn't convert me to their religion—they didn't even try—but I lived among them as a slave for all those months, and several truths were revealed to me during that time."

"Most spiritual leaders go through a time of trial before truth comes to them," Alexander pointed out. He was in his forties, and his dark hair had receded almost completely. He needed a trim, however, and his remaining hair stood out like a mane on an aging lion. One of his hands shook slightly. Kara wondered if he had palsy.

Kara gave the room an uneasy glance. A sizeable group was still listening to the exchange, hanging on every word. Suddenly she wished Lee was there, and that thought made her even more uneasy. Lee would be a bright, solid presence in this place where words spun around like shadows. Peter stood in the center of the room, a sun god surrounded by lesser, darker beings. Kara realized she was in the center with him. As a consort? She pushed that thought aside. Conflicting emotions tugged at her like restless children. She wanted to stand by Peter, feel his warmth and wallow in their shared sexuality. She also wanted to run away, leave his strange ideas far behind and bury them in the shadows.

And then a server announced dinner would be served and everyone needed to take their seats. The little crowd dispersed. Peter showed Kara to a chair at his right, and Kara decided to let him. No point in giving up a good meal over someone else's blasphemy.

The table itself was set with a linen tablecloth and linen napkins. The water glasses were thick, heavy goblets, and the silverware shone like clear water captured beneath a monstrous chandelier. Even during times of struggle, you could find luxury if you looked hard enough or had good enough connections. Earlier in her life, Kara would have felt out of place and uncertain in such grand surroundings, but a military officer quickly learned manners proper for any occasion. When in doubt, pretend the host was your commanding officer and everything else would follow.

Servers brought bowls of salad—fresh algae—and Peter took up a spot at the head of the table, where he addressed the room. He raised his water glass.

"A toast," he said. "First, to Kara Thrace for saving my life, leading me to all of you, and showing me that I don't need to feel lonely or afraid. Long may she live!"

"Long may she live!" repeated the room.

Slightly mollified, Kara nodded to everyone as they thumped their glasses twice on the table and drank to her health. Peter flashed her his trademark wide grin. But she was still unsettled. What the hell was this about? Had Peter made this many friends since she had brought him into the Fleet? She supposed it was possible. He was a celebrity, and celebrities rarely had trouble finding friends—or acquaintances and suckups, anyway. She glanced down the long table, trying to see what, if anything, everyone had in common. Almost everyone was her age or younger. The sole exceptions were Louann and Alexander. Both sexes seemed to be equally represented.

Kara took up her fork and tried a bite of salad. It was dark green and cold, with a slight salty tang. Surprisingly good. It was the first fresh greenery she had eaten in weeks, come to that. As a teenager, Kara had rebelled against eating anything resembling good nutrition. Once she was on her own, the diet of junk food and alcohol had continued, more out of habit than necessity. On *Galactica*, of course, fresh food was at a premium. Kara hadn't realized how much she'd missed the stuff until she had some in front of her, and she dug into the salad with delicate relish.

"We don't have much time tonight," Peter said, resuming his seat. "So we'll start."

Start what? Kara wondered, starting to feel uneasy. Her annoyance returned, and she found herself glaring at Peter. He had dumped her into an unknown situation without warning, without even telling her there would *be* a situation. She felt like he had tricked her.

"Most of you have been asking questions about my spiritual leanings. I'm here to make some of those clear." He coughed slightly and took a sip of water. "I believe I am the Unifier mentioned in the Book of Glykon. We humans fight among ourselves. We bicker and bite each other's backs. All humans once belonged to a single tribe living in splendor on Kobol until they argued and split into thirteen tribes. One of those tribes was lost forever, but instead of learning from this lesson, we still fight among ourselves. We rage over who should get what food and clothing. We bicker over sleeping quarters and medicine. We fight over who should be in charge. Laura Roslin, the dying leader mentioned in the Book of Pythia, actually had to flee the military. How did it happen that such an important person should have to run for her life?"

Kara set down her fork in surprise. Peter must have been busier than she knew. President Roslin's imprisonment and escape had happened long before he had shown up. Possibly Louann and Alexander had filled him in on the major events of the last few months.

"The Cylons were able to destroy the Colonies because they were united under a single god with a single belief," Peter continued. "Our belief in many gods and many tribes weakens us, creates us-against-them among our own kind. The Cylons will eventually win by default—we ourselves will finish the job they started."

Kara found herself leaning toward Peter, listening hard as a child sitting at the feet of her grandfather. Peter's smooth voice dripped hypnotic gold, his handsome face shining with an inner light. His words made sense. How much time had she spent fighting with other people instead of fighting Cylons?

"We need to reunite ourselves," he said. "Stop thinking of ourselves as Capricans or Geminese or Librans. We are all human beings. We are—"

"Heretics!"

Startled, everyone twisted in their chairs. Sarah Porter was standing in the doorway, her face dark with fury. Five or six more people stood behind her, all dressed in Geminese clothing. Kara tensed.

"How can you listen to this filth?" Sarah demanded of the room. "You so-called Unity people bring chaos and disruption at a time when we need to be focused. And you, Peter Attis." She stabbed a furious finger at him. "You and your music spread lies that poison everyone who hears."

"How dare you!" Alexander said, leaping to his feet. "You can't barge in here and—"

"No." Peter held up a hand. "No, it's all right. I welcome the dialogue. Though I'm afraid I can't invite you to dinner, Representative Porter—we seem to be out of plates."

Sarah folded her arms. Her followers remained stoically in place. "I wouldn't break bread with a poisoner."

"Please." Peter spread his hands. "Exactly what are your objections? I'd love to talk about them with you so everyone here can decide for themselves."

"You claim that all the gods are facets of a single god," Sarah said. "And that path only leads to damnation. It's what started the exodus from Kobol. The Sacred Scrolls say, 'One jealous god desired to be elevated above all the other gods, and thus the war on Kobol began.' You and your single god will destroy us all."

"The One isn't a jealous god," Peter countered. "The One is *all* gods, and can't be above or below them. Don't twist what I say."

"You twist what the Scrolls say," Sarah snapped.

Louann leaped to her feet. "Leave him alone! Peter's going to save us. Remember? 'The Unifier shall have a Voice of Gold, and He will save Humanity with the Plague of the Tongue.'"

"Nonsense," Sarah scoffed. "The Book of Glykon was declared apocryphal during the Third Conclave of Kobol."

"Only because the Oracle of Arachne was feuding with the Priests," Alexander retorted, also jumping up. "They knew she favored Glykon's writings, so they declared the book apocrypha to discredit her. That Conclave was a galandine takil from the very beginning."

A chill ran through Kara's body. What had Alexander said?

"Arachne was a disgrace to her office!" Sarah growled, not seeming to notice Alexander's odd language. "Your so-called Unifier has no place in our society!"

"Ah ha!" Alexander pointed at Sarah. His hand was shaking. Kara stared at it, remembering Kat and Hot Dog. "So you acknowledge that Peter is the Unifier! You recognize our existence, our power. There are more of us than you know, and thanks to Peter, we're growing. People listen to him, and to us. There are more than five hundred of us now."

"Perhaps I'll have Peter arrested," Sarah snapped. "For inciting a riot."

"Peter isn't our only leader," Alexander said darkly. "And you jail the Unifier at your own peril. By throwing him in jail, you acknowledge who he is."

"People, please," Peter interjected. "I don't want a fight."

Sarah ignored him. "I acknowledge no such—"

And then Alexander toppled over. He landed on the floor, twisting and writhing. A string of nonsense words streamed from his mouth. Louann clapped her hands over her mouth. Everyone else, including Peter and Sarah, stared. Kara recovered first and dashed over to kneel beside him. Alexander continued to yammer.

"He needs help," Kara said. "Call a medical team! Get Dr. Cottle!"

"It's a miracle!" Louann clasped her hands together. "The miracle of tongues! It's proof that Peter is here to save us!" She dropped to her knees and raised her hands high above her head. Most of the dinner crowd did the same. The salads sat on the table, half-eaten and ignored.

"Oh mighty One!" Louann shouted.

"Oh mighty One!" the kneeling crowd echoed.

"You who are all in one!"

"You who are all in one!"

Louann's eyes were shut, and she swayed like a willow in a wind storm. The crowd followed her movements as if tied to her. Alexander continued to writhe and babble.

"We thank you for this miracle!" Louann said.

"We thank you for this miracle!"

Kara's skin crawled. She ignored the people as best she could and tried to straighten Alexander's limbs to keep him from hurting himself. He seemed unaware of her presence. His eyes stared at nothing, and he continued to spout nonsense, just as Kat and Hot Dog had. Kara couldn't see Peter.

"Call a team!" she shouted again, hoping someone would *do* something. "Peter!"

"Blasphemy!" Sarah hooted.

The door exploded open and a platoon of marines poured into the room.

CHAPTER 10

Howls of indignation echoed through sickbay. Peter Attis shouted and bellowed and wrenched at his restraints. Kara stood next to his bed, feeling uncertain. One bed over, Alexander twitched quietly in medicated sleep. Dr. Baltar stood to one side, watching with a look of vague distraction. He kept turning his head, as if someone were standing beside him.

"Hold still," Cottle barked. "You'd think I was pulling out your fingernails."

"Let me go!" Peter snarled. "What the hell are you doing?"

"I just want to draw some blood." Cottle held up the empty syringe. "See? Simple blood. Just hold still."

"This was a trick, wasn't it?" Peter said, eyes wild. "You're all Cylons. You just made me *think* I'd escaped, and now you're playing with me some more."

"Shut up, Pete," Kara snapped. "And dump the martyr pose. It doesn't look good on you."

He stopped struggling and stared at her. Cottle used the moment to insert the syringe and start drawing blood. Peter winced. "Ow! What the frak—?"

"Peter," Kara said. "You need to listen to what the doctor is saying. They've found a disease that attacks your brain. It makes you babble and shake, and then it puts you in a coma. It started just after you arrived, which probably means you have something to do with it."

"I didn't do anything wrong! I didn't make anyone sick!"

"Not on purpose," Baltar said from his corner.

"Not on purpose," Kara agreed, resisting the urge to stroke Peter's forehead like a concerned wife or mother. She didn't like seeing him tied down, knew it upset him more than it would most people. "But it's happening anyway."

Peter slumped back against the thin mattress of his sickbay bed. Other patients groaned in other beds. A few babbled nonsense. Peter took a deep breath, visibly trying to calm himself.

"The people will recover eventually," he said.

"What makes you say that?" Cottle asked sharply.

"Because I did. I shook and babbled in a Cylon lab for hours, but I recovered. I told Kara—Lieutenant Thrace—about it. It's not a disease. It's a miracle."

"You'll pardon me if I don't completely take your word for that," Cottle said.

"You're just prejudiced," Peter shot back. "Anything that differs from your point of view must be evil or blasphemous."

"I don't give a damn what you believe, kid," Cottle told him. "I believe my tests and my microscope. If they tell me it's a disease, it's a disease."

"Then why am I not sick?" Peter asked pointedly.

"It's possible," Baltar put in, "that the Cylons used you to infect the Fleet. You said you spent considerable time in a laboratory, after all. If they wanted you to carry a disease, they would almost certainly want you to be immune so you could spread it as far as possible. Say, for example, by putting on a rock concert?"

And then everything clicked at once. Kara stared down at Peter as the pieces came together, creating a terrible picture she wanted to deny but couldn't. It was like staring at a picture of a beautiful young woman and abruptly seeing an ugly old crone occupying the same space. "That's what happened, isn't it?" she said. "Frak, we should have seen it."

"Seen what?" Peter asked. The fight seemed to have gone out of him.

"The Cylons created this disease and infected you with it," Kara said. "Then they showed up at Planet Goop and attacked us with a half-assed force. They *wanted* to lose—it was the only way to make sure you'd end up here. When I was flying that Cylon raider with the nuke back to the basestar, it sent a signal. We thought it was warning the basestar not to fire on me because that would set off the nuke and destroy the basestar, but that wasn't it. The raider was telling the basestar to get ready for a big kaboom and make sure that you were on the escape pod. Frak, the Cylons knew from the beginning exactly what was going to happen. Otherwise you and your Mistress Eight wouldn't have been able to make it to the pod in time. Hell, she must have hit the engines a few minutes before the explosion. Otherwise you'd have been too close to survive."

"I . . . no," Peter said. "That can't be. Why would they kill hundreds—thousands—of their own kind on purpose, even to destroy the Fleet?"

"Cylons don't exactly die," Baltar said. "When one . . . expires, its consciousness is downloaded into a new body. So sacrificing an entire basestar full of them is more like wrecking a car than killing people. And the Cylons have wonderful auto insurance."

"It also explains why they didn't come back to Planet Goop," Kara said. "At least, not at first. They needed to give the plague time to spread. And then when they *did* show up, it was with a tiny force. They weren't playing to win—they were playing to see how well we could hold the game. Kat and Hot Dog broke down in the middle of the fight, which told them the plague was working, so they left. Now all they have to do is sit back and wait for us to die."

"So why aren't *you* sick?" Peter asked. "You're one of the first people I ran into." Then he added quickly, "I'll tell you why you aren't sick. It's because the One hasn't chosen you to see the truth yet."

"A more scientific way to put it," Baltar said, "is that the disease's course runs differently in different people. It's the nature of such brain disorders. One person succumbs quickly, another goes unscathed for weeks or, in some cases, months. It seems Lieutenant Thrace is one of the lucky ones."

Cold water seemed to trickle over Kara's skin. With all that had happened in the last few days, it had never occurred to her that she might be infected.

"Do you think I have it?" she forced herself to ask.

"Almost assuredly," Baltar said wryly. "And it's likely I do, too, and Dr. Cottle, and everyone else in the Fleet. Why do you think we haven't bothered with quarantine protocols, Lieutenant?" His voice took on a shrill note. "Mr. Attis's concert—and there's no doubt in my mind that the Cylons chose him because they knew he'd give one— would have spread the disease to thousands of people. We've learned that Mr. Hyksos over there was on the third or fourth tier, and *he* caught it. Perhaps he even caught it from you, Lieutenant Thrace, during your excursion into—what's it called? Crowd surfing?"

Kara's mind fled back to the night she and Peter had shared, to the number of times they had kissed. Her insides shrank from sudden, cold fear. You couldn't fight a disease. It got into your blood, hooked your cells with tiny, invisible claws, and tore you to bits from the inside out like a rabid dog in a henhouse.

"Dr. Cottle said I was free of bacteria and viruses," Peter pointed out. "So it can't be a disease. It's a miracle, like I told you."

"Actually it seems to be a prion," Baltar said. "A protein fragment that in some ways acts like a virus but doesn't look like one. That's the theory, anyway."

Cottle held up the scarlet vial. "Then let's test it."

Gaius Baltar pushed himself away from the microscope and almost backed into Number Six. He shot her an annoyed look, then ignored her. She ignored him, just as she had been doing from the moment of her appearance. Yet, she remained, perched on one of the work tables like a slighted cat. She looked at the ceiling, she looked at the equipment, she looked at Cottle. She never looked at him. Gaius shook his head. It made him nervous, but he really didn't have time to ponder Six's strange behavior. His work was vitally important to the safety of the Fleet. There were other considerations as well. A trickle of sweat skimmed along his hairline, and his mouth was dry. A few minutes ago, he had slipped a sample of his own blood under a microscanner and set it to search for the prion he had found in Hyksos's blood. Now that he knew what he was looking for, the test was easy.

And it had come back positive.

Now every tiny tremor, every slip of the tongue made him break into a cold sweat. He was infected with a deadly scrap of protein, and he was going to die. He, Gaius Baltar. Struck down in his prime by a terrible disease. It wasn't fair. After everything he had done to save humanity from the Cylons, he was now going to die in a Cylon plague. Fear knotted his stomach and made his hands shake. Or maybe it was the prions already. He had been one of the first people to examine Peter Attis. Hell, he had helped persuade Adama not to space the man. Well, *that* had clearly been a mistake.

This was all Kara Thrace's fault. If she had just kept her mouth shut, Adama wouldn't have changed his mind and Peter Attis and his stupid prions would be floating in space, freeze dried for all eternity.

"Are you seeing what I'm seeing?" Cottle asked from his own microscanner. Gaius came to himself, realizing he had been staring at a computer screen without reading it.

"What are you seeing?" he asked.

"Peter's blood," Cottle said, "has three different prions."

"All right, we're listening," Adama said.

Gaius stood at the front of the conference table with a pointer in his hand. An overhead projector cast a harsh square of light onto the screen. At the long conference table sat Commander Adama, Colonel Tigh, President Roslin, Captain Adama, and Dr. Cottle. With a small start, Gaius realized he had never learned the doctor's first name. By now there was no way to ask it without being socially awkward. He cleared his throat.

"Dr. Cottle and I have run extensive tests," Gaius said. "And this is what we've found."

He slid the first transparency onto the overhead, which cast the picture of a prion onto the screen. It looked similar to the infectious one, except its ribbons were wrapped tightly around a body that was now slightly curved. Strange that it should look so innocent and pretty, like a tangle of bright ribbons on the dresser of a young girl.

"This is a prion, which is short for 'proteinaceous infectious particle,'" Gaius said in his Lecture Voice, the one he would have used if it hadn't been for Peter Attis. Peter Attis—the source of this plague and of Gaius's public humiliation. Anger rose up and threatened to burn away Gaius's fear like a forest fire swallowing a firebreak. He let it happen—anger was always better than fear. "A prion, if you haven't heard yet, is a long, complicated protein which isn't quite a virus. We've named this one Prion H, for 'harmless.' This prion is actually inert. Your body ignores it, and it ignores your body. This is the natural state for most prions, or PrPs. They're everywhere in animal tissue, to tell you the truth, and it's likely that this particular one was with us long before Peter Attis showed up on our doorstep."

The people at the table sat in rapt attention. A bit of pride gave Gaius's movements a bit of snap. They were enthralled, just as the audience at his ruined lecture would have been. Gaius was in charge of the room, and he liked that. He removed the first transparency and flipped a second onto the overhead's glass platen. Another protein molecule came up on the screen, this one a bit smaller and less complicated.

"This is another prion," Baltar explained. "We call it Prion T, for transformational. It's the one that's causing problems. It gets into your neural tissue and creates a form of transmissible spongiform encephalopathy."

"Could we have that in English, Doctor?" Tigh asked.

"Sorry," he said. "The prions attach themselves to a patient's brain cells and interfere with brain function. Eventually, the prions begin to actually *destroy* the tissue—encophalopathy. This opens up thousands of tiny holes, and after a while the brain takes on the form of a sponge—spongiform. And the condition is transmissible from one person to another. Transmissible spongiform encephalopathy."

He paused to take a drink of water. No one moved or spoke.

"There's a theory called the Protein X hypothesis. It says that harmless prions like Prion H are transformed into their dangerous form by yet another prion. In other words, Prion H meets with Prion T and the two combine to form—" He twitched a third transparency onto the overhead. This one was the prion he and Cottle had seen in the lab before, its ribbons twisting about it in all directions, like strands of bright taffy on a bender. "—this prion. It's still Prion H, but this one interacts with brain tissue. It's deadly."

"So the Cylons created this Prion T, and it changes Prion H, which we already have in us, into a deadly form," Roslin said. "Is that it?"

Gaius nodded. "Yes. Prion T is designed to replicate itself in the human body, and your immune system ignores it. Prion T is hardy, and easy to transmit. A triumph of biological engineering, really, if you don't mind that it kills you."

"What are the symptoms, exactly?" Roslin asked.

"They vary in degree and intensity," Gaius said. "Early on, the prions are only interfering with the brain and not destroying it. Symptoms include light palsy that eventually becomes full-fledged tonic-clonic seizures. Some people show strange slips of the tongue. Their brain-to-mouth filter malfunctions, and they start saying whatever occurs to them, rather like a bad stream-of-consciousness novel. Others sprinkle nonsense words into otherwise normal sentences. And still others will do both. These speech symptoms eventually worsen into an inability to say anything that makes sense— once the language centers start breaking down, the only thing the patient can produce is mindless babble. For some people, the progression is slow. For others, it's quick. Eventually, the patient lapses into a coma and dies." He cleared his throat. "We know this because the first patient we diagnosed—Mr. Hyksos—died a few minutes ago."

The room fell silent. No one present had known Hyksos personally, but so few humans were left that even the death of a stranger was reason for a twinge of fear. Gaius more than anyone knew the difficulties and dangers of a small gene pool, and he didn't like the way the odds were shrinking every day.

"So what's the good news?" Lee Adama asked at last.

"I'm afraid there isn't any right now," Gaius told him. "Unless you count the fact that we have Peter Attis so we can study him."

"Where is Attis now?" Adama asked.

"In sickbay," Kara said. Her voice was quiet, completely unlike her usual brassy self.

Laura Roslin raised a finger in a tired gesture. Even in the semi-darkness of the room, Gaius could see that her face was pale. "Is there a cure or treatment for—what is the condition called, anyway?"

"I gave you the proper name," Gaius said. Didn't these people pay attention? "It's a transmissible spongiform encephal—"

"Everyone else calls it the plague of tongues," Cottle interrupted with a wave of his cigarette.

"Oh, frak me," Kara muttered.

"Seizures and babbling," Tigh observed sourly. "Shit."

"It's taken on a religious connotation?" Roslin asked.

"Sounds that way," Commander Adama said. "This could cause a problem."

"A *problem*?" Tigh said. "It's a frakking disaster."

"I never thought I'd say this," Kara said, "but I agree with Colonel Tigh."

A startled look crossed Tigh's face, but he hid it quickly. "It's because I'm right."

Kara looked ready to snap at him, then seemed to change her mind. "Look, I've seen some of these people. They think that Peter's a savior. Hell, *he* thinks he's a savior." And she gave a short description of the events at the restaurant. "When the marines broke in and hauled Peter away, his . . . his followers reacted as if the marines had shot him." She gave Saul Tigh a hard look. "With all due respect, Colonel, it might have been better if you—if the marines—had been more subtle."

"We had to get him fast, Lieutenant," Tigh replied. "No time to pussyfoot around just because he's a prettyboy who can wiggle around on a stage. He's a danger to the Fleet."

"Not his fault," Kara said with cold calm. "He didn't *ask* to be infected."

"How do you know?" Gaius interjected. "The Cylons might have agreed to send him back to his own kind provided he carried this prion."

"So he would be the only living human on the entire Fleet?" Kara scoffed. "Not likely."

"He may not have known the prion was deadly," Gaius pointed out. "He might have—"

Roslin held up a hand. "This is immaterial, and it doesn't answer my initial question. Is there a cure?"

Everyone turned to look at Gaius, who hesitated a tiny moment. "No," he said.

The word landed on the table like a lead paperweight. A long silence followed. No one seemed willing to speak, as if more words might make the situation worse. Gaius waited.

"So we're all dead?" Lee Adama said at last.

"Not necessarily," he said, relishing the relief, however small, that came over their faces. It swelled him, made him feel important the way they turned to him for answers. "No one's ever cured a spongiform encephalopathy, but it doesn't mean it can't be done. Peter has clearly been carrying both the T and the H prions for quite some time, but he shows no symptoms. He claims to have had the disease and recovered from it, despite the fact that no human being has ever successfully fought off a spongiform encephalopathy. Peter did say that all the other humans who had been captured with him had died somehow. Perhaps they were test cases. In any case, Dr. Cottle and I are operating on the assumption that the Cylons infected Peter, then somehow cured him and made him immune."

"Don't want to kill the carrier too fast," Adama observed.

Gaius nodded. "Exactly. Peter's blood contains a third prion. If it has a function, we haven't figured it out yet, but it may be the key. Dr. Cottle and I have made this matter our top priority."

"So," Roslin said, "the fact remains that we have a deadly disease that masquerades as a religious plague along with the other touchy situation on our hands."

"What touchy situation?" Commander Adama asked, clearly concerned.

Roslin gave a wan smile. "There's an entire auditorium full of people who are expecting Peter to sing, but he's obviously not going to."

"Heaven forbid," Gaius muttered.

"We should initiate quarantine protocols," Tigh said. "Stop all ship-to-ship traffic and confine civilians to their quarters until we can spread the cure around."

"Not much point in that," Cottle said from his end of the table. "The prion's widespread by now. Might just as well shut the coop after the chickens get out."

"Are we all infected, Dr. Cottle?" Lee Adama asked.

Cottle shrugged. "Probably. You've all had close contact with Peter or with someone who did. Prion T was created to be easy to transmit. Breathing the same air will do it, really."

Another long silence fell across the room. Gaius felt his own heart beating heavy, pumping the prion to every part of his body. It seemed like he could feel them sliding through his endothelial cells, permeating his brain. Utter nonsense, of course, but emotions didn't listen to logic.

"So we're all dead, then," Tigh said into the silence. "Is that what you're saying?"

Alarms blared. Everyone jumped, including Gaius. Every time that damned alarm went off, it took five years off his life. Sometimes he felt two hundred years old.

"*This is Lieutenant Gaeta,*" crackled the PA. "*Set Condition One throughout the Fleet. Repeat, set Condition One. Commander Adama, please come to CIC.*"

"From one thing or another," Adama said, "we're all dead."

Kara Thrace's pulse pounded in her body while her legs pounded down the corridor. She'd been cooped up in the *Galactica* for two days now, and she was still feeling a little pissed off at Peter for the dinner—or lack of one. She also wanted to throw him down on the floor and get a good, solid frakking out of him. And she wanted him to hold her for a long time and stroke her hair. And she wanted to crack him across the jaw for probably infecting her with some weirdo disease that was going to dissolve her brain into gelatinous goo, even if the cure—maybe—was right around the corner. Peter filled her with dichotomies thick as mud, and Kara didn't like dichotomies. They reminded her too much of life at home with her parents, of her father in particular. She unconsciously flexed her fingers, the ones Dad had broken. Over years, he'd broken all of them.

"*You're a little frak-head. A worthless little slut, you got that? Gods, you can't do anything right!*"

"*Daddy! Please. Please . . .*"

"*I'll show you what it means to frak up. I'll show you. Go get the hammer.*"

"*Daddy, please. I won't do it again. Please.*"

"*I said, go get the frakking hammer, you little brat. Now!*"

Kara stumbled slightly. Her feet wanted to drag. She tried to banish the memory, but it wouldn't go. For a moment, she could only see her father's face. Love and loathing both tried to take command of her heart, and neither would give in. She wanted him to say, just once, that he was proud of her, that she wasn't a frak-up. She also wanted him to beg for mercy, to plead for her to stop the pain she was inflicting on him. It was unfair, and it was wrong that her dad was both father and foe to her, but that's the way it was. Kara set her jaw and quickened her pace toward deck five. Dichotomies.

The solution was simple enough. Out there, in her Viper, she was free. Out there, everything was black and white. Everything she encountered was either a friend or an enemy. No one was both. The certainty and security of that fact brought a rush of exhilaration that not even fear of death could dampen.

A hand grabbed her arm from behind. She wrenched around and found herself looking into Lee Adama's blue eyes. Other *Galactica* personnel rushed and bustled around them, intent on their own Condition One errands.

"Where do you think you're going?" Lee demanded.

She stared, honestly confused. "To kill a bunch of Cylons. You know—bang, bang, kaboom?"

"You're not going anywhere," Lee said. "You're grounded."

"What?" Kara barely kept her voice below a shriek. "For what reason?"

"You were one of the first people to encounter Peter. And you've been . . . close to him."

"You mean I frakked him."

Lee flushed slightly, then got angry. "Yeah. You frakked him. That means that he probably injected you with his little prion."

"It wasn't that little," Kara said with a deliberate smirk.

"Get your head on your job, Lieutenant," he snapped, stung. Kara was a little surprised to find she felt a little bad about making the remark. "You've had this prion longer than most of the people on this ship, which means it isn't safe to put you in a cockpit."

"I haven't shown any symptoms," she said sharply, denying a chilly tinge of fear. "Nothing's wrong with me."

"Yeah? Hold out your hands."

She did. After a moment, the left one trembled just a bit. Kara stared at it. Her entire world shrank to that one tiny tremor. "No."

"I noticed it in the conference room," Lee said gently. He held up his own hand. It trembled ever so slightly. "We can't fly, Kara. Not until Baltar or Cottle finds a cure. Simes is CAG until then."

Without a word, Kara spun on her heel and stomped away. Lee, caught off guard, ran to catch up.

"Where are you going?" he asked.

"To CIC so I can see how the fight goes," she said. "And then I'm going to sickbay."

CIC was busy, hushed, and tense. The steady growl of the DRADIS undercut every quiet comment. Kara shot the readout a glance. A handful of Cylon raiders was sliding toward a flock of Vipers. Distorted radio chatter filled the silent spaces. Adama and Tigh stood at the light table in the center of CIC, their eyes also on the DRADIS.

"Why don't we just Jump?" Lee asked.

"*Colonial One's* Jump computer crashed," his father replied shortly. "They have to reboot and recalculate. It'll take almost half an hour."

"Frak." Lee pursed his lips. "Was it a Cylon virus?"

"Sharon," Kara said without thinking. "She got over there somehow and did it."

"For once, we can't blame the Cylons," Tigh said. "It seems to be an ordinary old computer crash."

"Galactica *Actual, this is Lieutenant Simes. We are about to engage the enemy.*"

The voice was distorted by distance. Kara watched the display as the Vipers closed in on the Cylon raiders. She found herself leaning this way and that, trying to make the Vipers fly in the direction she wanted, like a Pyramid fan trying to get the ball to move a particular way.

"Only six raiders?" she said. "They're just testing us again."

"Which means you didn't need to be out there," Lee said.

She shot him an acid look. He was trying to be nice to her, she knew, but that only pissed her off. Lee was the CAG—or had been until now. He wasn't *supposed* to be nice to his pilots. He was supposed to give an order and watch it carried out. Niceness, however, seemed to be hardwired into him. It was too bad some of Tigh's bitter acid couldn't mix with Lee's milky niceness. Between them, they might make a fine commander.

The Vipers crawled across the screen until they were nose-to-nose with the raiders. Kara found she was holding her breath.

"*Watch your flank, Mack,*" Simes said.

"*I see it.*"

The soft thump of weapon fire came over the radio, and one of the raiders vanished from the readout.

"*Nice one, Mack!*"

"*Thanks! It was my first piggy bank withdrawal from fighting with a bloody—*"

"Shit," Tigh breathed.

"*Mack! Return to* Galactica *immediately!*"

"*Immediately now once upon a time is flying.*" On the display, one of the Vipers weaved erratically. A raider dove at it. Kara leaned forward and put out a hand, as if she were one of the Lords of Kobol, able to cup the Viper in her hands and protect it from a distance. Her jaw was tight, and she felt helpless, completely impotent. All she could do was watch. Was this how Adama felt all the time? Her hand was shaking again. The Cylon on the screen dove.

"*Mack!*"

"*Is a great big flying fishbowl full of milk for the cats . . .*"

The Viper vanished from the display.

"*Frak!*"

Kara looked at Lee for a long moment, then turned and fled CIC. She didn't let herself run, quite, but she didn't let anything get in her way, either. People moved out of her way instinctively, like schools of fish scattering before a shark. She refused to let herself think; she just reacted. In a few minutes, she was at Peter's bedside down in sickbay. Restraints still held him down. Kara had mixed feelings about this, too, and she refused to examine them. She was sick of being mixed around like a frakking martini.

A red tube ran from Peter's left arm to a machine. The tube emerged from other side of the machine and ran down to Peter's right arm. Red liquid flowed sluggishly through both tubes. Dr. Cottle stood at the machine, adjusting dials and checking readouts. He and Peter looked at Kara when she came in.

"What are you doing to him?" she asked without preamble.

"Hi," Peter said from the bed. "Nice to see you, too."

"We're taking some blood and plasma," Cottle said. "We won't take too much, and we'll return a chunk of the red blood cells to his body."

"How soon before you find a cure?" she asked.

Cottle blinked at her. "Not right this instant. We're barely—"

"Sure is nice to be treated like a human being instead of a science experiment," Peter put in. "I never realized how much I missed being on the Cylon ship until now. Maybe this is another test of my faith. 'And the Unifier shall walk among the Enemy, and He shall return both changed and unharmed.'"

"Shut up," Kara snapped.

"Kara!" Lee stood framed by the curtains that separated the sections of sickbay. "Are you all right? You took off like—"

"I'll be fine, Lee," she snarled. "Just as soon as the good doctor finds a frakking cure, I'll be even better."

"I told you it'll take a while," Cottle said. He took a drag from his cigarette and tweaked one of the dials. Blood filled four vials. He capped them and picked them up like a bouquet of scarlet glass flowers. "And that's assuming there's even a cure to find."

"That makes me feel so much better." Kara said.

"Will you people quit talking about me as if I wasn't here?" Peter demanded, trying unsuccessfully to sit up. "I'm the frakking Unifier, after all."

"Shut up," Lee said, and Peter sank back into his bed, a defiant look on his face. "Kara," Lee continued, "I wanted to tell you—the Cylons jumped away again. Looks like it was another test. All the pilots are returning."

"Except Mack," Kara pointed out. "If I'd been out there, he wouldn't have died."

"You would both have died," Lee said. "Your hand is getting worse. I can see it from here."

Kara put both hands behind her back like a small child in a glassware store. She could feel one of them shaking, defying all commands for it to stop. How much longer before she lay writhing on the floor babbling junk and nonsense? Anger flared. Peter had done this to her. She knew he hadn't done it on purpose, that he would have stopped it if he could, but that didn't make her feel any less angry. She wished she had just blown the rescue pod to dust. The old saying was true—no good deed went unpunished.

"I'll be able to get out there once I get the cure," Kara said, gesturing at Peter. "If the Doc here would just get off his ass and do some work."

"Stop ignoring me!" Peter howled. "I'm not a thing!"

The sickbay curtains burst aside and the alcove was suddenly full of people. Kara found herself staring down the barrel of a pistol. Lee was doing the same. Cottle's cigarette fell from his lips, and he took a step back from his machine, a startled and frightened look on his face. Kara noted in a flash that the assailants—there were seven of them—all carried service revolvers. Two carried pulse rifles. And all of them wore red masks that covered their faces and hair but left their eyes exposed.

"What the frak?" Lee said.

Cottle moved with astonishing speed. He thrust the blood vials into Lee's startled hands and interposed himself between the intruders and Peter, his patient. "What the hell are you doing? Get out of my sickbay!"

"Freeze, Dr. Asshole!" one of the intruders barked. It was a woman's voice, muffled by her mask.

"Look, I don't care who you are," Cottle said, "but you can't—"

The woman swept him aside with easy strength. Cottle fell heavily against a medicine cabinet. It tipped over backward with Cottle on top of it and crashed to the floor.

"Hurry, now!" the woman said. "Let's do it!"

"What's going on?" Peter asked, pulling at his restraints again. "Frak! Let me go!"

Two of the masked figures holstered their pistols and snatched long knives from their belts. They moved toward the bed, blades glinting in the fluorescent light. Kara's heart jerked and a new fear trilled through her. Her hand continued to shake even as she held it up. The pistol that kept her in place hadn't moved. Peter stared at the blades like a bird hypnotized by a snake.

"You don't need to do this," Kara said evenly. Adrenaline zinged through her like the blade of a hot knife. "Leave him alone."

"I'm afraid we can't, Lieutenant." The leader woman snapped her fingers. The blades flipped down. Peter gasped as they slashed his restraints open. Then he sat up, rubbing his wrists. The two masks helped him off the bed, and Peter pulled the tubes from his arms. A grimace crossed his handsome face, and a thin line of blood trickled down the inside of both elbows.

"Let's go," the leader said.

"You can't take him," Cottle said. "We need him to—"

"Shut up!" said the mask holding the pistol on Kara. "We're the Unity and he's the Unifier. He doesn't belong in a prison. He belongs with his people."

"Listen to me," Lee said in a reasonable voice, his hands in the air, still holding the vials Cottle had given him. "Peter's important to the entire Fleet, not just to you."

The eyes above the mask holding the pistol on Kara flicked toward Lee. Kara took advantage and moved. She swept the pistol out of her assailant's grip and punched him under the chin with the heel of her hand. She felt his teeth crash together, and he staggered backward. Lee dropped the vials—glass shattered on the floor—and grabbed his own attacker by the wrist. In a quick, practiced move, he disarmed his opponent and twisted the man around in front of him, turning him into a human shield. The pair with pulse rifles were fumbling them into firing position, and Kara mentally marked them *civilian*. They were probably more dangerous to themselves than to the people they aimed the rifles at. The remaining two stood next to Peter, apparently unwilling to leave his side. Their pistols were still holstered. Cottle had fled, and he would doubtless raise the alarm, evening the odds considerably.

Kara was reaching down to snatch up her opponent's dropped pistol when Lee stiffened and released his prisoner. The prisoner stumbled away and Lee, looking vaguely surprised, dropped unconscious to the floor. The leader was standing behind him. How the hell had she done that? No time to think about it. Kara's hand closed on the pistol—

—and a heavy foot came down hard on it. Kara stared stupidly down at it even as crushing pain made her cry out. She looked up. The leader's masked face met her gaze with hard brown eyes.

"Don't even," the leader said.

Kara, who was still kneeling, yanked her hand back, feeling the scrape of skin on metal and hard rubber. She tried to punch upward, but the leader caught her hand in a cruel grip.

"Not worth it," the leader said.

"Don't hurt her," Peter gasped.

"We need to go," said another mask. "Now!"

Kara whipped her free hand up and managed to snag the leader's mask just under the eyes. The fabric was soft and stretchy. She yanked downward even as the leader caught Kara's other wrist with terrible strength. The mask snapped back into place. Kara caught only a glimpse of the leader's face, but it was enough.

"Satisfied?" asked Sharon Valerii.

CHAPTER 11

A flash of pain hit the back of Kara's head, and the world sagged. Her muscles went limp as old molasses. She was vaguely aware of her own feet stumbling beneath her as someone half dragged her down an endless series of wavering corridors. Twice she heard gunfire and Peter's voice, and the hand that gripped her arm left bruises that her father would have been proud of. A hatchway closed, and she realized she was on a shuttle. It was small, and red-masked people crowded in tight on the deck plates. The grip on Kara's arm relaxed, and she was allowed to slump to the floor. Her head ached, but at least the world wasn't moving. The deck plates thrummed and sudden motion threw Kara off balance again. She caught a glimpse of blurred whiteness through the canopy up front. Then the view abruptly shifted to a blackness studded with bright stars. They had left the *Galactica*. Kara tried to take in her surroundings despite her wooziness. The shuttle seemed to be a civilian vessel, not military, and it was apparently used for cargo instead of passengers—the only seats were for the pilot and copilot. The back was a large empty space where the red-maskers, Peter, and Kara squatted or sat. Another wave of pain washed over Kara's head, and she had to stop thinking for a while.

"Where are we going?" Peter asked.

"Into hiding," Sharon said behind her mask. She was flying the shuttle. "I'm sorry, but it's not safe to tell you more right now, Unifier."

"So you guys are members of the Unity," Peter said. "My followers."

"That's us." She turned to the person sitting in the copilot seat. All Kara could see was the top of a head covered by red fabric. "Launch probe."

"Launching." Kara felt a small tremor. "Launch successful."

"Now hang on back there," Sharon called. "I need to do some fancy flying."

The shuttle dipped, and Kara automatically braced herself against a bulkhead as best she could. The armed and masked Unity members all tried to do the same, with mixed results. Two people lost their balance and caromed into other people, who in turn slammed into Kara. More pain exploded across her tender head and her stomach swooped inside her, but she clamped her lips shut, refusing to give her captors the satisfaction of a sound. She hated being a passenger instead of a pilot, and it wasn't any fun being a captive, either. Put the two together, and she found herself poised above a well of misery that threatened to suck her down into cold, dark water like a—

Oh, frak off, she told herself. *You've been in worse positions, Thrace. Way worse. You're alive, and they clearly don't intend to kill you. Those are two major advantages. So work on your next move.*

The shuttle continued to dip and weave. No one was able to regain their balance, and everyone yelped and howled in protest as they tumbled about the shuttle. All thoughts of her next move were driven out of her by force. Kara felt as if she had been tossed into a clothes dryer with a bunch of puppies. Sharon was a better pilot than this, wasn't she? Maybe she was doing it on purpose, a small gibe at the humans.

At last, the shuttle stopped moving. Kara cautiously sat up, pushing aside Peter's leg to do so. "Where the frak are we?" she demanded.

In answer, a hood came down over her head and restraints clamped her wrists behind her. Unseen hands jerked her to her feet and hustled her off the shuttle.

"Hey!" Peter said. "Don't hurt her! What are you doing?"

"We're not hurting her, Unifier," Sharon's voice said. "We're protecting you. We can't afford to let her know exactly where she is." Kara felt someone—Sharon—lean in closer to speak in a low voice as other hands hauled Kara down what was probably a corridor. "The only reason you're still alive, sweetie, is that Peter likes you, and we need his

cooperation. But we can probably figure out a way to get his cooperation without you. You're a convenience, not a necessity. Got it?"

Kara clamped her teeth around a retort and merely nodded her
head instead. A frakking *convenience?* She'd show Sharon how convenient she could be. Any vestiges of positive feeling she'd had toward
the Cylon woman were evaporating faster than water poured on a cac-
tus. Except none of this made sense. Despite weeks of incarceration,
Sharon had been helpful, even conciliatory. No matter how much
abuse had been heaped on her, no matter how often people called her
a toaster or put her in chains or slapped a restraining collar around
her neck . . .

Kara grimaced. In that light, maybe Sharon's actions made perfect
sense.

Kara's captors and Peter fell silent as they hauled her down a series
of pathways, stairwells, and corridors. All Kara could see was red, and
it came to her that she was wearing a Unity mask, but it was on backward, so her eyes were covered. She strained to see something—
anything—through the finely woven mesh, but couldn't. She tried to
keep track of the number of footsteps she took and which direction
she turned, but Sharon—she assumed it was Sharon—kept giving
Kara sharp jerks, which threw off her count. The dull, persistent ache
in her head didn't help, either. Eventually, she gave up, which was
probably what Sharon intended. Instead, she tried to figure out what
she could about her captors.

The Unity. Louann—or was it Alexander?—had said that there
were more people in the Unity than anyone knew. They had to have
contacts in the military—it was the only way they could get their
hands on pulse rifles and get a shuttle docked at *Galactica* without
awkward questions. It was likely they knew how to jam or confuse
military scanners, at least temporarily, so they could get away. Kara remembered the probe Sharon's copilot had launched. It probably put
out a false signal. It wouldn't fool *Galactica* for more than a minute or
two, but that's all it would take, especially if Sharon knew how to
switch the transponder codes on her own shuttle to make it look
like another ship entirely. A couple of minutes and Gaeta would see
through that, too, but once again, that's all it would take.

Sharon jerked Kara again, throwing her off balance and making
her take several quick steps to regain her balance. A surge of hatred
boiled and hissed inside her like a snake dropped into hot water. How
might this little band of fanatics react if they knew the leader of their
little expedition was a Cylon? Wouldn't it be fun to watch the fallout if

Kara told them? But almost as quickly as it came up, Kara discarded the idea. The fact that the *Galactica* had—or once had—a Cylon in her brig wasn't well known around the Fleet, and it was quite likely that the Unity simply wouldn't believe Kara. Kara had to admit that she'd find it hard to believe. Peter knew, though. He must not have seen Sharon's face. Kara didn't think he'd react well to learning that a copy of his Mistress Eight was one of his . . . rescuers? Captors? Kara was a captive, but was Peter one too? The idea hadn't occurred to her before. Peter had been treated like a captive on *Galactica* twice now—once when he'd arrived and once after Dr. Cottle had determined he was Patient Zero. Would he care that he'd been rescued by a Cylon as long as he'd been rescued? Sharon had once rescued Kara, and at that moment, Kara wouldn't have cared if Sharon was a human, a Cylon, or an insurance salesman. Peter might well think the same thing, no matter what his experiences with his Mistress Eight had been.

There were too many uncertainties. Kara decided to keep her mouth shut about Sharon's identity until she knew more.

Besides, the information might be worth something in trade.

The hands moving Kara along shoved her into an open space that echoed. The hood was yanked from her head. Her hair crackled with static electricity, and bright lights made her squint until her eyes adjusted. They were in a storeroom. Battered plastic crates sat in blocky piles amid freestanding wire shelves. A door in one corner opened into what Kara assumed was a walk-in refrigerator. Harsh fluorescents provided stark light, and the floor was cold gray tile. One of the maskers pressed Kara's shoulders with firm pressure until she slid to the floor, her back to one wall. Her hands were still cuffed behind her. Blond Peter stood nearby, surrounded by red maskers. He looked like a sunflower in a rose garden.

"So what's the plan, Petey boy?" Kara asked.

He looked at her for a long moment, and Kara realized she was dreading the answer. Had he really bought into this Unifier thing? And what would he do with her, an unbeliever?

"I haven't a clue," he said at last. "I didn't ask to be rescued. None of this was my idea."

"The Unifier must have a plan," intoned a woman's voice which Kara now recognized as Louann's. "The divine speaks through you."

Peter shrugged helplessly and Kara found herself trying not to laugh. "Looks like the divine took the day off," she said.

Pain smashed through her mouth as the masker standing closest cracked Kara across the face. "Don't blaspheme."

"Hey!" Peter snapped. "I want something clear here—hurting Kara is like hurting me. You got that, buddy?"

The masker instantly dropped to his knees in front of Peter, his fingers trailing the floor in absolute obeisance. A muffled sob came from behind the mask. "I am sorry, Great One. I am ready for you to strike off my head."

"What?" Peter said, startled.

"It is written," Sharon intoned from behind her own mask, "in the book of Glykon: 'And the Heads of those who defy the Unifier shall tumble to the Ground.' "

"Heads will roll, huh?" Kara said.

"Shut—I mean, the consort will be silent," Sharon said, and Kara filed away another fact—the consort had some leeway, even when she was a captive.

"So Petey, I ask again," Kara said, ignoring Sharon. "What's the plan? Now that you're free, what are you going to do? Raise a rebellion? Throw down President Roslin and Commander Adama? Take over a bunch of ships and Jump away on your own? Skulk in the shadows for the rest of your life? What?"

Peter took a step back as the realization of his position finally sank in. He clearly hadn't thought past his rescue. "I . . . I don't . . ."

"You people," said a new voice, "clearly have no idea how to run a revolution."

Kara jerked her head around. Standing near a pile of crates was the dark-haired form of Tom Zarek.

"I'm guessing they ran to another Geminon ship," said Lee. He was still holding a cold pack to his head, even though the Unity had attacked sickbay over three hours ago. Bill Adama studied his son without seeming to and told himself over and over the injuries were minor. Thank the Lords of Kobol for that. A small part of Adama was glad Lee hadn't been kidnapped even while the rest of him was worried sick about Kara—and the Fleet.

"What makes you say that, Captain?" Tigh asked, his voice harsh.

"So far the Unity have been active only on Geminon ships," Lee replied. "That's where their supporters are and that's where they'll find people to hide them."

"We've quarantined all six Geminon vessels," Adama mused. "Including the *Kimba Huta* and the *Monarch*. I want each one of them searched."

"We don't have the manpower to search them all at once," Lee said.

"Why not?" Tigh demanded. "We have lots of marines and the ships aren't that big."

In answer, Lee held up his hand. It shook visibly. Adama's stomach tightened into a cold ball of ice. Lee was getting sick. Adama remembered a time when Lee was five years old and had come down with flash fever. The sickness struck quickly, bringing on high fever and hallucinations, and Lee had been hospitalized with a clear plastic quarantine tent over his bed. Adama wished he could say he had never left Lee's side, but that wasn't true. Caroline, his first wife and Lee's mother, ate, slept, and lived at the hospital. Adama found he couldn't bear to spend more than half an hour at a time in Lee's room. He requested a temporary assignment that allowed him to remain closer to home and he told Caroline that he simply couldn't get away more than that for fear of being brought up on charges of insubordination. The truth was, the hospital room made him feel panicky, and the sight of his son lying there, twitching and muttering to himself under a plastic tent, stabbed him with a fear he could neither identify nor fight. So he blamed his job. Caroline knew Adama was lying about his reasons for staying away but pretended she didn't, and he could see unspoken resentments and rebukes in her eyes whenever she looked at him.

Lee's fever eventually broke, and he made a full recovery. Adama's knees went weak with relief at the news, but his only visible response was to ruffle Lee's hair, give him a quick kiss on the top of his head, and flee the room. Caroline had watched him go. Adama suspected the entire incident was one of the many reasons she divorced him a few years later.

Now Lee was sick again. Various events in the recent past—including the Cylon attack on the Colonies—had forced Adama to become more adept at recognizing and dealing with the depth of feeling he had for Lee, his only surviving son, but that only meant he had to face fears for Lee's safety instead of burying them. Perhaps facing them was healthier for everyone concerned, but burying had been a hell of a lot easier. He watched Lee's palsy-ridden hands and tried not to panic.

"A lot of the marines are shaky," Lee said. His voice remained steady, but Adama detected the slight quiver of fear in it, and it ripped at his heart. "They can't fire weapons until we find a cure for the disease. Cottle and Baltar think Peter is somehow immune to it, which means he's the key to curing it. But . . ."

"But what?" Tigh said.

"But they didn't get much blood from Peter before the Unity grabbed him. Cottle gave me four vials, and two of them broke during the attack. That's barely enough for anyone to study, and that's assuming they don't make any mistakes."

Adama and Tigh both fell silent. Adama's mind raced, trying to see options and finding none.

"So you're saying," Adama said slowly, "that the only person who might hold a cure for the plague of tongues is a captive of the Unity, and we're not sure where he is."

Lee nodded reluctantly. "That's the long and short of it."

"Shit," Tigh muttered.

"How many more cats?" Adama muttered to himself.

"Commander," Dualla said. "President Roslin is on the line for you."

Adama sighed and picked up the phone. He had to ask. "Madam President. What can I do for you?"

"*I see you've placed the Geminon ships under quarantine,*" came her tired, breathy voice. "*Is it to do with Peter's kidnapping?*"

"Yes. We think he's hiding on one of them."

"*Hiding. So you think he was in on the kidnapping?*"

Adama pinched the bridge of his nose. Frak. The woman was too perceptive for his own good. "I don't know, Madam President. It's crossed my mind, but I have no proof of it."

"*Any word about Lieutenant Thrace?*"

"I'm afraid not."

"*What about the escaped Cylon?*"

"Nothing there, either, I'm afraid."

His answers, while short, were carefully polite. Not that long ago Adama would have told Laura Roslin that he was too busy to talk to her, but these days, with her worsening health, he couldn't bring himself to be rude, or even brusque. He wondered if Roslin knew this and was using it. Probably.

"*Bill, you're aware that the majority of the algae harvest is still on the* Monarch, *right?*"

"I hadn't thought about it," he admitted. "Why?"

"*The algae can't leave the ship now that it's under quarantine. Some of the other ships were counting on that algae, and they're feeling the pinch. And we still need those antibiotics to counter the strep infection.*"

Adama had a brief image of himself standing in a canyon between two granite cliffs. On one cliff was the prion plague of tongues and

Peter Attis. On the other was a bunch of hungry children sick with strep throat. The cliffs were moving steadily together, with him trying to sail a ship between them.

"I'm hoping the situation will be resolved quickly," was all Adama could say.

"*I know, Bill. I just wanted to make sure you were aware of everything.*"

"You're very good at that, Madam President," he said without a hint of the irony he was feeling. Roslin's only response was a small, tired laugh before she hung up.

"Sir," Dualla said abruptly, "I think you should hear this."

And before Adama could respond, she twisted a dial on her console. Music filled CIC. It was a fast tune with a military beat to it. Peter's voice, throaty and strong, sang the lyrics. Peter sang about choices, about religious freedom, and about the need to rise up against oppressors. The song was fast and the chorus was catchy. A few seconds into it, Adama discovered to his horror that he was tapping his foot in time to it. He stopped and glanced guiltily around, hoping no one had noticed. No one had—everyone in CIC was listening to the music. Several people nodded in time to it and Adama caught Dualla humming along with the chorus. He glared at her, and she stopped.

"Where is that signal coming from, Mr. Gaeta?" Adama demanded.

"The *Galactica*, sir."

"What?" Tigh said, coming around to look at Gaeta's screens and controls.

"It's scrambled, sir, and by an expert," Gaeta explained. "So it looks like it's coming from us. I could unscramble it if the signal continues for the next two or three hours and I drop everything else to work on it."

The song ended. "*This is Peter Attis,*" the singer said. "*Earlier today I was kidnapped on the orders of Commander William Adama because of my religious views. Because my followers speak in tongues and because he needed to justify his actions, Adama claimed that I spread a disease. My friends, the disease is a sham cooked up by Sarah Porter and the military to keep me from spreading the truth about the One. The fact that Adama is persecuting me proves that he fears me, that he thinks there is truth to what I preach. Many of you have heard my followers speak in tongues, proof that the One has blessed them.*

"*My friends, you've heard me speak of how all the gods are merely facets of the One. The Cylons have a similar belief, a belief in one God. It's the reason they continue to attack us. But belief in the One would shelter us, my friends. The Cylons won't attack those who believe in the One. I call on all right-thinking people to oppose the military's illegal restrictions of our freedom. I call on all people to stand up for their rights! I call on all people to stand up and take shelter in true belief!"*

Music swelled, and Peter started singing again. Adama made a curt motion at Dualla, who shut it off.

"Dammit," Adama muttered.

"I don't give a boar's tit if that bastard worships the cockroaches in his bedroom—I want him found and dragged back here by his short hairs," Tigh raged. "We need Attis back on *Galactica* and we need him here now!"

"Do you think he really believes the disease is a sham?" Lee asked. "Or that the Cylons will leave us alone if we believe in his god?"

Adama shook his head and stole a glance at Lee's shaking hand. "Hard to tell. It doesn't really matter, does it? What will matter is whether other people believe him or not."

"Sir," Dualla said, "I'm receiving numerous requests from reporters who want to interview you. Sixteen, at last count."

"Tell 'em to shove their requests up their collective asses," Tigh snarled. "Tell 'em—"

"Thank you, Colonel," Adama said. "I think she gets the idea." He took a deep breath and turned to Lee, his only surviving son. "Are you well enough to lead a strike force?"

"I can't fire a weapon, but my tactics are just fine," Lee said. "Where to? We don't know where Attis is."

"The *Monarch*," Gaeta put in.

Everyone turned to stare at him. He took an unconscious step backward.

"How," Adama asked, "do you figure that?"

"Exhaust trail," Gaeta said. "Harder to trace, but not impossible. I've been working on it since I realized the first signal was a fake. The ships have moved around, of course, and I had to extrapolate a little, but the trail could lead to one of two ships—the *Celestra* or the *Monarch*. The *Celestra* is an Aeron ship and it's small. Hard to hide there. The *Monarch* is a Geminon ship and it has most of the algae harvest on it. He could hold the food hostage if he wanted—another advantage. So I figure the *Monarch* was the shuttle's the most likely destination."

"Well done, Mr. Gaeta," Adama said, then turned to Lee. "Assemble your strike force."

• • •

"Much better," said Tom Zarek. He leaned casually back against a bulkhead between two shelving units, his arms crossed. "Raising a revolution is much more effective if you get the people on your side. And having a good fighting song is a real plus."

"You are so dead," Kara growled from her position on the floor. Her hands—still shaking—were bound behind her. "You're going straight back to jail once this blows over."

"Really?" Zarek raised his eyebrows. "What for?"

"For aiding an escaped felon," she snapped. "For inciting riot."

Peter set down the microphone, his face hard. "So I *was* under arrest. Even though they told me that it was a quarantine thing."

"It *was* a quarantine thing," Kara protested. "Peter—"

"There you have it," Zarek interrupted with a grin Kara wanted to smack. "If Peter wasn't arrested, then I'm hardly aiding a felon. And if he *was* arrested, it was done illegally, since he's broken no laws. We still have freedom of speech around here, last I looked. It's not against the law to exercise our civil rights, no matter how inconvenient they may be for those in power."

Peter knelt in front of Kara. "Look, I can't deny it anymore. I'm the Unifier. My time among the Cylons was meant to show that to me, show me that the One exists. I see the One's touch in so many people. The Scrolls say that I'll save humanity with the gift of tongues, and I'm doing it."

"What are you saving us from?" Kara asked hotly. "The Cylons? Give me a break."

"I'm saving us all from lies. Kara, all our lives we've been told about the Lords of Kobol, and they do exist, but not as we've thought of them." He leaned closer, and Kara could feel the heat emanated from his body. His eyes burned with a fervor that until now she had only seen when he was on stage. "We were like children, learning simple lessons. But now we've been thrown out of the nest and into the greater universe. The One will show us the way we need to go, but first we need to believe in the One's existence."

Kara tried to swallow, but her mouth was dry. Peter's handsome face and earnest, hypnotic voice lent credibility to his words. She actually found she *wanted* to believe him, would have been willing to at least consider what he was saying—except that she'd been kidnapped and tied up and her hands were shaking from the prions he had infected her with. His words meant nothing to her now.

Still, he had given her an opening, however small.

"Peter," she said, "your ideas are pretty far out there, but . . . I have to admit that sometimes I wonder how the Lords of Kobol could possibly have let the Cylons destroy the Colonies. Maybe you're right and there's something more out there. I . . . I don't know."

"Of course there is, Kara," Peter said, his blue eyes filling the world before her like a tropical ocean. "You've seen how the One smiles on me and my followers. I'm the Unifier."

"Maybe," Kara said, careful not to agree suspiciously fast. She glanced around the store room. Some of the Unity people had gone off, leaving only two guards behind. They were clearly civilians, and probably not good fighters. A couple of quick moves, and Kara would have one of their pistols. Tom Zarek was standing by himself, watching and listening with an amused expression on his face. He was unarmed and no threat. Sharon was Kara's main adversary. The Cylon, still masked, was packing up the radio transmitter and jamming device. Where the hell had she gotten that? Must have stolen it while she was wandering the ship. At Sharon's feet lay a large red duffel bag, and Kara had no idea *what* that contained. She had the feeling it wouldn't be fun finding out.

"Look," Kara said, "this whole Unifier thing just seems kind of . . . I don't know." She shrugged and winced. "Ow! Frak, this hurts."

"Here," Peter said, reaching around behind her. His body pressed against hers, but with none of the intimacy they had shared in his room. This time, his touch made her want to throw up. "Let me get those off you."

Kara held her breath as Peter's hands found her restraints. In a few seconds . . .

"Hey!" Sharon grabbed Peter's hands and pulled them away. "She's toying with you, Peter. Unifier. They're all trained for this—get you to trust them, and then when you untie them—pow! You're on your back, and not in a good way."

Peter stepped back uncertainly, and Kara glared at Sharon. "What's your stake in all this, anyway? You're not even . . ." She trailed off pointedly.

Sharon's almond eyes crinkled above her mask. "I want to see the Unifier succeed. The established priesthood feels threatened by anything different, even when it's the truth. Or maybe *because* it's the truth."

"That there's only one god," Kara said.

"That's exactly it," Sharon agreed. "The truth."

The door to the storeroom opened, and some two dozen people

entered. Peter turned to face them. Their expressions were alternately fearful, apprehensive, and skeptical. A few looked confident. Some wore red masks, and Kara scrutinized each. Were any of them in the military? Anyone she knew?

One of the masked Unities came forward. "These people want to hear the Unifier speak. They want to hear the truth."

"Of course, my brothers and sisters." Peter upended a crate and climbed on top of it. He seemed to have forgotten all about the truth Kara had wanted to tell him.

Kara strained against her bonds. Even though she knew it was futile, she couldn't help it. "Why don't you tell Peter your own truth, then? Or maybe I should."

"Go ahead." Sharon picked up the duffel bag and set it on the floor in front of Kara. "Just be prepared to pay the consequences."

Kara automatically looked down at the bag's contents. Her eyes widened. "Where the hell did you get missile ordnance?" she asked. Her heart was pounding again. She was sitting bare centimeters away from enough explosive power to wipe out a small ship or punch a hole in the side of a big one.

"There's always someone willing to dicker," Sharon said. "Especially for the chance to get close to the Unifier." She squatted down beside Kara and said softly, "You know what they say, Lieutenant: 'Loose lips blow ships.' Though your lips blow something else."

Kara automatically tried to take a swing at Sharon, and her wrists jerked painfully against her restraints. Peter, meanwhile, was speaking to the crowd.

". . . and know that you, too, are chosen by the One. You are special, part of the force that unifies us all. You can help us end the suffering, end the strife and war. You have the same power I do, if you just believe in the One."

Although he was speaking in a scruffy storeroom in the bowels of gods only knew what ship, his powerful voice and silvery earnestness made it seem like he was standing on a windswept mountain, preaching to the masses below. The people listened, rapt and staring. When Peter gestured, they swayed in time to it, as if they were an orchestra Peter was conducting. Kara didn't believe a word he was saying, but the power in him was undeniable. She saw the people's expressions shift. Instead of fear or skepticism, she saw hope, and even happiness. The four people closest to Peter fell to their knees. Kara understood exactly what was going on. The civilians in the Fleet had few choices and certainly no control over anything major. They ate what they were rationed, went where their ships took them, died when the Cylons fought them. And the priests could do nothing but offer empty prayers. Peter was offering something better. He made them feel powerful and special, gave them hope for control over their own lives. Kara sympathized, but she wasn't foolish enough to fall for false hope. Not again. Zarek leaned against the walk-in refrigerator door and watched the goings-on, a look of admiration on his face. Sharon watched also, her expression unreadable through her mask.

"Maybe my lips will blow your secret," Kara said to her. "How would the Unifier react to learning one of his followers is a frakking Cylon?"

"You want to tell Peter who I am, be my guest." Sharon gestured at the duffel bag. "But there'll be a price if you open your mouth, honey. Tick tock, tick tock, boom. A boom from Boomer. Get it?"

"You can't set that thing off," Kara said, ignoring the stupid joke. "Not without the access code. And I'm sure as frak not going to give it to you."

"What if I torture you?" Sharon's tone was so idle, so gentle. It made Kara's skin grow cold, and she remembered her father.

"Meh," she said, trying to shrug. "Been there. Besides, Peter won't cotton to you pulling out his consort's fingernails."

"It was just a whim." Sharon leaned closer. "I already have the code, sweetie. The guy who gave me the ordnance provided it. I was just frakking with you."

"Sure. Your lies are getting thinner, sweetie."

"Okay. Go ahead and blab about me to Petey-boy. You do, I'll enter the code. Poof! We're nothing but a cloud of bloody debris."

"Don't forget that 'we' includes you."

Sharon shrugged. "I don't have much to live for and so I don't care if I die. What about you?"

"I'm dying already," Kara hissed back. "Plague of tongues, re-member?"

"Ah, but you're not a fatalist," Sharon countered. "You think there's a possibility the prions won't kill you. The ordnance, on the other hand, will *definitely* kill you. A chance of life versus a definite death. I think you'll keep your mouth shut."

Kara glared at Sharon but kept her mouth shut as Sharon predicted. A small part of her wanted to shout the truth to Peter and his followers just to prove Sharon wrong, but the rational part of her knew better. She would have to keep Sharon's secret.

For now, anyway.

CHAPTER 12

Lee Adama arrived in the rec room just before the fight started. He was winding his way through the section of the *Galactica* that housed the marines. The entire area smelled of sweat, gunmetal, and old blankets. Corridors were narrow, and the rooms were lined with bunks and lockers. A song echoed through the hallways. Lee paused to listen, tracking the source. It came from the rec room a ways down the hall, and the song in question was the revolution song Peter had broadcast over the radio. An angry rumbling sound provided a background. Lee tensed and hurried his steps.

He didn't need this. He still had a throbbing headache from getting clocked in sickbay. It pierced his skull like a lead stiletto. And a desperate worry twisted his insides so tight, his bones felt as if they would break under the pressure. Kara had been snatched straight out of sickbay a few hours ago and seemed to be in the hands of a religious nutcase. Every detail of the events in sickbay was branded into his brain—Peter's howling, Kara's annoyed expression, the scarlet masks of the Unity kidnappers. He hated to admit it, but those masks had really creeped him out. He couldn't explain why, even to himself. Masks always creeped him out. Once, when they were kids, his brother Zak had found a full-face mask made of translucent plastic. It gave the appearance of a perfectly smooth face with human flesh tones. Zak had jumped around a corner with it on and made ghost noises. Lee couldn't comprehend what he was looking at, this blank-faced thing menacing him just outside his own bedroom. Utter terror had made his bladder let go. Zak had laughed at Lee and Dad had thrashed Zak for it.

And then had come the robotic Cylons.

The Unity were only people, Lee told himself, not inhumanly mechanical Cylons. But you could see robotic Cylons for what they were, and you could identify the human ones once you knew what their faces looked like. They shouldn't be any more frightening than any other enemies Lee had faced. But the masks were still creepy. And he was still worried about Kara. What the hell were they doing to her? She would be both scared and pissed off. A part of Lee smiled at the thought of Kara held prisoner by religious fanatics. Why rescue her? Who cared what happened to the kidnappers?

But Lee continued to worry.

It seemed he worried a lot about Kara Thrace. More than he

should. After all, she was just a friend. A close friend. Who was seeing someone else. A religious someone else. Lee's head throbbed again. He had seen the picture of Kara kissing Peter in *Person to Person*. He had closed the magazine carefully, as if it might sprout teeth and snap off his fingers. Then he had pointedly put it out of his mind. No point in thinking about it. Kara didn't matter to him in that way. She was more like a cousin or sister.

Definitely. A sister. Lee shook his aching head, trying without success to convince himself the lie—no, the *statement*—was true and that he wasn't jealous over Peter Attis. He couldn't be. He loved Kara, yes. But he wasn't *in* love with her.

Sure. Of course not.

A few more steps down the corridor, and Lee entered the rec room. The place was crowded with off-duty personnel. A group of eight marines was pounding the table and singing Peter's revolution song. Another group was half shouting at them to knock it off.

"Kill that shit," one of the dissenters barked. "You want to preach blasphemy, do it in vacuum."

"Frak off," snarled one of the singers, advancing on the dissenter with clenched fists. "If you can't handle the truth, get the frak off *Galactica*. The Unifier lives!"

Lee felt his mouth fall open and he halted dead. Unity factions among the marines? That was something he hadn't even considered. Obviously the Unity was spreading farther and faster than anyone had anticipated. Before he could say anything, the dissenter rose to his feet and snapped a punch at the singer's jaw. Taken by surprise, the singer dropped to the floor. There was a tiny moment of silence as everyone stared at everyone else, and then the room erupted into chaos. Fists and feet punched and kicked. Tables and chairs scattered and flew. Lee snatched a phone off the wall.

"This is Captain Adama in rec room seven," he barked. "I need peacekeepers down here. Now!"

The brawl continued. The dull smack of flesh punching flesh thumped through the room, punctuated by grunts of pain and howls of outrage. Furniture crashed against walls and floor. Lee stood in the doorway, unable to halt the fracas by himself. Helpless anger suffused him. He could bark an order for everyone to freeze, but he doubted anyone would hear him, and being ignored like that would undermine his authority. He ground his teeth. The Cylon plague was succeeding in ways no one had anticipated.

"Holy frak! Look!" someone shouted.

And a hole opened up in the middle of the brawl. Two marines lay on the floor, twisting and convulsing. Nonsense fell from their mouths in a stream of babble. The fighting slowed and stopped as people turned to look.

"It's a miracle!" said the singer. "The Unifier's touch brings a blessing."

"It's a disease," shouted someone else. "It's not a blessing. The Lords of Kobol have cursed us for blasphemy."

The two marines continued to babble. One was frothing at the mouth.

"You can't call a miracle blasphemy," the singer said, clenching his fists again. Blood flowed from a split lip. "You can't—"

"Quiet!" Lee bellowed, taking advantage of the semi-calm. "That's an order!"

Everyone in the room turned to look in surprise, noticing Lee for the first time. The afflicted marines convulsed and jabbered, lost in their own private, painful worlds.

"I should have everyone in this room arrested for conduct unbe-coming," Lee boomed. "Line up at attention!"

Several of the marines looked defiant and Lee wondered if they would actually disobey orders. What the hell would he do then? But the defiance lasted only a moment. They lined up just as a group of MPs burst into the room. They took in the situation quickly, and the sergeant turned to Lee.

"Sir?" he asked.

"I think we're calmed down," Lee said. "But those men need med-ical attention. Get them to sickbay. The rest of you need to remain here and make sure the situation stays calm."

The marines stayed at attention while the MPs hauled the two bab-blers out of the room. Lee walked up and down the row of marines, the broken furniture forming a strange backdrop behind him.

"Hold out your hands, palm down," Lee ordered.

The marines looked mystified but obeyed. Lee watched. Twenty marines held out forty hands, palm down. Two shook noticeably. An-other five trembled, and three more started to shake a few seconds af-ter Lee gave the order. Lee kept his own shaky hands behind his back.

"The Unifier's touch," said the singer in awe. He was one of the tremblers.

"No," Lee said. "It's a prion, a disease that Peter Attis is spreading." He pointed at the ten marines whose hands weren't shaking. "Report to the briefing room in ten minutes. The rest of you report to sickbay."

• • •

"He's so handsome, Gaius," Number Six murmured. "Have you ever wondered what it would be like to be that good-looking?"

"No," growled Gaius. "It's not an issue with me."

"And he's talented. When he speaks or sings, everyone listens. Even Laura Roslin."

The words popped out of Gaius's mouth before he could stop them. "I'm her vice president," he snapped. "She should listen to me."

"What's that?" Cottle asked from the other side of the lab.

"Nothing," Gaius said quickly. "Just thinking out loud."

Cottle gave him an odd look, then turned back to his instruments. Gaius shot Number Six a harsh glare. She was sitting upright on one of the tables, one knee drawn up, a lot of smooth leg showing under a red dress.

"It must be difficult to be pushed into the background," Six said in a low, silky voice. "It's not fair of them to ignore you, Gaius. You're worth more than that."

"Frak you," he muttered, and managed to wrench his attention back to the protein scanner. So far it was showing very few similarities between Prions T and H and Prion C. He was hoping for *something*, some kind of link between the three. Prion H, the harmless prion, linked with Prion T, the transformational prion, and became the deadly prion. Their link was well established. But what was the third prion for? Gaius knew it was artificial—there was nothing like it in any of the databases, and it was present only in Peter's blood. He hadn't found it in any of the other random samples he had taken from other crewmembers, which also meant the prion wasn't communicable. It was, in fact, rather fragile. Once removed from its host plasma, it fell apart. The samples of Peter's blood and plasma, in fact, had to be kept at body temperature and in near darkness, or the mysterious prion simply melted away. But what did it *do*? It had to be connected to Prion T and Prion H somehow, though it shared no structural similarities. Prions T and H had several similarities that let them hook together like pieces of a jigsaw puzzle so Prion T could unfold Prion H into its deadly form. But if Gaius was reading the scans right—and he was— the mysterious prion had a single marker in common with Prion H, which meant they might hook together in one spot. Gaius furrowed his brow. If that happened, and Prion H linked with the mystery prion, they would form an enormous, ungainly macromolecule. And that would mean . . .

And then Gaius had it. It was so simple, so obvious. Quickly, he assembled slides filled with Peter's plasma. He had to be careful—Cottle had only extracted a few hundred cc's of plasma before Peter's kidnapping. Escape. Whatever you wanted to call it. And some of the vials had shattered on the floor when Lee Adama dropped them. Fortunately, two had remained intact. Now the entire supply rested in a pitifully small collection of sealed test tubes kept in a warmer set at precisely thirty-seven degrees—human body temperature. Gaius took care to return the tubes before the fragile mystery prion could be exposed to temperatures outside its viability range. He would have to hurry, in fact, because the prions he took out of the plasma would only survive a few minutes.

"Onto something, Gaius?" Six asked archly. He ignored her. Cottle shuffled papers from the work area he had carved out of Gaius's lab.

Without bothering to take proper notes or make proper documentation—no time—Gaius dropped samples of Prion T and Prion H into a single slide. Then he slid them under a microscope and watched. It didn't take long for the copies of Prion T to find partners among the Prion H samples. They clicked together like little magnets, and the tightly-wound Ts unraveled, just as Gaius had seen them do a thousand times. His skin crawled with cold worms, and it seemed as if he could feel the same unraveling process happening in his own body. All his life, Gaius had been blessed with a whipcord body that required little maintenance and which held a certain amount of charm, if he said so himself. But in the end, his body was merely a home for his mind. It was his mind that had made him into a celebrity, his great intelligence that had elevated him above other humans. Having such a mind was a terrible and heavy responsibility, and it was his duty to preserve his mind so that the rest of humanity could benefit from it. And now that mind was under attack by a rogue bit of protein that would eat holes in it until it looked like a lumpy gray sponge. It would leave nothing of Gaius Baltar but a babbling, incoherent fool, and the thought filled him with a cold terror that twisted his gut like a snake.

"All right, you little bugger," he whispered to himself, "let's see what happens when I do this."

With careful fingers, he introduced the mystery prion to the mix and watched carefully. At first nothing happened. The mystery prion floated in the thin plasma, bobbing about the white blood cells, water, and other flotsam like a complicated beach ball floating among the detritus of an ocean shipwreck. Then a mystery prion intersected an unfolded Prion H. Instantly, it linked ribbons with its deadly cousin, forming as Gaius had predicted, a long, lumpy macromolecule of protein. The moment that happened, a nearby white blood cell engulfed the molecule. In a few moments, the macromolecule fell completely apart. The component amino acids drifted harmlessly away.

Exultation swelled in Gaius Baltar, banishing the fear. The mystery prion was the cure to the plague of tongues and he, Gaius Baltar, had discovered it. Pride inflated his chest, and he felt strong enough to punch through a metal bulkhead. See if anyone would avoid his lectures now!

"Are you finding what I'm finding?" Cottle said behind him.

Gaius jumped and jerked away from the microscope. "Gods, you scared the bleeding shit out of me."

"Sorry." Cottle exhaled a stream of smoke. "Just wanted to see what you got."

"The third prion is the key to Peter's immunity," Gaius said triumphantly. "It bonds with the deadly prion and turns it into a form that the body's immune system recognizes as a threat. I just observed a macrophage consume and destroy an unfolded Prion H."

"Interesting," Cottle said. "I just finished examining a bunch of Peter's B cells. B cells produce antibodies, right?"

"I know what B cells do," Gaius said shortly, annoyed that Cottle hadn't acknowledged his breakthrough with appropriate fanfare.

"Just setting the stage," Cottle said, unruffled. "Peter's B cells produce antibodies, but currently they're also producing—"

"The mystery prion," Gaius finished.

"Brilliant," Six commented dryly from the table. Didn't she get cramped from sitting in one position for so long? "Too bad you have to share this discovery with the good doctor, Gaius. The credit should go to you."

Gaius didn't like Number Six very much at that moment, but he had to admit she was right. Cottle might grab credit that belonged to Gaius Baltar.

"So in summary," Cottle said, "if you inject someone with the mystery prion—let's call it Prion C for 'cure'—it bonds with Prion H and changes it into a form your white blood cells crunch down like potato chips. Prion C also convinces your B cells to make antibodies against the transformed Prion H, which further boosts your immunity. You continue to carry the prions, but they don't bother you."

Gaius ran a hand over his face, feeling suddenly tired. "Except our only reliable supply of Prion C was kidnapped by a bunch of religious fanatics. Every time we find a solution, it only reveals another problem."

"Then we'd better get back to work," Cottle said, turning back to his own instruments. "Before we start shaking in our own booties."

The fear took hold of Gaius again. He couldn't afford to get sick—he had to finish his work here or thousands of others would die along with him. A small sob tried to escape and he choked it back. It was so unfair!

"Have you examined your own blood lately, Gaius?" asked Number Six.

"Not half an hour ago," Gaius muttered, wishing she would go the hell away and leave him to his fear and misery.

"Check it again, Gaius."

"What for? Nothing's changed."

"You never know." A small smile tugged at the corners of her red lips. "Not until you look."

Gaius looked at her, but her face remained a beautiful mystery. "Fine," he snapped as loud as he dared. "But it's a waste of time."

He glanced at Cottle to make sure the man was occupied, then pricked a fingertip and dripped several scarlet drops onto a slide. He capped the sample and slid it under a microscope.

"What am I looking for?" he whispered. "What do you think I'm going to find?"

"It's what you don't find that's important, Gaius," Six said from her table. "Go ahead."

He looked. It was a perfectly normal blood sample. Erythrocytes, thrombocytes, lymphocytes, leukocytes. All to be expected.

"What am I . . . not looking for?" he asked.

"Keep looking. Focus closer."

A suspicion crawled over him, and he adjusted the focus on the microscope. He spent considerable time searching, and found . . . nothing. He backed away from the microscope, feeling abruptly weak and wrung out.

"No prions," he said in a hushed voice. "I don't have the prion."

"You're observant, Gaius," Six said.

He turned to face her. "But how? No, scratch that. It's obvious how." He started to pace, oblivious to whether Cottle was paying attention to him or not. "In any case of infection, there's always a certain percentage of the population who is naturally immune. I'm simply one of those cases."

"Poor Gaius." Six slid off the table and sauntered toward him. "You still don't believe, do you?"

"Believe what?"

"In miracles." She put her arms around him, breathing her breath into his mouth. "Isn't it clear? God wants you alive for a purpose, Gaius. He took the prion from your blood so you can fulfill your purpose."

Gaius felt a strange combination of uncertainty and gratification. This wasn't the first time Number Six had told him he was special, that his destiny was for something more than puttering around a laboratory and signing paperwork. It was immensely gratifying to hear this. To a certain extent it was a relief, further proof that his own estimation was right—that his innate intelligence and talent made him more valuable, more important than the masses of humanity who scurried through their ordinary corridors living their quiet, desperate lives. On the other hand, it was a little unnerving to think that a Cylon deity—assuming such a being really existed—had its eye on him.

"What purpose am I supposed to fulfill?" he murmured.

"That will come clear in time, Gaius," Six said, backing away. "And in less time than you think."

"Oh, that's helpful," Gaius complained. "Why is it the people who hand out predictions never say exactly what is going to happen? It would be nice, for once, to hear something like 'You'll find an inhabitable planet in a few weeks, so don't worry,' or 'Run for president and you'll win.'"

"Just concentrate on the cure, Gaius," Six said. "It's in the blood."

Gaius was about to argue when a thought crossed his mind. He turned to Cottle, who was still bent over his own instruments and appeared to have noticed nothing. "Peter's blood type is O negative, right?" Gaius asked.

"Yeah," Cottle said. "We caught a break there. O negative is rare, but it's the universal donor. Anyone can receive his blood—and the cure. We're just stuck with the fact that we don't even have two hundred cc's of Peter's blood left."

"We can create more Prion C," Gaius said. "We have the samples. We just need to use the right incubation methods, feed Prion C the appropriate nutrients in the right medium. Shouldn't take more than a few hours. A half-trained beagle could do it. What do you think?"

"That had occurred to me. But I think we need to do more tests first."

"Dammit, we don't have time for that!" Gaius smacked a tabletop in a melodramatic gesture. "Let's just get to work, shall we? You know I'm right."

Cottle looked at him, then shrugged and started pulling petri dishes from a shelf. Gaius was a little surprised he had given in so fast and with so little argument.

"It's funny, when you think about it," Cottle said.

"What's that?" Gaius crossed his arms as he stood next to the plasma warmer.

"Peter's turning out to be the savior he's been claiming to be all along. His blood is going to cure everyone." Cottle set the stack of dishes on a work table and ground out the stub of his cigarette in one of them. "We're going to do all the work, but you know how it always goes. Peter Attis will be famous for saving us while we toil in foggy obscurity."

Gaius felt his jaw slowly drop as Cottle laid out the dishes in preparation for the incubation medium. Number Six's soft hands slid over his shoulders, and her warm breath moved against his ear.

"He's right, Gaius," she said wetly. "You and Cottle will labor here in this dim, cramped lab while Peter Attis, handsome Peter Attis, rakes in the glory. If only you could find a cure completely on your own. It isn't fair or right."

The thought made his jaw go from slack to tense. It *was* unfair. How many times had he labored to save the Fleet, and how many times had his hard work gone unnoticed? Once he had spent hours working up calculations on how much food and water the Fleet would use on a weekly basis, and when he had presented Commander Adama with the information at a meeting, Adama had stared at the startlingly high figures for a moment, then turned to discuss the matter with Saul Tigh and Laura Roslin, as if Gaius were a child who had brought home average marks on a report card. As vice president, he had been saddled with idiotic paperwork and given lectures no one attended while people like Kara Thrace appeared in full-color magazines because she kissed a rock star in public. Fury clenched his fists.

"I could do it," he said softly. "A prion is just a protein, and I have a model to work from. Reverse engineering is much easier than creating something from scratch. I know my way around a molecule. It wouldn't take that long to create my own Prion C."

"Except you don't need to," Six pointed out. "Peter's prion will replicate itself in his rare, heroic blood. As long as his material exists, the world doesn't need you, Gaius."

Gaius stared down at the little plasma warmer. It was the size and shape of a microwave oven. The temperature readout on the front indicated that the internal temperature was a precise thirty-seven degrees. A few degrees too hot or too cold, and Prion C would disintigrate. Cottle, meanwhile, was pouring careful amounts of liquid nutrient medium into the Petri dishes. In a few hours, the cure would be ready. The dial that controlled the warmer's temperature seemed to stare at Gaius, daring him.

"Do it, Gaius," Six goaded. "It's the right idea."

"No," he whispered. "People might die in the time it takes me to replicate the original. One person already has."

"Do it," she said firmly. "It's your destiny!" She took his hand and pulled it toward the dial. He resisted, hand trembling, but she was strong, stronger than he had ever been. His fingers found the ribbed surface of the dial. It would be so easy. One little twist, and his position in history would be assured while Peter Attis was forgotten.

"No," he whispered again.

"Yes," Six said, and twisted his hand. The dial slowly clicked counterclockwise, and the readout indicated a falling temperature. Thirty-six degrees. Thirty-four. Thirty-one. No! This was wrong. Gaius reached out to turn the dial back, but Six's hand snaked out and grabbed his. She wrenched it aside, and he gasped with pain.

"Leave it!" she barked. "Be a man, Gaius! Grab the opportunities God and I send you!"

He stared at her, comprehension dawning. "Did you . . . did you arrange this, somehow? Start this plague of tongues so I could cure it?" His back was now to Cottle, who was still engrossed with the Petri dishes.

"Think, Gaius," Six snarled. "Does anything in the universe happen by accident? Do you think I'm here, with you, by random chance? I've told you before, Gaius—you have a destiny, and you can't ignore it. God cured you for a reason. Fulfill your purpose!"

"I . . . I can't . . ." he whispered. But he made no move to turn the dial again, and the temperature continued to fall.

Galen Tyrol held up his hands. Both were shaking. His mouth went dry and fear squeezed his heart, but he didn't panic. Not yet. That would come later, when he was lying in his bunk with the curtain drawn and his trembling hands crammed against his mouth so no one would hear him whimpering in the dark against an enemy he couldn't see, hear, or touch but was coming to kill him nonetheless.

Lined up on the floor in front of him were dozens of people. Deck five—Tyrol's deck—had been turned into an impromptu sickbay because sickbay itself was full. The people lay on stretchers, blankets, towels, and hard, bare floor. Some twitched and writhed and babbled, others lay perfectly still. Two harried-looking medical technicians did their best to tend them, but there wasn't much they could do except try to keep everyone comfortable. Half the Viper pilots were among the patients, as were several of Tyol's people, *Galactica*'s "knuckle draggers." Tyrol squatted next to Cally, who lay on an old rug Tyrol had scrounged for her. She twisted like a dancer whose tendons had been halfway cut, and long strings of nonsense syllables fell from her mouth. He took her cool, squirming hand in his shaking one. The air around her was tainted with the sour smell of sickness.

"I wish I could help," he said. "I'm sorry."

"She doesn't need help," said a man Tyrol didn't recognize. He was similarly holding the hand of a male patient who was babbling just like Cally. "None of them do. They've been touched by the Unifier. When they awaken, they'll have seen the face of God. You should be happy for her."

An urge to punch the jerk in the face made Tyrol's hands into shaky fists. Blasphemous nonsense—and hurtful. Cally wasn't in a divine state. She was sick, and this frakking bastard had the nerve to tell Tyrol he should be happy about it. But he kept his hands to himself and pointedly turned his attention back to Cally. The look she gave him was uncomprehending. She didn't even know he was there. Tyrol pushed down more panic. He liked Cally—as a friend. As someone who worked under his command. Nothing more than that. But the intensity of the distress he felt at her pain startled him. He was the guy everyone came to when something needed fixing. Vipers, Raptors, conveyer belts. Hell, once he'd even fixed a sewing machine. This, however, he couldn't fix.

Abruptly, he got up and strode away. The only solution was to keep busy. Or try to. There wasn't much to do, wasn't much he *could* do with his hands the way they were. Only five pilots hadn't been grounded, but it was only a matter of time. Emergency flights were the only ones running. It meant that the repair crews didn't have much to do, but that didn't matter—with no ships out, Tyrol didn't have much to repair. If the Cylons found and attacked them now, they'd be dead.

Of course, even if the Cylons *didn't* find them, they were dead. No matter what, the Cylons won. Frak.

The escape pod caught his eye, and his feet took him toward it. His footsteps echoed, mingling with the babbling behind him. A little itch at the back of his mind nagged at him every time he looked at it, but he hadn't had the time to examine it much. Until now. Figuring out what was bugging him about it might take his mind off his own impending death—and Cally's.

First he made a circuit of the outside, walking around it and examining every centimeter. It was the standard gray ceramic, no major cracks or visible blemishes. Some scorching from the explosion that had destroyed the basestar. A few scratches, either from the explosion or the landing.

He cranked the door down—it took a while with his hands shaking as they were—and inspected the inside. Nothing had changed. The basic control panel was still there, the porthole was still there, the CO_2 scrubber was—

Tyrol put a quivering hand on his chin, then pulled a measuring tape from his tool belt. He tried to extend it, but his hands shook too much. Frustrated, he flung it against the bulkhead. It hit with a loud clang. His body was breaking down, becoming undependable. Then he set his jaw. He hadn't lost everything yet. He put his arms out like a tightrope walker and paced from one end of the pod to the other, going heel to toe. His body made an adequate measuring tool, and no disease could change *that*. Tyrol counted fifteen of his own feet. After that, he went outside, started at one corner, and measured off the outside.

Eighteen feet.

Ah ha! Excited, Tyrol went back inside. Even assuming the thickness of the bulkheads added up to one of his feet, that left two of his feet unaccounted for. He retrieved his measuring tape and used it to tap on the bulkheads, something even his shaky hands could handle. The bulkhead opposite the door, the one with the scrubber hanging on it, had a hollow ring. Carefully Tyrol examined the scrubber. On the underside, his palsied hands found a switch. He flipped it.

Near the floor, a rectangular section of the rear wall a meter high and two meters long moved inward slightly. Cautiously, Tyrol pressed on it. It gave way, sliding inward and revealing a long, low chamber with a light set into the ceiling. A blanket and pillow lay on the floor. Tyrol's mouth set into a pale, hard line. Someone besides Peter and the dead Cylon had stowed away on the pod.

"I don't know what the hell happened, Commander," Cottle said in the conference room. "All I know is that the temperature in the incubator fell to twenty-eight degrees and all our samples of Prion C fell apart."

Commander Adama's face remained as impassive as rusty iron.

"So you're telling me that we have no samples of Peter's blood to work with."

"Yeah." Cottle lit a cigarette with a practiced flick of his lighter. "Frak. I put the samples in the incubator myself, and I'm sure I set the temperature right. But I may have misread the dials. Or maybe the dial snagged on my sleeve and I didn't notice. Hell, I don't know."

Gaius studied both Cottle and Adama's faces, but neither of them seemed to suspect the incident with the blood was anything but an accident. "It could have happened to anyone," he said magnanimously. "However, we do have computer mock-ups of all the prions. I'm sure, given time and supplies, I could come up with—"

"Let me get this straight," Adama interrupted. "With the samples destroyed, the only source of the cure is Peter himself?"

"That's pretty much the situation," Cottle said.

"Though I'm quite positive I can recreate Prion C," Gaius said. "It'll take a little time, but—"

"Time," Adama interrupted, snatching up a telephone, "is in short supply. Dualla," he said in the receiver, "get Captain Adama on the line."

A few moments later, Adama said, "It's me. I need an update on the strike force and you need an update on the prion situation. In the conference room."

Cottle excused himself and left. Gaius knew he should follow suit and get into the lab, but he was feeling an utter lack of urgency. If Adama wasn't all that interested in Gaius creating a cure, then Gaius could just trundle along at whatever pace he liked. He was already immune, and his fear of the disease had evaporated. Besides, he wanted to know what was going to happen between captain and commander, so he pulled out a small notebook and sketched amino acids instead. Adama seemed too preoccupied to notice. Ignoring him. Lee Adama arrived after a few minutes and took the chair Adama indicated. Gaius stopped sketching.

"I haven't even been able to round up a dozen people who aren't shaking," Lee said. "And I'm running into . . . other factors."

Adama removed his glasses and polished them with a white handkerchief. In that moment, he looked more like an exasperated grandfather than the commander of a military fleet, though he looked nothing like Gaius Baltar's grandfather. The vain, randy old bastard wouldn't have worn glasses in public if you'd paid him. Gaius wondered what it would have been like to have a grandfather that soaked up the sun in a rocking chair and carved charming little toys out of

wood instead of jetting about the world attending conferences and seducing anything that walked on two legs. One of Gaius's earliest
memories didn't involve walking in on his parents. It involved walking in on his grandfather and three of his bedmates.

"What other factors, Captain?" Adama asked quietly.

Lee grimaced. "The quarantine of the *Monarch* started up the food
shortage again, which is making people unhappy. Everyone in the
Fleet seems to be singing Peter's revolution song now, and lots of
them seem to think that you're a . . . a tyrant who's trying to step on
Peter's civil rights—and on the Unity's. It's making people remember
the—uh, the 'incident' on the *Gideon* again."

Gaius added another amino acid to his sketch without comment. It
was a challenge, sketching a three-dimensional molecule in two di-
mensions. The "incident," as Lee put it, had happened while Commander Adama lay in a coma, recovering from the near-deadly
wounds Sharon had dealt him. Saul Tigh had taken over Adama's
command, and he had sent armed marines to "liberate" food supplies
from the recalcitrant ship *Gideon*. An unruly mob had greeted the
marines, and the situation quickly devolved into a riot. One marine
had panicked and opened fire. Four civilians had died. For days, the
media had shown videos of a little girl crying over the bloody corpse
of her father. Gaius mentally shook his head. Saul Tigh was crafty in
some ways and stunningly stupid in others.

"And I'm learning the Unity has more sympathizers than I knew,"
Lee finished. "They see Peter as a savior."

"Savior from what?" Adama said in a dead-even voice.

"The Cylons." Lee cleared his throat. "The Cylons seem to have a
monotheistic system of belief, and they won the war. Peter is preaching monotheism, and a chunk of the listeners are thinking that our situation would improve if we had the same belief system. It's just as he
said on the radio, with the added 'fact' that his touch makes people
speak in tongues, and that only makes him more believable."

"I don't give a damn one way or the other about the civil rights of
Attis or his followers," Adama snapped. "He has the cure for this
prion disease, and that's why I need him in sickbay, whole and unharmed."

"But a growing number of people see the disease as a blessing,"
Lee countered. "Cure not desired or required. They think they'll recover and be blessed somehow."

"We'll worry about the Unity's attitude toward the plague of
tongues after we extract enough blood from Peter to cure it," Adama

said. "Get back to assembling the strike force, Captain. Bring Peter Attis back to *Galactica*."

"I think I'll need two forces, sir," Lee said. "And I'm afraid I'm going to have to use personnel outside the marines. Too many of them
are down."

"Whatever you think is necessary, Captain," Adama said. Lee left,
and to Gaius's surprise, Adama turned to him.

"You should work on creating that cure, Doctor," he said. "In case
we can't find Peter—or in case something happens to him."

Ah. So he wasn't worthy of being ignored after all. "Of course,
Commander." Gaius gathered his sketches and rose to go. It hadn't escaped his notice that neither commander nor captain had mentioned
Kara Thrace in their final exchange, but it was equally obvious to him
that both had been thinking about her.

The group of Unity people ended the final verse of Peter's song just as
three of them landed on the floor, twitching like half-dead fish. Those
who remained standing cheered and clapped each other on the back.
Peter stood on his packing crate, lapping up the attention like a starving cat left overnight in a milkhouse. Several Unity members helped
the fallen ones to a place near a bulkhead where ten others squirmed
and babbled. Kara watched with a mixture of fear and bafflement.
How could these people believe this was anything except a curse?
They'd have to be desperate, clutching at straws made of starlight.

She sighed inwardly. How many times had *she* been just as desperate? No, it was all *too* understandable.

Her hands, still tied behind her, were shaking even worse now, and
she caught one of her legs beginning to tremble. Fear made her mouth
dry. The disease was taking the slower course with her, but it still was
progressing. How much time left?

"Left and right of way for fifteen dozen eggs came first—"

Who the frak was talking? No new people were twisting on the
floor. It took a moment to realize that the nonsense words were pouring from her own mouth.

"—second in line for muffins and butter with apple pie in the
kitchen—" Kara clamped her mouth shut and managed to stop the
flow of words. Her heart pounded faster under a fresh spurt of adrenaline. It was happening. It was happening to her.

Not yet, she prayed. *Just let me hold out a little longer.*

Peter was talking to individual members of the Unity crowd now.
This was the fourth set that had come in. Tom Zarek, the bastard, re-

mained standing near the walk-in, smug in the knowledge that he had fomented this chaos.

Where the frak was the cavalry? The military knew Kara was missing. Lee had been standing right there when the Unity had kidnapped her. So why hadn't they tracked her down? Kara "Starbuck" Thrace set her jaw. She was tired, so frakking *tired* of having to rescue herself—and everyone else—from everything. It would be nice if once, just once, someone would ride to *her* rescue. Lee, for example. The stupid frakhead was ignoring her, leaving her to face the wolves alone.

Kara pursed her lips and shook her head. Time to get a grip. No one had forgotten her. Least of all Lee Adama and his father the commander. When her Viper had come up missing, Commander Adama had put the entire Fleet in danger by refusing Jump to a safer location until Kara was found. Lee—or someone—would come. In the meantime, it would be better if she were in a position to help whoever showed up. Once again she pulled and twisted at the bonds that held her hands captive. Hot pain made raw ropes around her wrists, and her hands were shaking so much that she couldn't tell if her bonds were getting looser or not.

"Not on a good day for fishing in the watering hole back on—" Kara shut her mouth hard and stopped the flow. How much longer before it became uncontrollable?

Sharon, still clad in her jumpsuit, abruptly knelt down in front of Kara, blocking her view of the goings-on. "I heard that," she said. "Sounds like your mouth has a case of the runs."

"Frak you very much to my own—" Kara clapped her teeth so hard together she was sure she had cracked one.

"Yeah." Sharon reached over and pulled the duffel bag closer to her. The missile ordnance peeped out from the interior in a deadly game of peekaboo. "Now that you've joined the Chosen and are babbling like a lunatic, I think it's safe to let you in on a secret."

"Secret lies within the fallen angels of—"

Sharon pressed a cold finger to Kara's lips. "Shush. Here's the deal." She leaned closer and whispered, "I lied. I don't have the ordnance access code."

Tom Zarek fished a wireless communicator out of his pocket. He listened, then dashed over to Peter and said something to him. Peter stiffened, then disentangled himself from his Unity groupies and got back up on the crate.

"My friends," he said, "I have disturbing news."

The crowd fell silent except for the quiet babbling of those caught in the throes of the plague of tongues. Words bubbled up inside Kara, and she bit her lip to stop herself from joining the babblers.

"I've received word," Peter said, "that a group of marines is burning its way through the hull of this ship."

CHAPTER 13

Gaius Baltar worked quickly in his lab, his movements swift and firm. No sign of the shakes, no desire to spout nonsense. Just him and a pile of amino acids. It was only a matter of putting them in the right sequence, snapping them together like pieces in a very tiny puzzle. It should have been a fine thing to be in control again, should have felt like he was master of his own world. Instead, he was beginning to fear he had bitten off more than he could chew. The prion was far more complicated than he had originally thought. Oh, he could put one together, that was certain. But a mounting alarm was saying it would take days instead of hours, and he was filled with a growing certainty that he would perfect the curative prion only after everyone else was dead.

A computer monitor showed a growing Prion C blown up to the size of a multi-colored octopus. Gaius manipulated sensitive controls, and a microprobe nudged an amino acid closer to the proper position. It touched the prion and attached itself. It seemed to Gaius that he heard a *click*, though the idea was preposterous. He allowed himself a small sigh of relief, then checked his prion against the computer mockup of Prion C and nodded. Perfect so far. He wiped some sweat off his forehead, then dipped the microprobe into a different amino-acid bath, brought out a few samples of the next sequence he needed, and transferred them into the medium that contained his slowly evolving prion.

"Better hurry, Gaius," Number Six said behind him.

Startled, Gaius jerked his hands. The probe skittered sideways and sheared off several amino acids from his prion. They floated off into the liquid medium like fish frightened by a shark. A slow smile slid across Six's face.

"Dammit, that's not funny," Gaius snapped without looking around. "Look what you made me do. That's two hours' work right there."

A hard pair of hands grabbed him from behind and spun him around. "Don't ignore me, Gaius. You know what a terrible thing that can be."

And Gaius lost it. Six had been yammering at him non-stop about being ignored, interrupting him, embarrassing him, slowing or stopping his work. Days of constrained frustration exploded like a cracked pressure cooker.

"Shut up!" he snarled. "Just shut the frak up! I've had it with your petty complaints, your sly comments. If you aren't going to say anything useful, get the hell out of my lab."

Six didn't seem the least bit fazed by this outburst. Her impossibly beautiful face remained impassive, her platinum-blond hair hung in perfect tendrils, her scarlet dress flowed around the perfect lines of her body. At times like this, she *looked* like a robot, or maybe a mannequin. But even here, with him angry and her robotic, he found himself attracted to her. A part of him wanted to fling her to the lab floor and tear the clingy dress away. Sometimes he hated that part of himself. Now, for example.

"I'm not being helpful when I tell you that you're being tracked?" she said. "That within four hours, a Cylon basestar will jump into this sector and wipe all of you out?"

The anger drained from Gaius like blood from a felled ox. "What are you talking about?"

"Someone on board the Fleet is transmitting a signal, Gaius. Once your position is pinpointed, you'll be so very vulnerable. Think of it— an entire Fleet of humans too paralyzed by prions to fight back. The slaughter will have its own scarlet beauty, wouldn't you say? We'll wash away your sins in your own blood."

Gaius stared at her, a cold chill washing over him. He had no idea where Six got her information, but it was always accurate. Back when he thought he had a chip embedded in his head, he had assumed the Cylons were transmitting Six's image straight into his brain, making him think he saw and heard and touched a woman. Since then, he'd learned he had no chip in his head and he had assumed that Six was some strange facet of his own subconscious, a weird waking dream brought on by the trauma of the first Cylon attack on Caprica. It made perverted sense—his conscious mind was so much stronger than a normal person's, so it followed that his subconscious would be equally powerful. That didn't explain the source of Six's information, however. It was possible his own subconscious was figuring out things his conscious mind couldn't and was using Six as a messenger to feed him information that would keep him alive and well. In the end, he supposed, it didn't matter. Six often gave him information he could use. What difference would knowing the source make?

He reached for the phone. "I'll tell the Commander about this. We can Jump to a new location."

"And how will you explain the source of this information, Gaius?" Six purred. "A hotline to the Cylons?"

That stopped him. He paused, confused.

"Besides, Gaius," she continued, "if you check with the Commander, you'll find that more and more of the crew are speaking in tongues. You're short-staffed. Performing a Jump now would be difficult at best. Some ships have no one well enough to calculate a Jump. Another person's hand might shake at the wrong time and . . ." She made a puffing noise and flicked her fingers to indicate an explosion. Gaius felt his stomach knot like tense tree roots.

"So what do you want me to do about it?" he said at last.

"Stop ignoring what's important, Gaius."

"And what might that be?" he said, giving the video screen a curt gesture. "This prion is all that's standing between us and extinction, and I'm *trying* to give it my full attention. Hell, I don't even know if this cure will work. The prion is more complicated than I thought."

Sudden anger twisted Six's mouth into a red sneer. "You think that's what this is about? You think this is about your microscopic problems?"

"Then what is it about?" Gaius raged, thankful he was alone in the lab with the door locked. "Tell me! You've been lording it over me for days now. Just spit it out."

Six grabbed his tie and pulled his face close to hers. He smelled warm, minty breath. "You're ignoring the One," she hissed. "And he's pissed off."

Gaius's mind seized up. For a long moment he couldn't do anything at all except stare into Number Six's face. Was this one of her tests of faith? Six liked to spring these little surprises on him, forcing him to admit to a spirituality that made him feel uncomfortable. She had once threatened to allow the President to learn of his connection to the Cylon attack if he didn't admit to a belief in her version of god, and he had admitted to it. More than once since then, in fact.

At last, his mouth started to work again. "Are you testing my faith again?"

"I'm not. God is. Or the One."

"The One? The One has taken notice of me?"

"Oh, Gaius. Think, for once. You've seen what a terrible thing it is to be ignored. The One doesn't like it any more than you do."

"You engineered everything that's been going on so I could see what it was like to be ignored?" he said in disbelief.

"Peter brought you a message of faith, and you've been ignoring it all this time—and ignoring the One. Now you have the chance to ensure that everyone in the Fleet listens to his message."

"What message?"

"That Gaius Baltar cannot be ignored."

Gaius felt his ego rise to the bait and he struggled to keep it in check. "I didn't catch that part in Peter's song lyrics."

"Because no one else is listening, either. But now you have the chance to make them listen."

"By curing the plague?"

"Oh, Gaius. You think too simplistically. I'm telling you *not* to cure it."

"That's insane! If I don't cure it, everyone will die except me and Peter Attis. Wouldn't we make a fine couple, floating alone through space? Or perhaps you'd care to join us in a ménage à trois."

"Perhaps you should take some time out and pray instead," Six said.

"I'll pray while I work, thanks. Even though it slows me down."

"And what will you pray for?"

"That I find the frakking cure before your people show up to attack," he growled. "It's harder than I thought, and frankly, I'm not sure I can do it in time for it to do any good. Now if you aren't going to help, kindly disappear."

"I'm helping more than you know, Gaius. But right now, I need to tell you a little secret."

"Oh goody. And what might that be?"

Six leaned into his ear and lowered her voice to a whisper. "There is no attack."

He stiffened in shock and outrage. "What? Then why did you tell me—?"

"It was a test of faith, Gaius," she said patiently. "You should have seen that. God wants you alive. Why would he allow anyone to destroy the Fleet unless *you* were saved first?"

"That's outrageous!" Gaius sputtered. "You think you can just toy with me whenever you—"

"If you like," she interrupted, "think of it as God answering your prayer. Or half of it, anyway. Now"—she spun him around and pushed his face back into the microscope—"get to work. And pray as you go."

Commander William Adama looked down at his left hand. It lay palm down on the light table, fingers splayed. Motionless. He stared at it for a long moment. Then a little tremor ran through it. Just a small one. No more than a one on the palsic scale. But it was enough.

"I saw that," Saul Tigh murmured.

Adama carefully and deliberately put his hand behind his back. "Keep it to yourself."

"Keep what?"

Adama gave him a tight smile and Tigh moved on. Then Adama decided to do a quick circuit of CIC. Many of his people were tired, he knew. So many crewmen and officers had come down with the plague of tongues that the unaffected people had to pull double shifts. Dualla had bags under bloodshot eyes, and when Adama wandered by her station, she hid her right hand, but not before he caught the tremor. Dammit! He should send her off duty.

On the other hand, so to speak, he should also remove himself from command. He gave Dualla a nod and continued on his way as if he had seen nothing. As long as she was able to function, he would let her remain at her station. There wasn't anyone to take her place. He thought about calling down to Baltar's lab for an update, then decided against it. Baltar would find a cure or he wouldn't, and interrupting him for a status update wouldn't do anything except delay the man.

Baltar. Adama passed by Gaeta's station with a nod and a hidden grimace. He hated the thought that everyone's health might well rest in the hands of a crackpot who kept up conversations with himself. Adama knew very well that about half the population talked to itself. Adama was in the half that didn't, but he had caught Lee at it numerous times over the years and knew what it sounded like. Baltar, however, didn't simply vocalize internal conversations—he held raging debates that involved full-blown body language. It was as if he were caught up in a child's game of cops and robbers, getting pushed around by imaginary enemies. Baltar probably thought he was hiding it, but Adama had seen him. So had many others. But with quarters so tight and cramped in the Fleet, a new sort of privacy law had evolved. If it didn't involve you directly, you pretended not to notice it. Adama suspected that if they stayed out here long enough, people would go from pretending not to notice to actually not noticing, the way people did in societies that had little or no physical privacy. According to anthropological texts Adama had read, the tribes of the Numinol Islands on Caprica had once lived in large caves with nothing but lines of pebbles to indicate where one family's living space ended and another's began, and the inhabitants of such caves lived, ate, fought, and frakked with each other in full view of their fellow tribesmen, but only those within the stone boundaries saw or heard a thing. Adama wondered how long it would take before the current tiny handful of human survivors got to that point.

Adama didn't like Baltar's obvious instability and would normally have tossed the man from any discussion group or advisory board, but he couldn't deny that Baltar's knowledge and contributions could be—had been—helpful, even necessary. So Adama went for a middle ground. He ignored Baltar when he could and used him when he had to.

Adama realized he was standing at his light table in the middle of CIC again. He looked up at a monitor that showed a computer image of all the ships in the Fleet. The symbol for the *Monarch* was outlined in red. Lee and his force of marines were burning through the hull even as Adama waited. They were keeping radio silence, which aided secrecy but kept Adama in the dark about the team's progress. He looked down at his slightly shaky hand again and for a moment he was seized with an overwhelming urge to whine. He wanted to whine that the prion infection was unfair, that his only surviving son's life was in danger again, that the only person who could assemble a cure for this disease was a frakking lunatic, that the only other source of a cure was about to be attacked by a military force, that everyone expected him to have answers and solutions to everything when he didn't. For an unsettling moment, he imagined himself with his head in Laura Roslin's lap while she stroked his hair and told him, in his first wife's voice, that everything would be all right. He banished the image.

"Dee," he said, "any way to get an update on Captain Adama's team?"

She shook her head. "Negative, sir. They're still keeping strict radio silence."

"All right," he sighed, "maybe we can—"

Galen Tyrol stumbled into CIC. His gait was uncertain and his eyes were wild. His hands were shaking like butterflies in a windstorm. Everyone, including Adama, turned to stare at him. He tripped and almost fell against Tigh and Adama, who helped him back to his feet. Adama tensed. Tyrol only rarely came to CIC, and never for anything less than a full-blown emergency.

"Commander," Tyrol said in a hoarse voice. "Commander, I found a lost ocean breeze in the tropics for—"

Tigh slapped his face hard. Tyrol stopped babbling and stared at the colonel with startled brown eyes.

"Calm yourself, Chief," Tigh snapped. "Concentrate. What's so damned important?"

Tyrol's expression shifted from dislike to a look of concentration. "I f-found . . . found a peanut in the . . . no. I found . . . in the pod of peas . . . dammit!"

"Can you write it down?" Adama asked in a moment of inspiration.

Tyrol wordlessly held up trembling hands and shook his head. "I was looking in the pod people of Caprican gardens who—frak! It's important to tell the audience that we can't fin mey beldin trassinell—"

Tigh slapped him again. Tyrol slammed a fist into Tigh's gut, then backed away with a look of horror on his face. Tigh bent over the light table, then dropped into a chair, gasping.

"I'm s-sorry," Tyrol stammered. "I'm s-so frakked in the bedroom with Dina melsh zaraform." He shook his head. "It's . . . it's a-about the Cy—the Cylon. There's someone else cooking my mother's yudin asp terring . . ."

He crashed to the floor, twisting and babbling. Gaeta rushed over and tried to help Tyrol to his feet, but the convulsions were too much for him. He lowered Tyrol back to the floor and picked up a phone to summon a medical team—if one was to be had. Colonel Tigh sat in his chair, still panting for breath.

"What . . . the hell . . . was he saying?" Tigh gasped.

"I wish I knew," Adama replied, and steadfastly turned back to his light table.

"Passive!" Peter boomed. "Your resistance must be passive! Go limp. Block the way. Get underfoot. It will take two of them to drag one of you aside. But don't make any aggressive moves. Don't make a fist or reach for a weapon or even put your hand in your pocket. Don't speak, either. Sing, if you want. Let your faith give you strength. The One will protect us because our faith is true!"

Peter raised a fist, and the people cheered.

"Our love for the One is strong!"

Another cheer.

"We are the Chosen few!"

A third cheer. Peter started to sing his revolution song again. Kara had heard it so many times she was sick of it, but the crowd of thirty-odd swayed in time with the music and sang along. About a third of them wore red masks. How many people were on this frakking ship, anyway? This was the third group of Unity followers Peter was sending out to fight—or resist—the marines. Kara had overheard one of the

Unity women mention that this was the *Monarch,* so she knew where she was, though she hadn't been able to escape. She couldn't imagine that the Old Man hadn't quarantined the ship before sending over the marines, and there was no way all these people were part of the *Monarch* crew. So where were they coming from?

The answer, when it came, was obvious. The plague of tongues was no doubt grounding military personnel left and right. Kara suspected few pilots remained steady enough to climb into a cockpit, let alone pilot a Viper on patrol.

Kara scanned the group as they boiled out of the room, and her stomach knotted. Some of these people had brought children with them. The kids sang with their parents. Kara watched, her shaking hands still bound behind her. As the song progressed, a sense of determination filled the room. Kara knew the feeling—it filled her every time she went out to fight Cylon raiders. And she was forced to admit that Peter was doing a good job stirring them up.

"How's it going?" Sharon asked in a patently false chipper tone.

Kara refused to answer. Pent-up words boiled around inside her, pressing against her pursed lips like a riot pressed against a police barricade. Once the torrent started, she didn't think it would ever stop. And Peter—the frakking idiot. He seemed to have forgotten all about her. Gods, what had she ever seen in him? The thought of listening to another Peter Attis song made her stomach ooze with nausea.

"Yeah," Sharon said, as if Kara had answered. "Getting hard to hold it in, isn't it?"

Kara couldn't stand it anymore. "Why . . . are . . . you keeping the barn door open for . . . keeping me here?" she said with aching slowness and deliberation.

"Because Peter loves you, stupid," Sharon said. She was sitting beside Kara, her knees up, wrists resting on them. Between her feet sat the duffel bag and its explosive contents. "Or lusts you, anyway."

"No way for bright red robins to—" Kara bit back the words, took a breath, and tried again. "No. You . . . know I won't . . . give up the fight for freedom that we've—no! I won't give you . . . the access codes. You can . . . torture me, but I'll . . . I'll be . . ."

"Dead before I can torture you enough to get them out of you?" Sharon finished. Then she laughed. "Don't be stupid, Kara. Peter wouldn't let me torture you. Not that he could stop me. It's just I know an easier way to get the codes."

Kara didn't answer. She had a terrible feeling she knew.

Sharon put an arm around Kara's shoulders, drew her close, and gave her a sisterly kiss on the temple. Kara cringed at her touch. Her whole skin tried to crawl away from it. Sharon brought her lips so close to Kara's ear that she could feel Sharon's warm breath.

"What's the access code for missile ordnance?" she asked.

The answer popped into Kara's mind and rushed toward her mouth. She clenched her jaw, but she found the treacherous words spilling out. "Five six eight—no!" Kara clamped her lips shut.

"Five six eight," Sharon prompted.

"Eight chi frak you in the—"

"Now, now," Sharon interrupted. "Try again. "Eight chi . . ."

Sweat broke out on Kara's face and she bit her tongue until it bled, but the words still came. "Omega two four six eight ten twelve fourteen—"

"Nice try," Sharon said. "But ordnance has only six code words. The four-six-eight thing was a silly try at fooling me."

Kara slumped back against the cold wall. Her legs were shaking now and exhaustion pulled her muscles into limp rubber bands. To her horror, she felt tears gathering in the corners of her eyes. Dammit, she wasn't going to cry. Not in front of a frakking Cylon.

"Are those cuffs painful?" Sharon asked like a nurse in a doctor's office. "Make you weepy? Let's see what we can do."

Kara braced herself, expecting a devastating blow to go with the sarcasm. Instead, Sharon reached behind Kara and, with a flick of her fingers, released Kara's hands. Instant anger seized her. She whipped her fists around and smashed them both into Sharon's smiling face.

Or tried to. Her hands and arms wouldn't obey. She managed to get her hands around in front of her, but they only lay in her lap, twisting and flopping like half-dead fish. Her legs joined in the terrible dance. Kara stared down at them in disbelief. She could almost hear her father's voice echo inside her head.

Little slut! That's what you get for frakking around.

"See?" Sharon said. She rose to her feet, the better to loom over Kara. "You're perfectly safe to keep around now. No chance for betrayal. Even if you tell anyone my secret, they'll put it down to babbling."

Meanwhile, Peter's followers finished the revolution song. "Go!" Peter said. "Show them your faith!"

The crowd marched out of the room, many of them still humming. Several people dragged the forms of those who had fallen victim to the plague of tongues. Some were comatose, others squirmed and shook, but all of them would serve to bolster the human barricade. The other people chatted and laughed, as if they were on their way to a picnic. Then the crowd abruptly spread apart, creating a hole around a young woman who was writhing and babbling on the floor. With a cheer that set Kara's teeth on edge, they helped her up and streamed for the door again, taking her with them. Kara was left alone with Peter, Sharon, and Tom Zarek.

"Idiots," Sharon murmured. "They mistake conviction for faith." She took a step away from the duffel, then another. Kara's eyes were drawn to it. Marines might be burning their way into the ship, but the *Monarch* was a big place, and there was no easy way for them to find her unless she could shout for help. And the ordnance might just be the key.

Sometimes missiles overshot their targets, either because the target dodged or the missile's guidance system failed. In either case, there was a small chance that it might hit something else, which meant unexploded ordnance had to be recovered. Or it did in the days before the Cylon attack. Nobody much cared now. Despite this, missile ordnance still carried a homing signal that allowed it to be tracked. It was activated automatically after the missile launched, but there was a manual switch as well. Now that Sharon had untied her, Kara might be able to activate the thing.

If she could distract Sharon. If her body would cooperate.

"What's the . . . difference," she stammered, "between cold snow and hard hail to the—"

"The difference between faith and conviction?" Sharon interrupted. "Conviction comes only with proof. Faith comes from within."

"Does P-Peter think the same wish for a good—"

"Who cares what Peter thinks?" Sharon said. "He's nothing but a toy. Cute, too, and damned good in bed, after he was trained."

"You've never frakked a big baloney sandwich on white—"

"Oops!" Sharon put on a patently false girlish pose. "I've gone and said too much."

Kara gritted her teeth. She didn't care about Peter anymore, or who he might have frakked around with. All she cared about right now was that damned bag of ordnance. "You never," she managed to say without babbling. "Not good enough for him. Be like putting his dick into a toaster slot instead of a Cylon slut who—"

The slap rocked Kara to the base of her spine. She cried out, long and hard, much louder than the blow actually called for. Peter, still standing on his box as the last of his people streamed away, heard the sound. So did Tom Zarek, who was working on some electronic equipment over in a corner. Kara collapsed into tears that were only half faked and covered her face with shaking hands, though she peered through her fingers. Peter jumped down from the box and ran over. Zarek followed.

"What the hell are you doing?" Peter snapped. "Get away from her!"

"She's a mouthy bitch," Sharon said.

Kara managed to raise her middle finger at Sharon. This time the Cylon woman drew back a fist. Peter stepped between them and pushed Sharon back. The move caught Sharon by surprise and she backpedaled several steps, her eyes wide above her red mask.

"I said to leave her the hell alone," Peter snarled. "She's my consort."

"Watch it, Petey-boy," Sharon snarled back. "I don't know who you think you are, but—"

"I *think* I'm the Unifier," he spat. "Do you doubt who I am?"

Kara forced herself to move while Sharon was distracted. She managed to pull the duffel open and locate the switch that activated the homing signal, but her treacherous fingers wouldn't grab hold of it. Twice, she felt the smooth metal of the switch, and twice she felt her fingers slip away from it.

"Don't get a swelled head," Sharon was saying into Peter's face. "The One may have chosen you, but that doesn't mean you rule everyone you see."

Heart pounding, Kara hooked a finger under the switch. *Come on,* she prayed. *Come on!*

Her finger slipped off. Kara wanted to howl in frustration.

"My followers do as I say because they believe the One speaks through me," Peter said. "Don't you believe it?"

Sharon seemed to realize she was breaking her cover. She swallowed hard and visibly forced herself to take a step backward and bow her head. "I'm . . . sorry, Unifier. I lost my temper. My apologies."

"We all make mistakes," Peter said magnanimously.

Kara made one more try. Her mouth was dry as a raisin. If this didn't work, she was frakked. Her finger found the switch—

—and Sharon saw her. With inhuman quickness, she spun, knelt, and grabbed Kara's quivering wrist. Kara tried to pull free, but her body wouldn't obey. Sharon shoved Kara's hand away with contempt.

"Now just what are you up to with that?" she said.

"That's missile ordnance," said Tom Zarek, speaking for the first time. "What the hell is that doing here?"

"Missile ordnance?" Peter echoed. "You mean a bomb? You have a frakking *bomb?*"

"All part of the plan, Unifier," Sharon said calmly, pulling the duffel bag out of Kara's reach.

"Whose plan?" Zarek said. "I don't remember talking about a bomb."

"It's an insurance policy," Sharon told him. "Those marines won't close with us if they know we have this. It'll keep them at a distance, if necessary."

"We can't blow up the ship," Peter said, clearly shaken. "Shit! Passive resistance, remember?"

"*They* don't know that," Sharon returned. "For all they know, we're a bunch of religious suicide terrorists who'll kill a whole shipful of people rather than be captured. I'm not going to set it off, for frak sake. I'd die, too."

"Bluffs aren't worth the air it takes to make them," Zarek said. "Good players usually call them, and Adama's very good."

"So what? I'm not *counting* on Adama and the marines believing me—us. If they do, it's a nice break and it'll make it easier for us to escape. If they don't, we still escape."

"Where?" Peter said. "How?"

"The less you know, Unifier, the better," Sharon said. "Just in case."

"Wait a minute," Zarek said. "We already discussed this. I told you that the marines won't fire on civilians, so you're supposed to use passive resistance to wear them down and convince them to leave you alone. And if that doesn't work, Peter is supposed to get caught. He hasn't done anything illegal, so he'll become a prison martyr like I was. The press will keep Peter and his music alive until his trial and acquittal. I've already tipped off some of my press contacts about the possibility."

"I'm not willing to go to jail for my beliefs just yet, thanks," Sharon said. "Even if I have a key to the back door." She nodded at the monitors Zarek had set up in the corner. "Check out phase one of the plan, there."

Peter looked torn between the contents of the duffel bag and the monitors Zarek had set up in the corner. At last he said to Sharon, "Don't touch Kara," and strode away. Zarek went with him.

Sharon looked hard at Kara, then calmly reached into the bag. Kara tensed. Sharon tilted the duffel so Kara could see every movement. Wiggling her eyebrows for comic effect, she deliberately flipped the switch that sent the signal. Kara couldn't keep in a gasp.

"Surprised?" Sharon said to Kara.

And suddenly Kara wasn't. The Cylon's actions made perfect sense.

"I . . . know what . . . mish nar—no. Know . . . your plan," Kara managed.

"Really?" Sharon looked down at Kara, a small smile on her face. "What plan would that be?"

"You don't . . . care . . . care about Peter or . . . galimaufry Alice has a blue—dammit! Or about . . . the One."

"No shit."

Kara shoved hard, and the words spilled out the way she wanted them to for once. "It's a trap. You want the armed force to board and find us so you can blow up Peter and what few soldiers we have who aren't sick and you'll die but just be downloaded into a new body because you don't care anymore that you'll lose your . . . your . . ." She trailed off.

"Lose my what?" Sharon said.

Kara looked up at Sharon, but not at her face. From this angle, she could see Sharon's stomach. It lay perfectly flat beneath her stolen gray jumpsuit. There was no hint of roundness, not even a tiny bulge.

Sharon Valerii—*this* Sharon Valerii—wasn't pregnant.

CHAPTER 14

The acrid smell of burning ceramic scorched Helo's nostrils. It felt strange to be kneeling on the outer hull of a spaceship without a vac suit for protection, but he kept his mind on his job. The marine ship had clamped itself to the *Monarch* like a barnacle and Captain Adama himself had opened the floor hatch, revealing the gray ceramic. Helo kept his hands steady and his eyes on the white-hot flicker of flame that was burning a careful circle through the hull of the mining ship. Goggles protected his eyes. The strike force gathered behind him, bodies tense and weapons ready. Helo could hear their body armor creak as they shifted position.

The final bit of ceramic gave way. Helo jumped back as a human-sized circle dropped into the ship and landed with a loud clang. He extinguished the torch. Captain Lee Adama dropped the end of a cord into the space beyond. The other end was hooked to a small monitor clipped to Lee's belt. It showed a dim, empty corridor.

"No apparent resistance," Lee reported. "Move in!"

Moving with trained precision, the strike force members dropped into the hole. The first ones scurried out of the way, weapons drawn to cover the ones who came next. Helo and Lee Adama were the last.

"They have to know we're coming," Helo said in a low voice. "Why aren't they meeting us?"

"Maybe they don't want a fight," Lee murmured. "Maybe this'll turn into a game of hide-and-seek." He holstered his rifle across his back and unrolled a long square of paper, specs for the *Monarch*. "Gaeta said that since we stopped enforcing the quarantine, something like ten ships have docked with the *Monarch*. The only place where all those people could be gathering is the main processing area here. But that's just a guess. I wish we knew for sure."

"Sir," Racetrack said. "I'm getting a signal."

Lee spun like a small tornado. Helo wondered if the captain was thinking about Kara like he was thinking about Sharon. "From who?"

"No one in particular." Racetrack held up her radio so Lee could see the readout. "It's a missile ordnance tracking signal."

"Kara," Lee breathed. "She's found a way to tell us where she is and make it look like an ordnance signal."

"I don't know, sir," Helo said doubtfully. "What if the Unifiers really have ordnance?"

"Doesn't seem likely they'd activate the homing device," Racetrack said. "It gives away their position."

A series of clanks and thuds rang through the corridor. Everyone, including Helo, readied their weapons, rifle barrels pointing in a dozen different directions like an angry porcupine. After a moment the noises faded.

"Mining ship," Racetrack said as another set of sounds started up, further away this time. "Lots of weird noises around. Let me get to work and we can get moving."

Helo let himself relax. A little, anyway. Lighting in the corridor was dim, and the whole place smelled of algae and engine oil. Helo shifted inside his flak armor. A belt hung with ammunition and equipment dragged at his waist, a helmet covered his head, and he carried a pulse rifle. The back of his head wouldn't stop itching. The helmet wouldn't let him scratch, which made it worse. Doc Cottle had been too busy with plague patients to look at him, and now Helo was on a strike force, where an itchy head was considered something you sucked up.

Technically Helo shouldn't be here. He was combat-trained, yes, but he wasn't trained to sneak aboard an enemy ship and track down terrorists. But Captain Adama, faced with hundreds of people whose hands shook too much to fire a weapon, had been forced to augment marines with other personnel. At the moment, that included Helo. So far his hands had proven plague-free and rock-steady, though he found himself checking every few minutes.

The search for Sharon had been suspended. No one was available to look for her. Helo couldn't decide if this was a positive or a negative. In the end, he had decided to stop thinking about it altogether. If she turned up, she would turn up.

But he also wondered about the baby.

He was going to be a father. The idea ambushed him at odd moments, like a mugger whacking him over the head and dragging him into an alley. A baby. A little girl or boy who would look at him and say, "Daddy!" First steps, first words. First date.

From a prison cell. How would Adama handle this? It wouldn't be fair to the baby to keep it in a cell, and it wouldn't be right to keep it away from Sharon. Adama would have to make some sort of ruling, and that pissed Helo off. Every other time a baby was born, people celebrated. New life was precious and valued and loved. Except his. His baby would be born in a prison to a lifetime prisoner. His baby would be born to a hated enemy. His baby would endure a life of stigma. His baby's birth would be decided by military law, his parenting held up to military scrutiny. The baby had committed no crime, but already it was being treated like a criminal. Helo got angrier and angrier just thinking about it.

Racetrack jostled Helo's arm, bringing him out of his seething reverie. He almost jumped, realizing how foolish it had been for him to lose himself inside his own head when he was in enemy territory.

"Careful," Racetrack said. She had opened a wall panel and was tearing at the nest of cable inside. "Pass me that shunt, would you?"

Helo obeyed. Racetrack selected a cable and attached the shunt while the rest of the platoon stood guard. Racetrack, an adept ECO, flipped on a portable screen. Helo peered over her shoulder. At first the screen remained blank, but she flicked dials and switches and eventually came up with an image of a large room crammed with people. Several of them wore red masks.

"I've broken into the security cameras, Captain," she reported. "I think we're looking at the main processing area."

"Crowded," observed a marine Helo didn't know.

Captain Lee Adama checked the schematics. "It's also on the only path from here to where the signal is coming from."

"So we have to go through them to get to Kara?" Helo said.

"Looks that way."

"Sir," said one of the marines, "our orders are not to shoot or attack civilians. How are we going to get through those people without attacking?"

Lee Adama looked at the people on the screen, then at the schematic in his hand, then at the hole in the bulkhead above him. "We're not," he said.

"Commander," said Felix Gaeta. "Lieutenant Edmonson is beaming a direct signal to us. We have video of what's happening on the *Monarch.*"

"Put it up, Lieutenant," Colonel Tigh ordered.

Bill Adama turned his eyes up to one of the monitors above his head. Lee was out there, leading the *Monarch* strike in an attempt to rescue Kara Thrace, and Adama had to stand there in CIC and pretend he wasn't worried, that his heart wasn't leaping in his chest, that he wasn't sweating under his uniform. No reason for distress, everyone. The Old Man has everything under control.

He adjusted his glasses and peered at the monitor. It remained blank.

"There a problem, Mr. Gaeta?" Tigh asked.

"Just . . . taking a little longer to get the telemetry right, sir." Gaeta, flushing, worked at his controls, his hands hidden by the rim of the console. Adama knew what was causing the delay, and he kept his face carefully neutral. He shot Tigh a quick glance to let him know that the colonel should keep his mouth shut. Tigh gave a tiny nod in acknowledgment. Dualla busied herself at her own console, as did everyone else in CIC. Their work was similarly slow and laborious and several stations were unstaffed, but no one took note. Yep, no reason for distress. Everything's under control. Ignore the elephant standing beside you. We all know it's there, we all know why Gaeta can't work his console, and we're all going to pretend we don't. The marines will bring back Peter Attis alive, healthy, and chock full of curative protoplasm to cure the disease we aren't talking about. We won't mention that the Cylons could pop up at any time and turn the Fleet into an expanding cloud of gas and debris. We won't mention that the prions are turning our brains to sponges and that our only hopes are the leader of a religious movement that kidnapped one of our best pilots, and a scientist who isn't known for his stability.

A wave of anger suddenly swept over Adama. He was dying, dammit, dying for the second time in as many months. The frakking asshole whose life Adama had spared had repaid Adama by infecting him with a deadly disease, creating a religious cult that fomented chaos wherever it went, kidnapping a pilot who was like a daughter to him, and disappearing into the bowels of a mining ship with the disease's only cure. Gods, Adama had even attended the man's concert. And what an evening that had been. Laura Roslin had clung lightly to his arm like a half-solid ghost, and the two of them sank into lawn chairs set up specifically for them, like a king and queen attending the revels of the commoners. Billy Keikeya hovered nearby like a cup-bearer. And gods help him, Adama actually enjoyed the show. The music wasn't his usual thing—as he grew older, the classics became more and more appealing—but Adama recognized good showmanship when he saw it, and Peter Attis had a hell of a voice. Laura Roslin sat next to him, unabashedly enthralled, and Adama found himself feeling pleased and proud, as if he had somehow arranged Peter's rescue and subsequent concert for her benefit. Anything that reduced her pain was, in his book, a fine thing, and no more than Roslin deserved. As for himself, he'd forgotten for a while about juggling cats, about the death of his wife, about Cylon attacks. He'd even caught himself pretending that he was out on a date with a beautiful woman. Adama blushed slightly at that memory. Laura Roslin was the president of the Fleet and a good friend, nothing else. But his treacherous mind, the one that had been hungry for female company for too many years now, planted the idea nonetheless.

But the concert, it turned out, had become a major venue for spreading this plague of tongues and the point of a terrorist attack by Caprica Sharon. Billy had hustled the president away the moment that news came down, and Adama had snapped from civilian mode into commander mode. It was as if an old, heavy weight had smacked down on him with contemptuous familiarity. He had dealt with the crisis, and only later had he realized he hadn't even bid Laura Roslin good night.

And Caprica Sharon was still at large, Adama couldn't spare the personnel to look for her, and gods only knew what she was up to. Still more cats to juggle.

He banished further thought with firm discipline. Right now, he had to deal with the *Monarch* and Peter Attis. The Sharon problem would have to wait.

The picture on the monitor was silent and fuzzy, despite—or perhaps because of—Gaeta's ministrations. A group of helmeted marines, their face plates down and their weapons holstered, burst into a roomful of people. Adama had no way of telling which one was Lee. His muscles tightened. Beside him, he sensed Saul Tigh tensing up as well. Adama understood why. Tigh had been in charge of the Fleet during the *Gideon* incident—the civilians called it a massacre—and Adama knew the man lived under a cloud of guilt over it. Tigh covered it well and acted as if the entire incident had never taken place. Adama wondered sometimes if it wouldn't have been better for him to show guilt or other public feeling about the *Gideon*. There were times when the commanding officer needed to be a god and times when the commanding officer needed to be human. The *Gideon* might have been one of the latter times. Well, it was too late now. Tigh making any kind of public statement about the *Gideon* would only tear open wounds that hadn't fully healed yet.

On the screen, the people in the processing room swarmed toward the marines like ants on a pile of sugar. Several of them wore masks over the lower half of their faces, creating two groups of masked, anonymous people thronging toward each other. Army ants and worker ants, heading for the clash. Adama held his breath. If the people attacked, the marines had the right to defend themselves, but that could quickly devolve into something worse. Another *Gideon* loomed.

But the people just surrounded the marines and stood there, unmoving. The two groups froze, staring at each other. Then one of the marines, the one in the lead, tentatively tried to nudge the woman in front of him aside. She didn't fight back, but she didn't give ground, either.

"Can we get sound on this?" Adama asked. His hands were shaking again, a situation that made his mouth go dry with a fear—

the prion is chewing on your brain

—that he refused to examine closely.

"I'm sorry, sir," Gaeta said. "The security cameras on the *Monarch* aren't wired for sound, and the marines are still keeping radio silence in case Lieutenant Thrace's kidnappers are listening in."

Adama nodded acknowledgment and went back to watching. The marine—Lee?—tried pushing forward again, but the woman still didn't move. Neither did the people standing on either side of her. Another moment passed, and then the lead marine—Adama was more and more sure it was Lee—signaled, and the entire platoon tried to push forward.

The people didn't resist, but neither did they get out of the way. They fell against the marines or went limp or formed human barricades. The marines were easily outnumbered ten to one, and their progress through the crowd slowed to a maddening crawl. Adama recognized the technique, of course. Passive resistance. There was no riot, no attack, nothing the marines could really fight against, but it hindered progress nonetheless. Against an opponent willing to kill, it was almost worthless. The Fleet marines, however, didn't want to kill anyone, and the civilians knew it. It made an effective wall between the marines and Peter Attis, wherever he was.

"Why don't they fire off some tear gas?" Tigh said. "That'd clear the area right fast."

"It would get into the ventilation system," Adama pointed out. "In a ship that small, the gas would fog the entire place in just a few minutes, and there'd be nowhere to run to. Then you'd have a shipful of angry civilians in pain. Bad combination."

"Right, right," Tigh said, clearly disappointed.

On the screen, the marines tried to wade through the mass of people, but were unable to make progress. Every person they pushed aside was immediately replaced by another, and then another. Every so often, one of the resisters fell twitching and convulsing to the floor. When that happened, two of the masked Unity followers hauled the victim into the path the marines were trying to take. The symbolism was clear—the people touched by the One opposed the people who fought for the Lords of Kobol.

"Frak," Tigh muttered. "They're going to have to open fire if they want to get through."

"They have orders not to," Adama said. "And I'm not going to change them."

"Then we're all dead, Commander," Tigh said. "If they don't get Attis back to sickbay, the prions and Cylons win."

"I won't have an—a massacre on my watch, Colonel," Adama said, dropping the word "another" just in time. But another voice inside his head said he might need to issue killing orders. A hundred civilians might die, but it would mean the rest would live. He frowned hard. Why did so damn many of his choices come down to letting a few die so many could live? Why couldn't it ever be that *everyone* gets to live?

The marines continued to wade through civilians, making no real progress but also inflicting no casualties. Adama's left hand was seriously shaking now, and he wondered how long it would be before he joined the masses writhing down in sickbay and on deck five.

"Commander, Dr. Baltar is on the line for you," Dualla said.

Hope and relief washed through Adama. If Baltar was calling, it could only mean he'd finished a cure for the plague. He could order the marines to return to the *Galactica*, and Peter Attis could sing and preach blasphemy to his heart's content. End of problem. He felt the weight of stress lift. Even Saul Tigh looked relieved. For once, the solution would be easy. He picked up the receiver with his right hand, the one that wasn't shaking.

"Hello, Doctor," Adama said. "What can I do for you?"

"Commander, I'm afraid I have bad news," Baltar said.

Adama's stomach tightened again, and the weight crashed back down on him as if it had never left. "What is it, then?" he asked with resignation.

"Prion C, the cure prion, is far more complicated than I anticipated," Baltar said regretfully. *"I can eventually synthesize it, but . . . I doubt I can do it before the majority of patients become terminal."*

Adama's insides turned to liquid and he almost dropped the phone. "What are you saying, Doctor?"

"I'm estimating that by now, over ninety percent of the Fleet's population has been infected with the plague prion and that by the time I've finished creating the curative prion, close to eighty percent of the Fleet's population will have died."

Baltar delivered this news in a calm, flat voice. A thousand different thoughts swirled through Adama's head, making him dizzy. Or was the prion affecting him? He wondered how much time Baltar had wasted calculating how many people would die and how fast, and he wondered if more people would die because Baltar was talking on the phone instead of working in his lab.

"How long before you have the cure, Doctor?" Adama asked, his voice betraying none of these questions.

"Two or three days," Baltar replied.

"Thank you, Doctor," Adama said evenly. "Don't let me keep you from your work." Then he hung up.

"How long?" Tigh asked.

Adama didn't see any point in concealing the truth. "Two days, maybe three."

"But we'll all be dead by then," blurted Felix Gaeta, violating the unwritten rule about mentioning the elephant in the room with a commander who juggled cats.

"Then we'd better hope Captain Adama and those marines bring us Peter Attis," Adama said. With that, he hid his shaking left hand under the light table and turned his attention back to the marines on the monitors.

• • •

Nonsense fell in long strings from Kara's mouth now. The only way she could stop it was to bite her lips shut like a child refusing to take medicine, but her treacherous muscles didn't always obey her. Most of her body trembled with earthquake aftershocks, and the moment she stopped concentrating, more bullshit tumbled from her mouth. It wasn't even real words. She could say real words if she worked at it, but she was so tired. All she wanted to do was pass out. Except her twitching, jerking body kept her awake on the cold floor.

Peter sat cross-legged with her head in his lap. He stroked her hair and said things that he probably thought soothing. "Everything's going to be fine. I know it's bad now, but eventually you'll see the One and you'll recover, like I did. You'll be fine. Just fine."

Kara had never wanted to hit anyone more in her entire life.

Sharon, meanwhile, was kneeling over the red duffel bag, dipping tools in and out of the ordnance that squatted inside like a malevolent toad. The red mask still covered most of her face. Except it wasn't Sharon's face. It wasn't the Sharon Kara knew. She was someone else, another copy of Caprica Sharon. Kara should have realized it. Caprica Sharon wouldn't endanger her baby by escaping and trying to commit acts of terrorism. *This* Sharon, a different one, had somehow gotten on board, probably hidden somewhere in Peter's escape pod. There had been one Sharon on it—why not a second? The pod had been searched, but a secret compartment would be easy enough to add, especially since the Cylons had been in possession of the stupid thing for months. And if this Sharon was caught and executed, so what? She'd get a brand-new body and probably spend her remaining days lazing around a Cylon swimming pool bragging about how she put one over on those idiot humans.

The bitch had certainly outfoxed Kara by convincing her to keep silent about Sharon's identity as a Cylon. Black, tarry anger bubbled like pitch, and one of Kara's hands actually managed a fist for a couple seconds before losing it again. Sharon, glancing up from the ordnance, noticed and flashed Kara a quick thumbs-up before turning back to her work.

A monitor set up on one of the shelves showed a troop of marines trying to force their way through Peter's followers. They made almost no headway. The Unity members created a solid wall of bodies five and six people thick. They flung themselves down on the floor. They draped themselves over the invaders like boneless lovers. And the marines clearly had orders not to kill. Or if they did, they hadn't acted on them yet.

"Still silence on the radio," Zarek said. He was fiddling with a frequency scanner, his face serious. "They either know or suspect that we can listen in on what—"

"—*change your orders, Captain,*" said the scanner. Kara's heart jumped. It was Commander Adama's voice. "*Dr. Gaius says he can't replicate the cure prion in time for it to do us any good. Peter's blood is the only cure, and we need him back on* Galactica *no matter what the cost.*"

Kara gasped. So did Peter and Tom Zarek. Peter's blood would cure the plague? Kara's limbs shook with a terrible, all-encompassing palsy, and the cure was standing only a few feet away. Kara wondered what would happen if news of this hit the entire Fleet. She imagined hordes of people stampeding toward Peter, all of them hungry for his blood.

"*I have new orders for you,*" Adama continued on the scanner. There was a pause, and Kara held her breath, knowing what was coming next, praying she wouldn't hear it. "*You are authorized to use force against the civilians. Deadly force, if necessary.*"

"*Sir? I didn't quite copy that.*" It was Lee's voice, and the sound swelled Kara with a bright elation she didn't think was possible. Lee was leading the force that was coming to help her. Help was coming. *Lee* was coming. For a moment, she felt Lee's arms lifting her, holding her and keeping her safe. The hard-bitten part of her, the part that let her survive broken fingers and bruised skin, told her that no one could ever keep her safe, but the part of her that was tired ordered it to shut up. Lee was coming, and she could relax.

If he could get through the civilians.

"*I said, use deadly force if you need to,*" Adama said. "*Peter Attis is your top priority. Nothing else matters, Captain.*"

There was a pause. Then Lee said, "*Understood, sir.*"

"You frakking bastard!" Zarek shouted at the scanner. "Didn't you learn anything from the *Gideon?*"

Kara licked dry lips. Lee wouldn't shoot unarmed civilians. Would he? But she knew the answer. He would have to. Peter carried the cure for the disease. If sacrificing a hundred people meant several thousand would live, what choice did Lee have? Kara thought about the image of the little kid crying over her daddy's chewed and bloody corpse on the *Gideon* and wondered how many more kids would be crying over their parents in just a few minutes.

"Sounds like our time here is limited," Sharon said, still working on the duffel bag.

Peter stared at the scanner. "What did he mean when he said my blood would cure the plague?"

"I didn't think that remark needed interpretation," Sharon said. "But I'm betting that once word of it gets out, there'll be a whole lot of people wanting to go vampire on your ass."

"People like me," Zarek said coldly. "Frak—this explains . . . Look, are you telling me this is a real disease? I thought it was religious fervor. Your groupies were the ones who came down with it."

"It's . . . it's real," Kara managed to gasp out. "Real service gets good tips for—"

"The plague doesn't need a cure," Peter said. "I was out cold for a while, but I recovered. Everyone else will recover."

But Tom Zarek was already rummaging through a first aid kit. He came up with a syringe. "Let me have some of your blood, Attis."

"You're not a doctor," Peter protested.

Zarek held up shaky hands for a moment, then grabbed Peter by the front of his shirt and shoved him against a wall. He was older than Peter, but his arms were heavy with muscle. "No. I'm just a man who spent twenty years in a prison that taught me a dozen ways to cause someone serious physical pain. You let me draw some blood right now, or I'm going to pound you into a frakking pancake."

Peter shot Sharon a glance, but she just returned his gaze, an amused look in her eyes. He finally nodded. Zarek pushed up one of Peter's sleeves and jabbed the needle into the man's elbow. Peter yelped.

"Watch it!"

"Shut up, god-boy." Zarek filled the syringe despite his shaky hands, then jabbed the needle into his own arm and depressed the plunger. Kara stared hungrily at the syringe, but Peter and Zarek seemed to have forgotten she existed. She wanted that syringe more than anything she had ever wanted. Life in a few cc's of human blood.

"*ATTENTION CIVILIANS!*" boomed a voice from the scanner. Kara didn't recognize the speaker. "*IF YOU DO NOT VACATE THIS AREA IMMEDIATELY, WE WILL BE FORCED TO OPEN FIRE!*"

Zarek tossed the syringe to Peter, who caught it automatically. "You can frak your revolution," he said. "Your religion isn't real, your followers are deluded, and you're as empty as your music. Those people out there are going to die for a cause that doesn't even exist."

Peter looked frantically around the room, as if his world were coming apart. Kara supposed it was. "They're going to kill my people. I should be with them."

Faint shouts came over the scanner. Clearly someone had left their radio open. "*Up with the Unity!*" someone shouted. Someone else started singing Peter's revolution song.

"Not that piece of shit again," Zarek muttered as Peter headed for the main door. "Gods, I can't believe I thought this was a group worth helping."

"Stay here, Peter," Sharon ordered without looking up from the duffle bag. Her voice was cold and brittle as a knife made of ice. "Don't frakking move."

He stopped and looked at her. "Exactly what are you doing with that?"

"I'm putting a timer on the ordnance so we can set it off properly."

"But we don't *want* to set it off," Peter said, growing more and more agitated. "We don't *want* anyone to die!"

"The marines don't know that," Sharon said calmly. "It's a much better bluff if they can see the countdown. And don't try to pull the timer out once I'm done. If you do, you'll have ten seconds to live before the ship-shattering kaboom."

"THIS IS YOUR SECOND WARNING. MOVE ASIDE AND BRING US PETER ATTIS, OR WE WILL OPEN FIRE."

"Why not remove the explosive part, attach a timer to the rest, and bluff with that?" Peter said.

Sharon paused.

Ha! Kara thought, feeling a moment of triumph seep through the fear and exhaustion. *He's frakking got you!*

"There is that," Sharon said slowly. "But I don't think we'll do it that way. We need to move out."

"Move out?" Peter echoed. Kara wanted to roll her eyes. Peter seemed to spend most of his time repeating what other people said. "We're staying here to confront the marines if they get past my people."

On the monitor, one of the marines looked up at the camera. He raised a pistol and fired at it. People ducked and screamed. The monitor image dissolved into static.

"My people," Sharon said, a smile in her eyes. "I like the way you say that, Peter. As if you own them."

"I don't own anyone." He took a step toward her. "Who are you, anyway?"

"Someone who's telling you we have to get the frak out of here," Sharon said. "Grab your girl-toy and we'll go. Tommy's already left. Didn't you notice?"

Kara, still shaking on the cold floor, managed a glance around the storeroom. It was empty except for the monitors in the corner. They still showed that the marines weren't making much headway against the room packed full of people. Tom Zarek was gone. Kara wasn't in the least surprised. She raised her hands, trying to wave them and get Peter's attention, but she didn't have the coordination. He still held the syringe, and it was half full of blood.

"THIS IS YOUR FINAL WARNING," the scanner said. "MOVE ASIDE AND BRING US PETER ATTIS OR WE WILL BE FORCED TO OPEN FIRE!"

"The marines are wrong," Sharon said. "The schematics they're undoubtedly using to get around are telling them that the only way into this part of the ship is through that room your people are guarding. Problem is, when the *Monarch* was modified to take on algae, the workers added another access passageway to make air circulation easier and to simplify transporting goop around, and those changes aren't on the schematics yet. That means we can get out of here just like Tommy did and put the bomb someplace where it'll do some good. It's not close enough to the outer bulkheads here to cause a breach."

"We aren't setting off the bomb!" Peter shouted at her.

Kara mustered all her willpower, forcing her lips to move the way she wanted them to. "*Peter!*" she gasped.

He turned and looked at her. Instant realization came over him. "Frak! I'm sorry, Kara. I'm so sorry." He dashed over to kneel beside her and push up one of her sleeves. Kara felt the sharp prick as the syringe pierced her skin.

But Sharon was already there. She grabbed Peter's wrist and twisted. He yelped and dropped the syringe, though it remained stuck in Kara's arm. The plunger hadn't moved.

"None of that," Sharon said. "We're getting out of here. Now."

"Who the hell are you, anyway?" he gasped.

"The less you know—"

Peter lunged. He caught the bottom of Sharon's mask and yanked. Caught by surprise, Sharon didn't react in time, and her face lay revealed. The mask made a crumpled red beard beneath her chin, though her hair was still covered. Kara continued to shake on the floor, the syringe sticking out of her arm, but she saw Peter's face go pale as milk. His face looked so horrified and stricken that Kara would have felt sorry for him if she weren't twisting in the final stages of a disease he had given her. She looked down at the syringe poking into her arm.

"Mistress Eight," Peter whispered, rising to his feet.

"One of them," Sharon said, also rising.

Cracks of gunfire came over the scanner. People screamed. Kara's blood went cold at the sounds, but more of her attention was focused on the syringe. The needle had pierced her deeply—Peter wasn't a medical technician and had just jabbed it in. A thin bit of blood trickled down the side of her arm. Hers or Peters? Kara gathered her strength. She probably had one chance to make this work. If she frakked it up, she was dead.

"Oh gods." Peter backed up a shaky step, his attention on Sharon. "Oh gods, what have I done?"

"So much for faith," Sharon said. "Or maybe you're swearing to your multiple gods out of habit." She caught up the duffel bag with easy strength and set the timer inside. Kara, still on the floor, couldn't read the numbers, but she heard the familiar beeping of a countdown. "I suppose this is where I bow out. There's a lot more I can do, but not if I'm dead or captured."

Kara made her move. She half rolled, half flopped onto her stomach. The motion drove the syringe deeper into the meat of her arm. It was like being stabbed with a thin knife. Kara bit her lip at the unexpected pain and flopped onto her back again. The syringe fell out of her arm and clattered to the floor. The plunger had been pushed all the way in.

"Resourceful as ever, Starbuck," Sharon said, noticing for the first time what Kara was up to. "Now I *really* have to go."

"Where's . . . groll delk karoledd—frak!" Kara tried again. "Where's . . . real Sharon?"

"I'm perfectly real," Sharon said. "More real than the One. More real than Peter's faith."

"There is no One, is there?" Peter said slowly. He was wrapped in his own fear and misery. The self-centered bastard wasn't even trying to fight Sharon. Not that he had a hope of hurting her, but Kara thought he should at least *try*. "You all just fed that religious stuff to me, made me believe it. But it's all shit."

Sharon cocked her head. "You think so? God exists, Peter dear. How you see God is up to you, really. But we don't care what you humans believe. The prions will kill most of you and leave the rest so weakened that you'll be easy prey. Thanks be to God. And to Peter."

More gunfire over the scanner. More screams and shouts. Kara found that the shakes were already lessening. How long before she could get up and walk?

"I need to get out there and help all those people!" Peter said. "Maybe if I surrender, they'll stop shooting!"

"No, Peter," Sharon said, putting a hand on his shoulder. "You aren't going anywhere."

Peter twisted out of her grip. "I'll kill you," he snarled.

"Will you?" Sharon drew herself up to her full height. Even though she was half a head shorter than Peter, she seemed to tower over him. "I could beat you to death five times before you threw a single punch at me. Now back away."

Peter stared at her for a long moment. *Try, Pete!* Kara thought, pushing herself up to hands and knees. *I'll back you! Or try.*

But Peter dropped his eyes and backed away. Kara's heart sank. Sharon snorted and gave him a contemptuous glance. The crack and pop of gunfire boomed from the scanner, and Kara tried not to imagine bleeding corpses piling up on the deck. Sharon, meanwhile, grabbed Peter's arm. Something metal flashed in her hand. In a single swift movement, she clicked a handcuff to Peter's wrist and snapped the other inside the duffel.

"What the hell?" Peter gasped, shaking his wrist.

"You're a hostage now," Sharon said. "Actually you've always been one—you were just too blind to see it. It won't take those marines long to chew through your people, so let's get moving." She hauled him unprotesting toward the door leading to the other exit—the newly made one, Kara assumed. The scanner continued to spout the cold crackle and crunch of an ongoing massacre. Sharon reached the door. Kara tried to get to her feet, using the wall for support. The cure for the plague was in the hands of a bomb-toting Cylon, and she had to do something. She pushed herself from hands and knees to just knees, then got one foot on the floor. So far, so—

Her legs gave out and she crashed back to the floor. Too much too soon. Sharon laughed at her and opened the door.

"Fight her, you frakking coward!" Kara shouted in a last-ditch effort. Or she tried to. What came out of her mouth made no sense at all.

"See you on the other side, Starbuck," Sharon called over her shoulder. "Wherever that is."

Then main door burst open and a dozen helmeted and face-plated marines poured into the storeroom, rifles at the ready. "Freeze!"

It was Lee's voice. Kara wanted to collapse with relief, but all she could do now was shake. Sharon turned to face them in her own doorway, wrenching Peter around in front of her.

"Go ahead and fire," she said. "But Petey here is between you and me. So how good is your aim? Feeling a little shaky? Want a bit of babble?"

"I said, freeze!" Lee barked. "We've got you, Sharon. There's nowhere to go."

Sharon yanked open the duffel bag and showed Lee the ordnance inside. Peter was cuffed to it, and the timer showed a countdown of twenty-two minutes and ten seconds . . . nine . . . eight.

"Let's play hide and seek, Captain Adama," she said with a winsome smile. "Just you and me. You need Peter alive to cure the plague. I want a shuttle off this ship. Count to a hundred, then come find us to talk about it."

And she vanished into the dark beyond the door, dragging Peter with her.

CHAPTER 15

"Two days' worth of work, Gaius?" said Number Six.

Gaius Baltar continued to peer into the microscope. "That's what I told the Commander. Having you repeat it doesn't change anything."

"Liar. Words have power, Gaius. You just need the right thing to say at the right time."

"Also true. Completely and totally true." He pushed himself away from the microscope and, swiveling on his stool, reached for the telephone. His face was scratchy and unshaven, his clothes were wrinkled and disheveled, but his movements snapped with energy. This often happened to him when he was midway through a project. A sort of manic power crackled through him and he could go for days without sleep—or last for hours in bed.

Six's hand landed on his and pressed them into the dialing pad before he could punch more than two numbers. "Wait. Who are you calling?"

"The president. She needs an update on the situation."

"Don't you think Adama can tell her?"

"I'd rather tell her myself, thanks," he said with a little smile.

She slid her soft hand up his forearm, his shoulder, his neck. A tingle of electricity followed her fingertips, and a coppery taste tanged Gaius's mouth. She leaned down and whispered in his ear, "Call her later. You've been working so hard, Gaius. Don't you think you deserve a break?"

"I have so much to do," he murmured back, though his hands stole up her sides, caressing the cool, smooth fabric of her high-slit dress. "So much work to save the Fleet."

"Will twenty minutes matter in the grand scheme of things?" she said, slitting her eyes like a hungry cat. Her hand reached beneath her own buttocks, opened his fly, and slipped inside. Gaius gasped, then let out a long, rumbling sigh. Her touch made little shudders of pleasure ripple up and down his entire body.

Gaius glanced over his shoulder at the microscope, then at the telephone. He was vice president of the Colonies and their pre-eminent scientist. He was a powerful man with equally powerful appetites, and he needed to indulge them. He *deserved* it, especially after everything he had done for the Fleet. His hands slid up Number Six's smooth thighs.

"Yes, Gaius," she panted against his mouth. "Oh, yes."

His groin tightened, and desire slid over him in a hot rush. He pulled her down into his lap and kissed her, devouring her mouth like a wildfire consuming a forest. He half expected her to push him away, but she met him with a ferocity so powerful, she growled. The sound rumbled in her breasts, and he felt them move against his own chest. His groin ached, and he felt like he could push into her, push *through* her, until the two of them were a single being.

"Twenty minutes?" he said. "I was thinking sixty."

Lee Adama pointed impatiently at the door. "You six go after her and Peter!" he told the marines who had entered behind him. "The rest of you secure this room. Go go go!"

The marines hurried to obey. Lee pulled up his face plate and ran across the room to kneel next to Kara. She had never been so glad to see anyone in her life. But his hands were shaking. Concern, fear, and relief all mixed together inside her and made her entire body feel weak. Or maybe that was still the plague. Lee gathered her into his arms, and she let him. Hard muscle made a barrier around her, sealing out the rest of the world. For a short, blissful moment, she let herself feel safe and cared for. She felt tears welling up, and she forced them back. Lee looked down at Kara and she looked up at him. His eyes were so blue and full of . . . what? Concern? Love? She wondered what he was seeing in her eyes.

And then he was kissing her. His lips were warm on hers. The move surprised both of them, and Kara's eyes opened wide. A second lasted a thousand heartbeats. Kara wanted this and didn't want this. Too many things could go wrong—*would* go wrong. Best to end it before it began. Kara tensed to push Lee away, but a howl of pain followed by gunfire jerked them apart. Thuds, more shots, another scream. Lee scrambled to his feet and hauled Kara up beside him with an easy strength that left her a little breathless. The other marines in the room had spun and were pointing their rifles at the door Sharon had used.

Sharon appeared in the doorway again, holding a pistol to Peter's head. The ordnance was still cuffed to his wrist. Kara swallowed.

"Hold your fire!" Lee barked.

"See what you did?" Sharon said. "Now I have weapons. I said I'd talk just to you, Captain, and to Lieutenant Thrace there. The both of you. Anyone else follows me, I kill Petey. If both of you don't come, I kill Petey." She vanished back into the darkness.

"Frak!" Lee muttered. "Can you stand by yourself, Kara?"

Kara checked. The shaking had ended. She also felt no desire to babble nonsense. Her voice was her own again. She felt weak, but strength was already returning. Lee's hands, however, still trembled.

"I think I'm okay," she said in a tight, tired voice.

"Helo!" Lee shouted. "I want you and the others to check the hall for wounded. And dead."

"Those people," Kara said as Helo and the others obeyed. "I heard the orders on the scanner. You killed them?"

Lee looked at her, and Kara's heart suddenly felt like a bruised apple. A wave of revulsion made her stomach roil. The arm that held her up had just killed a score of innocent people.

Then Lee shook his head. "We didn't hurt a single person. Adama broadcast those orders, figuring Peter would hear them and come out of hiding to surrender himself. We fired into the air to make it sound like we were shooting. People screamed, so that made it even more realistic. Or so we thought—it obviously didn't work."

Relief swept Kara in a powerful wave that weakened her knees. Lee tightened his arm around her shoulders. "It almost did work," Kara said. "How did you get in here?"

"I asked the Old Man to let me bring two forces," Lee said. "I sent one down to the great room as a distraction," Lee said. "The rest of us got back into the Raptor, flew around to the other side of the ship, and burned through over there. That got us around the crowd. We figured the perpetrators would think all the marines were wading through the passive resistance people, letting the rest of us sneak up on them. But we got lost—the schematics are wrong. Eventually, we had to home in on the ordnance signal. Then Da—Commander Adama gave the killing orders, hoping to flush Peter out into the open and maybe distract the bad guys some more. I just wish it had worked."

"I told you it almost did. Peter was about to run out there and give himself up, but Sharon stopped him."

"Yeah. Sharon." He ran a shaky hand over his face. "What the frak is that bitch doing here?"

Helo trotted up. "Sir, we have six dead. She—" He swallowed, and Kara could see the distress on his face. "I'm sorry, sir, but she killed them all. Sharon . . ."

"That wasn't your Sharon," Kara said quickly. Both Lee and Helo stared at her in surprise.

"What do you mean?" Helo asked, his voice full of hope.

"That's another Sharon copy. I saw her close up, and she isn't pregnant."

Helo grabbed Kara's free shoulder. "Are you sure?"

"Absolutely. She—this new Sharon—must have been hiding in a secret compartment on the rescue pod. I don't know what happened to *our* Sharon, but that wasn't her, and I'm betting our Sharon wasn't behind the attack on the concert, either."

The love and hope that crossed Helo's face was so clear, Kara's heart ached for him. She hadn't loved anyone like that since Zak.

Really? said a treacherous little voice in the back of her head. *What about his brother?*

"So where is our Sharon?" Helo asked. "And why did she escape?" Behind him, marines were dragging dead bodies into the storeroom, clearing out the doorway. Some were missing their weapons.

"No idea," Kara said. "But the Sharon who has Peter is definitely someone else."

"Wait a minute," Lee said. "What happened to you? Why aren't you shaking anymore?"

"Peter . . . cured me." She bent down, freeing herself from Lee's hold, and picked up the syringe from the floor. "With his blood. Lee, we have to get him back. He's the only cure for the prion."

Lee visibly relaxed. "Thank all gods. If he injected you, Kara, then we're fine. Your body will start making the cure prion and—"

"No," Kara interrupted. "My blood's AB positive. It's really rare, and I can only give blood to other AB positives. Peter's O negative. He can give blood to anyone."

"Baltar and Cottle might be able to synthesize the cure prion without using your blood," Lee said. Then his face fell. "But not before most of the Fleet dies. Dammit, we need Peter."

"Shit," Helo said. "Nothing is ever easy around here, is it?"

"Sir," Racetrack approached, raising her face plate, "do you want us to go after her?"

Lee checked his watch. "No. She said she'd kill Peter if anyone but me and Kara went in there. Call the Old Man and tell him what's happened. You think you can fire a weapon, Lieutenant?"

Lee's words filled Kara with a new strength. She suspected it was mostly adrenaline, but right then, she didn't care. Her hands were blessedly steady, and the thought of filling that bitch Sharon with chunks of metal made Kara itch to get moving. She held up her hands.

"I'm solid like a rock, sir," she said.

Lee handed her his own pistol and rifle. Helo gave her his kevlar armor, and she belted it on. It felt solid and comforting, despite the stiff weight. Kara accepted an equipment belt and a helmet.

"What do you think her game is?" Helo asked. "There's nowhere for her to go. Now that we know she's on the *Monarch*, there's no escape. Even if the Old Man gives her a frakking shuttle in exchange for Peter, she has to know we'll blow her out of the sky the minute she's clear of this ship."

"I don't know." Lee tried to check the firing mechanism on his own pistol, but his hands were shaking too much and he couldn't get the slide action to work. "Frak!"

"Maybe you should stay here," Kara said. "I'll go alone."

"Like you always do, is that it?" Lee said. "Noble Starbuck, the maverick, on her own again. Well, not this time."

"Lee," she protested, "you're sick. You should—"

"I should get my ass moving," Lee told her. "Sharon—bad Sharon—said she wanted to talk to me and maybe you. We don't know what she'll do if I don't come, so I'm coming."

"Fine," Kara said. "Just keep your pistol in the holster, buddy. You fire with those hands, and you're just as likely to hit me as her."

They trotted toward the door. On the way, they passed the six bodies the others had laid out. Kara carefully avoided looking at them. If there was a friend among them, she didn't want to know it. Not yet.

"Go get her, sir," one of the marines said, and Kara wasn't sure if he was talking to Lee or to her, so she nodded. Pistol drawn, she stepped across the threshold into the blackness beyond.

The darkness wasn't absolute, and her eyes adjusted in a few seconds. They were standing in a metal corridor barely wide enough for the two of them to stand side by side. Something dark and sticky stained the walls and floor, and Kara caught the coppery smell of drying blood. She pursed her lips and felt abruptly glad that Lee was beside her, close enough for her to feel his body heat. The darkness pressed around her, close and frightening. Her heart beat faster and her mouth went dry. Shapes moved just at the corner of her eye, reaching out to pluck at her with cold fingers, but when she jerked her gaze around to look at them, they disappeared.

Kara had never liked the dark very much, even as an adult. She knew exactly why, though knowing the source of the fear didn't make it any less intense. When she was little, her father had used the dark. Like most small children, darkness made Kara nervous, and Dad knew it. He thought it was absolutely hilarious to hide in her closet just before bedtime and bang the door open while she was climbing into bed. His harsh laughter at her screams of terror still echoed in her head. Her pleas for him to stop doing it fell on deaf ears. She needed a sense of humor, she needed to be toughened up. After a while, she took to checking the closet when the lights were still on. Once, she had searched the house, padding around in her nightgown and bare feet, unable to find Dad anywhere. At last, Mom had told her to get her butt into bed and no excuses. Sure she knew where Dad was, Kara had thrown open the closet door. The space beyond was empty, except for her clothes and a few toys. Puzzled, but feeling safer, she had turned out the light and scurried over to her bed before anything in the dark could get her. Something furry shot out from under the bedstead and grabbed Kara's ankle in a monstrous grip. Kara's bladder let go and she almost fainted from sheer terror. The monster, of course, had turned out to be Dad wearing a furry mitten. He had roared with laughter, and then had whipped her for wetting her underwear.

As an adult, Kara knew there was nothing coming to get her in the dark. Or she *had* known that. Now Cylons attacked from the dark of space. And there had been that time a bunch of robotic Cylons had gotten aboard *Galactica* and cut the power. Now the darkness hid Sharon. There *were* monsters out there.

But this time, Kara was armed and armored, and she wasn't alone. Beside her, Lee squinted down the hallway. "Helmet lights?" he whispered. "Or would that give our position away?"

"I think Cylons see pretty well in the dark," Kara muttered back. "We may as well use the lights."

They switched them on, and twin beams of light speared the darkness of the corridor and put sharp edges on the shadows. "Come on," Lee said.

They moved cautiously along the corridor. Their cautious footsteps clanked faintly on the ceramic deck plates, and the damp air smelled of salt water and algae. A part of Kara wanted to hurry, hurry, hurry—the Fleet needed the cure that only Peter could provide. Another part of her urged caution. Sharon might have already killed Peter and just wanted to frak with her and Lee. It wouldn't be the first time the Cylons had screwed around with someone's mind.

The corridor ended in a door that was so new, it still smelled of solder. Lee tried to crank it open, but his hands were shaking too badly, so Kara took over. The hinges creaked, and the sound seemed to boom through the entire ship. Lee flinched. Kara waited until her heart slowed down again before stepping through, trying to cover all directions at once with her pistol. Darkness pressed in on all sides like black cotton, and Kara felt exposed and vulnerable despite the kevlar. Her breathing sounded too loud in her ears, a beacon for bombs or bullets.

The space beyond the door felt big and echoey. Kara and Lee shined their lights around. Huge shapes loomed like black beasts, and catwalks made lattices far overhead. Kara made out trucks and loaders and giant equipment she couldn't name, all motionless, and found herself tiptoeing past them as if they were asleep and the slightest sound might bring them snarling awake.

"I think this is the spot where one of us is supposed to say, 'Let's split up, we can cover more ground that way,' " Lee murmured.

"Frak that," she scoffed.

"Well I wasn't actually going to say it," Lee replied.

Kara smiled in the dark, feeling a little better. A lot better, actually. Having Lee beside her felt good, felt right. They were a great team, both on missions and off duty. And when he had kissed her earlier . . .

She slammed the brakes on that line of thought. They had to find Peter, and fast, or Kara would be one of the few people still alive the next time the Cylons showed up. The thought sent cold shivers over her entire skin.

Something clinked in the darkness above and to the right. It sounded like chains. Kara thought about ghosts as she and Lee both swept their helmet lights across the underside of the catwalk above them. Nothing moved, though Lee's beam was a little shaky. He tried to hold it steady and failed. The light danced around like a malicious fairy. Lee made a small sound in his throat, then coughed, trying to cover it. Kara's heart ached for him. She knew exactly what he was thinking.

"Lee," she said softly. "We'll find her. We'll get you cured."

"I know," he replied in an equally soft voice. "I can always count on you when the chips are down and my hand is shitty." He paused. "*Especially* when the chips are down and my hand is shitty."

Kara slowly reached out, found his hand, and squeezed it. Her heart was pounding as if she were facing a hundred Cylon raiders by herself. Lee's hand was shaking badly, and she couldn't tell if he was squeezing back, but it was warm.

Lee suddenly dropped her hand and swept his light to their right. "You hear that?" he whispered.

Kara listened, still feeling the warmth of his hand in hers. She heard a faint shuffling in the darkness, but her flashlight beam picked up nothing but a giant conveyer belt. "Footsteps?" she whispered back.

"I'm not sure," he murmured. "I can't quite—"

"Why the frak are we whispering?" Kara interrupted. "She knows we're here." She cupped her hands around her mouth. "Hey, Sharon, or whatever the hell your name is! I'm here! Lee too! Get your ass out here!"

Lee flinched, then seemed to realize Kara was right. "Come on!" he bellowed. "Let's get this over with."

"Up here, guys. And no insults, please. I've had a hard day."

Kara's beam stabbed upward toward the voice, and she saw Sharon's face looking down at them through the mesh catwalk two stories above them, not far from the place they had checked earlier. She was kneeling on a kevlar vest and peering over the edge of it. Next to her on the catwalk sat Peter. A long chain was wrapped several times around his body. His hands were tied in front of him with more chain, and the missile ordnance, now minus the duffel bag, was still cuffed to his wrist. He was gagged with a blood-soaked piece of cloth. Kara realized the cloth was a strip torn from the uniform of a dead marine, probably the same one Sharon had taken the vest from. Anger tightened in Kara's stomach like a screw. She thought about taking a shot at Sharon, and instantly discarded the idea. Even if the bullet didn't carom off the catwalk mesh, it would probably just hit Peter or the kevlar vest—a fact Sharon no doubt knew very well.

"Hi!" Sharon called down to them, as if they were meeting to go shopping. "I've got your medicine. It's all here."

"What do you want?" Lee said.

"First, I want you to take off those kevlar vests and the helmets and your equipment belts," Sharon instructed. "Toss them far away. Now! Or I'll slice a piece off of Peter here. Set the helmets on the floor with the lights pointing up so you can see—and I can see you."

Reluctantly, the two pilots obeyed. Kara felt naked and vulnerable once the armor came off, and she had to force herself to toss it into the gloom beyond her flashlight beam. She set her helmet on the floor and pointed the light as instructed. The helmet looked like a decapitated head.

"Now your rifles and your pistols," Sharon said. "And the knives you're keeping in the ankle holsters. Move it! Or I'll cut off a couple of Peter's fingers."

Kara gritted her teeth and tossed her rifle and her pistol away. Lee did the same. He also pulled a knife from an ankle holster and threw that away. It clattered in the dark. Kara wasn't wearing an ankle holster. She pulled up her trouser legs so Sharon could see them. Lee shot Kara a knowing look, and Kara felt a tiny bit better—Lee was hiding more weapons somewhere.

"So you *can* follow directions," Sharon said. "Good. Now take off your shirts. Both of you."

"Our shirts?" Lee said.

Sharon flicked open a knife of her own and gestured at Peter with it. His wide eyes fixed on it. "Do it, Apollo!"

Grimacing, Lee peeled off his shirt. Well-defined muscle rippled in the dim light. Kara, who lived in close quarters with Lee, had seen him undressed any number of times, but never had she seen him strip for a kidnapper.

"Turn around," Sharon said, and Lee reluctantly obeyed. A pistol was stuck into the waistband of his trousers at the small of his back. "That's what I thought. Toss it, Starbuck. And don't get funny ideas while you're doing it."

"Dammit," Lee muttered under his breath as Kara plucked the pistol out of his belt line. Her hand brushed against his back. The skin was warm and smooth, and she remembered how he had cradled her back in the storeroom. His capacity to help her, protect her, was diminishing by the moment, and wasn't that the way it always went? In the end, it came down to just you.

"Now Starbuck," Sharon ordered. "Lose the shirt."

Rather than put off the inevitable, Kara whipped off her shirt and dropped it. The sports bra she wore underneath covered more of her than most bathing suit tops, but still she felt exposed. She caught Lee not looking and knew he was a little embarrassed, even though he was wearing less than she was.

"Turn."

Kara turned, showing she had no weapons. "Okay, fine. We're unarmed and half naked down here. What the hell do you want?"

"A trade, duh," Sharon replied. "Here's how it's going to work. I'm going to send Peter down, and you, Captain Adama, are going to come up. You'll take me to the Raptor that brought you over here and we'll both get in. Then I'll pilot us away. When we're a safe distance from the Fleet—and by that, I mean, 'when you can't blow me out of the frakking sky'—I give little Lee a transponder and shove him out the airlock. I make a Jump, you fly out to pick him up, everyone wins."

"Except Lee, who'll be sucking vacuum," Kara scoffed.

"He'll be in a vac suit," Sharon said with exaggerated patience. "Cylons still follow safety regulations. Sheesh."

"Forget it," Kara said. "You're stuck here, with nowhere to go. Why should we deal with you?"

"Because there's only ten minutes left on the timer," Sharon said, gesturing at the bomb. "You better take the deal, unless you want to be licking your plague cure off the walls and ceiling."

"So you're giving us Peter?" Kara asked. "I thought the point was for the plague to kill all of us. You kill Peter and the mission succeeds. That's what you were trying to do at the concert, wasn't it? I thought you just wanted to hurt a bunch of humans, but your real objective was to kill Peter after he infected everyone but before anyone realized he was carrying the cure. Though that doesn't explain why you didn't just kill him in sickbay during the kidnapping."

"The longer he stayed alive, the more people he infected," Sharon said. "And it was way more fun watching his followers do what they did. You humans are willing to believe anything that sounds like the truth, even if it's false."

"So why not kill Peter now?" Lee asked. "You put one bullet through his head and a second one through yours. We all die and you get home faster."

"True," Sharon sighed. "But death frakking *hurts*, you know? I'd way rather avoid it."

Kara caught Lee's eye and shook her head. "There's more to it," she said just loud enough for him to hear.

He gave a tiny nod of agreement. "We need to play along," he mouthed back. Then, louder, "So you want to take me hostage."

"That's the plan. I don't think Adama will shoot at me if I have his pretty-boy son Apollo chained up beside me."

"How do we know you won't just kill him and Jump away once you're aboard the Raptor?" Kara asked.

"You don't. And maybe that's exactly what I'll do. But you'll still have Peter and the cure." Sharon paused. "Now there's an idea. He could start a new group—Peter and the Cure. Assuming you all survive this. You only have eight minutes and thirty seconds left on the timer." She pulled Peter to her and gave him a kiss on the forehead. "You're so cute when you're tied up. Maybe I'll just keep you anyway."

Above the bloody gag, Peter's eyes were wide with fear, horror, or both. Kara thought about what it would be like to be gagged with someone else's blood and shuddered.

"All right," Lee said. "I'll do it."

"No!" Kara said, stepping in front of him. "I'll go instead."

"What?" said Lee and Sharon at the same time.

"Lee's sick," Kara pointed out. "He's already shaking. Soon he's going to start babbling, and then he'll die. He won't be worth much as a hostage if he's dead. Besides—I've had practice being a hostage already."

"No," Lee said firmly. "You stay here, I'll go with Sharon."

"Actually, I'm the one in charge here," Sharon reminded them from above. "But this is so cute—the two lovers quarreling over who gets to be in danger."

"We're not lovers!" Kara said, with Lee echoing a fraction of a second behind her.

"Sure, sure," Sharon said. "In addition to easily believing a false truth, you humans refuse to believe a real one." She tossed a pair of handcuffs over the catwalk, and Lee caught them. "Starbuck wins the hostage lottery today, I think. Tell me where the Raptor's parked, Apollo."

Lee gritted his teeth. "Aft, starboard side at ninety degrees to the axis."

"Good boy. Now I want you to—what was that?"

Both Lee and Kara froze, listening.

"Who followed you?" Sharon said sharply. "I said, if anyone came with you—"

"I don't hear anything," Kara said.

"No one followed," Lee called upward. "I gave orders."

Sharon narrowed her eyes, then continued. "Just remember I have a knife and about six liters of plague cure up here just waiting to rain down on you. I want you to cuff one end to Kara's wrist, Captain. A little to your right, you'll see the end of a chain. Cuff the other end to one of the links. If you know what's good for you, Kara, you'll grab the chain. And hurry—you've only six and a half minutes left."

Peter made noises around the gag as Lee obeyed. The cuff was cool on Kara's wrist, and she kept swallowing her own heart to keep it from leaping out of her throat. Despite her show of bravado, fear gripped her chest with a cold hand. Lee looked like he wanted to say something but didn't know the words. The muscles on his broad back bunched and moved as he fumbled around in the dim light until he found the chain Sharon had mentioned. He brought one end over to Kara and fastened the free end of the handcuffs to one of the links. It clanked. Kara looked up, trying to trace the line of the chain, but she lost it in the gloom. She grabbed it with both hands.

"Ready-set-go!" Sharon said, and she shoved Peter off the cat- walk. Kara tried to shout, but sound died in her throat as she was yanked upward. Chains clattered, and pain wrenched her shoulders. Peter rushed down past her as she flew dizzily up toward the cat- walk. Kara got a glimpse of Peter's frightened expression and of the ordnance still cuffed to his wrist. Red numbers flashed, but she didn't have time to read them. Her feet dangled over nothing. Sharon grabbed Kara's belt and hauled her onto the catwalk. Below, Lee was already unwrapping Peter's chains. The moment Kara's feet touched down, she tensed to attack, but Sharon spun her around with terrifying speed and forced both of Kara's hands behind her. The chain clinked again. There was a click, and both of Kara's hands were cuffed behind her.

"Don't try to kick me, either," Sharon said. "I'll whack you over the head and carry you if I have to, and you won't like it very much."

"Is Peter all right?" Kara called over the edge.

Lee and Peter both looked up. Lee had freed Peter from the chain and the gag, but Peter's left hand was still handcuffed to the missile ordnance. The timer was counting down toward five minutes.

"I'm fine, Kara," Peter called. "Gods. Are *you* okay?"

"How do I disarm the bomb?" Lee said. "I don't recognize this setup."

"Well, that's part of the problem," Sharon said. The timer hit five minutes and the numbers suddenly jumped. The minutes counter read zero and the seconds counter read thirty. They were counting back- ward. "Looks like you got to save your girlfriend's life after all, Cap- tain. And you, Starbuck, get to see both your lovers die."

CHAPTER 16

Kara stared in shock, then fought against her restraints. "No! Lee! Peter!" she cried through the catwalk floor. It felt like she was a mile away from them both.

Peter looked up, stricken. Lee tried yanking at Peter's handcuffs, but they didn't budge. The timer continued its deadly countdown. Lee grabbed it, and his hand shook visibly.

"Pull the timer off and it blows right away," Sharon called down, and Lee froze. "Have fun with it. Come on, Lieutenant." And she began to haul Kara away by one elbow.

"Lee!" Kara shrieked. "Lee!"

Below, Peter's face hardened. Abruptly, he shoved Lee away and sprinted off into the darkness. Lee, still shirtless, snatched up one of the helmets from the floor and pointed its light toward him. The timer, glowing an angry red in the dark, showed six seconds. Peter was already climbing into the heavy metal scoop of a loader. He shot one more look up at Kara. She stared back, feeling completely helpless.

"I'm sorry, Kara!" Peter called. There were tears in his voice. "I'm so sorry."

He dropped into the loader bucket. Lee dove to the floor. Even though she was two stories above it, the explosion knocked Kara off her feet. It was like being slapped by a giant hand. She landed beside Sharon, the latticed metal of the catwalk scraping her bare arms and shoulders. Automatic alarms blared. Sharon recovered her feet first, yanked Kara back to hers, and towed her toward a set of stairs that led downward. The heat sucked the air from Kara's lungs and shriveled her hair. The hot smell of scorched metal stung her nose and acrid smoke clawed at her eyes. Then she heard the scream of tortured metal, and a section of the catwalk behind them crashed to the main floor. The section Kara and Sharon were standing on tilted backward. Kara, her hands cuffed behind her, lost her balance and fell heavily to the latticework. She slid backward with a yelp, losing more skin to the catwalk.

"Frak," Sharon said, and managed to grab Kara by the hair. White pain ripped Kara's scalp and she screamed. Sharon, who had hooked an arm around a strut for support, hauled Kara closer, then managed to get a hand under Kara's arm and yank her along until they came to a level section of the catwalk near the stairs. Kara felt like a bruised bag of meat. She coughed and stumbled, but Sharon yanked her down the steps anyway. Twice she stumbled and fell, and both times Sharon hauled her roughly to her feet.

"Lee!" Kara called over her shoulder. "Lee!"

"Shut up," Sharon ordered. "We have to get to the Raptor."

"I'm not going with you, bitch," Kara spat. "You had that planned from beginning, didn't you?"

"Well, yeah." Sharon opened the door. "You didn't honestly think I'd wreck a plan we've been perfecting for months, did you? This way, Peter's still dead, the cure is destroyed, the only other person whose body makes the prion is with me, and I still have a hostage that'll get me clear of the Fleet. If you're very nice to me, I'll give you a vac suit before I dump you out the airlock, and if you're *really* nice to me, I'll let you put it on first."

"So why did you tell Lee to come along? Why kill him?"

Sharon shrugged. "Someone had to handle the chains."

Kara decided not to respond to this. Sharon shoved her into the corridor beyond the doorway and shut the hatch. The heat vanished, letting Kara breathe more easily. They were standing at a well-lighted T intersection.

"All right, let's see," Sharon said, "assuming Captain good-boy Apollo wasn't lying about the Raptor—and your life expectancy will be really short if he did, honey—we need to go . . . this way."

"I'll frakking kill you," Kara gasped. "I swear I'll find a way."

"Sure, sure," Sharon said, towing her along. "Even if you managed it, I'd be alive and kicking humanity's ass again before long. Not that there'll be much ass to kick now that Peter blew himself to bits and took the cure with him."

"He didn't do it," Kara snarled. "That was you."

"Whatever. Let's see. Left up here, then right, and the ship should be—ah-ha!"

They came across a hole, perhaps a meter and a half in diameter, that had been cut into the bulkhead. Lying on the deck in front of it was a big circle of ceramic. It looked like a mutated round drawbridge. Sharon pushed Kara toward the hole. Kara ducked to get inside and found herself in the familiar interior of a Raptor transport. Sharon also ducked to follow. The moment Kara crossed the threshold, she straightened, spun, and kicked Sharon in the head before the Cylon woman could straighten. Sharon grunted and went down to her hands and knees. All the anger and fear Kara had been carrying with her exploded like a missile. She swept Sharon's arms out from under her with a sweep kick and jumped forward. The back of her foot came down on the back of Sharon's neck. Kara pressed down.

"Now who's the hostage, toaster?" Kara panted.

"Don't call me that," Sharon growled. In a flash of movement, she grabbed Kara's ankle and yanked. Kara lost her balance and crashed to the deck on her side. Sharon scrambled to her feet and kicked Kara under the jaw. Her teeth clacked together and Kara saw stars through an explosion of pain. The Raptor spun around her.

"Frakking human bitch," Sharon spat. "I should shoot you right now."

Running footsteps pounded down the corridor toward the hole and the hatchway that framed it. Sharon started to shut the hatchway, but an arm interposed itself. It was shaking.

"Wait!" said a male voice. Kara was too groggy from Sharon's kick to recognize it, but Sharon seemed to. She let the hatchway open again just far enough to reveal a dark-haired man crouching over to peer inside the Raptor.

"Helo," Sharon said. Her hand dropped to her belt and toyed with a small control Kara hadn't noticed before. "This is a surprise. Trying to delay me long enough for the rest of the troop to catch up?"

"No," Helo said. His dark eyes were serious. "Sharon, please don't do this. Leave Starbuck here."

Sharon looked genuinely puzzled. "Why would I do that?"

"I know you aren't . . . aren't *my* Sharon," he said. "But you have to know how much I love her—you. Please leave Kara here. Everyone over at CIC is too sick to chase you. Leave Kara here."

"So you can try to synthesize a cure from her blood?" Sharon scoffed. "I don't think so, Helo."

Kara tried to sit up, but the pain in her head and her bound hands made it impossible. She could only lay with her cheek pressed into the cool floor.

"Then do it for me," Helo pleaded. "I've talked to my Sharon a lot, and it sounded like all of the Sharons . . . all of *you* . . . share some of the same memories. Don't you remember any feelings for me?"

"Your Sharon never died, Helo, so her memories were never downloaded anywhere. You're just another human." Sharon started to push the hatch shut again. "One who made the stupid mistake of falling in love with a superior being."

A pistol appeared in Helo's hand. "I gave you a chance," he said, and fired.

Sharon, however, was already moving. She ducked, and her foot came up in a sideways kick that slammed into Helo's midriff and flung him backward. He hit the opposite wall with a terrible thud. The bullet ricocheted off a strut in the interior. Kara heard a cracking noise, but lying on the floor as she was, she couldn't see much. Helo slid to the deck, clearly dazed.

"I could kill you, Helo," Sharon said, her hand once again on that strange control at her belt. "But I won't. The plague can take you. Maybe there's something to the whole 'feelings for you' thing after all."

She slammed the hatchway shut, spun the wheel to lock it, and reached into a storage closet to remove a white vac suit. With practiced

BATTLESTAR GALACTICA TRILOGY

ease, she slipped it on and sealed the helmet. Kara was too groggy to do anything but lie there. And what did it matter if she fought back, anyway? Lee was dead, Peter was dead, the cure for the plague was destroyed. Almost everyone in the Fleet would die within the next two or three days, and the Cylons would be able to mop up the remaining handful at leisure. A single tear ran from the corner of her eye and down the side of her nose. Everything she had worked to preserve, everything she had fought for, was gone. Her life was a waste.

And you're a waste of life, said her father's voice. *Just a scared little nothing.*

Sharon, fully suited, took up the pilot's seat at the front of the Raptor, and switched on the radio. "*Galactica* Actual, this is Boomer. Anyone over there well enough to give me a high sign?"

There was a long pause. Kara tried to remain hopeful. If there was a way to negotiate her release, Commander Adama would find it. Sharon didn't wait for an answer. She released the clamps holding the Raptor to the side of the *Monarch*, and the bright stars beyond the pilot's canopy began to move.

"*This is* Galactica *Actual*," came Colonel Tigh's voice, and Kara's heart sank. The man was as diplomatic as a hammerhead shark. "*Just what the hell do you think you're doing?*"

"Hey there, Colonel," Sharon said, as if this were a perfectly normal day. The Raptor picked up speed. "The Old Man too sick to come on the line himself?"

"*None of you goddam business,*" Tigh snapped. "*You just bring that Raptor back, missy, and we'll call it even.*"

"Nah. Thought you might want to know I'm making off with one of your star pilots," Sharon said. Her voice was tinny over the suit's intercom. "Lieutenant Thrace is lying here on my deck, stunned but in one piece. She'll stay that way unless you try to fire on me with those shaky hands of yours."

"*How do I know you're telling the truth?*" Tigh countered.

Sharon got up from the pilot's chair and hauled Kara to her feet. Pain slashed through her head, and she felt warm blood dribble down her chin from a cut she hadn't noticed before. Sharon plunked Kara into the copilot's chair and said, "Say hello, Lieutenant."

Kara remained silent.

"If you say hello," Sharon said sweetly, "I promise to give you a vac suit of your own before I shove you outside."

"Frak you," Kara said.

"That could be a recording," Tigh said.

"Repeat what the good Colonel just said, Starbuck," Sharon ordered. "If you want the vac suit, that is."

"That could be a recording," Kara said through gritted teeth. Every movement only made the pain worse.

"There you are, Colonel. So hold your fire and everything'll be just fine. I'll stick Starbuck here in a suit, give her a tracking transponder, and toss her outside. Once I've Jumped away, you can come and rescue her."

The lie was so transparent, even Tigh had to see through it. Kara had no illusions about her eventual fate at Sharon's hands, but the pain in her head made it difficult to think.

"Where's Peter Attis?" Tigh demanded.

"Back on the *Monarch*," Sharon said.

"Where, exactly? The Monarch *is a big place."*

"I guess you could say he's all over the place, really. Boomer out."

A tiny crackle came from the canopy in front of Kara, and a hairline crack ran across the Plexiglas. Kara's blood chilled as she realized what had happened—Helo's ricochet had chipped the canopy and the resulting weakness was getting worse. Sharon, however, didn't seem to notice. She was busy plotting a Jump.

"Okay," she said, putting in the final numbers and standing up. "While the computer's finishing that up, you and I have things to do."

She hooked a hand under Kara's elbow, tugged her out of the co-pilot's chair, and hauled her toward the closed hatchway.

"No suit?" Kara said, already knowing the answer.

"No suit," Sharon agreed. "I was lying. Hell, I'm doing you a favor. Better to die now than watch all your friends die while you live."

"Don't do me any favors," Kara said half-heartedly. Sharon's grip was steel-strong and Kara couldn't break the handcuffs. Her mind came up with a dozen ideas, each one more desperate and unworkable than the last. Sharon let go of Kara and put her hands on the wheel that would open the hatchway and evacuate the air. The resulting blast of wind would shove Kara straight out into space. Kara swallowed, trying to hold on to every sensation she could because they would be her last ones. The air rushing through her lungs, the heart beating in her chest, the pain stabbing through her head. It didn't seem fair, having pain as her final sensation. Sharon started to turn the wheel—

—and then another Sharon rose up behind her, both hands laced together in a double fist. Kara stared, not comprehending what she was looking at. The second Sharon brought both hands down on the back of the first Sharon's head. The thin fabric of the vac suit head covering was no protection, and the first Sharon staggered in pain and surprise. The second Sharon hit her again and again and again, a dizzying rain of blows that thudded against the vac suit. The first Sharon collapsed to the deck.

"Sorry it took so long," the second Sharon said. She was wearing a prison jumpsuit, and her stomach was a little rounded. Pregnant. It was Caprica Sharon. "I had to wait until she was in a vac suit before I made a move."

"What?" Kara said, confused. "Why?"

The Plexiglas crackled audibly. Caprica Sharon spun in surprise. A spider web of cracks was spinning a network across the canopy.

"Oh frak," she whispered, then flew into action. She leaped behind Kara and snapped the handcuff chain. Kara winced, but she was growing used to pain by now. Every part of her body hurt by now. Caprica Sharon pulled Kara to her with easy strength, and both of them groped through the storage closet for vac suits. The canopy crackled again and the web of cracks grew larger. Kara thought she heard a faint hiss of escaping air. Gods, nothing ever came easy, did it? She should be in the clear now, but she was still struggling for life.

"Could we make it back to the *Monarch?*" Kara asked.

"That canopy's going to go in less than a minute," Caprica Sharon said. "So that would be a 'no.'" She thrust a suit at Kara, who pulled it on with chilly fingers. Neither human nor Cylon spoke further. The first Sharon lay on the floor, still unconscious. A trickle of blood ran from the corner of her mouth. The canopy made a soft popping sound, and this time the hiss of escaping air was clearly audible. An alarm beeped on the console, in case no one had figured out that the Raptor was losing air. Kara checked the fastenings of her suit and reached for the helmet. A slight breeze caressed her cheek, bringing a reflexive stab of fear. A breeze was a fine thing outdoors on a still summer day, but on a ship, it heralded death by decompression. Kara yanked on the helmet, sealed it, and inhaled the rush of plastic-scented air. Caprica Sharon, meanwhile, had put on her own vac suit, but she set the helmet aside.

"What are you doing?" Kara asked, her voice close and muffled inside the suit. The canopy was by now nothing but a network of cracks.

Caprica Sharon wordlessly reached down, unfastened the other Sharon's fabric helmet, and ripped it free. She put it on her own head and fastened it, then shot a glance at the canopy. Now Kara understood. She supposed she should have felt some sort of pity or reluctance, but all she felt was glad relief.

The first Sharon's eyes popped open and she vaulted to her feet so fast, Kara couldn't react. She caught Caprica Sharon by surprise as well. The first Sharon plowed into Caprica and knocked her face-down to the deck with the first Sharon on top of her.

"I'll kill him *and* you," the first Sharon snarled for no reason Kara could see. Who the hell was *him*?

"You can't reach the control while you're in that vac suit," Caprica Sharon gasped back.

The first Sharon got her fingers under the fastenings of Caprica Sharon's cloth helmet. Damage alarms and air alarms blared through the Raptor's cabin. Caprica Sharon couldn't get the leverage to fight back. The first Sharon ignored Kara entirely.

Wild anger roared over Kara. The first Sharon was responsible for everything that had happened—the plague, Kara's sickness, Peter's death, Lee's death, the destruction of the cure. Strength she didn't know she possessed thundered through her. She grabbed the first Sharon's vac suit by the back of the neck and at the small of the back and lifted.

The first Sharon weighed less than Kara had anticipated. Startled, the first Sharon came free of her victim with an indignant yelp.

"Grab something!" Kara shouted inside her own suit. Without waiting to see if Caprica Sharon had heard, she swung the first Sharon once to gain some momentum, then flung her straight toward the canopy. Sharon hit the weakened Plexiglas face-first dead between the pilot and copilot chairs. The canopy exploded outward, and Sharon blew into space. Her scream was lost in the rush of air.

A hurricane blast knocked Kara off her feet from behind, and she found herself flying toward the empty canopy. She desperately grabbed for one of the chairs and missed. Then an iron hand caught her ankle. Caprica Sharon, her other hand firmly clutching a handhold, towed her back to safety. Kara caught a glimpse of the first Sharon as she drifted through uncaring vacuum, twitching and clawing at her own face as bloody vapor burst from her mouth and nose. The pain and horror of her expression made Kara look away, despite her earlier feelings of anger and hatred. The Cylon may have deserved the death, but Kara found she didn't want to watch it.

The blast of air was short-lived on such a small vessel, and it died quickly. Once the women were sure neither of them was injured or leaking air, they both carefully climbed into seats, Caprica Sharon in the pilot's chair and Kara in the copilot position. It was unnerving to sit in a Raptor, looking at the stars without a Plexiglas barrier between herself and vacuum. She felt as if she could float off into the emptiness. Maybe she should. Everyone in the Fleet was either dead or dying, and she didn't want to be the only one left behind.

Lee was dead. The thought hit her like a punch to her already-sore gut. Frak. She felt tears well up and blinked them back. Crying in a vac suit was almost as bad as throwing up in one. To distract herself, Kara shot Sharon a glance. The Cylon's face was calm inside her vac suit helmet.

"Thanks," Kara said hoarsely. "For saving me. Twice."

"Thanks for saving me once," Sharon replied with a small grin. "Why don't you radio *Galactica* and tell them we're coming? I have the feeling they won't believe anything I have to say."

Gaius Baltar filled a pipette with fluid from a Petrie dish, prepared a slide for it, and slipped it under the microscope. He peered through the lenses.

"Well, Gaius?"

For once, Gaius didn't jump or yelp or spin around. He had sensed Six's presence before she spoke. "I've been listening to the radio news," he said without turning around. "Quite a lot's been happening aboard the *Monarch*."

"And a lot's been happening in this lab," Six said smugly.

This time Gaius glanced over his shoulder at her. No matter what they did together, no matter what happened, Number Six remained perfectly beautiful. Her white-blond hair was never mussed, her makeup never smeared, her dress never wrinkled. Her legs never prickled with stubble, her breath never smelled of garlic, and the only time she sweated was during sex, which Baltar found a turn-on. She was physically perfect in every way.

"So are you here to tell me something useful or just kibbitz while I work?"

"Work?" She gestured at the incubator. It was the size of a small refrigerator and filled with warm test tubes. "Looks like the machines are doing the work for you."

"Mmmmm." Gaius changed slides and looked again. "I don't suppose you'd be willing to lend a hand."

"Why not call Dr. Cottle in to help you?"

"Cottle is a doctor, not a research scientist. Besides, he's shaking too much to be of any use. Looks like it's just me."

"Chosen by God," Number Six said, "and working like a devil. That's you, isn't it, Gaius?"

"Just hand me that box of syringes, would you?"

"I think it would be more appropriate if I just watched."

"That's not what you said half an hour ago," Baltar teased.

Six smiled. It wasn't a happy smile or a sensuous one. It was the sort of smile Baltar had come to dread over the months. His good mood faltered.

"What?" he asked.

"There's something you're forgetting, Gaius."

Kara was in a frak-it mood by the time the Raptor was safely aboard the *Galactica* on Deck Five, so she pulled off her vac suit helmet and climbed out the shattered canopy instead of exiting through the hatchway. Only five people were waiting for her—the plague was getting worse. Three of the people were combat troops Kara didn't recognize. Their rifles were at the ready, and she assumed they were there for Sharon. The fourth was Karl "Helo" Agathon. His face was pale and his uniform was dirty.

The fifth was Lee Adama.

At first Kara's mind couldn't process what she was seeing. The bomb had gone off. Lee was dead. But there he was. Bruises and burns mottled his face and arms. He had replaced his shirt. A bandage covered one cheek. But there he was. Gladness as wide as a rainbow poured over her, and she grabbed him in a hard hug.

"Ow!" they both said as the embrace aggravated their injuries. They backed away from each other, unable to repress the grins that stretched their faces.

"You bastard!" she said. "I thought you died in that explosion."

"I thought so, too," Lee admitted. "Piece of machinery shielded me. That, and the fact that the bomb went off inside the loader scoop. If Peter hadn't run when he had, I *would* be dead."

"Peter." Emerging sorrow dampened the gladness. "He saved us both, then."

"Yeah," Lee said grimly. "Maybe." And he held up his hands to remind Kara that they were still shaking.

Helo stepped forward and gave Kara a hug of his own, but gently. Then he said, "Was Sharon—*our* Sharon—really on board the Raptor with you?"

"Sure thing," Sharon said, emerging from the Raptor, her vac suit already removed. Before anyone could react, Helo grabbed her in a hard embrace and kissed her. She kissed him back. Kara shot a sidelong glance at Lee and caught him shooting a sidelong glance at her. A moment passed and Lee took a step toward her. Kara leaned in.

Then she kissed him quickly on the cheek. He smelled of metal and sweat. "I'm glad you're okay," she said brusquely.

"Uh, yeah," he replied. "Thanks."

The three marines, meanwhile, moved in on Sharon and Helo, safeties off, expressions tense. Sharon noticed them and stepped away from Helo, hands raised. "Don't shoot. I'm not going to make any sudden moves or hurt anyone."

One of the marines brandished his rifle. "Toas—"

"Don't finish that phrase, soldier," Kara interrupted. "Unless you want a world of trouble from an unexpected direction."

The marine shut his mouth.

"What the frak happened?" Lee said.

"How's the Old Man?" Kara countered.

"Barely functional. Tigh's mostly in charge."

"Aw, frak." This from Sharon. The Cylon allowed the marines to put shackles on her wrists and ankles. Around her neck, one of them fastened a man-catcher—a collar with a stiff pole instead of a leash. Helo watched, a pained look on his face, but he didn't interfere.

"I won't let him hurt you, Sharon," Kara said. "But we all need to catch up."

"The President's already in the CIC conference room with the Old Man," Lee said. "Come on."

They made a strange procession through the corridors of the *Galactica*—Lee and Kara both limping and sore, Sharon hobbling at the end of the man-catcher, the grim-faced marines with their ready weapons. The corridors, however, were mostly empty.

"Where is everyone?" Kara asked. "Down with the plague?"

"I guess," Lee said. "Helo and I grabbed one of the *Monarch*'s shuttles and rushed over here after Helo talked to Sharon—the other Sharon. Helo can still fly, and we were hoping to get him into a Viper or another Raptor, something faster than a shuttle, so we could intercept you. But all the combat ships are down—not enough knuckle-draggers to keep them running. Everyone on the *Galactica* is either too shaky to do anything but lie in their bunks, or they're trying to run three and four duty stations at the same time."

"Have you told them about . . ." Kara trailed off, not sure how much she should say.

"No," Lee said. "I've talked to CIC, but I haven't been up there yet."

Helo muttered something that sounded like, "We're all ass-frakked," but he didn't elaborate. Kara concentrated on staying upright. Exhaustion was weighing down on her like a lead blanket. How long had it been since she'd had a real rest? Or sleep? She couldn't remember. Escaping from the other Sharon hadn't been the end of her problems—or the Fleet's.

CIC was almost empty. Kara counted six people, none of whom she knew, desperately trying to run stations designed for twenty. They barely glanced up as the group passed through on their way to the conference room. Kara swallowed. If a Cylon basestar showed up now, they were dead.

Though the same was true if a basestar *didn't* show up.

The CIC conference room was hushed and dimly lit. At the table sat Commander Adama, Colonel Tigh, and Laura Roslin. President Roslin's hands were on the table, and they trembled only slightly. Adama, on the other hand, was clearly fighting to keep himself upright and his mouth shut. Tigh was trembling but seemed functional. They all eyed Sharon as the marines herded her through the door. Sharon was keeping her face impassive, and Kara wondered how she felt about being hauled around like an animal. Did she get angry? Or maybe she found all the extra security flattering, along the lines of "only someone truly dangerous rates this kind of treatment." Kara decided that if she were ever in Sharon's position, she'd try to feel flattered.

Everyone took a seat except Sharon, who stood to one side.

"We don't have time for preliminaries, so I'll just ask about the bad news now," Roslin said. Her voice was soft and tired as an old blanket. "I don't see Peter, so I assume he's dead."

Kara gave a reluctant nod, and felt cold fear and hopeless despair settle across the room. "Sharon—a different Sharon—killed him." She briefed them on what had happened to her since the kidnapping and was surprised to learn she'd been gone for less than a day. It felt like a week.

The table remained silent for a moment after Kara's briefing. Adama was sweating with the effort of remaining silent, and Kara wanted to comfort him. Unfortunately, there was nothing she could do.

"Sharon," Roslin said at last. "Tell us what happened to you." Roslin's voice carried an edge of ice. The President loathed all Cylons and had never warmed to Sharon, even after repeated demonstrations that she meant the Fleet no harm and was, in fact, helping as best she could.

"Where should I start?" she asked.

"From your jailbreak," Roslin said levelly. "When you killed that marine and sent the other to sickbay."

"I didn't kill anyone," Sharon said, though her tone said she expected no one would believe her. "The other copy did."

"Thank gods," Helo said with a small sigh.

Sharon gave him a small smile. "She wiped out the guards at the cell and broke me out, but she wasn't offering to get me off the *Galactica* or anything like that."

"What *did* she offer you?" Roslin said.

"Nothing. She said there was a secret compartment in the escape pod on Deck Five and that I'd better find a way to get there and hide." Sharon paused and licked her lips. "She was going to use me as a scapegoat or a distraction or both. Commander Adama would order search teams to look for me, and that would take extra time and resources and allow her to do what she wanted more easily. They also know that I've been helping the Fleet. If I got caught and was blamed for killing the guard, you'd never believe another word I said. My so-called escape was a way to neutralize any further help I might give the Fleet."

"She could have just killed you," Roslin said.

"That would kill the baby, too," Sharon replied. "Not what she—or any other Cylon—would want."

"Why didn't you just come forward?" Tigh demanded. "Let yourself get caught?"

"Him," Sharon said, nodding toward Helo. "She knocked him out just after the escape and stuck a microdetonator under the skin on the back of his skull. She told me she'd blow Helo to pieces if I got caught."

Helo's hand stole to the back of his head. His face was pale. "That's why my head's been itching lately?"

"Probably. I'm so sorry, Helo."

"Is it going to . . . you know . . . go off now?"

"If it hasn't by now, I'd say you're safe," Sharon said. "Like Kara—Lieutenant Thrace—said, the other one is sucking vacuum, or vacuum is sucking her."

"Why didn't she pop it off outside the Raptor?" Helo pressed. "When I had the pistol?"

Sharon shrugged within the man-catcher. "Who knows? I'd guess she thought you weren't a serious danger to her, and it was more fun to play with you. The detonator was aimed more at me than you any-way."

"Yeah," Helo muttered. "Gods."

"That's what you meant when you said you had to wait until the other Sharon was in a vac suit," Kara said with new understanding. "If she was wearing the detonator on her belt or something, she wouldn't be able to set it off with the suit in the way."

"Yeah," Sharon said. "I hid until I was sure Helo would be safe." She shifted position within her shackles and the chains clinked. "Any-way, I didn't know what to do after the other Sharon sprung me, so I hid for a while. But Chief Tyrol found the secret compartment in the pod, and I couldn't stay there anymore. I snuck on board the Raptor that transported the marines to the *Monarch*. Once you all boarded, I slipped out and tried to get the other Sharon alone, but I couldn't."

"Those were *your* footsteps we kept hearing," Lee said.

"Probably. I couldn't think of a way to get Peter out of there without getting me and Helo killed, so I just waited. Once I realized the other Sharon was going to take Lieutenant Thrace back to the Raptor, I ran ahead. You know the rest of it."

"Nothing . . . matters of state on the steps of—" Adama clamped his teeth together and tried again. "Nothing . . . matters. All dead soon."

That silenced further conversation. Kara bit her lip. The Com-mander was completely right. Within a day or so, everyone Kara had worked so hard to save would be dead. It would be her, Sharon, and maybe a few other people rattling around in the ships.

Something occurred to Kara. "I can help a few people," she said. "Anyone who has AB blood can get the cure from me. No one else, though."

"That's about four percent of the population," Lee said. "It'll help. Every life will help."

He didn't say what his blood type was, and Kara found she couldn't bear to ask.

"And maybe someone can extract the cure from my blood and help others," Kara said instead. "Tom Zarek was also cured, so maybe we can use his blood, too."

"We'll have to try," Lee agreed. "Though Dr. Baltar said—"

The phone buzzed. Adama looked like he wanted to pick it up, but held back for obvious reasons. Everyone glanced uncertainly at every-one else. At last, Kara reached across the table and snatched up the re-ceiver with her steady hands.

"CIC," she said. "Lieutenant Thrace."

"*Doctor Baltar here,*" said a familiar voice. "*It's good to hear your voice, Lieutenant. How are you?*"

Kara kept her voice neutral. She had been trying to forget that she and Baltar had shared a brief, torrid bedroom session, but every time she saw him, the memory surfaced. She still couldn't believe she had done it.

"I'm just dandy," she said, aware that every eye in the room was on her. "What's going on? Commander Adama's . . . indisposed right now, if you're looking for him."

"*Is he there? I know he probably can't talk reliably.*"

"Yes. What do you want, Dr. Baltar?" She added the latter so everyone would know who she was talking to.

"*Just to see if everyone is there. I have . . . I have more news about the plague.*"

Kara closed her eyes. She didn't know if she could handle more bad news. "What is it?"

"*It'd be easier to show you than to tell you,*" he said. "*If everyone is there, I'll just come up.*"

Kara relayed this to the others. Laura Roslin took charge and gave assent. A few minutes later, Gaius Baltar entered the room. His lab coat was neat and pressed, his face shaven, his hair combed, his tie straight. Kara wondered where he found the time and energy. She also noticed that his hands weren't shaking at all. How had he escaped the plague?

Baltar was carrying a tray covered by a black cloth. He glanced at Sharon in surprise but didn't comment on her presence. Instead, he set the tray down at the head of the table and took up a position there.

"What is it, Doctor?" Roslin asked softly. "How much worse can it get?"

"Actually, the news is rather better than you might think." He whipped the cloth aside with a flourish, revealing a row of syringes. The needles gleamed in the dim light of the conference room. "Ladies and gentlemen, I give you the cure for the plague of tongues."

CHAPTER 17

Confused babbling broke out around the table. A fair amount of it was literal nonsense. Commander Adama lost his fragile control and jabbered, a look of shock on his craggy face. Tigh joined in. Until now, his speech had been clear, but being startled seemed to push him over some sort of edge. Roslin and Lee both shouted questions. Only Kara, Sharon, and her guards remained silent, though Sharon's guards stared at the syringes as if they were a rich pile of emeralds and rubies. Through it all, Gaius Baltar stood at the head of the table, his arms folded across his chest, a look of triumph on his face. Kara found herself distrustful instead of glad.

At last, Lee bellowed for quiet and the room fell silent. Or nearly so. Adama and Tigh babbled gibberish for a few seconds before managing to quiet themselves.

"Thank you, Captain," Roslin said. Her body was shaking now. Kara wondered if the plague was worse for her because of the cancer. "Doctor, if those injections will cure the plague, I think you should administer them now. We'll have the explanation later."

"Of course, Madam President." Baltar moved quickly about the room with the tray. He started with Commander Adama, then followed up with Tigh and Roslin. When he reached Kara, she held up her hand.

"I'm good," she said.

Baltar gave her an odd look, but continued around the table. He also injected Sharon's guards. He didn't offer one to Sharon and she didn't ask. Cylons had red blood, that Kara knew—she had seen enough of it over the months—but she doubted it was compatible with human biology.

"You should begin to feel better almost immediately," Baltar said. "The prions fasten onto your nervous tissue early on, and that starts the shaking and the babbling, but they don't do permanent damage until later in the cycle, when the patient is in a coma."

"How, Doctor?" Roslin asked. She was rolling her sleeve back down. "You said it would take you two or three days to manufacture the C prion."

"True," Baltar admitted. "But I found a . . . shortcut in the middle of the process." He paused and made a tiny shudder before continuing. "I had also been operating under the assumption that I would begin to shake as well, which would slow me down. It never happened. I seem to be part of that tiny percentage of a given population that is naturally immune to any given disease."

"Lucky for us," Tigh said.

"Indeed," Baltar said. "Even as we speak, the incubator in my lab is making enough Prion C to innoculate the entire Fleet. I have enough to start on the military—and the government, Madam President. They can handle distribution."

Tigh got up and clapped Baltar on the back. "You're a hero, Doctor. A real hero."

And then everything fell into place. Kara knew. Her jaw tightened and her stomach oozed with nausea. She rose abruptly. "I have to go," she said. "I can . . . I can help with the distribution process. I'll go down to sickbay and see to it. Commander?"

"Dismissed, Lieutenant," Adama said hoarsely. As Kara turned to go, he added, "Lieutenant."

She stopped and turned.

"I was sorry to hear about what happened to Peter," he said.

A lump formed in Kara's throat. Peter had infected her with a disease, aided in her kidnapping, and duped hundreds of people into joining a monotheistic little cult. But before that, he had been funny and kind and fascinating. A few minutes before his death, Kara had hated Peter, found him weak and self-centered. But when the timer was counting down those final seconds, he could have stayed with Lee in the hope that the Captain would find a way to disarm the explosive at the last moment. Instead, Peter had given up the hope in order to save Lee's life. Kara didn't know how to feel about Peter right then, but she did know his bloody death made her sad in a way she didn't want to explore right then. So she nodded acknowledgment to Adama and left the conference room.

Lee caught up with her in the hallway outside CIC. "What was that all about?"

Kara glanced around. The corridor was empty. When people got sick and shaky, they slipped off to their beds to hide rather than collapse in the hallways. "The frakking bastard *lied*."

"Who do you mean? Baltar?"

"No, the frakking High Priest of Geminon," Kara snarled. "Of *course* I mean Baltar. Who else?"

Lee held up his hands. They only trembled the tiniest bit. "His cure seems to be working. I can't tell you how relieved I am. We were all heading for death's gateway, including my dad."

"He lied about how long it would take to make the cure," Kara explained, overly patient. "He said creating the cure prion would take a couple days when he frakking *knew* it would only take a few hours. He lets us all think we're dead, and then he strides in to announce that he has the cure after all, applause and adulation, please. Frak him!"

"That's a serious charge, Kara," Lee said. "Can you—"

"No, I can't prove it," she sighed. "And there wouldn't be any point now." She took off down the hallway again with Lee tagging after her.

"How do you know, anyway?" he pressed. "You haven't even been on the *Galactica* for the last several hours."

"How long does it take to grow a prion?" Kara countered. "I'm betting it takes a couple hours. He had enough on that tray of his to cure everyone in CIC. That means he had the cure prion while I was still with the Unity on the *Monarch*, right? If he had come forward right then, it wouldn't have mattered if we got Peter back or not, and the entire situation would have changed. Peter might still be alive."

"We still needed to get you out," Lee reminded her. "And once word got out that we didn't need Peter anymore, Sharon—the bad one—would have just taken you hostage earlier."

"Maybe," Kara acknowledged. "But Peter"—her voice caught—"would still be alive. Meanwhile, Baltar saves the Fleet."

Lee put a hand on her shoulder, halting her in mid-stride. "Look, we can't know what would have happened. Maybe Baltar lied, maybe he didn't. There's no point in chewing on it right now. We have to get the prion out to the military and then to the public. And you won't be any help by walking this way."

"What do you mean?" Kara asked.

"Sickbay is that way."

Kara managed a small laugh and was surprised at how much better she felt for it.

It was two hours later. Commander William Adama sat once again at the conference room table, but he had managed a shower and a change of uniform. Between that and the lack of shakiness in his limbs and his voice, he felt bright as a new-minted coin. Laura Roslin, also seated at the table, looked more like her old self. He knew the cancer gave her good days and bad days, and she seemed to be having a good day now that the prion had been cleansed from her system. He felt gladder about that than about himself and Lee.

Lee, Kara, and Baltar had set about administering Prion C to Dr.

Cottle, his medics, and the rest of the sickbay staff. Once they were well enough, they headed out into *Galactica* proper with more syringes. Adama had ordered skeleton crews for all shifts. The cure worked, but people were still tired and needed rest before becoming completely well.

Once *Galactica* was inoculated, Adama ordered Raptors to carry the cure to the rest of the Fleet.

Unfortunately, casualty reports were also coming in. So far twenty-one people, including five children, had died, and twelve had gotten the cure too late for it to do any good, meaning death would eventually come to them as well. Adama pursed his lips at the report of each new death. Every single life was precious now, and every single death whittled a little more away from humanity's chance of surviving.

Gaius Baltar was also in the room. The rest of the cure had finished incubating and he wasn't needed in his lab anymore. "There's going to be a problem," he said.

Adama sighed heavily. "What now?"

"The *Monarch*, the *Phoebe*, and some of the other Geminon ships are absolutely rife with Unity followers," Baltar said.

"So?" Adama said.

"Oh!" Roslin put a hand to her mouth. "I should have foreseen that."

"Seen what?" Adama said, beginning to get annoyed. Nothing was ever easy on the *Galactica*.

"Peter's death makes him a martyr," Roslin said. "It will only strengthen the beliefs of some—perhaps even most—of his followers."

"And they see the plague as a blessing instead of a curse," Baltar finished.

Adama took a moment to rest his forehead on his now-steady hand. "So you're thinking that they'll resist inoculation. Even though they'll die without it."

"I'd bet a year's salary on it," Roslin said. Adama wasn't sure if that was meant as a joke or not—Roslin hadn't been paid for anything since the attack. Neither had he, come to that.

His tired mind, now overly sensitive to crisis, was already running scenarios. Forced inoculation would take large amounts of personnel and practically guarantee someone would get hurt. It was difficult or impossible to persuade someone caught in the grip of religious fervor. Maybe they could trick at least some of them into thinking the injection was something else?

"This," Baltar said, interrupting Adama's train of thought, "is why I took a small liberty. I hope you don't mind."

"What's that, Doctor?" Adama asked warily. Roslin looked uncertain as well.

At that moment, a knock came at the door. Baltar rose to open it. In walked Sarah Porter, closely followed by two men in priestly robes and another man with a video camera slung over his shoulder. Porter held a double scroll. Roslin kept her seat, but Adama got to his feet.

"Doctor?" he asked.

"You know, of course, Representative Porter of Geminon," Baltar said. "And this is Remus Tal, a Priest, and this is Nikolas Koa, an Oracle. They're also from Geminon."

Greetings were exchanged. Roslin still didn't rise, and Adama suspected she was feeling tired again.

"Some of the people in my jurisdiction are resisting inoculation," Porter said.

"As I predicted," Baltar put in.

Porter shot him a hard look at the interrupting, then continued. "However, Dr. Baltar here has pointed out something which may be of interest in solving the problem." She spread the scroll across the table. Adama put on his reading glasses. They made him feel like a grandfather, but he really had no choice. Roslin got up to join him. Her movements were slow and careful, so Adama resolved to keep this short.

"The Book of Glykon?" Roslin said. "I thought you considered this apocryphal."

"Just between us," Sarah said, "I do. But Dr. Baltar has pointed out something very interesting that just might solve this one last problem."

Kara lay sound asleep in a sickbay bed, dreaming of explosions that hurled chains in every direction. A dark figure loomed over her, and a sixth sense told her this wasn't a dream, and she jerked awake, hands in a fighting stance. Lee Adama backed up, his own hands raised.

"Just me," he said.

"Frak," she said, and sank back into the thin mattress. After injecting maybe a hundred people, Kara's body had finally given out. Darkness closed in and she felt herself falling. She remembered careful hands helping her along until she ended up someplace soft. A bed in sickbay. The place was crowded. Every bed was occupied, and most of the privacy curtains were open. She caught sight of Dr. Cottle bending over a patient in another bed.

"Why am I here instead of in my bunk?" she asked.

"Someone was already sleeping there," Lee said wryly, "so I brought you here. The person who had this bed had recovered enough to walk, so Doc Cottle kicked him out to make space for you."

Kara grimaced. "I feel like I could sleep for a month—and I'm frakking *starved*. Don't ever get kidnapped by the Unity. They don't feed you." Her stomach growled, emphasizing the point.

"I'll see if I can scrounge you something to eat in a minute," Lee said. "Got lots of algae."

"I'll take a big plate of it, as long as you add a steak, some fries, and a hunk of corn on the cob dripping with butter and loaded with salt."

"Maybe after you've had more rest," Lee said. "Even the mighty Starbuck needs sleep once in a while."

"So why'd you wake me up?" she growled. "And how long was I out?"

"Couple hours. I woke you up because there's a news conference coming on I thought you might want to see." He reached up to a video monitor hanging in a corner and switched it on. A well-dressed reporter with braided auburn hair was talking earnestly into a microphone.

"—here on the *Phoebe* where riots have broken out over the military's attempt to inoculate the population against the so-called plague of tongues," she was saying. The picture cut to scenes of angry civilians, some of them clearly in the shaking, babbling stage of the disease, throwing small objects at wary soldiers, who ducked behind shields and dodged around corners. Several carried signs that boasted slogans: PETER ATTIS WAS A MARTYR! WE ARE BLESSED! THE UNIFIER WILL SAVE HUMANITY! THE ONE IS THE ONLY ONE!

The soldiers in the scenes were clearly unwilling to engage the civilians, but it was equally clear that they weren't sure what to do.

"Rioting isn't limited to the *Phoebe*," continued the reporter in a voiceover. "After the explosion on the mining ship *Monarch* killed Peter Attis, the large gathering of Unity members who were opposing the military's attempt to free Attis's lover Lieutenant Kara Thrace—"

Kara bolted upright in the bed. The movement earned a jolt of pain from various injuries, but she ignored it. "How the frak did they learn about this so fast?"

"Hush!" Lee said.

"—refused inoculation," the reporter continued. "Many other Unity members and sympathizers are also refusing to cooperate. President Laura Roslin has enacted a new law requiring all people in the Fleet to receive the injection, which was developed by Vice-President Gaius Baltar. Despite this, Unity members and sympathizers continue to fight being inoculated."

"What idiots," Kara said. "They want to die, that's their business. After everything we've been through to get that cure, I say screw 'em."

"We're talking several hundred people," Lee said. "And several children."

Kara sank back into the bed again. "I know, I know. It's just . . ."

"I know." Lee patted her arm, and Kara realized that out of all the friends she had in the Fleet, Lee probably understood her the best. She felt comfortable with him, even safe. So why the hell did she feel pulled in two different directions about him all them time? Even now, part of her wanted him to take her hand and part of her wanted to shove him away. She settled on ignoring his touch and fixing her attention on the television. More angry civilians vied with uncertain soldiers. Then a newscaster broke in.

"We've just received word that President Roslin will be addressing the Fleet," he said. "We take you to her now."

Billy Keikeya appeared on the screen. He looked pale and wobbly, probably still recovering from the plague of tongues. "Citizens of the Colonies," he said, "I give you our president, Laura Roslin."

He stepped aside, and Roslin, also pale, came on camera. Kara realized with a small start that the background was not the usual podium on *Colonial Fleet One*, but the conference room off CIC.

"Good evening," Roslin said. "By now all of you know of the plague which has struck the Fleet and the fact that we have an inoculation developed by our vice president, Dr. Gaius Baltar. The inoculation will cure those who have the plague and grant immunity to those who don't. However, some people are seeing this plague as a blessing, as the touch of some divine being brought by Peter Attis. These people are resisting inoculation. I am here to tell you that the plague is no divine blessing. It is a prion developed by the Cylons. They infected the late Mr. Attis with it in the hope that as an entertainer, he would come into contact with great numbers of people and spread the plague farther and faster.

"I also know that many people believe Mr. Attis was a person called the Unifier come to save humanity by uniting everyone under a single god. This position seemed to be supported by certain passages in the Book of Glykon. I am here to tell you that this interpretation of the passages is an error. Peter Attis is not—was not—the Unifier fore-told there."

The camera pulled back, revealing that Roslin was standing behind the conference table in CIC. The chairs had been pulled away to make room for her and for Sarah Porter and Gaius Baltar, who were stand-ing next her. Baltar looked cool and calm, almost smug. Also present were two men Kara didn't recognize, though she assumed by the clothes they wore that they were clergy. On the table in front of Roslin lay a partially unrolled scroll.

"What the hell is this about?" Kara asked.

"Just watch," Lee said. The expression on his face was rigidly neu-tral and gave Kara no clues. Was the news good or bad? She couldn't tell, and that annoyed her. Why couldn't Lee just tell her?

"The main passage that the Unity members quote," Roslin said, stabbing a finger at the open scroll before her, "reads as follows: 'He—the Unifier—will save Humanity with the Plague of the Tongue.' This is taken to indicate that Peter Attis would bring a dis-ease that would make people speak in tongues, and this plague would save everyone by uniting humanity. There are also rumors that the Cylons will stop attacking us if we profess to believe in a single god, rumors that further feed the idea that Mr. Attis is the Unifier.

"In light of recent events, I have consulted with Representative Sarah Porter of Geminon and with Remus Tal, a Priest, and Nikolas Koa, an Oracle. They pointed out that Peter Attis and his followers read the Book of Glykon incorrectly, an easy mistake and com-pletely understandable, but a mistake nonetheless. The Book of Glykon indicates that the Unifier will save humanity with the plague of the tongue. This doesn't mean the plague will be the tool that saves humanity. It means that the Unifier *will save people who have the plague*. In other words, the Unifier will cure—save—the people who carry this sickness. The identity of the true Unifier can now be revealed."

"Oh, frak," Kara whispered. "He didn't."

"Yeah," Lee said. "He did."

Roslin stepped aside so that Tal and Koa could come forward. Between them they held a rectangular piece of gold cloth with two strings at the upper corners. The camera followed them as they solemnly processed to Gaius Baltar, who wore a humble, slightly overwhelmed look on his face.

"The Scrolls of Glykon are clear," Koa intoned. "Gaius Baltar is the Unifier who saved people with the terrible plague of tongues."

"Blessings on Gaius Baltar!" Tal said. "Blessings on the Unifier!"

Kara stared. "Is this . . . are they really doing this?"

"It's the best way," Lee said. "If it works, and Baltar is recognized as the Unifier, people will stop resisting inoculation."

"It's twisting one of the scrolls," Kara protested. "Baltar isn't the Unifier."

"How do you know?" Lee said philosophically. "This might be exactly what the Scroll of Glykon meant. It's hard to save humanity if it's dead."

"—to accept this honor," Baltar was saying from the screen. "I often felt that an invisible hand guided me during my work on the inoculation. I sincerely believe I was touched by a greater power, and I am humbled by this grave responsibility." He paused dramatically. "As the Unifier, I ask my followers to receive my touch and allow the inoculation to continue."

"Turn it off," Kara said. "I'm tired."

Lee obligingly shut off the monitor and turned to go. Kara watched him move away, leave her behind as everyone in her life seemed to do. And suddenly the thought of being alone was too harsh to bear.

"Wait," she said. "Lee, hold on."

He returned to her bedside, a quizzical look on his face. "What's wrong?"

"Nothing." Acting on impulse she reached out and took his hand. "Thank you."

"For what?" He looked genuinely puzzled.

"For coming after me. For bringing me here. For checking on me."

"That's what friends are for, Kara."

"I know." She continued to hold his hand. It was warm in hers. "And sometimes I think you and I . . ."

He leaned down to kiss her. But she turned her head at the last moment and the kiss landed on her cheek. Lee pulled back, looking confused and not a little angry.

"Kara," he said, "I don't know what you—"

"I don't either," she interrupted. "Look, Lee—everyone leaves. Zak. Sam. Peter. I don't want you to join those ranks. I'd rather keep you around."

"I wouldn't leave you, Kara," he said.

"How can you be sure?" she countered.

"Nothing's sure around here," he said, half wry, half sullen. "Absolutely nothing."

"Exactly. Maybe one day I'll feel different, but right now . . ." She squeezed his hand again, then carefully and firmly put it down. Lee gave her a long look with his blue eyes and a hurt look on his boyish face. Then he nodded once, turned, and left.

Something twisted in Kara's chest. Not only had she ruined any chance of a deeper relationship with Lee Adama, she had also killed their friendship.

You're stupid. A stupid, ugly cow. You don't deserve to be happy. You don't deserve to live. You don't deserve anything at all.

And she couldn't tell whether the inner voice was her own or her father's.

She turned over, squeezing her eyes shut against the tears. Sleep. That was what she needed now. The sounds of a busy, bustling sickbay swirled around her, but the military taught you to sleep through anything, and sickbay sounds were as soothing as a seashore lullaby. She would sleep and forget all about everything. Kara was just drifting off when the clank of dishes brought her awake again.

"What the hell?" She sat up and found Lee there. He was looking at her over a tray of covered dishes.

"Supper," he said. "You said you were hungry." He lifted lids as he spoke. "Algae soup. Algae salad. Algae bread. And for dessert, algae tapioca pudding. Yum yum!"

Kara stared down at green piles of glop, then burst out, "You frakhead!" She scooped up a spoonful of goo, ready to fling it at him, but Lee had already fled, the sound of his laughter trailing behind him. Kara put a hand to her mouth to stifle relieved laughter of her own. Then she sniffed the tray and picked up the spoon again.

The tapioca was surprisingly good.

President Laura Roslin slumped into a chair and leaned back with her eyes shut. The CIC conference room was empty of people except for Bill Adama. Baltar, the clergy, the camera crew, and even Billy Keikeya had left, thank gods, and that meant she could slouch all she wanted. Bill Adama wouldn't tell anyone. Laura suppressed a snort as she realized that the only two people in the Fleet who she felt comfortable showing weakness to were both named William.

"How are you feeling?" Adama asked from his own chair.

"Like I could sleep for a century," she said.

"Want a drink? I got the good stuff."

She opened her eyes. "No, thanks. That would really lay me low.

Wouldn't do for the president to conk out on her way to *Colonial One.*"

A moment of silence fell between them, a comfortable silence Laura enjoyed sharing with him.

"Did we do it right?" Adama asked at last.

"No way to know for sure," Laura said. "I mean, the riots calmed down almost immediately after Dr. Baltar's broadcast, and people are accepting the inoculation, so that's a plus. But declaring Gaius Baltar the Unifier . . . I don't know. He took to the role a little too well for my taste."

"I suspect that part of it will die down after a while. After all, the Unifier has already performed his duty by saving humanity. Nothing else for him to do, really."

And Laura Roslin laughed.

Helo put a hand to the wire-enforced Plexiglas barrier that separated him from Sharon's cell. She sighed, then pressed her own hand to it. Helo tried to pretend they were touching skin-on-skin, but it didn't work.

"Are you okay?" he asked.

"I feel like a dog who slipped her leash for a while and then got thrown back into the kennel," Sharon said.

"I'm going to try to get you out of there, Sharon," he said. "I am. Commander Adama will listen to reason eventually."

"Right," Sharon scoffed. "What do you think's going to happen? That I'll put on my uniform again one day? That Adama and I will sit at a little table together all buddy-buddy and he'll tell me his personal problems?"

"Who knows?" Helo said, trying to remain calm, though his voice was cracking. "It seems like something weird happens every frakking week around here, and you can never tell one day to the next what's going to happen."

"Easy to be optimistic when you're outside the jail instead of in it."

"I know."

"Be honest, Helo," she said, and he detected a hint of nervousness in her voice. "Did you really think I killed that marine?"

"No," he said promptly. "I did wonder how else he could have died, but I knew it wasn't you. Even when other people were calling me toaster-lover and giving me shit, I never thought it was you."

Some of the tension visibly went out of her. "Okay. Thanks."

"I have to go," he said reluctantly. "I have to get some sleep before I go on duty again. I love you."

She nodded. "I love you, too."

He turned and left the brig, not at all sure that he had told Sharon the truth but knowing there was nothing else he could have said.

"No, no, really. I have work to do. Thank you for coming. Really! It's quite all right. Yes, yes. Blessings on you all. I'll be giving a lecture just as soon as everyone's on their feet. Thank you again. More blessings, more blessings! Good day!"

Gaius Baltar closed the door to his laboratory, locked it, and leaned his back against it. Muffled knocks and faint pounding thudded on the metal. A smile stretched Gaius's face. Ah, the price of fame. Never a moment alone, even in his lab.

"That went well, Gaius," said Number Six. She was leaning against the door beside him, but her posture was casual.

"*I* liked it," he said with a grin. "Being the Unifier could have its advantages."

"Even though you lied about how long it would take you to find the cure so you could swoop in at the most theatrical moment and save everyone," she said.

He faltered. "Well, I *did* find the cure."

"And they won't ignore you ever again." Her gaze was hard and penetrating.

"I thought that was the whole idea."

"It was." Six swayed seductively toward him. "How did you put it? 'An invisible hand guided me'?" She put both hands on his shoulders, then slowly slid them down his chest, past his stomach, past his waist. Her voice dropped to a whisper. " 'I was touched by a greater power'?"

He shuddered deliciously as her fingers worked. "Yes. Yes, I was."

"And it's a good thing I reminded you to set up that little display with the priests."

"Yes, it was."

"But you haven't remembered everything, Gaius."

He sighed. "Now what?"

"The other parts from the Book of Glykon. How did they go? 'And the Unifier shall walk among the Enemy, and He shall return both changed and unharmed.' "

"I . . . I suppose that fits me, doesn't it?"

Her fingers continued working on his body, playing it like an instrument of pure pleasure. " 'The Unifier will bring together all Humans into one Tribe under one God.' I wonder what that could mean?"

"I haven't the foggiest."

"Don't forget the best one. 'And the Heads of those who defy the Unifier shall tumble to the Ground.' "

Her caressing fingers made him shudder. "That has a poetic ring."

"Just so you never forget it, Gaius," she murmured. "Never, ever forget who you are and who got you here."

"I," he said with a sudden grin, "am Gaius Baltar."

He took her into his arms and danced her across the room, swirling in gleeful circles all by himself.

ABOUT THE AUTHORS

CRAIG SHAW GARDNER is a *New York Times* bestselling author best known for his movie tie-in novel based on *Batman*. His impressive list of tie-ins also includes books based on the TV series *Angel* and *Buffy the Vampire Slayer* and on the movies *The Lost Boys*, *Batman*, *Batman Returns*, *Back to the Future II*, and *Back to the Future III*, in addition to tie-ins for comic books and video games. His original works include the Ebenezum trilogy, the three-part Cineverse Cycle, the Dragon Circle Trilogy, the three-part Changeling Saga, and many others. He lives in Boston, Massachusetts.

PETER DAVID is the author of dozens of works of fiction, including novels, comics, and screenplays. His most recent novels are *Tigerheart* and *Darkness of the Light*. He has worked with both Marvel and DC comics, and has penned many bestselling *Star Trek* books. In addition, he has written for several television series, including *Babylon 5* and *Crusades*, among others, and was the cocreator of *Space Cases*, which ran for two seasons on Nickelodeon. His other novels include *Knight Life*, *One Knight Only*, *Fall of Knight*, *Howling Mad*, and the Sir Apropos of Nothing series. He lives on Long Island.

STEVEN HARPER lives in Michigan with his wife and three sons. When not at the keyboard writing books and short stories, he sings, plays the piano, and collects folk music. He maintains that the most interesting thing about him is that he writes novels. All four books in his Silent Empire series were Spectrum Award finalists. Visit his Web page at http://www.sff.net/people/spiziks.